THIS WAS THE SITE OF A GALLOWS.—Tyburn Tree once stood where the policeman is directing the traffic near Marble-arch, at the junction of Bayswater and Edgware roads. A triangular stone tablet fixed in the road by the London County Council in 1909 marks the exact spot. Tyburn was a place of execution as early as the end of the twelfth century. Among the notorious people hanged there were John Felton, murderer of the Duke of Buckingham, and Jack Sheppard, the highwayman. The last execution at Tyburn took place in 1783. Oxford-road (now street) has been described as being in the days of Tyburn "a deep hollow road full of sloughs, with here and there a ragged house, the lurking place of cut-throats."

TYBURN TREE;

OR, THE

MYSTERIES OF THE PAST.

BY JAYHOHENN DEEHISEEKAYESS, ESQ.,

AUTHOR OF "PEN AND PENCIL SKETCHES," "THE OLD MANOR HOUSE," &c., &c.

LONDON :—
PUBLISHED BY R. S. SWIFT, 6, LITTLE NEW STREET, SHOE-LANE;
SOLD BY A. VICKERS, 5, HOLYWELL-STREET, STRAND.

TO

THOMAS KNOX BESSENT, ESQ.,

AS A TRIBUTE OF RESPECT AND FRIENDSHIP

THIS WORK IS MOST RESPECTFULLY DEDICATED

BY THE PROPRIETOR.

TYBURN TREE.

THE MYSTERIES

OF THE PAST

No. 1.

TYBURN TREE;

OR, THE

MYSTERIES OF THE PAST.

INTRODUCTION.

Long ago—so long ago, that generations have passed since he died who last remembered it, there stood a few miles out of London, on a wild common, a tall and stately Elm. Unlike other trees, this one was an object of dread, for from its branches, at certain times, condemned criminals swung, and the rustling of its leaves were blent with the groans of expiring wretches.

This was the original gallows — Tyburn Tree!

That tree decayed; its branches withered! —a curse seemed to cling to it. It at last was rooted up, but only to make space for a more convenient instrument of death.

Three uprights, and three cross-beams, now occupied the place of the Elm. Unlike its predecessor, it did not spring *from* the Earth, —it was driven *into* it: but, as of yore, from those triple beams malefactors swung, and guilt and innocence alike were punished miserably.

This was the second and the last Tyburn Tree! And what thrilling tales could both, were they erect, tell! Were there tongues in those trees, how would they reveal stories which would shame the pen of the most popular writer of fiction! The records of real life far surpass the dreamings of romance; and, in the exercise of a high moral purpose, we commence chronicles which will throw no little light on The Mysteries of the Past!

In the following pages, then, our aim will be to show how, in the history of great criminals, is exemplified the facts, that, though Vice and Crime may triumph for a-while, that Virtue is the only safeguard: that, though cunning may assume a thousand disguises, it will in the long run over-reach itself: that great talents may become great curses; and genius prove the destruction of its possessor: that beauty may be vain, and that learning may be rendered contemptible Not that we intend to be sentimental, or sophistical, —such reflections we leave to the reader. Abhoring cant, then, we intend painting a series of pictures from real life, and place them in the dark frame of Tyburn Tree!

CHAPTER I.

THE THIEVES' "CHAPEL."

In or about the year 1700, there was situated near Long Acre, an hostelry of notorious ill-fame, as being the safe abiding-place of highwaymen, burglars, prigs, and prostitutes; and from the security its walls afforded them of evading the officers of justice, as well as of concocting robberies' &c., gained for it both among thieves and thief-takers, the name of "The Chapel." It was towards this den of infamy, two young men, well-dressed, and well-mounted, coming from the neighbourhood of Knightsbridge on the evening in question, (an awfully wet one, by the bye) directed their steeds. Having arrived opposite a gateway leading to the stablery of "The Chapel," the younger of the two drew a small silver whistle from his pocket, and breathing gently through it, it omitted a note not unlike those of a thrush, but so low as only to be heard on the spot where it was breathed.

Almost immediately the sound was give , a small slide shot back from the stout oaken doors, and a pair of human eyes stared through the aperture; the slide was instantly shut to again, and the celerity with which the gateway w s thrown open, showed that they were not only expected but welcome guests.

"Rough night, Captain," said the man,— a short, thick-set, muscular fellow, with shoulders neck and head like an ox, and with a face that bore a very strong resemblance to an English bull-dog; for his nose was flattened upon his cheek, and his chin considerably protruded beyond the average of human jaws, which, coupled with his deep-set, wild, ferocious eyes, certainly entitled him to the soubriquet he had gained of "Beauty."

"Rough night, do you call it, you dog?" said the young man who was designated as Captain, "you've got no taste, Beauty. 'Tis a lovely night—charming night, you dog!" and he cut at the man playfully with the silver-mounted riding-whip he carried.

"Hap you've had a shower of guineas to-night, Captain," said the man, with a knowing leer. "People what have, werry seldom care about a shower of rain, so long as a good shower of shiners precedes it."

"Chalk up your last words as a proverb, Beauty," said the highwayman, gaily, "but your first surmise is incorrect. I have got no guineas; but look you, here's a whole host of flimsies!" and he pulled from the capacious pocket of his laced coat a complete handfull of bank notes.

"My precious eyes and limbs!" muttered Beauty, as he led the two reeking steeds into a stable, "but it's a first-rate business. Damme! I'll turn highwayman myself!"

"You turn highwayman?" roared the Captain, having overheard the soliloquy. "Ha! ha! ha! why, Beauty, your conscience is like the Bank of England—an inexhaustible mine, by Jove! You turn highwayman—ha! ha! ha?"

"Aye, for the matter of that, why not me, eh?" questioned Beauty.

"Why not you, you dog?" said the Captain, almost beside himself, by what he considered the absurdity of the idea. "Why, they'd fancy you were a stray baboon and shoot you, by Jove they would!"

"Oh, handsome men is always lucky, no doubt!" growled the serving man.

"A good-looking young man, my dear fellow, generally is," said the Captain. "More depends upon good looks than you are aware of; 'pon my soul, it does. The essence of politeness is absolutely necessary in the stopping of a gentleman's carriage. First of all, with pistol in each hand your pal stops the post-boys. Next, yourself, advancing to the carriage window, beat a gentle rat-tat upon it, and with the politest bow in the world, beg of his lordship, or her ladyship, or both, as the contents of the carriage may turn out to be, to let down the window. Of course you are obeyed. If my lord makes a fuss, and begins searching for his fire-arms, all you have to do is to raise your hand deprecatingly, thus!" and he suited the action to the word, "and to say in your quietest manner, with your very blandest smile, 'my dear lord, now really, why will you be so absurd? You are very imprudent—very ungallant to wish to shoot me before your lady's eyes; you are, upon my soul! Now, come, let's settle this little affair without bloodshed. Of all colours, I do most eternally detest scarlet. So, pray be kind enough to pass your purse, or my comrade, who has no such objections, will certainly make a target of that blessed carcase of yours.' The name of a comrade, and the least glimpse of your pistol's bright barrel, does it, Beauty; you find the swell's purse in your hand in one minute and three seconds less than no time. You turn you then, my friend, to her ladyship, who a hundred chances to one has her purse, watch, and trinkets, in her hand, waiting your taking. These dear ladies are ever most considerate. Press her lilly fingers to your lips, or your lips to hers, if you can get near enough, doff your *chapeau* politely, and hey! for a good bold canter for town! There, you dog! what do you think of that?"

"Think! you're a regular rum-mums,* and

---

* Great Beau.

worthy to be our Captain, that's all!" answered Beauty, adding in a half whisper, "who's that man there? he's precious quiet! A foreigner—a green 'un, eh!"

"He is a brave man, and a gentleman!" answered the Captain, with warmth. "I should not be here now, were it not for him!"

"How so, Captain?"

"The person from whom I obtained the booty, fought desperately; and by this time I should have been dead and d—d, had not his good sword been interposed. He struck aside the fatal blow, and thus he saved my life."

"Then he's a friend of mine; I ain't werry pretty, but I'm precious strong; I ain't werry bouncible, but I can fight: can't I, Captain? Tell him that—tell him that! Tell him I feel grateful for his saving you, and if he is to be one like you, tell him if he ever gets into trouble, here's a fellow will die to rescue him!"

"Here, Beauty, I know your faithfulness before to-day, you old English bull-dog, I do! Here, man, here's a guinea for you! I'll tell him of your offer, for I know he might have a worse friend at his elbow than Beauty Ellis." And saying these words, the Captain rejoined his companion, who wrapped in his cloak, had been sullenly pacing to and fro in the yard.

"Come, sir," he said, "I must apologize for my rudeness in leaving you, but that fellow has detained me."

"Mention it not, friend," replied the Unknown, in tones singularly sweet; I was so wrapt in contemplation, that the time passed like———"

"A flash of blue lightning!" said the vivacious highwayman, breaking in, "here now—there now—and nowhere in a jiffey; gone, by goles, in a thundering hurry! But, come, sir! unused, as you say you are to such sights, I am about to introduce you to one of the mysteries of this City of London—an organised gang of thieves, and so organised, that one is dependent upon the other, and each upon the whole; so that you will confess after five minutes' introduction, that sterling honesty—none of your silver-gilt—but real sterling honesty, is only to be found here—here in this den of thieves!"

"Den of thieves!" repeated the other, instinctively drawing back. "Suffer me to depart from this place; I like not this fellowship—I bargained not for this."

"You bargained for a supper and a bed;—I proffered my hospitality; and again I pledge you my honour you shall sup here to-night sumptuously as a prince; and prince like, that wearied form of yours shall repose upon a bed of down; when morning comes, if you will leave me, you shall depart unmolested! You waver, sir! Upon my honour—nay, sneer not at it, honour is allowed to exist among thieves," said the highwayman in a tone of unaccustomed seriousness. "So follow and fear not!"

"I can, Captain,—for so others calling you, I take your name—where your gang twenty times as powerful, aye, and twenty times as villainous, for the matter of that! Fear! it is a feeling I would scorn;"

"Scorn!" echoed the Captain, with a scarcely perceptible sneer.

"Aye! scorn is the word, sirrah, and if you doubt, take me before your villainous gang—tell them to kill me by piecemeal—and, if I quiver one muscle, even an eyelid, may I be shot!"

"You proved yourself a brave man tonight, but allow me to tell you, sir, you are now proving yourself a boaster."

"A boaster!" said the unknown, in a tone of bitter sattire, "an' you think so—lead me on, I'll follow."

"So be it," said the highwayman, and following each other with rapid steps, they mounted a winding, intricate staircase, until coming at length to a dead wall, the Captain paused, and again produced the silver whistle before mentioned, and repeated the self-same note; almost instantaneously the whole wall broke, as if by a charm, and a door became apparent, guarded by Two Soldiers, with carbines and long bayonets formidably protruding at the end.

"Who comes here?" was the challenge.

"One, who knowing all, commands all," was the reply.

The soldiers dropped their weapons, and simultaneously raising hand to helmet, said, "All right—pass on!"

The Captain and the Unknown moved on the bidding, each without uttering a syllable more than had been spoken to the guards, and still pursuing a winding course, came at length unto another door, which being iron bound and strongly fastened would have held the mastery against any attack the constabulary might have chosen to have levelled against it.

The Captain took a pistol from his pocket, and rapped loudly thrice with the butt-end upon a certain spot in the door; the echo of the sound had scarcely died away, ere an aperture was opened, and a pair of eyes, for one single moment, became visible; the next, there was a sound of the shooting back of bolts and bars, and the massive door, creaking upon its hinges, showed them another passage to be explored.

The man who opened this door, bent his head in respectful defference to the visitors, but spoke not one word.

The Captain led the way to a trap-door, so closely fitted to the floor, as to be entirely imperceptible to the naked eye. He struck his foot upon a small brass spot in the furthermost corner, and immediately a trap-door fell, revealing unto the astonished companion of the highwayman a long flight of stairs. For one moment the Unknown hesitated.

"Comrade, you fear to follow," said the Captain.

"Lead on!" was the short, stern reply.

Without further comment the highwayman descended the narrow staircase, slowly and cautiously, and so closely followed the Unknown at his heels, that the front of his boots more than once came in contact with the silver spurs that decorated the heels of the highwayman. At length they reached the bottom of this flight of stairs.

"Now, signor," said the highwayman, "I shall try your courage, the den of thieves of which I spoke is before us. If you prefer to return, you must find your way back from whence we came; but, if you will follow me again, upon the word of a man—upon the honour of a gentleman—upon the sacred feelings of a friend, I swear to you, you are not only safe, but that you shall never have cause to regret trusting upon the honour of Captain M'Cleane."

"M'Cleane," said the Unknown, utterly astonished, "are you indeed that desperate man, for whose capture one hundred pounds already have been offered?"

"I am that man," said the Captain, "who, despising—hating life, while I was beholden to the mercenary power of man for the support of it, turned courageously brave at last, and determined, instead of wasting what little talent I possessed for the general good of mankind—that the public should support me by the payment of such contributions as their persons might hold when necessity bade me make a levy; and I tell you, Sir Stranger, the shivering hand, which first cowardly, tremblingly—honest trembling!—forbade to hold an empty pistol in its faltering grasp, can now boldly go forth and threaten only what it dares perform! But, come, I see you are tired—wearied—hungry; come, all your wants shall be supplied, and if you had a very woman's curiosity, that too shall find its level. Again I bid you follow me."

"Look to your spurs, my comrade," said the Stranger, in a tone of gaiety; "for, by'r lady, if you move not quickly, I shall damnably damage my boot-soles upon the rowels of them!"

At this juncture a sharp voice bid them—"Stand!" And in another instant the query was put—"Who goes there?"

"One, who knowing all, commands all," was again given in reply.

"Long live the Captain!" cried the sentinel instantaneously, in a loud voice.

"Long live the Captain!" was again repeated by many a stentorian lung, and immediately two massive folding doors were simultaneously thrown open, and Captain M'Cleane and the Unknown found themselves in a spacious and richly furnished saloon, wherein, seated upon soft cushioned chairs, and still softer ottomans, at the least fifty men and women, of every variety of age, and in every variety of costume, were lounging, some with liquor glasses, some with "blue ruin," some with sparkling champagne, and others with foaming mugs of ale standing before them.

The Unknown cast a keen, searching glance around him, a bright colour flew to his hitherto pale cheek, his heart beat wildly, and with burning desire—for never had he beheld such manly beauty—such exquisite, rare feminine loveliness as was there exhibited—there, in that den of thieves.

"Lasses all! Heaven's blessings on your lovely faces, I drink your good luck and health, and here's an eel each night for a bed mate."

"An eel for a bed mate!—heaven forefend I should ever be troubled by such a slippery blade as that! Dick Flybynight there, is bad enough," cried a very pretty damsel.

"Quite—quite, I'm sure," exclaimed half a dozen lasses, simultaneously.

"Ha! Dick, you rascal," said Captain

M'Cleane, bending his eye upon a fine dashing young fellow opposite, "you're going too far a-head, man a-live; come now, cool down a bit—cool down a bit. That's advice for yourself, Dickon; as for you my dearly beloved, would that I had a hundred arms to embrace you all at once.

"But an eel has not an hundred arms, has he Captain?" said Gipsey Betty—a lass with a brown skin, coal black hair, and eyes dark as midnight.

"Nay, sweetheart, I proposed an eel, not because he is a slippery blade, you know," and the Captain bent a glance on Dick, "but because beyond all others we may call him a cove fond of a movement, and as eels are everlastingly on the move, and ladies everlastingly pining for the same, I thought I could do no better, sweet lasses, than to wish you an eel for a companion through night's consoling rest;—for, begad; I know full well he's a devil of a cove at a wriggle. But stop! I see my modest friend here blushes, and, before I proceed further, I have, members, one and all, to introduce him to you as a friend."

"If our Captain welcome him, we too have welcome for him," said the gang as it were in one voice.

"That, thanks to past proofs, I firmly believe; yet has this gentleman greater claims upon you, friends, than fortune has ever before given me to bring before you for your thanks and applause."

"What has he done, then," said a fellow with bushy whiskers, and face so hair covered he would have made a lovely monkey-man.

"He saved my life, comrades brave!—saved it at the dire hazard of his own."

"Long—long may he live! shouted every voice; and every voice blending so musically together that one appeared only to have spoken in that spacious saloon.

"And that is not all, brave companions. We have to thank him for this,"—and M'Cleane threw the roll of notes upon the table. "Yes, my brave compeers, I have three hundred pounds in good Bank of England notes, thanks to this gentleman's extreme daring and bravery."

"Nay," said the Stranger, "you extravagantly overrate my abilities and my services to you. When I found you were attacked by two, I felt that could not be right; so I bared my sword to protect you, and right glad I am now my help was effectual; although, as to procuring yon pile of wealth, in justice to you I must say I had no hand in it."

"No hand in it?" cried M'Cleane, "by'r lady but you had, and a right bold one too. For had you not after disarming your antagonist, seized mine by the w zen, the devil's in it but before this I should have been in Hades; and the consequence would have been, instead of yon pretty pile of flimsies lying as they do, my brave fellows, the prettiest pieces of transparencies in the world, because the most valuable—the real owner, poor Pill Garlick, would have marched home with them, and blazoned forth about town that most uncommon feat—'Money saved and killed a highwayman.'"

"Not this time exactly—damme!" said Dick Flybynight, surveying his person in a mirror (and evidently to his own gratification), then turning, he said "Curse me! we're treating our new friend somewhat scurvily; allow me to suggest he does descend from that cloak, and appear, as our players say, in *propria persona;* and having to thank him, at the least, if not for the flimsies, for what is still more valuable, the life of our gallant commander, I do propose we drink his health with three times three, in goblets of golden sherry."

A burst of applause, in which the Captain joined right heartily, followed this announcement.

The Unknown threw aside the military cloak that enshrouded his form, and stood before them in the gay and graceful costume of a courtly cavalier of the day.

M'Cleane started when the person who had rescued him from the jaws of death, stood openly and boldly before him, his handsome features, looking doubly handsome as the silver light of the saloon fell upon them, and the rich and fashionable attire in which he was robed, setting off to the best advantage his slim but graceful figure.

"God of Heaven! is it indeed Sir Richard ———?"

Ere he could finish, the Stranger's hand was raised imperiously waiving him to silence.

"What I was," he said seriously, "matters not; sufficient for all be it, when I say, the laws of England have declared me a bastard—confiscated my estates—have robbed me of the title I once held; my own extravagance has done the rest; and you now behold in me a man without a name, credit, or a single stiver in my purse."

"Then are you a thousand times the more welcome from those very evils," said M'Cleane, "and, at least, you will own that gentlemen of the road, thieves, and burglars though we be, we have yet hearts to sympathize with misfortune, yet power to extend a helping hand to those in need; but, come, the pledge! Lift high your wine glasses, and drink, bright eyes and noble hearts, to the welfare of our gallant unknown friend."

The pledge was drank as enthusiastically as given, and three loud and prolonged cheers echoed again through those dark and intricate corridors.

Enjoyment now began with right good spirit, and M'Cleane, advancing gallantly towards a blue-eyed damsel, led her to the table at the far end of the room, and which was groaning under the costly luxuries heaped upon it. The Unknown, fascinated with the beauteous faces and bright eyes of the lasses around him, seemed for a time uncertain which to choose so beautiful was each and all; at length his eyes fell upon the dark lustrous eyes of Gipsey Betty. To this dark skinned beauty he attached himself, and the pair, with graceful motions, moved towards the supper table. Full justice was done, both by the robbers and their mistresses, to the rich viands set before them, and right merry was their ringing laughter as the jest and the glass went round. Ere, however, the clock had chimed the hour of midnight, a deep toned bell broke upon the ear. Each gazed wistfully in the other's face, for that was a signal that something of deep importance was about to transpire.

CHAPTER II.

TREACHERY IN THE CAMP.—ITS PUNISHMENT.— HURRAH FOR THE ROAD!

THE echoes of the bell had scarcely died upon the ear before M'Cleane, placing his hand upon a knob which secretly communicated by means of a wire, with a bell beyond, gave an instant and intelligible answer to it. For a few moments there was a silence deep as the grave itself, and each and all of the company assembled listened attentively to the responding signal.

In a few moments it came, and the bell of the deep tone before mentioned clanged sharply once upon the ear.

"All is right!" said M'Cleane, who, pale with fearful expectation and eagerness, had been almost faintive from the strong beatings of heart: "yes, all is safe." Then turning to those around him, he said, "Secrete those arms!" for, instantaneously upon the sound of the warning note, the men had bared their shining blades, anticipating a deadly attack, and the very women, true to their clan and to their comrades, stood pistol in hand, with eyes flashing fire, and with tiny feet firmly pressed into the downy carpet, determined to fight to the very last— even death before surrender!

The arms, obediently to M'Cleane's orders, were stowed into a secret place immediately, and the swords whose glittering blades had flashed so brilliantly beneath the rays of the lamps, were once again harmlessly, securely, and bloodlessly encased.

These necessary preparations had scarcely been completed, ere a signal of sufficient significance to warrant immediate attention reverberated through the saloon.

"Open doors!" said M'Cleane, briefly and sternly. They were opened immediately, and in walked, with a swaggering gait, a man whose stature could not have been less by an inch than six feet, and whose pimpled and bloated countenance bore undeniable signs of the habitual drunkard.

"Ha! Ben Culls, how fares the world with you—how goes times?" Then without waiting for an answer, he turned to M'Cleane, "What, Captain, are you once more here, after your long absence from us? I'm right jolly glad to see you; tip us your palm, my —— fine fellow!"

M'Cleane took no notice of this course request, except the retreat he made of a pace or two might be unequivocally taken as a strong dissent from such a proceeding.

"You won't? damme! you are strangely wanting in courtesy to-night;—but never, never mind," said the drunken braggart, "I can do without it—set you all at defiance, blast you!"

"That remains to be proved," said M'Cleane, in a tone of cool indifference.

"That he has attempted it, can be proved now," said a girlish voice in deep tones. "I can prove that."

All eyes were turned up to a young beauty, whose age could not have exceeded eighteen summers: yet she looked more, for her form was well matured, and her handsome face, now cast into a firm decisive mould, from the passion under which she shook, and the scorn which lightning-like, shot forth flashes from her jet black eyes. She was indeed faultlessly beautiful—features full of soft feminine beauty—and a countenance so rich in its delicacy, and now a face so bold and defying in her anger, she was indeed a perfect study —a perfect model of scornful, ireful beauty.

"You know, my pretty damsel," said M'Cleane, "from whence came you? I cannot remember ever having seen that pretty face before."

Flybynight Dick here spoke.

"She was introduced to our fraternity during your absence, Captain: Madame Charlotte gave her an introduction, and I myself saw such specimens of her ability as induced me in the first instance, and without your knowledge, to administer to her the oath, and the secret countersigns of the gang."

"If she be but as good as she is pretty, you have acted wisely Dick, and great praise is due to you for your promptitude in making so desirable an addition to our society."

"I bow in deference to that observation, said Dick, gaily.

"Well, now, what is it? This is a——pretty caper, I don't think! what does this young lass know that you turn your eyes so suspiciously this way,"

"I know you are a treacherous villain, and that you are already in league with the magistrates to sell the gang; and more, all would before this have been done, had they raised the blood money to the height your cupidity set—a thousand guineas!"

At the sound of treachery, every sword simultaneously flew forth, and the betrayer found himself surrounded by an armed host of those whom he would have betrayed. At this moment the Unknown also followed, but merely to strike down the blades pointed so threateningly to the denounced one's breast.

"Gently!" he exclaimed, in a tone of authority; "do you execute the sentence before the guilt is proved? If you do, come on,— I side with the weakest!"

With a companion to his back, the man of treachery grew bold and audacious.

"The cowards would kill me on suspicion —let that lying minx prove my guilt—I defy her to it—she cannot."

"She both can and will!" said the girl, advancing, "or she herself is willing, in case of failure, to bear the punishment, or which else you will."

"That is but fair," said the Unknown; "bring her to the test, Captain."

M'Cleane turned towards her—"Speak on, madam, without hesitation or fear; we are here to help the truthful, and punish the false!"

"So be it," responded the girl, and she immediately commenced her important revelation in these words :—"Sir, by the kindness of Madame Charlotte, and the urbanity of this gentleman, (indicating Flybynight Dick) I became a member of this fraternity. The oath of allegiance—the solemn oath that I would be faithful unto the end, and forward the interests of the gang, was at my heart, and ever will be, sir, to the end, even though that end should be a leap from Tyburn Tree."

"Bravo!" shouted all, with one exception, with startling enthusiasm.

"In pursuance of these principles, sir, I started forth to see whether Providence would bless my intentions by granting me a prosperous fly-faking. Madame Charlotte gave me a basket of flowers, and I started to the theatre to sell them, of course."

"Of course!" cried Flybynight Dick, "and devil a one in the world could suppose—would suppose, begad, you could possibly mix in a crowd for any less innocent motive!"

"I thank you for the compliment; but to proceed: I mixed in the gay crowd, and although a poor innocent Irish girl, who has only received but a few lessons in the art, I managed to extract from the pocket of a gay old buck, who insisted upon kissing me, this purse. (and she threw a well filled one upon the table) from another old bloak, I managed to get a snuff-box—see!"

M'Cleane took it from her extended hand, and examining it minutely for a moment ere he laid it on the table, remarked, "Fine gold —real diamonds."

"I made a tug at a lady's watch; she felt the tug and turned, but seeing a poor innocent flower girl, she thought it was an accident, and pitying my poverty-stricken look, she kindly gave me a shilling for one of my posies. I had unhooked her watch and would have had it, but the kindness of her manner —her kindness in giving the coin without solicitation, overpowered me. I did wrong, I confess; but so unaccustomed have I been through life to aught or anything in the shape of kindness, that by God I could not rob that generous lady!"

"You are a noble-hearted girl!" said M'Cleane, with warmth, "and are worthy of a far better path through life than the one that now lies before ye! Ye acted quite well in obeying the dictates of your grateful heart; and now learn that it is not the generous-hearted or the poor that we wish to rob, but those who are fattening upon the works of a poverty-crushed people—or debauched, purse-proud aristocracy!—those are the victims for us!"

These ennobling sentiments are blasted fine in their way; but while you're spinning these everlasting yarns, I'm in a funk to know what I have done, that you set upon me like a pack of hungry hounds, as you are!—ain't I mean?' said the fellow, correcting himself with the coolest insolence.

The girl fixed her flashing eyes upon him with a glance that made the villain cower. "Your turn is coming, sirrah! and if not sooner than you expect, sooner perhaps than may be pleasant for you."

"You be ———!" said the scoundrel with brutal coarseness. The girl took no notice of the oath, or of the dark look of fierce hatred that accompanied it, but quietly resuming the thread of her narrative, she proceeded calmly on.

"Shortly after the lady had left me, I found myself in a deserted street, for playgoers had entered the theatre, and a drizzling rain having come on, such as had money in their pockets, took their way to a tavern—the poorer to their homes. I, too, set out for the "Chapel;" for unaccustomed to so much riches, I felt contented, thinking I had reaped a rich harvest. Opposite the gateway to the "Chapel," standing under the portico, were two men. What induced me to act so, I cannot define; but as I was passing a stray word caught my ear, and unnoticed during the rattle of the rain, I listened to their conversation."

'I don't see why I should stand here guarded, 'cos you choose to play eves-dropper to a couple of fools who stood chattering in the wet.'

"But if that person you so courteously and appropriately call a fool, happened to be yourself—how then? And if the conversation happened to be full of deep, treacherous intentions—how then?" and the girl looked enquiringly around.

'You were fully justified in the course you pursued, and merit our very warmest thanks for the same."

"I know in my own heart my intentions were just and honourable towards you all; and I swear to you by all that's just and sacred, I would die even a death of ignominy, rather than falsify the oath I took—rather than betray those whom I am, by promise freely given, firmly bound to aid and serve. I tell you," continued the girl, "I listened to this man and the other's conversation."

"What was it?" said M'Cleane; "this dear lump of innocence," he added, in a tone of bitter irony, "seems most anxious for the tidings. I pray then let's have it quickly, not for our sakes, dear miss, but for his."

"I dally no longer, then, upon preliminaries, but will at once proceed to re ate facts."

She paused for one moment—rinsed her mouth with a glass of wine, and then continued :—" the man to whom this villain was speaking was a stout elderly man, encased in a cloak, whose ample collar sufficed to conceal his face, but, nevertheless, his long grey hairs hung pendant over his collar. And thus I calculated he was an aged man. The first words I heard him say were, 'Then it is in your power to furnish us with directions—in fact, to lead, if we go disguised (a matter of little moment that) into the secret hiding, the hitherto impenetrable strongholds of this infernal chapel of vice?' That man who now faces me answered," said the girl, "'Yes, I will introduce you by such secret means that your constabulary shall be astonished at the intricacies of the vast strongholds, and the astonishing means of defence they have—such means,' yon villain added to his words— "look to his pale face," said the now excited girl, "a guilty conscience needs no accusation, and if that fellow's countenance is not a proof of guilt, may I die this minute."

"His countenance shows the villain," said M'Cleane, "that we all confess. He was a handsome baby, and such beauties you know generally grow ugly with their growth; but we need positive proofs of his base duplicity, mademoiselle, and I cannot guarantee you help in this painful affair unless we have it."

"My word is mistrusted then," said the girl with eyes full of indignation.

"Nay, my fair friend," said the Captain, composingly; "we have all faith in you, but in a case like this, where life or death hangs, we have need to have stern full proofs of all."

"That you shall have, be assured; and if I fail, bring me to the test of which I spoke; kill me, you have weapons here."

"Nay, we would avoid so bloody an extreme," said M'Cleane, "though thieves, we are not assassins."

More composed, the girl continued,—

"The older man then asked that villain how many men would be necessary for the attack. He answered 'Twelve,' for he could lead them by a secret route to the saloon early in the evening time, they should there lie in ambush, and pounce upon the gang as they came in, as he said we generally did so in one's, two's, and three's. That these parties, as they straggled in, could be securely handcuffed and carried under escort before a justice of the peace, and for this act of justice yon villain claimed as reward one thousand guineas. Five hundred were promised him upon the gentleman's own responsibility, but that was refused, he would have a thousand—not a guinea less, or he would keep the secret. That would enable him to finish his days in comfort and peace in a foreign land—comfort and peace, good God; bought at the price of fifty human lives."

"A rare life to lead, truly;" said M'Cleane. Then turning to the villain, who stood trembling before him at his discovered villainy, he said, sternly, "What have you to say to this charge?"

"That 'tis a lie—a d—d infernal lie," he answered.

"It is truth," said the girl, undauntedly, "and I can prove it."

"How?" questioned M'Cleane.

"There is a constable, an elderly man, who was pointed out to me by Madame Charlotte, and one in whom, so she stated, I could safely confide, for he aided and abetted the gang to the utmost of his power. As soon as this man and the Justice had done talking, which they did in a few minutes, the Justice promising to meet that man at the same place on Wednesday night, and if possible, to bring the reward with him. I followed the fellow until both him and I came upon the constable. I could tell it was him not only because I had a perfect knowledge of his features, but also in passing they used some words of slang one to the other. I allowed this fellow to go on, and then I accosted the constable, and informed him of my fears that a conspiracy was on foot for the total annihilation of the whole gang. He said more than once a suspicion of

that man's faith had crossed his mind, and now he swore, if there was treachery he would seek it out and uproot it. In pursuance of this plan, we together proceeded into the city, the direction the Justice had gone; being an old man, we soon caught him, and the constable said, "All right," which was a signal I should leave him, which I did, and came hither."

"Brave, indefatigable, Charlie!" exclaimed M'Cleane, joyfully, "that then was the reason the signal of warning was given this night. We shall have the truth at last; and you, you treacherous scoundrel, shall meet with a just reward; Guard well that man!" he said to his followers, and the fellow was again surrounded with bared swords. "You, Sir Stranger," he said, "and you also, Dick, will accompany me as witnesses of what is now to follow. "Come! as time is precious we will ascend by the shaft."

He advanced as he spoke to the fireplace, in those days so capacious as to be quite as large as many a modern room. By the side of the fireplace was an oaken pannelling; this, upon touching a spring, instantly flew open, discovering an aperture sufficiently large to admit the body of a man. Into this, in close succession, M'Cleane, Dick, and the Unknown entered—the former bearing a dark lantern in his hand. The Unknown found himself in a circular room, walled-round with bricks. Upon gazing upwards a faint light was discoverable, and the thought instantly occurred to the Unknown that this was a dry well sunken to afford means of escape to the robbers in the hour of peril. M'Cleane blew three notes upon his whistle, and in a few seconds the head of the ostler we introduced in the first chapter, was beheld peering down from above.

Without any observation being made, pro or con, a large dark substance was observed descending, as it were, upon their heads. It stopped, however, very considerately when within a few inches of them, and the two highwaymen, seizing the substance, drew it to the ground. It was a large well-bucket, capable of holding two men. Dick and the Unknown, at the bidding of M'Cleane, got into it, each standing upright and seizing the chain by which the bucket was connected; upon a signal from M'Cleane's whistle, found themselves slowly and securely upon the rise. Having reached the top they were drawn to terra firma, and the empty bucket was again lowered for M'Cleane. In a few minutes he reached the top, and was also safely landed.

"Follow me," said M'Cleane. The pair followed him with profound silence up a flight of steps that stood at the far extremity of the yard. It brought them by a secret doorway into an old deserted and delapidated mansion. Here, by means of a phosphorous bottle and match, a light was obtained and a taper lit, which served more, in addition to M'Cleane's dark lantern, to show the utter desolation around them.

The Stranger shuddered involuntarily, the place was so cold, so cheerless, so desolate.

"A pleasant place this for a believer in ghosts to pass a night in," observed Dick, "by my hopes, sceptical as I am of such matters,

I fancy the unhappy spirit of some departed wretch lurks in every passing shadow."

"It is indeed a cheerless place, and if but one-half of the traditions are true that are told of it, it may right well be haunted. But come, we must begone; there is but one chamber in this mansion inhabited, and that is by our ghost-defying friend, Charlie, who for the sake of living rent free, would, I verily believe, accept the apartments of the devil himself. But here we are." A few minutes elapsed, and they stood before a small door, through the chinks of which a light, as from a taper, was visible. M'Cleane opened the door and entered without ceremony. An old watchman was crouched before a miserable fire warming his shrivelled hands.

"Holloa Charlie, my boy; what, down on all fours; come, rouse thee, man, bring forth that bottle of Hollands; we are shivery rather."

The man sprang up at the sound of the Captain's voice, and his dull leaden eyes sparkled with satisfaction.

"Ha, my noble Captain, your servant! Yours, too, noble gentlemen! Hollands, did you say? By the blessed virgin I've a gallon as good as
No. 2.

good can be, the best that the Dutch can make and pure as a maiden of twelve.

He took down a bottle, and pouring each out a glass, reserved also a drain for himself.

"You rung the warning bell just now, Charlie, at the 'Chapel;' what mischief is brewing, lad?"

"Horrid—werry horrid doings; you are all to be hung; all, every man jack of ye."

"Indeed!" said M'Cleane; "and when is this celebrated tight rope dance to come off?"

"When they can catch you," tittered the man; "he! he! he! but that won't be this week."

"Nor next, so far as I am concerned. I wasn't born to be scragged, so I'm safe," said Dick Flybynight.

"As usual," said the old Charlie, looking admirably at the dashing highwayman; "as usual careless, happy, and free."

"And so shall remain until some random bullet lays me low; but come to the tac, M'Cleane; I have an appointment with a young baronet to-night, and time flies."

The question was then plainly put to the Charlie, and his answer was—

"It is all true, Captain; all true, every

blessed word! I followed the justice home, and on the plea that I had tidings of M'Cleane and his gang, I gained a knowledge of the plot; oh, it is werry horrid—werry horrid!"

"What decision did the magistrates come to?" asked M'Cleane.

"To get him to accept a less reward if possible, but, if not, to give him a thousand guineas, and arrest you all—it was cleverly managed—cleverly managed—and if I hadn't a happened to have been let into the secret your lives would not have been worth that!"

"Not even a d—d solitary snap of the fingers, eh?" said Dick; "decidedly too cheap to be good that!"

"You are certain," said M'Cleane, "they would have effected their purpose?"

"Sartin, sure," answered the Charlie; "why, God bless me, he was to have furnished 'em with a plan of the whole building—they were to have got in by secret means, and when in, to have secured you as you came straggling in, and if you made the least resistance——"

"Which we should a trifle," said Dick.

"To have shot and stabbed you without mercy," continued the Charlie.

"Well," said M'Cleane, "I am deeply grateful to them for their good intentions, but as a plan of the building up to the present time does not happen to be in their possession, and as I shall place a double guard upon the secret entrances known to that villainous informer, we have nothing to fear. No, Charlie, for the time being, at least, we can cope successfully with the law! There is a purse for your services," said M'Cleane, throwing a well lined one upon the table; "now get you to your duty, and plant a couple of officers at the north door of the 'Chapel,' give them a description of Blackmoor, and immediately he sets foot without let him be arrested. Leave the rest to me." And so saying, they left the old Charlie to his meditations, and returned to the 'Chapel' by the route they had left it.

Eager eyes greeted their return, and eager exclamations burst from lips anxious to learn if he who was so strongly guarded was guilty or innocent, and when the word "guilty!" fell upon their ears, the eyes of the more gentle were dropped, for they knew the crisis of a dread tragedy was at hand!

"Guilty!" the wretched Blackmoor's visage turned ashy pale as the word of condemnation fell upon his ears, for he knew that word was synonymous with death!

"There remains but one question for us," said M'Cleane, "and that is, what shall be the sentence of this man.

"Death!" exclaimed all simultaneously.

"Yes, that must be his portion; he sought to slay us, and are we not justified in defence of our own lives, to sacrifice his?"

"Yes!" responded every voice.

M'Cleane turned towards the culprit—"You must prepare for death, for die you must in a manner fitting to punish the damnable treachery you have been guilty of towards us; us, who, on your solemn oath, you swore to help to aid, and to assist."

M'Cleane went to a book, a perfect chronicle of crime, for it contained a record of every robbery where, when, and by whom perpetrated, and turning over a few leaves, he said,

"I find, upon reference, you were concerned in the robbery in March last, of a Mr. Welsh, at Hampstead, and that you not only committed the robbery, but with a bludgeon did so murderously assault, that he died of the wounds there and then received. Who were the witnesses of this crime?"

"I was," said a young man, stepping forward; "but I declare, before God, I had no hand in the murder!"

"Of that I can adduce proof; a servant who witnessed the deed is still living, and attested the same in her examination before a magistrate. Now bend your ear to me," and M'Cleane whispered a few hasty instructions in his ear.

"I am bound to obey you, Captain—it shall be done," said the young man.

"But is it done willingly?"

"Yes!" was the reply.

"That is well!" he turned towards Blackmoor and those who held him, and when the young had left the room, he said, "Release him—he is free to depart from hence." M'Cleane threw the doors open with his own hands, and pointing to it, said, "If you can guide officers in the house you can guide yourself out; begone, villain!"

Almost paralysed by the sudden change in his fate (for he had anticipated instant death,) he stood for one moment stupified, the next he bounded forward to the doorway, and turning, he shook his fist at the girl who had betrayed his baseness, and in a voice, almost inarticulate from excitement and passion, he exclaimed, "D—n you, we shall meet again!"

She pressed her ripe red lips the closer together as in defiance, and replied,

"We shall!"

This had happened in a moment, and the gang, astounded by the unexpected liberty granted the villain, crowded round M'Cleane with murmuring words—

"You are making the devils own mess of it!" said Dick, "after taking all the pains you have to let the villain loose. I'd have had his heart out first!"

"Nay, comrades, watch the sequel ere you complain: we wish not to make a catacombe of the "Chapel," so I thought I would bring him to the death he would have doomed us— "the cord."

"But how can that be done? the villain is at liberty, and can now wreak his vengeance upon us."

"Watch the sequel!" repeated M'Cleane, talking with evident admiration of the flower girl.

"Well, begad! morning's breaking, and whilst you are dallying with the lasses, I must be on the road."

"What's in the wind now, Dick?" inquired M'Cleane.

"A mere trifle," answered Dick, "a hundred or so!"

"But the victim that is to be—who is he?"

"Sir James Town, the gambler and debauchee. I have had tidings that he has been winning heavily; and as I know him to be a thorough villain, and I am determined for my especial fame and general benefit, to drain his pockets this night!"

"Where is he to be met with?" inquired M'Cleane.

"At Harrow-on-the Hill: by the bye, said Dick, looking round, "I hear he always carries fire-arms, and has had tolerable practice in the way of using them; who will accompany me? I need a comrade, but let none stir who fancies cold lead indigestible. "Now, blast you! don't all speak at once!—who will come?"

"I will!" said the Unknown, rising and gathering his cloak around him.

"You!"

"Ah, me!" said the Stranger. "Why not!"

"For two reasons: you may be a brave man, and are, by God! that none can dispute; but notice the lauding, there is something more than courage, that cool effrontery, a reckless dare-devilry which you possess not—at least so far as personal appearances are concerned."

A smile of scorn crossed the handsome face of the Stranger.

"And that is one reason;—I prythee give me the other."

"Oh! it's quite at your service!" said Dick. "I am not allowed to companionship with one who is not a member of the band."

"And if I become a member, and after my installation as daring and dashing a knight of the road as you yourself are, what then, do you still refuse?"

"Why no!" said Dick, frankly.

"Then swear me in, and let me go!" said the Stranger impetuously. "I have set my heart upon this expedition;—I know the villain well; he has robbed me of many a thousand, and I would ease him of a particle back!"

"Bravely said, my bold fellow! Come, it's agreed; let's to horse; for good or ill we'll share this adventure to-night!"

A loud cheer arose to greet the new member of the "Thieves' Chapel," for brave men were they—soul's delights—they worshipped them!

"Then by what name are we to know you, Captain?" said the pretty gipsy to the Unknown.

"Name! I have forfeited my own for my country's good—now to raise another by my country's ill! Hurrah for the road! Name! my pretty Bessy, call me Dick, Tom, Harry, ought you like, all are henceforth the same to me!"

"But it is necessary we should know you by some name—we need not your real one; you know a fictitious one will suffice," observed M'Cleane.

"Then, I'll name him," said the pretty gipsy, "let's call him HANDSOME JACK!" and "Handsome Jack," he was thenceforward called.

"We have another to christen," said M'Cleane; "here is my sweet friend here up to this time nameless."

"By Jove! I can name her!" said Dick; "she is a thorough Jenny Diver!* Art satis-

fied with that name, my pretty face!" and he would have chucked her under the chin, but she drew herself proudly up, and put his arm down. "Now come not so coy!" but all his coaxing was without avail; so calling Handsome Jack, they both strode from the room, and passing through the intricacies described at the commencement, they passed into the stable yard, and in a very few minutes the sound of their horses hoofs awoke the echoes in the quiet street as they cantered on their way.

"A lovely night, Jackey, especially with the prospect of a dashing exploit, and full purse for our pains! By my soul! ours is the profession of professions for carelessness, riches, and hilarity. Hallo though, what have we here—a row!"

This remark was called forth by a party of constabulary, who were dragging two men to the round-house.

"Hallo, there! what's the matter now—what's up?" exclaimed Dick, as he rode in the midst.

"Only a couple of prisoners, sir," replied a Charley; "one on 'em, sir, is charged by the other with the murder of an old man at Peckham : Mr ——— dash my wig, I forget his name, but he had his pimple cracked awhile ago!"

"Push on, Jack," cried Dick, "or Blackmoor may recognise us, and a hue and cry might be raised too warm to be pleasant."

"Is that the villanous spy there, the Captain dismissed?" asked Handsome Jack.

"The very same," answered Dick; "M'Cleane has done it beautifully, by God! and poor old Blackmoor has put his foot in it, as the farmer did who had a passionate love for man-traps, and spread them so plentifully that he got his foot in one the very first night. Come, Jack, tip that lagging beast of thine a little cold steel, or we shall miss the prize, and that, for my own part, I would not do for the best hundred guineas ever coined."

Jack dug the rowels of his spurs into his horse's side, muttering as he did so between his clenched teeth, " Nor I, for all the world!"

Forward they went at a brisk gallop up the road that led to Harrow-on-the-Hill, and in an incredible short space of time reached the desired neighbourhood.

"Gently, Bessy, gently," said Dick, reining in the noble animal he bestrode, "we'll see now if this humbug has passed;" and he accordingly rode up to a little way-side inn, that offering "good accommodation for man and beast," stood invitingly forth.

"Hillo, there! house ahoy!" shouted Dick, his voice echoing again in the distance. The challenge was answered by a portly person coming forth with a red cotton nightcap on his head.

"What may'st want?" said the man.

"A tankard of thy very best, old Redhead, and that in half a jiffey!

"Ay, ay, sir," said the fellow, as he shuffled into the house, returning presently with the foaming liquor. It was duly drank and paid for.

"Has Sir James Town's carriage passed this way to night, Redhead?"

* "Mary Young, *alias* Murphew, *alias* Webb, *alias* Jenny Diver, was so great a proficient in her art that she got the name among her companions of Jenny Diver, *alias* Diving Jenny, from her great dexterity in picking pockets." "Annals of Newgate." She was executed at Tyburn, March 18, 1741.

"Ar'nt seen him, sir, he arn't stopped here."

"I thought he made a point of always stopping here?"

"So he do, sir, when he's sober; but he's come home lately so infarnal lushy, he arn't known nought about what he has been doing."

"Oh, he lushes, does he? Well, we'll ride on, I was only waiting for company's sake; for I have heard this road is infested with highwayman—is that a fact?"

"'Tis indeed, sir," said the man. "Sir James himself was stopped last week."

"Indeed, did they take much?"

"More than they bargained for I believe, sir, one on 'em took an ounce of lead home in his cocoa nut — Sir James don't travel without outriders now."

"Phew!" whistled Dick, as they rode off. "What do you think of that, Jack?"

"Think!" echoed Jack, "with your kingly namesake, Dick, I've bet my life upon the cast, and now I'll stand the hazard of the die."

"Bravely said, by goles!" exclaimed Dick enthusiastically, "and spite of his outriders we'll win—we'll win!" and he flourished his riding whip triumphantly over head.

"Comrade, your hand," said handsome Jack, drawing rein. "I know you to be a brave man. I find you to be truthful, aye, truthful verily to the back-bone! My hand but obeys the dictates of my heart, I pledge you on my honour for true friendship from now until the end."

"You do?—then blessings on you! Here's a fist, lad," Dick exclaimed, as he extended his hand, "honest by its own free will, but dishonest from dire necessity. If it ever proves traitorous to you in that moment, may it wither and become useless to its owner."

Handsome Jack wrung the hand that was extended to him in grateful silence, and they then proceeded at a gentle trot towards Harrow-on-the-Hill.

"So, so, gently," said Dick, reining in his steed, "if my ears be not at fault our friends are on the road."

"On my soul I hope they are!" said Jack in deep, stern tones; "the sooner we meet now, the better 'twill suit my complaint!"

"And mine," said Dick. "I was never very famous for long patience, and to-night, Jack, I am like yourself, eager for the fray. By my sword if 'twere not for a spree of dare devilry, the life of a highwayman would not be worth a rush. Hist!"

The clatter of horses' feet could now be plainly heard mingling with the sound of carriage-wheels.

"Look to the priming of your pistols."

"That I have already done," answered Handsome Jack.

"'Tis well," said Dick: "now, friend Jack, which do you choose? Here come the outriders — a couple of lubberly loons; see how they sit their horses! Like bags of peas jolting hither and thither with the animals every step. An' they be not drunk, by yon pale moon they are lovely riders. Come, Jack, choose you—take these outriders and leave me the carriage; more danger lurks inside those cushioned seats than in yon couple of mounte-

banks, were they armed to the teeth. I'll wager my share of this night's adventure on the truth of what I say."

"I choose the carriage," said Jack briefly.

"You do, then by my faith you've a bad taste. You'd better, on this your opening night, have chosen the less dangerous attempt; come, leave the carriage to me! But shout lustily at these boobies, and if they ride not hastily off at full speed I'll eat my shoes, buckles and all."

"Have I not told you I have a motive in this night adventure?"

"Yes," answered Dick carelessly; "but you havn't given me any very definite information as to what that motive is."

"It is revenge," answered Jack with startling earnestness, "revenge, deep and deadly! Lounging in yon advancing carriage is my bitterest foe—a man who has robbed me of wealth—has made a beggar of me; and not staying there his hellish malice, by lies as deep as they were sinister, has stigmatized the name of my dead mother with the loathsome name of frailty, and has dubbed me with the honourable name of bastard!"

"Just enough—to the very tittle—to rouse a brave man's blood," said Dick; "well, friend Jack, it shall be even as you say—the carriage yours, these outriders mine!"

"Thanks! — a thousand times," answered Jack. "See, they come!"

"Right wheel," said Jack, turning his horse round, the bridle of which he held between his teeth, whilst he grasped a pistol in each hand. "Come on! Let us dash past these outriders, I can then play a prank with them should they endeavour to harm you during your amiable work at yon carriage door."

This advice was obeyed to the very letter. The outriders had not passed the highwaymen twenty yards ere, at the stentorian voice of Handsome Jack, the carriage suddenly stopped. The inmate, secure in the comforting idea that he was perfectly save from all attacks of highwaymen or other disreputable persons disposed to knight errantry, threw open the window with a bang, and with sundry and divers oaths touching eyes, limbs, souls and bodies (and which for the sake of morality we do not set down here) demanded "What the d—l was the matter."

If none of my readers have experienced the delicious sensation on a dismal night, of having the cold barrel of a pistol in close contact to their noses, they really cannot conceive the celerity with which the unfortunate occupant withdrew his nose from the connection described, nor his rage and astonishment when, in spite of his outriders, a bold, determined voice gave vent to those ominous words—"your money or your life!"

"What, villain?"

"Your money or your life, Sir Charles," repeated Jack, in stern, distinct tones.

"I don't feel inclined to part with either to-night, rascal! and if you stand more from that window I'll rob the gallows of its due; for I'll shoot you like a dog."

It was well for Handsome Jack at this juncture that his horse moved a pace backward;

for a bright flash, followed by a sharp report, came from the interior of the carriage, and a ball, which grazed his ear in its flight, would inevitably have found a lodgment in his brain, but for that fortunate movement the animal made. Staggered for an instant by this unexpected attack, and unable for the same short space to curb the alarm of the spirited animal he bestrode, it was not until the smoke had blown away that Jack could ride again to the carriage, which he did calmly and boldly with a pistol in each hand.

"A good shot, Sir Charles, but a *leetle* too high. Now, Sir, if you do not instantly throw the contents of your carriage into the road, I'll blow your brains out; and mark me,—this is no idle threat—you are playing a desperate game with a desperate man."

While this was transpiring, Dick Flybynight was not inert. At the sound of his master's pistol one of the outriders imprudently turned. Dick knew if he withdrew his eye from them, even if it were but for one short minute, the game might be lost: he, therefore, bid the man, "stand!" The fellow, heedless of this injunction, was wheeling round.

"'Twill never do," muttered Dick between his clenched teeth, "to let this fellow get to his master's side." Impelled by these thoughts, he shouted,—"mind! if you move one step I'll fire!"

The man moved. True to his promise, Dick's extended pistol belched forth fire and smoke—true to its aim the fatal bullet sped its short but deadly race, and the stricken man, uttering a cry of anguish, was thrown violently from his prancing horse. The other outrider tried in vain to curb the mettlesome steed, which, true to its own blood, finding itself riderless, started forth in a frenzied gallop. The companion of the dead man—(for Dick's ball, too well directed, had hit "home")—by the frantic leaps of the fallen man's steed was dragged from the horse's back upon which he rode by the impetuosity of the first animal,—sprang in a desperate leap upon the affrighted animal's back and bravely rode for assistance.

In the meantime Handsome Jack was far from idle, the words he had given produced the required effect—a stout canvass bag, filled with a thousand glittering guineas, was handed to Handsome Jack. Jack dropped them as though the precious coins were valueless as the soil on which they fell.

"You have rings upon your fingers, Sir Charles, if I mistake me not, one which you received from a venerable uncle of your own, by due rights it belonged to that uncle's son; and I, on behalf of that son, do, quite disinterestedly, but most earnestly, claim that ring."

"You shall have my life first!" exclaimed Sir Charles.

"Nay, had I returned your compliment I should have had both. See you not these?" —and his pistols, not only well loaded, but upon full cock, were exposed to the other's view.

"Yes," answered Sir Charles, with a shudder; "and may the devil take me if I ever wish to see them again. Here, take them;" and he threw some half-dozen rings into the highwayman's outstretched hand.

"Many thanks," said Handsome Jack, with a low obeisance. "At the same time, Sir Charles, if report has not most irreverently belied you, you are in the habit of wearing about your person a diamond-hilted sword,—will you be pleased, with the complaisance that has governed your actions these last few minutes, to deliver that also."

A little oath came from the helpless Sir Charles's lips, as he passed the valuable weapon through the carriage window.

"It is well," said Jack, "and becometh me well, I verily believe," as he coolly buckled it around his own waist. "All I want now, my dear Sir Charles, is a good laced coat to set such an excellent ornament off to the best advantage, and as I am sure you would be deeply grieved if you found so goodly a weapon in so poor companionship,—I'll even trouble you to doff that coat."

"My coat! Zounds, man alive, you'd better have my skin!"

"Everything but your skin will suffice to night, my friend. I beg your pardon, my dear Sir Charles,—so, come! dallying is dangerous, again I bid you pass the coat."

"'Tis thine, rascal; and I only give it because I hope to see thee hung in it."

"So! so! a goodly wish, but ill-timed, inasmuch as it puts me in mind if I must go to the gallows, it is necessary for the honour and dignity of my family, I should appear there in genteel costume,—therefore will I trouble you for your vest, Sir Charles."

"Take it in the devil's name,—and now let me go! Drive on, you scoundrel, there," he shouted to the servant.

"Nay, we must not part thus shabbily. Coat and vest of superfine quality, in excellent keeping and of first-rate cut, I cannot sufficiently admire your superlative taste in choosing such elegant articles of apparel. Allow me to compliment you thereon,—at the same time, Sir Charles, I must beg you will favor me with your breeches, that I may have the suit complete."

"My breeches, you scoundrel, I'll see you ——."

"Gently, gently, good Sir Charles! The genteel society in which I have passed my life absolutely abhors swearing."

"But I shall catch my death of cold sirrah!"

"May be you will of cold lead an' you obey not my injuctions, — your trowsers, Sir Charles."

The shivering baronet crouched down from the extended pistol, and with hands trembling from the chilly night air and the mingled feelings of rage and excitement, unloosed his nether garments and confided them to the care of the avaricious highwayman.

"Good!" said Handsome Jack, parenthetically. "Now sir, your boots and hose."

"I shall catch my death of cold as it is, you scoundrel."

"Your boots and hose," repeated Handsome Jack, in fierce decisive tones. "Come, Sir Charles, no dallying—out with them."

Sir Charles passed them out.

"I have but one more favour to ask you, sir."

"Speak it, in the devil's name, and let me go!" said the trembling baronet, his teeth chattering from the incessant cold.

"Your shirt."

"My shirt!" cried the astounded baronet, "I should think you have enough without that,—come, come, you are joking!"

"Not I, faith!" returned Handsome Jack; "I never jest, and being in an unusually serious mood to-night, I beg you will not attempt to jest with me,—indeed it would be barbarous, for in the new appearance which, thanks to your fine clothes, I shall now make in the metropolis,—would it not be extremely absurd in me to go forth in any but fine linen? Your silence proves the truth of what I utter, therefore I again and for the last time request your shirt."

"Never!" exclaimed Sir Charles. "Send me home naked to be the laughing stock of every fool in my house:—I'll see you d——d first!"

"Hollo, Jack," said Dick, who having succeeded in winging one man and frightening the coachman, and another outrider away, now came up to his companion. "How goes luck, lad, won't that bloat shell out?"

"No, my dear fellow, he's very obstinate."

"Is he by God!" said Dick, "hold my bridle, Jack, I'll fetch him out!" and suiting the action to the word, Dick plunged into the carriage and dragged the wretched baronet into the road. A loud and boisterous fit of laughter almost took Dick's breath away, as seeing the whole joke in the instant he caught sight of the baronet's really pitiable plight.

"Ha! ha! ha! He! he! he! Oh, Jack, you devil, this is rich!',

"Off with his shirt, Dick," shouted Jack.

"Now, sir, doff that yard of linen — you won't? By the powers I'll make you then; since words are empty and valueless, s'pose we try whipcord—take that! and that!" and Dick, suiting the action to the word, cut him sharply with his whip at every exclamation.

The Baronet uttered a long yell of anguish, and tearing the shirt from his back with frantic eagerness, he fled like the wind, urged on by one extra cut from Dick's sharp lash.

The two highwaymen burst into a loud roar of laughter at their victim's discomfiture, and 'twas full five minutes ere their shouts subsided even to a titter.

"Oh Jack—oh Jack!" was all Dick could utter as the shouts of boisterous merriment left his lips.

Gradually quieting at last, he turned to business—to cut the traces of the baronet's horses and set the animals free, was his first act. A sharp cut sent them gallopping away far from the scene of action.

"So far, so good!" cried Dick, "Now, Jack, for a gallop to town, the sooner we quit this place the better, there will be the devil's own row over this adventure;" and saying these words, the agile highwayman vaulted into his saddle.

"Gently a moment, Dick, there is a money-bag hereabouts. Ah! I have it; and full weighty it seems too; now lad," he said, as soon as he had fastened both them and the Baronet's clothes securely to the horse's back, "I'm your man—forward."

"Hark! I hear horses' feet—the fool has raised an alarm, we are followed."

"We are!" said Jack, his blood fired by his successes on this his first night on the road. "Then we'll give them a race for it, come on!"

"I'm following," shouted Dick, "but it grows too late for a ride to town; no, Jack, we must not try it; but quickly forward, we'll give them the slip, and roost to-night at our country house at Highgate; a cross country ride will do us good—forward, lad!"

"Country house," muttered Jack.

"Ay, sir, and a right good one too," answered Dick. "It's a private branch of the 'Chapel,' another mystery connected with our gallant fraternity.

CHAPTER III.

MADAME CHARLOTTE SHOWS HERSELF IN HER TRUE COLOURS, AS DO ALSO CAPTAIN M'CLEANE AND JENNY DIVER.

IMMEDIATELY after the departure of Dick Fly-bynight and Handsome Jack, the gang filed off to their different chambers in the "Chapel," with the exception of M'Cleane and Jenny Diver, they both proceeding by another private route to the hotel portion of the extensive building, the one to enjoy a social chat with Madame Charlotte, the keeper of the establishment, and the other in accordance to her duty as the last new comer, to wait upon that lady.

She was a portly dame of some forty summers or thereabouts, with a fair complexion, pleasant countenance, and a pair of bright roving eyes. Her reception of the handsome Captain was most unequivocal, and showed the friendly footing upon which they stood.

"Ha, James!" she exclaimed immediately she entered her private snuggery, throwing her plump round arms around his neck as she spoke, and impressing a loud kiss upon his lips, "I am delighted to see you! How late you are, my love, I thought I should have had to go to rest all alone this night!"

"It has been quite unavoidable, my dear Lizzy," said M'Cleane, returning the embrace with warmth. "I have had a sharp tussle to-night, and have been most infernally annoyed, for a case of foul treachery has been exposed to-night."

"So Betty was telling me," said Madame Charlotte, "and not to my great surprise, M'Cleane, for I have had my fears of that man for a long time; but I am astonished, James, utterly astonished, you should have let him loose. Where is he? do you know?

"Yes, my love," answered M'Cleane, "he is safely caged in Newgate by this time, and there he'll lay, sweetheart, until he leaves it for Tyburn Tree."

"I'm right glad to hear it," answered Madame Charlotte, "and cannot sufficiently praise your ingenuity in capturing him so gloriously. It is fit such knaves should be hung in the halters they weave themselves. Gipsy Betty tells me, James, you obtained your information from our new assistant—her whom you christened so appropriately to-night Jenny Diver."

"By my faith 'tis a capital name for her; she's a shrewd, clever girl, and, if she lives long enough, will be a gem of the first water. She's devillishly pretty."

"Pretty! do you think so?" said Madame Charlotte, carelessly.

"I think, Lizzy?" answered M'Cleane, "by my hopes I got past that at one single glance; I call her handsome—devillish handsome!"

"And you'd have no objection to revel in her beauties?" said Madame Charlotte, with a peculiar glance at M'Cleane.

"Not the least in the world, Lizzy, dear, if it can be comfortably managed."

"I, faith! out upon you for a doubter, have I not always done these little affairs for you to your satisfaction?"

"You have, my dear Lizzy, and I owe you an endless amount of gratitude for being so excellent a caterer for my pleasure; but, in this case, I fear for your success.'

"Fear!" cried Madame Charlotte, laughing merrily. "It is the first time I have ever heard the redoubtable Captain M'Cleane confess himself capable of such weakness. Fear! what, you who can meet your man on the road to fear a woman in a little love dalliance; fie on you, M'Cleane, I blush for your manhood. Never fear; one dose of this little white powder, dissolved in a glass of wine, and she is thine to work love's charm upon. Say, is it agreed?"

"Nay, gently, Lizzy, there is a fire in that girl's dark eye I love and respect in spite of myself, a nobility of nature by which my better feelings are roused, and I cannot but think 'twould be a dastardly act to do a wrong to one so good and beautiful as she is."

"As you like, M'Cleane," said Madame Charlotte; "mind, I was seeking your gratification, not my own."

"I know that, and feel grateful for it, Lizzy; but, in this case, I feel as though I could not sacrifice one so brave and spirited to a fit of licentiousness. No, no, Lizzy! much as I should glory in such a prize—much as I should love to have her throbbing breast meet mine,—those ruby lips in heavenly connection, I cannot do it this time, I must forego that pleasure."

"For my own part I see no *must* in the matter, you can pluck this flower—say the word—it is thine."

"That I would you well know," said the Captain, and I only hesitate from the fear of making this Jenny Diver an enemy for life."

"Tush man! with all your boasted experience I see you have no knowledge of woman. That a few tears for nature's sake would be shed at first, I grant ye; but are there not ways of soothing such griefs? Kiss them away, man—swear you love her—promise to marry her, and if she jump not at the offer, and in her joy at possessing so great a gallant as yourself, forgive you for the trick you have played her, I'll eat my head."

M'Cleane shook his head dubiously.

"What! you doubt me, do you?" asked Madame Charlotte; "well come—we'll prove it!"

"But I say no!" exclaimed M'Cleane.

"And mean yes all the time—why you are even now shaking with uncontrolable desire. I know your motive well, man. Come, we will try this experiment. This powder is perfectly harmless, and will produce only a deep sleep. We will invite her in to take a glass of wine and have a friendly chat, as soon as the powder shows its somniferous properties I will leave the room. If you can then withstand the temptation, I'll give you courage for more chastity to-night than ever before I believed your benedict breast could hold."

She arose when she had done speaking and rang for Jenny Diver. That bell met with no response—again Madame Charlotte applied her hand vigorously to it, and at the same instant Jenny entered, and dropping a profound curtsey, said in a tone full of ripe, rich melody—

"Did you ring, Madame?"

"Yes; come in," said Madame Charlotte, in her most friendly tone, and with a most assuming smile; "both the Captain and myself are so well pleased with your conduct, we desire nothing better than a glass of wine and an hours' social chat with you."

"But the hour is late, Madame," said Jenny, "and after the events of the day, I feel tired, worn, and dispirited."

"That is what the Captain foresaw, my pretty damsel, and hence his generous invitation. Come, we can take no excuse—you need be under no apprehension for the morning; the hour that will suit you to rise, will suit me to receive your services."

"I am deeply grateful," said Jenny, advancing as she spoke, to the table, and placing herself confidently between the highwayman and Madame.

"Well done!" exclaimed M'Cleane, joyfully, for he was entranced by the brilliancy of her beauty. "Come, Lizzy, fill each a glass of sparkling Burgundy!'

"You shall have your wish, Captain," said Madame, rising, and reaching down a bottle of Burgundy and three glasses, into one of which totally unperceived both by M'Cleane and Jenny as she thought, she dropped the narcotic.

"Come!" said M'Cleane, rising, an example that was followed by the other. "Let us drink success to the cause!"

"Success to the cause!" added Jenny, enthusiastically, but still without lifting her glass to her lips; Madame Charlotte suspended hers when she saw Jenny so act, and laughed inquiringly at her.

"Will you favour me with a rusk?" said Jenny.

"Most certainly," answered the complaisant Madame; "pardon my stupidity in forgetting it."

As Madame turned away, Jenny, with the rapidity of lightning, changed the glasses, passing hers to Madame and taking Madame's unto herself. So quickly and cleverly was this change effected, that M'Cleane, although looking on, noticed not the movement. The rusk was brought: Jenny curtsied as she received it.

"Come, the toast!" exclaimed M'Cleane, "the toast! and mind its heel taps. Success to the cause."

"Both Madame and Jenny repeated the words, and the next instant the three wine glasses were set down in an inverted position to show they were empty.

Madame's eyes sparkled again at the supposed success of her scheme, and, lolling back in her easy chair she seemed prepared for a gossip. The potent power was but a short time effecting its change. Her eyes closed, her breath came more hardly drawn, her hands fell listlessly by her side, and Madame Charlotte was in a deep and profound sleep. M'Cleane looked fixedly at Jenny, and from the girl's sparkling eyes he half guessed the secret of the mistake.

Anxious to satisfy himself, however, he approached Madame, and shook her for the purpose of recalling her to herself; but Madame was wrapped in a sleep so deep it was a counterfeit of death.

"This is strange!—d——d strange!" muttered M'Cleane, "what in the devil's name ails the woman."

"A lethargy, sir," said Jenny, rising from her chair and drawing herself to her full height, "to which she would for a base, treacherous purpose have doomed me; but which, thanks to yon key-hole and a quick ear—yon glass and a quick hand, have fallen most deservedly upon herself."

"You know all then," said M'Cleane, a deep crimson covering his cheeks.

"Yes, all," answered Jenny, sternly.

"And can you forgive me my share in this base conspiracy—can you pardon me for the presumption—for the folly I have been guilty of in heeding such thoughts," said M'Cleane, with emotion.

"Yes," answered Jenny, "I can, because more honourable than yon sleeping beauty you would have spared me.

"Thanks! thanks! a thousand thanks!" said M'Cleane, falling upon one knee and pressing burning kisses upon the hand of Jenny Diver. "I am to be pitied," he said, after a pause, "for I have loved you—madly loved you from the first moment I beheld you. The desire to possess you was gnawing at my heart—I was burning to possess you, and such was the tide of passion, as Heaven is my judge, I could not resist the temptation.

"And I, too, have loved you, M'Cleane," said Jenny in a gentle whisper, "yes! the same mercurial power that has awakened your wishes has also run through my veins."

"What do I hear?" said the amazed M'Cleane, almost beside himself with this unexpected news.

"That I am thine," answered Jenny, as she threw herself into his arms and pressed warm kisses upon his handsome brow, "thine, thine, for ever!

"This is joy unutterable," said M'Cleane, as he caught her ardently to his breast, "I am beside myself—almost mad with joy. But are you indeed mine—willingly mine?"

"Yes, willingly," answered the girl, pressing many warm kisses upon his handsome face. "For oh! M'Cleane, though you may think lightly hereafter of me for this freedom——"

"I swear to you no!" exclaimed M'Cleane vehemently. "No! on my soul."

"Yet I do assure you," she continued, "the force of my deep love is uncontrollable."

"Then you so love me?" asked the Captain, almost doubting his senses, so totally unexpected was this declaration.

"Yes, M'Cleane—dear M'Cleane, I do!—I love you because you are good and generous—because in opposition to that woman's seductive counsellings, you would have sacrificed your own gratification, rather than have injured me. Yes, M'Cleane, I love you for that dearly."

M'Cleane wound his arms about the supple form of the girl as she so confidently reclined herself upon his bosom, and kissed her in his fit of transport again and again, until their very lips in that ecstatic time seemed glued together.

"Release your hold for a moment, love," said Jenny; "my heart throbs so violently I scarce can bear it."

M'Cleane loosened his arms, but still kept the pretty one reclining upon his knee.

"Are you frightened, Jenny, dear," asked M'Cleane in a whisper.

"Frightened of you, dear M'Cleane!" exclaimed Jenny; "oh, no! But for maiden timidity you can surely make some allowance."

The only allowance M'Cleane made, was to strain Jenny Diver more closely to his breast, and to press innumerable kisses upon her ruby lips.

At this moment Jenny started, and said, "Saw you not that? Madame Charlotte revives:" this supposition was, however, an erroneous one, the potent powder, true to its work, was stealing over the organs of the sleeper, and Madame Charlotte, with a deep sigh, fell forward from her chair upon the rug insensible.

"The mischief she had in store for you, Jenny dear, has fallen upon herself."

"In such a case, Captain, said Jenny, with a wicked smile, "you cannot do better than take the same advantage of her, that under a different phase, I scarce dare say you would have taken of me."

"By all that's good, Jenny, I would not, if I could resist, but I should indeed fear to trust myself, you are so attractive—so beautiful—'tis heaven itself to be encircled in your arms;" and he advanced with an impassioned look and gesture towards her.

"And to lie in hers?" said Jenny, levelling her finger at the fallen woman.

"Has been pleasant enough heretofore, but in comparison with you, is as the thistle to the rose!"

Jenny noted the words with a smile of triumph; and in an instant a brightening glance like a flash of light, came from the depths of her jet black eyes. It was a look full of love and desire!

"Madame Charlotte destined that couch for my resting-place for the night, did she not?"

"She did," answered M'Cleane.

"But I think she did not mean to repose upon that rug herself—do you think she did, M'Cleane?"

"Not a bit of it!" answered the Captain.

"Then why not remove her to her bed—third parties in love affairs can always be spared."

M'Cleane's heart beat tumultuously, as, in reply to the arch hint, he looked earnestly into the girl's face, which was now suffused with a slight blush, a blush which added fresh charms to that fascinating countenance. A long—long kiss of passion in all its intensity followed, and again he clasped her to his bosom.

At that moment the lovers rioted and revelled in delirous excitement: heart throbbed against heart, and told tales of love,—although for a few moments the tongue of each was silent.

"Shall I ring for some of the people to remove our snoring friend?" asked the young girl.

"Not for worlds," replied M'Cleane, and tearing himself from Jenny's ardent embrace he rose, and lifting Madame Charlotte from the rug with as much ease as though she had been an infant, carried her into his bed-room, and then returned on the wings of love to his new charmer.

No. 3.

With all a pretty woman's artifice, Jenny Diver had, during the brief interval which elapsed between M'Cleane's leaving the apartment and his returning to it, resorted to some of those little wiles which seldom fail to snare the heart for whose capture they are brought into requisition.

On a luxuriously cushioned sofa, reclined the bewitching creature, her face radiant with smiles, and her jet-black eyes flashing with intense desire: her raven hair, parted on her alabaster brow, flowed like glossy waves from her forehead, polished and pure as Parian marble, and streamed in luxuriant clustering ringlets down her swan-like neck, until at length they rested on two panting breasts, which rivalled in colour the snow on some mountain's summit, when faintly gilded by the rosy dawn. Her dress was low—so that nearly the entire of her magnificent bust was exposed to view; less of it indeed was concealed by drapery than by those ebony-coloured tresses which dallied with the bewitching maiden's charms.

On one faultlessly shaped arm and white and delicately moulded hand the girl's head reclined; her eyes were filled with a delicious langour, and from between her half-parted and pouting lips, behind which teeth of a pearly hue appeared, her breath exhaled in fragrant sighs. A foot of fairy-like shape and dimensions, and an exquisitely turned ancle, with the gently upward-swelling portion of a leg which suggested ideas of still more tempting and concealed charms, peeped coquettishly from beneath her quilted petticoat. To Captain M'Cleane's eyes, as they rested on her perfect form as he re-entered the room, Jenny appeared angelic indeed.

Throwing himself on the couch beside the willing syren, M'Cleane, passing his arm around her taper waist, drew her close to his side.

"Madame Charlotte," said he, in a voice quivering with excitement, "is safely enough bestowed,—and now dearest Jenny for love and happiness."

Nothing loth, Jenny reclined her head on her gallant's shoulder, and for a few seconds the breath of the lovers came short and quick. Growing bolder, as the intensity of his desire increased, M'Cleane's hand wandered upon the deliciously soft, yet firm breasts of the girl; as he dived into their charming recesses, and pressed the rosy tips of those hills of pleasure, the hot blood ran like lava through his veins, and one long burning kiss from Jenny proclaimed his hour of triumph to be near.

Nor was Jenny Diver less susceptible to the influences of that universal master-passion—love. The pressure of M'Cleane's hands on those lovely and delicate globes, which until now had never known the touch of man, sent a thrill of pleasurable delight through every fibre of her sensitive frame. A delicious langour stole over her, and her large dark eyes gleamed with passionate fire. A sensation, as delicious as it was novel, bound her as with a voluptuous charm, and when M'Cleane proceeded still further in his endearments, she resisted not, but willingly yielding to his ardour, sank unresistingly into his eager arms.

* * * * * *

"My beloved James!" faintly murmured the now somewhat agitated girl; and again and again she imprinted burning kisses on the brow and lips of her lover, who was by no means slow in returning with interest her caresses.

"Mine—only mine!" breathed M'Cleane into the girl's charmed ear, and again they reclined upon the capacious couch, her warm breath fanning his flushed cheek, whilst his hand wandered amidst the mazes of her luxuriant and now somewhat dishevelled tresses.

And thus, in amorous dalliance, two hours flew, scarcely heeded by,—for Madame Charlotte had by no means over-rated the power of the narcotic with which she had impregnated the wine. Still, much to the delight of the happy pair, who now seemed all the world to each other, the buxom and blue-eyed keeper of the establishment lay wrapped in profound sleep,—and from her prolonged nap she even now gave no intimation of waking.

"Madame Charlotte is an adept in her art," remarked M'Cleane, as he pointed to the apartment, from whence came forth a very audible proof of the sleeper's state. "Had you taken the dose, dearest Jenny, my happiness would have been a tithe of that with which your waking moments have blessed me. To my thinking, the possession of a fortress which surrenders at discretion is far more to be prized than that one which is taken whilst the sentinels sleep!"

Jenny Diver blushed as she replied: "And the conqueror likely to retain a more exclusive and permanent possession."

Whilst engaged in conversation of this kind, the snoring of Madame Charlotte ceased, and the rustling of that lady's hooped petticoat was heard. M'Cleane and Jenny exchanged meaning glances, and in a moment or two afterwards the matron entered the room.

Women have sharper eyes and quicker perceptions than creatures of the masculine gender. So it is not to be marvelled at therefore, although pretty Jenny—the little minx! pursed up her ruby lips, and looked as modest as she possibly could, that the sagacious keeper of the "Chapel" saw at a glance that the Captain had added another to the list of those whom his manly person and noble bearing had fascinated.

"Why, Lizzy!" remarked the Captain, "you have had a most convenient nap."

"Something," chimed in Jenny, maliciously, "must have ailed Madame Charlotte—perhaps the wine disagreed with you;—for my own part I have taken several glasses and found that it rather kept me awake than sent me to sleep."

The truth of the matter, however, flashed on the lady's mind, but she said nothing; and giving the Captain a kiss, she slapped him heartily on the back, as though in approval of some accomplished feat, a movement which was perfectly understood by all present.

An elegant supper consisting of the most recherché viands, and of the richest wines, was now served up—after the luxurious enjoyment of which, at a sign from M'Cleane the elder of the ladies retired, which, sooth to say, she did not much relish the idea of doing: but in that place the Captain commanded all, and was always obeyed. She had fondly hoped, as we have seen in the commencement of this chapter, that her bed that night would not have been companionless—but she was for once doomed to disappointment, for she occupied a companionless bed—and the reader will easily guess with whom Captain M'Cleane passed the night.

We hear every day of our lives words of condemnation or censure uttered against those of the stronger sex, by whose machinations, the fairest specimens of humanity are induced to quit the paths of virtue and abandon themselves to sensual pursuits; but it strangely enough happens that not a syllable of blame is ever breathed against those women, who by their wiles entangle many a manly heart. With all due respect to the female sex, we declare it to be our firm belief that in multitudes of the instances of *crim. con.* and seduction, which afford material for actions in our law courts, the lady performs the part of Potiphar's wife—and her paramour that of Joseph, in part only it is true, for that virtuous young gentleman fled. But, alas! there are few Josephs in the present day,—although there may be quite as many Potiphar's as of yore. It is no trifle to slight a woman: some one has said that she is worse than the devil to have to do with—for resist the evil one, and he will fly *from* you—but resist a woman, and she will fly *at* you!

"Earth has no rage like love to hatred turned,
And hell no fury like a woman scorned."

Our fair Jenny's advances, it has been seen, were met with anything but coldness, so that we need not trouble ourselves for the safety of M'Cleane, to whom the dark-eyed flower girl's amours were more than welcome.

CHAPTER IV.

THE COUNTRY HOUSE AT HIGHGATE.

LEAVING Jenny Diver in the arms of her gallant—Madame Charlotte pondering, not without a tinge of jealousy, on the effects which the charms of the new-comer might have on the affections of M'Cleane as regarded herself; and all the other members of the gang, excepting those whose special duty it was to keep watch and ward, asleep in their different dormitories, we must now follow the fortunes of Dick Flybynight and Handsome Jack, whom we left at the close of the second chapter on their way to Highgate.

It was evident, as Dick had intimated, that the party who had just been relieved of his bag of guineas, and stripped to the skin also by Handsome Jack, had, either himself, or by means of his outriders, given the alarm; for the stillness of the night was only broken by the dull, distant sounds of the feet of several horses on the high road—sounds which became every moment clearer and more distinct, to which, before many moments had elapsed, the shoutings of men were added.

Turning into a cross-road which led by a circuitous way from the coach-road to Finchley Common, the highwaymen, Dick Flybynight taking the lead, proceeded at a hand gallop for two or three miles, and then drawing rein, remained for a moment in the deep shade caused by the over-arching branches of a huge oak tree, and listened intensely in order to ascertain whether their pursuers were on their track.

Not a sound, however, fell upon their anxiously attentive ears, except the sighing of the breezes of early morning through the gnarled and mighty branches overhead, or occasionally the melancholy hooting of an owl from the ruins of an old mill at a little distance from them.

Satisfied that, for the present at least, they had baffled those who doubtless had despatched parties towards Harrow-on-the-Hill, as well as towards London, in order to intercept them should they have ventured to return to town with their booty, one of the knights of the road—Dick Flybynight burst into a hearty laugh, at the recollection of the ridiculous figure cut by Sir James Town, when in a state of almost utter nudity, he fled howling with pain from the well-applied lash.

Handsome Jack, however, did not share this time in his mirth—and as they resumed their ride, at a slower pace than before, his silence was so profound that it at length attracted the attention of his companion, and we may add, his suspicions also, for robbers are ever apprehensive of mischief in some shape, and it is a part of the business of their lives to guard against it.

"By St. Nicholas! Jack, and that saintly old gentleman, it is said, hath a great regard for the brave members of our fraternity, thou seemest as dull as though thou were preparing to dance a hornpipe in fetters at Tyburn! Cheer up, man, in God's name! Dost repent of thy first perilous exploit on the road? If so, Dick Flybynight here offers thee his silence on the subject, and the liberty to leave the profession so lately embraced—taking also half of the booty."

Handsome Jack bit his lips with vexation, and then replied:—

"I should have thought, Dick, that I had this evening, in my first venture, afforded you sufficient proof that fear is a stranger to my heart; and if you suppose that I am anxious to quit the company of which I was made a member last night, you are greatly mistaken. I have risked all in this venture, and am resolved to stand 'the hazard of the die.' No, no! other—far different feelings occupied my mind, and caused that silent sadness which (and Jack's lip curled with ineffable scorn as he spoke) you have mistaken for cowardice and vaccilation."

In an instant Dick Flybynight stretched out his hand, as if by way of deprecating any further intention of misconceiving, and so wounding the sensitive feelings of his brother highwayman; for, though Dick by practice was a robber, and since the last rencounter—a murderer also—possessed a frankness of nature which would not allow him for a moment to harbour a suspicion of one, who so boldly asserted his freedom from dishonourable motives.

"Pardon me, Jack," exclaimed Dick, eagerly, "I meant not to impute to you aught base or mean. Tush, man! I might well have considered, after what you revealed last night in the 'Chapel,' that the very sight of that villain Townley was sufficient to stir your bile. Egad! 'twas no bad joke either to make him the subject of your maiden effort!" and the highwayman burst once more into a cheerful peal of laughter.

It is scarcely necessary to state that the proffered hand of Dick was cordially grasped in amity by Handsome Jack, and then the pair fell once more into easy conversation.

By this time they had arrived at the edge of that well-known shooting-ground for highwaymen, Finchley Common;—a place which even to this day is frequently the scene of depredations. The gay, dashing, and reckless highwayman, to be sure, has long since ceased, on his blood-mare to gallop over its surface—and carriages are driven fearlessly by its boundaries. The gibbet, too, no longer looms gloomily against the red evening sky or the grey east—its rattling burden swinging, and its iron work creeking, as shrill gusts sway the bleaching carcass to and fro: all these things have passed away; and the solitary footpad alone ventures there now-a-days on his predatory excursions. Even these are but few, and their victims, instead of being lords or ladies, are for the most part feeble old men, or forlorn washerwomen.

A faint streak of grey which appeared in the eastern horizon—the crowing of early cocks, from their roosts in the yards of farmhouses round about, as well as other rural sounds, warned the two highwaymen that if they wished to reach Highgate undiscovered by any of the rustics who would soon be on their way to the fields, they must hasten onward. They therefore put spurs to their now somewhat jaded steeds, and before long, after again taking, as a measure of precaution, a circuitous route, they reached Hampstead Heath, in an unfrequented part of which Dick Flybynight hinted at the necessity of their again halting for a few minutes, in order that he might reconnoitre, and ascertain whether the way to the "Country House," as he had before termed it, was clear.

Alighting from their horses, they led them into a grove formed by a plantation of young trees, where they could be effectually concealed from observation, and tethered them to the branches. Dick Flybynight then requested Handsome Jack to advance with him to the edge of the copse, and there remain out of sight until his return. He also gave him an injunction on no account to stir from the place until he saw him coming back—and then to release the horses and lead them out; he went forth slowly and with watchful eyes, upon the yet dimly-lighted heath, which was then far more abundantly dotted with trees, and less with human habitations than now; for on the spot to which this conducted the reader, instead of there being such as Handsome Jack and Dick Flybynight, pic-nic parties enjoy themselves; artists quietly sit and sketch; donkeys gallop by with laughing girls or screaming children on their backs; and splendid structures are situated. Such are the inevitable results of time and change.

Left alone, for the first time since the hour when he so opportunely saved the life of Captain M'Cleane, by interposing his practised weapon when the latter was almost overpowered by the resolute person from whom a large amount of property had been forcibly taken, Handsome Jack began seriously to reflect on the singular and very unsafe position which he at present occupied. For years before, and until a very recent period, he had moved in the most glittering and exclusive circles which the Goddess of Fashion chooses to monopolize as her empire. Gifted with a person rich in its attractions—attractions which then, even, should not principle guide their possessor, would have been a passport to the gorgeous halls and glittering saloons even of royalty itself; he also might,

had he so chosen, have boasted of rare powers of mind. But it must be added that he was gay, rash, and impetuous, strong in passion, self-willed, and self-indulgent. There was not a gay cavalier of the day amongst those of higher, as well as those of lower rank than his own, who did not look up to Sir Richard ——— as the "glass of fashion and the mould of form;" and every hour the glances of admiration which flashed from many a brilliant eye and the smiles which dimpled many a bewitching cheek. No party was considered complete did not Sir Richard ——— make his appearance — no elegant trifle was admired unless he stamped it with the seal of his approbation. He was, in one respect, the Count D'Orsay of a former day; for he was universally allowed to be one of the most accomplished arbiters of taste, and masters of opinion. And he was rich, too—immensely rich.

Perhaps, after all, his wealth was the great key to his immense popularity; for with all his manifold attractions, there was that about him which repelled more than it attracted. Contradiction he would not brook; and when most courtly he was most imperious. His sensuality in the matter of women, especially, was very great, and many a polished town belle, as well as many a simple village maid, had tested the faithfulness of Sir Richard ———, and found it to have evaporated with the last promise, and the last kiss. Such was, or rather had been, the man who now leans gloomily against the trunk of a tree on the heath of the pretty suburban village of Hampstead, awaiting the return of Dick Flybynight.

His arms were folded on his capacious chest, his legs crossed, and his eyes bent on the earth as he mused.

"And, so, it has come to *this*," he muttered to himself from between his firmly-set teeth, "to *this*," and, as he repeated the two latter words, he ground his iron-shod heel into the soft moss, as if the green tuft had been the spot occupied by some mortal enemy, and the primrose which grew from it, had been that enemy himself. "But yesterday," he continued, although stripped of my inheritance, and proclaimed a *thing* in whose veins base blood ran, I was, at least, safe from the Lion of the Laws—I was not a criminal: at the very worst, a lodging in the Fleet and an exclusion from the cursed circles of dissipation would have been all that could have befallen me; but *now*," and the strong man shed tears, which, for worlds, he would have let none else see; now I must be content to be a fugitive and a vagabond; ever to be in peril, never to dare my fellow-creatures gaze; and live in constant fear, never to lie down again to refreshing slumber, never to rise from my bed with that hope of success imparted by honest industry, and always to see my Future bounded by the distant prospect of TYBURN TREE!"

Did no other thoughts than these chase each other on that still morning, through his heated and bewildered brain? Yes! Well he knew that at that moment, in all likelihood, one for whom he felt the only *real affection* his roving heart had ever known, was thinking of him whom she so dearly loved to call *her* Richard.

This was the pang which afflicted him the most of all—which nearly maddened him; indeed, when he remembered the desperate career he had but a few hours since commenced.

Would she—his gentle and affectionate Emilia—ever consent to be the bride of one who had entered into a compact with law-defying men—with one who, himself had by main force stolen another's gold? Would *she* be inclined to palliate his crime, because he had been previously wronged by the man whom he had robbed? He knew in his innermost heart that much, and intensely as she was attached—devotedly attached to him—she *would not.* Well aware was he that her pure mind would shrink from an alliance with aught dishonourable. She might have pardoned and pitied his follies, but she was too pure to look with an eye of love upon his crimes.

All at once he started, as if a serpent had rested its fascinating eye upon him; his countenance turned of an ashy paleness, and large beaded drops of perspiration stood on his broad and high forehead. For a moment he firmly believed that the law's vengeance, swiftly following on the heels of crime, had already overtaken him, for he felt a hand heavily laid on his shoulder. A chuckling laugh, however, and the voice of Dick Flybynight dispelled his fears, although his knees quivered again, and his heart still beat to an unpleasantly quick time.

"What! musing on the fate of yonder worm which is just crawling out, poor fool! to be the prey of the first sparrow which eyes it, instead of being a vigilant sentinel! Why, Jack! after all you seem to have watched, the Philistines might have been on us: had a strolling countryman surprised you thus, the matter might have been serious, friend," said Dick.

"I was not exactly thinking of the worm," replied the now relieved Jack, "but now you have mentioned it, I might have foreseen in its fate something similar to what my own may one day be. There are beaks who prey upon men as well as upon worms, Dick! I may as well confess that I fancied when you touched me that ——"

"The rope was round your throttle! was that it?" gaily remarked Flybynight. "Damn it man! a goblet of clear canary will wash away such qualms as these. But, come, get some more colour into those ghostly cheeks, and don't shake so much; no man ever exhibited his pretty person on the tripple-tree of Tyburn on the occasion of his first robbery! See, the sky begins to redden, and now no time must be lost in gaining our quarters.

Again mounting their horses, they, with extreme caution, left their place of temporary concealment, and, avoiding the open ground, proceeded along secluded lanes and through hollows between the rising portions of the heath, towards Highgate. Several times they were compelled to turn from their path in order to escape the notice of troops of ploughmen and milkmaids, who thus early were going blythely to the scene of their peaceful labours, forming a striking contrast as it referred to their feelings and occupations, to those of the two daring men who were skulking through bye-paths to a place of secret shelter.

At no great distance from the spot where the Gate-house in the pretty village of Highgate now stands, was situated the private branch of the Thieves' "Chapel" of Long Acre; or, we should rather say, one of the offshoots of that infamous place which, itself, was the headquarters of that extensive gang, whose organization was so complete that they almost defied detection, and laughed at the laws. The "Chapel" was the centre—the great rendezvous—the seat, so to speak, of government; and the metropolis of the nefarious community, places, such as that to which we are about to accompany Dick Flybynight and Handsome Jack, being used as refuges when, as in the present instance, an immediate return to town after a robbery might be thought unadvisable, or when it was deemed necessary for a member of the community to retire for a time from practice until some affair in which he had been recognised as an actor should have blown over. In nearly all these "country houses" there were apartments furnished in the most sumptuous manner, for they occasionally served the purposes of voluptuous or riotous pleasure, as well as that which the gang considered to be business.

To allay suspicion as far as possible, the "Country House" at Highgate was considered to be, and indeed was, used as a hostelry; this was absolutely necessary; as houses of public entertainment were places of great resort, and parties going to or coming from them would be less likely to excite dangerous attention and curiosity, than had they been seen to visit or depart from establishments of a private class.

Externally, it presented the usual appearance of a village, or road-side inn of second or third-rate respectability. Between the trunks of two lofty elms which stood in the front of the building, swung a sign on which, beneath the rude representation of a lion of a remarkably sanguinary hue, the handy-work of some country artist, was an inscription which informed travellers that within might be obtained "GODE ENTERTAYNMENTE FOR MANN & HORS." A rustic porch, with benches, afforded a lounging place for idlers; and on each side of the door was a diamond-paned window, one of which admitted to the large kitchen, and the other to a parlour especially kept for the use of the better sort of customers. Before the inn was that usual addition, at the time we are writing of, a bowling-green; at one extremity of which a May-pole, on which still hung hoops with the blackened garlands of the last May day, hanging like melancholy memorials of departed pastimes. The building which adjoined the hostelry on one side was a large uninhabited, and very old-fashioned mansion, in which—so the good folk of Highgate asserted—years and years ago a foul murder had been perpetrated. Its grimy windows, many of them broken, and all stained by time and curtained by cobwebs; its door, battered and blistered by the weather; its steps, over-run with weeds, and its neglected patch of ground, all proclaimed that it had long ceased to be tenanted. It had a painted-house sort of look; and the superstitious rustics of the place told a hundred tales of horror connected with it. On the other side of the inn was a lane, which separated it from other dwellings.

Of the interior of the place we shall presently have occasion to speak.

Just as the clock of Highgate church struck the hour of five, our two highwaymen rode slowly up the lane at the side of the hostelry, and stopped at the door of the stable yard. Producing a pass-key from his pocket, Dick Flybynight opened it, and immediately afterwards both he and Handsome Jack were in a place of safety.

The same key admitted them into the stable itself; where they disposed of their horses, using all precaution as to silence.

"Follow me," said Dick, in a low voice to his companion; "and whatever you may see, say nothing—I know full well you will fear naught. You will see a rather different company here to that you were introduced to last night at the 'Chapel.'"

The inmates of the hostelry appeared to be buried in profound slumber as the two highwaymen crossed the yard in the direction of the uninhabited house. A low wall separated the inn-yard from what was once the garden of the mansion; this they leaped, and in another minute were descending a flight of steps which led to the lower portion of the building.

With the butt-end of his whip, Dick Flybynight pressed firmly against the head of one of the nails which studded the door, to select which particular one he had recourse to the light afforded by his phosphorous box. The nail yielded to the force applied, and sank into the woodwork. Not a sound was heard, for some few minutes afterwards, but then, a sliding panel in the roof of the low porch overhead was cautiously drawn aside, and a voice, no part of the owner of which could be seen, in a low tone challenged the visitors:—

"Who comes here?"

"Birds that fly by night seek their perch in the morning," replied Dick.

"In whose name?" again asked the invisible questioner.

"In his who, knowing all commands all," was the answer.

"But you have a stranger with you?"

"And a comrade—a new night-bird has been hatched at the 'Chapel'—Dick Flybynight and Handsome Jack hunt in pairs."

"Handsome Jack! enough!"—said the concealed sentinel. "His name has already been enrolled in the lists of our brave fraternity; I know him to be one of us."

Handsome Jack started involuntarily on hearing this assertion. By what means had it been made known so speedily to the inhabitants of this lovely place that he had become one of the gang?

He asked no questions, however, bearing in mind Dick Flybynight's caution against saying a word until he was given liberty to do so.

The sliding panel overhead closed as quietly and mysteriously as it had been opened; and presently the stealthy withdrawal of bolts, and the shooting of locks was heard. Then the door silently opened, and another voice said, "Enter!"

They did so; the door closed after them, and they found themselves in a damp narrow passage. No one, however, was visible. A dim light afforded by an oil lamp showed them another door which effectually prevented them from proceeding further. A shrill whistle was now given by Dick, and the same questions and replies already mentioned having been asked and given, this barrier also ceased to impede their progress, and the two men found themselves in a large apartment, which, from the appearance of the huge fire-place, and the rusty hooks, yet fixed in the ceiling had evidently once been the kitchen of the haunted house.

"You may now safely unloose your jaw-clapper," said Dick; "and to enable your red-rag to wag the better, suppose we moisten it with a stoup of canary."

"With all my heart," replied Jack; "but how in the devil's name, Dick, did that invisible porter of yours, here, know of my connection with your honourable society; I confess that to me the affair is most mysterious."

"So perfect is the organization of our body," replied Dick, " that nothing transpires in one portion of the community which, by secret and safe means, is not communicated to the others. Within two hours after you took the oath in the 'Chapel,' your real name, your assumed one, and your personal appearance was as well known to the officials here, as to yourself."

"By the way, Jack, before we proceed further it may be as well to conceal that nest of canaries which sing so pleasantly in the bag you carry as——"

Handsome Jack handed to Dick Flybynight the booty he had obtained from Sir James Town.

"Stay, Jack! take from the lot, a handful or so of the guineas—they will be serviceable to you before long;—the fraternity always expect garnish from a new hand, and you must be liberal to-night."

"Use it all, and as you think best," exclaimed Jack, hurriedly; "the booty is not mine but the property of all. As to the guineas, I value them not, but this diamond ring which belonged to one I dearly loved, I confess I should like to retain."

"In God's name, man, retain all the diamonds, but they must be concealed at present; that diamond-hilted sword, should it be found on you, would be your death-warrant. The coin could not be sworn to."

"I perceive that I have much yet to learn," remarked the novice, as after having taken a number of guineas from the bag, he handed the remainder of the night's proceeds to Dick.

"See here," said the latter, as he pressed the end of a particular plank in the flooring. The board jerked upwards. Dick then drew it aside, and a small trap-door was revealed. By means of a second spring this was opened, and the treasure placed in an iron box; the plank was then replaced, and all being now safe, Dick Flybynight gave a shrill and peculiar whistle, which summoned to the kitchen an old woman of hideously repulsive appearance.

Let the reader imagine a human being of the feminine gender, with a countenance indicative of a heart hard as the nether millstone, and of a breast in which all the milk of human kindness had long since been dried up. But we must be more minute in our description. The hag's thin grey hairs streamed in disorder from beneath a dingy cap; her eyes were bloodshot, and distilled a disgusting rheum at their corners; over a hawk-like nose was strained yellow skin, which puckered into folds and wrinkles around her bloodless lips and sunken cheeks; two yellow fang-like bones were all that remained of her teeth, and her chin was long and peaked. Her attire was a mere bundle of dingy rags, huddled on carelessly, and streaming in tatters around her thin sinewy limbs, as sea-weed dangles from the timbers of some long stranded wreck. Yet this woman was amazingly active and acute, and well adapted for the situation which she held in this imfamous place.

Such was the party who Dick Flybynight saluted by the somewhat inappropriate name of Sweetlips.

"Welcome, my noble lieutenant!" said the hag in a shrill voice; "'tis an age since the gallant Dick Flybynight honoured us with a visit—and what's in the wind, Dickey dear—eh?" asked Sweetlips in a wheedling tone.

"Egad! dame," replied the highwayman, "there's a plaguy deal of wind in my stomach, and my gallant companion has the same complaint—so a beaker of the best the house can afford, and then we must join the company who, I hear, are merry-making in Deadman's Chamber."

"Aye, troth, are they! for lily-faced Polly and Bill the limmer turned two into one a little while ago, and the people are drinking health to the young couple; but here's the canary, Dick, and——You're a trump, Handsome Jack," as at a hint from his friend the former dropped five guineas into the crone's shrivelled fist, intending, as he did so, that it was for "garnish."

Giving directions to the old woman that their horses should be looked to, the highwaymen now prepared to join the party, the sounds of whose merriment had reached the quick ears of Flybynight.

The house in which they were, was remarkably well adapted for the purposes to which it was now appropriated. Built many and many a-year before, it abounded with secret passages leading to mysterious staircases, which in their turn led to apartments unknown even in the days when the house was regularly inhabited but to the initiated. That portion of the structure below the surface of the ground was almost as spacious and commodious as the upper part, and was of course in times of trouble, an admirable place of refuge and concealment. To Captain M'Cleane and his companions therefore it possessed peculiar recommendations; and the very circumstance of its being the reputed resort of supernatural beings rendered it the more secure, since the villagers would be the less likely to be intrusive or prying. As we have seen, it was closely connected with the hostelry with which, it was also joined by a subterranean passage.

A portion of this passage Flybynight and Handsome Jack now traversed; at its extre-

mity they descended a long flight of winding stone steps at the foot of which was a door at which Dick gave three distinct knocks.

"Who claims admittance?" asked a surly voice from within.

The necessary pass-word having been given, all obstruction was now at an end. Greeting with a nod and a shake of the hand, the last of the line of sentinels, Dick strode onwards, and immediately afterwards he and his companion were received with vociferous shouts of joyous welcome by a motley company who, in a large and brilliantly illuminated apartment, were doing ample justice to a well-stored board.

Although the room was not so gorgeously furnished as was that which we have already described in the "Chapel;" there was much in it to dazzle and startle the beholder. Here also were to be seen many of the loveliest of womankind; exquisite creatures, the glances of whose lustrous eyes sent the blood dancing again through the gazers veins. The gay and fashionable saloons of the metropolis might have been searched in vain for beauties such as adorned this hot-bed of iniquity. The wine which it was evident had been flowing without stint appeared to have heightened their charms. Some reposed on fantenils of exquisite workmanship, their eyes beaming with passion, and their snowy breasts heaving with voluptuous desires; for it may easily be imagined that the occasion of the banquet, Bill the limmer's wedding, had occasioned many a piquant jest and warm insinuation.

"Welcome — welcome— illustrious Dick!" cried a middle-aged man, who wore a dark patch over his eye; "and thou hadst not paid us this visit, I should have began to think that my services were to be called to thy aid."

"Not so fast, master Dashpen," returned Dick; "I shall not need thy advice for some time to come I believe," and whispering aside "he informed Handsome Jack that the party who had just spoken was a well-known forger, who, whilst hiding here, acted as secretary to the fraternity."

"Comrades! I introduce to your honourable society a new member of our body—Handsome Jack! who on his first exploit, an hour or so since, has given such proofs of his skill and bravery, that we may well be proud of snch an acquaintance. We will drink his health."

This was done with right good will, and then the two new arrivals having taken seats at the upper end of the table, the merriment which their arrival had interrupted, was resumed.

A song!—a song!—Jem Starlight's song!" shouted a dozen voices.

"You shall have it, comrades, with all my heart," returned Jem, a dashing looking young fellow, whose feats on the road had already rendered him one of the terrors of the town.

JEM STARLIGHT'S SONG.

Come, let's drink in canary as bright as ere flowed,
A health, my gay boys, to the knights of the road;
To our comrades who canter o'er heath and o'er wold,
Whose seeds are lead bullets, whose harvest is gold.
Brave fellows, who scorning to flinch or to falter,
Defy full-wigged beaks, and don't care for the halter;
Who taxes alike spendthrift, miser, and churl,
Then is off with light heart to his crib and his girl.

CHORUS.

Come, let's drink in claret as bright as e'er flowed,
A health, my gay boys, to the knights of the road.

Oh! a highwayman's life is the life which I love!
When the sun has gone down, and no moon shines above,
To leap on the back of my beautiful mare,
And skim o'er the road, fleet as a bird through the air.
In ambush I lie, till advances my prey,
Then I pocket the flimsies and gallop away;
Past tree, town, and village, I speed like the wind,
And laugh as I leave my pursuers behind.
                          Come, let's drink, &c.

Let the asses who choose drive the plough or the spade,
Let the noodles of commerce get guineas by trade,
Let the sailor for wealth skim the wild raging sea,
I envy not either—the high-road for me!
If to day I am poor,—why to night I have wealth,
And the breeze of the heath keeps my body in health;
If my girl pines for trinkets, a carriage I check,
And diamonds and pearls grace her beautiful neck.
                          Come, let's drink, &c.

Then come, let us empty the bright flowing glass:
Success to each lad, and a health to each lass:
Long life to our captain, as gallant and brave
As e'er snapped a trigger, or trolled out a stave;
And if, boys, at Tyburn our exit we make,
A curse on the sneak who shall peach, or shall shake;
Let's swear to be faithful, if such our end be,
And manfully, drop like ripe fruit, from the tree.
                          Come, let's drink, &c.

Uproarious was the applause which followed this effusion of Jem Starlight's, and when it had ceased, Handsome Jack was complimented by a request that he would sing.

"Comrades!" he remarked, "I beg that you will consider these goldfinches my substitutes, inasmuch as I am not musical,"—and he flung a handful of guineas on the table.

"However, with your permission," he resumed, "I will drink the health of the young bride:—the health and happiness of lilly-faced Polly!"

The pretty girl blushed in acknowledgment of the stranger's politeness. She was indeed a lovely young creature, so fair and fragile looking, that Handsome Jack could not help wondering to find her in such society. She was evidently somewhat embarrassed by her novel position, and blushes mantled her cheek and neck, as one of the revellers, who was far gone in liquor, wished her "a happy wedding," a wish which had the effect of hurrying her from the room.

Shall our rude hands dare to draw aside the veil which hangs before the entrance of the bridal chamber? Yes—we will just look within!

The girl was attended to her bed-room by the old woman to whom we have already introduced the reader, and what a contrast did the pair present, the face of the one wrinkled and dry as that of a mummy, the other plump and of a pearly transparency; the old woman had long ago ceased to be warmed with the fires of passion,—the young girl's heart was throbbing with tumultuous ecstasy.

"Well!" exclaimed the old crone, as she surveyed the blooming creature, "Bill, the limmer, will be a happy man this night. Now, you had better let me undress you;—there,"—and she loosed the maiden's gown, which fell on the floor, leaving her gracefully-turned shoulders, budding breasts, and rounded hips fully developed.

A few more articles of attire were removed, and then, having clad her in her bridal night-dress, the old woman led her to a bed situated in a recess.—The blushing girl reclined her cheek on the pillow; and there, the woman having withdrawn, we also leave her, waiting with trembling anxiety for the arrival of her husband, and return to the apartment in which the revellers are still seated.

They were in the last stage of inebriety.—Madness had succeeded to merriment, and coarse jokes were bandied from lip to lip.

"Captain!" said one, "I should like to know who *is* Captain here? I like not these new-fangled troopers who take a peep at the king's highway, only to laugh and not be found when they are most wanted;—*who* is Captain?"

"*I* am!" said Dick Flybynight, and he enforced his claims to the title by the production of a pair of pistols. "In the absence of Captain M'Cleane, *I* act as *master* here; a traitor to him, is an enemy to me!"

The fellow who had spoken was completely cowed by the determination of Dick.

"Brothers, will you protect me?" asked the man who had disturbed the peace of the place; "am I, because I am a beaten-down burglar, to be betrayed?"

"Rogues are always suspicious," murmured Dick Flybynight.

"And always rascals and spies," echoed Handsome Jack.

"Who says *I* am a spy?" asked a member of the gang.

"I do!" and Handsome Jack boldly faced the questioner.

"Is it true that Blackmoor has escaped?" asked one of the now drunken revellers.

Had a person been near enough to one of the company in that secret place, he might have heard a low murmur:—

"He has!"

"I heard of the escape of Blackmoor," chimed in another; "he made friends with the watch, and when they were quietly dosing, he walked out of the Round-house,—and, by the way, there are as big rascals here now as the watchman."

"Rascals!" echoed Handsome Jack.

"Rascal?" asked Dick Flybynight.

In a moment all was uproar. Rapiers flashed—and they who but a few moments since were dear friends, were now deadly foes. The horrible influence of liquor had extinguished all feeling of friendship, and the robbers fell upon each other remorsely. Blood would inevitably have been spilled had not the newly-made wife rushed from her bridal-bed with her lost virginity apparent in her countenance.

Suddenly the door was opened—the watchful sentinel was there; but noiselessly came in a man who assumed authority.

"*You* here," he asked of Dick Flybynight.

"Here, Captain, to obey you." was the reply.

"And you, Handsome Jack?"

"To obey him who commands me."

"Blackmoor has escaped from the Round-house, and our welfare depends on his capture. I knew him to be a crafty villain; one who will stick not at trifles to ruin us; and I *know* that the traitor is now in this room."

The last remark was made by the man who Handsome Jack had denounced as a spy.

"In supposing that Blackmoor is now in this apartment," remarked Captain M'Cleane, for he it was; "you are mistaken. Our emissaries are already on his track, and he cannot, I think, escape. I heard of the affair whilst at the 'Chapel,' and came hither immediately to apprize you of the event."

The sudden entrance of M'Cleane acted like a charm; every weapon was sheathed, and peace reigned instead of discord.

"Comrades! we must be more than ever united now," resumed the extraordinary man who had obtained such a powerful influence over his desperate companions; "every member of the fraternity must avoid petty discords, and join heart and hand for the protection of all. Are you willing to do so?"

No. 4.

A deep shout of "All" rang through the apartment.

"Good!—then let each of you act as though on your single arm, and head hangs the safety of our centre body. And now let us consult as to our future proceedings."

The bride, who had been frigtened from her nuptial couch, having returned thither, a sort of council of safety was held, after which all of the gang retired save Dick Flybynight, Handsome Jack, and M'Cleane.

Then the former related to the Captain the adventure with Sir James Town, at which he laughed heartily, and highly commended the maiden exploit of Handsome Jack. He regretted, however, that blood had been shed.

It was arranged that Flybynight and Handsome Jack should remain at Highgate until the darkness of night should enable them to return to the "Chapel" in safety. M'Cleane then took his departure, with as much privacy as he had made his appearance, and within an hour afterwards the whole of the inmates of this mysterious place were buried in slumber, except those, of course, whose duties were to watch over the safety of the community.

M'Cleane did not depart from Highgate, altogether unobserved. As he slowly rode down the hill, on the summit of which the village is situated, he was closely watched by a man who was concealed behind the trunk of a large tree. The fellow grasped a pistol, and just as the Captain arrived opposite to him, he cautiously levelled it, and pulled the trigger; fortunately it missed fire, or M'Cleane would have bitten the dust. Having failed in his object, and fearful of renewing the attack, as some travellers were seen approaching, he slunk away, muttering curses on his weapon.

It was the escaped traitor—Blackmoor.

CHAPTER V.

ROBBERY AND MURDER IN BUCKLERSBURY, AND APPREHENSION OF THE PERPETRATOR— THE ESCAPED TRAITOR BLACKMOOR.

IT will be remembered that after Blackmoor had been detected in his villainy through the agency of Jenny Diver, he was, by the order of M'Cleane, set at liberty, much to the surprise of his comrades, who fully expected that the sentence of death passed upon him would have been immediately carried into execution.

So admirably managed, however, had been the plans of M'Cleane, and so well were they carried out by his subordinator—that almost before the traitorous scoundrel could felicitate himself on having escaped with his worthless life, he was pounced upon as he wandered through High Holborn, by two of the Watch, who a few minutes previously had received some private information from a young man who had been dogging Blackmoor's footsteps, ever since he quitted the "Chapel."

In spite of a most desperate resistance he was taken to the round-house on a charge of murdering an old man at Hampstead, some time before. His situation, therefore, was little better than it had been an hour ago, when his life was threatened by his former comrades.

But the desperado determined not to perish without a strong effort. He, therefore, no sooner found himself alone than he began to make a minute examination of the place with a view to escape.

Fortunately for him, the guardians of the night had omitted to search his person, and a large knife remained in his possession—this, and an iron bar which he managed to wrench from the chimney, by the exercise of prodigious strength, was his only hope.

He now commenced an examination of the round-house, or cage, which, though strong in its construction, was far less secure, than are similar edifices in our own day. It was a stone building, with a circular roof and strongly grated windows, and consisted of three apartments, two of which were allotted to prisoners, and the third to the accommodation of the constables.

These latter worthies were very far from being always faithful to the trust which was reposed in them; and it has been said, doubtless with truth, that they gained more by letting their captives escape than by securing them as they ought to have done. This was well known, of course, to Blackmoor, who, on an old Charley's appearance with a jug of water and a loaf of bread, began to sound him as to the probabilities of his escape.

Blackmoor was not unprovided with gold, that universal agent; and the old Watchman, who had him in charge, was by no means proof against its magic influence. It was not long, therefore, before an agreement was made that the gaolor should take a convenient nap; and within a very brief period of his departure from the cell, the guardian of the place was snoring audibly.

Blackmoor needed no further hint. Chipping away with his knife, the mortar from between the intertices of some large stones, he gradually loosened them with the iron bar, until at length the breeze from without blew through the chinks. Soon the stones were removed, and he peeped cautiously out. All was safe, so creeping out of the aperture he was in a few minutes at large.

Sneaking along, in the broad shadow cast by the neighbouring houses, and diving through obscure lanes, he soon gained the open fields, and it was when concealing himself from some passing labourers, that he observed Captain M'Cleane riding down Highgate Rise. All the malice of the man was aroused at the sight of his late chief, and he determined to revenge himself by his death. We have seen, however, that his attempt was futile.

It may appear strange that M'Cleane should so soon have heard of Blackmoor's escape, but it must be remembered that he had scouts in all directions, who suffered nothing to elude their vigilance.

The traitor, compelled to live, had now no resources but those which his nefarious profession afforded; he therefore hurried to one of his old haunts, where he was heartily welcomed by his former associates in crime.

On the day succeeding his escape a burglary was planned. There resided in Bucklersbury, an old man of great reputed wealth; but no one, to outward appearance, was more miserable than Abraham Blake. As he walked to and from his cheerless abode, his rags fluttering in the breeze, he loooked like a personification of misery itself. Meanness was visible in every line of his countenance, and avarice lurked about the corner of his cunning mouth.

His house was one of those dingy old places in which rats and mice rejoice, and in the single room which he occupied, Abraham was one evening seated, rubbing his bony hands together, in order to warm them—for coals would have been too much of a luxury.

In one corner of the room was a large iron chest, trebly locked. This was the depository of the old man's affections; for all that he loved on earth was within it.

The night was wild and tempestuous. The wind whistled down the chimney, and moaned as it swept through the dreary passages of that ancient habitation. The sudden gusts, shaking the doors and window-sashes, made the old man start and look at his chest;—not that he feared the weather— *that* he knew could not deprive him of his gold. But the continual fear of being robbed of his wealth, rendered him nervous.

It was midnight: unlocking the strong box, the old man drew from it several bags of guineas, counted them carefully, and replaced them. Then he drew forth some small packages, which he opened, and his eyes flashed with delight as costly gems reflected the rays shed by the rushlight.

Having satisfied himself that all was right, he closed the box, and then lay down to rest on his bed of rags.

His sleep, however, on this evening, was strangely disturbed, and he tossed to and fro beneath the influence of distressing visions. For some time he was thus tormented by his fears. All at once he jumped in alarm from the bed.

He had heard footsteps outside his chamber door. How his heart beat with terror! Well he knew that no friendly visit was about to be paid him, for none were permitted to visit that house save himself.

Again he heard footsteps—and also a low whispering. Some one, too, was evidently trying the door, which was well secured within.

Abraham Blake was completely paralysed by terror—his tongue refused to utter a syllable. In another minute a sound as of some cutting instrument was heard, and the door flew from its fastenings.

Three men entered the room. Each of them had his face covered with crape, and one of them held a dark lantern.

"Mercy—mercy! for God's sake have mercy on a poor old man!" screamed the miser.

"That won't do, old fellow!—if you had been poor, you would not have had the honour of a visit from us," exclaimed one of the ruffians. "Come, hand us out those guineas which we know you have—or it will be the worse for you."

"Gentlemen—dear gentlemen—as God is my judge, I have nothing! Do you think if I had gold, that I would live in such a hovel as this?"

"Come, come! our time is too precious to be taken up with your cant, you cunning old scoundrel!—your money or your brains!—Be good enough to save us the trouble of opening that box."

Abraham shivered like an aspen leaf. That box! why it contained his very soul,—and he determined to make a desperate attempt to save it.

The window of the room, was his sole hope. Could he but open that, and raise the watch, all would be well, thought he.

But in his anxiety to guard his money safely, he had nailed up the sashes, and he bit his nails to the very quick as he perceived that he had shut assistance out.

The burglars laughed again, as they saw their victim in his self-constructed trap. One of them—it was Blackmoor—caught the miserable man by the throat, and forced him towards the chest.

"I will *not* unlock it!" he cried. Then, he muttered, "I have not the key."

Blackmoor instantly thrust his hand inside the miser's waistcoat, and with a villainous laugh drew forth the instrument for opening the treasure-box.

And now commenced the work of plunder. The lid of the box having been lifted, the canvas bags filled with gold were drawn forth with savage delight. The parcels of diamonds were thrown aside, as though they had been but bits of glass; even the articles of old plate were left: gold, and nothing but gold, was what the miscreants coveted.

The despair of the old man was somewhat mitigated by the sight of the diamonds—they at least would remain to him. He lost his prudence, however, whilst gazing on the gems; for just as the robbers were quitting the room, he exclaimed:—

"One of you infernal devils, at least, I know —and Justice Fielding shall know it too."

The words were scarcely spoken, when Blackmoor confronted Abraham.

"And which is the one you know?" he said. "Answer—or you are a dead man!"

"*You!*" said Blake, "*you*, Blackmoor, the burglar."

"That fools tongue of your's must be stopped!" cried the robber, and with one blow he struck the old man to the ground.

There was a low moaning—a short gasp as if for breath — a convulsive heaving of old Blake's chest—a bubbling noise, as though water was gushing forth from some hitherto pent up channel—and then the miser slept, unconscious of his loss.

Blackmoor had cut his throat—and there lay the old man—his grey hairs floating in a pool of his own blood. The murderer looked ferociously at the corpse—kicked the senseless clay, and then urged his comrades to depart.

They were not slow to leave the room in which the murdered man lay. Softly creeping down stairs, they reached the front door, which on entering they had locked inside. To their utter surprise and consternation, it would not yield to their efforts;—again and again they attempted to open it, but it was as firm as a gate of adamant.

"Damnation!" muttered Blackmoor, "we are entrapped;—our only chance is the back door."

They tried that mode of exit, and were foiled—although they could force the lock, they could not open the door.

They were now in utter despair, and consulted as to the best means of proceeding. While so engaged, the front door suddenly fell in with a crash, and Blackmoor's shoulder was grasped.

"Villain!" said Handsome Jack,—for he it was,—"your time has at length come."

Blackmoor vainly tried to escape, and a terrific struggle ensued. The other burglars had been easily secured by Jack's companions.

Blackmoor, however, was not one to be easily taken. He knew well enough that he struggled for life—and he struggled desperately.

At length he was secured, and conveyed outside the house, where a posse of Charleys were in waiting. He and his confederates had no sooner been placed in their safe-keeping, than Handsome Jack and his party disappeared.

The burglars were conveyed to Bow Street, and thither we must accompany them.

On being placed in the dock, Blackmoor was charged with the Hampstead murder—the witness against him being the young man who had been his accomplice in that robbery, though not in the sanguinary deed; and who had been admitted as king's evidence.

Just as, loaded with irons, he left the presence of the magistrates, he heard a voice whisper in his ear, "such is the reward of a traitor."

CHAPTER VI.

THE EXPLOITS OF JENNY DIVER.—AND A SCENE IN NEWGATE.

THE security of the "Chapel" was guaranteed by the capture of Blackmoor, and having effected this object, M'Cleane breathed freely again. With renewed eagerness he sought the embraces of the fascinating flower-girl, who evinced no lack of warmth in her reception of the handsome captain.

"Adorable Jenny," murmured M'Cleane, as he imprinted a passionate kiss on her pouting and ripe lips, and strained her to his heart.

Madame Charlotte, who was present, seemed by no means pleased with this excess of tenderness, for she addressed M'Cleane in not very amiable tones:—

"Fresh faces have, it seems, great attractions for you. There was a time when no eye was so bright, or no lip so tempting as mine."

At that moment she bitterly repented that she had ever attempted to aid M'Cleane in his amour with Jenny.

"Nonsense, Lizzy," exclaimed M'Cleane. "Why, my girl, I think I have given you sufficient proofs that I can prize *ripe* fruit. Surely you would not have me confine my appetite to one dish. Here, sit on my knee, and then, with Jenny beside me, and you embracing me, I shall be indeed doubly blessed."

Madame Charlotte needed no further invitation; for, with a smile, she flung her arms round M'Cleane's neck and repaid his burning kisses with interest.

"I must leave you now," remarked Jenny Diver, "*I* am not greedy, and besides, I have to prepare for business on the morrow."

And with an arch smile she tripped lightly out of the apartment, gaily saying to herself, "It is Madame Charlotte's turn now."

No sooner had she closed the door, than Madame Charlotte's lips were again eagerly pressed, and M'Cleane's unresisted fingers toyed with her voluptuous bosom. She was delighted at thus recovering the influence which she half imagined she had lost, and more than half-met the Captain's advances.

"Both parties revelled and rioted in intoxication of passion. Gently drawing M'Cleane closer to her, she looked into his face with an expression of intense desire. The lamp burnt dimly, but light enough remained for the purposes of pleasure; and soon nought but broken murmurs and deep breathings were heard. Then M'Cleane, having tenderly kissed the plump and beautiful housekeeper, with an air of languor, sank almost powerless on the sofa.

We must now follow Jenny Diver.

It was on a bright and beautiful Sunday morning that, having quietly emerged from the purlieus of Long Acre, a young and lovely girl was seen proceeding along the Strand towards the church of St. Martin's-in-the-Fields. The female looked a very pattern of pious propriety. In one hand she carried a splendidly bound prayer book, and with the other she sufficiently raised her petticoat to allow two of " the prettiest ancles in the world" to be seen. With great demureness she approached the sacred edifice, and entered the porch, where she waited until the sexton should conduct her to a pew.

While she waited, she watched closely the parties who passed by her—though no one would have suspected that she was doing so. Her pretty face was pursed up into a modest bashfulness, but her dark eyes were actively employed.

A pompous-looking woman having entered the gates, she at once attracted Jenny's notice. She was a fat and richly-dressed person; a gold watch of huge dimensions rested on her abdomen, and rings glittered on her red fingers. Behind her stalked a man in gorgeous livery, who carried a prayer book almost as heavy as himself. A running page also followed her. Jenny at once marked her prey, and contrived to attract the fat female's attention by pretending to be overcome by a fainting fit.

The result was that she was invited to take a seat in the lady's pew, and shortly the service commenced.

Had Hogarth been there he might have made a happy sketch. The fat lady, through a pair of spectacles nearly as large as a moderate-sized saucer, looked out her prayer-book, and with great apparent devotion declared herself to be a "miserable sinner," while the young woman beside her was busily engaged in thinking what the pockets of the devout person might contain.

Jenny Diver's hands were clasped and laid modestly in her lap, when the parson commenced his extremely dull discourse; indeed, so dull was it, that before he had been speaking five minutes the fat lady was fast asleep.

Had a keen observer been present he might have seen another pair of hands than those which Jenny exhibited on the front of her person, busily at work in the old lady's pockets. The girl had, with great dexterity, constructed a pair of false arms; so that whilst the counterfeit limbs were in a state of repose, the genuine fingers were profitably enough employed. Suspicion was thus effectually diverted.

The girl, having with great dexterity abstracted a well-filled purse from the old lady's pocket, was again seized with a fit of faintness, and hurried from the pew. The old beadle, who was apparently sinking, hurried to her aid, and conducted her into the fresh air; when she speedily recovered, and was quickly on her way to the "Chapel" with her booty.

Great was the excitement consequent on the discovery of the murder of the old miser of Bucklersbury; and as the day of the trial of Blackmoor and his two companions drew near the public curiosity increased. The ruffian, himself, now that all hope of escape had departed from him, maintained a dogged silence; but remembering that he possessed information respecting M'Cleane and the "Chapel" which might be turned to his own account, he determined to avail himself of the last chance of saving his neck.

But he failed in his object; and on the appointed day of his trial he was arraigned on a double charge of robbery and murder.

Refusing to plead, he was reminded that if he persisted in his obstinacy he would be pressed to death. This threatened punishment, however, had not the effect desired, and he was forthwith sent back to his cell.

The next morning was appointed for carrying this horrible sentence into execution, and Blackmoor, still persisting in his obstinate course, was led into the press-yard of Newgate.

His irons having been knocked off, he was stripped of all his clothing except a pair of drawers, and the common hangman having laid him on his back, secured his wrists and ancles with stout cords to iron rings, which were fixed firmly in the pavement. His position, therefore, when his limbs were extended, was that represented by a Saint Andrew's cross.

Blackmoor beheld and endured those terrible preparations with an air of dogged indifference. Not a muscle quivered, nor did he exhibit the slightest symptom of fear.

The sheriff, having arrived, informed him that even then he might be saved from being pressed to death, by returning into court, and pleading "Not Guilty." His continued silence was the signal for his sufferings to commence.

Perhaps a more barbarous mode of torture was never devised than that of pressing a human being to death: it was only inflicted for one offence — that of refusing to either admit or deny guilt. Thank God! it has long since been abolished, as we trust the gallows will before long be. But we must not moralize.

A heavy flat board and a number of heavy iron weights were now brought into the yard, and the former placed on Blackmoor's chest. Then one of the iron weights was placed on the board.

And another and another was added, until the pressure on the chest must have been fearful. Still Blackmoor spoke not; but his face began to be frightfully distorted: a cold perspiration bedewed his temples, and his breathing was laboured.

Another weight, and his eyes almost started from their sockets; his tongue, black, and swollen protruded from his mouth, and the veins of his temples appeared ready to burst.

It seemed almost incredible that human nature could so long survive such torments. As if to increase his tortures water was now poured down his throat, some of the weights removed, and a short respite granted him; after which his misery again commenced.

Weight after weight was heaped on the board until many hundred weights rested upon his lungs. All at once a piercing shriek of mortal agony burst from the sufferer's lips. The point of nature's endurance had been reached at last.

The wretched man fainted, and it was at first thought that the vital spark had fled, but on the first sign of reviving consciousness, the horrible weights were again added to the board, and Blackmoor, at length, worn out with suffering, made a sign, by nodding his head to the Sheriff, that he wished to communicate something to him.

That functionary having attended to the summons, instantly ordered the weights to be removed, and the man to be unbound. The burglar had declared that he would plead. A cordial having been administered, he was removed to his cell there to remain until he should be sufficiently recovered to be again placed at the bar.

CHAPTER VII.

SIR JAMES TOWN RECEIVES AN UNEXPECTED VISIT.

NEAR unto Tottenham Court, was an old family mansion which the "oldest inhabitant" of the neighbourhood remembered to have been an old house when he was young. It was one of those substantial buildings which time takes a long period of years to destroy. There was a fine old entrance-hall, with a very ancient porter therein, whose occupation it was to sit in a monstrous bee hive chair, and admit visitors. On the brown oaken panels were heads of deer with branching antlers, and heads of foxes from all the cunning had long ago departed. A large fire-place, in which burned a mighty log of oak, gave a cheerful aspect to the place, which, otherwise would have been rather sombre in its appearance.

On the left-hand side of the entrance-hall was a door which opened into a large apartment, where is seated at a table covered with papers, a man in the prime of life, and of an elegant and polished exterior.

By his side, or rather near him, is sitting a rather vulgar looking man, who has a quick piercing eye, a remarkably red nose, and a visage—taken altogether, indicative of great sagacity.

On the walls of the apartment were many old family pictures. Grim looking men stared frightfully out of the canvass, and low boddiced ladies looked languishing and insipid. A clock of a costly kind adorned the mantel-shelf, and a multitude of nic-nacks, such as Sevres china and other articles of *vertu* were scattered here and there about the room.

The gentleman to whom we have referred was Sir James Town; the red-nosed man was one of the Bow-street runners, to whom the former was relating the circumstance of his robbery, near Harrow-on-the Hill, with a view to the apprehension of the highwaymen.

"There were two of the scoundrels I think you said, Sir James?" asked the Bow-street constable.

"Well I think there must have been more, for I scarcely imagine that two men would have made me run, or have induced me to part with my money," said the baronet, somewhat pompously.

"But you only saw two, Sir James?" enquired the Runner. "Should you, do you think, be enabled to recognise either of them."

"I should know, and could swear to the voice of the man who"——he was going to say horsewhipped me, but he saved himself from such a humiliating trip of the tongue by hastily adding——"demanded my rings, which were more valuable even than the bag of money."

"And did you hear no conversation pass between the man who shot your servant, and the one who waited on you in the carriage?"

"I only," replied Sir James Town, "heard one of them call the other 'Dick.'"

"Humph!" said the Bow-street Runner. "Dick—eh! was he a dashing sort of a blade, a kind of dare devil?"

The worthy baronet, felt at that moment a tingling sensation in the skin of his back, which convinced him that there was not a little of the devil in the arm of the man who had assaulted him. The point, however, was with him a very sore one.

"Yes; he seemed devilishly disposed, Mr. Watkins; and it is a money I escaped with my life."

"Dick Flybynight was on the road with a strange companion last night," said the Officer to himself, "with a man not known at Bow-street, but I'll wager my life," he uttered in a louder tone. "that before twenty-four hours I will be on the track of both."

"And if," said Sir James, "you succeed in recovering my diamond-hilted sword, and the other jewels, a large diamond ring especially I will most handsomely reward you."

The officer promised to exercise his utmost vigilance, and having received from Sir James a handsome gratuity, he left the house in order to prosecute his enquiries.

We will follow him as he proceeds on his anxious errand.

Cautiously avoiding the great thoroughfares, Mr. Watkins made his way into Westminster, then one of the strongholds of the metropolitan plunderers. Slipping into an obscure public-house, he made a certain signal to the landlord, who at once accompanied him to a private room where, he speedily changed his dress, and so completely was the metamorphosis which was effected, that no one would have recognised in the priggish-looking individual who sat down to take a pipe with the landlord, the celebrated Runner of Bow-street.

He next directed his steps towards the Almonry, and arrived without having been observed at the door of a well-known house of ill-fame, and gave a sharp knock.

Almost immediately afterwards, he was admitted to the interior by a woman, whose appearance was quite sufficient to indicate the nature of her avocations.

A slatternly cap which had once been gay with tawdry finery half covered a frowsy head of hair, whose colour might be familiarly compared to that of a carrot. Her dirty dress rather hung on her shoulders than enveloped her form. It was unlaced in front, and a pair of breast's, soft, and flabby looking, and not of the cleanest, by their full exposure repelled rather than attracted. One of her eyes had a villainous squint in it; her brow was low and receding, and her eye-brows almost straight. Her nose was turned up and very red, and her breath was strongly flavoured with Usquebaugh, to which beverage she was greatly attached. Like her face, her figure was anything but attractive, and she was slightly lame.

"And only to think of seeing Mr. Watkins!" exclaimed the woman, as she poured out a glass of strong waters for her visitor. "Well, what's in the wind now?"

"A trifling matter, Mother Sin," replied the officer, "but one in which I must have your assistance."

"That you shall be right welcome to," remarked the lady, who had been addressed by so flattering a name.

"Is Sall, the gonnoff, in the house just now?" inquired Mr. Watkins.

"Yes—she is with a young spark upstairs, and I'll engage she won't leave him till his purse is rather lighter than it was just now. But what may be your business with Sall, Mr. Watkins?"

"She must do a little job for me, that's all, Mother Sin, so just let her know that there is business on hand. In short, I must see her, and that soon."

"Well—well, you shall have your own way," said the woman, as Watkins slipped a guinea into her palm, and going to the foot of the wretched staircase, she bawled out to the girl, who at that particular time was engaged with her gallant.

She soon, however, made her appearance. An intimation that Mr. Watkins required her attendance being quite sufficient to hasten her. It would have been by no means politic on her part to have kept him waiting.

At that period, as well as at the present time, an extensive system of espionage was carried on by means of females, such as Sall, the gonnoff. Many a criminal was traced in consequence of information procured by girls of the town, who, when their sparks were in their arms, wormed from them their secrets, and for gold betrayed them. Hogarth, in one of his manifold pictures, has finely illustrated this fact.

"It is necessary for you," said Mr. Watkins to Sall, to procure me some information respecting a robbery which has recently taken place; if you succeed, you shall be well rewarded; but, if you deceive me in any way, you know that you are in my power."

"I am well aware that I am," replied the girl—too well aware; and what do you wish me to do now?"

" To help to put a man's neck into the halter," drily replied Watkins.

The girl clasped her hands, and tears gushed into her eyes, which, bleared and blood-shot as they were with Hollands and dissipation, still retained some of their former beauty.

" Now, don't be a cursed fool," said Watkins, " you know you hanged Bill the Tobyman; you know you did, and I should like to hear why you hesitate now? Do you see these?" and drawing from his coatpocket a pair of small handcuffs, he placed them on the table.

" Yes—yes, I see them—and ever since I saw poor Bill in the cart up Holborn Hill, I've had no peace of mind. I wish to God I had perished with him on Tyburn Tree. Better that than to have sold him as I did."

The Bow-street runner grinned. Years ago all humane feeling had died in his breast; so it cannot be expected that he should have sympathised with the girl. He would have thought no more of hanging a man than he would of winding up his watch, both were matters of every-day business with him. An occupation such as his must have a tendency to harden the heart and deaden the feelings. In Watkins's case, the heart had become morally petrified.

" You know Dick Flybynight, Sally. Now mark me: you must find him out, and draw from him where he was very early yesterday morning. And just try if you could not persuade him to make you a present of a ring, or some trinkets to adorn your pretty person. I suspect he has had luck lately."

" Dick!" exclaimed the girl—and she was on the point of peremptorily refusing to obey the mandates of Watkins, when she suddenly remembered that she might be the means of warning him of the pit-fall which the constable was digging. " I will do your bidding," she said.

" Good," replied Watkins. " And now here's an earnest of what you shall receive if you succeed." Saying this he slipped some coin into her hand.

Quitting the house with the greatest privacy, the man of Bow Street returned to the tavern and resumed his ordinary apparel, feeling convinced that he should soon be put on the right scent.

Let us now return to Sir James Town, whom we left in his study engaged in the examination of various documents relating to the estate which he had recently succeeded in getting possession of.

Whilst doing so, he was startled by a violent knocking at the door of his chamber. Hurridly placing some papers in a cabinet, he opened the door, which he had taken the precaution to lock. Had he seen a ghost, he could not have been more startled than he was on beholding the man, whom he had compelled to abandon the title of his house.

" You here, Richard!" he exclaimed; and he rushed to the bell rope in order to summon his servants; but Handsome Jack was too quick for him, and prevented the alarm being given.

" Your business, fellow?" demanded the infuriated baronet. " And by what means have you gained admission here?"

" My business," replied the other, coldly, " is to denounce you as a villain.—How I entered the house, to which I have a better right than yourself, I do not choose to inform you."

" Begone, sir?" exclaimed Sir James, " baseborn bound that you are."

The last words had scarcely been heard by Handsome Jack, before his rapier's point was at Sir James's throat.

" Yet I scorn to take advantage of you," cried Jack. " Draw, reptile, and defend yourself;" and he retired some few paces from the baronet, who drew his sword and stood on the defensive.

A few passes were exchanged, and both then fought with great fury. The anger of Sir James, however, overcame his discretion; for he was an excellent swordsman, and before long he was disarmed.

Jack did not, however, further injure him; but as the baronet lay on the floor, he demanded from him certain documents which he knew he had in his possession.

" I would rather perish first!" exclaimed the baronet, " my rights I never will relinquish."

" Rights?" asked Handsome Jack, sneeringly, " I am not aware, Sir James Town, that a forged deed can confer any. By the God who made me! unless you deliver up to me the forged document which I know you have in that cabinet, even at the risk of my own neck, I will sacrifice yours."

The baronet's colour faded from his cheek, which became of an ashy paleness as he heard these words.

" I am no forger," was all he said, as he slowly rose, and staggered to a chair.

" Liar, as well as scoundrel!" said Jack, seizing him by the throat, " circumstances have within the last hour occurred, which throw a light on your proceedings of late. If you will not give me the deed, I will take it by main force."

Still Sir James refused—but his agitation was terrible.

Advancing to the cabinet, Handsome Jack extended his rapier towards the baronet with one hand, while with the other, he opened a drawer in its interior, from which he drew forth a parchment which he just glanced at, and then placed in his pocket.

" I have now," he remarked, " in my possession damning evidence of your guilt. Proceed one step further in your endeavours to apprehend the men who attacked your carriage last night, and you shall die the death of a forger on Tyburn Tree!"

With these words he stalked out of the room, leaving the baronet in a state of the utmost alarm.

What Handsome Jack had asserted was indeed true enough. Sir James Town, in order to secure to himself the title and estates which he enjoyed, had resorted to the basest means. A deed had been concocted by him and a petti-fogging lawyer, and certain fraudulent signatures attached to it. Whilst this parchment remained in his possession, he was comparatively safe; but now he was completely at the mercy of a man whom he had deeply wronged.

Wrapped in these unpleasant meditations, he sank into a chair, and looking round the room, and beheld in imagination all its splendour passing away. Then he imagined himself the inmate of a felon's cell, and dismally loomed up the gallows on his mental horizon. His torture was dreadful. At any moment the officers of juctice might seize him and deliver him over to the hangman! What was to be done?"

Taking a bottle of brandy from a side-board, he filled a large glass, and emptied at a draught —but had the potent spirits been only water, it could not have effected him less. Glass after glass he poured down his parched throat, but it was of no avail; Conscience could not sleep, and his anxiety increased momentarily.

For hours he remained in this state, when he was thrown into still greater perplexity by the arrival of the Bow Street officer, who informed him that he had succeeded in finding a clue, which he firmly believed would lead to the discovery of the Harrow Road desperadoes.

Greatly to Mr. Watkins's surprise, the baronet expressed his wish that the matter should drop. The acute officer instantly suspected that a screw was loose somewhere, and he determined to fathom the secret. Besides, he had no idea whatever of losing the reward which he had been promised.

"It's werry odd, Sir James," he remarked, "but may I ask your reason for this sudden change in your intentions? Here a few hours ago you were has hot as blazes on the subject, and now, all on a sudden you are as cool as a cucumber. One of my chums tells me somebody had some one here.—Perhaps you've got back the mopusses?"

Every word the constable uttered was like a dagger in Sir James' heart. He simply replied that he had changed his mind. Was it possible, he thought, that the possessor of the deed had imparted to Watkins his dreadful secret?

Pleading an engagement—he dismissed the officer with a handsome gratuity, and felt excessive relief when he had disappeared. He then locked himself in his bed-chamber, and threwing himself on a couch, endeavoured to devise some means for securing his safety.

In vain did the harrassed baronet seek to drive from his mind the dread which hung over and clouded it; at length he made a desperate resolve. He would rid himself of his woes and of his life at once; and with the intention of procuring sufficient laudanum to effect his purpose, he walked out.

In order to evade suspicion, he purchased on various pretences at different shops small quantities of the deadly drug, and when he had collected as much as he considered necessary he returned, and once more locked himself in his room.

Pouring the contents of the different phials into a wine glass, he sat down in order to write some last letters. Having, with a steady hand, accomplished this, he took the deadly draught in his hand.

But he had not as yet sufficient courage to drink it off. So to screw his courage to the sticking point, he drained bumper after bumper of brandy, and at last, half maddened by his repeated libations, he seized the poison cup with frenzied energy and drank it off with desperate emotion.

The brandy, however, which he had previously taken, prevented the laudanum from doing its office, and it was long before he sunk into insensibility. When he at last did, he slept long and soundly, but his sleep was not that of death. For many hours he was relieved by insensibility from the horrors of his situation. When he awoke they returned with re-doubled power.

CHAPTER VIII.

A NARROW ESCAPE.

AFTER Blackmoor was removed from the press yard of Newgate, he was allowed to remain for some time in his cell, and then was again placed at the bar, where he pleaded, " *Not Guilty!* "

It was, however, proved beyond the possibility of a doubt that he had committed a foul murder on the person of the old miser, Abraham Blake, of Bucklersbury. To his horror and surprise the two men who had accompanied him in his midnight's excursion, were, as they had not committed the fatal deed, admitted as witnesses against him. Their testimony, added to that of the young man who also had been one of Blackmoor's companions in villany decided his doom, and the judge passed sentence of death upon him, without giving him the slightest hope that mercy could be extended to one whose career had been of such enormous crime.

His frequent escapes from previous places of confinement had rendered it necessary that he should be heavily ironed; and he was therefore taken from the bar to the press-room where his limbs were fast fettered; and he was then conducted to the condemned cell.

He refused the office of the Ordinary with many an oath, and his greatest trouble arose from the fact that he had not been enabled to carry his traiterous intentions with respect to M'Cleane and his companions into effect. He determined, however, that before he died he would give such information to the authorities as would lead to their utter ruin.

Day after day passed swiftly on, and at length the last day but one of his mortal career arrived. Seeing now that all hope had well-nigh departed, he sent for the sheriffs.

And now, indeed, the terrors of an ignominious death began to effect the wretched man's mind. The hours he counted, and every sound of the bell as it boomed along the passages of the dreary prisons, sounded like his death-knell. The shorter grew his time the swifter seemed the minutes to fly.

The last night had arrived, and the miserable man, sat in an attitude of deep dejection, when the door of his cell was opened, and a female entered.

As she caught the eye of the criminal, she placed her finger on her lip in token of silence, and then dropped a guinea into the hand of the turnkey, who retired from the cell.

It was no other than Jenny Diver.

"Blackmoor," she said, "I promised you that we should meet again—that promise I am now come to redeem."

"To torture me more than is necessary," growled the ruffian.

Had his limbs at that moment been unfettered, he would have flown at Jenny, and tore her in pieces. As it was, he darted at the girl a glance of savage ferocity, which almost appalled her.

"Blackmoor," she exclaimed, "I come to make you an offer—it remains for you to say whether you will accept it.—Do you wish to live?"

"Do I wish to die a dog's death!" he mut-
No. 5.

tered, "why come here to mock me?—By this time to-morrow I shall be carrion!"

"Not if you comply with the terms I am about to propose," said the girl. "Even now you may be saved."

"How, in the devil's name?" gasped Blackmoor, who like a drowning man at a straw, caught at the hope of life."

"It is rumoured," said Jenny, "that you intend to make a communication to the sheriffs which will perhaps ruin Captain M'Cleane and his brave comrades. I come from the Captain with the offer that if you will seal your lips on the subject—you shall not be executed tomorrow morning."

"And how am I to know that he can save me?"

"Once already he has spared your life when that life was in his power, and it is equally in his power to save it again; but before I can explain to you the mode in which you will escape the rope, I must have your solemn oath that you will not divulge the secrets of the "Chapel."

"I am ready to give you that promise," said Blackmoor. "I will be as silent as the grave on all that concerns it."

"That is sufficient," returned Jenny Diver, "and now listen:—When I am gone, do not allow your manner to be changed, or suspicion of our intentions will be aroused. Act in every respect as though not a ray of hope remained, and keep up your fortitude. When the cart in which you will ride towards Tyburn tomorrow morning (the man shuddered involuntarily) shall have arrived," continued Jenny, not heeding his agitation, "at a certain part of the road, at a given signal a rescue will be made. The arrangements already made are so perfect that it is impossible they should fail. When the disturbance commences, leap from the left side of the cart, and a person will instantly cut the cords with which your arms are pinioned. You will then be conducted to a place of safety, and your deliverance be complete."

A smile played over the traitor's swarthy brow as he listened to these arrangements; and having again promised to observe secrecy, he grasped the girl's hand, and pressed it warmly.

It was as if an angel had visited the condemned cell; for hope now dwelt where before despair was the tenant.

"And now," said Jenny, "fear nothing—you will certainly escape. The ride in the Tyburn Cart will be on the road to liberty!"

The girl then departed, and the prisoner was left alone once more.

Morning came, and found the criminal full of hope, though he took especial care to conceal his feelings of exultation. At the appointed time he was taken into the press-yard, where his irons were knocked off.

He was pinioned by the Hangman, and the sheriff having demanded his body of the jaoler—the cart, with the coffin in it, was drawn up to the door of Newgate.

The cart was open behind, and the criminal sat with his back to the single horse which drew it, and his back rested against the coffin, in which, after he should have become a senseless corpse, his remains were to be placed.

By his side was the Ordinary of Newgate, in full canonicals, and with a freshly-powdered clerical wig surmounting his jolly round face. Had he been about to officiate at a stylish wedding, he could not have paid more attention to his attire. Indeed, in those days, the morning of an execution was rather a festive time, and the long ride from Newgate to Tyburn an occasion for display. In one hand he held a book,—with the fore-finger of the other he pointed towards heaven, and he appeared to be whispering in Blackmoor's ears exhortations to make his peace with God.

Blakmoor, whose arms were pinioned at the elbows, and had a white cotton nightcap on his head, as also a halter round his neck, appeared to pay the utmost attention to the divine's pious teachings; but every now and then a keen observer might have remarked a peculiar expression in his face, which augured more of hope on earth than of confidence in heaven.

Seated on the coffin, which served him as a sort of throne, was a sinister looking personage. He wore a low-crowned three-cornered hat, a shabby coat, buttoned closely up to his chin, and seedy velvet breeches, with tarnished knee buckles. From his coat-cuffs hung faded lace ruffles. He looked like a villain dressed in the cast off suit of some ruffling spark, and indeed such was the case. From the pocket of his coat dangled the end of a rope—and he, with the utmost composure, smoked a long pipe as the cart moved slowly onward.

This was Jack Ketch—the common hangman; the suit which he wore had formerly belonged to a dashing swindler, on whom he had performed the duties of his revolting office; and the rope which he carried in his pocket was provided in case that which encircled Blackmoor's neck should prove too short, or chance to break.

Then, as now, this functionary was regarded by the people with the utmost abhorrence, and the instant he made his appearance in the street, he was saluted with groans and yells from the populace; a reception which he treated with the most stolid indifference.

Before the cart went the sheriff in his state carriage—with three gaudily attired footmen behind, and six javelin-men on either side; and behind it on horseback the Recorder of London, and four of the aldermen, similarly guarded. A posse of constables brought up the rear of the procession.

It was a brilliant morning, and had it not been for the cart and the coffin and the chaplin and the criminal, a stranger looking on the cavalcade as it slowly proceeded up Holborn Hill, might have imagined it to be some comic gala-day. The shops in the line of the procession were all closed, and every window whence a view of it could be commanded, was crowded with eager faces. The women were dressed in their holiday apparel—and appeared to take more interest in the matter than those of the sterner sex, for they waved their handkerchiefs to the murderer, and felt themselves complimented if they got a recognition in return. With the men, it appeared as if business was not to be thought of for that morning at least; and the very children feasted their eyes on the sight, and longed to be allowed to go to Hang Fair.

A dense crowd of persons of all classes and conditions, preceded and followed the cart, which slowly proceeded until it reached High Holborn, where it halted for a moment, in order that the Bellman of St. Sepulchre's might recite his execution rhymes to the convict. This having been done, once more the sheriff led the way to Tyburn.

The mob all this while had not been unobservant of the conduct of Blackmoor, who, and the reader will not wonder at it, evinced great fortitude in his awful position.

"Isn't he a sweet gallows-bird?" said a young woman to a man whose sturdy arm was employed in helping her through the crowd. "Tis many a long day since I saw such a gay woodcock going to the springe!"

"Damny'ee, Nell," replied the fellow," "don't stop admiring the Ben Cull now, or we shan't get near to the three sticks. I wouldn't miss the ladder jump for a purse of shiners!" and the man dragged along the girl until they cleared the crowd where it was densest, and then both jogged merrily on towards the Edgware Road.

"Too bad, by my soul! to string up such a jolly blade as that, only for knocking a cursed old miser on the head," growled a savage-looking fellow, as he trudged amongst the crowd.

"Ain't it!" chimed in an old woman, who, aged as she was, carried a little child in her arms—"but we must all die one day or another, and to my mind, 'tis more pleasant like to die in one's shoes. My husband was tied——"

Here she was interrupted by a decent-looking man, who upbraided her with bringing the child into such a huge mob.

"That child's father—aye, and that child's grandfather, neither on 'em died in their beds —and mayhap he mayn't, too.—I always takes him to see the croakers, that he may learn to die game if ever his time should come to travel this way in a cart;—besides, I want that brave fellow in the cart to cure him."

"To cure him—cure that child?" asked the stranger in astonishment.

"Yes, and he will do it, after he's dead—not afore though; them sort of doctors can do what none of your 'potecaries can—no nor all the men in Surgeon's Hall put together."

The stranger was absolutely puzzled, and began to think the woman was out of her senses.

"Look here!" exclaimed the old dame; and so saying, she unwound a roll of flannel from the child's neck, and displayed to view a large wen which shockingly disfigured it.

"Well," observed the stranger.

"No, it ain't well yet—but I hope it soon will be—I only hope to God that I shall be able to get close to the gallows after he's turned off!" observed the old woman, with great energy.

"Why are you so anxious?" asked the man.

"Because if that wen is rubbed or stroked by a murderer's hand, when he's hanging from the gallows, and before it is cold, 'tis a certain cure for things like these.—I know it, for I've tried it more than once."

At that period, one of the chief sources of emolument to Jack Ketch was derived from this superstition which will doubtless remind the reader of the supposed efficacy in the reign of James, of the monarch's touch for the cure of scrofula, which from that circumstance obtained the name of the King's Evil.

Onward still proceeded the cart, which now drew very near to the Edgware Road—and Blackmoor, for the first time, began to fear lest he might have after all been deceived by Jenny Diver, for the purpose of throwing him off his guard, and so, until too late, preventing his divulging to the sheriffs the mysteries of the "Chapel."

By degrees he began to pay less attention to the prayers of the Ordinary, and to pray less fervently—at least so far as outward show went—himself. His eyes wandered searchingly amongst that sea of faces, nearly each of which was upturned towards him; but though he gazed with all the earnestness of a man whose life was hanging on a thread, and which might possibly before another hour be hanging on something stronger,—to wit a rope,—not one friendly feature could he discover.

Every turn of the cart-wheel made his heart beat faster, and at length he became so restless that the Ordinary observed it, and besought him to attend more closely to his spiritual duties. It was of no use, however, for the wretched man began to fear the worst.

Was it possible, he thought, that they had been sincere, but that their plans had failed? or, on second consideration, had they abandoned their project, as one fraught with too much danger to themselves?

A thousand such thoughts passed with the rapidity of lightning through his mind; but again entered his bosom when the cart entered the Edgware Road, and he remembered that Jenny Diver had said that in some part of that thoroughfare the rescue was to be made.

But that spark of hope too, was speedily quenched, as it struck him that even were the attempt made—the chances were that it would fail.

The procession proceeded a little way farther, and then halted opposite a road-side tavern.—It was a very ancient hostelry, called "THE THREE PUNCH BOWLS." Immediately on the cart stopping directly in front of the door, the mob set up a great shout, and at the same moment, a short, fat, jolly-faced man, habited in a suit of holiday clothes—his small-clothes half concealed by a little square white apron, and his head covered with a red peaked cap, was seen at the inn door with a steaming bowl of canary punch in his hands—the bottom of the bowl resting on his capacious stomach. Beside him was a drawer,—as waiters then were designated,—with a tray, on which were several small glasses, and one of very large dimensions. Behind both was the landlady, a comfortable buxom looking dame, jauntily dressed in a bran new quilted petticoat, and silk fordingall; and still further in the rear, a host of curious servants—men and maids, who nearly strained their eyes from their orbits to get a view of the man who was going to be hanged.

At a signal from the sheriff, Boniface advanced towards his carriage and presented him with a small glass of the punch; he then in turn administered similar potations to the chaplain, the javelin-men, Jack Ketch, and lastly he filled the large goblet, and offered it to Blackmoor.

"Take a glass of this, my valiant master; 'twill marvellously comfort thee in the long journey thou art about to undertake. Drink—man, drink!"

Blackmoor mournfully shook his head.

"What!" exclaimed the host in surprise; "never knew I but one who refused a parting draught at the three cups, and he was hanged for losing his drink. To my mind, friend, he served him right.—Tush, man, don't be [...] craven!" and again he offered the canary punch.

"No," said the culprit, "I need it not however, friend, there's a guinea, with which thou may'st drink mine!" and he threw Boniface a gold coin.

"That will I, my noble nob-breaker!—b[...] while there's life, there's hope."

Blackmoor caught spirit from the last r[...] mark, and determined to delay as much as possible; he therefore took the goblet—his arms being released for the occasion, and half emptied it.

"Good!" said the host; "and now, friend, I'll tell thee—for thou tarryest here yet ten minutes longer, while the sheriff and chaplain take their cool tankard within—how Nimming Jem Wildfire lost his life through leaving his glass. He was going to Tyburn, and stayed here, as thou hast done; but on my offering to him his parting cup, he dashed it to the ground, and commanded the driver to go on. He was taken at his word, and was hanged. In ten minutes after he was turned off, a reprieve arrived; but it was too late. You see, friend, had he lingered over his cup, he might now have been as merry as I am." And the land-lord chuckled heartily at his story.

Again the procession moved onward—and Blackmoor's anxiety rose to the most agonising pitch. The Edgware Road was nearly traversed, and all was quiet: not the slightest symptom of a disturbance appeared. The cart seemed to go at a fearful rate of speed, though in reality it went at an extremely slow pace. Still no rescue.

The crowd now became denser and denser, and temporary erections, crowded with people, were seen on either side of the road. Not a hundred yards off the cart, was a woman bawling out in the criminal's very ears, "The last dying speech and confession of the cruel murderer Blackmoor," and the Ordinary became still more energetic in his endeavours to induce Blackmoor to pray. By a strange oversight the hangman had omitted to pinion the wretched man's arms after he had drank at "The Three Punch Bowls," and now, he, by an impulse for which he could not account, suddenly started to his feet, and turning round, gazed forward.

God of Heaven! what a sight met his startled eye! He had not noticed that they had left behind them regular rows of streets, and that now the road was bounded by open fields—these fields covered with a mighty multitude of people; but he looked not at them, for high above their heads, mocking the glad sunshine with its hideousness, was a spectacle which drove the blood with a shock back to his heart.

It was Tyburn Tree!

There it stood—its three uprights and triple crossbeams standing out in black relief against the clear blue sky,—looming up like a dark spirit, all the darker for the brightness with which it was surrounded. All hope then was gone—he had been cheated, betrayed, and ruined, and——

No; not yet—there was yet hope. As he

[...] ng [...] the dismal sight, he [...] of the left side of the cart and recognised [...] ry Diver's face. She smiled encouragingly [...] it was a smile which at once banished [...] hope—it was not lost yet.

In a few moments afterwards that dense mass of beings began to rock to and fro, as the surface of the ocean heaves just before the outbreak of a storm; and in the distance and at the edge of the crowd was observed a man on horseback, waving a white handkerchief.

"A reprieve—a reprieve!" shouted the mob, many of them in no very pleasant mood; for after tramping so far, they did not feel inclined to be cheated out of the sight.

The sheriffs' carriage stopped—so did the cart, and in an instant afterwards both were surrounded by a band of desperadoes, armed with bludgeons and pistols. The suddenness of the movement was such, that the officials were completely dumbfounded, and rendered almost incapable of resistance.

"To the rescue!—to the rescue! my brave fellows!" shouted a voice well known, to the prisoner, and which sounded sweeter to his ear than would have done the music of the spheres.

Almost before the words had left his lips, the cart was completely surrounded —- the hangman, by one vigorous blow from a bludgeon, sent sprawling amongst the people, and the chaplain unceremoniously tumbled out of the cart. A desperate struggle now took place between the javelin-men and the assailants.

"Now then, quick!—for God's sake, lose not a moment!" said the leader to Blackmoor, snatching the cap from the head of the latter; "jump!"

The murderer made one desperate leap and was caught in the arms of a man, who instantly wrapped a cloak round him, and pressed a three-cornered cap over his head. Struck with surprise, the crowd parted right and left, as fifty men and more fought their way through them, and gained the open space; there stood several horses, on one of which at a sign the freed culprit leaped; his companion also mounted his steed, and exclaimed, "Follow me."

Away they went, and not until they were far beyond the reach of pursuit did they pull up their jaded steeds.

We must for a moment return to the neighbourhood of the gallows. The sight of the pair of horsemen galloping away, so absorbed the attention of the sheriff and javelin-men, and of the mob also, that the other persons concerned in the attack found it an easy matter to conceal their weapons during the confusion, to separate, mingle with the crowd, and thus escape detection.

Fruitless as the effort would have been, the Sheriff commanded his coachmen to drive after the fugitives with all speed; but on the servants attempting to obey the order, it was discovered that the traces had been cut. In this dilemma he ordered the best-mounted javelin-man to follow the escaped prisoner; but this was impossible—every one of the steeds had been ham-stringed.

Nothing, therefore, was to be done but to return to Newgate, whence when the sheriff arrived there, he issued a notice offering a reward of five-hundred guineas for the re-capture of Blackmoor, and the like sum for the apprehension of his rescuers.

Unobserved, however, by all, even by Blackmoor and his deliverers, one person, well mounted, had started in pursuit of the daring fugitives, and he was close on their track before they became aware of his purpose.

CHAPTER IX.

THE LAWYER AND HIS CLIENTS.

WHERE is the man who in his wanderings either of business or of pleasure, through this huge brick and mortar Babylon, called London, has not at some time cast a curious eye upon one or other of those human hives in which lawyers congregate, and where they wait like rapacious spiders for clients, who "bleed freely enough" to satisfy their enormous powers of suction?

In a well-known lane, leading out of Holborn and to which thoroughfare it gives its name, is a huge and unsightly pile of buildings—at the period in which the scene of our tale is laid, it was more unsightly still, so far as it regarded the mere materials of which it was constructed —but the neighbourhood around was far more cheerful. Within a short distance from its walls green fields commenced and stretched away in northerly and westerly directions, and on calm summer evenings sober citizens might have been seen gravely walking after business hours to the "Lamb's Conduit," or towards Primrose Hill and the village of Hackney. Prudent tradesmen, however, never passed by the walls of Gray's Inn without casting furtive glances at the place, and blessing their stars that they had nothing to do with law.

In one of the chambers of this celebrated Inn of Court resided a personage, who will be by-and-bye found to have exercised an important influence over the fates of certain persons connected with our history.

This person occupied three rooms in Gray's Inn; one he used as a sleeping apartment— one as a private office, where he transacted all his business, for he kept no qualified assistant —and the third, a small chamber opening into his office, and separated from it by folding doors, was during the day answered by a snub-nosed boy who was dignified by the name of "Clerk."

These apartments were situated in the uppermost story but one of the house in which they formed a part: it will be necessary to remember this in order that subsequent events may be fully understood.

On the sides of the door-posts, as one entered from the street, might have been read, printed in small letters, as if they were half-ashamed to show themselves, the name of the occupier of the apartment immediately under the attic:—

MR. WRIGGLETON DOOM, Attorney-at-Law' ☞ Right-hand door, 6th Landing.

And pointing directly in the direction of Mr. Wriggleton Doom's door on the landing specified was another board, with another ☞ and another direction, "Mr. Doom," so that if any stupid fly of a client had felt inclined to turn back, he would not had the least excuse in the world for not rushing headlong into the legal cobweb.

Mr. Wriggleton Doom was one afternoon sitting in his office, his slippered feet planted on the fender, and his arms folded on his chest, he was in such deep meditation that he had suffered the handful of fire in the grate to go almost out, when he was suddenly started by a tap at his green baized door.

But before we admit the visitor, whoever he may be, we must take a sort of pen-and-ink sketch of the attorney-at-law.

He was a long, lanky, bony-faced man;—his nose was beak-like, and over its sharp ridge was strained parchment-coloured skin ; hair of an iron-grey colour, and much resembling short bristles in texture covered his head, just as the said bristles rise from the wood-work of a hard scrubbing brush. His forehead was very high and very narrow, with dark hollows over the temple bones : eyes small and cunning peered suspiciously every where, and his mouth had a habit of compressing its thin lips until they looked like two thin blue lines, curved downwards between his nose and his receding chin. He was dressed in a suit of seedy black, carefully brushed ; around his neck was a white cravat with long ends; and extensively thin legs, the thighs encased in black plush breeches; that part below the knee (which was calf-less), wrapped in thick worsted stockings, and feet fixed into buckled shoes completes our portrait of the man and his costume.

"Come in," said the Attorney, as the knocking at the door was repeated.

The face of a boy who had a terrific obliquity in his left eye, and a twisted nose, a mouth of amazing dimensions, was immediately visible—the door was not sufficiently open to admit of a view of his body.

"Well, Snarley—any one want me—eh, Snarley?"

"Watkins," said Snarley.

"Humph! Watkins— Newgate-job, eh?" muttered Mr. Doom; "tell Watkins to come in, Snarley."

Snarley gave a grin and vanished—in another moment Watkins entered.

Snarley who opened the door to admit him, made a sort of pantomime sign as the Bow-street Runner greeted Mr. Doom, which said as plainly as signs could say, "You're a nice pair." He might perhaps have continued his dumb commentary, but observing that Mr. Doom was shifting his chair, he bolted in the most respectful manner possible.

"Werry odd business of this of Sir James Town, Mr. Doom," remarked Mr. Watkins.

The Lawyer started.

"I say," continued Mr Watkins, who never

did anything in a straightforward manner, " as this robbery of *Sir James Town, Baronet*," he laid a very strong emphasis on the " Sir " and the " Baronet." " beats me somehow."

Mr. Doom looked at the officer in the utmost astonishment—" What, my honoured patron, Sir James Town, plundered?" he asked, and his cadaverous countenance turned of an ashy hue.

" And a werry serious affair it is too—for sommat is gone as he'd give any money to get back again,—I thought as you does little odd jobs for the cage chaps now and then, you might have heard something about the missing ———"

" By God, Watkins! I know no more of it than you do," eagerly exclaimed the Attorney. " I had nothing to do with it."

" Well, Mr. Doom, who the devil said you had—who'd ha' suspected you of stopping a Baronet on the King's High Road, and robbing him of a thousand guineas and his diamonds, I should like to know:—You lawyers does all your little *business* at home," and as he spoke, the Bow-street Runner cast his eye round the office and smiled knowingly.

" Oh! Mr. Watkins—it was *only* diamonds and guineas, eh?" remarked the lawyer.

Mr. Doom, from some cause or other felt inexpressibly relieved, and leaning back in his chair he breathed more freely.

" *Only?* " repeated Mr. Watkins. " Only!—why now, Mr. Doom, I fancy you wouldn't much relish to have your silver spoons and odd matters of that sort taken—old parchment deeds, I'll be bound for it, you wouldn't mind the rascals grabbing.

A suspicion at once flashed on the mind of Mr. Doom.

It was best, he thought, that he should know more—so he said as coolly as he could:—

" Has Sir James Town lost any deeds—surely he did not carry his parchments, as well as his guineas, with him in his carriage?"

" Well, I cannot tell that," said the wary Officer—I merely called to know whether any one in Newgate had engaged you as lawyer, and let you into the secret of having a diamond-hilted sword, and some rings—and as you were Sir James's solicitor, you know, I was certain you would feel some interest in the matter."

" Of course I do," remarked Doom. " But I assure you, that should anything come to my knowledge, I will not fail to let you know of it."

Mr. Watkins awkwardly bowed his thanks and retired. After he had closed the door, the lawyer flung himself on his chair in a state of the utmost trepidation—something had shaken him terribly.

As Mr. Watkins went down the stairs, he muttered to himself, " I'm cursed if there isn't something werry odd in this business," then putting his fore-finger on one side of his nose, he seemed to ponder for a moment: a sagacious wink and a nod, however, indicated that he would solve the enigma, whatever it might be.

While Mr. Doom was yet wrapt in thought, another visitor ascended the staircase. It was Sir James Town.

The baronet entered unannounced into Mr. Doom's private office as was his custom. The lawyer was still absorbed in meditation, and did not hear him come in. Sir James walked slowly towards him and touched him on the arm.

" My God!—Oh! bless me—You! Sir James—I beg your pardon—pray be seated. You are the man whom I least of all expected, and him of all others I was most anxious to see," said Mr. Doom.

" So far—well," remarked Sir James, if you are not engaged I have some rather important business to transact with you. Are we quite alone?"

" Stay," said Doom, as he moved towards the door.

" Snarley!" he cried, " Snarley!"

" I'm here," said that amiable youth—Must I come in?"

" Not now—Did you serve that writ on Widow Griggs this morning?"

" No, master, I didn't; she said as she'd sure to pay you to-morrow, and thought I'd leave it till then."

" *You* thought, sirrah! A pox on your impertinence—go and serve it without loss of time, and hark ye! you dog—as 'tis near your home you need not return again—I'll lock up."

Snarley snatched his hat, whistled all the way down stairs, and sped away in the direction of the Westminster cockpit, where a main of cocks was, he knew, to be fought that afternoon.

Doom then carefully locked the outer-door, and returned to his visitor.

" You don't look well, Sir James," he remarked.

" It would be wonderful if I did, after the loss I have sustained," replied the baronet. " Have you heard of it, Doom?"

" Yes—not an hour since," replied the man of law.

" And do you know the extent of the robbery —I suspect not," inquired the baronet.

" Well—Sir James, I was told you had lost a thousand guineas besides some valuable family diamonds—Is that so?"

" Yes; and something which troubles me far more than either—something which may be the ruin both of me and of yourself too, therefore I have come to consult you as to the best mode of proceeding in this exceedingly awkward dilemma."

The lawyer's doubts were now dissipated, and his mind harboured a fearful certainty—He felt himself in the broils, but the wily man determined to exercise his utmost ingenuity to free himself from them.

" Doom," said Sir James in a low voice, " the deed which enabled me to wrest the title and estates from Richard—the deed which you and I forged is now out of my possession, and our necks are not worth an hour's purchase."

" Be good enough, Sir James, to say *you* forged—I had nothing whatever to do beyond drawing it up, and when I did so, I had not the slightest doubt that I was acting under proper directions."

" Liar and scoundrel!" exclaimed the baronet, in a towering rage, " it fortunately happens that, though you thus meanly attempt to get your neck out of the noose and leave me to dangle alone, I have ample proofs in my possession of your being an accomplice—all your letters to me on the subject—aye, every one, and the very original draft of the deed too, with your tracings will rise up against you if you choose to attempt to sneak out of this business."

The attorney was fairly taken aback, but he was not yet beaten.

"And who," he asked, "would believe the word of a man like Sir James—I beg his pardon—Mr. James Town? If a man avails himself of a forged document to gain possession of the title and estates of another, it is not unlikely that he would not forge documents also which might implicate others."

"But supposing there are *living* witnesses of your share in the transaction, Doom?" asked Sir James, coolly.

The lawyer burst into a scornful laugh.

"*Living* witnesses," he almost shrieked, "there are none! Flitchman, who so cleverly counterfeited the handwriting of the will, and the old woman who we got to swear at Doctors Commons that she saw old Sir Richard Town sign it, are both dead. Flitcher was transported to Virginia for shoplifting where he died, and no one for years has heard of old Mrs. Larkin."

"Flitchman is *living*, Doom! he escaped long since from the plantations, where he had spread for obvious reasons a report of his death; and so is the old woman Larkin; and I know where to find them."

The lawyer gasped in agony. "Damnation," he muttered between his clenched teeth.

"Aye, and more than that," continued Town, "the nurse who substituted me for the true heir to the title and estates, is still alive and in London! so you see that both of us, unless we work together, are on the brink of ruin."

There was no way of escape now; and the villains offering each other their hands, sat down to consider what was best to be done.

To what conclusion they come, the subsequent events of our tale must develop. After a long and earnest consultation, Sir James took his leave and the lawyer was once more alone.

Mr. Doom was destined to have one other visitor that day. About an hour after Town had departed, the knocker of the outer door sounded.

For a few minutes,—so shaken were his nerves by his two previous encounters—he hesitated whether he should obey the summons; but again the knocker rattled, as if he who grasped it was in no mood to be kept waiting.

It was now growing dark, but without waiting to light his lamp, Mr. Doom, labouring under a sense of new ills to come, proceeded to the outer door and opened it.

"Mr. Wriggleton Doom, I presume," said the person who was standing without.

"That is my name, sir—Wriggleton Doom at your service."

The speaker was, so far as could be observed in the gloom of the evening, tall; but his figure was entirely concealed from view by a large cloak which completely enveloped his person. His address was courteous, though firm.

"Then, perhaps, sir, you would favour me with a few minutes' conversation," insinuated the Stranger.

"Really, sir," replied the lawyer, "I don't know; 'tis past business hours—my clerk is absent, and if you would call to-morrow it would be rather more convenient to me."

"But not to me, sir; and if you are alone—why 'tis all the better; for my business requires your private ear."

"More trouble!" thought Mr. Wriggleton Doom. Seeing that to put off his unwelcome visitor was a matter of impossibility, he made a virtue of necessity, and invited him inside.

The instant the Unknown had crossed the threshold, he coolly closed the door, locked it, and put the key in his pocket.

"Really, sir," remarked the lawyer, "this is"—

"Somewhat strange, you would say," interrupted the Stranger; "but I assure you that both for your sake and mine, it is absolutely necessary that every precaution against surprise should be taken."

Mr. Doom invited the Stranger to take a chair, when they had reached his inner office. He flung himself into a chair, and the lawyer was about to light a lamp, when the mysterious visitor laid his hand on his arm and prevented him.

"We had better talk in the dark," said he. "When I have to do with knaves I use every precaution, and perhaps it would be quite as well if you ever met me by chance, that you should not know me again."

It now struck Mr. Doom that the Stranger had visited him for the purpose of plunder, and he assured him that if such was the case, he would most certainly be disappointed in obtaining a booty, as he left all his money and valuables at his private residence.

"On that score you have nought to fear, Mr. Doom—I came here for a far different purpose. You are, I believe, the legal adviser of Sir James Town?"

"Until," said the lawyer, somewhat emboldened by the assurance Handsome Jack had given him—for Handsome Jack in reality it was—"until I know who you are, and by what right you ask the question, I do not feel disposed to answer it."

"Then," said Jack, drawing two pistols from the belt beneath his cloak, "perhaps you need a little persuasion. I asked you a simple question, and, mark me, Mr. Doom, to that question—aye, and to some others, too, I *will* have positive and distinct answers;—so no quibbling or evasion with me, for I know you."

"Well," said the lawyer, who by no means relished the sight of the formidable weapons, "and suppose I am engaged in some trifling matters for Sir James Town—what then?"

"Much—very much," returned Jack. "Pray, sir, have you any remembrance of drawing up a certain deed—a will, in fact, for one Sir Richard Town; by means of which Sir James, your client, came into possession of his title and estates?"

"I remember nothing of the kind," said Doom, who was scarcely able to conceal his agitation. It was fortunate for him, he thought, that the room was dimly lighted, or the quivering of the muscles of his face must ha... ...throwing ... the window he gave a low whistle, ...observed. ...which was answered from below.

"And you do not remember a ... ...Flitchman, and a woman named ... ...urged the Stranger.

"In the devil's name, sir! who ... ...thus question me?" cried the lawyer.

"I represent the legitimate owner of the title and estates, the young Sir Rich... ...who has been most cruelly and ba... robbed of his rights by James Town;—you, ... in-famous tool, and your wretched subor... ...who I am, it matters not; but that you ... one day know."

"Assertions do not prove what you say," ...observed the cunning Wriggleton.

"I have the proofs of your infamy, ...returned Handsome Jack; "there is ... suffi-cient light for you to behold a damn... proof of it," and he drew from his pocket the deed which he had taken from the cabinet on the night of his visit to Sir James Town.

The lawyer put on his spectacles, placed his eyes close to the parchment, observed the sig-nature, and suddenly he attempted to snatch the document from Handsome Jack's hand.

But he had to do with the wrong man—in an instant it was raised high beyond his reach, and a scornful laugh proclaimed the triumph of the stranger.

A fearful shriek burst from the lips of the lawyer—staggering for a moment, he fell sense-less on the floor.

Seizing a jug which stood near, Handsome Jack dashed its contents on the face of the fainting man, this recalled him to conscious-ness, and Jack lifted him to a sofa, muttering as he did ...

"...God knows, were it not necessary to do so, I would rather chop off these hands than place them in contact with aught so vile as this mis-creant."

Doom being now recovered, he gazed wildly about him, and then asked in convulsive ac-cents,

"Where got you that deed?"

"That it concerns not you to know—the ob-ject of my visit to you at this unseemly hour, is to demand from you a written acknowledg-ment of the share you had in this affair of the forged deed—that I am determined to have; unless you give it I will instantly deliver you into the hands of justice, but if you fully and freely confess your share in this transaction, I pledge you my word that Sir Richard Town will use his best endeavours to secure your safety."

"I accept the terms," said Doom.

He then procured paper, pen and ink, and drew up a formal acknowledgment of his share in the transaction, and was about to sign it, when Jack exclaimed,—

"Stay, sir;—we must have two witnesses to your signature, or the confession will be worth-less."

"But it will be impossible to procure them now," remarked Doom; "if to-morrow would——"

"Damn your to-morrows—you slippery spin-ner of subtleties. Think you I came here un-provided with witnesses of my own;" and

Footsteps were then heard ascending the stairs, and Handsome Jack having unbolted the door, two persons entered the room, a man and woman. The moon had risen, it was dimly shining into the place, affording sufficient light ... through ... ...which by the ... concealed.

"I have obtained, friends," said Handsome Jack, addressing them, "that for which I came ... This infernal villain has drawn up a document, which I wish you to witness and sign, for he is as slippery as an eel, and as crafty as the devil. Now then, Mr. Doom, please to read over what you have written to these friends of mine."

With much mortification Doom did this; and at Handsome Jack's command he affixed his nature.

Then the latter desired hi... friends to place their's also on the face of the document, and by the side of the signature of Wriggleton Doom appeared those of James M'Cleane and Mary Young.

"And now," said Handsome Jack to the un-happy lawyer, "we will leave you to your me-ditations, which will doubtless be of no very pleasant nature, and in order to afford you an opportunity of pondering on the fate which will inevitably be yours if you inform Town of what has passed,—I will take the liberty of locking you in."

The three then departed, Jack locking the outer door behind them, and flinging the key on the landing.

"A good trick, i'faith, Jack," said M'Cleane, when they had passed the street. "You have now got the game in your own hands, for Town dares not prosecute you should he ever discover it was you who robbed him of his jewels ——"

"I beg your pardon, M'Cleane," said Jack, interrupting him, "I did but help myself to my own; for in my pocket I have that which, did I choose to use it, would at once re-instate me in the portion of which I was unjustly de-prived."

"Then, mayhap, you will soon be tired of our company, Handsome Jack? asked Jenny Diver with an arch look.

"Not so, by Heaven!" replied Jack, quickly, "I freely chose my present vocation, and while the profession boasts of such brave men as Captain M'Cleane, and such pretty girls as Jenny Diver, I shall be in no hurry to quit it."

The party having arrived near Little Turn-stile, now deemed it prudent to separate, and having done so, Jenny Diver proceeded towards the "Chapel," while Handsome Jack and M'Cleane strolled towards Chancery Lane on their way to Hanging Sword Alley, in Fleet Street, where at that time resided Williams, one of the most noted "fences" of the day.

CHAPTER X.

THE FLIGHT—THE PURSUIT—AND THE SECRET TRIBUNAL.

It will be remembered when Blackmoor, through the agency of his old companions, had been in so extraordinary a manner rescued from the doom which he had almost given over all hopes of evading, that, accompanied by a single horseman, he rode off at full speed, never daring to look behind him, until the panting steeds, and the assurance of present safety, induced both to draw rein and take a few moments rest after the excessive excitement of the last few hours.

They were now far away from Tyburn—but still, as they stood upon a rising ground, concealed from observation, however, by a cluster

No. 6.

of large trees, they could see far away, and below, so clear was the atmosphere, the gallows.

"Look yonder, Blackmoor," said M'Cleane, "had it not been for those whom once you would have betrayed, where and what would you have been now?"

"Dangling like a dog from one of the cross-beams, and food for worms, my noble Captain," replied Blackmoor.

And falling on his knees, he poured forth protestations of gratitude to the man who had twice saved his life; in the latter instance at the expense of his own.

M'Cleane listened; but believed not in the scoundrel's sincerity for a moment. He had, however, his game to play, and therefore appeared to confide in the promises of gratitude which Blackmoor uttered.

"Are you willing, Blackmoor, to again join

us, and be true to the oath of fidelity which you will, if you agree to my proposition, again have to take?"

The escaped murderer gladly embraced the offer and eagerly renewed his protestations of unflinching devotion to the interests of the community.

"Good!" returned M'Cleane. "We will return together to the chapel this evening. But we must wait until dark, for I imagine that you have no desire to be recognised and so take another ride to TYBURN to-morrow morning."

Blackmoor turned pale and unconsciously put his fingers to his neck. It was odd enough; the halter was still round it, the long end having in the struggle got within his loose waistcoat.

"Rather ominous!" observed, or rather sneered M'Cleane, "but never mind, Blackmoor, remove that hempen cravat and give it me. I'll hang it up in my cabinet of curiosities at the "Chapel."

Blackmoor handed the halter to M'Cleane, who carefully coiled it up, wrapped it in his handkerchief, and deposited it in his pocket.

Having now somewhat recovered their coolness, and the horses being relieved, they persued their way with extreme caution; at length, at a turn of the road, a carriage was perceived advancing towards them.

After cautiously surveying it for a few moments, M'Cleane exclaimed:—

"It contains only women—what say you, Blackmoor, to beginning business again? Now just to keep our hands in, we'll even try what mettle those women are made of."

Blackmoor instantly assented—the wretch had scarcely been snatched from the jaws of death, before, with avidity, he again entered upon the path of crime.

"You take care of the post-boy, and I'll pay attention to the ladies," said M'Cleane; "and here—here is a barker for you!"

By this time the carriage was close upon them. Blackmoor drew his pistol, and putting its muzzle close to the face of the terrified creature, threatened him with instant death if he moved an inch. At the same moment Captain M'Cleane rode to the side of the carriage, which was an open one.

Politely removing his hat, he made the gentlewomen, who were very young, and pretty, a profound bow. One of them had a romance in her hand, which she appeared to have been reading to her companions, who all seemed to regard the interruption as a very pretty incident, similar to those which they had been reading of, and which was got up for their special amusement.

"Ladies," said M'Cleane, who had eyed the book and its title, again bowing, "as a patron of the fair sex, I am at this moment travelling purely for the sake of winning the favour of a heard-hearted mistress!"

The young ladies tittered, and appeared to be mightily pleased with the adventure, especially as M'Cleane was such a handsome gallant.

"But, ladies," resumed M'Cleane, "I am at this time reduced to the necessity of asking relief, having nothing to carry me on my intended prosecution."

At this the girls began to think that they had met with some Quixote or Amadis de Gaul, such as all of them had read of and admired, in real life, and who was saluting them in the extravagant, but then rather fashionable style of knight-errantry.

"Sir Knight," said one of the prettyest and pleasantest amongst them, "we heartily commiserate your condition, and are very much troubled that we cannot contribute towards your support; for we have nothing about us but a sacred deposition, which the laws of your order will not suffer you to violate."

Captain M'Cleane, whose practice on the road had not hitherto been of the most peaceable and gentle character, was not a little pleased to think that he had met with such pleasant folks, and for the sake of the jest was half induced to let them pass unmolested; but Blackmoor was present, and to have ridden away without any booty would, he thought, have looked like a failure. This he could not brook, so he again addressed the gentlewomen.

"May, I, ladies, be favoured with a knowledge of what this sacred deposition which you speak of is, so that I may employ my utmost abilities in its defence, as the laws of knight-errantry require?"

The lady who had spoken before, and who suspected least of any in the company, replied, that the deposition she had spoken of was £3,000, the portion of one of the company, who was going to bestow it upon the knight who had won her good will by his many past services.

"Then," said M'Cleane, bowing more courteously than before, "pray present my humble duty to the knight, and be pleased to tell him my name is Captain M'Cleane; that out of mere necessity I have made bold to borrow a part of it; that for his sake I wish it were twice as much, and that I promise to expend the sum in defence of injured lovers, and the support of gentlemen who profess knight-errantry."

"M'Cleane!" the ladies exclaimed; "what! are you the famous Captain M'Cleane, the highwayman!"

"The same ladies, at your service!" replied the Captain, again bowing; "and as I do not wish to deprive you of all, I will thank you to hand me a part only. Show me the money."

One of the ladies produced three canvas bags, in each of which she said were a thousand guineas.

M'Cleane took one, bade them not to fear, for he would not further molest them, and then requested the post-boy to drive on.

"A lucky windfall, by St. Nicholas!" exclaimed the Captain, as he and Blackmoor rode off again at full speed.

"Pity that you left behind you those two bags of gold-finches!" said the traitor, as they gallopped along.

"If I had taken them," returned M'Cleane, "I should deserve to be put into the noose from which you have escaped.—Blackmoor, you cannot understand generosity, and even in our profession there is much of it."

Blackmoor bit his lip at the rebuke, and was silent.

"It has been before stated that, although when the traitor and murderer was rescued, the sheriff's men were prevented from following the daring perpetrators of the act, one individual, well mounted, followed on their track.

This individual was a man of about thirty years of age—of middle height, and of a frame which appeared to be capable of much endurance. His physiognomy was indicative of indomitable perseverance in any project which he undertook; and of an unforgiving and relentless disposition.

This was the only son of Abraham Blake—the old miser who was murdered by Blackmoor in his dwelling-house in Bucklersbury.

The old miser had long ceased to hold communication with any member of his family save this son, who was his favourite, if ever a love for anything save a love for gold, could harbour in his dried-up bosom; and him, he would not allow to enter his house. And even this scanty portion of affection was returned; but interest may have had something to do with it, for old Blake had intimated his intention of leaving the young man the whole of his property.

Revenge was a predominating principle of Ephraim Blake's heart; and it was with a view of beholding and gloating over the dying agonies of the murderer of his father, that he had mounted horse, and followed the procession to Tyburn.

With savage delight he had feasted his eyes upon the sufferings so evident in the face of Blackmoor, when that man's fate was trembling in the balance: with demoniac glee he had seen the cart near the fatal spot; and with infernal satisfaction he looked on the coffin which was soon to contain the hated remains of the murderer of his father.

Little as he truly loved that miserly parent, he felt as he stood over his senseless and mangled corpse, and marked the crimson pool in which his grey hairs were dabbled, that his blood cried for vengeance.

Judge then, of his feelings, when he was the murderer leap from the cart, and in company with another, escape from his punishment. His teeth literally gnashed with passion at being disappointed of the treat which he had promised himself.

As soon as he recovered from his surprise, he determined to go in search of, and, if possible, re-capture Blackmoor; and this resolution he immediately carried into effect;—with what success we shall hereafter be acquainted.

Threading his way through lanes and bye-woods, now losing sight of and again catching glimpses of M'Cleane and Blackmoor, as they swiftly pursued their way; he managed to keep them in view, and partly to ascertain what course they intended to take. Whilst they were resting their steeds and themselves at the brow of the hill, he was at its foot; but he deemed it prudent not to attack two such daring men as he knew both must be.

When they quitted their covert he was again on their track, as stealthily, but as surely as the Indian on the trail of his enemy, or the bloodhound on the path of its prey.

When they were robbing the young gentlewomen in their carriage, he was watching them;—and when, that business concluded, they again pressed onward—he marked their course, and though unseen, was not very far behind them.

But we will for a time leave the pursuer and rejoin the pursued. The sun had gone down—the last red tinge had died on the west, and the mists of evening began to render objects around shadowy and indistinct, when, as M'Cleane and Blackmoor were gently walking their distressed horses along the old Bath and London Road, which they had gained by t king a very circuitous route, and were anticipating a safe return to the "Chapel," the quick ears of the Captain caught the sound of horses' hoofs clattering along the road, and of voices shouting "A highwayman! a highwayman!"

"Hell and furies!" he exclaimed, "they have raised the hue-and-cry. Blackmoor, as you value your safety, keep close to me, and follow my example in everything."

"I am bound to obey you, Captain!" returned the traitor.

"This is no time for talk; see that your pistol is primed—and now remember we both ride for our necks!"

Clapping spurs to their horses, they commenced the desperate race. The shouts of the people behind became more distinct, and the word "murderer" as well as "highwayman," was plainly heard.

"Heard you that?" asked M'Cleane, significantly.

"For God's sake! let us push on!" said Blackmoor, in reply; "I feel as though the halter was once more round my neck."

On the horses dashed at the very top of their speed, their riders caring nought for any obstacles which might be in their way,—and swiftly followed the pursuers. The whole country seemed to be up, for it was evident that every moment the numbers of those who sought to capture them increased.

Still nearer—house after house as they passed by them, looked like mere shadows; from their windows, however, the inmates, startled by the shouts of young Blake and his companions, anxiously looked out.

Nothing for a time interrupted their progress, until they reached a turnpike, the gate of which was closed.

Flinging the toll-man a guinea, M'Cleane hurriedly exclaimed:—

"Keep the change, and bolt the gate after us!"

A wink from the toll-man assured M'Cleane that his order would be attended to.

"We shall gain time at least by that ruse," said the Captain; but by the devils in hell, we have not a moment to lose!"

The pace was not in the least slackened, and at length they no longer heard the cry of those who followed them; a hill now lay before them, and it became absolutely necessary to walk their horses to the summit. Still all remained quiet, and they were hugging themselves on their success after they had descended the other side, when to their suprise and consternation, their enemies, who had skirted the rising ground, were seen approaching from a cross-road.

"Follow me!" cried M'Cleane, and grasping the bridle rein of Blackmoor's horse, whose rider was now almost stupified with terror, he turned its head in the direction of a lane which fortunately lay on their left, and nearly opposite the place from whence their pursuers emerged.

This sudden movement was the means of somewhat disconcerting Blake and his party, and before they could re-unite their scattered forces, M'Cleane and Blackmoor were galloping furiously down a narrow lane which led they knew not whither.

Both the Captain and his companion were now almost in despair, for their relentless enemies were heard plunging through the lane; and what made the matter worse, their horses, which had been hard worked, and had had no provender since the morning, began to show symptoms of breaking down.

Suddenly a gate, dividing the lane from a ploughed field, arrested their further progress. It was high, and on the other side of it was a deep descent.

"There is nothing left for it," said M'Cleane, "but to trust to these poor devils of animals to take the leap;" and backing his horse, he dashed forward and cleared the barrier in safety. Immediately afterwards Blackmoor also attempted to gain the field, but his steed struck her fetlocks against the upper bar of the gate, and man and horse rolled on the ground.

M'Cleane was at his side in an instant.

"It is of no use to trust to four legs," said he; "we must abandon the horses, and conceal ourselves as we best may. Then seizing Blackmoor by the arm, he doubled as it were, on his course, and skirting the hedge, both crept softly towards the very point where Blake had surprised them.

The high-road again gained, they had the satisfaction of hearing the voices of those who had caused them so much anxiety gradually growing less and less distinct; and now, though regretting the loss of his horses, M'Cleane pursued his way towards London.

They had not travelled far before they met two countrymen, who they compiled to part with their farmers' frocks and hats, M'Cleane liberally remunerating them for them. Throwing the former over their habiliments, and otherwise disguising themselves, they walked on unmolested until they arrived, about three o'clock in the morning, in St. Giles's Fields. From thence to the "Chapel" was a way comparatively easy to be traversed, the dim lanes and crooked streets, being far more favourable to concealment than the king's highway.

The gateway, which led to the stablery of the "Chapel" having, after their toils and anxieties been reached, M'Cleane with his whistle gave the usual low and expressive signal; and "Beauty" having rapidly surveyed the parties without, quickly opened the strongly-barred gate.

"Safe at last!" ejaculated the Captain, as he flung off the farmer's frock, and directed Blackmoor to do the same.

"Werry glad to see you, Master Blackmoor," remarked Beauty, as he recognized the traitor; "who'd have thought of your visiting your old quarters, arter the ride up Tyburn way?"

Blackmoor growled out something—and at a sign from M'Cleane, Beauty disappeared.

Shortly, he returned with Dick Flybynight, who grasped his hand with great fervour.

A short conference took place between the pair—and then Dick retired. Presently the sound as of a troop of men on march was heard, coming towards the door which communicated with the interior of the "Chapel." The door flew open, and twelve men, dressed in black garments which reached from their necks to their feet entered, and saluted the Captain.

Dick Flybynight, who was their leader, addressing M'Cleane with the utmost deference, observed in respectful tones:—

"We are at his command, who knowing all, commands all!"

"Black Guard!" ordered M'Cleane, pointing to the traitor, "there is your prisoner,—convey him to the SECRET TRIBUNAL, where he shall be judged!"

"Was it for this you saved me?" exclaimed Blackmoor, turning pale; "was I saved from one death, only to endure another?"

"Away with him!" ordered M'Cleane, waving his hand;—and Blackmoor, cowed and terrified, was hurried from the place.

M'Cleane, having given Beauty some private orders, then proceeded to that part of the building where Madame Charlotte and Jenny Diver were to be found.

"Oh, James!" shrieked Madame Charlotte, "Jenny and I were in despair lest some evil should have befallen you;" and flinging her plump arms round his neck she burst into tears, and almost smothered him with caresses. Jenny Diver, who, hearing M'Cleane's voice, rushed into the room while the scene was enacting, also fell upon his neck, and the gallant highwayman was in almost as much danger from suffocation between that pretty pair, as he had a few hours previously been from the pursuit young of Blake, the murdered miser's son. The predicament in which he was now placed, was, however, by far the pleasantest of the two, if his sparkling eyes and flushed cheeks might be believed.

"Kisses are very sweet, my beauties!" he remarked, "on a full stomach; but when a man has fasted twenty hours or so, a cold capon and a goblet of canary, would not be unwelcome. Since I quitted the "Chapel" this morning, I have tasted nothing."

Madame Charlotte and Jenny Diver immediately unloosed their wiry arms from his neck, and soon placed before him a meal to which he did ample justice.

"We have been terribly anxious for your safety, dear Jem!" said Madame Charlotte, who sat on one side of him, Jenny Diver leaning fondly on his shoulder on the other. "And have you got the villain?"

"He is in the vault below," answered the

Captain; "I have had tough work to get him here—but now he shall no longer be a source of anxiety to us. Had I not secured him when I did, before this, instead of being snug in the 'Chapel,' we should all have been whistling between the stone walls of the Compter or the Marshalsea': for the rascal told me that he would, even with his last breath, have betrayed us!"

"You are a brave fellow, M'Cleane!" murmured Jenny—a sentiment which was echoed by Madame Charlotte, and enforced by soft caresses from both.

"Unfortunately," said M'Cleane, to whom these feminine endearments were anything but disagreeable, "unfortunately, my charmers, I must dismiss you to your pillows, without this night doing myself the pleasure of accompanying either of you; for a Council of Safety sits in the Secret Tribunal, and I must repair thither to join them. Important business is in hand."

As neither of the ladies were to be favoured with the Captain's company, one had no reason whatever to be jealous of the other; so, pouting their pretty lips in concert, each indulged in lamentations for M'Cleane's forced absence. Kissing both of them, the Captain bade them adieu, and quitted the apartment.

If the "Chapel" possessed a magnificent saloon with its luxurious apartments, and its secret chabers, where splendour ministered to passion, it also contained within its mysterious bounds a place of secresy and of terror, in which the judicial part of the business of the fraternity was transacted. For even that company of robbers had laws which were binding on each member of the gang;—and so vigilant were they whose business it was to carry these laws into effect, that it was seldom indeed a transgressor escaped.

The "Court" in which all offences were tried—offences against the brotherhood of M'Cleane's band—was a subterranean apartment of the "Chapel," the entrance to which was only known to a few of the fraternity, and these were the oldest and most tried members. It was a large apartment, with a groined roof supported by stone pillars. At its upper end was a raised bench, on which was placed a single arm-chair and a table, on which reposed a skull. Sable draperies, which concealed the walls, and the black coverings of the table and chair, threw a sombre sort of solemnity over the place, which was lighted by three lamps. It somewhat resembled one of the courts of that infernal institution—THE INQUISITION. THIS WAS THE HALL OF THE SECRET TRIBUNAL !

Contiguous to it were several dungeons, with ponderous doors, in which those who were to appear before the Robbers' Court were confined, either until they should have been convicted, or acquitted. To one of these dreary places, was Blackmoor, the traitor, conveyed by the Black Guard, immediately after his being brought back to the "Chapel" by M'Cleane.

It was long past midnight, but had it been broad noon, not a single ray of sunshine could have found its way into that gloomy abode. The traitor lay on a heap of straw, pondering on the strange events of the day. In the morning he had been within a hairbreadth of the halter. By an almost marvellous interposition of those who had reason to rejoice in his destruction, he had escaped with life. Scarcely had he become free, than he committed a crime by which again his life might be forfeited. After a fearful pursuit, he had reached his old quarters in safety, only to be made once more a prisoner! As he thought of all this, he was bewildered; and he was only roused from his reverie by hearing the rattling of bolts and bars, and by the flinging open of his dungeon door.

The Black Guard—each one of whom wore a mask—drew up in front of his cell; each one of whom had a drawn sword in his hand. The Chief ordered Blackmoor to come forth; and shivering with anxiety, the traitor quitted the cell.

He was conducted into the Secret Tribunal, and placed in front of the person who occupied the chair;—this was M'Cleane.

Twelve members of the gang, also masked, stood near the table;—they were the heads of the twelve distinct bands into which the community was divided.

The Captain, as soon as Blackmoor entered, whispered to the Captain of the Black Guard:—"Has the master of the vessel arrived according to my orders?"

"He is here," was the reply.

"Good!—now, then, to our business!" M'Cleane then addressed Blackmoor:—

"Traitor! you will doubtless be surprised to find that you were not brought here for the purpose of being again enlisted as a comrade. With the brave men of our ranks you will no longer be associated. For the sake of these gallant men, you were this day rescued from a fate which you richly deserved;—but for their sakes, also, you must now be doomed to a punishment which will effectually secure all within the 'Chapel' from your villainy, and at the same time make you wish that you had never been delivered from the hands of the common hangman. Your life, henceforward will be one of misery and degradation. Did we choose, we might now shed your blood, and so dispose of your miserable carcase as to defy detection; but this Tribunal prefers that you be disposed of in a different manner; and before morning light you will be on your way to perpetual chains, and terrible slavery."

The traitor, somewhat relieved to find that his life would be spared, muttered an oath of defiance—and with desperate energy shook his clenched fist in the face of the judge.

"Bind him, hand and foot!" said the Captain, sternly.

The order was instantly executed, and Blackmoor lay helpless on the floor of the Court.

"Comrades!" asked M'Cleane, addressing the twelve leaders—"are you content?"

"We are content!" said each, as with one voice, at the same time bowing their heads with respectful deference to the Captain and Judge.

"Let Captain Grawler be brought hither," said M'Cleane.

The Chief of the Black Guard retired, and in the course of a few minutes returned with a man who was led into the place blindfolded.

The stranger was habited in the garb of a sailor. He was tall, very powerfully built, and seemingly possessed of herculean strength. His bronzed countenance indicated that he had defied all weathers, and visited many a climate. Across his right cheek and on his forehead were two deep scars, which looked as though they had been inflicted by a cutlass, or some such weapon. Great daring and ferocity were expressed in his countenance, as well as an utter recklessness of danger, and his glance assured one that he was mercenary, cruel, and relentless.

"Your servant, noble Captain!" said Grawler, addressing M'Cleane, with whose person he appeared to be perfectly acquainted. "By G——! walking blindfold along these cursed winding passages, and down the dark staircases, is worse than going to the masthead on a cold night in the Bay of Biscay. What's in the wind, now? and I'll thank you to run out the line quick, for it's now flood-tide, and the "Maryland Trader" only waits for me."

"And one other, Grawler,—that is, if you have room for a passenger."

"Well, Captain, that depends on the terms we come to.—Now, a good chap, who can work hard in the tobacco plantations in Virginny, might fetch a fair price over the water; and if you've one to sell reasonable, why I don't care if—"

"What d'ye think now of that fellow?" asked M'Cleane, pointing to Blackmoor.

Grawler looked at the traitor much as a jockey would regard a horse he was about to bargain for.

"Why," said he, after a careful survey, "he *might* sell there, if he keeps in good condition during the voyage; but I don't know whether I've room for such a big 'un. There are already thirty men, and forty-five boys, who we've managed to kidnap, aboard the 'Maryland Trader.' D—n 'em! I wish I'd got 'em safe off, for they don't like the idea of sailing with *me* at all, and make the devil's own fuss about their wives and families. But what d'ye ask for this great animal, Captain;—if we can come to terms, we'll soon gag him, and find him a nice master elsewhere."

"We are neither kidnappers nor man-sellers here!" said M'Cleane. "Our object is to get that fellow out of the country, and, d'ye hear, *kept* out of it. He is a traitor, and if you choose to take him, and sell him to some planter who will watch him narrowly, and not be over kind to him, we will not only make you a present of him, but present you with fifty guineas into the bargain."

"Sell him to a planter as is not *over kind!*" grinned Grawler; "why, if there's devil's incarnate, it's them planters! and a man had better be in hell than in their clutches! I'll accept your offer;—and you may depend upon it that this fellow here shall never trouble you more."

"Enough!" said M'Cleane; and he placed in Captain Grawler's hand the sum he had mentioned.

The miserable Blackmoor was now completely cowed. The atrocious system of kidnapping men and children by captains, for the sake of disposing of them to the cotton and tobacco planters of Virginia, Maryland, and the Carolinas, was then in full operation, and constituted an offence punishable by death. The unhappy wretches who were thus sold into slavery, endured the most dreadful suffering,—sufferings from which they could never, excepting in rare instances, escape with life. Blackmoor had formerly heard from one of the fortunate few who had returned, maimed, and emaciated, the story of his horrible sufferings; and, therefore, now that he was doomed to undergo similar tortures, his very heart-strings quivered with agony.

"Pity — pity, Captain M'Cleane, for God Almighty's sake!" shrieked the traitor, as he observed Grawler's cold and calculating eye fixed upon him.

"Pity, be d——d!" said Grawler. "Here, some of you, just cast off these lines, and my fellows who are in the place above stairs, will soon make this beauty aul taut!"

"Stay!" remarked M'Cleane — "Captain Grawler, you must submit to be blindfolded, and led from this place. Your purchase shall be delivered into your hands when you next see me."

Grawler's eyes were then bandaged. He was led through intricate passages, and up many winding staircases, until his conductors halted and requested him to remove the handkerchief.

When he did so, Blackmoor was standing bound and gagged by his side, as helpless and passive as an infant.

"Four of our people will accompany you as far as the Tower Stairs, where, I am given to understand, that your men await you with the boat," remarked M'Cleane. "By the way, when do you sail?"

"We shall drop down with the first of the ebb, and by this time to-morrow the 'Maryland Trader,' wind and weather permitting, will be dashing merrily through the waters of the Channel."

"God speed you, Captain," said M'Cleane, grasping the sailor's hand. Then darting a look of scorn on the trepanned traitor, and issuing a few orders to his men, he departed.

"There you go, old devils-rib!" exclaimed Beauty, as the traitor passed him on his way out of the Thieves' Chapel. "Give my love to the Blackymoor's in Virginny"—and as he spoke, Beauty Ellis's jaws moved like those of a bloodhound's, and his deeply set, and blood-shot eyes gleamed ferociously.

Blackmoor heard, but could not reply except by a glance of hellish hatred, the more demoniacal in its expression, because the rage which it indicated was perfectly impotent.

It was necessary in passing through the thoroughfares which led to the water-side to use the utmost caution, for in consequence of the daring rescue of the morning, the sheriff had directed the aldermen to double the watch in their respective wards, and especially in those localities contiguous to the river;—the very parts through which it was necessary that Grawler and his prize should pass.

A contrivance, however, suggested itself to his mind, by means of which he hoped to gain his ship in safety.

Passing his arm through that of Blackmoor, and whispering a few words to the men who had left the "Chapel" with him, he commenced trolling a bacchanalian song, and at the same moment the whole party appeared to be under the influence of the rosy god.

Staggering and reeling—they passed through Eastcheap, without interruption, but when they had got in Upper Thames Street, a posse of the watch surrounded them, and demanded whither they were going?

Blackmoor, at that moment knew not whether he could be best off in the hands of the watch or the gripe of the captain. As it was he could not speak, and a timely and cunning push from Grawler made him appear so remarkably tipsy that his silence was fully accounted for.

"Where are we going, my worthy masters!" said Grawler, "going to the next tavern to drink your healths in a bowl of steaming punch, if you worthy guardians of the night will honor us with your good company—or, if you won't, why here's a broad piece to drink ours."

"Some roysterer's from the stews," remarked the chief of the watch; "pass on, noble gentlemen, and beware of the blowens of Tower Hill."

"Come on, you drunken owl," shouted Grawler to Blackmoor—and the party hurried on towards the Tower Stairs, which they reached without any further adventure.

There a boat and four brawny sailors were in waiting. Without a moment's loss of time, Blackmoor was hurried from the shore, and sternly ordered to lie down in the stern-sheets. The sailors then took their seats, and Captain Grawler, after having dismissed the men of the "Chapel" with a reward for their services, jumped on the gunwale, and from thence to midships thence aft, when he grasped the tiller in his huge hand.

"Now then, men," said he in low tones, "pull like devils for the ship—are there any watches about?"

"We have seen none," replied one of the sailors, and then they all bent to their oars, and pulled so vigorously that the tough spars bent and quivered again as they swept through the dark waters. Keeping in the shadow of the numerous vessels that thronged the Pool, and occasionally gliding between their hulls, the boat silently approached the 'Maryland Trader' which lay at anchor in the stream, and was shortly alongside the vessel. At a low "Ship a-hoy!" from the Captain, the Mate flung a hawser over the ship's side, and the boat was fast.

Blackmoor looked up, and as he saw the black tracery of the spars and ropes standing in sharp relief against the sky which was partially lighted by the early moon, his heart sunk within him; but little time was allowed him for reflection, for no sooner was the boat moored than he was forced on board the ship, and instantly pushed below, where he found a miserable lot of companions who, like him, were about to be voyagers against their will.

The tide was now running down rapidly, and the anchor having been heaved with as little noise as possible, the 'Maryland Trader' dropped down the river, when the day dawned she was abreast Gravesend, and long before the sun set she was, with her daring commander and crew, and her wretched cargo of human beings, gliding amid ripple and spray, over the dark blue waters towards the shores of the Western World.

CHAPTER XI.

MOTHER SIN AND SAL, THE GONNOFF.

AFTER Mr. Watkins, the Bow Street runner, had quitted the house of Mother Sin, in the Almonry, Westminster, to which place, it will be remembered he had gone for the purpose of securing the services of Sal, the gonnoff, to aid his investigations respecting Dick Flybynight, that unfortunate girl sank into a chair, covered her face with her hands, and wept bitterly.

"I know it—I know it!" exclaimed the wretched girl, "I am in Watkins's power sure enough, and that is why he makes a tool of me; but Dick Flybynight did a kind action for me once, and, by G—d, I won't be ungrateful."

"Ungrateful! you faggot!" said Mother Sin, who entered the room time enough to hear Sal's remarks. "Ungrateful, quotha? What have such as you to do with gratitude, I should like to know? And why shouldn't you do that civil man, Mr. Watkins' bidding? I believe Mr. Flybynight doesn't pay you to keep his secrets. And what did that decent gentleman give you, my dear?" continued Mother Sin, in a wheedling tone.

"This," said the girl, and she flung down with scorn, two bright guineas on the table.

"And very handsome of him too," said the hag, "but you know, my dear, you won't want to spend it all at once, so I'll take care of them for you, and here are five shillings for you to spend; you might lose the gold, you know, if you carried it about the streets."

The girl made no objection, and Mother Sin, who was as covetous as the gentleman in black, himself, was emboldened to still further rob Sal, the gonnoff.

"And what a smart gallant, my dear, you had with you upstairs. By my troth, Sal, but you are the most attractive girl in all the house, and you can't tell what a regard I have for you. Did the spark behave handsomely, my dear—a pox on him an' he didn't say I, for there's not a girl in all the Almonry equal to Sal, the gonnoff, for taking the stiffening out of a rake's body, or the shiners out of his purse."

Sal was not altogether insensible to flattery—what woman is? and coarse as Mother Sin's eulogium was, it was not without its effect.

Drawing from her bosom a purse, through the silken network of which the glitter of guineas was perceptible, she shook it gaily before the gloating and covetous eyes of Mother Sin.

"That's a good Sal," quoth the woman,

didn't I say you was the jewel of the place: why there's that good-for-nought, Edgworth Bet, who hasn't earned a shiner these three days. But she shall tramp! Out on the lazy w——e, she shan't be idle here; she shall go to the streets—the streets, and good enough for her too."

Sal was about to replace the purse in her bosom, when Mother Sin requested to look at its fine workmanship. It was handed to her.

"Marvellously pretty Sal," said Mother Sin, "Let me see, how much have you got in it?—One, two, three, four, five guineas! as I'm a Christian woman. Well, Sally, how lucky it is for you that you are now able to pay my little score—isn't it, and not to be in danger of being bundled out like that dishonest hussey, Edgeworth Bet? Here, Sal! take this glass of Hollands, 'tis right good Nantz, girl, for the Dutch Skipper, Kepferhausen, brought it from Rotterdam on his last trip." And she handed the girl a glass of neat spirits, which was disposed of in a twinkling.

"But I don't owe you *one* guinea, much less five, Mother Sin, so I'll just thank you to give me back my purse and money," exclaimed the girl.

"To think of that now!" cried Mother Sin, lifting up her hands and eyes in seeming astonishment. "Only to think of that now—why my dear, there is four guineas of it plump for lodging and victuals——"

"But," said Sal, interrupting her, "you know that when ——— was here not three weeks ——— gave you a ten ——— support till he came back his journey to the north; you know that, I say, and let's have no more words about it. Give me my money!"

"And suppose I was to say, that I choose to make you pay your honest debts with it, madam?" asked Mother Sin, not heeding in the slightest degree the allusion to Rakehelly Joe and the flimsy.

"I believe you're bad enough to say it," retorted Sal, "but if you commit such a base action, you will do that for which you shall have cause to be sorry, and that before long."

"Hoity-toity! so Miss Vixen, you threaten do you? Now, suppose I sent for Mr. Watkins, and told him about a certain person's faking the gold watch from a certain baronet—eh? Why, you minx, I could hang you any day."

The old wretch, as she spoke looked like a malicious fiend, and the poor girl shuddered as she timidly remarked:—

"But, cruel woman that you are! you know I did it at your instigation,—and more than that, you received the booty."

She might as well, however, have appealed to the stones beneath her feet; the fascinated bird might as well have appealed to the tender mercies of the rattlesnake, as that girl to that hard-hearted and abominable mother of harlots.

Sal knew well enough that she was completely in the power of Mother Sin, and therefore deemed it prudent to appear satisfied, and to pretend to go on the errand assigned her by Watkins, the Bow Street runner. Dressing herself, therefore, with more than ordinary care, she fortified her spirits by another dram, and quitted the Almonry.

She had determined in her own mind not to betray, even had it chanced that she should be enabled to do so, Dick Flybynight, who had once rendered her a signal service by rescuing her from a set of brawling roysterers, who were grossly ill-treating her;—but rather to put him on his guard against the wiles of Watkins. But how to procure an interview with him—that was the question?

Suddenly she remembered that Dick had a mistress who resided in Shire Lane, near to Temple Bar; and to her, with whom she had some acquaintance, she resolved to apply.

Arrived at the place, she discovered, to her chagrin, that the mistress of Dick had gone no one knew whither; the woman of the house, however, managed to draw from Sal the object of her visit.

"I should advise you to make application to Jonathan Wild," she remarked, "and if Dick Flybynight is above ground, that's the man to find him for you."

"And where may that famous thief-taker reside?" asked Sal.

"Why, his country-house is at Dulwich," replied the woman; "but you had better go to his office in Newtoner's Lane, and if Jonathan is not there himself, you'll see his man, Abraham, who'll do your business just as well."

Quitting Shire Lane, Sal proceeded in the direction indicated, and soon arrived at the residence of the notorious Jonathan.

It was a dingy-looking old structure, well suited, however, to the purposes of the designing man who carried on his nefarious business there. The entrance was by a narrow passage, dark, and lighted by a single oil lamp, the smoke from the half-trimmed wick of which, had begrimed the walls and cieling. Midway in this passage was a door, furnished with a sliding panel, at which, as she had been directed by Mother Mobbs, she tapped gently.

In an instant after she had done so, the sliding panel was withdrawn, and a pair of keen, dark eyes, gleamed through the aperture.

"Vell, ma tear," said a wheedling sort of voice, "and vat may pe your pusiness here—eh?"

"Can I see Mr. Wild?" asked the girl.

"Vy, perhaps you *can* see Mishter Vildsh, and perhaps you can't, mine tear; but if you have de fee, I think as he could be prevailed upon to see such a nicsh girl as you," and the Jew chuckled as though he had given utterance to a capital joke.

"Take this, then," said the girl, handing the five shillings which Mother Sin had given her. "It is all I have now, but if I get the information I want, you shall have five lots of gold in addition to-morrow."

"Vell—vell, I suppose you must," said the Jew; "but vat ish your name, mine tear?"

"I am known as Sal, the gonnoff," replied she, "and I life with Mother Sin in the Westminster Almonry.

The door was instantly opened, and Abraham directed the girl to follow him.

He led her through a long passage, from which a flight of stairs led upwards. Ascend-

MOTHER SIN, AND SAL, THE GONNOFF.

ing these a door was reached, at which the jew gave three taps and a low whistle. Presently it opened, as if by its own accord, and a pair of folding doors were seen.

"Enter!" said some one within. And Abraham and the girl were the next instant in a large chamber, fitted up with shelves and drawers, from ceiling to cornice, on, and in, which were deposited hundreds of parcels of goods of almost every description.

At a table, with a large account-book before him, sat a man of apparently about three or four and thirty years of age. His face, which was puffed and bloated, as if from the effects of strong drinks, wore a most peculiar expression. Great sagacity, and ferocity, appeared to struggle for the mastery. There was, too, a strange keenness in the glance of his eye, as he surveyed the girl narrowly. His dress was

No. 7.

that of a respectable tradesman, and his whole appearance indicated that he was a shrewd man of business.

This was the well-known Jonathan Wild, who at that time was in the very zenith of his prosperity as a negociator between persons who had been plundered, and the parties who committed the depredations.

"This nish young voman has paid de garnish, Mishter Vild," said Abraham — "not mush, to be shure; but dersh more to come, and she's got a honesht face." And the jew having winked his eye knowingly at Jonathan, retired.

"Now, to your business," said Wild.

"It is this, sir," observed Sal; "I am very anxious, for a most particular reason, to ascertain the whereabouts of a party, who may be trapped and haltered, if he is not put on his guard."

"His name?" demanded Jonathan.

"Dick Flybynight," replied Sal; "and the Bow Street runners are after him."

"Let me see," said Wild; and referring to a book before him, he searched it carefully for a little time, and then remarked:—

"Aye, I have the gentleman's name here, my dear! and I'll wager a guinea to a farthing that Watkins wants him for the robbery of Sir James Town, at Harrow."

"It was Watkins, the officer, who bribed me to seek him out and betray him. That I would never do;—but I am desirous of putting him on his guard."

"That I will do,—and protect him, too," added Wild; "so, my girl, you had better leave the business in my hands. I know where to find Dick, but it would be imposible for you to trace him; I will see him to-night.—Return hither to-morrow with five guineas, and you shall know the result."

Sall then took her departure, and no sooner had she turned her back than Wild rung a small hand-bell, and the Jew once more made his appearance.

"Abraham," said Wild, "here is a delicate bit of business to be transacted; and if it is manged well, we shall reap a golden harvest. Sir James Town, who was here yesterday, was robbed lately of a valuable diamond-hilted sword, a thousand guineas, and some rings, by two men, one of whom, from the description, I know must have been Dick Flybynight, of the 'Thieves' Chapel.' The other man I know not; but the baronet asserts that this same man has entered his house, and forcibly robbed him of a valuable deed, for the recovery of which he offers me five hundred guineas—and another five hundred for the jewels. Abraham, you must see Dick, and order him to be here this evening. If he refuses, tell him his name will be put down in my Black Book, and he well enough knows what that means."

"It shall be done, Mishter Vild," said the Jew, grinning with satisfaction at the prospect of such a handsome reward.

That night Dick Flybynight was closeted with Wild, and the next morning the sword was in the possession of the thief-taker, as also were five hundred of the guineas which Handsome Jack had taken from Sir James Town.

CHAPTER XII.

MR. DOOM TAKES A DESPERATE STEP.

After Handsome Jack, with Jenny Diver and M'Cleane, had quitted the office of Mr. Wriggleton Doom, the Lawyer of Gray's Inn, that worthy sunk into a chair in a state of perfect stupor. He was completely surrounded by his own coils, and how to extricate himself from them he knew not.

Had the door been unlocked, he would have followed Handsome Jack, in order to have been acquainted with the whereabouts of one who had placed him in such a perilous position. But as it was, he was a caged bird;—imprisoned in his own office.

He endeavoured to force the door, but that he found to be an impossibility; so, after due consideration he threw up the window, and after waiting some time he called to a watchman, told him that his clerk had locked him in by mistake whilst he was asleep, and by this means he effected his liberation.

There was only one course he could pursue which he thought would promote his safety, and that was to have an interview with his former clerk, Flitchman, who, it will be remembered, assisted him in the concoction of the forged deed, and either to bribe him into silence, or to get him out of the way. A similar course he also resolved to pursue with Mrs. Larkin, who had witnessed the signature to the same document.

Determined to lose no time, he at once set about the important business on hand, and remembering that at Lockatt's Ordinary he might find some of his old clients, whom he had assisted out of the fangs of justice, he, late as it was, proceeded thither.

Crossing Holborn, he walked through Lincolns Inn Fields, and arrived at Charing Cross. He then walked on to Whitehall, and speedily reached the place of which he was in search.

Locket's Ordinary was a well-known place of resort for dissipated characters of all grades: the aristocratic blackleg—the dashing highwayman, the footpad, the burglar, and the pickpocket, here all mingled with each other, and over the cards or the dice speedily dissipated their ill-gotten gains.

On entering this place of iniquity, Mr. Doom quietly took his seat in one of the boxes—ordered a stoup of sack, and peered cautiously around him. It was not long before he recognised among the dicers a face familiar enough to him.

"The very man for my purpose," said Doom to himself, and then calling the drawer aside, he slipped a gratuity into his hand, called for a private room, and requested the man to invite the person whom he had selected to follow him.

"Aha! my worthy friend, Master Doom!" said the fellow, as he entered the apartment, "and what's in the wind now? for the devil must certainly have some black business to do, when the Thieves' Lawyer, and Galloping Jerry meet at Lockatt's!"

"Why, you're not far out, Jerry," said Doom; "the fact is, I want you to trace out a party for me, and if you succeed in doing so without loss of time, you shall be handsomely rewarded."

"I'm your man, Master Doom! Wherever gold chinks, you will generally find Galloping Jerry in the neighbourhood.—And who is this bird whose nest you wish me to pounce on?"

"You remember being in Newgate some five years ago, for that little cut-throat affair in Drury Lane, Jerry?" asked the lawyer.

"Yes—I'm not likely to forget that, Mr. Doom—nor what a slip I made out of the halter!" replied Jerry.

"Nor who got you out of it?" suggested the lawyer.

"Well, by St. Nicholas! Master Doom, you managed that matter with your hard-swearing witness, nicely. No—no; I am not likely to forget that either, for it cost me a tidy sum, as you know."

"But your neck was saved from stretching! Now, then, Jerry, I want you to remember something else?"

"Well, what may that be?" inquired the man.

"At the time you were in Newgate," said the lawyer, "a man was also confined there, who had formerly been a clerk of mine. He was sent to the plantations, but I hear he has escaped, and is now in London. For certain reasons I wish to find him out, and that is why I am come to consult you."

"I know the man to whom you refer," said Jerry. "His name is Flitchman."

"The very individual!" said Doom, rubbing his hands.

"And he is now seeking refuge in the Sanctuary of Whitefriars," continued Jerry; "for I happened to be there when he claimed the protection of the Prior of Alsatia."

"Good!" remarked Mr. Doom. "Now, Jerry, you must contrive some means of getting me an interview with that man, and to-night. Here are ten guineas as an earnest of what I will do when the job is done."

"It would be odd if I could not manage such a trifle!" growled Jerry, "so we had better be off at once;—but where will you meet him, for it would be quite as well for you not to venture into the Sanctuary."

"I know it," said Doom; "and as it would be quite as advisable for our meeting to take place where no prying eyes, or sharp ears could see or listen, I will engage a boat at the next landing, and wait for you at the Temple Stairs; you can bring Flitchman there to me, and promise him that he shall be well rewarded."

This arrangement having been made, Galloping Jerry proceeded on his errand, and soon entered the precincts of the Sanctuary of Whitefriars — or as it was generally called, "Alsatia."

This singular place of refuge for those who had the fear of constables and bailiffs before their eyes, had been chosen by Flitchman when he returned from the plantations and from slavery. Under the protection of the Prior, he was perfectly safe, for no watchmen or officers of the law dared to show their faces in this part of the metropolis.

Jerry, having penetrated into the interior of the place, proceeded at once to a vintner's, where he knew it was likely that he should find his man. Here he was welcomed by his former companions with uproarous glee, and the glasses were passed freely round.

Seeking the private ear of one of the revellers, he slipped a guinea into his hand, and learned from him where Flitchman lodged. Having acquired this important intelligence, he proceeded down a narrow and ill-lighted lane, and stopped in front of the house which had been described to him. It was one of the worst even in that miserable locality: the door was unfastened, and a light in one of the

uppermost storeys acted as a sort of guide to Jerry in his search. As he mounted the ricketty and creaking staircase, the sound of his footsteps aroused the dwellers in the different apartments, who eagerly looked out from their half-opened doors, but who, on hearing a flash password given by the intruder, retired gladly again to their wretched beds. Arrived at the topmost landing, Jerry knocked at a door, which after some delay was opened by a man, whose pallid face expressed the terror with which this nocturnal visit had inspired him.

"D—n it, man! don't look so much like a scare-crow!" said Jerry; "I've come to put a job in your hands, and not to clap a pair of hand-cuffs on your wrists. How fares it with you, my chanting cove? To judge of your looks, the air of those plantations was anything but good!"

"Things are wretched enough with me," said Flitchman; "and I should be glad enough of a job—that is, if it's night-work, and all safe; for, as a returned transport, the hangman might tie me up any day."

"Never mind pattering that way!" said Jerry; "an old acquaintance of yours wants a little conversation with you — that's all, for which you'll get well paid."

"Who is it—and what does he want with me?" asked Flitchman.

"Your old employer—Mr. Doom—and he's waiting to speak with you now in a boat at the Temple Stairs, to which we can get through the back slums, without venturing into Fleet Street."

"I don't much like trusting to him—he is an infernal villain! for I've learned since I came home that it was through him I was sent across the herring-pond."

"Tush, man!" exclaimed Jerry; "you needn't fear;—see, here is gold for you, and he will give you more."

The poor, half-starved wretch was not proof against the temptation held out to him, and he consented to go, although he had yet some fears of foul play.

Threading, with the utmost caution, the labyrinth of lanes and alleys between Fleet Street and the river, the two men soon reached the Temple Stairs, where, true to his appointment, was Mr. Doom, seated in a boat, which was moored to a stake near the bank.

"Is that you, Jerry?" he asked, as the pair came to a stand still.

"Yes—and the other party, as well," replied Jerry; "and, now, I suppose I may receive the remainder of my reward—and go!"

"There it is," said Doom; — "and now, Flitchman—who, by the way, I am very glad to see again — you had better step into the boat, as I have a few words to say to you."

Flitchman did as he was requested, and then Mr. Doom handed a crown piece to the boatman, and told him to go and drink his health at the nearest vintners.

"We may as well get a little further out into the stream and fasten the boat to one of those barges—and then we shall be out of ear-shot," said the lawyer. And taking an oar, he pushed from the bank, and speedily reached a barge, to which he moored his little craft.

"I have sent for you Flitchman, to talk with you about that little affair of Sir James Town's, having heard that you had returned to England. Has any one seen you on the subject?"

"Yes," replied the man—"Richard Town has sought me out respecting it, and he has promised that if I come forward at the proper time, and confess the whole of the transaction, that he will use his influence to procure me a free pardon from the crown."

This was another unexpected blow for the lawyer—but he parried it as well as possible, for the game he was playing was a desperate one.

"Don't be deceived!" said the lawyer; "Flitchman! he cannot and will not do it. It will be far more to your advantage to be guided by me in this matter."

"You have deceived me before, and he never did," said Flitchman, gloomily. "Doom! what is it you propose I should do?"

"If you will sign a paper which I have brought with me," replied the lawyer, "I will give you a hundred guineas, and see you safely out of the country."

"And the purport of that paper?" asked Flitchman.

"That you were the only guilty party in the forgery. You know when you are far from England, such a statement cannot effect you!"

"No—no—Mr. Doom!" said Flitchman, shaking his head; "once for all, I say I will not trust you! Did I sign that paper, I should be at your mercy—and I might as well be in the hungry tiger's den!"

"The tide was now ebbing swiftly, and having exhausted all his persuasion and cunning in the endeavour to induce his companion in iniquity to sign the paper, Doom cast off the boat's painter, and endeavoured to scull the boat towards the stairs. A drizzling rain which had commenced falling, had, however rendered the bottom of the craft so slippery that he lost his footing, and whilst stumbling, his single oar fell into the water, and the boat shot like an arrow down the Thames.

Doom inwardly cursed the unlucky accident, for as a measure of precaution he had previously engaged three Crimps to kidnap Flitchman, and in some way dispose of him, if he declined to accede to his views.

A violent storm now raged—and onward swept the boat adown the rushing, roaring river. Narrowly escaping being dashed against the buttresses of Blackfriars Bridge, the unguided craft swiftly passed the arch beneath which it had been hurried. Swiftly flew the lights in the house windows by them, and now they plainly heard the rushing of the water beneath the dangerous arches of London Bridge—where the water had a rapid fall, and where the navigation was extremely difficult for well provided boats, much more for one utterly rudderless, and without an oar.

Just as they plunged on the surface of the boiling and eddying surf, Flitchman leaned over the side of the boat, and made a desperate

endeavour to stop its mad career by grasping at some sticks which stood close to the abutment. As he was thus more than half-balanced on the gunwale, Doom observed him, and a deep thought flashed across his brain. He might now rid himself of the man who he had reason to fear so much. The idea had no sooner occurred to him, than he hastened to put it into execution.

Suddenly and softly as a serpent creeps on its prey, did Doom approach Flitchman. A sudden push, and the deed was consummated! for the unfortunate man fell headlong into the stream. There was no time for him even to make any alarm. Doom saw him no more, and his boat having safely shot the fall, her speed began to abate, until at length she floated among the crowd of ships in the Pool, and he was enabled by their means to get to the shore, near Billingsgate.

Passing through Thames Street, a guilty, fearful man, he called a hackney coach, and desired to be driven to the foot of Holborn Hill, where he discharged the vehicle, and then hurried to his office, where he lay down on some chairs—but not to sleep, for the voice of Flitchman was in his ears, and he fancied he saw his reproaching face close to his own.

All the next day he remained in his office, fearful, lest should he quit it, that every stranger would read the word "murderer" on his forehead; but as soon as it was dusk, he made himself a strong glass of punch to revive his spirits before he ventured into the dim streets, and he was sipping it when a knock was heard at the door.

How it made him start—and his heart to beat! Were the officers of justice already on his track? Summoning up his courage, however, he withdrew the bolt, and requested the stranger to enter.

Miserable man! he gave but one glance, and then uttered a shriek so appalling that it might have been uttered by a damned soul! His eyes were fixed, and his face ghastly—his limbs tottered, and he seemed death-stricken as he gazed at the face of the man, who there, living and breathing, confronted him.

It was Flitchman!

For Doom, although a murderer in intention, was not one in reality. By a remarkable incident he had been snatched from the very jaws of death, and he now stood opposite the miscreant who would have murdered him.

"Villain—doubly dyed villain!" he exclaimed, "was I wrong in saying that I would not trust you? Thank God! your wretched scheme was frustrated—and I have braved detection in thus visiting you, for the sake of telling you how terrible and how complete shall be my revenge!"

"Mercy!" shrieked the wretched man.

"Curse you, Doom! it's little mercy you would have shown me. For all you cared, I might by this time have been feeding the fishes."

"'Twas an accident, Flitchman—upon my soul it was," exclaimed the lawyer, deprecatingly.

"Pooh—pooh! man, that won't do for me—the man who dragged me out of the waters saw you push me in, and he will at any time swear to it. Now, if you wish me to be silent, you must pay me to hold my tongue."

"I am poor—Flitchman—poor," said the lawyer; "how much do you require?"

"One hundred will do at present, Mr. Doom, and mind me, I won't take less—our relative positions are changed, so remember that I am master now."

"And if I give that sum to you, will you sign the document I spoke of last night?" asked the lawyer.

"To get your neck out of a noose, I put my own into one?" remarked Flitchman; never!—so, without more ado—hand me the shiners!"

Seeing that he was at the mercy of his former clerk, Doom made no further objections, but taking from an escritoiré a canvass bag, he counted out the sum and handed it to Flitchman, who eagerly clutched the gold.

"When this is gone," said the latter coolly, "I shall pay you another visit—that is, if you are not hanged in the meanwhile. Farewell!"

And quitting the office, he walked towards the Sanctuary, leaving Mr. Wriggleton Doom in, by no means, a pleasant state of mind.

Flitchman had just arrived at an obscure part of Fetter Lane when, looking cautiously about him, and seeing the way clear, he determined to make up for past privations, by an hour of enjoyment. He therefore sought the shop of a vintner, near Clifford's Inn—one of those places where, when wine had furnished the means of excitement, there were not wanting some of the frail sisterhood to gratify desire. It was a shop he had been in the habit of frequenting before he had quitted England for the plantations; but flushed by the possession of gold, he trusted to the change which a foreign climate and great hardships had made in his appearance, to escape recognition.

First peering through the window, to observe whether any of his old companions were present, he was not only gratified by convincing himself that such was not the case, but also by seeing, in the person of the landlord, a fresh face. Without any fear, therefore, he boldly entered in, called for a dram of Hollands, and asked whether he could be provided with supper.

The landlord eyed him narrowly, for Flitchman's appearance was none of the gayest. Flitchman rather winced under this examination.

"Yes, my queer gallant! Supper, quotha! If you cannot get a supper fit for Captain M'Cleane himself at the Golden Key, by my troth, I know not where you can. But the reckoning, master, doth not always follow the refreshment."

Mortified by the sarcasm of the vintner, Flitchman thrust his hand into his pocket, and drawing forth a handful of guineas, exhibited them. Then returning them to his pocket, he slapped his thigh.

"D'ye hear those goldfinches chirrup, master Vintner?" asked Flitchman.

"Aye — and pleasantly they chirrup, too, noble sir!—and what does your honour lack?

By my troth, I saw at a glance that you were a right valiant gentleman,—though mayhap you like not to sport so much point lace as Dick Flybynight. Won't your honour take your supper behind, where a few choice spirits are assembled?"

After artfully inquiring who were present, and being informed that only a few city 'prentices, and some rakehelly roysterers, were there discussing sack possett, together with some doxies, Flitchman fortified himself with a few more drams, and boldly joined the company.

His supper having been dispatched, he called for a bowl of sack possett, and was about to fill his glass, when the drawer entered, and Flitchman demanded the amount of his reckoning.

This point ascertained, he drew a number of coins from his pocket in a rather ostentatious manner, and flinging a guinea on the table, told the drawer to keep the change.

This unnecessary profuseness was not unobserved: by one of those present it was particularly noticed.

It was a young woman of remarkable personal attractions, who was sitting on the knee of a dashing blade, with one of her arms wound about his neck.

"Invite that simple galliard to join us, Jenny; he won't refuse you, I know;—his pockets seem well lined—though his coat be somewhat of the seediest; and if you do not ease him of his guineas, why James M'Cleane will never cry 'Stand and deliver!' again.

"I'll coax 'em out of his possession—only don't be jealous, dear Jem!" whispered the girl.

"Never fear, my sweet Jenny!" said Captain M'Cleane; "Handsome Jack and I will play a game or so, while you dive into the fellow's pockets!"

Quitting the Captain's knee, Jenny approached Flitchman, and with a fascinating smile, drank to his good health.

"I' faith!" said she, as though she were somewhat piqued, "those sparks yonder seem to care more for the dice-box than for a woman's smile. An' it be not intrusive, my fine fellow, I would share your company!" And she sat by Flitchman's side.

"Suppose," said Jenny, who saw that her company was anything but disagreeable; "we leave those roysterers yonder to their game, and quaff a bowl together in the next room. The vintner is accommodating."

"With all my heart!" said Flitchman, on whom the liquor now began to take effect, "and we'll seal the bargain with a kiss from those rosy lips!"

"Not here!" said Jenny, softly—"yonder blade carries a rapier. But as they are now deep in the game, and as I know they won't leave it in a hurry, I will quietly slip out, and do you as quietly follow me."

A nod of assent was given by Flitchman, whose eyes now flashed with passion; rapturously pressing Jenny's little hand beneath the table, he whispered her to depart.

With a footstep as light as that of a fairy, the bewitching creature glided away, followed by Flitchman. At a signal from Jenny, the vintner showed them into a private room, which contained a bed. He then placed a steaming bowl of Arrack punch on the table, and quitted the apartment.

Flitchman was perfectly intoxicated with love and liquor. All fear of detection had vanished, and he yielded himself up to the delirium of the moment.

They sat side by side on a couch—Flitchman's arm around Jenny's waist. In reply to his amorous hints, the Diver plyed him with the Arrack punch, and hinted at favours in expectancy.

"B-better go to bed, you charming c-creature!" stammered out Flitchman.

"Surely," said Jenny, with a seductive smile, "you would not have me undress before a man? besides, time is short.—See, now," said she, as though a sudden thought had struck her, "I'll just slip outside the door, while you remove your clothes, and then——"

"And then—you little angel!" cried Flitchman, who had toyed with the girl until he was half wild, "and then——"

"For God's sake—be quick!" said the girl, interrupting him, and disengaging herself from his ardent embrace. "Don't waste a moment, for should that gallant surprise us, his rapier might make a hole under your waistcoat!"

And with a smile she opened the door, and left Flitchman to his anticipations.

Quietly turning the key in the lock, Jenny Diver glided down the stairs, and in a twinkling was beside M'Cleane, triumphantly holding before his eyes the pocket containing Flitchman's guineas, which she had dexterously cut out of his breeches.

"By all that's jovial!" said M'Cleane, "but you are the Queen of Cut-purses, Jenny!" And he pressed her ripe, cherry lips to his own.

"And he didn't get as much for it as that, Jem!" said the girl, laughing merrily.

"But, my Ben Culs!" she immediately added, "that amorous spark is waiting my return; and unless, M'Cleane, you would prefer my sharing his bed to yours, and to see me with a rope round my neck, instead of your arms, I think it would be quite as well to shift our quarters. Come!"

"By Heavens! Jenny is right!" said Handsome Jack; "'tis no time, M'Cleane, for fooling now."

"To the 'Chapel,' then!" said M'Cleane; and passing the bar, they paid the reckoning, and made the best of their way to Long Acre.

Meanwhile Flitchman, having divested himself of his attire, had rolled into bed, where he lay in anxious expectation of the young girl, who seemed in no hurry to make her appearance.

"Her excessive modesty, no doubt," muttered the intoxicated man; but as the said modesty lasted rather longer than it generally does under similar circumstances, Flitchman grew somewhat restless; and when a full hour, as far as he could judge, had passed away, he rose, dressed himself, and attempted to open the chamber door.

In this, of course he failed. Violently ringing the bell, therefore, he summoned the vintner, who speedily released him from durance, and Flitchman was about to depart, when the host politely informed him that the last bowl of punch, and the room, were not paid for.

"That trifle is easily settled!" said the dupe. "Give me change against a guinea!" and he thrust his hand into the aperture where his pocket had been.

"Hell and furies!" he exclaimed, as his hand went to a considerable depth without coming into contact with a single coin—"I have been betrayed and robbed!"

"Gently, my master!" said the vintner; "mean you to damage the character of my house?—Are you pay me not the reckoning, I will call in the watch. I fancy you're nought more than a Dymber Mort?"

The mention of the watch was quite sufficient to sober Flitchman, who bestowed hearty curses on his own folly in risking the loss of the money which he had earned at so much peril to himself. Again he searched his pocket, but without success. Availing himself, therefore, of an opportunity when the Host's back was turned towards him, he rushed towards the door, burst it open, and then with the speed of lightning gained the Sanctuary, where, penniless and wretched, he flung himself on his wretched pallet, there to devise schemes for the future.

CHAPTER XIII.

THE ROBBERY OF THE MAIL.

It was long past midnight when M'Cleane, Handsome Jack, and Jenny Diver, arrived at the "Chapel," inside the strong gateway of which, on the Captain's giving the usual signal, all three were instantly admitted.

"Good morning to you, Captain!—you look as gay as if you'd been out in a golden shower; but it's werry bad hours to be out with young women!" remarked Beauty Ellis, winking his savage eyes.

"Damn your insolence, Beauty!" said M'Cleane; "one thing is certain, the women will never be troubled with you;—but look at that, you hound!"—and M'Cleane rattled the pocket full of guineas in Beauty's face.

"Werry pretty sound—werry, Captain! I likes that sort o' music!" said Beauty, as his huge mouth became still larger with a grin.

"Suppose you give him an opportunity of playing it himself," suggested Jenny Diver to the Captain.

"Why, Jenny, as you nabbed the booty, 'tis yours to do as you choose with," returned M'Cleane, handing her the pocket.

"No more my property, Jem, than that of the meanest member of the fraternity. All are equal here!"

"You have spoken nobly, girl!" said M'Cleane, patting her cheek, "but you shall have your own way, here at least. Here, Beauty! Jenny Diver will give you a couple of yellow birds, and they're out of her own earnings, mind."

"Werry good of the lady, too!" and as two guineas dropped into Beauty Ellis's hands, he attempted to look amiable, an effort which, it may readily be supposed, made his bull-dog face look a great deal uglier than it did before.

"By the way, Captain," said he, "Dick Flybynight wants to see you on werry particular business."

"Then we will repair to the Saloon, where we shall most probably find him," said M'Cleane; "for Dick is a devil amongst the women! and when not on the road, is sure to be tied to some pretty girls apron strings.

Taking, therefore, the course which was described in our first Chapter, the three soon arrived at the Saloon, and the usual challenge having been given and responded to, the two folding-doors flew open, the sentinel repeating the words "Long live the Captain!"

The gang received him with delight, and congratulations were showered on him from all quarters.

"Ah! Handsome Jack—welcome!" exclaimed Gipsey Betty, her dark eyes glowing with animation; "why, I thought you had forgotten me!" and the lass drew him towards an ottoman, and poured him out a goblet of sparkling wine.

"My memory is not quite so treacherous as that, pretty one!" replied Handsome Jack, as he kissed the dusky beauty; "and before I leave, perhaps, I may give you convincing proofs that I have not attached myself to any other damsel in your absence."

Gipsey Betty only answered by laying her cheek on his shoulder, and drawing him closer to her by the arm with which she encircled his waist.

Supper was now served, and the usual orgies following it, were just on the point of commencing, when Flybynight Dick entered the saloon, and made a sign to the Captain, who accompanied him to a retired part of the apartment.

"What's in the wind now, Dick?" asked M'Cleane.

"Two things—one which may replenish our purses, and one which may work our ruin," replied Flybynight.

"Why you're not in spirits, Dick, to-night. But come, explain yourself!"

"In the first place, then, we are menaced with danger, as much if not more imminent than that which threatened us when Blackmoor was at large," said Dick.

"In what way?" anxiously demanded M'Cleane.

"That infernal hell-hound, Jonathan Wild is on our track."

The Captain started and grew pale,—"How know you this?" he asked.

"Because" replied Dick Flybynight, "one of his damnable spies, Quilt Arnold, by some means smelled me out yesterday, and left one of his notices with Madame Charlotte in the Hotel;—a notice which, for all our sakes I was compelled to obey."

"Damnation!" muttered M'Cleane between his clenched teeth. "And did you see the doubly-dyed villain?"

"Yes, Captain, and he demanded the sword hilt, and a portion of the money which Handsome Jack and I took from Sir James Town; had I refused to restore them to him, he swore

that not only my name, but yours, should appear on his condemned list—or, as he calls it—his Black Book."

"And he is just the man to keep his word, for he is a most implacable enemy. Dick, his requests must be complied with."

"Such, at least, to a certain extent has already been done. The gold and the diamonds are in his possession; but he wishes another demand, with which I know not how to comply."

"And what is that, Dick? If it be any more booty he must have it, though we leave not a guinea in our coffers," said M'Cleane.

"He says that Sir James Town was robbed by one of our gang of a very important document, to which he attaches more value than even to his jewels and gold; and it is the restoration of that parchment which he imperatively requires. For my own part I know nothing of it."

M'Cleane bit his lip and was silent, for Handsome Jack had confided to him the secret of the abstraction of the forged deed in confidence, and no one but himself, Jenny and Jack knew aught of the adventure at Doom's. He resolved, however, to speak to Jack on the subject, and to hide his embarrassment he enquired of Dick what the other matter of importance was, on which he wished to converse with him?"

"I have received information," said Dick, "that in the Bristol Mail, which is now on its way here, is a great amount of money in specie, which has lately arrived from the Colonies. It would be as well, perhaps, to transfer it to our own strong boxes."

"If," said M'Cleane, "there was time to get to Slough the matter might be arranged—know you if there are extra guards with the money?"

"I am assured not," said Dick, "and that two resolute fellows might succeed in the adventure. What say you?"

"Say, Dick?" exclaimed the Captain, "why, that we'll instantly saddle our nags, look to our barkers, and be off. Perhaps you will repair to the stables and there await my joining you; and, Dick, provide yourself with some strong cords, for we'll shed no blood if it can be avoided."

Dick departed on his errand; and M'Cleane advancing to the rest of the gang, said—

"I must bid you adieu, comrades, for a short time. There is a little job to be transacted on the road, and as it may prove rather a dangerous one, I choose to undertake it myself; Dick Flybynight will accompany me;—so, come, lads and lasses, drink success to our expedition in flowing goblets."

Every glass was instantly charged to the brim, and shouts of "success and long life to our brave Captain," resounded through the gorgeous saloon.

"I must deny myself the honour of your sweet society, my charming Jenny, for a few hours," said M'Cleane, as he sat by Jenny Diver's side, and wound his arm round her taper waist.

Jenny pouted her pretty lip a little, for she had made up her mind to enjoy M'Cleane's society that night; but the Captain whispered a few words in her ear which apparently contented her.

"Jem Starlight! after my departure you will double the guards at all the posts, and act as second in command until Dick Flybynight's return, and you, Handsome Jack, will please to be my deputy until I see you again.

Another uproarious shout of applause saluted M'Cleane as he quitted the Saloon.

Before he departed for the road, however, he considered it prudent, after what Dick Flybynight had told him respecting Wild's spies, that he should give Madame Charlotte a caution to be on the alert. He therefore proceeded to her chamber.

Madame Charlotte not expecting a visitor that night had retired to rest some time before, and when M'Cleane entered her chamber she was sound asleep. Her bed-room was fitted up with remarkable taste. A lamp in which the purest oil was consumed hung by chains from the painted ceiling, and diffused a softened radiance over all the objects around. Her bed was covered with a quilt of delicate colors, and the elegant muslin curtains of a delicate rose tint. But the greatest charm of the apartment, as M'Cleane stood by the bedside, was the sleeper herself. She had been dreaming,— probably of some lover,—for she lay with dishevelled locks, her left arm, bare almost to the shoulder, thrown above her head on the snowy pillow, and her right hand resting on the outside of the quilt. Her half-parted lips had a smile upon them, and her ivory breasts rose and fell, unrestrained by the bed-clothes. It was a sight which would have made a hermit forget his vows, and become a devotee at the shrine of Love.

"Lizzy, dear," whispered M'Cleane to the fair sleeper.

Madame Charlotte startled, and gently opened her eyes, as soon as she recognised him she threw her arms around his neck, and bestowed on him an ardent embrace.

"This is no time for toying, Lizz," remarked M'Cleane—"I have come to speak to you on an important matter, some other time we will devote an hour to love."

"What! only come to tantalize me?" asked Madame Charlotte, with a pretty frown.

"The fact is, Lizzy, I am cursedly annoyed. Dick Flybynight has just informed me that Quilt Arnold, Jonathan Wild's man, was here yesterday with a notice. Now, you must be on your guard, and use the greatest precaution, should any of his spies again visit you. Know nothing! As I am now off for a dash on the road with Dick, and know not when I may return, I deemed it necessary to caution you; for Wild is much more to be feared than was Blackmoor."

"Rely on it, I will baffle the devils, should they come here. Trust to a woman's wits, Jem."

"I have already to-night had a specimen of them. If another, you have seen how beautifully Jenny Diver dished out a bounding ruffler; but the lass herself must tell you the story, for the horses must be saddled and Dick waiting for me by this time."

"Then good luck to you, Jem," said Madame

Charlotte, and after a hearty kiss she suffered the Captain to depart.

M'Cleane now took his way to the stable, where he found the horses saddled, and Dick Flybynight already mounted.

"A glorious morning for the road, Dick," said M'Cleane, "not a star to trouble us. Let us urge our nags, for the devil a moment of time have we lose."

"This is the life for brave men, Captain," exclaimed Dick, as, having cleared the suburbs, they were going down the western road at a rattling pace.

"You are right, Dick. Who the devil would be chained to a dull shop to plod for paltry shillings, when he could jump on the back of his good steed—cry "stand and deliver" to the first he meets, and return to his girl and his glass with golden-lined pockets?"

"Ha! ha! ha! not I, by my faith," cried Dick; "but, M'Cleane, what the devil is that creaking sound which comes on the breeze every now and then—by all that's horrible, it's a dismal noise?"

"Faith, I know not," replied M'Cleane; "but as we seem to be nearing it we shall probably ascertain the cause."

At this moment, abruptly quitting the high road, they entered on a broad common covered with heath and furze. Not a human dwelling was visible, and they now put their horses to the top of their speed.

Suddenly the mare which M'Cleane rode shyed, and nearly threw her rider; Dick Flybynight's nag also showed symptoms of restlessness; for she shook her head uneasily, and appeared to snuff something dangerous.

At that moment the creaking sound, which had ceased for a short time, was again heard, and now it appeared to be immediately above their heads.

"I never knew the old girl," said M'Cleane, patting the mare's neck and in vain endeavouring to make her proceed, "show off a trick of this sort before. What, in the fiend's name, can be the reason?"

"The reason is plain enough, Captain," said Dick, "just glance over head, and you won't be long in doubt."

M'Cleane looked upwards, and there above his head, dangled by a chain from the arm of a lofty gibbet, the black, and disfigured form of a human being, encased in a sort of iron cage; the clothes of the unfortunate creature, reduced to mere shreds by the weather, streamed in the night wind; and the flapping of wings were heard as though birds had been disturbed by the highwaymen during their hideous meal.

"A pleasant spectacle, Dick," said M'Cleane, "and one which might deter less resolute dogs than you and I from our present purpose."

"The fellow has at least plenty of fresh air," returned Dick; "for my part, I should prefer being above ground after the breath is out of my body, than being cooped up in a coffin in a dirty hole."

They now succeeded in getting their horses on, and were off once more at a slapping pace: at the furthermost edge of the common was a small road-side public house.

A light proceeding from the window informed

FLITCHMAN CONFRONTING DOOM IN HIS OFFICE.

them some one was stirring, and outside the door were several horses, ready harnessed.

"I'll wager Jenny Diver's smile against Beauty Ellis's grin," said M'Cleane, softly, that it is here the Bristol mail changes horses."

While he was speaking an ostler came from the stables which adjoined the house. It would not have done to put the question direct to him; so, by way of drawing him out, Dick Flybynight asked if they could have a dram that morning?

"That can you, my master," replied the fellow, scratching his head.

"Quick, then," said M'Cleane, and threw the fellow a shilling.

"What the devil do they stick up yon scare-crow on the common for? My horse had nearly sent me on the road;—'tain't safe for honest men to pass it," said Dick.

No. 8.

"Why, for rogues neither, for the sake of that, master. That be the body of Jerry Shovelter, the highwayman—he as was scragged at Tyburn some two years agone, for robbing the Brister mail, the very mail as these 'osses is waiting for."

"And likely to wait some time, ha! ha! ha!" laughed M'Cleane, as, having taken their drams and put spurs to their horses, they took a cross road, and so rapidly did they ride that they soon reached Slough, where they learned from a countryman that the mail had passed about ten minutes.

Determined not to be foiled, they returned along the high road until they reached Langley Broom, without falling in with the object of their pursuit; nor did they do so until they had got about half a mile on the other side of Coln-brook, where they perceived the mail in charge of two post-boys and a guard.

"Now is the time," said M'Cleane, as he observed the guard who had been sitting behind the coach, lay his blunderbuss on the roof of the vehicle and descend for the purpose of easing the horses, as they dragged the lumbering and heavily-laden carriage up a steep hill.

The guard walked forward and conversed with the post-boys; and seizing the favourable moment, the highwaymen, who had walked their horses so as to approach the carriage quietly, dismounted, tied their steeds to a tree, and silently ran up the hill.

"You jump up—seize the blunderbuss, Dick, and then we will run round by the horses' heads, and take them by surprise."

This feat was scarcely suggested before it was accomplished. With the rapidity of a monkey, Dick Flybynight noiselessly climbed up the back of the carriage, and so noiseless was the proceeding that he possessed himself of the weapon without exciting the slightest suspicion on the part of the guard.

They now had to pass the post-boys unobserved, a matter of no great difficulty, inasmuch as these worthies were in deep conversation with the guard, towards whom their heads were turned.

"A pox on the highwaymen in England!" they heard the guard say to the post-boys who sat trembling on their seats as they were now going over a part which had been rendered famous as being the scene of many a bold adventure of the Knights of the road.

"Art sure," said one of the post-boys, "they didn't draw the charge of thy blunderbuss when we stopped last to change? I saw some knavish-looking villains about the tavern door."

"Thunder and lightning!" exclaimed the guard, "d'ye think I forgot that? Not ten minutes agone I drew the charge, loaded the old bull dog fresh, and new-primed to make all sure. Why, what be afeared of? Damme! I shouldn't fear if bold Cap'n M'Cleane was to come himself—I'd like to see un."

"Oh, Mr. Guard! for God's sake," said the other post-boy, who, at the name of M'Cleane, fell into a fit of terror; "for the love of God don't go on so—you don't know what may happen!"

"And I don't care," said the guard, "I'm a match for a dozen of the villains. Why I beat off half a dozen one night with no assistance; and rather than M'Cleane or any of his gang should sack the doubloons and broad pieces in this mail, I'd——"

He was interrupted in his valiant harrangue by the appearance of the Captain and Dick, who suddenly came round in front of the horses' heads and confronted them.

The guard instantly made a dash for his blunderbuss; but he was boldly stopped by Dick Flybynight, who coolly presented the weapon at his head and commanded him to stand, whilst M'Cleane ordered the post-boys to dismount.

The abject terror of the guard after all his braggadocia was absolutely ludicrous, and M'Cleane and Dick could not help indulging in hearty peels of laughter at his expense. They had no time, however, to banter him, but immediately proceeded to business.

"The ropes, Dickon, the ropes," said M'Cleane. They were produced—and in a trice the two post-boys were dragged down a lane hard by, tied back to back, and securely fastened to a tree in a ditch so wet, that they stood up to their knees in water; the guard they also bound to a tree, and then proceeded to rummage the coach.

Wrenching open the box which contained the treasure, M'Cleane drew from it twelve heavy leathern bags, each of which was filled with gold or silver coins. Whilst M'Cleane was thus engaged, Dick Flybynight brought up their horses, and then they placed the booty in saddle bags, with which they had been cautious enough to supply themselves. They then, from the Bath and Bristol bags, selected all such letters as appeared likely to contain bank-notes, and having cut the traces of the horses, and flung the guard's blunderbuss into a ditch, they crossed the Thames, and after riding a little way into Surrey, returned to London by way of Bermondsey.

"I'faith, Dick!—a good morning's work," said M'Cleane, as they dismounted from their jaded horses in the stable-yard of the 'Chapel;' "I wonder how our bragging friend, the Guard, feels now?"

"By St. Nicholas, Captain! but that was devilish rich." And at the recollection of the scene the robbers laughed till the tears ran down their cheeks.

"But of that we'll talk by and bye; now, for I need rest,—I have much to think of. Let the saddle-bags be safely bestowed in the chest, and after a snooze we will examine the letters, finger the flimsies, and burn what is useless," said M'Cleane.

"Werry heavy, these 'ere saddle-bags, Captain," said Beauty Ellis, as he lugged them into the "Chapel," after he had placed the horses in the stable. "Any one would think as you'd a been a digging in a goold mine this morning, only you ha'nt had time to go down and come up agin, for I hears they be precious deep."

"You'll get rich, Beauty, if we go on at this rate, you ugly dog, you;—two guineas a few hours since, and two more to keep them company," said M'Cleane, as he flung the fellow a couple of gold coins.

Determined to use every precaution, M'Cleane before he retired to rest, passed through the saloon, ascended by the shaft and saw that the North door of the "Chapel" was properly secured and sentinelled. Satisfied on this point, he sought the chamber of Jenny Diver, and in her welcoming arms soon forgot the troubles and the perils of the last few hours.

————

CHAPTER VIV.

MADAME SINGLETON'S SPECULATION FAILS AND HANDSOME JACK THIRSTS FOR REVENGE.

IT was nearly midnight. In the ill-paved and ill-lighted streets of London little other than the staggering footsteps of some rake returning from the tavern or the brothel, or the drowsy cry of the watchman at intervals was heard. Only these and a few unfortunate girls of the town—the worst of their class—lingered on the pavements, or stood shivering and cowering under the projections over doorways, or in narrow passages, which, though they kept them from the drenching rain, afforded no protection whatever from the driving wind. Decent people had long since been in bed. Who, save men-midwives, monthly nurses, and "Charlies" would have been out on business on such a night?

It might have seemed a sheer impossibility that one who had within his own walls all that luxury could furnish, or wealth command, should have chosen to quit his blazing fire and wander out into the cheerless streets.

Yet so it was. Just as the deep-toned bell of Saint Pauls Cathedral, followed by hundreds of others of lesser note, with iron tongues tolled the knell of a day. A man, closely wrapped in a large cloak, from beneath which the point of a sword-sheath was discernible, hurriedly walked down Tottenham Court-road, and then threading a narrow street, which led to a square near the church of Saint Giles's in the Fields, stopped before the gateway of one of the most respectable houses in that quarter.

He gave a gentle rap at the door, and presently a window above was cautiously opened; a female face appeared, and the survey appeared to be satisfactory, for almost directly afterwards the street door swung gently back on its hinges, and the gentlemen of whom we speak entered.

This was the house of Mother Singleton— one of the most celebrated Procuresses of the time.

"Madame Singleton will wait on you directly, Sir James," said the girl obsequiously, as she ushered him into a parlour, elegantly furnished, and brilliantly lighted. His visit had evidently been expected.

That apartment was the very temple of voluptuousness and sensuality. On its walls hung pictures, executed in the first style of art, every one of them calculated to excite passion even in the most frigid breast. Exquisitely drawn figures of females, in all the bloom of youth and beauty and but little encumbered with drapery, were alternated with marble statues of Apollo, Adonis, and Narcissus. Every picture and every bit of marble was a minister to desire. Couches of luxurious softness were disposed in various parts of the room, and on the tables were books containing plates, and descriptions suggestive of the pleasures of Love.

Whilst Sir James Town was curiously gazing on one of the most luscious of the naked Divinities, Mother—or as she was generally termed, Madame Singleton—entered.

Though passed the prime of life, she was yet handsome, though somewhat too much inclined *ent bon point.* She curtseyed gracefully to Sir James Town, who gave one of his most courtly bows in return.

"Ah, Madame!" said Sir James, laying his hand on his superbly embroidered waistcoat, "I should have been here earlier, but my varlet of a serving-man forgot to hand me your note. You know, Madame, I always fly on the wings of love hither. And have you, as you say, caged that pretty bird which I spoke to you of?"

"Yes, Sir James, and a sweet pretty bird it is. I had, however, the greatest difficulty in snaring it."

"Never mind, my dear Madame, here is a recompense I hope;" and the baronet placed a purse of gold in the procuress's hand.

"And where is the charming prize. I am all impatient to hold it in my arms," said Sir James with almost frantic haste.

"Patience, sir, patience; newly caged birds are apt to beat their breasts against the wires. I have prepared her for your coming and will fetch her immediately. But deal gently, Sir James, at first; maidens, you know, require wooing, and this one seems as though it would take time to win her.

"Know you her name?" asked Sir James.

"Emilie, so she informs me," replied the procuress.

"I have heard that name before, somewhere," said Sir James, musingly. "Did you acquaint her with my name?"

"No;" said Madame Singleton, I always leave gentlemen to use their own discretion in that matter."

"And you are right," he muttered.

"Are you ready, Sir James? if so I will introduce the young lady and then leave you. Should you require anything, if you will ring that silver hand-bell on the mantel-piece, a servant shall immediately be with you."

"Not only ready but impatient, Madame Singleton. Ever since I saw that matchless creature by chance, I have been burning with an unquenchable desire to possess her.

The procuress quitted the room, and Sir James quivered with excitement. Debauchee as he was, he had never yet so ardently desired to revel in any female's charms as in those of this young girl, who, by his gold and the artifices of Mother Singleton, had been entrapped, for the vilest of purposes, into that house of aristocratic infamy.

Once more the door opened, and Mother Singleton appeared, leading in a young and lovely girl, whose eyes were red with weeping. Giving a nod to the baronet the vile creature retired.

Approaching the girl with the most polished and respectful air, Sir James requested her to be seated. As she did not accept this offer, he took her hand and would have pressed it to his lips, had she not wrenched it from him by a sudden effort.

"Unhand me, sir!" exclaimed the girl; "and if you are a gentleman, release me from this place to which I was allured by artifice, and in which I am confined against my will."

"My sweetest Emilie," said the baronet in the softest tones.

The girl looked at him fixedly,—it was a look of utter and intense scorn.

"You seem to know my name, sir," she said; "and if, poor defenceless girl as I am,

I fervently hope you are—a man of honour—you will not refuse to give me yours,—for your voice strangely reminds me of one whom once I knew, and—loved."

"To show you that I *am* an honourable man." he replied, "my name I give you—it is an honourable one, and if you will be but mine *now*, you shall share it—I am SIR JAMES TOWN."

"Now I know you—infamous wretch—as the usurper of anothers title and fortune."

She could speak no more, but tottering, she would have fallen, had not Sir James flown to her assistance and caught her in his arms.

"Touch me not, villain!" she exclaimed, and she shrank from him as if he had been a fiend.

"Oh! Richard, Richard!" moaned the poor girl,—"why are you not here to protect your Emilie," and she sank fainting and senseless on a sofa.

"The betrothed of Richard Town, by all that's wonderful," said the baronet. Yet thunderstricken as he was by the girl's recognition of him, he could not avoid gazing on the senseless maiden with libedinous eyes. To relieve her throbbing heart he was about to unlace her boddice, but the mere contact of his fingers on her chaste bosom at once restored her to her senses, and rushing madly from the parlour she ran up stairs to the chamber whence she had been brought. After locking the door, she sat down on the bed and wept bitterly.

The baronet, half maddened by disappointment and surprise, rang the hand-bell, and a servant entered.

"Tell Madame Singleton I wish to speak with her immediately," he said.

That lady having made her appearance, he informed her of all that had transpired—and begged her to do her best to soften the obduracy of the poor girl. Promising to call the next evening, he took his departure in no very pleasant mood.

Emilie no sooner heard that all in the house was quiet, than she resolved to attempt to escape from that place, the character of which, the events of the last hour had but too well assured her. Her first step was to throw up the window and reconnoitre.

The room in which she was confined, looked into a narrow alley, which from its direction, she presumed led towards Holborn. The height was too much for her to attempt it by leaping, but what will not desperation do? Knotting the sheets of the bed together, she found that they reached nearly to the ground, and having dressed herself just as she was when she was enticed to the house, she fixed one end of the sheets to the bed-post, and with little difficulty reached the bottom.

Hurrying through the alley, she found herself in Broad Street, St. Giles's, and fearing her own shadow, she almost ran until scarcely knowing how she got there; she sat down on the step of a carriage-maker's door in Long Acre, trembling and breathless.

It was now nearly four in the morning. Never before had she been in the streets at such an hour, and every noise terrified her. As she sat shivering with cold and terror, and crying, "Oh, Richard! Richard!" a hand was laid on her shoulder, and a friendly voice exclaimed:—

"You don't look like one used to this sort of work, young woman."

The speaker was a dashing young fellow, and he spoke in so sympathetic a tone that he at once inspired confidence.

"Oh! save me, sir—save me!" said the young girl.

"Save you! aye, that will I, if you need it; but from whom, lass? for let me tell you there are many queer one's in this quarter."

"From that villain, Sir James Town!" cried the girl.

"Aye—that will I, as sure as my name is Dick Flybynight!" said the stranger, "and perhaps you're nearer a friend than you expect; but get up, my good girl, and damme—bah! excuse my swearing before a lady,—if my friend is, as I suspect, a friend of yours, you won't stand in need of a true heart, or a stout arm!"

The girl, encouraged by a word of kindness, rose from the step, and Dick placing her for a moment under the care of an old lady who kept a saloop stand at one of the entrances to Covent Garden, hurrried off to the "Chapel."

Handsome Jack was flirting with Gipsey Betty, when Dick Flybynight entered the Saloon, and motioned him to the door.

"D'ye remember, Jack," said Dick, "that when you and I were on our way to rid that rascal, Sir James Town, of his gold, we pledged friendship?"

"That I do, Dick!" said Jack; "but why speak of this now?"

"For a very good reason. Just now, as I was strolling through the Acre, a distressed damsel craved my assistance—and to what end, Jack, thinkest thou?"

"To relieve her from some Dragon, perhaps," replied Jack.

"You are nearer to the truth than you imagine," continued Dick; "the Dragon from whom she sought to be delivered, is no other than your beloved relative, Sir James Town!"

"Curses on him!" muttered Handsome Jack; "but, Dickon, I cannot be expected surely to fly to the aid of all who get into his clutches."

"But," returned Dick, "if I be not greatly mistaken, the lass I just left has a greater liking for one Handsome Jack, than for Sir James—for before I accosted her, she sobbed out 'Oh, Richard! Richard!' as if her little heart would break."

In compliance with Jack's urgent request, Dick Flybynight described as nearly as possible the person of the young girl.

"It cannot be!" Jack exclaimed; "and yet, merciful God! there are no bounds to the villainy of that man. Come with me, Dick;" and with rapid strides they soon reached the place where Dick had left Emilie.

"Thank God! thank God!" exclaimed the girl the instant she saw her lover's face, and falling on his breast, she swooned.

"Poor dear—she've had a heep o' trouble, know!" said the old saloop woman; "h give her a drop of this!" and she drew a of Geneva from her pocket—" 'twill revive her."

She soon recovered—and then Handsome Jack learned from her lips the whole story. He burned with indignation, but that was not the time for indulging in thoughts of revenge; so despatching Dick for a hackney coach, he informed Emilie that he would see her safely home to Islington, and that he would not sleep until he had revenged the insult which had been offered her.

The vehicle having arrived, Handsome Jack and the young lady entered it, and it rumbled off in the direction of Smithfield.

No sooner had M'Cleane quitted the arms of Jenny Diver, than he retired to a private room of the " Chapel," where it was his custom to transact the private business of the fraternity.

Touching a small knot near the fire-place, the faint tone of a distant bell was heard, and presently afterwards a panel of the wainscotting slid aside, and the bull-dog face of Beauty Ellis appeared.

" Your commands, noble Captain?" said the fellow, respectfully touching his forehead with the side of his right fore-finger.

" Take this sealed paper to Handsome Jack, Beauty;" and M'Cleane handed him a note which he had just written.

Beauty took the missive—again saluted the Captain, and vanished like a harlequin through the panel.

" If he refuses to deliver up the bond, I fear we are lost beyond hope of redemption," said he to himself; " but he is too generous—too noble-minded, to peril the safety of all, for the sake of himself. He must be tried."

At this moment a tap was heard at the door.

" Enter!" said M'Cleane.

And with a face pale and ghastly, Handsome Jack entered. He looked ten years older than when the Captain had last seen him; in fact, the change was so startling that M'Cleane was staggered.

" In the Devil's name, Jack, what has happened?" he inquired.

" Enough to make a man a devil himself!" said Handsome Jack.

" What!" asked M'Cleane, banteringly, ' has Gipsey Betty turned prude, or vixen, or——"

" Neither the one nor the other," exclaimed Handsome Jack, interrupting him; " with Gipsey Betty I had nought to do last night, or rather early this morning."

" Why surely, Jack—you, to whom I deputed the Captainship, did not quit the 'Chapel' during my absence?" asked M'Cleane.

" All the fiends of hell would not have kept me in it after I saw the person who required my services out of it!" replied Handsome Jack, with great vehemence.

" But that person you must have quitted your post to see?" sarcastically remarked M'Cleane.

" M'Cleane," said Jack, " you have no reason to doubt my faithfulness to the oath which I took on the night when you conducted me hither."

" Well—well, Jack," said M'Cleane, holding out his hand, " I did not send for you here for

the purpose of worming out your secrets; it is for a far different purpose I require your presence—and your aid."

" Command it, M'Cleane," said Jack, " and you shall see how ready I am to obey."

" Good," observed the Captain. " Now listen, Jack. We are in the clutches of Jonathan Wild, and if we do not manage to get out of them, we may as well hang ourselves and save the executioner the trouble: you must help us."

" That will I, right willingly, as I have sworn," said Jack; " but how?"

" By delivering up the forged deed which you took from the cabinet in the drawing-room of Sir James Town," replied M'Cleane.

Handsome Jack started.

" Do you hesitate?" asked M'Cleane.

" Not only hesitate, but I positively refuse," was Jack's reply.

" Then, for the sake of obtaining your own," sneered M'Cleane, " you would put a halter round all our necks?"

" Had you asked me to do this yesterday," exclaimed Jack, " I would not have hesitated—to-day I cannot and will not."

" Humph! a mere subterfuge," muttered M'Cleane.

Stung to the quick, Handsome Jack instinctively grasped the handle of his weapon.

" Pardon me, Jack," said M'Cleane, " I do not fear your sword, for I wear as good a one, and can use it as well; but I am sorry to have wounded the feelings of a brave man."

" Enough," rejoined Jack, somewhat mollified. " Perhaps, Captain, you will inform me why you desire that I should deliver up the forged deed to Sir James Town?"

" Because," replied M'Cleane, " the false baronet sold to Jonathan Wild, and offered him a handsome reward for its restoration. Unless Wild has it this day we are lost."

" At this moment, too," said Handsome Jack to himself, bitterly, " when I owe him so deep a debt of revenge, to be compelled to do him a service!"

Then he related to M'Cleane the events of the previous few hours. He had scarcely concluded his narrative when the echoes of the deep-toned alarm-bell vibrated through the chambers and along the passages of the " Chapel."

M'Cleane started, and exclaimed:— .

" This is no common danger which threatens us—the alarm-bell, never rung by day unless we are indeed in perilous circumstances."

The Captain then again pressed on the knob, and again Beauty Ellis made his appearance at the sliding-pannel opening.

" A lady in Madame Charlotte's room, as says as she must speak with Dick Flybynight," said Beauty.

" Her name?" demanded the Captain.

" She didn't tell that," replied Beauty; " but Madame Charlotte slipped this here bit of paper into my hand, with a werry pertickler look."

M'Cleane took the paper—it had only two words inscribed on it in Madame Charlotte's handwriting; but those two simple words did what a dozen pistols loaded to the muzzle and directed against him would have failed to do—

they made him feel sick and faint.—They were MARY MILLINER.

"Jonathan Wild's mistress, and right hand, by God!" he exclaimed.

"'She says as she won't go unless she sees Dick Flybynight, or he sends her something for Mr. Wild, as Dick knows he expects,'" remarked Beauty Ellis; and he added, "'for,' she says 'as the gentleman as 'tis for will call at Mr. Wild's for it at ten o'clock to-night.'"

"Go—and return hither in five minutes," ordered the Captain.

Instantaneously the sliding-panel was in its place, and M'Cleane and Handsome Jack were once more alone.

"She is come for that document," said M'Cleane, looking anxiously into Handsome Jack's face.

"M'Cleane," said the latter, "I cannot consent to peril the safety of you and my comrades. To show you my utter hatred for selfishness, I will give up this parchment," and he placed his finger in M'Cleane's hand.

"By heavens, Jack, you are a noble fellow!" cried the latter, as he grasped his hand, "You have saved us!"

"Here then it is," said Jack, drawing from his bosom the important document, and laying it on the table.

"And now," asked M'Cleane, "how to convey it to this Mary Milliner; for it would be the height of imprudence to let mine or Dick Flybynight's person be seen."

A pause succeeded, during which "Beauty" again made his appearance.

"Enquire," said M'Cleane to him, "of the woman, what reward Mr. Wild is willing to give if we comply with his wishes."

The messenger departed, and then M'Cleane said:—

"Jack, you must take this deed to Mary Milliner yourself—she does not know your figure; your face, you will, of course, take care to conceal with crape. All you will have to do will be simply this,—with one hand present the document—and hold out the other hand for the reward; for I have no idea of letting Jonathan grab all the fruits of your daring."

"Beauty" having returned, M'Cleane requested him to accompany Handsome Jack to the door of Madame Charlotte's room, and to wait there until he came from it.

Handsome Jack having cautiously concealed his features, and imitated a stoop of the shoulders and a lameness of one leg, soon reached Madame Charlotte's door: at a whistle from Beauty it opened, and Jack passed in.

In an arm chair, beside that of Madame Charlotte, sat a woman, who, had it not been for the effects of drink and prostitution, might still have been deemed handsome. She was dressed in matronly style, and had, or assumed to have, a most demure countenance. Nevertheless, there was a world of cunning expressed in her ever-roving, restless, grey eye. The instant Handsome Jack entered the room, she looked at him as though she sought to penetrate the disguise which she knew he had assumed; for those persons who resort to such expedients themselves, are invariably the first to suspect others."

"Have you brought the parchment for Mr. Wild?" she asked, in a clear, calm, business-like voice.

"I have—here it is," replied Handsome Jack, in a feigned voice; at the same time presenting it, and offering his palm for the expected reward.

"Wild will not be illiberal," she remarked, as she examined the parchment narrowly. "Yes," she resumed, when her inspection had ceased, "this is it—and here is the reward."

So saying she placed a small parcel in Handsome Jack's hand.

"You will always do well," she observed, rather carelessly as she rose from her chair, "to comply at once with Mr. Wild's terms; if you do you will have no reason to repent, but if you play him false, remember that his word can in a moment consign you to Tyburn Tree; but so great is his power that, even were the halter around your neck, he could save you."

Mrs. Milliner then, courteously declining the offer of a dram from Madame Charlotte, took her departure.

Handsome Jack lost no time in returning with "Beauty" by the secret way to M'Cleane's private room.

"And what did the hag give in return for the parchment, Jack?" asked the Captain.

"In truth, I know not the sum," said Jack; "but there is the parcel she placed in my hands," and he threw the packet on the table.

M'Cleane opened it—and a hundred guineas rolled on the floor.

"These are yours, Jack," he observed, sweeping them to the other side of the table.

"May they blister my fingers if I touch them!" replied Handsome Jack. "Mark my words, M'Cleane, by saving the gang, as you say I have, I have got my reward, and more than their and your good opinion I require not."

"Well said, Jack; and now that we can breathe freely once more, let us wash down dull care in the bowl. Here are some flasks of the purest Rhenish which once graced an alderman's cellar, but which shall now moisten the throttles of highwaymen. Drink, Jack, drink!"

"I have a little business to do to-night on my own account," said Jack; "therefore you must excuse me debauching my brains just now; therefore, by your leave, noble Captain, I will take an hour or two's rest, and then to work."

"Well done, Jack!" said M'Cleane, slapping him on the shoulder; "by my faith! thou wilt make a right valiant son of the road, and if thou accomplishest not some notable feat to-night, why I'll be content to lie in a condemned cell and howl out my paternosters."

"I have no idea of booty to-night, Captain," said Handsome Jack. "Mine is a mission of revenge—deep burning revenge—springing out of hatred of one of the veriest reptiles who ever crawled."

"Do not expose yourself heedlessly," said the Captain; "the life of so brave a man as Handsome Jack should not be lightly perilled. Do you require assistance in this business?"

"None," replied Jack, proudly, as he left M'Cleane, "the injury belongs alone to me, and I only will avenge it.

CHAPTER XV.

ROGUE'S MEETING—HANDSOME JACK'S REVENGE.

PRECISELY at a quarter to ten o'clock on the evening of the day when the events occurred, which we recorded in our last chapter, three men might have been seen in the neighbourhood of Newtoner's-lane, not far from the door of Jonathan Wild's house.

Each had so disguised himself that all three appeared strangers to each other, and each took up such a position as not to excite the suspicion that all of them were watching the same place.

One was a tall thin man in figure,—a handkerchief muffled about his mouth and chin, and a slouched hat completely concealed his features.

The second was wrapped in a short cloak, from beneath which a sword-scabbard emerged, his figure and bearing appeared noble, but like the former his face could not be seen.

The other man had a shuffling gait, and moved sneakingly about, every now and then he would look round and start, although not a living creature approached him.

These three men were, Mr. Wriggleton Doom, Handsome Jack, and Flitchman, the returned convict.

They were all anxiously watching for the appearance of Sir James Town, for by means, which will hereafter be explained, two of them had acquired the information that he would visit Jonathan Wild at ten o'clock that night. The reader is already aware how Handsome Jack became acquainted with the fact.

Each of these three men had a deep interest in watching the baronet's movements.

The lawyer had been informed through his emissaries that Sir James was to regain possession of the forged document that night; therefore it was of the utmost importance that he should wheedle himself into Sir James's good graces, in order that he might get it, in a professional way, into his own hands, and destroy it. In such a case the confession extorted from him by Handsome Jack would be valueless.

Flitchman was desirous of an interview with Sir James, in order that he might, from a deep-seated principle of revenge against Doom, on account of the attempted murder, reveal some of his designs against the baronet, and at the same time replenish the exchequer which Jenny Diver had so dexterously emptied.

Handsome Jack was actuated purely by revenge; he had now determined to fling away all notions of regaining his position in society, and of embracing the life which, however lawless, had, for dashing and bold men, a peculiar charm. The insult to Emilie on the proceeding evening he determined the villainous Sir James should atone for, and to that end he now waited his appearance.

As ten o'clock resounded from the belfries of the neighbouring churches, a handsome carriage, behind which were two powdered lacquies, and on either side several link-boys, drove up Newtoner's-lane, and one of the footmen having nimbly opened the door, Sir James, after whispering a few words in his ear, entered Jonathan Wild's dwelling.

Abraham, the obsequious Israelite, instantly admitted him, and conducted him into Jonathan's presence.

"And have you been successful, Mr. Wild?" asked Sir James; his face, as he spoke, although he uttered the words in a careless tone, betrayed to the scrutinizing eye of Wild the most intense anxiety.

"At this very moment, Sir James," he replied, with a cool, business-like manner, "I am now negociating with parties who I have reason to believe have the deed in their possession,—but a great price is demanded, Sir James—a very great price,—I assure you, Sir James, that my only desire is to serve you, for I see you are anxious about this matter—an old *family* document, perhaps?"

"Why yes—that is, no—not exactly; but it *is* of importance, nevertheless, Mr. Wild," stammered out the baronet.

Here Abraham entered the room and whispered something in Jonathan's ear.

"Too much—too much; I couldn't think of letting this worthy gentleman pay so exorbitant a sum for a mere bit of paper," said Wild to his man;—then, turning to Sir James, he continued, the deed *can* be had, Sir James; but they will not let it go under five-hundred guineas—'tis monstrous!"

And the hypocritical wretch turned up the whites of his eyes as if ejaculating a prayer to Heaven for patience to enable him to live in this sinful world.

"Try again, Abraham,—try again," said Wild.

"S'help me Got, Mishter Vildsh, it's of no use, the nimming villain shwearsh as rather as he'd take a shilling less he'd take it to Mashter Vatkins, the Bow-street officer, as gives goot prices for family things like dat, and vont hurt a hair of their headsh afterwards if its goot for anything."

At the mention of Mr. Watkins, and the idea of *his* getting hold of the forged deed Sir James became extremely uneasy.

"Well, I suppose I must give you the money, Mr. Wild," he said.

"As you please, Sir James,—as you please. Mind me, not one farthing shall I be the better for it. My aim is to do good, and if I accomplish that end I am sufficiently rewarded," said the consummate villain.

"There is my draft then for the sum, on my bankers in Old Change.

"Abraham," said Wild, "take five-hundred guineas from my strong box in the next room and pay the scoundrel, it would scarcely do to let Sir James's draft get into their hands."

Abraham then departed, and Wild placed the draft in his pocket-book; in about five minutes the Jew returned and laid the deed on Wild's desk.

"Is that it, Sir James," he said, presenting it to the Baronet.

"The very thing, Mr. Wild, and I am infinitely obliged to you," and in the excess of his joy he insisted on Wild's accepting fifty guineas by way of remuneration for his services.

"I have only done my duty as an honest man," said Jonathan, "and need not this—but since you insist on it, I will take it and distribute it amongst objects of charity."

It had been supposed by Flitchman and Doom that Sir James would have dismissed his carriage on entering Wild's—but they were mistaken. Handsome Jack, however, who had got hold of and treated one of the lacquies, having ascertained that Sir James would be driven towards St. Giles's in the Fields, instantly surmised that he intended to visit Mother Singleton's in the expectation of again seeing Emilie; and if practicable, of winning her over to his diabolical purpose. Nor was he wrong. For as yet Sir James was ignorant of the young lady's escape.

He therefore bent his steps in that direction, and having been informed by Emilie of the exact situation, and description of the vile house into which she had been inveigled, he was not slow to recognise it. Placing himself therefore in a position which commanded all the entrances to the thoroughfare in which it was situated, he impatiently awaited the coming of the man for whose blood he thirsted.

At length he perceived at a distance the link-boys. Suddenly, however, the carriage stopped, and its owner alighting, came towards Mother Singleton's house, alone.

From his place of concealment, Handsome Jack watched his approach, as the baronet came near, he drew his rapier, and just as the baronet had placed his feet on the doorstep—he strode forward—laid his hand on his shoulder and commanded him to stop.

"Insolent scoundrel!" exclaimed Sir James, "How dare a sneaking footpad like you accost a gentleman? Begone fellow, or I will call my lacquies yonder, and they shall lay their canes over thy mongrel shoulders."

"Utter one word of alarm, move but one step, and your vile life shall leave your worthless carcass on the instant," said Handsome Jack.

"This to me?" exclaimed the Baronet, and he attempted to draw his sword, but Jack wrenched it from him and flung it into the road.

"Yes; that to you, and that also," said Jack, as with the back of his hand he struck Sir James a violent blow on the face.

"Town," he continued, "I know your errand here—but you will be foiled—the bird you would have snared has flown!"

"What mean you?" asked the astounded Sir James.

"That, the young girl whose pure body you would have defiled has eluded your artifices—that she has exposed your profligacy, and that I am here to avenge her."

"Would you murder me?" said Sir James, who now gasped with terror. "If money would make reparation——"

"A curse on your ill-gotten gold! No I would not murder; I will at least give you a chance for your miserable life. There, sir, is your sword again—and now defend yourself, for by the God who made me, the attempted seducer of Emilie shall have no mercy from me."

Their rapiers now flashed in the dim light of the street lamp, and rapid were the passes, and fierce were the lunges of each. Both fought with the energy of desperate men, but the arm of Handsome Jack was too vigorous to succumb to the perhaps superior skill as a swordsman of Sir James—the latter seeing the tide turning against him, craved a parley.

The thought of what the girl he loved so dearly might have been at that moment flashed across Handsome Jack's mind, and hardened his heart.

"Parley!" he sneered, and he fought with re-doubled fierceness—at length Sir James's weapon was struck upwards, and the weapon of Handsome Jack passed through his sword arm.

As he fell to the ground, a roll of parchment dropped from the breast pocket of his coat. Jack instantly seized it, and burst into a laugh of triumph as he held it close to the conquered man's eyes. It was the forged deed, which he had but just before purchased at so exhorbitant a price from Jonathan Wild!

"For God's sake restore me that," shrieked the unhappy Baronet—but Handsome Jack, coolly securing it in his bosom, replied:—

"Wretch, you are now utterly in my power; I would have on this spot ended your loathsome existence, had I not lighted on this; your life shall now be such as to make death a welcome thing—and Emilie shall be well revenged. Dare but to inform your miserable tool Doom or of your love, and the result will be terrible; for I shall watch you and be near you when you little dream of it—and if you apply again to Jonathan Wild, you shall as surely be hanged as you have been outwitted to-night."

The sound of the watch approaching was now heard, and Handsome Jack, spurning with his foot the abject Sir James, strode away into the gloom.

What his thoughts were may be easily conceived. The deed, which he had deemed irrecoverably lost, was now, by almost a miracle, replaced in his hands. Yet, perhaps, to gain that document he had committed a murder!—had executed a revenge!

"Back again?" asked Beauty, as Handsome Jack entered the precincts of the "Chapel." "Well, its werry odd—it never rains but it pours."

And "Beauty Ellis" held out his hand for the accustomed fee.

Silently placing a bit of gold in his "itching palm," Jack proceeded inward, until he reached the Saloon.

McCleane had long since retired, and Gipsey Betty was the sole occupant of the sumptuous place.

She was lolling on a couch, in all the voluptuousness of unbridled passion—but Handsome Jack had, just at that moment, other fish to fry.

"I am going to the Captain's room," he said, "and, Bessy, darling! you must wait till business of lesser importance will enable me to spend an hour with you."

M'CLEANE ACTING AS FOOTMAN TO JENNY DIVER.

"Lesser importance," said Betty the Gipsey. "Aye—it's always the case with you men! You look after girls—manufacture them into women;—and then they are things of 'lesser importance.'"

"Lesser importance—women!" muttered Handsome Jack.

"I did not mean that—not exactly that, Jack; but I thought you might have spent five minutes with Gipsey Betty, who you led to the supper table on the first night of our meeting."

"Well, five minutes isn't much," said Jack, as he sat down by the side of the Lingaro of the gang.

"A great deal of mischief, Jack, may be done in five minutes," replied the girl, archly.

"But you wouldn't lead me into mischief, or into temptation either?" asked Jack.

No. 9.

"Of course not," she replied; and Handsome Jack, by some influence for which he could not account, fell into a dream which had nothing of trouble to annoy it. He fancied he was wandering with the Graces through the flowery groves of Paradise, and that the angel who led him along was Gipsey Betty. Hand in hand, and heart to heart, they pressed their way onwards, and inwards, until that temple was reached, at whose vestibule the pilgrims sink, faintingly—like thirsty and satiated souls, who, when they have drank enough, exclaim—"No more!"

"Jack!" exclaimed a stern voice.

"I am here, M'Cleane, and have news for you—news which you will be delighted to hear."

"To my room, then—this is no time to spend in idle dalliance. "Oh, Jack! Jack!"

"Blame me not, M'Cleane!" said Jack; "I am not the first who fell into a love-trap."

"I have no time for talk now!" said M'Cleane; "a man of the name of Flitchman is here.—Come with me."

"I am here to obey," said Handsome Jack.

They were soon domiciled in M'Cleane's room.

The two men sat silent for a time; each, for particular purposes, was anxiously watching the other. At length M'Cleane spoke:—

"You had an adventure to-night, Jack?" said M'Cleane.

"Yes, and I reaped the reward of it," replied Handsome Jack.

"I know it," said M'Cleane; "you found some fool who dropped that which did not belong to him."

"How! have you divined it?" asked Handsome Jack; "you must be as clever as Doctor Faustus, to have known this!"

"I believe," said M'Cleane, "if I am not misinformed, that you watched for Sir James Town to-night at Jonathan Wild's house—bribed his lacquey—hunted him to the door of Mother Singleton's, and that there you had a sharp encounter."

"Such is the truth," replied Handsome Jack.

"And you gained your own?" asked M'Cleane.

"I did," exclaimed Handsome Jack. "See here!" and he flung on M'Cleane's desk the parchment which had fallen from Sir James Town's pocket, when the baronet had sunk bleeding before Mother Singleton's door.

"The king shall enjoy his own again!" said M'Cleane, as he rose and summoned a messenger.

Beauty was not long in appearing.

"Send in the man," was the command.

Slouchingly, trembling, and confused with the novelty of his position, came into the apartment a man, who looked as though the world had used him, and much abused him.

He was abject—positively abject; much suffering had cowed the spirit which he might have once possessed; great changes had subdued him into an acquaintanceship with sorrow. There was something, however, good about the man, if any one had chosen to have been at the trouble of finding it out.

There are, in Venice, that City of the Sea, to whose marble palaces the sea-weed clings, numberless canals. In one of these a lady one day dropped a valuable ring; the waters rippled, and the seekers looked in vain for the jewel: a looker-on, wiser than the rest, suggested that if a little oil was thrown on the surface of the water, a clear medium would be established. Oil was cast on the troubled wavelet, and then, one of the humblest of the gondoliers saw the gem below, and recovered it. It is always thus in the canal of humanity. Pour on a little oil of human kindness, and however black may be the depths of the heart, some bright thing will be found there worth diving for.

"Flitchman," said M'Cleane, "are you willing to join us?"

"No!" said he, decidedly; "no!"

"Do you remember a little transaction in a certain inn, when you lost a hundred pounds, or very nearly that sum?" asked M'Cleane.

"Yes," replied Flitchman.

"And you know from whom you obtained that money?" asked M'Cleane.

"From Mr. Doom, the Lawyer of Gray's Inn," replied the man.

"The party who wanted to send you to heaven by water under one of the arches of London Bridge?" suggested the Captain.

"The very man."

"You love him, of course," said Handsome Jack.

"Just as much as I love Sir James Town," was the reply.

"And you will serve us?" asked M'Cleane, putting five guineas into his hand.

"If protected, I will; at present I am a Sanctuary bird——"

He was proceeding when M'Cleane interrupted him with:—

"A burglary is to-night to be perpetrated by some members of our fraternity; Jem Starlight will lead the party. Now, will you put crape on your face, and courage in your head, and join the burglars?"

"Not I!" exclaimed Flitchman, "it ain't my line—I'd scorn to be a burglar,—to break into peoples houses, and steal when they're asleep;—I've helped to do forgery, and I've had enough of that. No; give me the road—a pair of pistols—and a gentleman who has a pair too! There's something like courage in that."

The man spoke this with desperate energy. He had so long grovelled in the back-slums of crime, that he panted for a wider field in which he could display his peculiar talent of laying his appropriation-claws on what belonged not to him.

"We will protect you," said M'Cleane, "so long as you serve us faithfully. But if you are to share our gains, it is but fair that you should obey any commands of your Captain, and engage in any job, for the general benefit of the fraternity."

"Well—I am willing," remarked Flitchman.

"Administer the oaths!" said M'Cleane; and the late clerk of Mr. Doom was formally admitted a member of the gang.

CHAPTER XVI.

JENNY DIVER AND CAPTAIN M'CLEANE GO INTO PARTNERSHIP.

M'CLEANE had now so devotedly attached himself to Jenny Diver, that the latter acquired an amazing ascendancy over him; and at her suggestion it was arranged that the Captain should assist her in such depredations as those we have already recorded, and in the commission of which she had exhibited such marvellous dexterity.

"You shall act as my footman, Jem, and I will dress as a fine lady—and, my life on it, we will fleece the most cautious. You won't object to follow Jenny in livery—will you, Jem?" said the Diver.

" Anywhere with you, and in what character you like, my girl!" replied the Captain.

" I only feared," remarked Jenny, "that you would think it unbefitting your dignity as Captain of the band, to put on the habiliments of a serving-man, and to walk after her who has so recently become one of your loving subjects!"

M'Cleane replied by a laugh and an embrace, and the next day it was agreed upon that in their new characters they should sally forth in search of adventures.

And on the following morning, whilst Jenny Diver was dressing, M'Cleane entered her apartment. The young woman had just put on her stays, which she was about to lace, when M'Cleane proposed to perform that office for her.

" Wait a bit," said Jenny; "here, Jem, hand me that pillow from off the bed. I mean to wear it this morning."

M'Cleane stared in unaffected surprise, as he handed to Jenny the moderate sized pillow she had pointed out to him.

" Why, you won't want this till bed-time again," said he.

" Ah, M'Cleane!" she replied, laughingly, "you don't know half of Jenny Diver's tricks yet. What do you think now? I am going to wear that same pillow this morning."

" Wear it this morning?" asked M'Cleane.

" See here, Jem," said Jenny.

And carefully doubling the pillow, she placed it beneath the lower part of her stays, so as to produce a considerable prominence in the front of her person.

" Why, damn it, Jenny!" said M'Cleane, "is my mistress going to spoil that pretty figure of hers, by padding it?—better wear a hooped petticoat at once!"

" Don't you see, Jem, that I am going to act a new part this morning. I am going to be with child, Jem, without the troublesome prospect of bearing a baby. There, now! lace my boddice, an' you will. You will make an excellent footman!" said the girl, when M'Cleane had finished this rather exciting operation.

Jenny now drew on her quilted petticoat and outer garment, and presented the appearance of a pregnant woman so exactly, and laid her arms so naturally and demurely over her stomach, that M'Cleane, as he gazed, could not but indulge in a paroxysm of laughter.

" There, Jem!—now go and put on your livery, and then you shall follow your mistress to the park!" said Jenny, archly.

M'Cleane retired, and before long was equipped in a walking footman's rich dress. As he re-entered Jenny's chamber, he made a bow of mock humility, which was responded to by a nod of haughty recognition from Jenny.

Within an hour from that time, two persons might have been observed sauntering towards St. James's Park,—a lady followed by a servant in rich livery.

Amidst the fashionable throng assembled between the Park and Spring Gardens, none bore herself in a more ladylike, or, indeed in a more aristocratic manner than that female, who appeared to move through the children of fashion, as though she was one of the proudest of them all.

Her dress, although arranged with extreme modesty, indicated that she was in that interesting way, in which it is said ladies who love their lords long to be. Her eyes, when any one observed her situation, glanced downwards, as if with bashful confusion, and a blush overspread her beautiful cheeks.

" Who is she?" was a question asked by many an admiring man and envious woman. None could tell—but all agreed that she was a woman of fashion, and a charming one too.

Behind her, with a gold-headed wand in his hand, in a superb livery, powdered wig, cocked hat, and unexceptionable calves, stalked at a respectful distance, her lacquey. He followed her as faithfully as her shadow, and looked so handsome, that several footmen who saw him, fell instantly into fits of jealous admiration.

These parties were Captain M'Cleane and Jenny Diver; but little indeed did those who remarked them suspect, that in the person of the footman they saw the most dashing highwayman of the time, and in Jenny Diver, the most accomplished cut-purse of her day.

On that morning the king was to proceed in state to the House of Lords, and consequently the crowd was very great. M'Cleane and Jenny observed with great satisfaction that the greater portion were well-dressed persons, and that many of them wore rich ornaments, which they trusted ere long to transfer to their own pockets.

It should have been stated, that at some distance from the false mistress and man servant, lingered Gipsey Betty, whose aid as a female accomplice had been enlisted by Jenny.

When they arrived between the Park and Spring Gardens, Jenny observed a number of persons of quality lounging about, and judging that here a booty might be acquired, she resorted to an expedient which had been concerted between her and M'Cleane before they had quitted the "Chapel."

Whilst several persons were looking at her with evident admiration, she suddenly slipt down, and as she fell, she cunningly with a damp handkerchief rubbed the rouge from her cheeks, which now appeared of a lily paleness, and uttered a cry of pain.

Seeing such a catastrophe occur to his mistress, the footman rushed forward—and at the same moment a considerable number of persons of both sexes surrounded her, and offered assistance.

Feigning to be, however, in violent pain, she faintly waved them off, and expressed a desire to be allowed to lie on the ground until she should be somewhat recovered. Her apparent situation commanded the utmost sympathy, and two ladies volunteered to remain with her while her servant should procure a coach from the nearest stand.

The crowd still increased, and M'Cleane and Gipsey Betty were by no means idle, for by the time Jenny had somewhat recovered they had obtained a considerable booty.

" Here is a carriage, my lady," said M'Cleane, as he hurried to the spot where Jenny still lay,

"Will any gentleman be good enough to assist my lady to the carriage?"

A young gentleman instantly stepped forward, and offered his arm, which Jenny with some confusion accepted. As he held out his hand to her, she perceived a large diamond ring on his finger, and determined if possible to possess herself of it.

When they had reached the coach, she was placed in it. Gipsey Betty having offered to attend the lady home, was accommodated with a seat, and M'Cleane jumped up behind.

Just as the carriage was about to start, the young gentleman who had handed Jenny to it, expressed a hope that he might be allowed to visit so charming a creature. Jenny blushed, looked offended, and observed that the gentleman might suppose that she was not a married woman. In token, however, of her gratitude for the assistance he had rendered her, she extended her hand to him, which he eagerly seized; and at this moment she contrived to get possession of the ring without the knowledge of the gallant, who on leaving the coach and missing the jewel, never for one moment conceived that his innamorati had helped herself to it, but imagined that it must have been purloined from him in the crowd.

Dismissing the coach in a retired situation, M'Cleane, Jenny Diver, and Gipsey Betty adjourned to a vintner's of their acquaintance, where they were accommodated with a back room. Here they changed their dresses, as they did not deem it safe to appear with them again in the precincts of the "Chapel."

Having partaken of some refreshment, Jenny proposed that they should examine their booty.

"Here are two purses, containing upwards of forty guineas, and a gold snuff-box," said Gipsey Betty, placing the articles on the table. "The snuff-box I got from the waistcoat of an amorous old fool, who put his arm round my waist in the crowd, and chucked me under the chin with his skinny finger; one of the purses I filched from the pocket of a bullying bawd, and the other from the buttoned-up pouch of a snuffy old tradesman.

"Bravo, Betty!" exclaimed M'Cleane, "Handsome Jack shall be acquainted with your dexterity. Why, Jenny Diver herself need not be ashamed of such a morning's work. Now for my harvest!" continued the Captain.

He then placed beside Gipsey Betty's produce two diamond girdle-buckles, and a gold watch.

"These," he remarked, pointing to the glittering girdles, "I relieved two ladies of, who pressed against your handsome footman, Jenny, when you were in agony on the ground."

Jenny's laughter at this was long and loud, and rang out as clearly and as merrily as the song of a bird.

"And this gold watch I took the liberty of borrowing from one of the frequenters of Fop's Alley, whilst he was looking at the pregnant lady through his opera-glass!"

Again Jenny laughed until she cried.

"I can bring but little into the common stock," she said.

"The devil! how could you bring anything?" asked M'Cleane; "a person—even one so clever as Jenny Diver herself, cannot pick pockets

when they lie on the ground, groaning as if they were in labour."

"I never picked a pocket at all," remarked Jenny, slily—"and yet I did not come here with empty pockets!"

"I'll swear," said M'Cleane, "that from the time you slipped down, until you were handed into the carriage by that perfumed beau, you never touched a purse;—I saw your eyes, though, look rather covetously at the suberb diamond ring which the gallant wore on his finger. Pity you had no chance of filching it, for it was a diamond of large size and of the first water; and would fetch as much or more than all that I and Gipsey Betty have managed to pick up."

"There it is," said Jenny, handing the ring to the Captain; "You see I had a chance—and I didn't let it slip!"

M'Cleane stared in astonishment. Wonderful as he knew Jenny Diver's dexterity to be, he had not been prepared for such a startling display of it.

"Damme, Jenny! you must have the devil himself at your fingers' ends!" he said.

"And of course I hooked off that ring from the man's fingers, then, with old Nick's crooked claws, as he squeezed my hand, after he placed me in the carriage," said Jenny, laughingly.

Jenny then gave him the particulars of the affair, after which M'Cleane exclaimed:—

"By Jove! you are a wonderful girl. Jenny, dear, you must get into the family way again, if you get safely delivered of such brilliant babies as this!"

"And have such an easy delivery, too!" remarked the girl; and she resumed, with a cunning glance at the Captain:—"The best of it is, Jem, that bantlings of this kind bring their parents cash, instead of, like flesh-and-blood children, who take gold out of their pockets. Besides, you know, Jem, a pillow under one's stays, neither injures the figure nor requires a man-midwife and a nurse to relieve one of it!"

The trio were now in such high spirits, that calling the master of the house, they ordered a sumptuous repast, to which they did ample justice. At its conclusion M'Cleane sent the drawer for a bowl of Sherris sack, which beverage they were discussing when the vintner entered the room, and requested to have a few words in private with the Captain.

"What's in the wind, now?" asked M'Cleane, as he followed the tavern-keeper.

"Only want to give you a bit of advice, valiant Captain. Mister Watkins, the Bow Street runner, is a prowling about the neighbourhood. He's after summut, or he wouldn't show his nose near my door, I'll swear! so I thought it 'ud be as well if I gave you a bit of a hint to keep out o' sight an hour or two."

"You're quite right—and I'm much indebted to you, Master Bilkit; and mayhap 'twould be as well to follow your advice—not that there's exactly any occasion for it," he added, "but you know, Bilkit, it's as well to avoid bad company when you can."

"Sartinly, noble Captain! sartinly — I'm o' your opinion;—and what luck o' late? Do you know, Captain, that since I retired from 'Chapel' business, and set up as a vintner in this here hostelry—the 'Jolly Pedlars,' with the little I'd ha' managed to scrape up——"

"By *honest* industry?" asked M'Cleane, with a sidelong glance at the vintner, "with the fruits of a sober livelihood? eh, Master Bilkit?"

"Ha! ha!" returned Bilkit, "you're just as much of a wag as you were when you and I robbed the parson, and then made him pray for our soul's salvation, Captain! but as I was a going to say, in this here crib, I feels sometimes, werry lonesome like, and longs for the road again. If I didn't do a little with drunken kiddies who come here, now and then, I should be quite out o' heart; but that sort of thing puts me in mind of old times, and keeps up my spirits a bit."

"What's bred in the bone, won't come out in the flesh," said M'Cleane, laughing heartily at the last remark of Bilkit; "but, come," added he, "let us join my friends in the parlour, who will be uneasy at my absence, and you shall drink a beaker full of sack to your old friends, and I'll empty a goblet to the landlord of the 'Jolly Pedlars.'"

"With all my heart!" said Bilkit; "but you go in first, and I'll follow you as soon as I have set a watch on the motions of that infernal Watkins, the officer; for he's after no good—no, no more than the carpenter o' Newgate is when he is hammering nails into a brave fellow's coffin!"

Having delivered himself of this appropriate and eloquent simile, Mr. Bilkit went into his shop, and M'Cleane proceeded to join Jenny Diver and Gipsey Betty in the private parlour.

"Don't be afraid, girls," he said, as he entered, "there's not much the matter—it's only that rascal Watkins, of Bow Street, prowling about the neighbourhood; he can't however, be looking for us, for there has been scarcely time for what we've done this morning to get wind."

Jenny Diver's pretty lip curled with something of a disdainful expression, as she replied:—

"Afraid, Jem! why, you never suppose I would show the white feather, do you? Why, if the halter was round my neck, and my foot on the ladder, I would scorn to show one symptom of fear!"

"That's my noble Jenny all over!" exclaimed M'Cleane, as he caressed the girl, and took her on his knee. "You shall have a companion presently," said the Captain to Gipsey Betty; "an old friend of mine—one who was formerly a member of our gang — Tony Bilkit, our worthy vintner here, is coming to join us over a glass."

"I'd much rather 'twas Handsome Jack," said Gipsey Betty; "but if, as you say, he was one of us, Captain, why he must be welcome."

At this point of the conversation Mr. Bilkit made his appearance. He was a big, burly fellow—a man who, at one period, must have possessed prodigious strength. His occupation, however, of vintner, though it had tended to add to his bulk, had rather diminished than increased his muscular power. His head was bullet-shaped; from beneath a low forehead, peered forth two small dark piercing eyes; his nose was of that description known as "pug," and his mouth reached almost from ear to ear; when he smiled, it resembled a huge gash across his face; on his cheek was a mark where, years before, he had been branded for his villainies.

"I wish to my soul, I was along with you in the 'Chapel' again, Captain!—but as I ain't, all I can do is to drink success and long life to all them as is!" said Bilkit, tossing off immediately after the utterance of this bit of philosophy, a brimming glass full of liquor.

"We have a job now and then, when an extra hand might be serviceable, Tony," remarked M'Cleane, carelessly. "What do you say, now,—should you have any objection to amuse yourself now and then?"

"Not a bit on it—not the leastest objection in the world!" said Tony; "on the contrary, I should werry much enjoy it. Got anything on hand now?"

"Why, yes," said M'Cleane; "but how could you quit the tap of the 'Jolly Pedlars,' Tony?"

"Oh, I could manage that easy enough; Jerry Laggum, my man-servant, is as fly as I am myself, and he'd attend to the customers—especially to the bucks!"

At the last allusion Mr. Bilkit grinned with great meaning, and put his fore-finger to the side of his nose.

"Damme! if I could stand being cooped up here, after having been free of the road!" exclaimed M'Cleane, as he gazed round the dingy room.

"Do you know, Captain, as 'tis cheerful enough sometimes, though—for when business is slow, I sits in this darkish apartment, and thinks of all the pleasures I felt when I was in the exercise of my lawful calling."

The idea of burglary being a lawful calling amused Jenny Diver mightily.

Without heeding her merriment, Bilkit proceeded:—

"I'm a thinking this werry moment, Captain, of that Hackney Job—ah! 'tis really refreshing to remember such Toby-fakes as that was!"

"Was it very interesting?" asked Gipsey Betty.

"Werry, Miss, werry much so, there was three of us in it, Stiv Mallick, Dick Blowhard and your humble servant."

"Tell us something about it?" asked Jenny, who had a due share of that article common to females—called curiosity.

"Why, we got into a baker's shop, you see," said Tony, "and after we were inside all snug and comfortable, the journeyman and the 'prentice heard us, and came down stairs. They was soon settled, for we tied 'em neck and heels, and flung 'em into the kneeding trough. Stiv stood over 'em with a drawn sword, while Dick and I went up stairs to see what we could get. Lord you should ha' seen how the old feller started when he seed us!"

"Don't doubt it, Tony; I should have started too, for damme, man, you're by no means handsome," said M'Cleane.

"I was rather better looking then, Captain, though—for that cursed brand hadn't been put on my cheek, only for that job of taking a portmanteau from behind a coach. Lord—lord! how my skin hissed again, and how my whiskers singed up, when the hot iron came against 'em!"

"Well, never mind that," said Jenny, "go on with your story."

"The old chap wouldn't tell us where his money was hid, threaten as we might, and I was just going to try the thickness of his skull with the butt-end of my horse-pistol, when a werry happy thought struck me."

"What was that," enquired Gipsey Betty.

"Why, the obstinate old fool had a little child asleep in bed with him, a pretty girl enough, with eyes as blue as the sky on a moonlight night over Hounslow Heath; and curly hair of a golden colour. 'Twas a granddaughter of his, whose father and mother was dead."

"Well?" said Jenny, whose face betokened a deep interest in the narrative of Tony.

"Well," resumed Mr. Bilkit. "I catched up that little 'un, and, ordering the old baker to come down to the bakehouse; I carried it down stairs. Now," says I to the grandfather, who was shivering with terror, "if you don't hand over your money, as sure as I'm standing here I'll put this child into the oven; I said so, so help me God!"

"Wretch!" said Jenny Diver, in a low tone, for the young girl, abandoned as she was, had the feelings of a woman strong within her. With the man, because of his barbarity, she felt utterly disgusted.

"He couldn't stand that, so he told us where we could find the money, and we took seventy pounds from him that night. There," added Mr. Bilkit, in conclusion, "that's something to think on, ain't it?"

M'Cleane, who possessed much genuine humanity in his bosom, felt inclined to apply to Tony some such epithet as that with which Jenny Diver had honored him; but he refrained, for he well knew that it would not do to quarrel with the landlord of the Jolly Pedlars, who was in possession of too many of his secrets to be made an enemy of.

"Now, Tony," he said, "I don't think there is much fear of Watkins, if he'd been on the watch for us, we should have seen him before now," said M'Cleane.

"No you wouldn't though," returned Tony; "d'ye think I havn't got a snug place to hide my friends in when they wish to retire into private life?"

"Just follow me," said Tony to the Captain, and, rising, he touched a concealed spring in the floor, when a trap-door rose, and a ladder was visible. Bilkit, lighting a dark lantern, descended followed by M'Cleane.

At the foot of the ladder was a winding passage which led to a large chamber, on the walls of which were hung fire-arms and weapons of all descriptions. Near a large fireplace was a table and some benches, on the former of which stood some measures, which had recently been emptied.

"I would defy Jonathan Wild himself to find you here, if you didn't choose to see him," said Tony, with a grin of self-satisfaction. "One man might defend this place against one

hundred if he chose. 'Tis a werry convenient place too, for a private churchyard, and there aint no parson-croaller to pay for putting a body out o' sight."

"What mean you?" asked M'Cleane.

"Oh! nothing werry particklar—but can't you guess, Captain? Only just look in that corner."

M'Cleane turned his eyes to the point indicated by Bilkit's finger.

The place in which he stood was floored with large flag stones. In one corner these stones had been recently removed, for the earth between their edges had not had time to dry. A little mound of damp earth, too, lay in the angle formed by the junction of the walls; and a churchyard sort of smell arose from the spot!

"Why, you've been murdering some one, Tony, and have buried him there!" said M'Cleane, shuddering as he looked on that horrible place.

"I didn't do the job, myself—but 'twas some good customers of mine who did. The fool hadn't the sense to be quiet, after he had lost at dice, and demanded back his money, because he said he'd been cheated out of it; so they prewented his going to Bow Street and giving information, by slitting his weasand!—You'd have done the same yourself, Captain!" said the villain.

"By Heavens! I would have done no such thing, Tony;—if I am a robber, I take my booty like a brave man, and not like a sneak and an assassin!" said M'Cleane, indignantly.

"But you won't peach—will you?" asked Tony.

"I'll keep your secret, never fear—though I must confess that my heart sickens at such hellish doings!" replied M'Cleane.

"Well, now, Captain, we'll mount the ladder," said Tony.

"I'm much mistaken," said M'Cleane, interrupting him, "if you don't mount the ladder at Tyburn soon, if you go on in this way; but come—I must be off;" and he led the way through the winding passage.

They were speedily with Jenny Diver and Gipsey Betty—and it being now dusk, they left the "Jolly Pedlars" by a back door, and Gipsey Betty having been sent forward, M'Cleane and Jenny Diver proceeded through Covent Garden in the direction of the "Chapel."

CHAPTER XVII.

HOW GIPSEY BETTY PAID A VISIT TO THE FENCE—AND HOW SHE GOT INTO TROUBLE, AND ALSO OUT OF IT.

As Jenny Diver and M'Cleane were on their way homewards, their attention was arrested by the loud tones of the bellman of the Parish of St. Martin's-in-the-Fields, around whom a considerable crowd was collected.

The pair were half afraid to mingle with the throng, and therefore M'Cleane inquired of a by-stander what the bellman was crying.

He was informed that the man was giving

notice that two diamond girdle-buckles, a gold watch, and a gold snuff-box, had that day been stolen in the Park; that a considerable reward would be given to the party who should restore the property, and that no questions would be asked.

Having acquired this information, they repaired with all speed to the "Chapel," where a council of the gang was summoned, who should decide how the booty was to be disposed of.

Jenny's dexterity in abstracting the ring from the gallant in the Park, was the theme of universal commendation; and Dick Flybynight immediately proposed, that as a reward for her superior address, she should in future have an equal share of all the booties of the gang, even though she might not happen to be present when they were obtained.

This was unanimously assented to, and Jenny might now almost have been considered Empress of the nefarious band.

" And now," said M'Cleane to his confederates, " let us decide as to the disposal of these trinkets. They have been cried, and a handsome reward offered. Shall we run the risk of returning them, or send them to the Fence."

Several opinions for and against either course were delivered, and then M'Cleane said:

" In case we determine to restore them to their former owners, who amongst us will volunteer to be the messenger, of whom it is declared, no questions will be asked?"

There was a pause for a few moments; no one appeared inclined to undertake the dangerous task. They seemed to be of opinion, like the rats in the fable, that a bell should be put round the cat's neck to warn them of her approach; but no one seemed inclined to bell the cat.

In other words, each member of the gang feared to risk his neck, by returning the articles; for they well enough knew that the promise of "no questions," was quite as often broken as kept; and was also frequently a bait of the officers.

At length, as if ashamed of the fears of her male comrades, Gipsey Betty came forward and with something like a sneer on her pretty lip, said:—

" If none of these valiant gentlemen of the road will venture on this errand, I beg to volunteer my services."

" Bravo, Betty!" exclaimed several of the gang.

" It is my opinion," resumed Betty, " that I had better go on this errand, for the reward offered is much more than we should realise by the sale;—I am willing to run every risk!"

" No," said Jenny, " that will never do— there are too many keen eyes about. Gipsey Betty might be traced, and our association utterly ruined. How do we know but this may be a manœuvre of that villain Jonathan Wild?"

" True, Jenny!" said M'Cleane, " you are sharper-witted than most of us, It might, indeed, be one of Wild's devilish plots to get us into his power!"

" It would be by far more prudent," said Jenny, " to sell the things at half their real value, than to thrust our necks, perhaps into nooses, for the sake of a trifle more."

This course was ultimately decided on, and Gipsey Betty was deputed to dispose of them to a receiver of stolen goods.

" Shall I take them to Duke's Place, or to Hanging Sword Alley?" asked the girl.

" It is of little consequence which," replied M'Cleane; " Williams gives us the best prices— but old Ishmael, of Duke's Place, is perhaps the safest purchaser of the two, he having such fine opportunities of sending the property away to Holland."

It was not too late for the business to be transacted that night; indeed, it was conjectured that it would be better to dispose of the jewels at once, lest by any untoward chance they might be traced to their possession.

Gipsey Betty accordingly carefully disguised herself, and prepared to undertake her commission. Quitting the " Chapel," a thought struck her that she would, without the permission of the gang, first ascertain whether there really would be any risk in returning the property to those who had advertised for it; and she proceeded in the direction of Oxford Street, to a house in which thoroughfare reference had been made by the bellman.

Then it occurred to her that she should be perilling the lives of those with whom she was connected—and at the same time betray the confidence reposed in her by the gang. Suddenly, therefore, changing her mind, and obeying the dictates of that sort of honour which exists among thieves, she turned back, and walked as rapidly as possible towards Hanging Sword Alley, in Fleet Street.

When she arrived at the entrance of this thoroughfare, she looked cautiously about her, and perceiving to all appearance that the way was clear, she slid from the street into the alley.

She had not, however, noticed a man who, standing within the shadow of an old gateway, was with vigilant eyes watching her every motion, and who had done so from the moment she had quitted the " Chapel."

The thoroughfare which she now traversed with hasty steps, was gloomy and lonely. On either side of it stood old houses, whose upper stories so far projected over the ground floor, that it entirely prevented even a ray of noontide sunshine from entering the latter portions of the buildings; for, looking upwards, only a thin blue streak of sky resembling a ribbon, was visible. At night it was gloomy indeed, for only a few dingy oil lamps, and these at considerable distances from each other, flickered in the alley.

Its very darkness and dinginess, however, rendered Hanging Sword Alley a fit place for the deeds of iniquity which were there perpetrated. The greater number of the houses were brothels of the very lowest description, at the half-opened doors of which stood girls, in a half-naked state, and bawds in all their hideous ugliness. From the interiors of these temples of vice, sounded forth drunken screams and rude oaths; and every now and then a drunken rake would reel forth, with heated brain, languid limbs, and empty pockets.

Stopping near a door at the extremity of the alley, Gipsey Betty tapped once at a low window, and then rapped with her knuckles twice at the door itself. The window was almost immediately raised, and the frouzy head of a man appeared at it. With his small eyes, he peered curiously at the girl, who uttered a pass-word. The head was quickly withdrawn—the window closed—and presently the door revolved on its creeking hinges.

The person who opened it, was the man whose head had been seen from the window. He gave the girl a knowing look, which was quickly returned by one equally intelligible; and the girl having entered, the door was carefully locked and barred.

"Is Mr. Williams at home?" asked the girl.

"Sartinly, Gipsey Betty—to *you*, sartinly—for I know as you always comes on business. You *do* look tempting to-night, Betty!" And the ugly fellow with a sensual leer attempted to snatch a kiss.

"Come, Master Slogger! hands off, or you'll have a taste of my nails!" exclaimed the girl, as she slipped from his proffered, and to her, disgusting embrace.

"I'd much rather have a taste of those sweet pretty lips of yours, my lass!" said Mr. Slogger, amorously.

"Then you won't—and that's certain, you ugly old varlet!" replied the girl, giving him at the same time a saucy slap on his cheek.

"Come!" she said, sharply, "I must see Mr. Williams, and that immediately!"

"What have you brought, my pretty dear?" asked the man.

"That concerns your master, and not *you*," replied the girl.

"Ah! what nimble fingers you have got, Betty;—why, such a clever girl as you are, will soon make a fortune!"

"Tush!" said she, impatiently, "lead on—I have no time to spare for such idle talk!"

"This way, then, Betty dear! this way;" and unlocking a door, he led the way up a flight of narrow stairs into a small, unfurnished room, from the ceiling of which hung a single oil lamp.

"Stop a minute," said Slogger, "while I trim the lamp." Having done so, he proceeded to that side of the apartment opposite the door by which they had entered, and pressing a small spring, a part of the old oaken panel flew back.

In the opening thus made, was to be seen a machine of a rather curious construction. At first sight it resembled a cupboard without a door. In the recess, too, was a wire which Slogger pulled gently, and then requested Gipsey Betty to place the articles she had brought with her in the seeming cupboard aforesaid.

Gipsey Betty then put the girdle-buckles, the watch, and the ring in the machine, with a paper on which was writen the price expected, and Slogger having pulled the wire, the apparatus revolved, and to all appearance the aperture was again permanently closed.

In about five minutes a bell was heard to sound, and then Mr. Slogger informed Gipsey Betty that his master was ready to see her.

Following her guide, she proceeded through a secret door into the next apartment, where sat, with the articles she had just parted with in his hand, Williams, the notorious Fence.

At a nod from Williams, Slogger quitted the room, and the former requested the girl to be seated.

"You ask a large price for these, Betty," said the Fence; "bless you! I couldn't give half the sum. Money is scarce—very scarce; and if I did buy the trinkets, I do not know on earth how I could get rid of them."

"What is *your* price, Williams?" asked the girl.

"Oh! nothing like what you expect, my dear! Now, look at these diamonds, as you call them. Upon my soul and honour, I think they are only mock ones—what they call paste; and if they are rich stones, they're terribly off color;—that's not of the first water, my dear, like these."

And he took from a drawer of a cabinet a superb diamond necklace of great value—the size of the stones being prodigious, and their brilliancy absolutely dazzling.

"Now," said he, "I call these something like jewels—and yet, my dear Betty, you can't think what a low price I gave for it."

"There's the gold watch and snuff-box," suggested the girl, who now almost wished she had returned them to the real owners at all risks, "surely there can be no doubt of their goodness!"

"Let me see," said the cunning Fence; "these court gallants now-a-days wear such good imitations of gold, (for they drink and dice away their money so much, that they cannot afford to buy the genuine article) that only one who completely understands the tricks of trade, can tell what is almost worthless, from the precious metal itself."

The Fence rose, and after taking a small phial from a shelf, which contained a small quantity of a greyish powder, resumed his seat.

"You see this powder, Betty?"

The girl looked curiously at the bottle, and nodded assent.

"Our own eyes may be deceived," he continued, "but by the use of this powder we can always tell what is good and what is bad. 'Tis a rare invention."

"I ought to know what is gold and what isn't," remarked she, "for *I've* had a good deal of the stuff pass through my hands, as you know, Mr. Williams."

"Ah! you're a clever girl," said Williams, coaxingly; "now look you here, Betty;—I believe this watch and snuff-box to be nothing more than silver, gilded over; and if it is as I suspect, a little of this infallible powder will in an instant dissolve the gilding, and expose to view the silver underneath."

He then took a pinch of the powder, and rubbed it on the back of the watch-case, on the chain, and on the seals. In an instant those parts touched by the test assumed a shining silvery appearance.

The snuff-box was subjected to the same examination with a similar result.

"There!" he exclaimed, with an air of great

self-satisfaction, "you can now see for your-self;" and he handed the girl the articles.

She could not doubt the evidence of her own senses; it was as Williams had said—the thin coating of gold had disappeared, and silver appeared in its stead.

Mortified at the discovery, she laid down the articles, and demanded the price Williams was willing to give.

"I'll give *you* more than I would anybody else," he said. "Now I can't afford one far-thing more for the buckles, watch, and snuff-box, than twenty guineas—and that is their utmost value, so help me G——!"

"Well—give it me," said Gipsey Betty, "for I want to get back. I thought I should have carried home sixty shiners, at the least!"

"If they'd been real diamonds, and good gold, Gipsey, I'd have given you a hundred," he

No. 10.

said, as he told down the money on the table.

The girl then took her departure.

No sooner had she quitted the room, than a grin of huge satisfaction appeared on the face of the rascally receiver of stolen articles; and taking another phial which contained a white liquid, he poured on those parts of the watch and snuff-box which he had whitened, a few drops, rubbed them with a bit of leather, and in an instant the silver disappeared, and the gold shone brightly again.

Both these articles were of solid gold, as he well knew them at the first glance to be; but he had resorted to the aid of chemistry for the purpose of mystifying and cheating the girl.

The grey powder was a preparation of mer-cury, which, when rubbed on a gold surface, instantly covers it with a very thin coating of quicksilver, resembling silver itself—and the fuid was aqua fortis, which has the property of dissolving quicksilver, but which will not act on gold. From this explanation, it will readily be understood how the villain accomplished his purpose.

Holding up the diamond girdle-buckles to the light, he examined them with great glee.

"Of the first water!" he muttered; "worth a hundred and fifty guineas at least!"

Then he weighed the snuff-box, and minutely looked at the watch.

"Seventy guineas more, if they're worth a farthing!" And he rubbed his hands as he thought what a capital night's work he had made of it.

"Two hundred guineas in half an hour!" he exclaimed, as he had placed the treasure in an iron chest, "and if I can but find out the owner, mayhap I may make a hundred more."

He had scarcely deposited the articles in a place of safety, when again the bell rang, and the box in the wall revolved.

"More grist to the mill!" he cried, as he took a parcel from the apparatus, as also a paper on which a name was scrawled.

"Humph! a strange name to me," he said; and glancing over the rings, and other trinkets which the parcel contained, he wrote on a scrap of paper the price he was willing to give for them, and placed it in the box, which again turned its open side towards the outer room.

Presently it again turned, with the word, "Accepted" written under the offered price, Williams placed the stipulated sum in the box, which turned once more, and the unseen visitor departed.

Such were the precautions taken by Fences of that day in their dealings with parties with whose names and persons they were unacquainted. Neither the party who brought the stolen goods, nor the one who purchased them, saw each other's faces, nor heard each other's voices. All was conducted with the utmost secrecy, in order that, in case of treachery, neither might be enabled to identify the other.

Follow we now the footsteps of Gipsey Betty, who, labouring under feelings of mortification and disappointment, left the house of the Fence and entered Fleet Street.

She had not the slightest idea that Williams had cheated her; and so, instead of pronouncing maledictions on him, she cursed her own, and M'Cleane, and Jenny Diver's ill luck; but so far as she was concerned, the greatest of her misfortunes were yet to come.

The man who had dogged her steps, and who, from his place of concealment had seen her enter Hanging Sword Alley, had also stealthily followed her and had observed her go into the house of the Fence. When she emerged from it, he was also on the watch; and, like a cat watching its prey, he waited till a convenient opportunity presented itself of pouncing upon her.

She had just passed Temple Bar, and entered the Strand, when a heavy hand was laid on her shoulder.

Gipsey Betty started and turned, and to her utter consternation, beheld in the person who had so alarmed her, no other than Mr. Watkins—the redoubtable Bow Street runner himself. The officer's face was full of satisfaction as he seized the girl by the arm, and hailed two of the watch, who at that moment came hobbling by the church of St. Clement Danes, drowsily crying the hour.

"Let me go!" said the girl, endeavouring to shake off her captor.

Mr. Watkins replied to the girl's appeal by placing the fore-finger of his left hand along his nasal protuberance, and by a very cunning wink of his eye.

"Let you go, you hussey! eh?" he said; "no—no! I had rather too much trouble to catch you;—you slipped away this morning when you got out of the coach after you had eased that gentleman of his snuff-box. Damme! you young girls are as slippery as eels—but I fancy you're fast enough now! We must take this hussey to the watch-house," said the officer to the watchmen, "and I charge you in the king's name to aid and assist!"

"Why, Master Watkins," said one of the old men, "you be surely strong enough to take a young girl like that to St. Martin's round-house. I've known ye to collar a bouncing Toby-man, as though he were a baby."

"How do I know but that some of her Ben Culls are in the neighbourhood?" said Watkins; "I tell you, neighbours, that 'twas some of this girl's gang who cheated the gallows of that murdering cracksman, Blackmoor. And if they were to attack me with my prisoner here, I might be made worse meat of before the morning!"

At the bare idea of the possibility of their being such blood-thirsty villains in the neighbourhood, the old Charlies felt a greater disinclination than before to assist Watkins; but on the latter's threatening them with the law, and the loss of their places if they still refused, they reluctantly lent their assistance, and Gipsey Betty was conveyed to the watch-house, in which, spite of her remonstrances, she was locked up, on the charge of having robbed from the person.

The Bow Street runner having seen his prisoner safely bestowed, immediately proceeded to the house of the Justice of the Peace, where he procured a search warrant, armed with which document he went without loss of time (after having assumed the disguise of a thief) to the domicile of Williams, the Fence.

That worthy had not yet retired to rest; for the principal part of his iniquitous business was transacted during the hours of darkness.

Mr. Watkins had had great experience in matters of this kind, and the disguise which he assumed was perfect. He knew well enough if he made his appearance in his own proper character at Williams's door, that to effect an entry would be almost a matter of impossibility; but he trusted, and confidently, to his ingenuity to effect that which he desired to accomplish.

He had taken care to provide himself with some articles which he might pass off as plundered property; and after looking over his memorandum books, he selected a name by which he should pass.

His great acquaintance with thieves, and his accurate knowledge of their habits, rendered his task comparatively easy; that task was to recover the snuff-box which Gipsey Betty had just sold—which the owner valued as a family relic, and which he told Watkins he would handsomely reward him for procuring.

Having that morning seen M'Cleane, Jenny Diver, and Gipsey Betty in the Park, he immediately on receiving information of the robbery, judged from the manner in which it was committed, that the Gipsey was the robber, and thought it most probable that she would dispose of her booty at the earliest opportunity, he had, as we have already stated, watched her from the "Chapel," and dogged her to Hanging Sword Alley.

Having given the private signal at the Fence's door, the pretended robber was admitted by the man with the frouzy head of hair before referred to, and by him also conducted into the apartment next to the Fence's private room.

He then placed the pretended plundered articles and the name of the party he represented—who he knew was not known to Williams but by name—in the receptacle, and in a short time the signal was given and he entered.

"Werry glad to have the honour of making your acquaintance, Bill Moonflyer," said Williams; "I've often had the pleasure of hearing of your dashing exploits, and longed to do a little business with you."

"You're werry parlite—werry; I've been in the habit of taking my business to Duke's Place—but them jews is so uncommon sharp, I thought I'd try you."

Bill Moonflyre was a crack housebreaker, whom Williams had long wished to get in his clutches, and the good humour into which he had been thrown by his bargain with Gipsey Betty, was marvellously increased by the visit of this worthy man.

"How's business, Master Williams?" asked Watkins.

"Bad—shocking!" said the Fence; "either the honest people are growing poor, or rogues—I beg your pardon, Mr. Moonflyer—gentlemen of your profession are getting honest. You are the first visitor I've had to-day, and now you ask a deal more for what you've brought than I can afford to give. Money is so scarce."

"Oh! I don't want money so much," said Watkins, "I want to make an exchange. You don't happen to have such a thing as a handsome snuff-box?—I can pay the difference, you know!"

"Why, let me see—yes, now I think of it, to be sure I have; but I'm afraid it's too high a figure for you, Bill—I've been offered a cool hundred for it!"

"That is rayther too much," said Watkins; "but I tell you what I'll do—I'll give you my bill of exchange for the box!"

The Fence jumped from his chair, and fairly laughed in the officer's face.

"And where, in the devil's name will you be when your bill of exchange, as you call it, is due?" asked Williams, sneeringly.

"Not werry far from where I am at this blessed minute!" replied the officer.

"Why, man, you may be dancing at the end of a chain on some wild common—you know

you may, and then I think I may whistle for my money. No, no, Master Moonflyer, you're only joking—let's to business!"

"Oh! with all my heart," said Watkins; "as I made certain as you'd accept my offer, I've got the dockyment in my pocket; and as to my dangling from a gibbet—let me tell you, Master Williams, that you stand a much better chance of that honour than I do."

"You've been drinking, Bill, surely?" suggested the Fence.

"Oh! no gammon, Mr. Williams; if you don't hand out that snuff-box, I must make you, that's all!"

Then drawing from his pocket the search warrant, he handed it to the Fence, who shrank back as if a venemous reptile had been placed in his grasp.

"And look here, Mr. Williams," said the officer, as he removed the wig from his head, and the handkerchief which muffled his chin, and the huge black whiskers which half concealed his cheeks—"d'ye know me now?"

"Know you, hell and furies! yes, I know you—you are Mr. Watkins, of Bow Street!" answered the Fence, turning deadly pale.

"That's a werry near guess o' yours—werry! my name is Watkins. You bought that box this very night, and if you don't produce it, why that there 'bill of exchange' empowers me to look for it, and if I do, perhaps something else unpleasant may turn up."

"How know you that I bought a gold snuff-box this evening?" asked Williams.

"Didn't say 'twas a gold one—but you see you've jist let the cat out o' the bag your own self. So come, I've no time to spare; besides, if I find the box, you must go along with me, you know—and you might settle the matter quietly, you know. I tell you one thing, the girl you bought that box from is now in the round-house!"

"The devil!" exclaimed the Fence.

He knew it was of no use to resist, and deemed it would be wise on his part to avail himself of the hint which the officer had flung out. With a heavy heart, therefore, he placed the box in the officer's hand, who at once, from the description he received from the owner, identified it as the one stolen in the Park that morning.

"You'll allow me a trifle for it—won't you, Watkins?" said Williams; "I gave, as God is my judge! fifty guineas—it is worth double."

"That's werry likely," returned the runner; "I should rather think as you'll give me a dab in the fist to purwent this matter going further;—but perhaps you'd prefer going to the Compter along with me, to hushing it up? As I said before, the thing might be settled quietly."

Much against his inclination the Fence paid thirty guineas to the officer as hush-money, who immediately he received it quitted the place, and hurried to the round-house where Gipsey Betty was confined.

"Now, young woman!" said he, "if you goes afore the big-wigs to-morrow morning, they'll send you to Newgate, and arter that the Recorder 'll send you to Tyburn! How would you like that?"

"Not very well," said Gipsey Betty, with a

shudder—for she knew what the officer said was true.

"I know all about that box you ———— this morning. Here 'tis, you see, dead proof against you—for you were seen to take it, and I know where you sold it. Now tell me how much Williams gave you for it, and perhaps I may do something for you?"

"Twenty guineas," replied the girl.

"No more—are you sure?" asked the officer, eyeing her keenly.

"Not a farthing!" she replied, showing the money; "search me, if you will, and you will see that I speak the truth."

"Well," said Watkins, "which do you value most — that pretty neck of yours — or this money?"

"My neck, of course," replied the girl.

"Then I'll put these in my pocket, and I'll tell the officer of the watch as I captured you by mistake, and you can go."

"For God's sake take it!" said Gipsey Betty, starting up from the bench on which she sat, "and let me go."

"Wait a bit," said Watkins; "now I'll give you back ten of them guineas if you'll tell me the pass-word you use for getting into that ere crib of yourn."

The girl's eyes flashed with indignation. "If I had twenty necks," she replied scornfully, "I would let a halter be put round every one of them, rather than do so base a thing!"

Watkins saw it would be useless to urge her further, and therefore forbore to press her.

He then went from the cell to the place where the Captain of the Watch was sitting smoking, told him that he had apprehended the young girl by mistake, and desired that he would liberate her forthwith.

"That's more nor my place is worth, Mr. Watkins, and that you know," said the chief watchman.

"Nonsense, man!" replied Watkins; "'tis a pity for the innocent young creetur to lie there through my mistake."

"She must go afore a Justice of the Peace, and be discharged in a right and proper manner. I knows nothing 'bout her innocence;—she's in my custody, and there she must stay, for I can't, in my own mind, see my way clear to let her go."

Watkins, who knew his man well enough, slipped a couple of guineas into his hand, which he thought would act as a pair of spectacles to assist his mental vision.

"Now I think on it again," said the Charlie, "'tis a pity for the poor thing to be locked up all this blessed night, and 'tis so cold, too, in there!"

"Then you'll let her go—won't you?" asked Watkins.

"Well, Mr. Watkins, to oblige you, I suppose I must; but we must keep our own secret, you know."

"Of course!" replied the runner; "dog don't eat dog!"

And immediately afterwards Gipsey Betty was set at liberty, and on her way to relate to the Captain and her comrades the eventful occurrences of the evening.

———

CHAPTER XVIII.

MORE MYSTERIES. — MRS. SNOLLEY MAKES STRANGE DISCLOSURES, AND SIR JAMES TOWN FALLS INTO A TRAP.

WHEN Sir James Town (to whom we must now return) had recovered from the swoon into which he fell, in consequence of the loss of blood consequent on the wound which he received in the encounter with Handsome Jack, he found himself lying on a couch in the parlour of Mother Singleton, with his arm bandaged, and feeling excessively weak.

The mistress of the house herself was sitting near him, bathing his temples with sal volatile, while a young girl was burning feathers under his nose. For a moment or two he could not collect his scattered senses; but when consciousness fully returned, his fears so overcame him that he turned yet paler than before, and sank back on his pillow.

A surgeon who had been sent for now arrived, and examined his arm, which had been completely transfixed by the rapier of Handsome Jack. Fortunately the larger blood-vessels had escaped laceration, but still there was a sufficient degree of fever to render it necessary that for the present Sir James should be kept quiet, and not removed from the place in which he then was. The baronet's carriage and lacqueys were in consequence dismissed, and a bed was made up for him in the procuress's house.

Here he had ample time to reflect on the daring manner in which, for a second time, the forged deed had been abstracted from him; and, although in his luxuriously furnished bedchamber, he was surrounded by all that could minister to his naturally voluptuous temperament, he cast a passionless eye on naked statue and glowing portrait, and groaned in the very despair of his spirit.

Mother Singleton, who had been uninformed of the real cause of Sir James Town's agitation, not unnaturally attributed it to the loss of the young girl, Emilie, whose ruin he had so perseveringly sought. She therefore determined, as soon as he had a little recovered, to endeavour to banish recollections of the lost one, by the substitution of another, who would be quite as charming, and a little less unkind.

Nor was she without some uneasiness on her own account; for she felt it was in some measure owing to her own negligence that Emilie had escaped. It was, therefore, necessary that she should put all her wiles into action for the purpose of pacifying the baronet.

On the evening of the day following the encounter, Sir James was well enough to be removed from his bed-chamber to the drawing-room of the establishment; indeed, with the exception of a slight inflammation in the neighbourhood of the wound, all uneasiness on that score had vanished.

While he was sitting at the large window which overlooked a pretty garden, inhaling the fragrance of the flowers, Mother Singleton entered the apartment, bearing a tray, on which were decanters of choice wines, and some delicate viands.

"If Sir James Town has no objection," she said in soft tones, I shall feel pleasure in enjoying his society for a short time."

Sir James returned a courteous bow to the lady's proposal.

"I cannot but have observed," she said, after a pause, "that something has greatly vexed you—and I think, Sir James, I can divine the cause."

The baronet started. Had he, he asked himself, when raving with passion, after the encounter with the Unknown who attacked him, betrayed himself—divulged his own secret? But he was speedily relieved from this disagreeable surmise.

"I must confess, Sir James," said the old woman, "that it must be extremely mortifying to you, after having taken so much pains, to have lost that run-a-way upon whom you had set your heart."

The baronet breathed freely again, when Mother Singleton did not know anything respecting the lost parchment in ——.

"But," she continued, "there are plenty pretty girls in the world, who would deem it an honour as well as a pleasure to revel in the embraces of such a man of worth and parts as you are."

Sir James acknowledged the compliment by a smile, and a slight inclination of the head; the fact was, his vanity, of which he possessed an inordinate quantity, was tickled.

Mother Singleton saw that the bait had taken, and she determined to follow up the advantage she had gained; for Sir James was one of her best patrons, and she determined if possible to retain him on her list.

We have before intimated that Mother Singleton was by no means unattractive herself; and this evening she had arrayed herself to ——; and really, to those who prefer ripe and ready fruit, to the troublesome pleasure of gathering from the tree themselves, the lady we are referring to would have been rather a dangerous neighbour. And so indeed she appeared to be to Sir James, for after having sipped a few glasses of sparkling wine, he began to cast amorous glances on his fair and fattish partner, which she was not at all slow in returning.

"Those young chits are not always the most charming, Sir James," she said, in a soft voice, "at least so I have heard gentlemen say; for my own part, now, I should far prefer a gentleman in the vigour of manhood—yourself, for instance—to one of those impetuous young sparks who flit from flower to flower, and only sip a little from each."

"Do you know, Madame Singleton," said Sir James, "I have often thought the same thing. Now, do you know, I am not in the least sorry that that little minx escaped me; indeed, how can I be, when I am at this moment favoured with such charming company?"

Mother Singleton bridled up—flirted her fan —bit her lips, and looked unutterable things.

Sir James had now arrived at that state of intoxication which has been designated as "maudlin"—not exactly from the quantity of wine he had taken, but from the effects of a potent powder which the procuress had infused into the canary which he had drank.

"Have you seen these pictures, Sir James?" said the lady; "they are just arrived from Paris;" and she placed an elegantly bound volume before him.

Sir James turned over leaf after leaf—and every moment his face became more flushed, and his frame more excited. The pictures at which he was gazing were of the most luscious description, and what with the effects of the wine and of the Parisian pictures put together, the baronet was in a fever.

Rising from his chair, he took a seat next Mother Singleton on the sofa, and putting his arm round her neck, he imprinted a kiss on her not unwilling lips.

"O! Sir James!" said the matron, "allow me to call down one of the beauties up stairs!"

It is more than probable that Sir James would have refused this offer, but he was prevented doing so by a thundering knock at the street door.

Every sound alarmed him now—for that which might prove his ruin was in the hands of another; and, to add to his perplexity, of whom he knew not. Hastily requesting Mother Singleton to deny him from all, he almost thrusted her from the room, and bolted the door.

He sat listening anxiously, and a slight tap at the door made him again start and tremble.

"It's only me," said Mother Singleton; "here is one of your lacqueys, Sir James, who wishes to see you, he says on important business. I thought I had better not deny you to him."

"Certainly not!" said Sir James; "admit him."

A vague sense of something wrong flashed on his brain, for he knew his servants would never have dared to seek him; then slight ——

The lacquey entered;—it was Sir James's confidential servant.

"What now, Lawrence?" he asked.

"Here's a packet, Sir James," replied the man, "which I was ordered to give into no other hands than your own, and without fail to deliver it this evening." And the lacquey handed a note to his master.

Sir James opened it and read:—

"Mr. Wriggleton Doom presents his compliments to Sir James Town, and begs to request that Sir James will favour him with an interview this evening after ten o'clock, without fail, at his chambers in Gray's Inn, as Mr. Doom has matters of the utmost importance to communicate."

"Damnation!" muttered the baronet; "when was this note left, Lawrence?"

"Two hours agone, Sir James."

"Who was the bearer?"

"A tall thin man, as I think I've seen before somewhere, but where, I don't remember. He had a hook-nose, and——"

"That will do, Lawrence;—go and bring a hackney coach in half an hour from this time."

"Doom! it must be he!—What on earth can be his business?" said Sir James to himself.

The lacquey departed on his errand, and Mother Singleton re-entered the room.

"Unexpected business compels me to leave you, madame," he said, "and I do it with much regret; but in a few days you will see me again."

He spoke this calmly and decidedly, for the fright into which he had been put had completely sobered him.

Madame Singleton, though somewhat chagrined at having lost her swain, just at the very moment when she felt certain that she had secured him, saw that it was of no use to attempt to detain him. So, with a simple expression of regret at his departure, she assisted him to attire himself for his journey, and by the time this was done, the hackney coach lumbered up to the door.

Sir James desired his servant to return home, and then entered the coach.

"Where to, your honour?" asked the coachman.

"To Gray's Inn."

The streets were neither as well paved or lighted in those days as in ours; and it is not, therefore, to be wondered at that a full hour should have elapsed before the clumsy vehicle after immeasurable joltings in deep ruts, and frequent stoppages in dark places, stopped at the gate of Gray's Inn.

It wanted yet three quarters of an hour to ten o'clock, the hour Doom had mentioned in his note, but Sir James, unwilling to remain in the street, mounted the staircase which led to the lawyer's chamber. He had proceeded about half way upwards in the dark, when some one ran rudely against him.

"Who's that?" asked the baronet.

"Who is it?" replied a saucy voice, "why it's me—who else should it be, master; my name is Tim Snarley, a junior member of this honourable Society of Gray's Inn, and an ornament to his profession. I needn't ask who you are, 'cause I knows yer woice."

"Oh! Mr. Doom's clerk," remarked the baronet. "Is your worthy master at home?"

"I don't know as there be any worthy masters hereabouts, but if you means Mr. Wriggleton Doom, why, I should say he is," replied the boy.

"I'm going to see him—good night Snarley," said the baronet, and he was proceeding still further upwards, when Tim Snarley remarked, drily—

"No, you ain't—not yet, leastways; he can't see nobody now, he's engaged."

"With whom?" asked Sir James.

"With an old woman—a werry old woman," replied Snarley; "but Mr. Doom expects to see you at ten. Missis Snolley 'ill be gone afore then."

"Mrs. Snolley," gasped Sir James. "By Heaven there's some treachery here, Snarley!"

"Well, Sir James?"

"Here's a guinea for you."

"S'pose I be to do some job or other for it. People don't pay wages for nothing," remarked the boy.

"What are they talking about, Snarley?"

"Summat about chopping and changing a hinfant," replied the clerk.

"You can hear what passes in your outside room, can't you boy?" asked Sir James.

"Yes; if I puts my ear to a chink in the wainscotting which I made for the purpose," replied Snarley.

"Then I'll make that guinea five, if you'll let me put my ear to that chink for the next half hour," said Sir James, softly.

"But if Doom know'd of it, he'd murder me," said Tim, "for he's a very devil when he's angry; aye, and when he's pleased too for the matter of that. But give me the shiners, and I'll manage it."

"You'll find close to the chink a large closet, where I sleep when Doom keeps me werry late. When the old woman and master have done talking, you slip in there as he lets her out. He'll go back to his private room directly, and then you can let yourself out and knock at his door pretending you've just arrived."

"Excellent!" said Sir James, slipping another four guineas into Snarley's hand.

They now mounted the staircase with extreme caution, and, as they did so, Sir James heard the quarters of St. Andrew's, Holborn, strike half-past nine; he had, therefore, a full half hour for his purpose.

The lad with a latch-key softly opened the outer door, took Sir James by the hand, led him to the wainscott chink, and showed him where the cupboard of concealment was; and then departed homewards.

"Never thought that chink would turn out such a profitable investment," said Tim Snarley, as, under the first lamp he came to, he gazed at the five bright guineas; "but I wouldn't for five hundred as old Doom knew what I've done to-night."

Let us return to the Baronet.

The aperture in the wainscotting was so cunningly contrived that the party outside Mr. Doom's private room could see as well as hear what passed within without raising suspicion. So that it combined the wonderful properties of the eyes of Argus, with that of the ear of Dionysius; although, in all likelihood, the ingenious and curious Master Timothy Snarley, had never heard of those ancient worthies, when he constructed his chink. But every age has its own great geniuses; and it often happens that those of a later day accidentally stumble on very similar inventions to those which immortalized their predecessors, but without injuring a particle of the latter's fame.

Peering cautiously through the chink, Sir James observed an old woman bowed almost double with age and infirmity. Doom was at the moment writing, and the crone's face was turned towards him, so that the baronet could not be sure from ocular demonstration that she in reality was the party in whose existence he felt so deep an interest.

A few minutes elapsed, and then she turned round. All doubt was banished in an instant; for there, before him, sat one, who feeble, wretched and old as she appeared, could by one word precipitate him from the enjoyment of wealth and station, into poverty and disgrace.

"That villain, Doom, has over-reached me," he muttered. "How in the fiend's name did he find out that woman?"

"You will, then, if necessary, swear that you substituted the illegitimate son of the late Sir

Richard Town by one of his mistresses, at the urgent request of the latter, for Richard Town, who was the really oldest child of Sir Richard by his wife, and born in wedlock?"

"That's true enough: but wouldn't they hang me, if I confessed that I had anything to do with such a base transaction?" said Mrs. Snolley.

"Hang you?—nonsense." replied Doom. "I'll hold you harmless."

"Well, then, Lawyer Doom, I *would* swear to it: for 'tis a thing that has laid heavy enough on my conscience ever since. I never see that villain. Sir James Town, who's no more a Sir than I am, but my heart bleeds for poor Richard who they say is now a vagabone."

Sir James Town shuddered as he listened; he afforded an excellently apt illustration of the old adage, 'that listner's never hear any good of themselves.'

"And know you the object. Mrs. Snolley, which this mistress of Sir Richard Town had in view in having the exchange of children made?"

"Yes, yes—well enough," replied the crone. "The lady was very beautiful and very proud, and she could not bear the idea that her child by Sir Richard, should not inherit the title and estates; and in order that he should do so, she by a large reward induced me to substitute her child, for Lady Town's; for both were confined nearly at the same time, and a dangerous illness of Lady Town's made the matter easy, for she saw not the child for several days after its birth—she had the milk-fever."

"How then came the present Richard Town to assume the title; for it is certain that he enjoyed it for some time?" asked Doom.

"Because," replied the woman, "on her death-bed the mistress of the late Sir Richard, under the influence of remorse, confessed to the true heir, and the cheat which had been practised. At that time the present usurper of the title was abroad on his travels, and did not return until long after the death of old Sir Richard The younger Richard, possessed of the important secret, immediately on his father's death instituted law proceedings which terminated in his favor, and he succeeded to the name and estates. When James returned however, some years afterwards, he, by means which I know of, Mr. Doom, ousted poor Richard, and you know the rest"

"Have you any idea where a Mrs. Larkin resides?" asked Doom.

"Larkin—Larkin—Betty Larkin: I remember the name too; wasn't that her as witnessed the deed that you and Mr. Flitchman made up between you?" replied Mrs. Snolley.

"Not *me* and Flitchman! Flitchman you mean—Don't fancy, for Heaven's sake, that I had anything to do with it," said Doom.

"Infernal liar!" growled Sir James behind the chink.

"Try and find out this Betty Larkin, Mrs. Snolley, and you shall be well paid for your pains," remarked the lawyer.

The old woman promised to do so and prepared to depart. Doom rose to light her out, and at that moment Sir James Town sneaked into the closet, with what feelings may easily

he supposed. Some treachery was evidently intended to Lawyer, and he determined if possible to fathom it.

The lawyer had not long returned to his private office, when Town, emerging quietly from his place of concealment descended with noiseless steps a few of the stairs; then returned with heavy footsteps and knocked at Doom's door, just as a neighbouring clock was sounding the hour of ten.

"Punctual. Sir James, to the minute, my dear sir," said Doom, offering the baronet his hand.

"Why," remarked Town, "it's always well to be so, when business is on hand: indeed, Doom, I think that sometimes one had better be a little before one's time, than after it."

Sir James laid a slight emphasis on the last sentence; but the lawyer either would not or did not observe it.

"The business must needs be of importance, I should think, Mr. Doom, which requires my presence in your office at this hour," remarked the baronet, as he took a seat.

"Of the very last importance, Sir James, to each of us," replied Doom.

"Then we had better proceed to it at once," said Sir James, with as much calmness as he could assume.

"Read that letter, Sir James," said the lawyer, placing in his hands a document covered with those particular characters, in which lawyer's delight to convey their ideas.

Sir James drew the lamp near him, and Doom's eye keenly scrutinized him as he bent over the important document. It ran thus—

"*In the matter of Town v. Town.*

"To Mr. Wrigglesin Doom, Esq.

"Sir,—Understanding that you are the Attorney of James Town, falsely calling himself 'Sir James Town, Baronet,' I beg to inform you that an action-at-law will immediately be instituted against him by Sir Richard Town, the lawful son and heir of the late Sir Richard Town, for the recovery of the title and estates which he now illegally holds, unless he immediately and without reservation relinquishes them; and in case of vexatious opposition to the claims of my client, I have to state that proceedings will be instituted in a Criminal Court for fraud and forgery.

"My Clerk called at said James Town's residence this morning and was informed that he was from home; therefore, as the matter admits of no delay, I at once address you.

"I am, Sir,

"Your obedient servant,

"ROWLAND FERRETT."

When Sir James had concluded the perusal of this staggering epistle he looked intently in Doom's face; but uttered not a syllable.

"What is to be done?" asked the lawyer.

"Doom, you are playing a double game—this letter is a forgery!" said the baronet, slowly and emphatically.

"The charge of forgery comes with a good grace, indeed, from one who holds his title and his wealth by a forged deed," as coolly retorted the lawyer. "On my honor," he returned "the letter is genuine and you would do well to attend to it."

"*Your* honor!" sneered Sir James.

"Yes! *mine*, Sir James. It is well for you to taunt me now that you have to a certain extent a hold over me. Jonathan Wild has informed me that through him you have recovered possession of the forged deed."

"It was in my possession; but it is so no longer. I was waylaid in the streets, in the scuffle it fell from my breast-pocket, and what has become of it I know not."

This piece of intelligence startled Doom, who with all a lawyer's acuteness could now fully comprehend the meaning of the implied threat in Ferrett's letter.

"Something must be done, Sir James in the matter, for I fear it is but too plain that young Richard Town has a finger in this pie. If but one only knew where he was to be found matters might be arranged," exclaimed the agitated limb of the law. It seemed fated that both him and Town should be for ever falling into new dilemmas, spite of all the cunning of each.

"We will let the matter rest until to-morrow at least, Doom," said Sir James, and he quitted the office, promising to be there again on the following evening.

Doom shook his head doubtfully after his departure, and then sat down, made out a long lawyer's bill against Sir James Town, and threw himself ███████████████████

Sir James Town immediately hailed █████ and drove towards Tottenham Court. ██████ as he reached his ████████ he collected ██████ valuables together, arranged his papers ██████ ███ lay down wrapped in deep thought ██████ few hours. After breakfast he drove to ███ bankers, and, under pretence of needing money for the purchase of a large estate, he drew out the balance ████ ████████ over which lay in their hands. On ████████ home he informed his domestics that he ███ ██████ into the country for a few weeks, during ███ time they might absent themselves. ██ ████ as they had departed he sent to a ████ ██ whom he disposed of every stick of ████████ his carriages, horses, &c., and received ████████ for the same, depositing the keys with the purchaser that he might remove them ██ ███ convenience. All this effected, toward ████ ing he hired a coach and proceeded to ██████ Wharf, where a vessel bound for ████ ██████ was then lying, and in which he had ████ ██ passage.

The vehicle pulled up at the stairs, and Sir James hailed a waterman.

Just, however, as he was going to ████ ██ the boat a rude hand was laid on his ████████ and turning round he was confronted by a bailiff and his two followers.

"Beg pardon, Mr. Jeems," said the man, "but you must put off this trip for a time — werry sorry; but unless you settle ██████ ████ ███ costs you must go with me."

"At whose suit do you arrest me?" asked Sir James.

"That of Mr. Wriggleton Doom, attorney-at-law, for legal services rendered, four thou-sand, three hundred and ninety pounds, fifteen and eightpence; and then there's the costs, Sir Jeems."

The baronet was struck dumb with amazement at the rascality of Doom; but he felt that he was in the lawyer's power to a certain extent, and that he could not accuse him without criminating himself. It was impossible for him to pay the demand, and he had no other resource than to accompany the officers.

"Will you go to the Marshalsea at once, Sir Jeems, or to my house; 'tis a werry comfortable place, and you can stay there 'till matters are arranged. Accommodations werry good and charges moderate," said the bailiff.

Sir James did not much like the idea of a prison, so intimating his desire to accept of the bailiff's hospitality, for which he had sufficient to pay, the officer desired the coachman to set them down at his own domicile, in Shire Lane, Temple Bar.

CHAPTER XIX.

THE "CHAPEL" IN DANGER. — MORE OF JENNY DIVER'S EXPLOITS. — A COUNTRY TRIP. — ROBBERY OF THE FLY-WAGGON.

The prolonged absence of Gipsey Betty from ████████ up to Williams's, the Fence, in █████ Sword Alley, was the source of the ████████ McCleane and his com-███████████████████████, much more ███████████████████████ for her to ███████████████████████ a council was held to consult whether it would not be advisable to send scouts in search of her; but Handsome Jack opposed such a course, and declared that if she did not speedily return, he would take it upon himself to make the search; for, as he was a new member of the gang, and his person unknown to the constables, he was more likely to evade observation than any of the others.

Another hour went by, and Handsome Jack had already equipped himself for the purpose of going forth in search of his chosen lass — when Dick Flybynight entered the Saloon with intense anxiety depicted on his countenance.

"Hello! Dick," cried McCleane; "why, you look as frightened as a child of hell, Black-████████████████████ to Tyburn; what's in the wind now?"

"The devil's luck," replied Dick, who had just returned from robbing a gentleman's carriage, in Lincoln's Inn Fields.

The highwayman as he spoke placed his pistols on the table, threw down a purse of money and a watch, and then filling a large goblet with strong ale, emptied it at a draught.

"You can't call *that* devil's-luck, do you, my bold Dick?" said a pretty blue-eyed damsel to the dashing robber.

"I had a hard run for it though, and was compelled, in order to save my neck, to trust to my heels; for I had hardly left the carriage

THE WAGGISH OLD GENTLEMAN FEELING FOR JENNY DIVER'S MONEY.

when the patrol came up, and the hue and cry being raised I was compelled to dash down Chancery Lane into Fleet Street, to baffle my pursuers. And who should I see being lagged off to the round-house by that bloodhound Watkin's——"

"Who—who?" eagerly enquired fifty voices at once.

"Gipsey Betty," replied Dick Flybynight, wiping the perspiration from his face. "It would have been worse than useless for me to have gone to her assistance," continued Dick, "for two of the watch acted as a guard, and beside Mr. Watkins knows my face and figure rather too well."

"At all events I'll go and learn what I can," said Handsome Jack, and he hastily left the saloon.

All present were extremely anxious; the

No. 11.

Captain and the fair Jenny the most of all, as Gipsey Betty had been their accomplice in the morning, and she had gone to the Fence, simply to dispose of the plunder they had acquired on that occasion.

"If we are not doubly careful, this place will be too hot to hold us soon," said M'Cleane.

He had scarcely uttered these ominous words when a shout of joy resounded through the splendid saloon.

"Here she is—here she comes!" they cried, as Gipsey Betty pale, and almost fainting, in the stalwart arms of Handsome Jack, was borne into the apartment.

"I encountered her just at the door of Madame Charlotte's hotel," said Handsome Jack, "where I believe she would have fainted had I not fortunately been present to aid her."

They laid the poor girl on one of the sofas,

Jenny chafed her temples with an aromatic fluid, and poured a cordial down her throat. Gipsey Betty soon recovered and then the gang eagerly surrounded her, to learn the particulars of her adventure.

These are already known to the reader, it is, therefore, unnecessary to repeat them here.

The utmost indignation at the conduct of William's, the Fence, was expressed, and many a vow of vengeance uttered.

"I have not told you quite all," said Gipsey Betty, "I might, at least, have brought home ten of the twenty guineas I received from Williams, had I chosen to accept the conditions offered me by the Bow Street officer."

"What were they?" asked M'Cleane.

"To tell him the secret pass word by which we gained admission to this place."

"And you refused?" asked M'Cleane.

"Have I the money?" asked the girl, seemingly deeply hurt by the question. "No! I tell you as I told him, that had I a hundred necks and a halter round each I would not betray my friends."

A shout of applause rent the saloon. M'Cleane went to the girl, took her hand, and asked her pardon for having wounded her feelings, and Jenny Diver fell upon her neck and half smothered her with kisses.

The gang now proceeded to partake of supper; but it was evident that a sense of danger oppressed each and all. In vain did they drink deeply—in vain did they troll out lusty and lustful staves; from the Captain down to the meanest member of the gang—all felt that danger was at hand.

Besides this, the funds in the common treasury were getting low, and it was absolutely necessary that the strong box should be refilled.

After supper a meeting of the whole gang was called and after much deliberation it was decided that, within a week from that time, they should vacate the 'Chapel' for a time; that one part of the fraternity should retire to the Country House at Highgate, from which they might make profitable excursions into the surrounding country, and that the other portion should go into the provincial towns, in search of adventures.

"If I might be allowed to speak," said a girl, who had been but recently introduced, "I think I could mention a place where we should not fail to pick up a good amount of plunder."

"Speak out, Bristol Ann," said M'Cleane.

"Next week," said the girl, "the summer fair commences in Bristol, which lasts for ten days; and to that city, at that particular time, nearly all the wealthy farmers and graziers of the country round resort, with empty heads and full pockets."

"It's worth thinking of," said the Captain.

"I know all the flash cribs there, and all the swell tobymen, and there's not a few of 'em," added Bristol Ann, "and I volunteer my services to the gang as guide."

"Well spoken," was murmured through the saloon.

"Might do some business on the way down, too;" interposed Dick Flybynight, "there are plenty of stage waggons and carriages always on that road!"

"Right;" said M'Cleane, "I don't know that we can do better," and Bristol Ann's proposal was adopted.

The members of the fraternity then dropped off, one after the other, to their sleeping apartments, and the place was soon as quiet as if crime had never held its orgies in that singular place.

"We'll have one more ramble as mistress and servant, Jem," said Jenny Diver, as she lay in bed beside the Captain, soon after waking on the following morning.

"As you please," dear Jenny, "you know I am always proud to serve such a sweet mistress as you are," returned M'Cleane, as he laid his cheek on the fair creature's ivory bosom.

"I've conceived a new scheme," said she, "so don't fondle now; you know before we take this trip to Bristol we must provide funds, and thanks to that devil, Watkins, we have little enough just now."

"That's true enough," said M'Cleane, sighing as he jumped out of bed.

It was now eleven of the clock, and proceeding seperately to Mr. Bilkit's, at the Jolly Pedlar's, they resumed the dresses which they had cast off the day before. Here Jenny Diver explained her scheme to the Captain.

Taking a boat they proceeded eastward, and landed at Wapping old stairs; M'Cleane walking behind his mistress and both on the look out for prey. As they were passing through Burr Street they observed a gentleman come out from a very genteel looking house, his wife accompanying him to the door. The gentleman proceeded Citywards, apparently intent on business, and the lady, who was very amiable-looking, retired into the house.

"That's the place for us," said Jenny, turning round as though giving an order to her servant.

Onward went our heroine, until she reached the house in question, when she sunk down as if exhausted, on the door steps.

The footman, seeing his mistress in this plight, ran up the steps and knocked at the door. A servant answered his summons, of whom M'Cleane enquired whether the lady of the house was at home as his mistress, who was a lady of high respectability, had experienced a sudden fainting attack and begged she might be admitted until it had passed over.

"Certainly—with all the pleasure in life," said the lady, and with the help of her footman and the maid-servant, Jenny was helped into the parlour and placed on a sofa.

"If you will go down into the kitchen and wait till your poor lady is recovered, my maid and I will go up stairs and procure her some cordials, which I doubt not will relieve her."

M'Cleane, with many thanks, went down stairs into the kitchen, which, to his great joy, he found untenanted.

He did not remain idle, for in the course of a few minutes he pocketed six silver table-spoons, a silver pepper-box, a salt-cellar, and other articles.

The instant the lady and maid went up stairs

to prepare the medicine, Jenny picked the lock of a drawer, from which she took sixty guineas. She had hardly accomplished this feat, when the lady and servant returned; and while the former held a smelling-bottle to her nose, she picked her pocket of a purse containing about twenty shillings.

Jenny now appeared to be recovering, and although pressed to stay longer, refused, pleading urgent business, and requested her footman to be summoned from below.

"How shall I thank you, my dear Madam, or repay this obligation to a stranger?" said the artful creature.

The lady protested that she required no return whatever—she was only too happy to have been of service.

"I am," said Jenny, with a most engaging smile, "the wife of an eminent merchant in Thames Street, who will be delighted to see you!"

Jenny then handed the lady her card, and invited the lady and her husband in the most pressing terms to dinner on an appointed day, which invitation the lady having accepted, Jenny and her servant took their departure, and getting into the first coach they met with, were soon far from the scene of the impudent robbery.

The party who were selected to visit Bristol consisted of M'Cleane, Dick Flybynight, Gipsey Betty, Jenny Diver, and Bristol Ann; the remainder of the gang dispersed in different directions, some to Highgate, and others to different "Country Houses." In case of any circumstance of importance transpiring, likely to effect the interest of the entire community, a system of communication was organized, and the general rendezvous of all, at a fixed period, was the "Chapel."

This establishment was closed, and the keys of it deposited in the hands of Madame Charlotte, who wept bitterly on parting from M'Cleane, to whom she was in reality passionately attached.

"Keep up your heart, Lizzy," said M'Cleane at their parting interview, "I shall soon be back again, and then——"

"But what shall I do in the meantime?" asked the plump beauty, flinging her arms around M'Cleane's neck; "you, Jem, will have Jenny Diver to comfort you—whilst I, all alone shall be——"

"An old maid till I return!" said M'Cleane, interrupting her, and laughing heartily.

Madame Charlotte pouted her lip and looked grave, but said nothing.

"Oh! Lizzy, you mustn't be jealous of Jenny. Do you remember a certain lady, who once asked me if I'd have any objection to revel in her beauties?"

Madame Charlotte tapped his cheek with her little fore-finger, and replied—"Ah! Jem, but I only meant once, you know."

"But are not you aware, Lizzy, that one sweet morsel only acts as a sharpener of the appetite for another?"

"Then, Jem, there is one sweet morsel for you now," said Madame Charlotte; "let me see if your opinion is correct!"

As she said this, her bright blue eyes looked almost beseechingly into his, with an expression the import of which could not be mistaken by the Captain.

"It is now twelve o'clock, dear Jem! and you do not leave for Bristol until morning; surely you will not run away now. Come, you must drink a glass with me, at all events;" and she coaxed him to a couch.

"Perhaps you will put some of that somniferous powder in it—I mean the stuff you meant for Jenny Diver one night?" asked M'Cleane, archly.

"No, no, Jem!" said Madame Charlotte, "I want you to be awake and active to-night!"

"I must go, Lizzy," said M'Cleane; "I have many preparations to make—so give me one kiss, and then——"

"No appetite for another morsel?" said the witch.

M'Cleane was about to move towards the door, when Madame Charlotte rushed past him, locked the door, and put the key in her pocket.

"There, Captain M'Cleane, you are my prisoner!" she said.

"On what charge?" he jokingly asked.

"That of desertion, Jem! and you will not be liberated until you have paid the penalty."

"Desertion — do you mean of my sweet Lizzy?" asked M'Cleane; "I swear by all that's beautiful—by you, in fact, Lizzy, that if I have sipped the sweets from one fair flower, I have not forgotten the fragrance of another!"

"Very pretty, indeed, Captain M'Cleane!" said Madame Charlotte; "and so you swear by me, do you?"

"Yes, by all that's lovely — by you!" he replied.

"Then kiss the book, you sinner!" she said; and she put her lips so close to his that they acted like a charm, and so forcibly attracted his own, that a burning salute was the result.

Madame Charlotte failed not to follow up the advantage, which with a woman's tact she perceived she had gained; and so she commenced a series of dalliances, which in an extremely short time made M'Cleane forget Jenny Diver, and all the rest of the women in the world put together, save and except the warm-blooded and ripe beauty, upon whose panting bosom his hand rested.

"Then you won't let me press my pillow alone this last night of your stay, dear Jem!" she softly whispered.

In truth M'Cleane had now no inclination to depart, and the reader will not be at all surprised to learn that whilst Jenny Diver lay tossing restlessly on her bed, in expectation of her lover, that that gentleman was extremely happy in the embraces of Madame Charlotte, who on this occasion determined to condemn her prisoner to hard labour, as a pleasing punishment for the recent neglect she had experienced at his hands.

How Jenny Diver gently scolded her faithless swain the next morning—and how M'Cleane plausibly excused himself, by declaring that he had been detained from her arms by business of a private and pressing nature, needs not here to be set forth. Suffice it to say, that harmony was soon restored, and all were soon busied in making preparations for their departure.

To prevent suspicion, as to their being accomplices, it was agreed that they should not travel all together. Bristol Ann was therefore sent forward by a stage-coach, in order that she might first reach the scene of operations, and prepare her old comrades in iniquity there to act in concert with the members of the London gang, who being quite ignorant of the city to which they were going, deemed it good policy to admit into their confidence persons who were acquainted with the localities and the constables.

M'Cleane was to assume his old character of footman to Jenny Diver, who with Gipsey Betty were to assume the characters of merchants' wives.

Dick Flybynight undertook to personate a country trader, who was going to the fair on business; and they relied on the co-operation of those of the Bristol gang to whom Bristol Ann was to introduce them, for effectually carrying their nefarious schemes into successful operation.

None of these disguises, however, were to be assumed until they arrived at the place of their destination; but it was understood that, while on the road, they should lose no opportunities of pursuing their professional duties, if only by way of keeping their hands in.

Jenny Diver and Gipsey Betty determined to travel by the Bath and Bristol fly-waggon—a vehicle which, in those days, was supposed to travel with remarkable speed, as its name implied, but which crawled over the road so slowly, that the journey, which is now performed in less than three hours, then took almost as many days to accomplish.

Captain M'Cleane rode his horse—an excellent arrangement—as it would afford him chances of doing business in his own peculiar way on the road.

A similar course was adopted by Dick Flybynight, who was not a whit behind his Captain in the desire to pick up whatever good fortune might fling in his way.

The two highwaymen having concerted certain plans with Jenny Diver and Gipsey Betty, quitted London by different ways on the morning following the capture of M'Cleane by Madame Charlotte, and pursued their westward route.

Some hours afterwards, and when the glare of a summer's afternoon had softened into twilight, two soberly, though very respectably dressed, matronly-looking females, preceded by a porter, who carried two huge trunks, passed beneath the gateway of the Swan with two Necks, Lad Lane, and entered the yard of that hostelry.

There one of those picturesque scenes presented itself, which we now only realize through the medium of paintings. The yard was a quadrangle, around each side of which ran overhead, two tiers of galleries, with quaint, little corpulent railings, that afforded a ready communication with all parts of the tavern. The windows were small, with huge sashes, and diamond-shaped panes; below was a covered way, formed by the undermost of the galleries, which was supported by wooden pillars, with rings in them to which horses might be tethered; and above all, rose high and pointed gables, which in the gradually increasing gloom looked like a series of pyramids on a small scale, on the summit and sides of which sat pigeons innumerable, pluming themselves before they retired to their boxes, several of which were fastened to the gables aforesaid.

In the centre of the yard was the fly-waggon, a clumsy, cumbrous vehicle, with an arched roof, looking so high that one wondered how on earth it ever got into the yard, and that, having got in by a miracle, how it would ever get out again; and, in truth, it never did either without a scraping of the whitewashed roof of the gateway, and a slight damaging of the covering of the vehicle itself. To this vehicle, at the time of the entrance of Jenny and her companion, six stalwart horses were being harnessed—and the driver and his assistant were hurrying hither and thither like mad people, arranging luggage, and doing all those necessary things which it is not necessary here to mention.

At length all the preparations were completed—the huge lantern lighted, and hung in front of the waggon, and the passengers one by one mounted the ladder and reached the interior, which very much resembled a huge gipsey tent upon wheels.

A crack of the driver's whip—a sudden jerk which nearly threw every one of the passengers into each others laps—and the waggon rumbling through the gateway, commenced its journey.

The first thing Jenny did was to reconnoitre her fellow-passengers, and endeavour to ascertain whether any of them were fit subjects for her to practice her consummate art upon. The lantern, which was inside the waggon, rendered this a rather difficult matter; but Jenny Diver had sharp eyes—aye and ears, too, for what she could not make out by the quickness of one, she made up for by the acuteness of the other.

Soon after they had left the lights of the town behind them and emerged into the open country, which was not quite so far off from Lad Lane then as it is now, the gingling of the bells on the horses' harness began to have rather a lonely sound; and for a time no one spoke.

At length a very stout old lady, with a very small voice, ventured to say that she hoped the driver had brought his blunderbuss with him, for they had to go over Hounslow Heath.

At the name of Hounslow Heath, Jenny uttered a faint scream.

"Don't be alarmed, madam," said a young spark who sat next her, "no highwayman will venture to attack us, I'll warrant; and if they should—odds fish! madam, but I'll protect you to the last drop of my blood!"

"But I have a large amount of property with me, which I am taking to Bristol Fair, where I am to meet my husband; and should I be plundered, it will be his ruin."

"So too have I," chimed in Gipsey Betty; "and I persuaded my friend here not to risk so much in these dangerous times; but as she determined to venture, I determined to accompany her."

"My gold watch and money is in my bosom," said Jenny, artlessly, "and surely no highwayman would be impudent enough to look for it there!"

"They don't care what they do, madam," remarked a waggish-looking old gentleman, who sat in one corner of the waggon; "and, to say the truth, if I was a highwayman, and knew where your watch and purse were hidden, I think the temptation to finger them would be all the greater."

"Driver!" screamed out the old lady, putting her head through the covering of the waggon, which hung in folds over its front.

"Here I be, missis!—what do'ee want?" asked the fellow.

"Are you sure that your blunderbuss is loaded?" demanded she.

"E'es, to be sure I be—loaded un mysel' afore we started!"

One after another the passengers sank to sleep, and the night passed off quietly. As the grey light of the morning stole into the vehicle, Jenny was enabled to take a better survey of her fellow-travellers.

They were all, with the exception of the young spark who had boasted so stoutly of what he would do should the waggon be attacked, people of substance; and Jenny Diver laughed in her sleeve, as they described the precautions they had taken to prevent being robbed.

The waggon stopped about nine o'clock at a roadside inn to change horses, and to allow the passengers to breakfast. As Jenny was passing from the vehicle to the parlour, she observed the waggoner take his blunderbuss from a box at the side of the waggon, and deposit it in a corner of the stable.

The driver, his man, and the ostler, were soon cosily seated before the kitchen fire; and before taking her breakfast, Jenny, pretending indisposition, said she would walk in the yard for a few minutes, to refresh herself. The other passengers had already commenced, and were doing hearty justice to a substantial meal.

Watching her opportunity when the hostess was busy with her guests, Jenny slipped unobserved into the stable, and dexterously withdrew the charge from the blunderbuss; then pretending to be recovered from the effects of her night's ride, she joined her fellow-travellers at the breakfast table.

At this halting-place the number of the passengers was increased by several sturdy graziers, who also were bound for Bristol Fair, and who stated without reserve that they were going to purchase large quantities of cattle.

Again the horses were put to; and cheered by the fresh country air, and the change from the dark night to the pleasant sunshine, the travellers from London became more and more communicative.

For the present all dread of highwaymen was banished from every mind, even from that of the old lady; and to beguile the time, they began to tell rencontres on the road, which at night they would almost have shuddered to have thought of.

"I dispersed six with my own hand," said the young spark, who still sat next to Jenny. "Owns!" he remarked, at the conclusion of a boasting narrative, which only wanted truth to recommend it, "by my valour, I wish that I only had the opportunity of meeting with such scoundrels again!"

"I can't say quite so much as that," quietly remarked the waggish old gentleman, "but I once puzzled a highwayman by hiding my bank-notes in a place where the devil himself would never have dreamt of looking for them!"

"Bless me!" said Jenny, with a look of innocent wonderment, "and where in the world, sir, could that have been?"

"And more than that," continued the waggish old gentleman, "I've adopted the same plan ever since."

"And with success?" asked Jenny Diver.

"With entire success, my pretty lady," replied the waggish old gentleman.

"I wish I knew how to secure the little I have," sighed Jenny, looking tenderly at the ancient gentleman.

"You couldn't do it, my dear! with you it would be a matter of impossibility. Bless your pretty face! you dont wear the same sort of article that we men do;—there, don't blush!"

For Jenny, to keep up the modesty of her character, twitched her petticoats, and removed them from the close contact in which they had before been with the velvet small-clothes of the valiant gallant, who still pertinaciously kept close to her. By this simple movement, she conveyed a very delicate hint to all present, that although the wife of a man and a merchant, she did not wear the breeches.

"Quite mistaken, madam — quite so! I meant nothing of that kind," said the waggish old gentleman, who was rather 'cute, and not at all slow to take the hint.

"We will drop the subject, sir," said Jenny, looking as though she was offended by the gentleman's rudeness.

The long day wore on, and night succeeded. As the trunks of the trees began to throw long defined shadows across the road, Jenny observed that the bravadoes of the young man ceased—and his wishes to meet with highwaymen were no longer uttered. The waggish old gentleman—the stout old lady—and the graziers also, all began to fidget in their seats; and when the fly-waggon stopped suddenly at the last changing house for that day, the young spark, who had been indulging in a doze, started up in a fright, and exclaimed—"Good Mr. Highwayman, spare my life, and——"

The conclusion of his sentence was lost in a general laugh, in the midst of which, declaring he had been dreaming of a whole troop of blood-thirsty villains, the young fellow sneaked out of the waggon, and rushed into the inn, where he revived his courage by a glass of strong waters.

They were soon on the road again, with lighted lanterns to enable the waggoner to guide his horses safely, for the road was exceedingly bad. The courageous young blade, on re-entering the vehicle, which he did before any one else, had stumbled, whilst half drunk, by mistake, into the waggish old gentleman's seat, and the latter, not sorry to get near so pretty a creature as Jenny for the night, did not choose to notice the error; but was, in truth to tell, rather pleased than otherwise at a mistake which gave occasion for so pleasant an exchange.

They journeyed on for hours without the slightest alarm, and once more sleep fell on the travellers. The graziers snored loudly—the fat old lady wheezed and whistled in her sleep, and the tipsy gallant grunted.

None but Jenny Diver, Gipsey Betty, and the waggish old gentleman were awake.

The latter was very amorously inclined, as, indeed, many old gentlemen are; and as Jenny had a secret to discover, she did not discourage his advances, which were confined to pressing her hand, and whispering soft nothings into her ear.

All at once the fore-wheel of the waggon plunged into a deep rut; the shock awoke the sleepers, and put out the light in the lantern; luckily, however, although within the waggon all was darkness, there was sufficient light without to enable the waggoner and his man to extricate the vehicle and proceed onward.

All the travellers—save those we have already alluded to—were, as soon as they were assured that no real danger existed, again in the arms of the sleepy god.

"And so," said the old gentleman, "you hide your money in your bosom, do you?"

"Yes, sir," said Jenny, "but I beg you won't take advantage of my simplicity in telling you so."

"By no means, you lovely creature!—but I can hardly believe that you are not joking."

"Lend me your hand," said Jenny;—"feel here, and then you will be satisfied!" and she laid the palm of the old gentleman's hand on her dress, so that he could feel the watch beneath.

"Not quite, you darling!" he replied; "let me feel the watch, and then I shall be."

"But you have not told me where you hide your valuables," said Jenny, softly.

"I'll tell you what I'll do," said the old gentleman, and his breath came short and quick, "if you'll let me put my hand in your place of security for your valuables, you shall put your hand in mine!"

"Agreed!" whispered Jenny.

The old fellow was in ecstacies, and attempted to kiss his fair neighbour.

"No—no!" said Jenny, "I did not bargain for that; here, give me your hand!"

She allowed him to insinuate his finger for a moment beneath her dress, and feel the watch. He would have gone further, and the slight touch he had experienced of her budding breasts almost maddened him; but she would not allow him to dally, and drew his reluctant hand away.

"Now, then," she said, "as I have performed my promise, will you act up to yours?"

"You'll keep it a secret?" he asked, cautiously.

"As secret as the grave!" said Jenny.

"Lend me *your* hand, then!"

He took Jenny's taper hand in his, and guided it into something that felt much like the inside of a grease-pot, which had not been cleaned for a week or more.

"*That's* where I hide my money!" he whispered; "there are six hundred-pound Bank of England notes under the tips of your fingers—and if any highwayman should succeed in discovering the hoard, why I'll eat the article in which it is concealed!"

"But I can't tell what that article is—let go my hand," said Jenny.

The waggish old gentleman chuckled, and released her.

She now felt the outside of the article as well as the inside, and whispered in her companion's ear:—

"What an odd place to put bank notes in!"

"Isn't it!" said the gentleman; "who, in the devil's name, would think of searching my wig? Capital idea, that of stitching up bank notes in the lining of my wig—isn't it?—never knew it fail!"

Nothing was now heard but the gingling of the horses' bells, and the soughing of the night-wind through the trees. Even the amorous old fellow had dozed off, and Jenny Diver and Gipsey Betty were about to follow his example, when the fly-waggon came to a dead halt, and some confusion was heard in front of it.

"Stand! or I'll blow your brains out!" exclaimed a voice well known to Jenny and Gipsey Bet—but neither of them gave symptoms of recognition; on the contrary, they each fell into a state of insincerable alarm.

The whole of the passengers awoke as if by magic; and every one of them exhibited the utmost terror, excepting the waggish old gentleman, who winked at Jenny, pressed his three-cornered cap tightly down on his wig, and calmly awaited the course of events.

The waggoner was a courageous fellow, and the instant he found himself attacked he rushed to his blunderbuss-box—snatched out the weapon, and running after M'Cleane, just as the latter rode up to the back part of the fly-waggon, pointed it at him, and fired. It flashed in the pan, and the man cursing his mishap, threw it aside and rushed on the highwayman, whom he dragged from his horse.

"Dick! leave the horses—they'll stand quiet enough, and come here."

Dick Flybynight was by his side in an instant, and M'Cleane being disengaged from the grip of the waggoner, the latter tore a rope from a truss of hay which was suspended beneath the vehicle, and the two then firmly lashed the driver to one of the ponderous hind-wheels.

The fellow was about to shout for assistance, and M'Cleane seeing this, exclaimed:—

"Utter one word of alarm, and by the God who made me! I'll whip on the horses, and let your own waggon mangle your wretched carcass!"

The other driver was secured in a similar manner; and then ordering Dick Flybynight in a whisper, to stand at the horses' heads and prevent them from moving onward, walked with a pistol in one hand, and another in his belt to the tail of the waggon.

"Now, ladies and gentlemen," said he, very coolly, and placing the waggon-ladder in readiness, "I'll thank you to come down to me one by one, if you are quiet, your lives shall be safe."

"There's only two of them!" said Jenny, in despair, to the brave young fellow who had once frightened away six; "Oh! sir, save us—save us!"

"Lord ha' mercy upon me!" groaned the young fellow, who was in an agony of terror.

"Now, then—be quick, or I shall be under the unpleasant necessity of proceeding to violence!"

Jenny was the first to descend, and after her Gipsey Betty.

"Be good enough, ladies, to hand me any little money you may have about you!"

Jenny fell on her knees before him,—"I have only this, sir," she said, drawing a small purse containing two or three guineas from her pocket, and whilst handing it to him, and affecting the greatest terror, she managed to whisper—"The old man in the snuff-coloured coat has his money concealed in his wig!"

The fat old lady next made her appearance, quivering like a bag of jelly; without hesitation she handed her watch and purse, and was about to pull off her wedding-ring, but M'Cleane desired her, with a low bow, to retain it.

"This way, my galliard," said M'Cleane, as he saw the young man hesitating to descend the ladder; "make more speed, man!" and catching him by his coat-skirts, he jerked him into the road, which he had no sooner reached than he fell upon his knees, and besought for mercy in the most pitiable accents.

"What have we here?" asked the highwayman, as the young fellow produced sixteen shillings—a book of tailor's patterns—some tape measures—a thimble, and a needle-book.

"It's all, your honour, I've got in the world—I'm only a poor tailor! have mercy on me! oh—h—!"

M'Cleane kicked him aside, and burst into a fit of laughter, in which even the plundered parties could not help joining.

The waggish old gentleman now came from the waggon.

"As you're the last, sir, I presume you carry more match about you than the others," said M'Cleane, with a smile.

"There you are mistaken," said the gentleman quietly, and with a roguish twinkle in his eye; "I never carry more with me than is sufficient for my travelling expenses, and I hope you won't take that from me."

"All's fish that comes to my net!" said M'Cleane, "so just hand it to me, for I'm cursedly in want of money for travelling expenses myself."

With much seeming reluctance the old gentleman gave M'Cleane three guineas and some odd silver, with which, after searching his pockets, the highwayman appeared to be content.

"Now, ladies, let me have the felicity of handing you into your carriage;" and M'Cleane gallantly assisted the three females into the place which he had forced them to quit.

The discomfited tailor, more dead than alive, followed; and the waggish old gentleman was about to follow, chuckling at the manner in which he had escaped, when M'Cleane laid his hand on his shoulder.

"You'll agree with me, sir, that exchange is no robbery?" said M'Cleane.

"Certainly not!" said the little man.

"Then, sir, as I've taken a great fancy to that wig of yours—and as mine is none of the newest, I'll take the liberty of seeing whether the one you wear would not look as well on my head as it does where it now is."

"But, my dear sir," said the gentleman, "consider——"

"Though mine *is* an old one, it is sound, and you need not fear catching cold—there!"

And M'Cleane without more ado transferred the wigs; and then, not noticing the little man's agony, coolly told him to mount the ladder, or he would soon have no brains for a wig to keep warm!

"The passengers will unbind you," said Dick Flybynight to the waggoner and his man: then placing a huge stone under the wheel of the waggon, to prevent its moving onward and crushing the poor fellows before they could be released—they mounted their horses and gallopped towards Devizes, separating before they entered that town.

———

CHAPTER XX.

ADVENTURES AT BRISTOL—DICK FLYBYNIGHT AND THE DOCTOR—PERILOUS SITUATION OF DICK AND THE CAPTAIN—THE ESCAPE—THE GIBBET ON HOUNSLOW HEATH.

WITHOUT falling in with any further adventures, the whole of the party arrived in Bristol, and contrived to let each other know, through the medium of Bristol Ann, of their various places of residence.

To guard as far as possible against suspicion being attached to their movements, the several members of the gang took up their abodes at different inns; and it was arranged between them, that in case any of them should be apprehended, the others should endeavour to procure their release by appearing to their characters, and representing them to be persons of reputation in London.

In addition to this, they had adopted a code of signals, by means of which they were enabled to converse with each other as well by signs as by words. Thus qualified, they prepared to commence their Bristol campaign.

They had secured the services of an accomplished burglar of that city, who was well acquainted with the localities, to assist them in their operations; and late in the evening of the day after his arrival, M'Cleane and this worthy took their way over Bristol Bridge towards Temple Street, in which thoroughfare, and contiguous to where the fair was to be held, was situated the then far-famed cadging-house for thieves, called the Beggars' Opera.

Arrived at the opening of a dark passage with a low entrance, Jack, the Scragsman, whispered a few words in the Captain's ear, and then dived into the gloom, M'Cleane following him.

About mid-way in this gloomy passage was a flickering lamp, by the light of which was espied a house, at the door of which Jack, the Scragsman, knocked in a peculiar manner.

Soon the rattling of chains and bolts was heard, and a hideous-looking woman, with battered nose, frouzy red hair, and a pair of blood-shot eyes, made her appearance.

"What ruffler is that with you?" she asked, in a voice husky from the effects of liquor, as she peered inquisitively into M'Cleane's face.

The Captain here repeated the pass-word with which Jack had made him familiar.

"All right!" she exclaimed; "enter!"

The room into which they were shown was a far different one to that at the "Chapel" where M'Cleane's gang assembled, and for a moment the Captain stood in mute astonishment at the scene which met his view.

It was a long low apartment, the sides and ceiling of which were begrimed with soot and tobacco smoke. Instead of the luxurious apartments of the "Chapel," here a long deal table, notched and cut in all directions, with stools on either side; and a bench of the same material, fastened to the wall of one side of the room, was the sole article of furniture. At certain intervals, knives and forks were chained to the table; and at the upper part of the room was a huge fire-place, round which, at the moment of the Captain's entrance, a number of persons were engaged in cooking their suppers.

When Jack, the Scragsman, and M'Cleane had gained the centre of the room, every eye was turned upon the handsome and well-dressed stranger; and there were not a few who surmised from his appearance, that he was rather an enemy than a friend.

"My jolly pals!" said Jack, "I have the pleasure of introducing to our noble society one whose name is well known to every Ben Cull here. This is the brave Captain M'Cleane, and I call upon you to do honour to his visit!"

"Hurrah! for Captain M'Cleane, the bold highwayman!" exclaimed every one present, starting to his feet. If he had been a general just returned from a great victory, he could not have been received with greater enthusiasm.

Amongst the most uproarous of the applauders was a legless individual, who, perched on the table in his basket, brandished his pewter pot, and shouted until the roof rang again. This worthy officiated as chairman, and called lustily on his boon companions to drink M'Cleane's health.

This was done with a hearty good will, and when the Captain threw five guineas on the table as garnish, the enthusiasm was at its height.

The place on this particular evening was more than usually crowded, for as the fair was to commence on the following day, there had been a great influx of thieves and mendicants from all parts, Bristol Fair being in those times one of the great rendezvous of the begging and prigging fraternity.

M'Cleane turned from the scene almost in disgust, and accomplished as speedily as possible the object of his visit—an object with which the reader will by and bye be acquainted.

Having done this, he returned to his lodgings at the Bush Inn.

The next day M'Cleane Jenny Diver, and Gipsey Betty, in the disguise of dealers, proceeded to the Cloth Fair, where they met Jack, the Scragsman.

In that place were assembled clothiers from all parts of the country, and M'Cleane and his companions saw, with no little satisfaction, that most of these were furnished with well-lined purses.

They had not been long in the fair, pricing goods, and seeking after prey, when an important-looking Devonshire clothier attracted the attention of Jack, the Scragsman.

"If we could only manage that old bloak," said Jack, "we might might make a haul; but he's a devilish deep one!"

"How so?" asked M'Cleane.

"Never carries his mopusses 'long wi' him!" replied the Scragsman.

"Where does he bestow them, then?" asked the Captain.

"Why, look here, Captain M'Cleane," remarked the Scragsman, with rather a knowing air, "he comes to Bristol Fair to meet the coves as buys the cloth he makes; they pays him their bills, and directly he gets the shiners, he sends his man-servant off to the landlord of the inn with it to take care of."

At this precise moment M'Cleane observed the Devonshire clothier receive a sum of money from one of the factors, and place it in a canvass bag.

This operation was several times repeated at different stalls, until the canvass bag appeared to be pretty full. At last the important-looking clothier, with a remarkably satisfied look, securely tied it round the neck with a piece of pack-thread.

"Very hard to get hold o' that," remarked the Scragsman, musingly.

"It *can* be done, though," remarked M'Cleane.

"Ah! you Lunnun chaps may *try* at it," insinuated Jack, the Scragsman, "but dang me if you could manage such a job as that!"

"Why, it's mere woman's play!" remarked M'Cleane, carelessly.

At this moment Jenny Diver came in sight, and, at a signal from M'Cleane, was in a moment by his side.

"See you that fat man in the drab riding-coat?" asked M'Cleane.

"I've been watching him this half hour," replied the Diver.

"I need not ask why," smilingly observed the Captain; "Jack, here, says that it will be impossible for us to get possession of that bag of gold."

"Pooh!" said Jenny, with something of indignation in her pretty face.

M'Cleane then made her acquainted with the fact that the clothier, when his bag was filled, entrusted it to the care of a servant.

Jenny mused for a moment, and then winking at M'Cleane, exclaimed:—

"I have it, Jem! Jack must contrive to fall down in the man's way when he is hurrying out of the fair with the bag of money; you and the Gipsey must then do as we did when a

THE GIBBET ON HOUNSLOW HEATH.

certain pregnant woman fell down near the park, and you acted so well as a footman."

Jenny now left the two men, and took her stroll through another part of the fair, having previously fixed on a spot for their meeting within half an hour.

M'Cleane and Jack, the Scragsman, now narrowly watched the Devonshire clothier, and got so near to him as to hear him, as he delivered the bag into the man-servant's hand, give directions that the money should be delivered to the landlord of the "Bush."

The bearer of the gold was closely followed by M'Cleane and Jack, the Scragsman; and when the fellow had arrived at a crowded place convenient for their purpose, the Scragsman, who had contrived to get directly in front of the servant, M'Cleane being in the man's rear, made a false stumble and fell.

No. 12.

The man laden with the gold fell also,—and as he fell, clutched the treasure so tightly, that M'Cleane with all his address found it impossible to obtain possession of it.

Jack, the Scragsman, had also exercised his professional abilities, but with a similar result.

Without at all suspecting that an attempt had been made to rob him, the servant, as soon as he had got out of the gutter into which he had been tumbled, instead of making the best of his way to the inn, went into one of the beer-cellars, with which the place abounded, for the purpose of brushing his clothes.

"Damn him!" said M'Cleane, "the clown has beaten us."

Jack, the Scragsman, appeared to be rather pleased than otherwise at the idea of an accomplished London thief being foiled.

"Why, Captain," said he, "these west-country folk be devilish sharp—sharper than they be in Lunnun!" and the Scragsman grinned maliciously.

"Wait a little—you stay here until my return, and see that the bird does not fly; there is but one way of getting that money, and but one person who knows that way," said M'Cleane.

"And who is she?" asked Jack, the Scragsman.

"The girl we just now quitted, Jenny Diver," replied the Captain.

"What, then, be that the famous Jenny!" asked Jack.

"Yes — yes," returned M'Cleane, hastily; "but this is no time for talk—I will be with you again speedily."

M'Cleane hastened to the rendezvouz where, fortunately, he found his accomplished confederate. To her he explained how matters stood, and asked her whether she thought it possible to effect the robbery.

"Possible!" exclaimed Jenny, a disdainful sneer curling her pretty lip; "possible, Jem! I have done easier things than that—and trust me I will do this!"

"Nay, nay, I did not doubt your abilities, my sweet Jenny!" said M'Cleane; "but, come, I'll show you where the pigeon is roosted, and then I will leave you to——"

"Pluck him!" interrupted Jenny.

The two then made the best of their way to the beer-cellar, where they found Jack, the Scragsman, keeping watch.

It has been before stated that Jenny lodged at the Bush Tavern;—so also did the west-country clothier.

After a short consultation the plans of the three thieves were matured—and Jenny hastened home to her tavern, where she speedily disrobed herself of her walking attire, and seated herself at a work-table.

As soon as the servant-man quitted the beer-cellar, he left the fair, and hastily proceeded towards his master's lodgings; he had got about half way thither when he was accosted by M'Cleane.

"My good man," said the wary Captain, "has not your worthy master ordered you to carry a bag of gold to the landlord of the Bush?"

The fellow stared at M'Cleane, held the bag more firmly in his pocket, and was about to proceed without replying, when M'Cleane remarked:—

"Your master is waiting for you at the tavern; he has just purchased some goods, and wants the money to pay for them. You had better hasten with me."

Fearing that he should get blamed for not having gone to the inn with the gold earlier, the fellow without hesitation followed M'Cleane, who introduced him to the room where Jenny Diver was sitting, and then retired.

' Your master is just gone out on some business in the neighbourhood, but he will soon return, and he has left orders with me that you are to wait here for him," said the Diver.

M'Cleane having impressed on the servant that Jenny was a woman of great wealth and consequence, he looked remarkably sheepish as she begged him to be seated. After some

persuasion, however, he sat down awkwardly on the edge of a chair, and heartily wished himself with the ostler and his companions in the stable.

"Take a glass of wine, my good fellow," said Jenny, in her most winning manner, at the same time pouring out a tumbler full for her bashful guest.

The man repeatedly declined her offers; but what will not beauty and female art combined accomplish? Jenny's blandishments conquered his shyness, and one glass of sparkling canary quaffed, it needed but little persuasion to induce the fellow to repeat the dose.

And repeat it he did, and again and again he drank off the bumpers handed him by the treacherous Hebe, until his eyes became multiplying glasses—the chairs whirling dancers—the mirrors winking planets of rather a large size — and Jenny herself an angel without wings!

Unused to the effects of wine, drowsiness succeeded to delirium; and the last tumbler full was but half drained when the guardian of the gold fell back in his chair and snored prodigiously.

When Jenny Diver became assured that the servant was fast asleep, she gently opened the window and made a signal to M'Cleane, who was stationed on the opposite side of the street.

He was not long in obeying it; and when he entered Jenny's room, she pointed to the intoxicated sleeper and said, "We must remove him into the next apartment without noise."

This was speedily effected; the unconscious servant was laid on a bed—the bag of gold abstracted from his pocket — and then Jenny locked the door, and concealed the key.

The produce of the robbery was upwards of two hundred guineas.

M'Cleane was about to clasp Jenny in his arms, but she gently repulsed him, saying:—

"No time now, Jem, for dallying; this affair cannot long be a secret; so, the sooner we vanish the better."

M'Cleane then proceeded to the Beggars' Opera, there to reward Jack, the Scragsman; and having informed that worthy gentleman of the success of Jenny's scheme, Jack lifted up his hands in amazement, and declared, that after all, the Bristol thieves were no more to be compared to the Lunnun sharpers, than an apple was to an inion.

Gipsey Betty and Bristol Ann were then sought out by M'Cleane, and furnished with the means of returning to London, as it was deemed prudent by the Captain that the party should at once leave Bristol.

In the meantime Jenny Diver summoned the keeeper of the hostelry, and having been supplied with her bill, instantly discharged it,—assigning as a reason for her sudden departure the dangerous illness of a relative at home.

In half an hour afterwards she had quitted the inn and was once more a passenger in the fly-waggon. M'Cleane would have accompanied her, but he was compelled to wait for Dick Flybynight, who, tired of confinement to the town, had the night before set out on horseback to practise that branch of his daring profession in which he so much excelled.

Whilst M'Cleane is sitting in a secluded part of the coffee-room of the White Lion, anxiously awaiting his arrival, we will narrate the Bristolian adventures of the dashing Dick Flybynight.

From Jack, the Scragsman, Dick had gained a knowledge of those parts of the surrounding country where it was most probable that booty might be obtained; mounting therefore, his gallant mare, he informed the landlord of the house where he was lodging that he was going to visit a friend a little way in the country, and off he went in search of adventures.

Leaving the city far behind him, Dick was soon gallopping over Dardham Downs. It was as yet too light for him to commence operations; so drawing rein at the door of a village ale-house, he fastened his steed to a neighbouring gate, and entered the only public room which the inn could boast of.

At the inn door was another horse, the owner of which—a grave old gentleman, attired in a bag wig, a suit of black clothes, with spotless linen, and with a gold-headed cane,—sat thoughtfully smoking his pipe.

Dick called for a can of beer and some tobacco, and soon found an opportunity of entering into conversation with the stranger, who informed him that he was a physician.

After a long coloquy, Dick, placing his hand on his heart, made a profound obeisance to the medical man, and assured him that should he ever stand in need of professional assistance, he should apply to him.

This compliment was courteously acknowledged, and shortly afterwards the old gentleman mounted his horse, and rode away.

"That be a fine man," remarked the landlady to Dick, "that he be; there ain't no doctor roundabouts as makes such cures!"

"Then he's rich, I suppose?" asked, or rather insinuated Dick Flybynight.

"As a jew!" replied the woman; "why, he be going now to receive fifty guineas, for a cure he made on Squire Castle's dearter, out to Shirehampton."

"Rather a lonely place, damme! for an old man like that to carry so much money about on his person. I wonder he's not afraid of highwaymen," said Dick.

"Lord bless 'ee, sir, Doctor Squills ain't afeard of the devil himself! more by token, there beant no highway robbers in this neighbourhood now," chuckled the hostess.

Are there not? thought Dick, who happened to know a little more on that subject than the loquacious landlady.

"I've heard tell," continued the woman, "that on this very down, twenty year ago, as Doctor Squill was 'tacked by a footpad, who he shot dead;—and 'tis true enough, for the people as lived here before I come, seed the robber's body hanging in chains, after he was hanged on Mile Hill, and if you'll only look over the Down there, you'll see the gibbet now."

Dick looked through the window in the direction indicated by the skinny forefinger of the old woman.

The twilight was fast deepening into gloom, yet, so clear was the atmosphere that evening, that objects at a considerable distance were plainly to be discerned. One, in particular, rivetted Dick Flybynight's attention.

Looming up, in hideous relief against the western horizon, where there yet lingered a streak of departing daylight, was indeed a gibbet; and so sharp and defined were its outlines to the highwayman's vision, that he could actually perceive the chain dangling from the beam: the miserable body which it once suspended had rotted away peacemeal, years and years ago.

"And to think that I may swing from such a cursed contrivance one of these fine mornings," said Dick aloud to himself, unconscious for the moment that any one was near him.

"You! God Almighty forbid!" exclaimed the old woman, as she surveyed the handsome figure and features of Dick Flybynight.

Dick explained that his meaning simply was that many an innocent man had been unjustly condemned to so horrible an exposure.

After another pipe, and another can, Dick made preparations for his departure. It was now quite dark, and the highwayman, who had by adroit questioning learned how far Doctor Squills had to ride, and at what time it was probable he might return, mounted his mare, and rode away in the direction of Shirehampton.

He had at first intended to have stopped the physician on the road in the usual "stand and deliver" style; but as he slowly rode along, he suddenly came up to a small cottage, through the window of which he perceived a woman knitting.

A sudden thought now flashed across his mind: having heard that the doctor was always well armed, and the gibbet on which formerly hung one whom the old man had dispatched, being still fresh in his memory, he determined to obtain that by cunning, which in other cases he would have got by force.

Alighting from his horse, which he concealed in a thicket near, he knocked at the door of the cottage, and pretending that he had been thrown off and injured, requested permission to rest himself for a few moments.

This hospitality was willingly afforded by the woman of the house; but no sooner had Dick made himself sure that her husband was not expected back from the city for some hours than he drew a pistol, and threatened her with instant death if she did not lend him one of her husband's great coats, and conceal herself in the coal-shed.

This the poor creature was forced to do; and trembling in every limb with anxiety she obeyed Dick Flybynight, who promised her that if she remained quiet until he chose to release her, he would amply reward her for the inconvenience he put her to.

Then he disguised himself in the husband's great coat and hat, and setting the door ajar, listened intently to the sounds proceeding from the road without.

Presently he heard a horseman deliberately approaching, and cautiously peeping out, he beheld Doctor Squills leisurely jogging along the road. Dick suffered him to pass the door, but when he had gone about twenty yards or so, he called loudly after him.

"Be that Doctor Squills?" he shouted, imitating as nearly as he could the voice and gait of a countryman.

The doctor stopped—clapped his hand on the stock of a horse pistol, and turned round on his saddle.

"That's my name," he replied; "who asks?"

"For the love of God, doctor, turn back!—I've been a watching for 'ee," said Dick.

And so indeed he had, but for a purpose which the good doctor little suspected.

"Why should I turn back?"—what's the matter?" asked the physician, hastily.

"My wife be 'most a dying with the bloody flux, doctor, and poor soul! she can't live without 'sistance. Only come in for two or three minutes, doctor, and I'll pay 'ee as soon as I be able."

Doctor Squills was a benevolent man, and though anxious to be home, he felt he could not but do all in his power to aid a suffering—perhaps dying fellow-creature; he therefore walked his horse back to the door and alighted.

Before he entered the house, he placed the pistol in the holster, Flybynight having respectfully hinted that his wife was mortally afraid of the sight of fire-arms; and that in her present situation the mere glance of a pistol might put her into convulsions.

"God bless you, doctor!" said Dick, as he ushered the physician into the litte room, "for this kindness to a poor man."

"Pooh! pooh!" said the physician, "if it is in my power to render you any service I shall be very glad. Where is the patient?"

Here the woman in the cupboard, from excess of terror, uttered an involuntary groan.

"Up stairs, doctor; don't you hear the poor soul moaning?"

"Yes, yes, I hear!" said the physician; "show me to her chamber."

Dick led the way up stairs, and was closely followed by the physician; the instant the latter had entered the apartment Dick shut the door and drew out a loaded pistol, which he presented at the old gentleman's head as he was looking for his patient.

"Where's your wife, you infernal scoundrel?" thundered the doctor, who now found himself fairly trapped.

"This is her!" said Dick, holding an empty purse before the physician's eyes.

"I mean your wife with the flux, you villain!" said the doctor.

"This is the very one," replied Dick, coolly; "and she has had a flux so long that now there is nothing at all within her!"

The doctor turned aside with a jesture of disdain.

"And," continued Dick, not heeding the movement in the least degree, "I know, doctor, that you have an infallible remedy in your pocket for her distemper. Now, sir, if you do not instantly apply it without a word, this pistol shall make a hole in your body which all the doctors in the universe shall not be able to mend!"

The doctor by no means liked the appearance of his strange patient, and shook his head; but Dick was peremptory—and the more so as he was in great fear lest the master of

the house should arrive before he could get clear off.

Doctor Squills seeing that there was no way of escape, transferred, much against his inclination, forty guineas from his own purse to that of Dick Flybynight's, which forthwith presented a much more healthy appearance;—indeed, the cure might have been said to be complete.

"And now, doctor, as you have been so kind to my wife, I can do no less than put you in full possession of this house and all it contains. I hope you will be satisfied with the fee!"

Then, making a profound bow to the astounded son of Galen, he left the room, locked the door upon the poor doctor, and throwing aside his disguise, quitted the house.

He was speedily on horseback, and galloping once more over the breezy downs towards Bristol, which place he reached about an hour before midnight.

Knowing where he should find M'Cleane, he repaired to the White Lion, in the coffee-room of which establishment he discovered the object of his search.

"Why, Captain, you look as dull as a dispirited maiden," said Dick; "what's in the wind now?"

"Quietly, Dick!" said M'Cleane; "we must be off before the morning, or the place will be too hot to hold us!"

M'Cleane then informed Dick of Jenny's exploit of the morning at the neighbouring tavern; and Flybynight in return entertained the Captain with his adventure of the evening.

"We shall have time to laugh over that on the road, Dickon," said M'Cleane; "by the way, where is your horse?"

"Not in the stable yet, Jem;—I felt in such glorious spirits that I had determined after I had seen you, to take another ramble on the road, and follow up my luck."

"That is lucky," said M'Cleane; "mine is in charge of a confidential person belonging to the Beggars' Opera, at Templegate; Jenny and the girls have taken all our luggage with them in the waggon, so that we shall have nothing but ourselves to care for."

"And by all that's damnable," said Dick to M'Cleane, in a low earnest whisper, "we can't take too much care of ourselves."

"What mean you, Dick?" asked M'Cleane.

Dick spoke not; but significantly pointed his finger in the direction of the door of the coffee-room.

M'Cleane glanced that way, and turned pale. "The devil!" he said, between his set teeth.

"One who's likely enough to send you and I to that dark gentleman, Jem, if we're not careful," remarked Dick Flybynight.

Well might the Highwaymen be alarmed, for they were indeed in a perilous position. The individual whose arrival in the coffee-room had so roused their fears, was no other than the waggish old gentleman whose well-stuffed wig M'Cleane had pounced upon on the night of the robbery of the fly-waggon!

Fortune, however, in this extremity befriended them, for the waggish old gentleman went into a box on the same side of the room as theirs, so that they were entirely hidden from his view. But the slightest accident, or the most trifling inclination or whim on his part might lead to a discovery. What was to be done? The old gentleman having sat down ordered the drawer to bring him candles, a newspaper, and his supper.

"So then," whispered M'Cleane, "he will be in no hurry to go, we are in a precious mess, Dick."

Dick was of the same opinion, and so replied by nodding his head affirmatively.

To get out of the room by way of the entrance door would be a matter of too much risk to attempt. There was, therefore, nothing to do for it but to wait until the old gentleman should be engaged with his meal or had retired.

The drawer brought in the supper.

"There's a terrible draught in this box, waiter," said the waggish old gentleman, "I think I'll come into the next."

"There are two gentlemen already there," observed the drawer.

"Oh! never mind that, I'm sure they'll accommodate me when they know how unpleasantly I'm situated, till my new wig comes home. This handkerchief doesn't half keep the cold off; and pox take me if I'll wear that rascally highwayman's."

"Should you know the villains again, sir, if you were to see them?" asked the drawer, to whom the old gentleman had on some previous occasion related the story of the robbery.

"Know 'em! aye; if I was to meet them at the North Pole;—and something tells me that I shall meet them some day—yes, and that I see the rascals swinging for it too."

"There's a worse draught in the next box sir, because there's a window close to it which looks into the stable yard," said the drawer.

At the mention of the words window and stable yard M'Cleane and Dick Flybynight looked meaningly at each other.

"Oh!" observed the waggish old gentleman, "then I'll stay where I am."

The drawer then retired.

The real difficulty was now overcome; M'Cleane cautiously examined the window, which he found could easily be raised, and as the coffee-room was on the ground floor, a very slight effort was necessary to enable them to get into the stable yard; the chief difficulty was to evade the observation of the people of the house as they passed from the stable yard to the street.

The case, however, was desperate and they determined at all risks to make the attempt.

Gently raising the sash, the Captain peeped cautiously out. "Thank God, Dick, the coast is clear," he whispered.

"Now or never then, Jem," said Dick, and without noise he got through the window.

M'Cleane had almost accomplished the same feat when the draught caused by the open window blew the handkerchief off the old gentleman's bald head. Jumping up to recover it he observed the unusual spectacle of a gentleman going out of the room without making use of the door. Dick Flybynight was just giving M'Cleane a-hand, and his face was close to the window; and the Captain's physi-

ognomy became distinctly visible, just as the old gentleman came in front of the box which the highwaymen had so precipitately quitted.

"The two villains who robbed me, by God!" exclaimed the surprised individual; and rushing to the bell he rang it violently, and hallowed at the top of his voice, "thieves, murder, fire!" until his face assumed a purple hue, and he had altogether a decidedly apoplectic appearance.

"Said I should see 'em again," said the waggish old gentleman, pointing to the open window, to the landlord, the landlady, the chambermaid, the scullion wench, and the waiter, who came rushing into the room.

"See who?" asked the landlord.

"See who?" screamed the landlady.

"See who?" bawled out the waiter.

"See who?" shrieked the chambermaid and scullion wench in concert.

"Why the villains who stole my wig," roared the old gentleman, stamping his foot with rage.

"Where are they?" asked the landlord, the landlady, the waiter, the chambermaid and the scullion wench all at once.

"Gone out at the window," cried the old gentleman. Something like the real facts of the matter now flashed on the minds of the landlord and the waiter who rushed to the box, and the latter immediately missed the two gentlemen whom he had seen occupy it not ten minutes before.

"Damn the rascals!" exclaimed the now sensitive landlord, "did they pay their score, Tim?"

"God bless me master, no! The swindling wagabonds!"

"Oh, the wretches!" cried the landlady, "to think of having two bowls of canary posset, a loaf of manchet bread, and four chicken sandwiches, and then to sneak off without paying."

"The wagabones to bilk me out of my shilling," chimed in the drawer.

"Curse your scores and your canary posset's, and your fees. Why the wig they stole from me was worth five hundred pounds," cried the old gentleman, who was not a little enraged at the people of the inn lamenting so much their own losses; not caring a fig about his, and then losing that time which should have been occupied in pursuing the highwaymen, in vain lamentations.

Meantime M'Cleane and Dick Flybynight having almost by a miracle escaped capture, made good their escape from the tavern. The delay occasioned by the incidents which we have just related proved of infinite use to them, for by means of it they were enabled to gain possession of their horses, and leave the city before the hue and cry was raised.

"By St. Nicholas! Dick, but we have had a narrow escape to night," said M'Cleane, as they reined in their panting horses after a hard gallop of six miles. "A minute later, and that infernal wig would have been a hangman's night-cap for both of us."

"What the devil should we have done had it not been for the window?—that was a lucky thought of the drawer's, by Jove!" said Dick.

They were yet apprehensive of pursuit, and,

therefore, after having breathed their horses a little they again plied whip and spur, nor did they slacken their pace until the lights of Bath twinkled on the hill side to their left.

"It would be as well to avoid going through the city," observed M'Cleane. "I will, therefore, go over Widcombe Down, and you, Dick, take the road to the left; we can meet at the cross-road, about three miles beyond Bath."

The highwaymen then separated and each pursued his separate way. Neither of them met with any molestation or adventure, and they arrived at the cross-road within a few minutes of each other.

Taking advantage of the few short hours of darkness which remained they again pushed on, and when morning dawned our adventurers had reached Devizes. Here it was absolutely necessary they should remain to refresh their horses and take a few hours repose themselves; they sought out an obscure public-house on the outskirts of the town and informed the landlord that they had been riding for a wager, in order to account for the distressed state of their horses.

Here, however, they dared not remain long, as the mail from Bristol would pass through the town in the course of the day, and in all probability bring intelligence of the escape from the White Lion coffee-rooms.

They, therefore, after paying their score, again mounted their horses, and without, during daylight, appearing to use extraordinary speed, contrived by nightfall to have accomplished more than two-thirds of their journey.

Having once more baited their horses, they proceeded on their journey, and about midnight, so rapidly had they travelled, they entered upon Hounslow Heath.

"Thank God! M'Cleane," said Dick Flybynight, "we are on our own plantation again, and now I breathe freely."

"And pretty trees grow in this 'plantation' of yours as you call it, Dickon," said M'Cleane, "and brave fruit they bear too. Look yonder!"

The moon, which was now rising, shed a sickly light over the scene, as the two highwaymen cantered along. On the rising ground, a little way to their right, in all its hideous distinctness, rose the trunk of a lofty and leafless elm tree: from this trunk, every branch save two, at a considerable height from the ground, had been lopped off; and as the tree had been barked, to prevent the ascent of sap and the growth of foliage, these two blasted boughs stretched out at right angles to each other, like huge, shadowy, and spectral arms, from the gnarled trunk.

From these boughs hung two human forms—like scarecrows—the decaying remnants of their clothing fluttering in the wind; and the iron chains by which they were suspended creaking dismally.

Urged by some impulse for which they could not account, M'Cleane and Dick Flybynight left the horse-road, and rode directly up to the gibbet-tree.

The moon had now risen sufficiently high to render the forms of the dead men perfectly distinct, and both the highwaymen looked at them with a shudder.

Well might they, for the sight was horrible beyond description. The heads of the miserable creatures had been picked clean by fowl birds; the eyes had been picked out by raven's beaks, and their empty sockets presented a ghastly appearance. Their white teeth grinned in the moonbeam; and in various parts of their frames, where the clothing had rotted away, polished ribs, or arm and leg bones appeared.

"What a dog's fate!" said M'Cleane, with a sigh.

"Well, I hope, Jem," said Dick Flybynight, with forced gaiety, "if ever we should be strung up like those bold boys above us, that we shall like them hang in company!"

"'Tis no subject for joking on, Dick!" said M'Cleane; "I feel at this moment a presentiment for which I cannot account, that such (pointing to the dead men overhead) will be my fate!"

"Tush, man! cease this croaking, or you will make me as dull as yourself," said Dick Flybynight, slapping M'Cleane on the shoulder. "But let us be off, and at the first hostelry a goblet of good wine will drown all these vapours!"

Quitting the gloomy spot, the highwaymen rode onward in silence for some miles, until they reached a tavern, with the landlord of which they were well acquainted.

It was nearly morning, and all the house were in bed; but a shrill whistle from M'Cleane brought the host in his nightcap to the window.

"What chanting bullies are there at this hour?" asked the landlord, who at the same time protruded from the window the muzzle of a blunderbuss.

"What, Tim! don't you know us, you purple-nosed old publican? Why who should we be but——"

"Ah! Captain, God bless you! I know your voice. Wait a bit, and I'll be with you."

Admission was speedily obtained; and here M'Cleane and Dick determined to remain during the day, and return to the "Chapel" after dark.

CHAPTER XXI.

BLACKMOOR AT SEA—THE MURDER OF GRAW-LER—THE TRAITOR IS CAUGHT IN A TRAP—ANOTHER ESCAPE—A CONVERSATION IN THE ROOKERY—A STARTLING INCIDENT.

WE must now shift the scene of our story, and for a little time follow the fortunes of one who has already exercised no slight influence on the fates of M'Cleane and his comrades of the 'Chapel.'

We refer to the traitor BLACKMOOR.

It will be remembered that we left this man on board the 'Maryland Trader,' under the care of Captain Grawler, on her way to the American plantations, where he was to be sold to one of the Tobacco growers.

Scarcely had the vessel got out of sight of land, when the sufferings of Blackmoor and his unfortunate companions commenced. To the horrors of sea sickness were added those of the most barbarous cruelty on the part of Grawler, who was as great a ruffian as ever trod a plank.

It was of course to his interest as a trafficker in human flesh not to kill his victims outright, nor to injure so much as to lower their value in the market; but also to his interest to keep them alive on the smallest possible quantity of food and water, so that though the miserable creatures were not actually starved, they were as near to that dreadful condition as possible.

Seventy-six men and boys, all of whom excepting Blackmoor, had been torn from their homes and friends by the vile artifices of Captain Grawler, were huddled together between decks in a space insufficient to have comfortably contained a quarter of that number. Here they ate, drank and slept: and only once a day were they permitted in small parties to walk the deck and inhale the pure ocean breeze.

From some cause or other, which cannot be explained, Blackmoor was an object of especial hatred to Captain Grawler, who never failed, when opportunity offered, to treat him with savage barbarity.

Blackmoor was on his part, one of those desperate ruffians, who never, if they can help it, will suffer an injury to go unrevenged; and it must be confessed that he had sustained a great grievance at Grawler's hands.

It happened, when the vessel had accomplished about half her voyage, that one of the sailors in taking in the mainsail fell overboard and was drowned in spite of every effort to save him. Unfortunately for Grawler, at this juncture, the weather, which had hitherto been fine, changed, and a succession of gales set in, which caused the drowned seaman to be badly missed, for the Captain proceeding on a too economical principle had not shipped his proper complement of men; and now, there were really not sufficient to work the ship.

In this emergency Grawler thought of Blackmoor, who was by far the most able-bodied of the kidnapped people; he, therefore, summoned him on deck.

"Blackmoor," said Grawler, "I can't afford to keep such a damned lazy lubber as you are on board unless you work, so, during the remainder of the voyage, you'll just help the sailors, d'ye hear?"

"Yes, I hear; but I arnt used to sailoring, Captain," replied Blackmoor.

"Then, by G—, I will soon make you understand matters," remarked Captain Grawler.

The traitor by no means liked the idea of work, he had never been used to it; and he determined to shirk labour if possible. To this end he adopted a decided course, trusting to his native ferocity to gain the mastery over Grawler.

"Look here, Captain Grawler," he said, with dogged determination, "you brought me on board this ship against my own inclination; but I won't work against my will, and you can't make me."

"Can't I?" asked the Captain, with a sneer. "You won t work, eh? I shall see."

"And so shall I see, too," doggedly remarked Blackmoor.

"Aye, and feel into the bargain; but come, sir, just walk forward and take your turn with those men who are at the pumps!"

"I'll be d—d if I do!" said Blackmoor.

"Carpenter!" called the Captain.

"Aye, aye, sir!" said the carpenter, approaching the place where Grawler stood.

"Get three of the strongest of the crew, and let this fellow be lashed to the gratings. Quick! d'ye hear?"

"Aye, aye, sir!"

In a minute afterwards three stout sailors and the carpenter made their appearance, and seized on Blackmoor, who, strong as he was, was but as an infant in their powerful hands.

Almost before the miserable man could comprehend the real nature of his situation he was stripped to the waist, and laid with his stomach downwards on the gratings of the main hatchway; his wrists and ankles were secured by ropes, which were fastened to ring-bolts, so that strive and struggle as he might, he was utterly powerless.

"And so, Master Blackmoor, you won't work!" said Captain Grawler, as he came from the cabin with a cat-o-nine-tails in his hand; "now, I'll try if I can't persuade you!"

Drawing the knotted thongs through his left hand, he grasped the short handle of the instrument of torture with his right, then raised it over his head, and finally taking a step forward, he exerted all his strength in lashing the back of Blackmoor.

A scream of agony burst from the wretched creature. Again, again, and again descended the infernal "cat," until Blackmoor's back was one discoloured mass of quivering, jelly-like flesh. As soon as Grawler saw that the repeated floggings had produced a species of numbness, and that the intensity of the suffering had diminished, he ordered the man to be released.

With infernal cruelty he ordered salt brine to be rubbed on the lacerated parts, which produced excruciating agony. This done, Blackmoor was conducted to his hammock, there to meditate on schemes of revenge.

Day after day he continually brooded on the idea of vengeance, and at length it assumed something like a plausible form. The man who attended him was the second mate—a determined enemy of his superiors in command: to him Blackmoor confided his plan, which was that of murdering the Captain and first mate, seizing of the vessel, and after disposing of the cargo at their place of destination, turn pirates.

The second mate undertook to sound such of the crew as he suspected to be disaffected; and a day or two afterwards accomplices were secured, and their plan of operations arranged.

"Only let me do for Grawler," said Blackmoor; "I owe him a grudge for that flogging, and by G— I ll pay it!"

They were now within three days sail of the port of Annapolis, in Maryland, and therefore it was absolutely necessary that the business should be executed without delay; and the following night, when the second mate would take the watch, was fixed upon.

Captain Grawler had retired to his berth for more than two hours, and the first mate had turned in about half that time, when Blackmoor crept upon deck and joined his confederates.

It was as lovely a night as ever gladdened the bosom of the great deep. The full-orbed moon rose majestically from the bosom of the ocean, tinging every wave, as it rose and sank, with liquid silver. Myriads of stars, shining in the blue firmament above, were reflected in the glorious mirror below. Every spar and rope of the vessel looked like dark tracery against the clear sky; and everything around betokened peace.

Who would have thought, as that gallant vessel bounded over the waters like a winged thing, that she bore such a freight of guilt, misery and human guilt? that on that lovely night, men in such a scene were plotting scenes of strife and blood? Yet so it was, though the influences of the hour would have moved gentler natures to promote peace and good will to men.

At a given signal those men on the watch who were not favourable to Blackmoor's plans were secured; and this having been done, the second mate knocked at the Captain's door, and on pretence of seeing land, requested him to come on deck.

The instant he did so he was seized by Blackmoor, who was waiting at the top of the companion stairs, and who, with the aid of one of the sailors, securely pinioned him.

The first mate was also similarly disposed of.

"Grawler!" said Blackmoor, "I vowed to be revenged on you for flogging me; that revenge I will have—and it shall be deep, stern, and terrible!"

"Release me, you piratical villain!" exclaimed Grawler, "or, by the God who made me, I'll have every one of you hanged from the yard-arm on our arrival in port!"

"You shall swing from it yourself before we get there," said Blackmoor, with a fiendish sneer; "but first," he continued, "I'll give you a taste of the cat, in return for the kindness you showed me. Strip him!" he continued, beckoning two men who stood near.

They were not long in doing this, and Grawler was stripped to the skin.

Blackmoor then, spite of the wretched man's shrieks for mercy, flogged him in the most inhuman manner, and then ordered him to rise.

Grawler now fully comprehended the desperate nature of his situation; and when he saw his first mate bound like himself, he lost all hope.

"As for you!" said Blackmoor to the first mate, "as you never did me any mischief, we'll be contented with simply flinging you to the sharks—there were three or four fine lively ones playing about the ship just now; so if you've any prayers to say, be quick about 'em!"

The mate turned ghastly pale when he heard his frightful doom pronounced, and falling on his knees, implored mercy.

It was all in vain; five minutes only were allowed him, and then he was borne screaming and struggling to the stern of the ship.

"For the love of Heaven, save me!" cried the mate, as looking over the vessel's side, he saw indeed the fins of a large shark, following in the wake of the ship.

He might as well have talked to the voracious fish itself as to those men. Not a spark of pity was kindled in their bosoms.

"In with him!" shouted the second mate—and the poor wretch was hove over the vessel's stern; with such desperate energy, however, did he cling to the rail, that his hands could not be removed.

"Carpenter, give me your hatchet!" said the second mate.

It was brought, and at a blow the hands of the first officer were severed, and he fell heavily into the water.

He did not sink at once, but boldly struck out for life, his mute appealing face turned upwards to his murderers. This, however, was but for an instant, for the shark, which had dived when the man dropped into the water, was now seen through the clear element rising perpendicularly to the surface, its white belly gleaming like a pillar of silver. The voracious fish was quietly under the first mate; and, as it neared him it turned suddenly on its side, opened its fearful jaws, and seizing its prey by the leg, dragged it to the depths below. A bloody tinge on the surface of the water was the only thing that was left to tell the horrid tale.

"Now then, Captain Grawler, we'll have a little sport with you before the sharks pick your bones!" said Blackmoor.

A block was rove to the end of the yard-arm—through this a rope was run, and at its end a noose.

"Why you're not going to hang me, your Captain, you devil's imps, are you?"

"Yes, we are, though, Grawler!" said Blackmoor, "you know if you hang a little time the sharks will find you eat tenderer. You are certainly tough now, I fancy!" and the villain chuckled at his own coarse humour.

"Don't waste time!" cried one of the sailors; "we're getting near port, and may fall in with vessels, you know."

"True!" said Seaton; (such was the second mate's name). "Blackmoor, you had better finish him off at once!"

"Now then, Captain Grawler, let me have the pleasure of fitting your neck in this noose!" and he approached the Captain, who shrank backwards in horror, and declared that if they would spare his life, he would never divulge what had passed.

"We won't trust such an infernal villain as you are; besides, I'll have my revenge!" said Blackmoor; and he flung the noose over the Captain's head, and drew it tight.

The main hatchway was placed on the bulwarks and Grawler placed on it. Blackmoor and four other men then took the loose end of the rope. At his suggestion three cheers were given for the Captain, and they all ran aft, while the body of Grawler swung to and fro in the air, his eyes starting from their sockets—his tongue protruding from his mouth, and his blackened face hideously distorted.

"We won't let him hang till he's *quite* dead," said the ferocious Blackmoor; "no, no! let him feel the shark's teeth!"

BLACKMOOR AND THE MUTINEERS SEIZING CAPTAIN GRAWLER.

The very mutineers themselves shuddered at this atrocious cruelty, and murmured against carrying matters to such an extent.

But Blackmoor was resolute; and seizing a cutlass which happened to stand near, he severed the rope at a stroke, and the yet living body of the wretched Grawler plunged heavily into the water, which it had scarcely touched when a huge shark seized on it and bore it away.

Those of the crew who had at first refused to join the mutineers did so now from fear, and the vessel proceeded towards her destination.

Two days after the perpetration of these horrid crimes the vessel entered the harbour of Annapolis, in Maryland; but strict care was taken that none of the crew should go ashore, lest they should divulge the affair. Blackmoor and Seaton had concocted a story to satisfac-

torily account for the absence of the Captain and mate, and they soon succeeded in disposing of the cargo.

After everything had been arranged, and the vessel was ready to sail, Seaton proposed to Blackmoor that they should take a trip a little way into the country to visit a planter, a friend of his.

To this Blackmoor acceded—and on the day before their intended departure on a piratical expedition, the two proceeded to the villa of Seaton's friend, who was the owner of a large tobacco plantation. They were courteously received, and hospitably entertained; and on being pressed to stay the night they agreed to do so, as there would be time enough for them to join the ship in the morning.

That night Blackmoor, who was pretty well primed, retired to bed before Seaton, who remained with his host, having, as he said, to arrange some private matters with him. It was a bright, glorious morning when he awoke.

He dressed and descended to the breakfast parlour. On the table were the preparations for that meal, but it was evident that only one was expected to partake of it: one coffee cup and saucer, one egg cup, one knife, and one plate, were all that met his eye.

"Seaton is in the garden," he said to himself, "with his friend;" and he quitted the house and sauntered down to the shrubbery.

He had not gone far when he heard a voice calling to him; he turned and beheld Mr. Vanderslick, Seaton's friend.

On reaching that gentleman he was rather startled by his altered looks and manner. On the evening before he wore the aspect of a friend—he now assumed the bearing of a superior.

"My slaves breakfast at seven o'clock, in that log-house you see over there; so I reckon you'd better join 'em, or you'll get none. The overseer 'll tell you what work to do after breakfast," said Mr. Vanderslick.

"Work! overseer!" exclaimed Blackmoor; "why, what do you mean?—where's my friend Seaton?"

"A good many miles out at sea by this time, I guess; and as to what I mean—why he sold you to me before he went last night as a slave for five years; here's his recipt for the money," replied Vanderslick.

It was true enough—Seaton had on the preceding evening informed the planter who Blackmoor was, and the circumstances attending his shipment on board the Maryland Trader. Desirous to get rid of so dangerous a friend, he had offered him for twenty-five pounds to Vanderslick, and the latter jumped at the offer. Immediately after clenching the bargain, Seaton, instead of going to bed, had started off to join his ship.

"The damned—the doubly damned villain!" exclaimed Blackmoor; "but I'll be revenged on him yet!"

"And look ye," said Mr. Vanderslick, "our rules are rather strictish here: you must work hard—and the first time you attempt to escape I'll hand you over to the authorities for that little affair of Captain Grawler! Seaton has told me how you served him."

Blackmoor was thunderstruck; the very man who he had seduced into crime had proved too much for him, and had betrayed him. His case was indeed desperate.

After all his contrivances, then, he was a slave, condemned to toil in a foreign land under a burning sun, harder even than the beasts of the field.

He saw that it was his best policy to conduct himself well, and he so acted as to gain in some degree the confidence of his master, who granted him unusual indulgences. But from the first moment of his captivity, for it could be called little else, he determined on the first opportunity to effect his escape, and for that opportunity he was ever on the look-out.

He had been working in the tobacco fields for some months when, in the absence of the regular messenger, Mr. Vanderslick sent him on horseback to the residence of a neighbouring planter with a letter.

He now suddenly determined to put his long cherished design into execution; and, therefore, instead of performing his errand, he made off in the direction of Virginia.

He had no money, and without that he could do nothing. Towards the close of the second day, however, as he arrived on the Virginian border, he robbed a gentleman of a number of pistoles, moidores, and dollars; and on the following day he stopped a chaise, in which was a lady and gentleman, and a negro servant, and got from them twelve guineas, and some silver.

He now directed his course for the backwoods, where he hoped to fall in with some hunting parties; but his fate had otherwise decreed. Happening to wander to the banks of the Potomac River, he saw a vessel outward-bound; he agreed for his passage, and embarked. In a few hours after Blackmoor had touched the deck of the ship, she spread her canvass-wings and sailed for Old England.

*　　*　　*　　*　　*

Many years ago—aye, and within the recollection too of many a one who lays no claim whatever to being considered the "oldest inhabitant," there existed in the metropolis one of those neighbourhoods which vice and misery claim to be exclusively their own.

A vestige of it yet remains—but the greatest part of it has been swept away by the besom of modern improvement;—and where dilapidated dwellings, and dismal lanes were once situated — shops, brilliant as palaces, and streets, broad and noble, are to be seen.

The neighbourhood to which our narrative at this time especially refers, was that of Saint Giles's.

To one particular part of that locality the current of events bears us along. That part was known as THE ROOKERY!

It was here too that tramps, beggars, thieves of all descriptions, prostitutes, and bawds, took up their temporary or permanent residences.

Here too were the houses of many receivers of stolen goods, as well as regular academies in which young thieves might be initiated by experienced hands into the mysteries of their profession.

Dirt, misery in all its shapes, pestilence, fever, crime, agony, and death, were the constant occupants of this horrid place.

The houses were very old tottering affairs, only prevented from falling into the narrow streets by intervening spars of wood which stretched from front to front, and supported the crazy structures on either side. In the windows panes of glass were scarce, but bundles of rags were plenty; indeed nothing could exceed these in number, excepting perhaps the swearings of children, who played below in the filthy gutter, and swore quite as roundly, and drank gin quite as unwinkingly as their fathers and mothers.

In the large room of a low public-house in the centre of this sink of iniquity, a great number of persons were sitting one evening—or rather near midnight—smoking, carousing, and gambling. At one extremity of the apartment a blind beggar was playing on an old cracked fiddle, while two or three young fellows and some prostitutes were dancing. Scattered about in groups were some dicing, others singing ribald songs, and many leaning on the tables, or lying on the benches, in a state of stupid intoxication; and round the fire were huddled a group who, from their gestures, appeared to be conversing on some deeply interesting topic.

"It was a pretty sight—a werry pretty sight, indeed, Nimning Toby!" said an old man who was smoking a short pipe in the chimney corner, to a dissipated-looking young fellow who sat opposite to him.

"I'd valk twenty miles nor more this blessed night, to see such another to-morrow morning—I would!" returned the young man.

"To see how Crookfingered Ned wouldn't listen to the old pattering cove, and shoved away the book from under his nose;—he wasn't a going to be a snivelling cove!" chimed in a stout, bloated-faced young woman.

"Not he, Bouncing Moll!" said the old man; "you young 'uns here should take a pattern by such a wirtious example as Crookfingered Ned's. I hates a chap as shows a turnip mug when it comes to the pinch."

"Why, after all," said the young fellow, "scragging is only a nateral sort of death, and werry much pleasanter than lying on your back for a month, may be in all sorts of pain, and being drenched with 'potticaries stuff!"

"Werry true, young man," observed a middle-aged man, in a seedy suit of black ; "what you say is right: hanging is a natural sort of death, and it can't be a werry unpleasant one, for werry often people chooses to depart this life in that way of their own accord: they wouldn't do it if they didn't like it I 'spose."

This was a convincing argument to which all present assented to by audible grunts of satisfaction.

"I should werry much prefer it myself to being sent over the water," observed one of the party; "now, only suppose as Crookfingered Ned had a been transported instead of being hung. Why, he'd a been bad enough off—and now, as 'tis, he's out of his misery!"

"Lor! how I laughed when Ned kicked his shoes off!" said the bloated faced girl; and she indulged in another hearty laugh at the recollection of Crookfingered Ned's last witticism.

"Kicked his shoes off! how was that!" asked some one.

"Why, you see," said the girl, "Ned always swore as he'd never die in his shoes—for he thought he was clever enough to cheat the gallows; but he found out his mistake, poor lad! and because he wouldn't be worse than his word, just before he was turned off he kicked off his trotter-cases. So you see that though he didn't die in his bed, he didn't die in his shoes!"

"That was a good un!" said the young fellow; "it ain't every chap as 'ud thought o' that!"

"Ned was always a droll chap!" said the bloated faced girl, who, by the way, had been on very intimate terms with the Crookedfingered

one. "Why he robbed two quakers once in Maidenhead thicket, and then made 'em dance a hornpipe whilst he played, for he was very fond of music, and always carried what he called his whistling-pipe about with him."

The idea of two grave quakers dancing a hornpipe after having been robbed, was so exquisite a joke that all the company forthwith fell into convulsive paroxysms of laughter, the effect of which was to render them so exceedingly dry that it became absolutely necessary to spend another portion of the guinea which Crookfingered Ned had bequeathed to Bouncing Moll, in another bowl of gin punch, which soon stood reeking before them.

"Well," said the dissipated-looking young fellow, taking a glass of the liquor, "here's success to all honest Tobymen, knights of the road, footpads, cut-purses, and prigs,—and if ever they comes to the rope, may they be as fly as our friend Ned!" and after having tossed off the drink, he in the fulness of his heart exclaimed—"after what I seed this morning, I shouldn't mind being tied up myself—blowed if I should!"

"Yes—you would, though!" said a deep voice behind him.

The young fellow looked round—a stranger had silently and suddenly joined the group round the fire.

The stranger was a tall, stout, vulgar-looking man; but no one there remembered to have seen him before.

"How do you know whether I should or not?" asked the young man.

"Because you've never been near enough to scragging to know anything about it," replied the stranger.

"That's true enough," remarked the young man.

"But *I have!*" said the stranger, in a voice of deep meaning.

Every eye was instantly fixed on his face, but to the speaker's infinite satisfaction no one recognised him.

IT WAS BLACKMOOR!

———

CHAPTER XXII.

RETURN OF M'CLEANE AND DICK FLYBYNIGHT TO LONDON—TONY BILKIT IN TROUBLE—STRANGE DISCLOSURES.

WE left M'Cleane and Dick Flybynight at the roadside public-house, after their visit to the gibbet on Hounslow Heath.

At this place they remained during the whole of the day, and when the shades of evening fell they once more mounted their horses, and a little after midnight reached Hyde Park Corner.

Before proceeding to Madame Charlotte's Hotel, M'Cleane suggested that they should pay a visit to Bilkit's, the vintner's, in order that they might hear whether anything of importance had transpired in their absence, and where they might leave their horses.

They accordingly, by selecting the most retired thoroughfares, before long reached Mr.

Bilkit's establishment—the "Jolly Pedlars."

To their great astonishment the house was closely shut up, and all within was as silent as the grave. This was a most unusual occurrence, for Bilkit's house was one of that description which did more business by night than by day. In those times the laws relating to houses of public entertainment, were far less stringent than they now are. Indeed it might almost be said that they were not affected exclusively and especially by any laws whatever.

"This is cursedly strange, Dick!" said M'Cleane.

"I don't like the look of it at all," returned Dick Flybynight; "Old Bilkit isn't used to keep such early hours."

"He's either turned parson, or the devil has flown away with him!" muttered the Captain; "however, we'll knock at all events."

And M'Cleane with the butt end of his whip gave a smart rap at the door.

Presently a casement over-head was cautiously opened, and the head and shoulders of Jerry Laggum, Tony Bilkit's man, made their appearance.

Jerry surveyed the highwaymen for a few minutes until he had satisfied himself who they were, and then observing that he would be down immediately, shut the window.

"Something has gone wrong, Dick, or I'm much mistaken."

"I feel a strange misgiving too, Captain," remarked Dick. "I hope to Heaven that all's right at 'The Chapel.'"

At this point of the conversation the withdrawal of bolts was heard, and the door was cautiously opened.

"Lead your horses round to the back of the house, noble gentlemen, and I'll open the stable-door; be cautious, for things hereabouts is in a werry ticklish persition, I tell yer," said Jerry Laggum, almost in a whisper.

The Highwaymen did as they were desired, and Jerry having put their horses in the stable invited them to accompany him into the house.

"Where's Bilkit?" asked M'Cleane and Dick Flybynight, both at once.

"He's in Newgate, thanks to Jonathan Wild," replied Jerry Laggum with some bitterness.

"What for?" asked M'Cleane.

"A bad job, worthy Captain, a werry bad job; 'deed there's two bad jobs again him, and I don't know which on 'em is the worst of the two," replied Jerry.

"For God's sake don't keep us in suspense," said M'Cleane hastily.

"He's charged with murder for one thing, Captain," said Jerry.

The mound of damp earth in the cellar, the displaced flag-stones, and the charnel-house effluvium of Bilkit's cellar, immediately recurred to M'Cleane's memory.

"But that would never have been found out, if Tony Bilkit hadn't been fool enough to leave drawing liquor and go into his old line again," continued Jerry.

"Talking of liquor, Jerry," said Dick Flybynight, "reminds me that I am devilish thirsty, I suppose if Tony is out the wine aint."

"Plenty of that, Master Flybynight," replied Jerry, as he, with great satisfaction, pocketted the guinea which Dick had placed on the table; in a few minutes afterwards a flask of Madeira made its appearance.

"Sit down, Jerry," said M'Cleane, "and tell us the particulars of this affair, for our time is short, and we are devilish anxious to be at home."

"Why, 'twas just this," said Jerry. "Poor Tony Bilkit got werry unhappy here, though he was drawing as much liquor as would have made him a decent fortune in a year or two. He kept a hankering arter his old trade, and when he was in low spirits he'd come into this parlour here, all by hisself, take out his picklocks and jemmy's and all his other tools, and spread 'em out afore him on this werry table. Then he'd talk to 'em just as if they'd been his children, and I werrily believe he loved 'em quite as much as if they had been, for he'd act'lly cry over 'em. If ever a man was in love with his perfession, Tony Bilkit was that man!"

Jerry stopped for a moment, quite overcome by his tender feelings; he drank off a glass of Madeira and continued:—

"Three nights ago, two cracksmen, Yorkshire Bob and Black Sandy came here to meet a third party as they was going with to break into a watchmaker's in Drury-lane. Somehow it happened that their partner didn't come, and they was obliged to have three to do the job."

"What must we do?" said Black Sandy to Yorkshire Bob, "it won't do to go without our pal; for one must keep watch, and another guard the old watchmaker, while t'other bags the booty."

"Must give it up for to-night, I s'pose," replied Yorkshire Bob, "though 'tis a mortal pity, for the old chaps servants and 'prentices have got a holiday to night, and we may never have such a chance again. Tony Bilkit, Captain, heard all this, and 'twas too much for him; he couldn't stand it that such a glorious opportunity should be lost, besides he longed to go to work again, he hesitated a few minutes and thought as tavern keeping was safest; but as he passed by the half open drawer where his old tools was, he happened to look at 'em, and that decided him."

"I'll volunteer to go with you, my covies," said Tony, rapping down his hard fist on the table.

"Black Sandy and Yorkshire Bob knew well enough what a tip top cracksman Tony was, so of course they were delighted with the offer, and to make a long story short, Captain, he went with 'em, and they did the job in a manner as any cracksman might be proud of."

"Well?" said M'Cleane, as Jerry paused to take another glass of comfort.

"Well!" resumed Jerry, "it unfortunately happened that Tony, who'd been a long time out of practice, hadn't tied the crape properly round his face, and when they was in the old man's room it fell off, and before he could replace it the watchmaker had marked him. Tony didn't know it though for the man was wise enough to hold his tongue; if he hadn't

Tony would have purwailed on him to be quiet with the but-end of a barker."

"No doubt of it," remarked M'Cleane, remembering the grave in the cellar.

"The consequence was," continued Jerry, "that next morning he gave such information to Master Watkins as induced that gentleman to come here with a search warrant: and the consequence was, that he found not only the watches, which formed Bilkit's portion of the booty; but summit as they didn't expect, and which made it a great deal worse for poor Tony."

"What could that be?" asked Dick Flyby-night.

"Body of a gen'leman in a hole in the cellar below," replied Jerry, "with his throat cut from ear to ear."

Dick Flybynight, to whom M'Cleane had not communicated the secret of the cellar, looked aghast, for, highwayman as he was, he abhorred the idea of secret assassination.

"So," said Jerry in conclusion, "they lugged off poor Tony, and left me to mind the casks and bottles; and if master don't come back again," he added, with a grin, "I shall drop into a good business without paying any goodwill for it."

"Any news of the 'Chapel,'" Jerry, asked the Captain.

"Bless me! Captain," said Jerry, "I'd quite forgot, Mistress Jenny was here this morning, and left a note for you in case you should call."

M'Cleane took the note and tore it open. As he perused it, the shade of anxiety which had clouded his fine features when it was placed in his hand gradually passed away and gave place to a smile.

"All is right, Dick!" said he, turning to Flybynight; "but we must not go to the 'Chapel' to-night."

The contents of the note were as follows:—

"DEAR JEM,—You had better not go to the 'Chapel' before you see me or to Madame Charlotte's either, as something has happened to Tony Bilkit, and 'tis said he wants to turn king's evidence; and should he do so he might tell some of our secrets, though I hope he will not. I have hired lodgings at Number —, King-street, Covent Garden, where I beseech of you to visit me as soon as you reach London. From your loving
"JENNY."

"The artful jade," said M'Cleane, as he folded the note, "she's jealous of Madame Charlotte."

"Selfish animals, these women!" responded Dick Flybynight, "they must either have all or none."

"But;" laughingly, said M'Cleane, "but Dick, how precious few women are there who get all."

"Right!" remarked Dick, "that same constancy is a very pretty thing for a man to talk about; but you know as well as I do, M'Cleane, that it's a cursedly difficult thing to put into practice."

"It's time for us to be moving, Dick," said M'Cleane, "how do you intend to bestow your-self for the night, for I shall be off to Covent Garden."

"Oh! never heed me;" replied Dick, "I shall stumble across some blowen or other, I'll engage."

Leaving their nags in charge of Jerry Laggum, who they handsomely rewarded for the recommendation, M'Cleane and Dick Flybynight quitted the 'Jolly Pedlars' and strolled towards Long Acre.

They had turned from the well known locality into the broad space where the market was held, when the clashing of swords startled them; but the night was so intensely dark that they could not discern any object a yard before them.

"Some midnight brawlers from the Hummums, or one of the other coffee-houses in the neighbourhood," remarked M'Cleane, "we had better not interfere."

And they were about to resume their walk, when loud cries of "Help," "Watch," were heard.

"Some one in need of assistance; and by G—d! I'll render it if I can," said M'Cleane, as he rushed forwards in the direction whence the sounds proceeded followed by Dick Flybynight.

They had proceeded about twenty yards when by the dim light of a street lamp they perceived three men fighting; two were furiously attacking a third, who defended himself with all the energy of despair.

The instant before M'Cleane and Dick came up to them, the man who appeared to be the attacked party staggered and fell; the sword of one of his assailants having passed through his chest. Dick instantly flew to his assistance, while M'Cleane attacked the victor, for one person only now remained, the other having slunk off under cover of the darkness as soon as he saw the two highwaymen approach.

M'Cleane easily wounded and disarmed his opponent, who begged for mercy.

"I should never have drawn upon the gentleman," he said, "had it not been for Mr. Doom, who promised me a large reward to dispatch him."

"Doom—Doom," muttered M'Cleane, "surely I should know that name."

"Doom, the lawyer of Gray's Inn," added the would-be assassin.

"Jem!" exclaimed Dick Flybynight, "there is some mystery in this which I cannot understand; the wounded man here appears to know you and me, for before he swooned in my arms he mentioned both our names."

At this moment one of the watch came up.

The man whom M'Cleane had disabled, observing the guardian of the night approach, fell on his knees before M'Cleane, entreating not to be given into custody, and promising if mercy was shown him that he would divulge all he knew concerning the matter.

"More brawling—more swords drawing," said the Charley, "why, these tavern-gallants give us more trouble than all London besides. What have we here? a dead man; if so, it's a case of murder, and he who committed it must go to the watch-house."

Whispering a word of assurance in the ear

of the fellow who had implored his lenity, M'Cleane looked at the insensible person who lay on the pavement, with his head on the knee of Dick Flybynight.

By the aid of the watchman's lantern he at once recognised the features of Flitchman. This circumstance, connected with the name of Doom, and the information he had received from Handsome Jack respecting this man, coupled with the fact of his having been attesting witness to Doom's signature to the document drawn up in the lawyer's office, convinced him that some mischief was intended to Handsome Jack, with whose affair he felt certain the present affray was connected.

Slipping a gold piece into the hands of the guardian of the night, he informed him that the parties implicated in the brawl were some friends of his who had been taking too much wine at a tavern; and hinted that he would take care of them. The old charley was well enough pleased with the solid explanation, and went on his way crying the hour without further interfering in the matter.

M'Cleane was placed in a position of some difficulty. What to do with Flitchman and the other wounded man he knew not; but of neither he determined to lose sight. It would not do to take the stranger to Madame Charlotte's, and Flitchman's case required immediate surgical attention. How was he to act?

While revolving these matters in his mind, a young girl, attracted by curiosity, joined the group. She was evidently one of those unfortunates who, to gain a precarious subsistence, wander the live-long night, through the streets in all weathers, subject to the pity of none, the insults of many, and the contempt of all.

"Why, Dick," exclaimed the girl, "is that you? I've been looking for you this many a day, and to think now that I should have lighted on you at last!"

"Who's that?" asked M'Cleane of Dick Flybynight.

"What don't you know her, Jem?" asked Dick in return. "Why, it's Sal, the Gonnoff."

M'Cleane remembered in a moment that this was the girl who had, on some former occasion, performed with the utmost faithfulness a service of some importance to one of his gang, and a thought suddenly struck him that she might be of service in the present emergency, for he was well aware that she resided with Mother Sin, in the Almonry; and he himself possessed some influence over that amiable old lady.

After a short consultation, therefore, with Dick and the girl, it was determined that the two wounded men should at once be removed to Westminster; and a hackney-carriage having been procured, the five got into it, and ere long arrived at the house of the bawd.

Without entering into minute particulars it may be sufficient to state that, for a certain consideration, Mother Sin undertook to shelter and provide for the wounded men, and Sal, the Gonnoff engaged to nurse them.

Before, however, M'Cleane departed, he learned from Flitchman's assailant that he had been employed by Doom to perpetrate the infamous deed; for what purpose the reader will, in the course of this tale, be duly informed.

"I think I shall stay here with Sal, the Gonnoff, to night," said Dick, "and by so doing I shall effect a double purpose, please myself and see to the condition of Flitchman."

M'Cleane now once more took his way to Covent Garden, and having arrived in King Street he speedily found out Jenny Diver, who received him with open arms, and it may be easily conceived, that, after the fatigues and anxieties to which M'Cleane had been subjected during the last few days, the blandishments of the beautiful girl were not unwelcome.

After the first transports of their meeting were over, Jenny explained to the Captain the reason why she had engaged lodgings away from the "Chapel;" it was that she might be in the immediate neighbourhood of the large theatres, where she hoped to reap a golden harvest during the coming season.

"I have engaged a real footman now, Jem," she said, "and, therefore, you must drop the livery and assume a new character."

"And what may that be?" asked the Captain.

"That of a gentleman," she replied, "and it will be strange indeed, if we cannot make the public find you a handsome income."

"This is an awkward affair of Bilkit's," remarked Jenny, as she and her favorite sat down to a supper consisting of the most rare viands, and the choicest wines.

"But even that," observed M'Cleane, "I hope to turn to our advantage;" he then informed Jenny of the adventures in Covent Garden Market.

"Bilkit's mouth must be stopped, so far as we are concerned at least," said Jenny.

"And it shall be; this attempted assassination of Flitchman has furnished me with the means of doing so; but come, Jenny, let us to bed, for I must be stirring early. There is too much danger threatening us for me to be idle," said M'Cleane.

So drawing a veil around the mysteries of the exquisitely adorned bed-chamber of Jenny and the Captain, we leave that happy pair to themselves and proceed with our tale.

The first care of M'Cleane on the following morning was to visit Newgate for the purpose of seeing Bilkit. If it was true as Jenny had informed him that Tony intended to turn king's evidence, and reveal the secrets of many of his former accomplices, not a moment was to be lost.

So completely disguising himself in a sober suit of black, that his most intimate acquaintance would not have known him, he fearlessly proceeded to that dark abode of misery and crime—Newgate.

On reaching the gate he accosted a grim turnkey, and requested to be admitted to the interior of the gaol, accompanying his request with a guinea.

"Who d'ye want to see?" asked the turnkey, "Bob Burke who is to be hanged to-morrow for highway robbery, 'cause if you do you must tip another canary; he's in the condemned cell and in a werry comfortable state of mind."

"No, not him; I'm a lawyer's clerk," said

M'Cleane, "and want to see one Anthony Bilkit."

"Wants to get a job, Master 'torney, I s'pose, said the turnkey, "well now, you may save yourself the trouble, for Tony is going to turn king's evidence and peach all his old chums."

"But I suppose I may speak to him," said the Captain. "Go on, master, he's in the yard to the left of the passage," said the turnkey, gruffly; and M'Cleane entered the yard, where he espied Bilkit seated on a stone bench, and drinking merrily with some pot companions.

Taking an opportunity of catching Bilkit's eye, he made a private signal and Tony was by his side instantly.

"Come to some private place, Bilkit, and don't look as though you know me; I am come to serve and perhaps to save you."

They went into Bilkit's cell, and M'Cleane said—"Is it true, Tony, that you intend to blow the gaff on your old pals?"

"Why, damn it, Captain, I don't want to do it; but if I don't you see they'll string me up as sure as my name's Tony Bilkit," replied the prisoner.

"But suppose, Tony," suggested M'Cleane, "that you could be got clear off without peaching."

"That's impossible, it can't be done," said Bilkit, interrupting him; "why, they found the stolen watches in my house, and the murdered man in my cellar. If that aint enough to hang a man, I don't know what is, Captain?"

"But I tell you it can and shall be done if you follow my advice," said M'Cleane, with earnestness, for he knew that it was in the power of Bilkit to effect the utter ruin of him and his gang; Tony having formerly been one of its members.

"Your advice!" exclaimed Tony. "I must have a lawyer's advice to get out of this scrape, and a pretty 'cute one's too, for 'tis a tough case; but if I thought there was a chance, I'd run the risk and not turn traitor."

"Well," said M'Cleane, "to offer you a lawyer at my expense was the object of my coming here. What do you think, Tony, of Mr. Doom?"

"Why," replied Tony, "he's a most infernal rogue to be sure; but, then, if he wasn't he wouldn't do for a rogues lawyer."

"Would you be satisfied and decline to turn king's evidence, and avoid being despised by all honourable men of all classes if he undertook your case?" asked the Captain.

"That would I," he replied; "if there's any man as can get me clear through this, it's Doom."

"And he shall get you off, Tony; so we will if you please consider the matter settled," observed M'Cleane.

"Certainly," remarked Tony, "make yourself quite easy, Captain; I feels my spirits revived by this visit."

"Well, make yourself as happy as you can, my Ben Cul," said M'Cleane, "and here, take these goldfinches, they're capital birds to sing in a prison."

"Werry much obliged, Captain, 'specially as that sneaking villain of mine, Jerry Laggum, havn't sent me a shilling."

"If you are prudent you will not want friends," said the Captain. "Farewell, Tony, I'll go at once to Mr. Doom's and lay your case before him."

M'Cleane quitted the prison, and, taking his way up Holborn Hill, soon arrived at Mr. Doom's Chambers in Gray's Inn.

Tim Snarley was amazingly intent on a drawing from a design of his own, representing a gallows with his master suspended therefrom, when M'Cleane entered the office.

"Is Mr. Wriggleton Doom at home?" asked M'Cleane.

"Seen you afore somewhere," said Tim Snarley, looking earnestly into the Captain's face.

"Answer my question," exclaimed M'Cleane.

"Well, then, Mr. Doom is at home," replied Tim.

"I must see him, and that immediately," said M'Cleane, giving the boy a shilling.

The Captain was then ushered into Doom's office. The lawyer was seated at his desk, to all appearance deeply engaged in perusing a deed. He raised his eyes as M'Cleane entered.

"Your business, sir," said Doom, after having pointed M'Cleane to a seat.

"I wish to engage you to defend a friend of mine who is now in Newgate," said the Captain.

"On what charge," asked the lawyer.

"He has committed a burglary," replied M'Cleane, "and it is of the utmost importance that he should be got off. You are the man who can and who must effect this object."

"Must!" said Doom.

"Yes; I don't mince matters, Mr. Doom," remarked M'Cleane, "I say must."

"If a suitable fee be paid me, I'll do my best, and I've no doubt of succeeding," insinuated Doom.

"I shall not pay you one farthing, Mr. Doom," said M'Cleane firmly, "and yet this man must and shall be saved by you."

"Do you think me mad?" asked the lawyer.

"Not in the least," replied M'Cleane.

"Then I tell you at once," said Doom, now in a towering passion, "that I'll have nothing to do with the case."

"And I beg to tell you, Mr. Doom, that unless you undertake it, aye, and succeed too, I will let the Bow Street magistrates know something about a certain forged deed, and an attempt at murder," said M'Cleane.

"At murder!" exclaimed Doom, turning pale.

"Yes; and no longer ago than last night. Your tool is already in my power and has confessed all;—your intended victim is also at my disposal. You see, therefore, the necessity of your complying with my present request," said M'Cleane.

Doom was compelled to submit, and before M'Cleane quitted him he put him into possession of all the particulars of the case. Having thus far expedited the business he returned to Newgate and informed Tony that Doom had been engaged to get him off.

Mr. Bilkit, very much relieved in mind since the Captain had first visited him, had got so amazingly drunk that it was exceedingly difficult to make him understand that Doom would visit him next day. Having, however, at length succeeded in impressing that important fact upon his mind; M'Cleane hurried off to Jenny Diver's lodgings in Covent Garden.

CHAPTER XXIII.

LIFE IN A SPONGING HOUSE—THREE SHARPS AND A FLAT;—AND HOW MR. WOLLAND BE-FRIENDED SIR JAMES TOWN.

WHEN Sir James Town was first introduced into the Sponging House of the Sheriff's Officer, he shrank back in disgust, for the place was anything but pleasant. There was a reeking odour of tobacco smoke—there were countenances indicative of vulgarity and low cunning. Not one single man in that cage of unwhitewashed birds had an honest expression of countenance.

"Here's another," said a man who looked as though he had not shaved since the time when he first imagined a head.

"Don't be down, old cock!"

This last remark was accompanied by a tremendous slap on the shoulder from the speaker.

"You'll soon get out again; that is, if old Wolland will let you," croaked another voice.

"In for much?" drawled out a man with a long pipe.

"For more than I can pay at the moment," replied Sir James Town.

"P'raps I could help you," suggested the man with the long pipe.

"If you can I should be very much obliged to you," replied Sir James Town.

"Wolland can accommodate you I dare say; that is if you pay him well for the accommodation," said the man with the long pipe; "but he's a thorough villain. But here he comes," and the speaker sauntered away.

If ever any man's countenance was an index of his mind and character, that of Wolland's the Sheriff's officer was. He had a low receding forehead, from which grey hair was brushed stiffly up; a pair of small dark furtively glancing eyes, which were deeply set beneath black shaggy eyebrows; a nose of that description known as pug; a large mouth and under jaw. He was rather corpulent, somewhat knock-need, and taken altogether, a man whose appearance would have more unfavourably inspired, could not well be met with.

"Hope you are comfortable, Sir Jeems," said the officer, rubbing his hands, and grinning diabolically.

"And pray, what am I to pay for staying here?" asked the baronet.

"Only ten shillings a day for lodging; and you can order what you like to eat and drink, Sir Jeems," replied Wolland.

"Not over moderate that, I think," said Town; "but, at all events, I shall stay here for the present. But I should like to have a private room."

"That 'ud be a guinea a-day, Sir Jeems," hinted the officer.

"Will it!" said the baronet, "then I'll e'en be content with this;" and at the request of Wolland, having paid a week's lodging in advance, he took a seat in one corner of the room.

And bitter indeed were his reflections; there he was shut up with some of the vilest characters of the day; but this was not that which pained him most. He had been over-reached by the very man against whom he had employed his own stratagems; and he was at the mercy of the person, whoever he was, who was in possession of the fatal forged deed. Every time he shuddered with apprehension, for he knew not how soon he might be dragged to another and more terrible place of confinement to that in which he then was, and on a much more serious business.

Two long dreary nights and days passed away in a state of misery; but on the third morning of his imprisonment a visitor was announced.

"Here's lawyer Doom wants to see you, Sir Jeems," said Wolland, thrusting in his great head, "shall he come up here or will you have a private room to converse in?"

The Baronet by no means relished the idea of talking over delicate affairs in the presence of such persons as those by whom he was surrounded, so he informed Mr. Wolland that he would adopt the latter alternative.

"Five shillings, then, Sir Jeems, if you please," said the officer, holding out his great vulgar-looking hand for the fee, which having received he conducted Sir James into an apartment about the size of a decent cupboard, whose only furniture consisted of a table and two chairs.

"I'll bring Mr. Doom directly," said Wolland, as he left the cupboard, the door of which, as he departed, he carefully locked.

Presently the door was again opened and the lawyer made his appearance; he had an ironical smile on his countenance as he approached Sir James, who received him coldly.

"A pretty trick you've played, Mr. Doom," said Town, as soon as Wolland had retired and they were alone.

"And a pretty trick you were going to play me, Town, if I hadn't prevented you," returned the lawyer; "why, if I had not caught you on the wing you might have been in Holland, laughing at me in your sleeve at this moment."

"And how long do you mean to keep me cooped up in this damned hole?" asked Sir James.

"Till I'm paid my bill," drily returned Mr. Doom.

"That is impossible; I havn't as much ready money as would pay half of it, even were the charges fair, which you know are not."

"Why," remarked Doom, "when you get people to do jobs for you by which they peril their necks, you must pay extra of course. Now, I'm come to offer you fair terms, and if you don't accede to them you will adorn Tyburn Tree before you are three months older; if you do you shall have your liberty to proceed whither you choose."

"Name them," said Sir James Town.

DOOM'S VISIT TO BILKIT IN NEWGATE.

"You remember my showing you a few days ago a letter from Mr. Rowland Ferret, attorney-at-law, respecting the claims of one Richard Town," asked Doom.

"Perfectly," replied the baronet.

"Mr. Ferret has been to my chambers this morning," continued the lawyer, "and he is determined to prosecute Richard's claim; more than that he has the forged deed in his possession."

Sir James started and turned pale.

"In his possession?" he exclaimed.

"Exactly so; and he is on the track of Mrs. Snolley, Betty Larkin and Flitchman," said Doom.

This was indeed a shock to Sir James, and he now gave himself up to a paroxysm of rage and despair; but the lawyer hinted that there might be a way of escape after all.

No. 14.

"In God's name how?" ejaculated the agitated man of fashion.

"You see," said Doom, "you owe me a considerable sum, and that I am possessed of a dangerous secret. There cannot be a doubt but that Richard Town will succeed in this action and oust you out of all. Now, would it not be better for you to save a part, and by leaving the country, to save your neck into the bargain?"

"Undoubtedly," remarked Sir James in an agony.

"Then I'll put you in the way of doing it," insinuated the wily lawyer. You have houses and lands still at your disposal, and none can prevent your disposing of them. Give me a written undertaking to do so as payment for my bill, and you shall retain the ready money you now possess, have your instantaneous discharge and be free to go wherever you please."

"You are driving a hard bargain, Doom," said Sir James, "why, the houses and estates are worth ten times the amount of your bill."

"But what will they be worth to you if I choose to let you stay here until you are taken to Newgate, and from thence to Tyburn, as you certainly will if you do not accede to my proposal?" asked the lawyer.

"And how will you escape; you, an accomplice in the fraud?" asked Sir James.

"Leave that to me, Town," replied Doom, "I'll manage it depend on it. Have you decided?"

Sir James pondered deeply for a few moments, and then seeing that he had no other chance signified his assent.

Doom foreseeing this compliance had prepared and brought with him the necessary legal documents, and Mr. Wolland having been summoned to witness Sir James's signature, Mr. Doom presented the officer with the prisoners discharge, and he was at liberty to depart.

But whither was he to go; he dared not return to the mansion at Tottenham Court—his indeed no longer; and he did not feel inclined to join the circle of his former companions at the coffee-houses or taverns. He, therefore, determined to conceal himself at Madam Singleton's, until an opportunity offered of quitting the country. This resolution, however, he did not communicate to the lawyer, who wished the baronet farewell and went homeward, chuckling at the success of his scheme, for such it was, no such visit having been paid him by Ferret as he described; and as to the forged deeds being in that persons hands, it was entirely a surmise of his own.

And the once gay and rich Sir James Town had so far fallen as to be compelled to seek protection in the house of a procuress! Madame Singleton, however, he determined should not be aware of the real cause of his so doing, as he deemed it not at all probable that she would afford him shelter if she knew his circumstances, such characters only give their good offices for gold.

"Werry sorry to lose your company, Sir Jeems," said Mr. Wolland, as soon as the lawyer was gone; "but can stay till dark you know, and over a friendly bottle I might perhaps introduce you to one or two gentlemen who could put you up to a dodge or two if you're low in pocket."

Sir James was low in pocket. As he did not care to quit the Sponging House in the day time he determined to remain; so he requested Mr. Wolland to order a dinner at a neighbouring tavern for himself and his two friends.

"That's something like business, Sir Jeems," said Wolland, as he took some gold from the baronet's hand to pay for the repast, "you're a gentleman every inch, and as I said afore I'm sorry as you're going."

"I'll tell you some of my adventures by and by, Sir Jeems. Why, a man never need want money if he aint werry partick'lar how he gets it," said Wolland with a self-satisfied air.

"Will you," said the baronet, hardly know-

ing what he said, for his thoughts was engaged with Doom's affair.

"What's the use of being down-hearted. Why, look you here now, if I was like you, a baronet, and had a handle to my name, instead of being plain Will Wolland, I'd live in clover at other people's expense."

Sir James considered within himself that that was very much like what he had been doing, and his thoughts reverted to the man whom he had defrauded of his inheritance.

After this conversation Wolland left Sir James, but rejoined him again about three o'clock, when he introduced two persons fashionably attired, named Jesson and Cook, who he stated were merchants in the city, with whom he was in the habit of doing business, and who were anxious to be of service to Sir James.

It should be mentioned that Wolland was fully aware that Sir James Town had a few hundred pounds in his possession. Mr. Doom having informed him of that fact before the arrest.

The dinner having been dispatched with not a little gusto by the four gentlemen, the bottle began to circulate freely, and before long Sir James had forgotten all his troubles; in fact he reached that point of intoxication, when the senses begin to be affected although the judgment is not deteriorated.

This was the very state into which, for their own vile purposes, Messrs. Wolland, Jesson and Cook, had sought to bring Sir James; but these worthies had taken especial care not to exceed the bounds of moderation themselves; although each of them acted as though they were under the influence of the juice of the grape.

After a short interval of silence Mr. Jesson informed Mr. Wolland that they were getting devilish "slow," and asked the latter gentleman if they couldn't have in candles and amuse themselves in some way.

"I should like a quiet game at cards," said Mr. Cook, "what d'ye say, Sir James?"

"Why, to tell you the truth gentlemen," replied the baronet, "I'm not in the humour for play just now; besides I've not got much to risk, and——"

"Pooh—pooh, Sir James!" interrupted Mr. Wolland, "my friends don't play for the sake of winning; besides you're as likely to win as any of us; or if what every one says is true, you've cleaned out many in your time."

Sir James rather winced at this; for bad as he was he considered himself vastly superior to the respectable sheriff's officer, and his proud spirit could not brook being accused of cleaning out any one; although Mr. Wolland was not very far from the truth in his observation.

"Well! I don't care about a rubber or two, then," said the baronet; "but remember, gentlemen, I don't play high."

"Nor do we," chimed in Messrs. Cook and Jesson.

"Blowed if I do either," growled Mr. Wolland.

Candles and cards were then brought in, and after Sir James had been plied with a few more glasses of wine they cut for partners.

"You and I, Sir James," said Mr. Jesson,

when that operation had been performed to his satisfaction.

"And it's our deal," said Mr. Wolland, after another cutting to Mr. Cook, who sat opposite him.

They played the first rub for half guineas and Sir James Town won; the next game the stakes increased, and still the baronet was triumphant, and so he continued to be until his partner, Mr. Jesson, with a knowing glance at Wolland and his partner, which spoke as plainly as words, what muffs they are, said to Sir James—

"Suppose we make it five guineas a corner."

"With all my heart," replied the baronet, tossing off a tumbler of canary.

If Jesson had proposed fifty guineas a corner he would have assented, for success had vanished scruples, and the wine had inspired him with a dare-devil sort of courage. In fact the spirit of gambling had taken entire possession of his mind.

The tide of success now turned, and Sir James very speedily lost all he had won; but what thorough gambler was ever checked by a reverse? In the hope of recovering himself he proposed Twenty guinea stakes, then forty, then sixty, and still he lost.

"We must win presently," said Jesson, "such luck as theirs never can last long."

Sir James Town appeared to be of the same opinion, for the cash in his pockets, all indeed that he now had in the world, was fast decreasing, he put down stake after stake with a desperate energy, and with few exceptions was yet on the losing side.

He had now but fifteen guineas remaining; and, in the forlorn hope that even yet the luck might turn in his favour, he determined to risk that.

With a rigid brow, firmly set teeth, and trembling hands he commenced the game, for a time fortune seemed to favour him, and his hopes revived. To cheer his spirits and nerve him he quaffed more wine, and exercised his utmost skill, but in vain.

"Game!" said Mr. Wolland, as he threw down his last card. "Will you try another rubber, Sir Jeems," said that worthy as he picked up two of the heaps of gold, and pushed the other to his partner, Mr. Cook. ·

"D——n it, no," said the baronet, "I've lost every guinea; but stay, if you lend me fifty out of what you've won of me, Wolland, I don't mind taking another hand."

"Don't mind that, Sir Jeems, always like to oblige a friend; but it must be on one condition."

"What is that, pray?" asked the baronet.

"Your gold watch is worth say thirty guineas, and the diamond ring on your finger ten more, that's forty. Now, it's my wish to be liberal. I'll hand you fifty guineas on them and you see that's ten more than they're worth."

The watch was worth eighty guineas, and the ring thirty at the least; but Sir James accepted the terms, and handed the articles to Wolland, who gave him fifty guineas in exchange.

"'Pon my soul, partner, you must try and play more carefully," said Mr. Jesson to Sir James. "I can't account for this run of ill-luck, except that you play wildly."

Thirty of the fifty guineas soon changed hands; and the last twenty was on the point of departing, when accidentally looking at his partner, Mr. Jesson, he observed that gentleman turn the faces of the cards for a second towards Wolland and give him a look full of meaning.

Starting from his seat, and snatching up his twenty guineas which he deposited in his purse, he exclaimed:—

"Infernal fool that I was not to have suspected this before."

"Suspected what," cried Wolland, Jesson, and Cook, also rising.

"That each and all of you are scoundrelly cheats, and that you have been plundering me all the evening," said Sir James Town.

"Put down your money and finish the game, and then I'll settle this affair with you," said Jesson."

"Never!" said the baronet.

"Then by G—d! you shall never leave this place with it alive," roared the sheriff's officer.

"Who dares prevent me?" asked the baronet, drawing his sword.

"I do; and I am master here, I believe," said Wolland, "so the best thing you can do is either to hand over the shiners, or to finish the game and play for them like a man of honor."

"Begin the game again, then," demanded Sir James, who now perfectly sobered saw that he was in a trap from which he could only escape by finesse.

To this the other three agreed and they again sat down to the game.

From what has already been stated the result may be easily imagined. Sir James Town rose from the table without a solitary guinea in his possession.

The full horror of his situation now burst upon him. Abject and with want staring him in the face, his position was by no means enviable. With his money his pride was gone, and he even stooped so low as to beg the loan of five guineas from Wolland.

"Couldn't do it, Sir Jeems," replied the bailiff, "and if I could I should like to know when and how you could pay me again?"

"Then I'll go," said the baronet; and he was about to quit the Sponging House when he was interrupted by Wolland—

"I'm werry sorry, Sir Jeems; but you can't go just yet."

"How so," exclaimed the baronet in surprise, "the debt and costs of Mr. Doom are paid, are they not?"

"That's right enough, they are," replied Wolland.

"Then on what grounds do you dare to detain me?" asked the puzzled and terrified Sir James.

"There's a detainer put in against you," coolly replied Wolland.

"A detainer! and at whose instance," he enquired.

"A sort of half-and-half relation of yours, I believe," returned the officer. "One Richard

Town, Ferret's his lawyer, and 'tis for a swing-ing sum too, Master."

Sir James staggered to a chair, and burried his face in his hands.

"It arnt no use to snivel about it," said Wolland. "What d'ye mean to do? You've got three days to stay here as you paid for in advance; but that won't buy you grub you see, and arter that time you must go to New-gate."

"Why not the Queen's Bench or the Fleet?" asked Sir James Town. "Newgate is only a place for felons, I believe."

"It's the County gaol," replied the artful bailiff. "But, Sir Jeems, if you'll follow my advice, I think as I might get you out of your difficulties."

"How?" asked the baronet.

"I'll procure bail for you, and then we must work together, replied Wolland.

"What am I to do, then?" asked the per-plexed baronet.

"As soon as you are out I'll take a house for you a little way out of town, and recom-mend you to tradesmen who shall supply you with all you require on credit. A chariot will dazzle and delude them, and you may once more enter the circles of fashion," said Wol-land.

"But how on earth am I to pay for all this?" asked the baronet.

"Easily enough," replied Wolland, "there are plenty of heiresses who would jump at a man of your face and manners. Do you un-derstand me; long before you are called on to pay the debts you may make a fortune by mar-riage."

"I see," said Sir James, who, however, hesi-tated to give a positive answer.

"You must make up your mind at once, Sir Jeems," urged the officer, "for I can procure bail in an hour."

The offer was too dazzling to be rejected by one who had long since taken his first step on the pathway of crime; so taking Wolland's hand he said—

"I agree to your proposal, and if you thus serve me I shall be eternally obliged to you."

Alas! Sir James Town little thought of the pit which was being dug for him.

In little more than an hour a hackney car-riage was called, and Sir James, Wolland, Mr. Jesson and Mr. Cook all got into it, and pro-ceeded to the office of the Sheriff in Chancery-lane.

There Messrs. Jesson and Cook tendered themselves as Sir James Town's bail and were accepted; the whole four then returned to Wol-land's house to arrange their schemes.

But what those schemes were, and to what results they led, must be left for a future chapter to develope.

CHAPTER XXIV.

HOW JENNY DIVER LEFT HER LODGINGS—
AND HOW THE LANDLADY WAS PAID.

THE ready furnished lodgings which Jenny Diver now occupied in Covent Garden, were fitted up in the most costly and elegant style; and to support her claims to the character of a woman of quality, she now hired a real footman; Bristol Ann acting in the capacity of lady's maid.

M'Cleane, who had formerly supported the character of footman now laid it aside, and as-sumed the appearance of a private gentleman.

'The Chapel,' near Long Acre was once more occupied, for not being aware of the re-turn of Blackmoor and no further trouble hav-ing been given by Watkins or Jonathan Wild's emissary, Mary Milliner, it was not deemed necessary to adopt more than the ordinary precautions.

Although Jenny Diver had ceased to be a resident of the 'Chapel,' she still continued to be in all other respects a member of the fraternity, and always attended their business meetings. Indeed, her marvellous dexterity and success had acquired her so much influ-ence that her opinion was invariably called for, and her word was law.

There was something generous in Jenny's disposition which really endeared her to all excepting Madame Charlotte, who to tell the truth, had began to feel a little jealous of her young rival; not it must be confessed without cause, for before the introduction of the latter, M'Cleane, who she doated upon, had alone revelled in her charms.

At one of the meetings of the gang, Jenny proposed to her associates that a tenth part of the general produce should be set aside for the support of such of the members as might through illness be rendered incapable of pur-suing their iniquitous occupations.

This proposition was readily agreed to, and three cheers were given for Jenny, as she re-tired from the 'Chapel' for the purpose of proceeding to her lodgings.

We must now, for a time, follow the ever fertile and artful creature in her adventurous course.

Passing, one morning, attended by her foot-man, the Theatre in Drury Lane, she observed it announced that that evening the king would be present.

Such an opportunity was not to be lost; she, therefore, immediately sent her footman to se-cure her a box in one of the most fashionable and conspicuous parts of the house. This ob-ject having been effected she returned to her lodgings.

That evening, having dressed herself in the most elegant manner, and greatly heightened the effects of her natural charms by resorting to those aids so well known to women of fashion, Jenny had a chair called, and desiring her foot-man to follow her until she reached her box, and to wait outside its door until she required his services, she proceeded to the theatre.

The house presented indeed a brilliant ap-pearance, it was absolutely one blaze of light. To do honour to the sovereign nearly all the great and titled of the land, then in town were present, and the waving of feathers—the beamings of bright eyes—the flashings of in-numerable diamonds, rubies and other gems formed a brilliant *coup d'œil*. But amongst all that courtly and aristocratic assemblage there was not one, who in youth, radiance and loveliness excelled our adventuress, Jenny Diver.

During the interval of one of the acts she retired from the box, and summoning her footman, she mingled in the crowd of persons who assembled in the lobby and saloon, and contived to purloin a gold snuff-box, with which she got safely off to her place in the theatre.

She attempted to follow up her success when the next act was over, and repaired to the saloon for that purpose; but hearing it reported that the gentleman had discovered his loss and was making active search for the thief, she determined to abandon 'diving' for that evening, and trust to chance and her own ingenuity for a booty.

The play had nearly terminated, when her footman knocked at the door of her box and informed her that a gentleman wished to speak with her.

Jenny, with a dignified and modest air, requested that he should be admitted, and the gentleman, bowing profoundly to the girl, entered the box.

He was a very handsome young fellow, and attired in the first style of fashion. Jenny saw at once that he was a man of fortune, and slightly blushing, begged to know why she had been honoured with his visit, at the same time pointing the gallant to a seat beside her.

"Charming creature!" exclaimed the young fellow, "I could not resist the temptation to make the acquaintance of one who has made an absolute conquest of my heart."

"Sir!" said Jenny, half concealing her face with her fan.

"For the last two hours I have seen nothing but your lovely face, exclaimed the innamorata. "Pardon me, madam; but unless you comply with one request which I have to make I shall expire."

Jenny now saw that a chance offered itself of doing business in her own peculiar way; a fish was nibbling, and she determined to hook it.

"What is your request, sir?" asked Jenny Diver.

"That, at the conclusion of the performance, divine creature, you will grant me the felicity and favour of attending you home," replied the young spark.

"No, sir," said Jenny, "I am shocked and surprised at such a proposition from an utter stranger. If you knew who I am, sir, you would not venture to make such a request."

"Whoever you are, I am madly, irrecoverably in love with you; let me beseech you to listen to me; I am rich and influential, and I am—"

"But, sir," said Jenny, interrupting him, "I am a newly married woman, and the appearance of a stranger might alarm my husband."

Jenny cast such a tender look on the gallant as she said this that he redoubled his entreaties, and after much apparent hesitation she yielded.

The play being over, Jenny requested her footman to return home, and was then handed by her gallant to a hackney coach.

"You must not come to my husband's door," said Jenny, as the carriage drew near to her lodgings; "it is as well you should be set down here."

"But when shall we meet again, my charmer?" asked the gallant, pressing Jenny's hand.

"To morrow," replied the Diver, "my husband will quit town on business for three days; my residence is at No. — King Street."

"Shall I then have the happiness of visiting you to-morrow evening?" asked the impetuous young fellow.

"Yes; but be careful," said Jenny, "for should my husband hear of your visit I am a lost woman."

"For whom shall I enquire?" asked the delighted spark.

"Mrs. Young," replied Jenny.

The young fellow was then set down, and Jenny proceeded home; from whence, having changed her dress, she hurried to the 'Chapel.'

"What luck at the play, Jenny?" was the general question as the girl entered the saloon.

"Only a gold sneezer case," replied Jenny, placing the snuff-box on the table.

A universal murmur of disappointment followed this assertion.

"Why, Jenny, you havn't lost the knack, have you?" asked Handsome Jack, who was dandling Gipsey Betty on his knee.

"Nor beginning to grow funky?" enquired Dick Flybynight.

"Neither!" exclaimed Jenny, stamping her little foot on the soft carpet, and her eyes flashing with something like indignation at these undeserved taunts. "Neither! and you, Dick, and you too, Handsome Jack, ought to know me better, than to suppose I am less skilful than of late, or that I am turning more grave."

Here Captain M'Cleane entered the saloon.

"What's in the wind now, Jenny?" he asked, as he observed the girl standing in an attitude of scorn, and her lip curved with pride.

"A trifle, Jem, a mere trifle," replied Jenny; "but you would not have trifled with me as some here have done," and throwing herself on a sofa she burst into a flood of hysterical tears.

Handsome Jack and Dick Flybynight, who really meant not to wound Jenny's feelings, were much grieved at this effect of their remarks. Jenny Diver soon recovered her equanimity. Explanations ensued and all were at peace again.

The usual night banquet was now served, and during its continuance Jenny Diver informed her comrades of her adventure with the young gentleman at the theatre, and her determination to turn it to her and their benefit. This announcement thoroughly restored good humour, and Jenny was loaded with praises.

It was then arranged that Dick Flybynight and Handsome Jack should on the coming evening act as footmen, and in case of necessity that M'Cleane should play the part of the injured husband. All the preliminaries having been discussed and agreed to, Jenny, accompanied by M'Cleane, returned to her lodgings.

Shortly before the time in the evening of the following day that the gentleman was expected, Jenny, beautifully dressed, awaited his arrival in her drawing-room. Her two footmen, equipped in elegant liveries, were in attendance, and Bristol Ann appeared to be the very pink of lady's maids.

About nine o'clock a carriage drove to the door, and one of the footmen having opened it, admitted the amorous young gentleman, and conducted him through the hall, where the other false footman respectfully saluted him, and led him to the drawing-room.

The lover was superbly attired in a peach blossom coloured velvet coat, an embroidered waistcoat, and white satin breeches. He had a gold headed clouded cane in his hand, a golden hilted sword by his side, a gold watch in his pocket, and his fingers were half covered with diamond rings.

"That will do," said Jenny to herself, as the spark bowed himself into her presence.

A choice supper had been prepared; and after the young gentleman had further stimulated his passions by sundry draughts of geneva, he hinted, to his fair one, his wish to retire to a more delicate banquet than that which she had already provided.

Jenny then, with much seeming bashfulness, introduced him into her bed chamber, and handed him her own jewel case, in which he might deposit his watch, rings, money and valuables.

Pleased with this delicate attention, the young fellow placed all his treasures in her hands, and then commenced undressing himself. Jenny affected to do the same; but, as every one knows, gentlemen are much more speedy in matters of this sort than the softer sex, it is not to be wondered at that the gentleman was undressed first.

The gallant now jumped into bed, where he had not been two minutes before a rap was heard at the door.

"Mercy on me," exclaimed Jenny, huddling on her gown again, "who can this be," and she cautiously opened the door, when Bristol Ann, the waiting maid, made her appearance, her face filled with alarm, and her hands clasped in anguish.

"Good Heavens, Ann, what is the matter?" asked Jenny.

"Matter enough," said Ann, with an air of the greatest consternation, "Master is suddenly returned from the country and will be here in a few minutes."

"What is to be done?" cried Jenny, in a violent agitation of spirits. "Stay, sir," she exclaimed, "there is but one thing to save me and you. Cover yourself with the bed clothes entirely," she said softly, "and I will convey your clothes into another room, so that if my husband comes here he will see nothing to awaken suspicion. I will pretend to be ill, and prevail on him to sleep in another bed, and then return to your arms."

At this moment the step of a man was heard ascending the stairs, and Jenny having seen her swain snugly hidden beneath the blankets, rushed from the room.

She now descended to the parlour, where they examined the booty, which amounted in value to above three hundred guineas. It was then determined that they should pack up all their moveables and decamp. This resolution they immediately carried into effect, by leaving Jenny's lodgings in the most secret manner possible.

The amorous young gentleman waited in a state of the utmost impatience until morning. He had listened with the greatest anxiety all through the night for Jenny's footsteps, but in vain; and when, at last, the day dawned, he began to suspect that a trick had been played on him, nor was he far from the truth.

At length he summoned sufficient courage to ring the bell, and immediately afterwards the servant of the landlady tapped at the door; but could not enter, in compliance with his request, as Jenny had taken the key away with her.

The landlady herself now hurried up stairs, and demanded admittance. The young fellow hesitated to admit her; but laying her stout shoulder against the door she burst it open, and beheld the disappointed swain in a most pitiable plight.

It is needless to narrate the upshot of the matter. Suffice it to say, that although the young fellow affected to be highly indignant at the way in which he had been treated, the people of the house were deaf to his expostulations; and declared that unless he remunerated them for the loss and damage they had sustained by the flight of Jenny and her associates, they would circulate the adventure through the town.

Rather than hazard the exposure of his character the poor dupe adopted this mode of getting out of the scrape. He, therefore, discharged the debt Jenny had contracted, and having procured a fresh supply of clothes and money he quitted the house in Covent Garden.

CHAPTER XXV.

MR. DOOM VISITS BILKIT IN PRISON—CAPERS OF JONATHAN WILD—BILKIT FOUND GUILTY AND SENTENCED TO DEATH.

MR. TONY BILKIT had not slept long in the consciousness of quite "getting off" before Mr. Doom paid him a visit.

"I'll save you, Mr. Bilkit, if any body can save you," said Mr. Doom, in his softest voice.

"Thank you, Mr. Doom," said the agitated burglar.

"But you must tell me all your secrets—everything—you must conceal not even a thought," said Doom.

"It's a hard thing, Lawyer Doom, to pick bad thoughts out of your breast, and show to other people what you don't want to talk about yourself," observed the burglar.

"Do you want to be hanged?" was the severe and acute remark of the Gray's Inn practitioner.

"Life is sweet," was the only reply.

"And you may save it."

"How?"

"By following my advice."

A long consultation then took place; and Mr. Doom left the prison. As soon as he was out of sight Mr. Bilkit walked over to the grating of the cell in which the condemned prisoners were confined, and with a look of barbarous pity presented them with a guinea each.

"I'm safe," he said, "my trial comes on to-morrow morning, and so, my glo-carussers, don't be down-hearted. You'll hear the bell-man of St. Sepulchre's by and bye."

*   *   *   *   *

The old Court House of Newgate, at the period we write of, presented a far different appearance to either the new or the old court of the Old Bailey does at the present time, with one exception. The recorder set then, as he does now, in the judgment seat. But the costumes were so strange—the characters about so grotesque—the severity of Justice so severe, that we are rather glad a change has taken place for the better.

Close beside the gaoler, who had to deliver his prisoner, stood the public hangman. He was one of those miscreants who, for the sake of money, would have bartered his own soul. Whenever a culprit was brought to the bar he looked at him in a pecuniary point of view. He could have choked his own mother for a guinea extra.

The recorder sat upon the bench as calmly as though he had sat there from boyhood; but his calm, clear, discriminative eye was wonderfully alive; nothing escaped his observation, not even the bustle of Mr. Doom, who, dressed in his best suit, slided into court.

There were many ladies in the galleries, all anxious to hear the trial of a man who had been charged with murdering a gentleman and hiding him in his cellar.

"Put up Anthony Bilkit," said the clerk of arraigns.

In custody of the gaoler and two turnkeys Tony was placed at the bar. He looked round him with a dogged indifference, until his eye recognised two persons in the crowd; and then so malicious, so full of diabolical meaning was the expression of one of them that his heart sunk within him.

The individuals who produced this feeling of uneasiness in the breast of the prisoner were Jonathan Wild and his man Quilt Arnold. Near to them, and apparently awaiting the orders of the former, were several sinister looking men, whom also Bilkit regarded with a shudder.

The prisoner was arraigned upon two indictments; the first charging him with being concerned in the burglary (with Yorkshire Bob and Black Sandy) at the watchmaker's, in Drury Lane; and the second with the murder of some person unknown, in his own house—'The Jolly Pedlars.'

To each of these charges he pleaded Not Guilty.

The old watchmaker positively swore to Bilkit's being the man from whose face the crape fell in his room on the night of the burglary;—and Watkins, the Bow Street runner, deposed to the finding a portion of the stolen goods in the prisoner's house. Nothing appeared more clear than this case; and the jury had already quite made up their minds, when through the adroit management of Mr. Doom an entirely new aspect was imparted to it.

Witnesses at that time had their price; and from the small false swearer on a petit larceny case, up to the dare-devil perjurer in a matter of life and death, all of this class were familiarly known to Mr. Doom. And without entering further into minute particulars, it might suffice to say that, after the examination of three of the class of witnesses refered to—two of whom swore that Bilkit was, at the time of the robbery, drinking with them at the Sir John Oldcastle Tavern, Islington; and the other that he had heard a man ask Bilkit, in his vintner's shop, to keep the parcel of watches for him in a secure place, until his arrival from the country—the respectable landlord of the 'Jolly Pedlars' was acquitted.

The trial for the murder of the man whose body was found in the vintner's cellar was then proceeded with; but so skilful a web of sophistry did Mr. Doom throw around the case that it seemed, more than probable, Bilkit would be declared not guilty of this charge also. The identity of the murdered gentleman had not been proved, nor was it clearly shown whether the body had been placed in the spot where it was discovered, before or after Bilkit had taken the public-house. In short, the whole affair was wrapt in so much obscurity that the judge was about to direct an acquittal when Jonathan Wild stepped forward, and addressing the court, said that he had witnesses present who would, beyond a doubt, prove the guilt of the prisoner at the bar.

This announcement caused a considerable sensation in the court. Mr. Doom, who had scarcely less at stake than the prisoner himself, started as he heard the voice of the well-known and dreaded thief-taker. As for Tony Bilkit his face assumed a flurried appearance, and he seemed rooted to the spot on which he stood.

Tony saw clearly at once that his life was now not worth a straw, unless he could, by some desperate means, extricate himself from the toils of Jonathan Wild, who he knew in consequence of some former quarrel to be a most implacable enemy. Heedless, therefore, of his promise to M'Cleane, he earnestly addressed the judge—

"My lord!" he said in a tremulous voice, "my lord, I wish to turn king's evidence; if that privilege be allowed me I shall be enabled to make such disclosures as will—

He was proceeding; but the judge interrupted him by saying—

"That application, prisoner, should have been made before your trial commenced; it cannot now be entertained."

Jonathan Wild was then called upon to produce his witnesses.

The first of these was a stout, beetle browed, ferocious looking fellow. He swore positively to having seen the deceased, who was a young rake well known at the coffee and gambling-houses, in the company of Bilkit, at the house of the latter, about a month before the discovery of the body. He also deposed to a quarrel having taken place between Bilkit and the deceased while gambling, in the course of which the former had used violent threats towards the latter.

A second witness swore that the deceased had been last seen alive by him when he was going into Tony Bilkit's house, and that to the best of his knowledge, the gentleman was never seen to quit it.

Thus far, Doom felt that he had not much to fear, and leaning over the dock he whispered as much in the ear of Bilkit, assuring him that he need not tremble so, as the evidence Jonathan Wild had brought against him was purely circumstantial.

Wild, however, had only been playing with his victim, as does a cat with its prey.

"I have yet another and a more important witness than either of those who have been sworn, my lord," he said as he handed a slip of paper, on which a name was written, to the clerk of the court.

"Call Jerry Laggum," said that functionary.

And to the unutterable surprise and dismay of Tony Bilkit, his own confidential serving man entered the witness box.

Jerry Laggum avoided the keen eye of his master. The wretch, in order to secure to himself the business of 'The Jolly Pedlars,' and also to screen himself from the vengeance of Jonathan Wild, had resolved to betray Tony to the law, and his evidence as to the murder, and the disposal of the body by Bilkit was so villainously clear, that the jury hesitated not a moment in considering the matter, but immediately on the conclusion of the judge's summing up the foreman pronounced the fatal word GUILTY.

The judge then put on the black velvet cap, and sentenced the miserable man to death, and afterwards to be anatomised, without holding out to him the slightest hope of mercy; and Bilkit, rather cursing Jerry Laggum for his treachery than bewailing his own fate, was removed from the bar.

CHAPTER XXVI.

DOOM MADE THE TOOL OF M'CLEANE—THE CONDEMNED CELL—EXECUTION OF BILKIT— SCENE AT SURGEON'S HALL.

IN a most confused and distracted state of mind Mr. Doom slunk through the crowd, and was about to quit the court as secretly as possible, when he felt a heavy hand laid on his shoulder.

Hastily looking round he beheld M'Cleane, who gazed sternly into his face.

"You should have foreseen this," remarked the highwayman; "but as I do not believe that you have, in this matter at least, acted treacherously, as your interest prevented that, I will yet shield you from the consequences of your crimes, if you follow my directions in full."

"What are they?" enquired the frightened lawyer.

"You must see Bilkit, and hold out to him the strongest hopes of a reprieve."

"That would be useless—nay, cruel," said Doom, "nothing on earth can save him from the gallows now."

"I know that to the full as well as yourself, Doom. As to the cruelty of the matter," remarked M'Cleane, with a bitter sneer, "there was none I suppose in throwing a fellow creature over a boat's side on a certain dark night."

Mr. Wriggleton Doom waved his hand as if he would have M'Cleane waive all further allusion to so unpleasant a subject; but his tormentor remorsely continued—

"Or in having an unarmed man attacked by a hired assassin in the public streets after dark?"

"Well, well!" exclaimed Doom, "I'll do as you wish. Bilkit shall be buoyed up with hope until the very halter is round his neck."

"On your pursuing such a course depends the safety of your own," remarked M'Cleane, as the lawyer and the highwayman parted at the gate of Newgate.

The moment after sentence had been pronounced on Tony Bilkit, he was conveyed into the press-room of Newgate, where he was heavily ironed. His manners appeared to have undergone a complete change within the last few hours. Previously to his trial he had boasted, and seemed to be shielded from punishment by the ingenuity of the subtle lawyer of Gray's Inn, that of all the villains who thronged that receptacle of crime—Newgate, none appeared to be more reckless or hardened than himself. A change had now, however, come over him; for, as the fetters were being rivetted to his limbs, he seemed like some strong man suddenly smitten by paralysis. Speechless with astonishment and disappointment he was led, tottering from the weight of his double irons, to the condemned cell.

This was a gloomy chamber, situated at that angle of the old prison where Newgate Street joins the area, in front of that dreary place of confinement. Its tenants were not then, as now, completely cut off from communication with those without its walls, at least so far as hearing was concerned; for about ten feet from the floor was a grating in the Newgate Street portion of the wall; and by means of this the condemned criminals, fettered and pining, had their miseries increased by hearing the free footsteps, and the careless mirth of the ever flowing stream of human beings who paced the pavements outside. They were tantalized by the every day sounds—the merry laughter—the business hum of that world in which they had to play but one more public part, and then to quit it for ever.

Another grating, placed in the wall, at right angles with the one we have spoken of, but at a much less height from the ground, enabled the condemned persons to have a view of the common yard of the gaol, and this enlarged window, like the other, was a curse rather than a blessing to the condemned; for it was the

chosen place of resort of the very worst class of the prisoners, whose ribald language and blasphemous conversations were anything but calculated to soothe the feelings of one whose hours were numbered.

Bilkit had flung himself down on a heap of straw, and was moodily thinking on his approaching fate, when the grating of the window communicating with the common yard was slightly darkened.

He raised himself on his elbow, and saw a man's face pressed closely against the bars; the light from the other grating enabled him to see the features of the gazer distinctly. He was not long in recognising them; he had too often seen the features of Jack Price the common hangman, not to be fully conscious that that worthy officer of the law was now surveying him, much as a butcher would look

at a beast which was almost ready to be slaughtered.

"What's that you, Tony Bilkit? I declare that you'd have been the last cove as I should have thought to have seen in the black hole. Such a cracksman as you were too; lord, lord! nobody knows what we may come to ourselves!"

Jack Price's words were almost prophetic, for not many years afterwards he was suspended from that tree to which he had tied up such a number of criminals, for having in the most brutal manner assaulted a married woman, who, because she resisted him, he so ill-treated that her death ensued.

"When am I to be hanged?" asked Bilkit, gruffly, of Jack Price.

"This is Wednesday morning; on Friday morning, that is the day after to-morrow, I shall bring my cart for you to take your last ride in, Tony," replied Jack Price.

" And," continued the hangman after a pause, " I should advise you to have plenty of liquor to make the time pass away pleasantly. Good bye, Tony, I shall see you the day after to-morrow."

Doom did as M'Cleane had enjoined him, and on the evening of the day of the trial he entered the condemned cell.

Bilkit, who was lying sullenly on his straw bed, started to his feet as soon as he saw who his visitor was. With the glare of a ferocious tiger when it springs at its prey, he gazed into Doom's face:—his hands worked convulsively, and, but for the chain which confined him to the wall of his cell, he would have fallen upon and torn the lawyer limb from limb.

" I am come to bring you good news here," said the lawyer, retiring from the reach of the burglar and murderer as far as the limits of the cell would permit him.

" You have deceived me once, and I will not be cheated again," howled Bilkit, "begone!"

" Be calm," said the lawyer, " steps are now being taken by myself and a certain Captain for your safety. Despair not! you will surely be reprieved."

After much persuasion a ray of hope darted into Bilkit's bosom, and he began to think that after all he might escape the gallows. Doom took especial care to foster this feeling, and when the lawyer left the condemned cell the criminal was in a far less ferocious mood than when he entered it.

The next day M'Cleane visited him, and assured him that every exertion was being made in his behalf.

" I'm werry much afeard, Captain," said Bilkit, " that before this time to-morrow afternoon I shall be in Surgeon's Hall, with them cussed doctors cutting into me. That's what vexes me most, excepting one thing."

" What is that?" asked M'Cleane.

" That Black Sandy and Yorkshire Bob aint a going to keep me company," he replied gruffly. Damn it—to think as they got me into the scrape and left me to be lagged."

" But," said M'Cleane there is no fear of that, Tony, you know I got Blackmoor off when he was in sight of Tyburn Tree, and what was done once may be done again; however, you will not need such a desperate measure, for I have it from a quarter to be relied on that a reprieve will reach you, if not before, even at the foot of the gallows."

" Blackmoor!" said Bilkit, recollecting himself, " if I did not know, Captain, that you had sent him over the seas, I could have sworn that I saw him in the court during my trial."

" Strange," muttered M'Cleane. " Jenny Diver told me this morning that she had seen either Blackmoor or his ghost passing along Long Acre."

Here, however, the conversation dropped, as the Ordinary of Newgate entered the cell, for the purpose of imparting spiritual consolation to the culprit. Taking Bilkit by the hand, and whispering to him not to despair, the highwayman left the place.

The Ordinary having performed his solemn functions bade adieu to Bilkit, who was once more left alone.

After the sun had gone down, and when darkness began to render objects shadowy and indistinct, Bilkit sat with his chin resting on his hands, and his eyes staring upon vacancy. The sounds in the prison had entirely ceased, for the prisoners were locked up in their respective cells; and the streets without had gradually become quieter and quieter. At length night came on—his last night on earth, though he madly clung to the belief that escape was not impossible. He was left to his own thoughts, sad companions for one whose career has been that of perpetual crime, and whose life is ebbing rapidly away. The scenes and events of his childhood, the wasted and mis-spent days of his youth, the crimes of his riper years, all rose vividly to his memory, and haunted him like angry ghosts. He felt subdued and wretched.

Ten, eleven, twelve o'clock pealed from St. Sepulchre's sonorous bell, and as the last echoes of the midnight sounds died away, Bilkit was startled by the ringing of a bell like that of a city crier's, beneath the grating on the Newgate Street side.

The person, whoever it was, made a very doleful imitation of funeral tolling with the said bell, and after so doing a gruff voice began to speak.

" My God!" exclaimed Tony, " it's the bell-man of St. Sepulchre's going to say his verses over me." And then he remembered with a shudder how, when years before in custody in St. Sepulchre's watchouse that very bellman being present, the constable had warned him against evil courses, assuring him if he persisted in them, that that very bellman would one day wait on him under the walls of Newgate.

The gruff voice belonged to the bellman of St. Sepulchre's, and these were the verses which he recited—

" All you that in the condemned hold do be,
Prepare you, for to-morrow you shall die;
Watch all, and pray; the hour is drawing
          near
That you before the Almighty must appear.
Examine well yourselves, in time repent,
That you may not to eternal flames be sent,
And when St. Sepulchre's bell to-morrow tolls
The Lord have mercy on your souls!
          Past twelve o'clock!"

The heavy tramp of the bellman was then heard to die away in the distance; and nothing now broke upon the stillness of the night save the chiming of the quarters from the different church steeples, and the occasional crying of the hours and half hours by drowsy voiced watchmen. Still, however, the verses sounded over and over again in the miserable Tony Bilkit's ears, until at last worn out with fatigue and excitement, nature gave way, and sinking down on his bed of straw he slept as peacefully as if he had never committed a crime.

It was past seven in the morning, when he was awakened by a man shaking his arm. Looking up he beheld the grim face of a turnkey close to his own; for a second or two he did not fully comprehend the nature of his situation; but suddenly, with a stunning force, the appalling truth burst upon him.

Unless a miracle, or something akin to one, interposed in his behalf that day would be his last he thought, and yet when his breakfast was brought him he devoured it as eagerly as though he had to gather strength for a score or more years.

At nine o'clock the Ordinary of Newgate entered the cell, and remained with Bilkit until ten, when the door was thrown open, and the Sheriff appeared with the gaoler, of whom he formally demanded the body of the condemned man.

A procession was then formed, and Bilkit between two turnkeys was led to the press-yard, where, his irons having been knocked off, he was pinioned by Jack Price the executioner.

The morning had been clear; but just as Bilkit mounted the cart which was to convey him to Tyburn, the sky suddenly became overcast. Dark, ragged-edged thunder clouds which drifted along slowly overhead, were at brief intervals rent as it were into fearful chasms, from which darted flashes of forked and lurid lightning which almost blinded one, followed by such rattling claps of thunder, which seemed directly overhead, as made the walls of the grim prison to tremble.

Large drops of rain spotted here and there the pavement of the press-yard; these were succeeded by a tremendous shower of hail and rain of, however, but short duration, and when this had ceased, the heavens instead of being blue and clear, looked like a huge funeral pall.

The coffin was placed in the cart, the criminal made to sit on its lid beside the Ordinary, and Jack Price took his place in front of the vehicle. All being now in readiness, at a signal from the gaoler the great doors of the prison was opened, and the cart was drawn outside.

Tony Bilkit had his back to the crowd; but he started involuntarily when he heard the shouts and groans of execration which greeted his appearance. A turn of the cart having been made to allow of its falling into its proper place in the procession, he for a moment faced the vast multitude. Yet he did not quail as he returned the fierce glances from thousands of eyes, each of which was turned upon him. At that moment a supernatural power of vision appeared to have been bestowed upon him, for every single feature in that upturned sea of faces appeared to be as distinctly defined as the very nails of the coffin on which he sat. This distinct perception lasted but for a moment, and then a mist came between him and the multitude, and the seperate visages, with two exceptions, blended, as it were, into one.

Rapid as the glance had been, he had recognized in the crowd two persons whom in the bitterness of his heart he cursed aloud.

These persons were Jonathan Wild and Jerry Laggum.

Jonathan stood just within the railings of St.

Sepulchre's churchyard, just at that part where Giltspur-street forms an angle with Snow-hill. His face wore a most diabolical expression as he glanced with evident delight on the wretch who he had betrayed, because he had dared to thwart him in one of his projects. His arms were folded on his chest, and, with one foot firmly planted a little in advance of the other, he looked like what indeed he was, a fiend.

Jerry Laggum, Tony Bilkit's drawer, and confidential servant at the tavern, stood beside the thief-taker, without exhibiting the least symptom of remorse or of pity for his late master. On the contrary, he rather rejoiced, for the moment after Bilkit should have been turned off, he knew well enough that the stock in trade of 'The Jolly Pedlars' would be his own.

"You see what it is to cross me, Jerry Laggum," said Jonathan Wild, in a low stern voice. "Take warning by the example before you, for should you play me any tricks after you become landlord, as surely as you now stand upon that tombstone, so surely shall you ride up Holborn-hill in that cart."

"I know it, Mr. Wild, I know it," said Jerry, "never fear, Mr. Wild, not a plant shall be made at 'The Jolly Pedlars' but you shall know of it."

"It will be the worse for you if I do not," returned Jonathan; "but here they come."

The procession having been formed, it moved slowly from the door of Newgate, the sheriff and some javelin men preceeding it, and a detachment of the latter guarding each side of the cart; for, since the rescue of Blackmoor, additional precautions were observed to prevent the recurrence of such an event. A troop of the city trambands followed the vehicle which contained the doomed man, and a large posse of constables brought up the rear.

Immediately the sheriff's carriage moved onward, the bell of St. Sepulchre's church commenced tolling its doleful knell over the yet living man, giving a yet more melancholy character to the scene.

Just as the fatal cart came opposite to the place where Jonathan Wild and Jerry Laggum were standing, gloating over their infernal work, the crowd became so dense that it was impossible to proceed, and, therefore, it halted for a few minutes until the javelin men should have cleared the way. During the interval Bilkit happened to turn his face in the direction of the churchyard, and his eye fell and fixed itself on the men who had betrayed him.

Starting to his feet by a convulsive effort, he boldly confronted and looked at Wild, who with arms still folded, as boldly returned the stare of utter hatred. Jerry Laggum on the contrary, when the eyes of his late master encountered his, exhibited symptoms of extreme trepidation and endeavoured to avoid the piercing and scornful look of Bilkit.

"Villain—damnable villain!" he exclaimed aloud, "your time will soon come, Jonathan Wild, for as sure as you stand there before long you'll swing from Tyburn Tree."

The Chaplin besought Bilkit to die in peace with his enemies; but in vain, as long as Wild and Laggum remained in sight, for all obstacles having been removed the procession was now moving onward. Bilkit ceased not to pour forth the most horrible maledictions on the heads of both.

The lurking hope which he entertained of the reprieve, assured to him by Doom and M'Cleane, caused him to pay little heed to the admonitions of the chaplain. Closing his eyes to shut out from view the thousands by whom he was surrounded, he presented a dogged silence, which he maintained until the cart drew up at the Three Punch Bowls, when after gulping down the contents of the parting bowl, a ceremony described in a former chapter of this work, he besought an interview with the sheriff, who was speedily at his side.

A long and earnest conversation ensued, and it appeared to those around that Bilkit was making some important communication.

"A confession—a confession!" shouted the mob, as the sheriff quitted Bilkit; but they were mistaken. What passed between the official and the criminal will be known to the reader when the events of our history become further developed.

Denser and denser became the crowd as the procession drew nearer and nearer to the point of its destination. It was with the greatest difficulty at last that a passage could be forced for the Sheriff's carriage; and when Tyburn Tree came in view, as far as the eye could reach on either side, was one mighty mass of human beings, which with every new emotion or excitement surged too and fro like a living ocean.

The arrival of the criminal was the signal for a general commotion; the mob, which had followed the cart in its progress from Newgate, being now added to the multitude who had been waiting all day near the instrument of death, slight skirmishes for the purpose of on one side, keeping possession of, and on the other of acquiring good places for seeing the sight, occurred; so that what with fighting, tippling in booths, swearing, 'last dying speech' bawling, and orange vending, the place might well have been designated, as indeed it was 'Hang Fair.'

The Sheriff's carriage having wheeled off to the right hand of the gallows, the javelin men surrounded the horrible implement of death; and then the cart was drawn up immediately under the fatal tree.

Jack Price now quitted his seat, and by means of a ladder mounted to the cross beam, where he sat very composedly with a short pipe in his mouth, and occupied himself in fixing the rope to an iron ring. Having accomplished this business he folded his arms, puffed his tobacco with much complacency, and observing that his victim was engaged with the Ordinary, he crossed his dangling legs and leisurely surveyed the crowd, nodded familiarly to many whom he recognised.

"Is there no hope, then?" asked Tony, of the Ordinary, after that gentleman had urged on him to make the best of his few remaining minutes.

"None whatever, I assure you, on the faith of a christian man," was the reply.

Bilkit trembled violently, still he would not as yet abandon hope; spite of the urgent entreaties of the clergyman he strained his eyes with gazing towards the extreme distance, for he yet fancied a reprieve might arrive.

Determining to prolong the time as much as possible he requested another interview with the sheriff, who mounted the cart.

"There will be a reprieve—I know there will!" exclaimed the wretched man, "For God's sake give me another half hour."

"Impossible;" said the sheriff, "if you have been led to hope for such a thing you have been grossly deceived."

"Then by God!" exclaimed Tony, "I'll not die without my revenge."

He then conversed with the sheriff and ordinary, or rather he spoke to them for about a quarter of an hour. At the conclusion of his statement, the ordinary said—

"As you are a dying man, Anthony Bilkit, do you swear that what you have told us is true?"

"As God is to be my judge," replied Bilkit.

The crowd had now become exceedingly impatient, and their cries and yells were most discordant. As soon, however, as they observed the hangman, in obedience to a signal from the sheriff knock the ashes out of his pipe on the cross beam where he had been sitting, and descend the ladder to the cart, a silence as deep as that of the grave itself succeeded.

Seeing that it was utterly useless to attempt further delay, Bilkit now rose from the coffin on which he had been sitting, and the sheriff delivered him to Jack Price, who tightened the halter which was round his neck; he then put a nightcap on his head and mounted him on a plank which he had placed across the cart, at its tail; lastly, he connected the halter with the rope he had tied to the cross-beam, pulled the cap over his face, shook hands with Tony and left him, after whispering in his ear, "Die like a man, Tony, when you feel the cart moving give a spring up, and all your troubles 'll be over."

What Bilkit's thoughts were during this interval of horrible suspense, is not for us to enquire. He stood as firm as a rock and as motionless, to the great admiration of his old pals, many of whom were present.

A crack of the whip, a slight jerk, and the horse moved on; at the first feeling of motion Bilkit pressed his pinioned arms to his side, and was about to take the fearful leap, but his courage failed him and he was literally dragged by the rope off the plank.

The wretched creature's body, quivering with mental agony, swung to and fro for a minute or two, when Jack Price, leaving the horses head ran towards him, hung heavily on him by his legs for a short time, and the burglar and the murderer's corpse hung motionless from Tyburn Tree.

*   *   *   *   *

On the evening of the day of Anthony Bilkit's execution, the great room of the theatre of Surgeon's Hall, in Lincoln's Inn Fields was thronged to excess by a wonder seeking multitude. For it had been announced that a series of galvanic experiments were to be made on the dead body of the murderer; and to witness these experiments the most intense curiosity was excited amongst persons of all classes. Even women, throwing aside the modesty of their sex, disguised themselves in men's apparel, and were to be seen looking from the galleries, with unabashed countenances, on the muscular frame of the naked criminal.

On the table was a powerful galvanic apparatus, consisting of troughs filled with acids, metalic plates and wires.

The operator was a grave old member of the profession; he commenced his experiments by making an incission in the leg of the dead man so as to expose the nerve. The same operation he also performed in the neck. Then placing the plates in the acid troughs he fixed a wire to each end of the apparatus. With one of these wires he touched the nerve of the leg and kept it in contact with it. He then placed the extremity of the other wire on the nerve of the neck, and instantly, as if life had suddenly and by a miracle re-entered Bilkit's frame, the corpse stretched out its arms and legs, the former with so much violence as to knock down an assistant who stood near. The instant the wire was removed the corpse resumed its former death like appearance.

The operator then laid bare the nerve in the temples, and the effect produced were infinitely more startling and horrible.

For on the application of the wire the dead man sat bolt upright; the eyes rolled and glared in their sockets; the mouth grinned frightfully, and the muscles of the face worked in a ghastly manner. It seemed as though every evil passion of the criminal had for a time returned to give each its own peculiar expression to his countenance.

A scene of the greatest terror and excitement followed the exhibition. Many of the disguised women fainted, in consequence of which their sex was discovered, and even strong men were so terrified that they rushed from the spot.

But the crowning experiment was reserved for the last, a third nerve on the very crown of the head was opened, and a fourth on the sole of one foot. The effect produced when the wires were applied was marvellous.

On the exciting wires being applied, the galvanic fluid, with the celerity of lightning, darted through every fibre of the criminals frame; the chest heaved, the hands and feet became violently convulsed, and the whole frame quivered with agitation.

The power was still further increased, and then, as if by some convulsive effort, the dead man started to his feet, and standing as erect as when in life, stretched forth its arm and opened its dull eyes. The very operator himself was startled at the wonder he had produced, and in his trepidation let the wire slip from between his fingers. No sooner had he done this than with a heavy sound the body fell in a heap on the table.

The result of this last experiment was too much even for the strongest nerved person present, and the theatre of Surgeon's Hall was speedily deserted.

CHAPTER XXVII

THE ATTACK ON THE 'CHAPEL.'

THE man who walks through the streets of this huge metropolis, fancying that he sees all its wonders whilst gazing at what meets his eye above the pavement on which he treads, or the carriage road over which horses convey him, is vastly mistaken.

For beneath that foot pavement, and that carriage road is another and a most important portion of the world of London. The superficial gazer sees, only, as it were, the outsides of the giant; but he who dives or digs below the surface will observe the arteries and veins which supply it with aliment, and health and light; and the great chanels through which its impurities are carried off to the broad river, which, in its turn, rolls onward to deposit the refuse of millions in the whole absorbing ocean.

Besides these necessary canals there are many subterranean passages, little thought of by the careless or hurrying pedestrian, beneath the London streets. For the most part these dark avenues are now appropriated to the purposes of business; but some yet remain which are used by lawless men. At the period of which we write, however, these secret chanels of communication were numerous, and in all the low quarters of the town there was scarcely a house which had not its curiously contrived trap door, and its mysterious winding passages.

The uses of such private thoroughfares as these must be obvious. In houses where the vilest of mankind congregated, there were always some who had the fear of constables before their eyes, or, who were in need of a place in which to conceal the products of their depredations. Then, again, these underground passages often connected together houses at great distances apart, so that, without their inhabitants going into the public streets they could interchange visits with the most perfect security.

But one of the principal of these singular places will be better understood by a reference to some of the events which are to be narrated.

The clock of the church of Saint Giles in the Fields struck the three quarters past nine, one evening, just as Mr. Watkins, the Bow Street runner, walked leisurely along within the shadow of the churchyard wall. Having first cautiously looked around him, he approached the gate of the receptacle for the dead, and by means of a key opened it. Carefully and noiselessly closing it he took his way towards a secluded part of the burial ground, and sitting down on a tombstone where an over shadowing tree perfectly concealed him from observation, he gave a significant whistle.

The whistle was returned, and directly afterwards a dark shadow was seen by the Bow Street runner emerging from an empty vault near.

"Thought you'd never have come Mister Watkins," observed the man, who now sat wearily down on the tombstone beside the officer.

"Why, I'm to the minute, man, to the minute," said the officer, as he pulled out a watch which certainly, in point of size, might very appropriately have been compared to a turnip. It was so dark, however, that Mr. Watkins would have had some difficulty in proving to ocular demonstration, his punctuality. Fortunately he was relieved from an embarrassment of this kind by the church clock striking ten.

"Didn't I say I was to my time," said Watkins.

"Yes—yes, Mr. Watkins; but if you'd been lying in that damned dark vault all day, with dry bones for companions, you'd have thought the time long too."

"Is every thing ready?" asked the officer.

"Every thing," replied the man; "but you must make it all right with me first. D'ye understand?"

"Our agreement is this," said the Bow Street runner, "I engage to procure you a free pardon and a hundred guineas, if you lead me and my men through the secret passage which leads from the house next to Justice Dyott's, in Church Lane to your old shop."

"Just so," observed the other, "but, Mister Watkins, what security have I that you will keep your word?"

"Why, curse you," cried Watkins, "the best security; could I not, this very moment, walk you off to Saint Giles's roundhouse, and send for the old miser's son of Bucklersbury? Wouldn't he be glad to see you?'

The fellow trembled violently from head to foot. Mr. Watkins pitilessly continued—

"And couldn't I just inform the Sheriff of London that a certain bird which flew in the neighbourhood of Tyburn, might be caged again?"

"But you won't do that, Mr. Watkins; you couldn't do that," gasped Blackmoor, for he it was.

"But I would though, and I will if you either shrink or shirk. See here!"

The officer drew from his breast pocket a piece of parchment which he unfolded, and by the light of the moon which had now risen, Blackmoor read the king's free pardon for himself.

The moment M'Cleane and his gang are in my custody that document is yours and you will have nothing to fear," said Watkins, as he carefully put away the parchment.

"Enough! I'm satisfied," said Blackmoor, "and now the sooner we go to work the better."

"Are you sure that you know the windings of the subterranean passage, Blackmoor," asked the cautious officer.

"Every inch of it, every winding and every corner," replied the traitor. "How many of your men are to go with us?"

"Thirteen, and every one of them armed to the teeth," replied the officer, "they are waiting for me in Bloomsbury."

"Then," said Blackmoor, "I will, as soon as you leave me, go to the house in Church Lane and there await your arrival. The house

is uninhabited so there are no fears on that score; but it would be as well to let your men drop in by two's and three's, for that fellow, M'Cleane, has his scouts everywhere.

Watkins then quitted the churchyard with as much secrecy as he observed when he entered it, and Blackmoor slunk through the silent streets and safely gained the uninhabited house in Church Lane.

By means of a skeleton key he opened the door and entered, then placing himself in a position near the entrance, he listened attentively for the arrival of Watkins and his troop of officers.

Whilst he is thus occupied, and whilst Watkins also is engaged in collecting his forces, we crave the readers company whilst we pay another visit to the 'Chapel.'

Never, perhaps, had the splendid saloon of that den of iniquity presented a more brilliantly dazzling appearance than on the present occasion. Innumerable wax candles, in exquisitely cut glass chandeliers, shed a glare of light on the festal board, and were reflected in many gorgeous mirrors which lined the walls. Pictures of a luscious character gleamed seductively from the panels; and some, half concealed by drapery, made the blood to run more riotously than if every charm had been displayed, and nothing left for the imagination to dwell upon.

On the luxurious sofas and ottomans reclined, in attitudes of voluptuous languor, the many beautiful girls who belonged to the gang. Among them Jenny Diver was conspicuous, for that young lady had, since the affair with the gallant in Covent Garden, taken up her abode in the 'Chapel.' Jenny was attired in a dress which showed off her charms to the greatest advantage; and even when surrounded with such beauties as Gipsey Betty and others there—for none were present who had not claims to loveliness—she blazed forth as does a diamond of the first water when encircled by less costly gems.

M'Cleane, Dick Flybynight, Handsome Jack and the other members of the gang present, were this evening in excellent spirits. It was, indeed, a sort of gala night in the 'Chapel,' for, on that day a danger which threatened them had been removed, and the fraternity now considered themselves safe.

It was the evening of the day on which Tony Bilkit had been executed.

"He'll tell no tales now, Captain," said Dick Flybynight.

"Or if he does," replied M'Cleane, "he'll only whisper them about in the lower regions, where no doubt he is now, for Tony was an infernal villain."

"I hope from my soul," said Jenny Diver, "that his berth is as hot as that oven was to which he would have consigned the old baker's grand child."

"Don't doubt it," said Handsome Jack. "Now, I honour a brave fellow, who lives like a man and dies like one too; but such villainous scoundrels as Tony was I abominably detest.

"Give the devil his due, however," remarked Gipsey Betty, "Tony did not peach after all."

"That is a comfort," said M'Cleane, "and an immense relief to me. I never drew breath freely after his apprehension until I saw him dangling. One word from him would have blown us to the devil."

The banquet that night was partaken of with unusual zest, for every one felt a load taken of his or her mind; and after the company had quaffed many a goblet of sparkling wine. M'Cleane exclaimed—

"Who's for a dance to-night?"

Jenny Diver and the other girls started to their feet, their eyes beaming with pleasure. In an incredibly short space of time the tables were removed, the carpet rolled aside, and each gallant provided with a partner.

And merrily indeed they footed it to the music of a spinet, played upon by Jem Starlight, who possessed no mean taste for music. M'Cleane became completely fascinated by the voluptuous movements of Jenny Diver. Handsome Handsome Jack was no less delighted with the wanton graces of Gipsey Betty; and Dick Flybynight and Handsome Jack gave abundant evidence that the mystic mazes of the dance were rather exciting. But whilst they are nimbly and gracefully footing it we must return to Mr. Watkins and Blackmoor.

The latter, now doubly a traitor, had not remained long in the place where we left him before he heard the footsteps of Watkins approaching the door. On opening it the Bow Street runner, accompanied by two men, entered. Presently others came armed, and in about half an hour the whole thirteen men were safe in the uninhabited house.

They were all well armed with cutlasses and pistols; and several of them carried dark lanterns, and crowbars. Having seen that their weapons were primed and that everything was in order, Watkins directed Blackmoor to lead the way.

It should be here remarked that many years previously there existed between this uninhabited house in Church Lane, and some houses in the vicinity of Long Acre, a subterranean communication. When, however, M'Cleane and his gang took possession of the 'Chapel,' they carefully bricked up all the avenues leading from it, excepting those they deemed most convenient for their own use. It happened that Blackmoor, when in the confidence of the fraternity, had by accident stumbled upon one of these closed passages, through which the rats had made an aperture. Always on the watch to turn things to his own account, he enlarged the passage made by the vermin, and after creeping through, threaded his way along the secret passage until he discovered that it communicated with the house to which we have referred.

From that moment the idea of betraying M'Cleane, with whom he was no favorite, took possession of his mind. How he was thwarted in his first attempt is already known to the reader. On the present occasion a desire for revenge was his actuating principle; and so anxious was he to pay off the old debt he owed the Captain on account of the kidnapping transaction, that even the pardon and the gold offered as a reward for his treachery by Watkins were secondary considerations to him.

Blackmoor led the way down a long flight of stone steps, at the foot of which was a massive door, black, and half-rotten with age and damp. As it creaked on its hinges, hundreds of rats were heard scampering to their holes; the smell of the place was damp and oppressive, for, with the exception of Blackmoor's, human foot had never trodden there for years and years.

The grate had long before been removed from the fire-place, each side of which was lined with iron. Taking a crowbar Blackmoor inserted the end of it under the hearth stone, which he raised; and then it was an easy matter to pull open the iron door on the left hand side of the fire-place, for a door it in reality was.

Still leading the way Blackmoor proceeded, followed by Watkins and his party, along a passage which abruptly terminated. Stooping down, Blackmoor raised a trap door, but no sign of ladder or staircase was visible.

"How the devil are we to get down there?" asked Watkins.

"Thus," replied Blackmoor, "but one false step and you are lost."

The traitor, fastening his lantern to the belt which encircled his body, commenced the descent. At equal distances in the wall, and in parallel lines, about two feet and a half apart, were firmly fastened iron rings, which served for the hands to hold on by, whilst between these lines of rings, notches for the feet were cut out of the solid stone. The depth was about twenty feet

"And how are we, in case the tide should turn against us, to climb quickly up such an infernal ladder as that?" asked Watkins, after he and all his men had reached the bottom in safety.

"We shall not have to return this way, or I am much mistaken," replied Blackmoor, "and if we should have, this window here when closed behind us, would be an effectual barrier against an army."

Passing through the window alluded to, which was at the bottom of the shaft, the party walked for some time through a straight sort of tunnel, and then came to the top of a flight of stairs which they descended and entered another passage of a similar construction to that which they had just left.

They proceeded slowly in this way for nearly half an hour, until at last Blackmoor came to a dead halt.

"We are now drawing near to the brick-partion," he said in a voice scarcely above a whisper, "and the greatest caution must be used. One false step and we might be all caught and killed like rats, and no one above be any the wiser."

They soon arrived at the brick partion, and Blackmoor then announced his intention of getting through the aperture, and going on some way forward by himself for the purpose of reconnoitering.

Enjoining the strictest caution on the part of Watkins and his men, the traitor crept through the wall, and, in the course of a few minutes was lost to view.

We will, however, follow him, leaving Watkins and his companions on the other side of the partition.

With the utmost caution proceeded the traitor; and, indeed, he had every inducement to be vigilant, for he now drew so near to the saloon that he could distintly hear the sounds of the reveller's within, who, in their exultation at the fate of Bilkit, were forgetful of their usual prudence.

Little, indeed, did they imagine that, creeping like a venomous reptile almost close to them, was he, who at that very moment they fancied securely bestowed in the plantations of Maryland.

Blackmoor had now so nearly approached to the walls of the saloon that he could distinctly hear what was passing within. Only separated by a panel, from the revellers, he listened attentively.

It should here be mentioned that the existence of this panel was unknown to any of the gang excepting Blackmoor, by whom it had been discovered by a mere accident, when hanging some tapestry against the sides of the place. This knowledge he had carefully concealed, no very difficult matter, inasmuch as that part of the saloon in which it was, was so situated as to prevent any suspicion of danger from that quarter.

Suddenly, as he listened, Blackmoor heard his own name mentioned.

"Pity we ever suffered that ruffian, Blackmoor to escape," said a voice, which the traitor well knew to be that of M'Cleane; "but, however, it's not much matter, for he's quite as much _____ as Tony Bilkit. They _____

_____ laughed demoniacally as he heard this, and involuntarily muttered—

"He's a little nearer than you think for or would like him to be, Captain, as soon you will find to your cost."

"By the way," said another person, "what the devil could that rascal Tony Bilkit be whispering in the _____'s ear this morning just before he swung?"

"Oh! never fear about that, Dick," said M'Cleane; he didn't peach then, I can tell you, for even in that last moment he had hope. I knew what he whispered, for 'twas by my directions he did it."

"An exclamation of surprise," was uttered by Jenny Diver.

"Why, Jem," she said; "you are cleverer than ever I took you to be, if you are in that secret. You know a woman never likes to have a secret kept from her—so, for mercy's sake, let me hear what it was."

In this request she was joined by Handsome Jack, Dick Flybynight, and by the other members of the gang, more especially the female portion of it.

"It is simply this," said the Captain; "I had told Bilkit, whose life I knew could not be saved, that if a _____ failed to come whilst he was living, that _____ would be taken to bring him to _____ ere he was hanged."

"The devil!" said Dick Flybynight; "and was old Tony Bilkit fool enough to believe that?"

"He believed it implicitly," returned the Captain; "I furnished him with a silver tube, which I directed him to insert in his throat just before he ascended the fatal plank; and I also told him to request the sheriff to let him hang only half-an-hour—a permission sometimes granted."

"By Saint Nicholas, Jem! but that was a clever contrivance of yours to stop his blabbing," said Jenny.

"I also directed him, when the cart moved on, only to pretend to jump from the plank, and to let himself down from it as gently as possible. Poor devil! he little thought that Jack Price would give his neck such a twist as would prevent his tongue wagging again. There, now, Ben Culs, you have the whole story."

"Hurrah, for our brave Captain!" cried the whole gang simultaneously." And the crystal goblets were filled with the richest wines, which they all quaffed to the health of their chief.

Having ascertained by the most cautious and secret examination that the secret panel remained in its former state, Blackmoor took the opportunity of an hilarious burst of merriment to gently push it aside.

He was now only concealed from the view of those whose destruction he was plotting by the heavy folds of tapestry which hung before it.

Having accomplished this much, he retraced his way back to Watkins on the other side of the brick partition.

The Bow Street Runner and his little band of men had, whilst waiting in the subterranean passage, been agitated by no very pleasant feelings. They very naturally distrusted Blackmoor, who they justly considered might probably betray them as his former associates if he could profit by it. The traitor, in consequence of the conversation in the saloon, which we have just referred to, had been detained much longer than had been anticipated, and when a quarter of an hour elapsed without any tidings of him, Watkins began to feel much as though, instead of trapping others, he was in a trap himself.

At length, however, Blackmoor made his appearance, and having detailed his proceedings, a conference as to their future steps was held.

Like all traitors, Blackmoor proposed that he should remain in the back ground. Watkins, however, would not hear of this. "Blackmoor," he said, "had led them so far, and he should conduct them still."

"It will be necessary that I should remain in the rear," remarked Blackmoor, in order that I may secure your retreat."

"No," said Watkins, authoritatively. "No, you shall lead us."

"But I shall certainly be sacrificed if they see me enter first. M'Cleane is a devil with his rapier; and if I am cut down, and you and your party should be overpowered, I should like to know how you would retreat without my assistance?" said the coward.

There was a show of reason in this, as the Bow Street Runner was compelled to admit; and it was at length decided that the traitor should occupy a centre-place in the column,

and that Watkins should leap into the room followed by his men as rapidly as possible.

The whole party now, one by one, crept through the opening in the brick partition; and then, having looked to the priming of their pistols, moved silently and stealthily onwards.

They at length reached the opened sliding pannel, and each man drew his rapier, with the utmost caution.

Only the heavy and thick folds of tapestry now divided Watkins from the gang who he had so long sought to secure; and the Bow Street runner's eyes gleamed with an intensity of ferocious pleasure.

"Is each man provided with handcuffs?" he asked in a whisper.

An affirmative nod was the reply, for the place they now stood in was sufficiently illu-

minated for such signals, as the light from the many wax candles within, streamed through the tapestry.

"Are all ready?" whispered the Bow Street runner.

The same silent nods responded again in the affirmative.

"Then, follow me, men, and remember that this is an affair of life and death. We shall either lose our lives or make our fortunes. Come on!"

So saying Watkins placed his foot on the slight ledge which separated the saloon from the subterranean passage, and was about to enter when the deep sonorous tones of a bell pealed through the 'Chapel.'

Instantly following this the sounds of revelry within ceased, and where, a brief period of time before, all had been mirth and revelry, was now a silence as deep and unbroken as that of the grave.

"It is the alarm bell;" said Blackmoor, "by some means or other they have got scent of our proceedings.   Forwards! we have not a moment to lose."

Watkins, with a double barrelled pistol in his left hand and a drawn sword in his right, followed by his party similarly armed, rushed like tigers into the saloon. Sudden, however, as had been their entrance, they found the gang ready to receive them.

M'Cleane, and the men under him, never parted with their trusty rapiers, and on a stand, in the apartment, loaded pistols were always ready; to draw the one, and to sieze on the other, was the first impulse of each on hearing the alarm bell.

The opposing parties were, therefore, similarly armed, and nothing could exceed the surprise of M'Cleane and the rest of the robbers when Watkins and his myrmidons made their appearance in so sudden, unexpected, and mysterious a manner; and an equal degree of surprise filled the bosoms of the invading parties when they beheld the magnificence of the nest of the highwaymen and burglars.

That gorgeous apartment was about to become a scene of severe conflict; for each party felt that life and death were involved in the issue of the adventure.

"In the king's name, James M'Cleane, I call upon you and your comrades to surrender," said Watkins, approaching the Captain.

"By the God who made me, never," exclaimed M'Cleane. "Come on, my brave companions," he continued, addressing the gang, "we will, at least, sell our lives dearly."

A loud burst of defiance from the whole fraternity told how warmly they responded to the appeal.

"Stand near to the secret panelling in the fire place," whispered M'Cleane to Jenny Diver, "in case of need we can escape in that direction."

"No, Jem, said the heroic girl, "I will not desert you in this extremity, my place is by your side, and here I will remain."

"I command you!" exclaimed M'Cleane, "and this is no time for parleying—Go."

That which Jenny had refused to do on the grounds of affection, she complied with when urged by the oath of duty by which she had bound herself. Quitting the Captain, she whispered to the other females, and they took their station at the further end of the saloon, where the fire place was situated.

"M'Cleane," said Watkins, "drive me not to extremities; resistance will be utterly useless; once more I say obey this warrant," and he exhibited the document.

Dick Flybynight rushed forward to seize the obnoxious paper, and in doing so caught sight of Blackmoor who had contrived to hide himself behind some of Watkins's men.

He started back with astonishment depicted on his features—

"Look yonder," said he to M'Cleane, pointing his finger in the direction of the man, who they had firmly believed to be thousands of miles off.

Had the grave itself given up its dead, M'Cleane could not have been more astounded. With scarce power to move he rivetted his glance on the now trembling traitor, who perceived that nothing but a miracle could save him from the vengeance of the gang.

"Fool that I was to spare thy miserable carcass twice." he gasped, "but now, villain, thou shalt not escape my vengeance."

The traitor made a backward movement, as if he would have receded into the subterranean passage, but M'Cleane by a rapid movement, placed himself between Blackmoor and it, and so cut him off from all chance of escape.

Several of the gang were about to rush upon and tear him limb from limb; but M'Cleane perceiving their intentions, exclaimed in a voice of thunder—

"Hold! I alone will punish him."

Before Watkins or his men could interfere to prevent him, so rapid was M'Cleane's movement, a flash was seen, a sharp report heard, and the falling as of a heavy body on the floor.

When the smoke of the discharge cleared, the lifeless body of Blackmoor appeared, the bullet had passed right through his brain, and his eyes glared horribly in death.

"So perish all traitors," exclaimed the Captain, as he indignantly kicked the senseless carcass.

A desperate conflict now ensued; the death of their guide had rendered Watkins and his men furious, and self preservation appeared to be their aim rather than the capture of the resolute robbers.

Struck with a panic, more than half of the assailants retreated to the subterranean passage; three already lay weltering in their blood on the carpet of the saloon, and Watkins himself was wounded. The issue of the strife was no longer doubtful, for in a space of time, shorter than that which has been occupied in recording it, the battle was at an end, the gang of M'Cleane being triumphant.

On the side of M'Cleane, only Handsome Jack had been wounded, and that but slightly, for all the men were accomplished swordsmen. and some of the defeated party had been shot down by Jenny Diver and the other females present.

Seeing the utter impossibility of accomplishing his object, and feeling the danger of his position, Watkins now sued for a truce.

"You would have hanged me and my fellows," said M'Cleane, "but on one condition only will I spare your lives."

"Well, Mr. M'Cleane," said Watkins, with a rueful air, "life is werry sweet, I must say, so what do you propose?"

"First, that you and your bloodhounds swear a solemn oath that what has happened this evening, and what you have seen shall never be divulged to mortal. Secondly, that you never again attempt to molest us; and thirdly that you all be led from this place blindfolded. Unless you accede to these conditions you shall all be made as silent as the villain who led you here, and your fates will never be known."

"I agree, Mr. M'Cleane," said Watkins,

whose state of terror was now absolutely ludicrous.

The men who had slunk into the subterranean passage were now recalled by the Bow Street runner, and the necessary oaths having been taken, Watkins applied for permission to depart.

"You shall depart as I promised," said M'Cleane, "but not by the way you came, nor yet immediately, you have first some work to do."

"Blindfold them all," commanded M'Cleane.

This operation was speedily performed by Jenny Diver, Gipsey Betty and the other girls.

"Now," observed M'Cleane, "you are strong fellows, these eight dead men must be carried on your shoulders to a place whither I shall lead you."

At a signal from the Captain, the members of the gang lifted Blackmoor and the others who had fallen, on the backs of the blindfolded constables. Lights were then provided, and leaving the saloon, they traversed a number of dark passages, and descended several flights of stairs, when they entered a large vault, far beneath the place they had quitted.

The men's eyes were then unbandaged, and spades having been brought, they were compelled to dig a pit, into which their late companions were cast. M'Cleane, himself, kicking the traitor into the hole.

"He's safe enough now," remarked the Captain, as the last spadeful of mould was thrown in. "If he was the devil himself he couldn't escape from such a grave."

The constables having concluded their revolting and terrible task, were again blindfolded and led through many passages until they arrived at the cells contiguous to the Secret Tribunal.

"Here," said M'Cleane, "here you must remain for a few hours at least; but be at ease, for you shall not be ill-treated. Circumstances render it necessasy that you should not yet be set at liberty; but of that you shall not long, on my honor, be deprived."

A member of the gang was then appointed sentinel over them, and another deputed to supply them provisions. M'Cleane and the rest then sought the saloon, where a council of the whole gang was immediately called.

CHAPTER XXVII.

THE COUSINS—A CONFLAGRATION—HANDSOME JACK RESCUES JENNY DIVER, AND GETS HIMSELF INTO DANGER.

ONE dark and stormy night towards the end of October, in the year 17—, there sat in an apartment of an old house in the city, cowering over a miserable fire, or rather expiring embers of one, a man who appeared to be about forty years of age.

He was tall and gaunt in his appearance, his face was wrinkled; but this was rather the effect of the workings of evil and tumultuous passions than of age;—a cold grey eye glanced

at intervals, furtively at the various objects in the room; and as he rubbed his long bony hands together, to increase the little warmth given by the embers, he murmured to himself.

This man was Ephraim Blake, son to that old Abraham Blake who was murdered by Blackmoor, and the room in which he sat was the very one in which the atrocious crime had been committed.

"The abandoned scapegrace!" he muttered, "not content with bringing his father to beggary, he seeks now to rob me of what little I have, by extortion; but I will be fully and amply revenged."

We have, before, in the course of this tale, intimated that revenge was a leading and a predominating principle in Ephraim Blake's character. As he now awaited an unsought visit from his cousin the feeling increased, until it acquired an almost overwhelming intensity.

Ephraim Blake had succeeded to the enormous wealth of his murdered father, whose death, although it placed him in possession of great riches, he had sworn to avenge. How he had been disappointed in capturing old Abraham Blake's murderer, after he, through M'Cleane's interference, had escaped the gallows, has already been shown.

But by persevering enquiries, and unremitting exertions he had learned by whom Blackmoor's escape had been managed, and now his revenge was to a great extent transfered to those who had robbed him of his revenge.

Whilst he was yet musing, a knock was heard at the street door; it was a peculiar knock which Ephraim at once recognised.

Lighting a candle which was fixed in a battered old horn lantern, Ephraim proceeded down stairs, and on reaching the door, loosened the chains, drew back the ponderous bolts, and half opened it.

A man wrapped in a dark cloak, with a broad leaved hat shadowing his face, slid in almost like a shadow. No sooner had he done so, than Ephraim with great care secured the way of entrance.

"Follow me," he said, and mounting the stairs, the new comer and himself entered the apartment which he had just quitted.

"Will you never cease to trouble me?" asked Ephraim. "Am I so rich, that I can afford always to minister to your necessities, or support your extravagance, Joseph?"

"Why, cousin, "replied the other, "your father robbed my father of his inheritance, and it is nothing but just that your father's son should do a little for my father's son, when he needs assistance. Come, a'nt you going to give one a dram. By the foul fiend! but 'tis cold enough to freeze even a miser's vitals, and they can stand a good deal of cold."

"Drams—drams—drams!" ejaculated Ephriam, lifting up his skinny hands, and turning towards the cob-webbed ceiling his dull grey eyes. "Strong waters have been your ruin, Joseph! Will you never quit this evil course of life?"

"Yes, Ephraim, if you will provide me with a more profitable one"

"Your soul is as dark as your countenance,"

remarked Ephraim, as with great reluctance he placed a long, cracked, big-bodied, old-fashioned black bottle, and a glass on the table.

"As to my countenance, the colour of it is none of my fault, Ephraim, any more than it is that I have got the nickname of 'Blueskin'———"

"Blueskin!" said Ephraim Blake, starting to his feet. "Can it be that you are that notorious member of———"

"Jonathan Wild's gang, you would say! exclaimed Joseph Blake, interrupting him. "Yes, cousin, I am."

And as Joseph Blake—or Blueskin—as we will in future call him, made the avowal, he poured out a brimming glassful of nantz, and drank Ephraim's health.

"Where are your companions, Oak and Levy, who were concerned with you—I did not then know it was you—in the street robbery in Oxford Street?"

"Hanged—both of them—together with a few more, cousin."

"As you too assuredly will be before long, Joseph, if you persist in your present evil courses," rejoined Ephraim.

"That is nothing to the purpose," said Blueskin; "I came here for twenty guineas, and that sum I must have."

"You shall have that sum, Joe; and I will double it on one condition," remarked Ephraim.

"Name it," exclaimed Blueskin, who was actually staggered at this unwonted benevolence on the part of his cousin.

"There is a certain man to whom I owe a grudge—that man is crafty and powerful. Without powerful aid, it would be next to impossible so to entrap him into the commission of a capital felony as to place his neck in jeopardy. That aid you must put me in the way of procuring."

"Is it necessary," asked Blueskin, "that he should commit any offence at all?"

"Why how could he be punished if innocent?" asked Ephraim.

"Oh!" replied Blueskin, "that's an easy matter enough. Give me the forty guineas, and I'll engage that, for a similar sum, Jonathan Wild will tuck up any man at Tyburn, though he be as innocent as an angel."

Bad as his heart was, and bitter as his feelings were, Ephraim Blake shrank, as he heard this cold-blooded avowal; but what course will not hatred pursue in order to compass its ends!

A long conversation now took place between the cousins, which it is not necessary, nor indeed would it be a proper one to detail here. When it had concluded, Ephraim counted out forty guineas, which Blueskin secured about his person and then, with sundry minute instructions to his cousin, quitted the old house in Bucklersbury.

Twenty-four hours afterwards, Ephraim Blake also, after carefully locking up his treasures, left his dilapidated house—home it could scarcely be called; and stealthily threading his way through Cheapside, shuffled along in the direction of Newtoner's Lane.

He had passed through St. Paul's Church Yard, had descended Ludgate Hill, and had arrived near Hanging Sword Alley, in Fleet Street, when he became uncertain as to his future way. Not caring to call one of the watch for the direction to so notorious a locality as that in which the domicile of the celebrated thief-taker was situated, he determined to trust to his own sagacity for discovering it, and so turned at random up Hanging Sword Alley.

He had proceeded but a few paces, when he fancied he smelt something like wood in a state of ignition: he paused—looked upwards, and from a window, not far above his head, he noticed a dense, spiral column of grey smoke issuing and writhing like a shadowy snake. Not a soul but himself was about,—the inhabitants of the alley appeared to be in profound sleep, and as to the guardians of life and of property, none were to be seen.

Presently, a flickering light from within made the diamond shaped panes of the window visible: it increased, until it became of a dull red hue,—then it absolutely glared. By this time thin jets of smoke were creeping out of crevices, and broken panes in other windows above.

It was evident that a conflagration was commencing its ravages within, unknown to the inhabitants of that, and of the surrounding houses.

As yet the fire was entirely confined to the front of the house, which was only occupied as a warehouse, and, strange to say, the only person who witnessed it had failed to give the alarm. But that was not long in coming.

Ephraim Blake, who had never before beheld a burning house, had been so paralysed at the spectacle that he was actually spell bound; but when the windows cracked with the intense heat, and he felt the warmth himself, he shouted at the top of his voice for the watch, who, alas! were too snugly asleep in their boxes to hear him.

Window after window now sent forth its volumes of dense smoke,—at length, yielding to the enormous pressure of vapour within, they burst, and then, as if glad to meet with sustaing air, the flames belched forth.

And now the dark sky above assumed a ruddy tint; volumes of smoke rolled upwards, and people in the opposite houses, awakened by the glare of the flames, started in affright from their slumbers.

As yet a side window on the second floor gave no indications of fire within the apartment, or staircase, or whatever it might be which lighted it, and the people who now began to crowd into the alley, suggested the propriety of placing a ladder against it, and so, by effecting an entrance, to alarm the inmates, who all the while were unconscious of their extreme danger.

Roused by the increasing din, the watch now came pouring into the alley, and a ladder was after some delay procured.

Just as it was about being placed against the wall, the side window of which we have just spoken, was thrown open, and the frowsy head of Mr. Slogger, the assistant to Williams, the "fence," made its appearance. His usually small eyes were now unnaturally dilated; and he held out his hands as if imploring for assistance.

"For God's sake, save me!" he screamed;—the back of the house has caught, and there is no way out but through this window or over the roof. Williams and two more are gone that way, but the smoke is so thick that I cannot follow them."

The ladder was placed against the wall, but, to the anguish of Slogger, he perceived that full ten feet intervened between its uppermost rings and the sill of the window over which he leaned.

"Jump!" cried many voices; for smoke now began to pour forth from the side window.

The poor wretch, however, hesitated, and looked back as though he had a mind again to try the staircase, and gain, by a desperate effort, the roof, and so escape by means of the adjoining houses.

"Suddenly he disappeared from the window, and how eagerly did the crowd look for his return. Five minutes elapsed—five minutes—during which the flames within raged and roared like a blast furnace; and still the unfortunate man came not.

The opposite house—for the alley was very narrow—had now caught fire, and already baked by the extreme heat, the old timbers rapidly ignited. These houses, so dilapidated were they, had been prevented for many years from falling against each other by huge transverse beams of wood, and even these were licked by tongues of flame.

"Who are in the house?" exclaimed a stranger, who had literally fought his way through the crowd to the door of the burning habitation.

"Four, if not more than that," remarked an old Charley, who did nothing but hold up his lantern mechanically, though God knows there was little need of light.

By a few batterings at the door with a large stone, the stranger burst it open, and rushed in, calling in vain on the standers by to follow him: none moved an inch. They could not, however, help cheering the unknown for his bravery.

A minute after he appeared at the side window; and again called for volunteers. Still his voice was unheeded.

"Then, by Heaven!—you craven reptiles!—I'll save them or perish in the attempt," he cried, shaking his hand at the mob scornfully, and rushed from view.

Five or six minutes of agonising suspense followed, beneath the leaves of the roof the smoke now poured forth in denser volumes than ever, and jets of flame issued through the crevices of the gable end and the roof.

"That fool-hardy fellow has thrown his life away in trying to save that old rogue, Williams' goods," said a bystander.

He had scarcely uttered the words, when a terrific crash was heard: myriads of sparks set like stars in an atmosphere of dark vapour arose from the building, and then high above the house tops ascended the uncontrolled flames, illuminating the neighbourhood and making the numerous steeples appear like pinnacles of red hot metal.

"The roof is in, and they are lost!" was the universal cry and belief.

A shudder ran through the crowd;—it appeared almost impossible they could have been saved, for some persons present had remarked that the roof of the "Fence's" house was far higher than either of those which adjoined it—so much higher, indeed, that to get from one to the other alive was almost impossible.

All at once a shout of "there he is!" burst from the crowd, and a loud huzza rent the air; for on the parapet of the roofless habitation stood the stranger, with a female, apparently lifeless, in his arms.

"Brave fellow!—noble fellow!"—now exclaimed the very people who so lately had denounced him as being fool-hardy.

The stranger's position was now, however, more perilous than when he had rushed through the suffocating and blinding smoke in the rooms of the 'Fence's' house. Beneath him, on one side, was a yawning abyss, the bottom of which glowed like the lava in the crater of some volcano. On the other, were the crowds in the alley, scores of feet from the summit of the wall which, in consequence of the intense heat to which it had been subjected, cracked and crumbled as he trod on it: add to this, that he bore in his arms a lifeless burthen, and it will be readily imagined that danger beset him on every side.

Two other figures now appeared, who were readily recognised as Williams, the Fence, the owner of the dwelling, and his assistant, Mr. Slogger. These worthies crawled slowly along the parapet, their faces, which in the strong light were perfectly distinct, betraying the horror they felt.

"I've seen that face before," said Ephraim Blake to himself as he looked on the stranger who had so gallantly thus far rescued the female; "I cannot be mistaken, and it was on the day, too, when that devil, Blackmoor was rescued."

He looked again, and again, and became more fully convinced that his surmise was correct, but his father observations were interrupted by the exclamations of those around him.

"By Heaven!" said one "he is going to venture across that narrow beam,—'tis impossible for it to bear his and the girl's weight."

Only this one beam had been left—all the others had been so burnt and charred that their centres had fallen away, and only two blackened stumps projected from the walls.

The one on which the stranger now planted his foot already gave symptoms of weakness; but it was his only bridge of escape, and he ventured on it.

It was not a foot square, and had it been strong as iron would have afforded at such a giddy height but a precarious footing. Nevertheless, with the utmost caution he proceeded until he reached to nearly the centre when he halted, and whilst he balanced himself with his senseless burthen with right foot pressed on the beam to ascertain its strength.

It bent, and with the point of his boot he could scrape of the charred portion to nearly the depth of an inch.

The people below marked them, and a murmer and a movement of horror ran through the crowd. It was at once evident to the stranger that the very centre of the beam would not support,—what was he to do? A minutes' consideration determined him. Onward he must go, and reach the opposite house before its roof had given way, and that would not be long, for below him the flames in it were spreading fast;—backwards he could not go, for on that narrow bridge to turn was an impossibility; besides, if he could, what would it avail him? His course—a desperate course indeed—was shaped.

Summoning all his fortitude, he planted his left foot firmly on the last sound bit of the beam, and then bending forward, he, with great slowness advanced his right foot, so as to reach the sound end of the part of the timber on the nearest the beam to which he was going,—then, with a desperate energy, he drew forward his left foot, and in a moment had cleared the rotten part and that of greatest danger.

Pausing but for a moment to draw a long breath, he again moved onward, and in a few minutes gained the parapet of the house.

To mount it—(it was but two feet from the beam)—carry the girl he had saved to the roof of the next house, and then to return and endeavour to save the two men, by encouraging them to follow him, was but the work of a few seconds.

But, to his horror. on looking at the beam he discovered that the jerk caused by his suddenly quitting it, in his anxiety for his charge, had snapped it in the middle, and now no communication whatever remained.

As he gazed in silent horror on the spectacle, Slogger and Williams implored him to save them;—whilst they were yet beseeching, a column of flame from the ruins below, caused by the falling of the hitherto unconsumed portion of some flooring, shot up, like a pillar of fire, its point darting immediately in the direction of where they sat clinging to the parapet.

One wild shriek of despair, which almost curdled the blood in the stranger's veins, was heard, and then, as the miserable men fell back into the burning ruins, nothing but the roaring of the devouring elements was noticed!

Rushing immediately to the place where he had left the young woman the stranger had rescued, he again lifted her in his arms, and proceeded along the roofs of the houses until he arrived at an attic window which was open. Entering it without ceremony, he deposited his burthen on a bed, and then taking from a pitcher near some water, he removed a veil from her blackened face, and dashed some cold water on it.

Until now, he had not beheld the countenance of her whom he had snatched from the jaws of a horrible death. Through the soot and dust which disfigured her, he fancied the face was familiar to him, but in its present state he found it impossible to identify it. Unfolding his neckcloth, which was of the finest texture, he dipped it in the water, and with as soft a touch as that of a mother tending her infant, he commenced removing the effects of the conflagration from her counte-

nance, which, even when so disfigured, was evidently one of great beauty.

He had but just commenced his task, when the young woman opened her eyes, and fixed them on her deliverer.

"Handsome Jack!" she exclaimed clasping her hands in astonishment.

"Jenny Diver!" cried Handsome Jack, no less surprised than the girl herself.

"How, by what means, came I here, Jack?" asked Jenny," her eyes wandering about the strange room, for as yet she had not quite recovered her senses.

"I might ask you the same question," replied Jack; "but, my dear Jenny, you must keep quiet for a little time: compose yourself,—you know you are with a friend."

"Yes, I know that well;" but, oh! what a horrible dream I have had!" said Jenny, shuddering.

"Another time, Jenny, you shall tell all—another time—rest yourself now."

"No—no! I cannot rest. I dreamed, Jack, that I was at Williams', the Fence, when all at once flames—horrible flames—burst in upon us, blocking up any way of escape but by the staircase. I thought Slogger and Williams ran up those stairs, and that I, in the frenzy of desperation, tried to follow them, which I seemed to do as far as the third story, when they rushed forward and left me. Then I seemed blinded by smoke, and scorched by intense heat; my eyeballs glowed in their sockets; my tongue became parched; my brain dizzy; and—and then, Jack, all afterwards is a blank. My God!" exclaimed Jenny, putting her hands before her eyes, as if to shut out some frightful vision,—"what a dream of horror.!"

*   *   *   *   *

For some time after the perilous passage of Handsome Jack and Jenny Diver over the beam, Ephraim Blake lingered about the locality in the hopes of seeing the stranger, whose face had recalled a certain past transaction to his mind.

That he had escaped to the roof of the opposite house was plain, for he himself had beheld him mount the parapet, where, however, he lost sight of him; but further than that neither he himself, nor those whom he questioned knew anything.

As the roof of the second house fell in immediately after the feat of Handsome Jack's had been accomplished, it was generally supposed that he had shared a fate similar to that of Williams and Slogger. Ephraim, therefore, was about to leave the place and proceed homeward. determined to postpone his visit to Newtoner's Lane until a future opportunity.

He had scarcely walked a dozen paces towards Fleet Street, when his cousin's voice saluted him.

Anxious to avoid being seen with Blueskin in public, and knowing him to be rather difficult to shake off, he endeavoured to distract his attention by pointing out the recent scene of Handsome Jack's daring exploit.

Looking upwards for this purpose, his eye caught sight of the face of a man whose eyes were peering cautiously downwards as if to ascertain whether the way was clear.

"By God it is him!" said Ephraim.

" It is whom?" asked Blueskin.

"The man into whose arms my father's murderer fell when he leaped from the cart," replied Ephraim; and I'll give you twenty guineas, Joe, if you'll mark him and find out who he is."

"Agreed," said Blueskin. " I too, have seen him before; but where, I cannot just now remember."

The cousins then separated, Ephraim returning to his gloomy abode in Bucklersbury, and Joseph Blake remaining in Hanging Sword Alley to keep watch over the movements of Handsome Jack.

CHAPTER XXVIII.

EPHRAIM BLAKE'S INTERVIEW WITH ⬛LD.— JONATHAN WILD'S ATTEMPT TO MURDER MARY MILLINER.

On the morning succeeding the conflagration in Hanging Sword Alley, Jonathan Wild was seated in his private office in Newtoner's Lane, busily engaged in arranging and carefully classifying various documents, when his man, Abraham, entered the apartment.

"What now, Abraham?" inquired the thief-taker; for he saw by the expression of the Israelite's countenance, that he had something of importance to communicate.

"Good news !—capital news !—Mishter Vild!" replied Abraham, rubbing his hands with diabolical glee.

"Sit down, Abraham," said Jonathan, pointing to a chair next him; for, with his usual keenness of perception, he saw in the jew's countenance an indication of coming profit to himself.

"Have my emissaries tracked that deceiving villain, Wilson?" he asked.

"No, Mishter Vild; de newsh I have to tell is petter ash dat," replied Abraham.

"Then out with it, man!" said Jonathan; " I can't stay dilly-dallying all day!"

"'Tis a fire, Mishter Vild," said the jew; " a beautiful fire;—a fire as 'll make de poys and gals come to Newtoner's Lane, instead of taking dere goots somewheres else."

"Indeed," remarked Jonathan, musingly.

"And vere do you think it vas?" asked Abraham, looking marvellously mysterious.

"How should I know?" said Jonathan, replying thus to one question by asking another.

"Not far from an old friend of yours,—a Fence. Ah! Mishter Vild! you should have been in Hanging Sword Alley last night; Jerry told me just now as 'twas a peautiful sight."

"Hanging Sword Alley," repeated Wild. "Fire there,—why there's no one about that neighbourhood whose ruin would serve me, but that infernal villain, Williams."

"Vell, Mishter Villiams' house vas purned down last night as ever vas, Mishter Vild, said Abraham; who, as he he spoke, watched with the utmost anxiety his villainous master's countenance.

"Purned down — down to de groundsh, Mishter Vild,—all put de valls," said the jew.

"Thank God!" exclaimed Jonathan; the fellow won't oppose me any more."

"No, Mishter Vild,—no he von't; I'll shwear to dat, Mishter Vild! I know a capital reason vhy."

"Give it me," said Jonathan rather fiercely; for his curiosity, as well as his cupidity, was now raised to the uttermost pitch.

"'Cos Mishter Villiams was purned in his house, and some von else peside him, too."

"Williams burnt to death!" exclaimed Jonathan, starting to his feet. Thank God for this?"

For Wild was so thorough paced a villain that he could bless the Deity for the removal of those who stood in his way, even in so calamitous manner.

"Then, suddenly recollecting himself, he muttered:—

"But there was one associated with him, as Abraham is with me, who knew all his secrets, and who will perhaps set up on his own account, now that his master's gone,—just as Jerry has succeeded to the business of Tony Bilkit."

"He can't do that Mishter Vild," remarked Abraham, who had listened intently to the soliloquy; "he'll never set up for Fence."

"Why not?" sharply demanded Jonathan.

"Vhy, 'cos Mishther Slogger vas purned alive, too, along mit Mishter Villiams," replied Abraham.

"Thank God!" cried Jonathan; and then letting his chin fall on his chest, he clasped his hands behind his back, and paced the chamber in silence.

This was usually a signal to Abraham to withdraw; but on this occasion he pertinaciously retained his seat, eyeing with an intensely cunning expression the physiognomical development of his infamous master.

"You may go, Abraham," said Jonathan, after a few turns round the room.

"Not before I puts a goot job in your vay, Mishter Vild,—a shentlemans vants to see you' —he's vaiting pelow."

"His name?" demanded Wild.

"Vhy, he's a cunning rogue, Mishter Jonathan, and he von't tell it put to you; I tried to get it out of him, put he as fly as—as——"

"The devil, "suggested Jonathan, who perceived that his minion was at a loss for a suitable simile."

"As you or me, I was going to say; put 'tis all as von," replied Abraham, sneering.

"Admit him," said Jonathan, who felt no inclination whatever to bandy compliments with his accomplice.

Immediately afterwards Blake was ushered by the jew into Jonathan's presence.

"Your business, sir, said the latter, rising.

Ephraim Blake then informed him of the particulars of the escape of Blackmoor; and stated, that he had on the previous evening, on the occasion of the conflagation at the Fence's in Hanging Sword Alley, by mere chance, recognised the man into whose arms the criminal was received when he leaped from the cart.

"I have a person on his track," said Ephraim; "and what I want you to do, Mr. Wild, is this: to discover, if possible, the man and his associates; and, either by a true or a fictitious charge, to put their necks, and his neck, especially, into a noose."

On hearing this, Wild assumed the appearance of an insulted and indignant man; and said, with apparent warmth:—

"Fabricate a charge, sir! You do not, I hope, conceive me capable of such an atrocity. I would have you to know," continued the wily villain, "that my business is principally confined to the procuring the restoration of property to persons plundered; and even this I do from a sense of my duty to my fellow men; but no trumped up charge would I ever bring against any man. You have mistaken me, sir!"

"Tush, man!" said Ephraim, flinging a purse of gold on the table; "there is no need of this squeamishness,—my cousin, who is well known to you, has let me into too many of your secrets for me to doubt that you will accede to my wishes in this matter."

"Your cousin!—my secrets, sir!" ejaculated Jonathan, "what may be the name of this cousin of yours?"

"Joseph Blake," replied Ephraim.

"What, is Blueskin related to you?" asked Wild.

"I have said," replied Ephraim, "that he is my cousin;—and a villainous cousin he is. As it is, however, I make use of him for the attainment of my own ends."

"Well," said the thief-taker, "we may understand ourselves, Mr. Blake, better by-and-bye. If, as you say, I can serve you, and you are willing to pay for my so doing, I have no objection, as it is to oblige a friend. Know you the name of the man you are so desirous of—of?"

Jonathan Wild hesitated; for he did not exactly know how to express the intended proceeding against the stranger.

"Desirous of being revenged!" said Blake, suggesting the necessary phrase.

"For what?" asked Wild.

"For the barbarous murder of my own father," replied Ephraim, his cheeks turning livid with horror and deadly passion, as he recalled to recollection the spectacle of the old man lying dabbled with his own gore on the floor of his house in Bucklersbury.

"Ah!" said Jonathan, "that indeed alters the case, and it is quite right that those who assisted the murderer to escape should be brought to justice."

The sight of the well filled purse had wrought this change in Wild's opinions; but to this of course he did not allude: on the contrary, he affected not even to observe it.

"You say," he continued, "that you have set some on one this track. Who have you so employed?"

"My cousin, Joseph," replied Ephraim.

"Blueskin—hem! and have you paid him anything?"

"Forty guineas," said Ephraim.

Wild's eyes flashed angrily on hearing this. "So then," he muttered to himself, as he paced up and down the apartment, "Master Blueskin has dared to take my business into his own hands, and set up on his own account; this affair he never mentioned to me, though he was here an hour ago; but he shall suffer for his treachery, or my name is not Jonathan Wild."

"Then you will do what I require of you,—discover this man, and by fair means or foul, I do not care which, effect his ruin?" asked Ephraim.

"If my experience can be of any avail, Mr. Blake," returned Jonathan, "you may command my services in this matter; but I must first see your cousin, Blueskin, who may have some knowledge of the stranger's person. If such be the case, depend on it that before many days are past, your desire shall be gratified; but I candidly tell you, that it will be rather an expensive affair; for though I am willing to give you my services, it will be necessary to employ secret agents, and they are not over liberal."

"Name any sum you please, Mr. Wild," said Ephraim; "I am wealthy, and what I have placed on the table is but an earnest of what I will advance in the event of your efforts proving successful."

"Enough," remarked Wild. "And now, sir, if you will do me the favour to call on me again a week hence, I hope to be enabled to afford you the information you require."

The interview then terminated, and Ephraim departed from the celebrated thief-catcher's house.

For some moments after Blake had quitted the apartment, Wild sat with his chin drooping on his chest, and his arms folded, apparently absorbed in thought.

Suddenly he rose, rang a small silver bell which always stood on a table near hand, thrice, and shortly afterwards a female entered in obedience to the summons.

This was his well-known confederate, Mary Milliner, a woman with whom Wild had made acquaintance when he was confined for debt in Wood Street Compter. She was one of the most artful and abandoned of her sex, and and a fit tool for one such as Jonathan to work with.

It happened, that on the present occasion, Mrs. Milliner had been making rather too free with the contents of a bottle of Nantz—a failing to which she was remarkably prone. When sober, she always was obedient to the will of Wild, who exercised a wonderful influence over her; but with her, as is generally the case with others, the effect of liquor was to develope qualities directly opposite those exhibited when in a state of sobriety. She came into the room with a flushed face and an unsteady step.

Jonathan Wild did not at first notice her condition, for his eyes were still bent upon the floor.

"I have a job in hand, Mary," he said, "in which I shall require your assistance; and you must in this matter exercise more than your usual sharpness. Do you hear?"

"Yes," returned the woman, in a thick, muffled voice, "I hear; but what sort of a job is it—old fellow!"

"You must pump Blueskin, and draw him

on to tell all the information he possesses, relating to a certain person who saved a young woman from the fire at Williams' the Fence. You can do anything with Blake, you know; he will be here this evening, and I expect you to bring some intelligence in the course of the night."

"You make a pretty tool of me, Master Wild," said Milliner. "Now, I tell you, I don't like this job: Blueskin has always been very civil to me, and I'll be d—d if I play the sneak with him; so if you want any news from that quarter, you must e'en go and fish it out yourself."

Wild started from his chair in a transport of rage at thus being defied by one of his subordinates;—seizing the half intoxicated woman by the shoulder, he looked in her face savagely, and reiterated his command.

Mary Milliner, however, still defied him;

and, made bold by the liquor she had taken, assailed her partner in iniquity with the most opprobrious epithets.

Bursting from his grasp, she was about to quit the room, when Wild, whose passion now completely mastered him, seized a cutlass which stood near, and rushed furiously on the woman.

Uttering the most horrible oaths and execrations, he waved the weapon above Mary Milliner's head, and again demanded whether she would do his bidding?

And again did she deny his authority to dictate to her, throwing back taunts in Wild's face which put him into a complete paroxysm of fury: he foamed at the mouth, glared on her with his ferocious eyes, and then thrusting her from him with his left-hand, he lifted the murderous weapon with his right, and aimed a desperate blow at the wretched woman's head.

Had it fallen on the centre of her skull, so violent was the effort he made, that it must have been cloven in twain. Fortunately, however, he missed his mark; but so near was he to it, that one of the wretched woman's ears was taken clean off, and a deep gash was inflicted on her shoulder.

"Villain—murderous villain!" exclaimed the woman; "but I'll be revenged on you for this!" and she sank on the floor, fainting from the great loss of blood.

The noise occasioned by this transaction brought Abraham, the jew, into the room. "Take that hag out of my sight," said Jonathan, pointing to the still senseless and prostrate woman.

Abraham, who at first believed Mary Milliner was dead, on ascertaining the real state of the case, recovered somewhat from the fright into which he had been thrown, and without uttering a syllable, dragged the wounded woman from the room.

Then Jonathan Wild threw himself in a chair, and opened his black book, that volume in which he inserted the names of those who had offended him, and whose fate he had determined to seal.

To the already long list of doomed men he was about to add another.

"I at least thought Blueskin was faithful to me," he murmured, "but I am deceived it seems; he shall, however, reap the reward of his treachery, for no man ever escaped who braved the vengeance of Jonathan Wild."

Then taking a pen, he wrote in the blood columns the name of Joseph Blake: with a grin of diabolical satisfaction he closed the book, replaced it in a private drawer, and sat coolly down to await the arrival of the man whom he had determined to sacrifice.

There, for the present we leave him, for the purpose of returning to the imprisoned Bow Street Runner and his companions in the cell beneath the Chapel.

The reflections of Mr. Watkins were by no means of a very cheering character. The dungeon in which he was confined was low, so low that, excepting in the middle of it, and just beneath the crown of its arched roof, he could not stand upright; some foul-musty straw formed his bed; and the only light he had was given by a small lamp, the smoke from which nearly suffocated him.

On the score of his personal safety too he felt somewhat alarmed, for in spite of the promise made him by the Captain, he knew that he had to do with desperate men, who, it was reasonable to suppose, from the very nature of their professions would not be remarkably punctual in their performances. He was conscious, too, that he had made the first attack; and the recent loathsome affair of the interment of the bodies, and of the summary punishment inflicted on Blackmoor, led him to anticipate that evil might result to himself.

As his expedition had been planned and executed in the most secret manner, no persons whatever, excepting himself and those connected with him were aware of his position.

He could not therefore expect any aid from without; and he now bitterly regretted his not having admitted some party into his confidence; but there was no help for him, or the only chance of it that was afforded was by bribing the sentinels.

Establishing a communication with the man on guard, by means of the small grating in the door of his cell, he sounded him on the delicate topic; but he soon discovered that his attempts to shake fidelity in that quarter at least would be useless.

Still he had another resource—he determined to try what could be done with the man who brought him his food, with which necessary article he was abundantly supplied.

The man who had been been deputed by M'Cleane to carry the Bow Street Runner his meals was no other than our old acquaintance, Beauty Ellis, on whose fidelity he knew he could implicitly rely.

Watkins not being aware of the devotion of Beauty to M'Cleane and to the interests of the gang in general, awaited with much anxiety the arrival of Ellis. The constable happened to have about him a sum in gold large enough to tempt many a one in a far higher position than that which the old Charlie occupied, and he doubted not that so potent a key would open his prison door.

At the usual hour Beauty Ellis entered the cell of the constable with refreshments.

"Hope you're comfortable, Master Vatkins," said Beauty, as he laid the food on the floor, for there was neither bench or table of any kind.

"Can't brag on it," remarked the constable; "but I say, Mr. What's-your-name,—when's M'Cleane goin' to let us out?"

"When he's in the humour, and not a blessed minit afore," replied Beauty.

"But," asked the officer by way of a feeler, "ain't there no means of getting away without waiting till he chooses?"

"Not as I know on," returned Beauty.

"Oh! nonsense, man!" said Watkins. "Here, put these in your pocket;" and he put five guineas in Beauty Ellis's hand.

"Them's the sorts, Master Vatkins" said Beauty, as he surveyed the glittering gold by the light of the lamp,—"got any more o' that sort, eh?"

"Why?" asked Watkins.

"Because," replied Beauty, "they can't be of no manner of use to you down here, you know. You gets your lodging and vittles for nuffin, and what do a man want more?"

"Well, I have some more, and they shall be yours on one condition," said Watkins.

"Out with it, master!" exclaimed Beauty, jingling the guineas in his brawny hand. "I'm always willin' to 'arn these golden chaps."

"I have now about me twenty more of those golden chaps, as you call them," said the Bow Street Runner; "and if you will put me in the way of getting away from this abominable place, they shall be yours."

"Well, that's liberal, too," remarked Beauty Ellis; "and a very great temptation to an honest man into the bargain." he added.

"You must wait till to night, then," said Beauty, in a low tone, as though he did not wish the sentinel outside the gate to hear him.

"Shall I then certainly be set free this evening?" eagerly inquired the constable.

"As sartin as you're lying there," replied Beauty, "so hand us over the mopusses."

"But how am I to be sure you speak the truth?" asked the cautious constable.

"And how am I to know as when you get your liberty you'll pay me what you promise? If you won't trust me—I won't trust you,—that's werry much about the fact of the business," replied Beauty Ellis, a grin of something like honest indignation spreading over his singular features.

Watkins saw that it was no use to parley,—so once more impressing on Beauty the necessity of his keeping his word, he placed the twenty guineas in his hand.

"Sarve's you just right, Master Vatkins, for fleecing poor Gipsey Betty of her money when you let her out of the roundhouse the other day. I'll give the gal ten of these shiners, with your love and respects, and I'll keep the rest for your sake."

A gleam of suspicion that he had been "done" now shot athwart the mind of Watkins, who, as Beauty was quitting the cell, exclaimed:—

"Remember! to night! Now, you are sure that I shall have my liberty then?"

"Sartin on it. Why, Lord bless my soul," he exclaimed, as if suddenly recollecting himself, "Captain M'Cleane sent you a message, and I forgot it till this blessed minnit."

"What was its purport?" asked Watkins.

"Why, replied Beauty, "the Capt'n said as you was to lie quiet and comfortable for the present, and to night at eleven o'clock, or thereabouts, he will perform his promise to you and your men, of letting you out. A'nt he a gentleman of his word now?"

"Damn you!" roared Watkins; "why didn't you tell me this before I gave you those twenty-guineas?"

"'Cos your interesting conversation put it out o' my head, Captain. It's wonderful how gold affects my memory, too. Now, if you'd have said nothing about putting anything in my way for opening your cage-door, I should sure to have thought on M'Cleane's message. 'Tis your fault as I didn't, Vatkins, and no one elses."

"Then," said the constable, "of course you will give me back the twenty guineas, at least,—the five you are welcome to."

"Lor bless you, Mr. Vatkins!" said Beauty, jingling the guineas most provokingly in his breeches-pocket as he spoke, " ve never returns money in this establishment, that's quite contrary to the rools."

And so saying, with the grim smile of a man who would not break the "rools" of the place on any account. Beauty Ellis departed, leaving the over-reached Bow Street Runner in a towering passion.

About an hour before midnight the bolts and bars of Watkins' cell were again withdrawn, and the massive door having been flung back on its hinges, M'Cleane entered.

With him was handsome Jack, Dick Flyby-night, and several other members of the gang.

"I have come, Watkins," he said, "to perform my promise of setting you at liberty,—an act of grace you do not deserve for having attempted to bribe one of my people; but before you go I must have from you another promise, that nothing you have seen or heard here shall be divulged."

Glad to get off on any terms, Watkins, without hesitation, took an oath to that effect,—after which his companions were brought forth from their several places of confinement and subjected to similar binding obligations.

"To guard against all treachery on your part," said M'Cleane, "both myself, and all who have been in the habit of using this place, will immediately quit it. All of my people, but those you now see around me, have already departed. We shall follow them as soon as you are liberated. Remember this generosity of ours, Watkins, should any of us ever get into trouble; for we might easily have left you to rot in these dungeons, and none could have aided you."

"I know it," said Watkins, who was, or appeared to be rather touched by M'Cleane's conduct, "and from me you shall never experience harm."

"Blindfold them," said the Captain. This operation was then carefully performed, and the constable and his remaining men were led through secret ways to the stable entrance of the "Chapel," it was quite dark, and some of the gang led them until they arrived in Lincoln's Inn Fields.

Arrived in the centre of that then lonely place, especially at midnight, they suddenly removed the fillet from their late prisoner's eyes, and instantly disappeared in the gloom.

Within one hour from that time, the constable had reached Bow Street, and given information of the late transaction; but long before any steps could in consequence be taken, the "Thieves' Chapel" was completely dismantled and deserted.

CHAPTER XXIX.

HANDSOME JACK UNEXPECTEDLY MEETS WITH
A SAVAGE CUSTOMER.—THE COUNTRY HOUSE
AGAIN.—JENNY DIVER TURNS HIGHWAYMAN.
—NAN OF THE COMMON.

WHEN Handsome Jack looked out from the attic window of the house, in which he had sought refuge after his miraculous deliverance of Jenny Diver from the fire at Williams', the Fence, his keen eye failed not to detect the man who was watching him from below.

Instantly suspecting mischief, he retreated into the miserable garret to consult with Jenny Diver as to the best mode of making their escape unperceived from the house before daylight, as it was of the utmost importance that that they should be at the "Chapel" ere morning dawned.

Handsome Jack's resolution was soon taken.

Leaving Jenny in the garret to arrange her disordered dress, he descended the ricketty staircase and soon reached a passage on the ground floor, which terminated in a door at each extremity,—each of these doors were closed, but judging from their positions, he proceeded softly towards the one on his left-hand, and to his great joy found it merely fastened by a bolt: withdrawing this, he peeped out and discovered that it opened in a narrow court, which appeared to be like Hanging Sword Alley itself, a sort of back-slum thoroughfare.

He now groped his way back to the foot of the staircase, and was about to ascend to the garret, when the sound of voices from a room close to the front door, and from the chinks of which a feeble light streamed forth, attracted his attention, and he paused to listen.

"If he and the girl escaped," said a woman's voice, husky from the effects of gin, "they must be about the roofs now, and not far off either."

"I tell you they have escaped from death in the flames at least," remarked a rough and ruffianly voice, "for I saw the man afterwards, looking out of one of the windows of one of these houses—I'll swear to it."

"And more than that," he continued, "if I can get on the track of that man I'd give five golden guineas this minute," and Handsome Jack heard the chinking of gold pieces.

"Well, master," observed the woman with the husky voice, "when we've finished this bottle of max you shall go up stairs and get out of my garret window, you can go along all the roofs as far as Fleet Street then,—you know they couldn't have got away off 'tother way, lest they was salamanders."

Handsome Jack stood to hear no more, but nimbly as a squirrel he mounted to the garret.

"Quick, Jenny, quick, for God's sake! we must leave this crib without a moment's delay," he said eagerly.

"What on earth is the matter, Jack? surely the people of the house would not refuse us shelter after what we have gone through," said Jenny, who had not recovered from her fright.

"The woman of the house would betray us;" and then Handsome Jack rapidly informed her of what he had observed and heard below.

Jenny turned still paler than she was before, and hastily gathering her gown round her to prevent its rustling, she followed Jack as he began to descend.

They had reached the bottom in safety, and in that part of their progress the greatest caution was necessary,—a false step—a stumble; —aye, almost their hurried breathing might betray them.

They could distinctly hear the conversation. From what was uttered they knew that the bottle of strong waters was nearly drained of its contents.

"Now then, let's go on the roof, mistress," said the man. "I have no time to lose."

"Nor have we," whispered Handsome Jack to Jenny Diver; and he gently drew the girl towards the back-door.

Scarcely had they reached it, when the door of the apartment from which the sounds had proceeded was opened, and Joseph Blake came staggering into the passage.

"Here, give us a light, mistress," he growled, —"this place is as dark as the infernal regions."

On hearing this, Handsome Jack and Jenny shrank as far as possible within the deep shadow cast by the massive bannisters of the old staircase. The chances of their discovery when the woman appeared with the candle were as a hundred to one against them.

But to their great relief the man went up stairs followed by the woman; and as soon as they were out of hearing, Handsome Jack hastily opened the door, and they were about to step out, when an unforeseen obstacle interrupted their progress.

A huge bull-dog, which had been lying before the fire in the room we have alluded to, was aroused by the creaking of the hinges, and rushed forth just as Handsome Jack had opened the passage-door.

Jenny Diver was standing on the outside, but Jack had scarcely effected his egress; before he could completely do so, the huge brute sprang on him, and seizing the skirt of his coat within his powerful jaws, attempted with incredible strength to drag back the fugitive.

The noise of the animal had now alarmed the man and woman who had gone up stairs.

"What the devil is the matter with Belzy?" said the hag as she leaned over the bannisters, holding the light above her head, so as if possible to command a view of the bottom of the well-staircase.

In vain did Handsome Jack tug and strive, it was all to no purpose, and now he heard the man and woman descending the stairs. Unless something desperate was done his ruin was perhaps inevitable.

Drawing from its sheath a small Spanish dagger, which he always kept about his person, he suddenly drew it across the dog's throat, who instantly fell bathed in its life's blood; but even in death its fangs still held to the skirt of the coat, and it was impossible to extricate it.

Nearer and nearer came the man and his companion, when Jack, in desperation, severed with his dagger the skirt of his coat from its body, and with Jenny hastened from the spot.

On Blueskin and the woman of the house reaching the passage, the first object they observed was the now lifeless body of the bull-dog, Belzebub, weltering in his gore.

At sight of this the woman burst into loud lamentations, for the bull dog had been more beloved by her than any other living thing— her own relations not excepted. To bursts of grief succeeded the most fearful execrations on the author of his death, and now she became a hundred times more anxious, from a principle of revenge, than was Blueskin himself from the hope of gain, to discover the mysterious hero of the fire, for he it was she was fully persuaded who had murdered her beloved brute.

"What's this in his mouth?" asked Blueskin, who had been stooping over the dead dog, "a piece of the rascal's coat, as I'm a sinner," and disengaging it from Belzebub's jaws, he held it near to the light and examined it narrowly.

"The skirt of a coat, and by Heaven! a pocket with a pocket-book full of papers inside it! Ho! ho! but this may be of some use, Master Joseph Blake," and Blueskin deposited the prize carefully in his bosom.

"It's of no manner of use going up stairs again, Missis," said he; "and as the fellow has evidently gone out the back way, the best thing I can do is to follow in the same course, and mayhap I may find the rest of this coat and the man I want inside of it," and throwing the old crone a guinea he quitted the house.

In the mean time Handsome Jack and Jenny Diver had hastily threaded the alley, which they found to their great relief conducted them into Fetter Lane.

Directing their steps, by circuitous ways, with which each of them were intimately acquainted, they soon reached High Holborn. Once in a place of comparative safety, they ventured to slacken their pace, and then Jenny Diver informed him how she was surprised by the fire at Williams', to whom she had gone for the purpose of disposing of some jewellery, which she had purloined from a lady on London Bridge a few hours before.

Nor did the young girl fail to give vent to the most ardent expressions of gratitude to him who had so providentially appeared in her behalf at the moment of her last extremity. Handsome Jack, however, begged her to refrain, and declared that nothing had ever given him such unalloyed delight as that evenings' adventure.

"It happened," said he, "that I had been to visit a person who is now employed in the affairs of Sir James Town, who, as you already know, has cheated me out of my rights, for the purpose of obtaining for perusal some important papers connected with my claims; and as I was returning the alarm of fire drew me to the spot. Unable to restrain myself when I heard that life was in such terrible peril, I rushed into the house and rescued you, not knowing until you were saved who I had been preserving, therefore, Jenny, no great praise so far as you are concerned do I deserve."

The girl answered not—her heart was too full; but she gave him a look in which gratitude and tenderness were blended; her eyes were suffused with tears, and her beautiful lips quivered with emotion.

Suddenly Handsome Jack's cheek turned ghastly pale—he stopped abruptly—and felt in his pockets—a blank expression of despair succeeded when his search he found to be fruitless.

"Why, Jack! what has come over you?" asked Jenny; "you look like a madman."

"No wonder," was all he could say; and then he again went through a series of ineffectual diggings into his pockets.

At length he said, in a voice calm with despair, "when that cursed dog seized the skirt of my coat, I cut it off to expedite our escape. I, however, had better have remained, Jenny, and sent you forward alone."

"My God! why," exclaimed the girl.

"Because that skirt contained a pocket,—in that pocket was a pocket-book,—and in that pocket-book I had but just before placed the important documents, of which I spoke to you a few minutes since:—I am a ruined man!"

"And to think that through your anxiety to serve me such a misfortune should have befallen you!" exclaimed Jenny. "Let me go back and endeavour to recover the pocket-book, Jack?"

"Not for worlds," replied her companion,—"nor must I return either. Come along, Jenny, we must trust to chance now."

And they proceeded towards the "Chapel," which they reached just in time to accompany M'Cleane and the rest from that singular place to another place of refuge.

It need scarcely be narrated how much closer the bonds of friendship between M'Cleane and Handsome Jack were drawn in consequence of the brave conduct of the latter. The whole story of the escape was narrated to the Captain by his innamorata, for Handsome Jack was not one of those who cared to boast of his good deeds.

The whole of the gang were now assembled at the Country House at Highgate.

This place, they determined, for the present at least, to make their head quarters, as it had been determined, for reasons which the reader will readily imagine after what has been narrated, to abandon the "Chapel" for some months to come.

As has been before intimated, the Country House was admirably adapted to the purposes for which it was used by the gang of highwaymen, footpads, cut-purses, and burglars, of which M'Cleane was the head. Situated at but a short distance from town, it was easy when business was to be done in the metropolis, to proceed thither; and for country excursions it was a most eligible centre. The fact of a portion of it being occupied and extensively used as a roadside inn, whose landlord was now a member of the fraternity, while it operated as a blind to the real purposes of the gang, served also as the means of procuring with the utmost facility information respecting travellers which might be turned to account. In short a more suitable residence for such a society could scarcely be found.

Here then, on the evening following their arrival, the gang sat in council deliberating on the course to be pursued.

It would be a waste of the reader's time and patience to record at length the proceedings of this eventful night, as their results will be related in due order in the course of our tale. We will only state that Beauty Ellis was installed in his old post of porter, an occupation which was also coupled with that of spy in the tavern kitchen, where the servants of the neighbouring gentry used frequently to assemble for the purpose of discussing the public business in general, and that of their masters and mistresses in particular.

To enable him the better to procure information from these worthies, he assumed the office of under ostler or stable-helper, and when so employed, the old woman, to whom we introduced the reader in an early chapter, acted as the Country House Cerberus.

Beauty, in the exercise of his assumed profession, was one evening, after having littered down some servant's horses, sitting over his last pipe and tankard of ale in the huge chimney corner of the kitchen, when a servant in a shabby livery entered, and demanded bait for his horse.

Beauty Ellis, with extreme humility, hurried from his seat, and led the horse from the door to the stable, where having provided it with provender, he left it and returned to his tankard.

The livery servant having ordered and partaken of refreshment, Beauty Ellis contrived to draw him into conversation with him, and elicited from him the information, that he had been directed by his master to proceed to Barnet for the purpose of making preparation for his reception at a mansion which he had purchased in that neighbourhood, and where he was expected to arrive from Gloucestershire late that very night.

"He's as rich as a nabob," said the livery servant; "but such a precious old skinflint as he there never was the likes of. He a'most starves me and the old housekeeper—the only servants he keeps—for he and his niece, an old maid who's as bad as himself, does the gardening, which is only raising cabbages after all, and he won't trust his money in banks for fear they'll break."

"Then what do he do with it, in the name of marcy!" asked Beauty carelessly, as he lit his pipe, and listened intently.

"Why he carries a little gold in his pocket for fear of highway robbers, and dresses shabby like, to make 'em think as he's poor; but," and the livery servant put his lips close to Beauty Ellis's ear, and whispered something.

"You do not say so," said Beauty,—"oh lor', who'd ha' thought of that, now. Come you're a joking, ain't you?"

"I ain't, though; and I should never have known if our old housekeeper hadn't got tipsy one night in the still-room, and let it out as I was carrying her up stairs to bed. She had a quarrel that day with Miss Penelope, and told it out of spite."

The conversation now dropped, for the livery servant having finished his pipe, asked for his horse, paid his reckoning, and rode off in the direction of Barnett.

Immediately on his departure, Beauty Ellis proceeded to the great room of the Country House, an apartment which corresponded to the saloon of the "Chapel" in its uses.

On entering it, he found, to his surprise, that it was all but empty—there being but two persons present, viz: Handsome Jack and Jenny Diver.

"Where's the Captain?" asked Beauty.

"Gone out with Dick Flybynight," replied Handsome Jack; "there's some business expected in Epping Forest to night."

"So there is nearer home, if any one would look arter it;—werry sorry Captain ain't in. Seen Jem Starlight, or Lucifer Tim, lately?"

"They've all gone out to work, but me," replied Handsome Jack; "but here, Beauty, drink this glass of sack-posset and tell us what's in the wind now?"

"Aye, do, my pretty Ben Cull," chimed in Jenny, with her soft musical voice.

"'Tis summut werry pertickler," said Beauty, mysteriously,—one could do it, but two might as well be in it. Lots of flimsies and a few shiners to be had for the asking.'

"Then, Beauty, I'll go and ask," said Jack starting to his feet."

"And I, too!" exclaimed Jenny, following his example.

"You?" asked Handsome Jack.

"Yes, me, and why not?" replied Jenny. "In the expectation that something of this kind would one day or other turn up, I have provided myself with a complete suit of clothes for the road. See, Jack."

And the courageous girl opening a clothes press, drew from it a complete suit of man's attire, a wig, and other articles, by means of which she could completely disguise herself. With a merry laugh she threw them across her arm, and saying she should be ready in a quarter of an hour, retired to her apartment.

"Madcap! but she will I suppose have her humour. Beauty, you must saddle two horses, and now let me know the particulars of this affair," said Handsome Jack.

"Rich old miser and his niece, an old maid, comes through Holloway at about eleven o'clock to night, or before twelve, in a post-chaise."

"Well?" asked Handsome Jack.

"He has a few guineas; but the niece hides the load of flimsies in her——"

"What?" asked Jack.

"'Cant tell you," said Beauty Ellis, grinning; "I'll let Jenny know that,—you tackle the old miser, while the girl manages his niece." And Beauty left the room for the stables.

In a few minutes afterwards, Jenny, perfectly transmogrified, bounded into the apartment.

Handsome Jack started back in utter astonishment, and well might he be surprised, for never had he beheld so wondrous a metamorphosis before.

Jenny was so thoroughly disguised that it would have been impossible for a stranger to have recognised in her the famous Diver. A three cornered hat was jauntily placed on a wig which entirely concealed her own luxuriant curls,—a cravat of the finest muslin, and embroidered at the ends, enveloped her neck, and her coat, waistcoat, and breeches, were unexceptionable; in a pair of high boots she stalked about the room, flourishing a riding-whip in her hand: encircling her waist was a belt, in which were stuck her pistols and a glittering rapier hung by her side. She was rather *petite* in figure, to be sure; but in all other respects she appeared the very beau ideal of a highwayman.

Beauty Ellis now reappeared, and as well as Handsome Jack started on beholding the strange apparition. After a grin of satisfaction, he drew Jenny aside and imparted to her some information which seemed to afford her great and intense delight. Slapping her breeches with her whip, she gave a cheerful shout and expressed her eagerness to be off.

"How will you manage without a side saddle, Jenny?" asked Handsome Jack.

"As I used to do when I scampered over the Irish mountains—do without one," replied the gay creature.

In another moment she sprung into the stirrup and bestrode the horse, which she gave abundant evidence of being well able to manage.

With great secrecy they now quitted the Country House, and took their way down Highgate-hill. Gently trotting along they soon reached the "Castle," at Holloway, and passing it, drew up beneath the shadow of some trees, for the double purpose of listening and of avoiding observation.

"The niece," said Handsome Jack, "must be your prey, Jenny; I will manage old Griper."

"I know all about it," said Jenny, "Beauty has let me into the secret. You attend to your part of the work, and I warrant you I'll manage mine."

"Hush!" said Handsome Jack; "do you hear anything?"

"Here they come,—I hear the chaise-wheels I am certain. Now then, Jack, for my maiden effort on the road!"

The vehicle now drew near, and Handsome Jack directing Jenny to remain where she was, he himself crossed the road and stationed himself opposite her.

Immediately the chaise was abreast of them, Handsome Jack rode forward, placed a pistol before the boy's face, and ordered him on his peril to "stand."

He then rode to the side of the chaise, Jenny proceeding to the other window, and both demanded their money of the bewildered travellers.

"Here, good Mr. Highwayman, is all I have," said the old miser, handing Jack a few guineas; "the rest I placed in the bank before I left London."

"Pooh!" said Jack. "Comrade! see what the old rascal's mother has about her."

"It's my niece, not my mother," groaned the miser, "and she hasn't a penny but what I give her."

"We'll see," said Jenny. "Be good enough to step out of the chaise, Miss Penelope, I have something to say to you."

Forced to comply, the stiff and starched up old maid of a niece descended to the road.

"I'm going to draw a little money out of your bank,—don't be frightened, miss," said Jenny.

In vain did the wretched female protest that she did not possess a penny, and turn her pockets inside out to attest the truth of her statement. Nothing would convince the inexorable Jenny.

"It's by no means cold to night, miss," she said; "so be kind enough to take off your gown."

"What, before a man?" exclaimed the indignant prude.

"Yes," replied the amateur highwayman; "but 'tis very dark, miss, and if you please, to prevent a shock to your modesty you shall turn your back to me. Come, remove the gown, I say, or I'll do it for you."

Forced to obey, the prude did as she was re-

quested, and then her skirt was also banished from her angular form.

"Your boddice is much too tightly laced, miss," continued Jenny,—"allow me."

And drawing forth a sharp pen-knife, she with one sweep upwards, after having insinuated its point beneath the lowest lacing, divided all the rest so neatly and so suddenly that, as the boddice flew open, a report like that of a pistol was heard.

"See how much easier you are now, young lady,—stay, you'll be better when I remove the boddice altogether."

Then cutting the shoulder-straps, she quietly removed that article of dress, folded it so as to go into the pocket of her coat, or at least partly so, and then directing the unhappy creature to dress herself, mounted her horse.

Handsome Jack in the mean time had gagged the postilion and the miserable old miser, whose groans, when he witnessed the abduction of the boddice were pitiful to hear.

Satisfied that the road was clear, Handsome Jack and Jenny Diver now sought to return homewards by a circuitous way. Immediately, therefore, after quitting the parties whom they had plundered, they turned into a lonely lane and put their horses to the gallop.

"Capitally done, Jenny!" exclaimed the gentleman highwayman. "Why, Jenny, my girl, with a little practice you bid fair to be as remarkable on the road as you have already proved yourself in your own particular line," and Handsome Jack burst into a hearty peal of laughter.

"And why should I not, Jack?" asked Jenny, slily. "Don't you know that when a woman determines on doing anything she is certain to succeed? By the way, Jack; how d'ye think I sit my mare?"

"As well as if you had been born in the saddle," replied Jack; "but, Jenny, won't it be a standing joke against you, that on your first highway expedition your sole booty was a lady's boddice?"

"Wait till we get home, Jack, and examine the lining of Miss Penelope's boddice. I shall be much mistaken if it does not yield a pretty picking—rather more than you managed to procure from the griper's pockets."

Jenny, put into the very best spirits by her late adventure, now proposed to Handsome Jack that they should follow up their good luck by a ride on Finchley Common, from which place they were not very far distant.

To this proposal Handsome Jack offered no objection, as the night was favourable: he was, moreover, anxious to show his devotion to the interests of M'Cleane, by adding as much as possible by his own exertions to the common stock. Hitherto he had in reality done but little, and he felt this. Moreover, the strange loss of the important papers in the house in Hanging Sword Alley had, to a certain extent, rendered him reckless, and he determined to embark all his energies in the new and perilous line of life which he had adopted.

"Forward then, Jenny," said he; "who knows what adventures and what prizes Dame Fortune may throw in our way. We have three good hours before us, and it will be strange indeed if your usual good fortune does not favour you."

Leisurely trotting along the road they at length came to the verge of the common, which lay a bare and bleak expanse before them, and on either hand faintly illuminated by the fitful beams of the waning moon.

"What the devil is this?" exclaimed Handsome Jack, as his horse shied at a dark object which appeared on the common within a few yards of him.

Jenny's mare also exhibited symptoms of uneasiness, which were not diminished when the dark object gradually rose as it were from the earth, and assumed the form of a human being.

"The devil!" said Handsome Jack; "but be it what it may, I fear it not," and he was riding in the direction of the strange appearance, when the moon burst from behind a dark cloud and revealed the form and features of an aged woman.

Her dress was of the strangest and most fantastic kind,—a dark, tattered robe enveloped her gaunt, meagre, and tall figure: round her head was bound an old crimson scarf, and in her shrivelled hands she held a hazel wand: her scan gray hairs streamed wildly in the night-blast, and from her eye-balls gleamed an unnatural fire.

"Beware!" she said in a croaking voice, pointing the skinny fore-finger of her left-hand alternately at Handsome Jack and Jenny Diver, whilst she supported herself on her hazel staff with her right.

"And who the devil are you who tell us to beware?" asked Handsome Jack, angrily.

"One who can read both your destinies as plainly as if your whole lives from birth till death were written in a book before me," replied the hag.

Jenny involuntarily turned pale, for she was by nature a little superstitious,—as indeed who of us are not?

"Come along, Jack!" she exclaimed impatiently, gently walking her horse on.

"No," said Jack, peremptorily; "the old fool says she knows our fates, and, by Heaven! I'll make her tell me mine."

"Fool!" cried the woman, stamping her foot, "then you shall know it. Aye, and that scornful companion of yours shall also be told some of the Mysteries of the Future."

"Come hither, and fear not," said Jack, addressing himself to Jenny. "Why fear a crack-brained old idiot's chatterings."

Lifting her long arm towards the moon the old woman, in a low solemn voice, exclaimed, "Listen!" and then in a low, monotonous chaunt, repeated the following:—

Ere thrice twelve months yon orb of night
Has gemmed the earth with . . . . .
Ere thrice twelve months . . . . . .
His bright and sure career . . . .
From tree without a . . . . . .
Two members of a . . . . . .
Yon girl, who . . . . . . yes,
Though tricked out in . . . . disguise;
And yon, man, born . . . . . . hope,
Shall both be noosed in Tyburn's rope.

And having uttered this wild prophecy, the hag leaned on her hazel staff, with a look of bitter hatred and indeed menace on Handsome Jack and Jenny Diver, strode away, muttering "remember Nan of the Common," and was soon lost to view.

"By Heaven, Jack!" said Jenny, whose cheek was blanched and deadly pale, "the hag discovered me, even through my disguise. Would to God we had not encountered her!"

"Pestilence on the witch," exclaimed Handsome Jack, who himself was not quite exempt from a feeling of uneasiness; "but never fear, Jenny, 'tis but the common story of those cursed gipsies. But let us onward, for should M'Cleane have arrived at the Country House during our absence, he will be thinking that the devil has flown away with us both."

Then putting their horses into a gentle canter over the Common, they soon, in gay conversation, forgot the warning of the mysterious woman whom they had so singularly encountered.

They had reached about the middle of the common, when Jenny observed in the distance the figure of a horseman, gently walking his steed and approaching in a direct line towards them.

Flushed with their recent success, Jenny proposed to Handsome Jack, that she should encounter the traveller single-handed. To this, however, her comrade objected.

But Jenny Diver, with that wilfulness which more or less characterises all women, insisted upon following her whim; so setting spurs to her mare, she galloped off across the common, and saluted the stranger with the fearful monosyllable, "stand!"

Instead of exhibiting any signs of trepidation or fear, the person to whom this mandate was addressed burst into a loud laugh; and so hearty was his merriment that to control it within reasonable bounds he was compelled to drop the reins, and firmly plant his brawny fists on his shaking sides.

"What!" he exclaimed; "Dog eat dog? Why, my Trojan of the road, cannot you yet tell the difference between a sheep and a wolf? If not, just look at my teeth, which are to the full, I believe, as sharp as yours, and a little older into the bargain." And, as he exhibited his pistols, he made a peculiar sign with his whip, which was not, however, comprehended.

Jenny was puzzled; and, for a moment, her firmness forsook her. Rallying herself speedily, she demanded the stranger's purse.

"Why," said he, "I have so recently come into possession of it that, you surely would not have the heart to dispossess me thereof. And if I am to tell you my name, I fancy we should be good friends instead of foes."

"Your name then," demanded Jenny, promptly.

"I know but one voice like yours, and that belongs to one Jenny Diver," remarked the stranger. "It's strange, young man,—my name is Hawkins—John Hawkins."

"Hawkins!" exclaimed Jenny; "Was it you who robbed the Earl of Harrington and Lord Bruce in Richmond-lane of their watches and the sapphire ring—the ring which Jonathan Wild was so eager to clutch?"

"The same," replied Hawkins, for it was indeed that famous knight of the road, "but, Jonathan, the cunning villain, was foiled there, for I took it to Holland, and there disposed of it."

"If you are an enemy to Jonathan Wild, you are a friend of mine," said Jenny, frankly extending her hand; "come, I must introduce you to my brave comrade."

Handsome Jack at this moment joined them, and the three were soon engaged in familiar conversation; and, at the invitation of Jenny, Hawkins consented to accompany them to the Country House.

Arrived there, Hawkins was warmly welcomed by M'Cleane, and merrily passed the few succeeding hours. The account of Jenny's exploit was received with uproarious applause and the laughter was loud and long; when she

No. 18.

took from the lining of the boddice bank notes to the amount of one thousand pounds.

One third of this amount was, by universal consent, awarded to Jenny herself; the remainder being divided, as usual, among the members of the gang: but, over and above the share awarded him, Jenny, with her characteristic generosity, presented twenty guineas to him who had placed her in the way of such good luck—Beauty Ellis.

That worthy, delighted with the success which had attended Jenny, took no little credit to himself for the exploit from which she had come forth with such flying colours. As he carefully deposited the glittering reward in his pouch, he remarked:—

"It's a werry low sort o'life as I'm a leading here, and I'd like to know, why Beauty Ellis, as they call me, shouldn't ride the high horse himself now and then? Here's Handsome Jack and a young gal goes out for two hours and gets a fortin, while I only drops in for the small pickins. Every one for himself—and so the next chance I get, by St. Nicholas, I'll try my luck, for I'm gettin werry tired of this lazy sort of life ; and who knows but what the watchman of the Country House may, by and bye, be as famous as the captain himself."

And having delivered himself of these opinions, and made this desperate resolution, Beauty Ellis retired to the kitchen, and there falling asleep, dreamed of an adventure on the road.

CHAPTER XXX.

BLUESKIN IN TROUBLE.—HOW THE THIEF-TAKER BAFFLES THE LAWYER, AND MR. DOOM TAKES THE LAW IN HIS OWN HANDS.

Mr. Watkins, the Bow Street runner, had no sooner been released by M'Cleane, than, regardless of his promise, he proceeded to Bow Street, and deposed on oath to the facts connected with the recent imprisonment.

Warrants were the next morning issued, and a posse of constabulary were dispatched to see them executed. But, as the reader is already aware, the birds had flown. In vain did they interrogate Madame Charlotte, who still remained in the hotel department of the Chapel; that worthy lady utterly repudiated the idea that she had the slightest knowledge of M'Cleane and his associates; and as, by a most ingenious contrivance, the communication between the saloon and Madame Charlotte's apartment had been destroyed, Mr. Watkins, entirely as he disbelieved the landlady, was compelled to appear at least to give her credit for speaking the truth.

Determined, however, to use every exertion to effect the capture of the gang, Watkins resolved upon visiting Jonathan Wild; he therefore proceeded to the office of the thief-taker in Newtoner's Lane, and was immediately conducted to his private apartment by Abraham, the jew.

Jonathan was, as usual, engaged in poring over his books—books in which were registered the minute particulars of various robberies. So business-like were the entries in these huge volumes, that no city merchant's ledgers could have been, by any possibility, more methodically arranged.

"The very man who, of all others, I was most desirous of seeing," said Jonathan, as Mr. Watkins entered the room, and, pointing to a chair near him, he requested the Bow Street runner to be seated.

"Any little job for me there, Mr. Wild?" asked Watkins.

"Let's talk first of your business with me," remarked the wary Jonathan. "I hope, Mr. Watkins, I'm not selfish—I do indeed—you know, as well as myself, that I never think of my own affairs until after I have obliged my friends."

Had any one closely scrutinized the face of the Bow Street runner whilst Jonathan Wild was thus boasting of his disinterestedness, he would have observed a sly twinkle of the small ferret eyes, and an unusual protrusion of the right cheek, caused by the thrusting of the tongue thereinto. It was evident that Mr. Watkins had his own opinion on the subject, but he very prudently forebore to express it.

"My business, Wild," said Watkins is to procure your valuable assistance in ferriting out a gang of villains. with some of the members of which you are, no doubt, acquainted;" and then the constable gave to the thief-taker an account of his recent adventure at the Thieves' Chapel.

"Strange!" said Jonathan Wild, placing himself in a musing attitude. "It so happens that I possess some sort of clue—a faint one it is true—but still a clue to this mystery."

"Then you will assist me?" asked the constable.

"On one condition," replied Jonathan. Wild.

"Name it," said Watkins.

"You know," remarked Wild, "that there need be no secrets between us. I have, as you are aware, in my pay a man named Joseph Blake."

"Blueskin?" asked Mr. Watkins, interrupting him.

"The same," continued Jonathan. "This Blake, or Blueskin, has dared to cross my path, and in direct contravention of our engagement, to enter into a negociation with a certain party without my knowledge. He must be—you understand?"

"Perfectly," replied the Bow Street runner. "You meant to say, he must be got rid of—and you want me to assist you in the job."

"Yes ; but the greatest caution must be observed. In the first place, Blueskin has. I know not how, got hold of some papers which it is of the greatest importance should be placed in my possession. It is through your agency that this can be done—and done it must be this very day."

"But, how?" asked Watkins.

"Thus," replied Jonathan, opening his black book as he spoke, and taking from a little portfolio, constructed inside one of the covers thereof, a slip of parchment, which he handed to the constable.

"Why, this is a warrant for Blake's apprehension," observed Watkins.

"For a robbery attended with violence on a gentleman in St. Martin's Lane—you perceive," quietly remarked Wild.

"Strange!" said Watkins. "that I never heard of the affair, Mr. Wild."

"Why, to tell you the truth, Watkins," said Wild, with a villainously triumphant chuckle. "The robbery is one of those little inventions of my own, which brings grist to both our mills. Forty or fifty pounds, you know, is no bad pay for nabbing a man on such a charge. I've had this warrant ready for Blueskin some time, for I thought I might have to put my thumb on him some day. The opportunity has now arrived—the spider has crawled into my path, and, by G—d, I'll crush him."

Jonathan Wild's face, as he spoke these last words, was absolutely diabolical in its expression—every feature of his hard countenance combined to form the very incarnation of hatred and revenge.

"There's the warrant—take it Watkins," and folding it in a twenty pound bank note, he handed it to the officer.

"Know you where I can find him?" inquired Watkins, upon whom the flimsy had wrought the desired effect.

"Yes ; in two hours from this time he will be at the house of his cousin, Ephraim Blake, in Bucklersbury, you cannot mistake the place, it is where the old miser was murdered by Blackmoor, some months ago."

"I know it well." said the officer.

"As he leaves his cousin's, seize him, and instantly get possession of all the papers he may have about him; then bring them to me, and I will double the sum I have now given you."

"But," asked Watkins, "are you ready with the proofs of the St. Martin's Lane robbery; in the event of his demanding to be taken before the justice at Bow Street?"

"Quite," replied Wild. "The old gentleman will swear through thick and thin if necessary; but I do not imagine we shall be driven to this course of proceeding."

After some further conversation, the Bow Street runner left Newtoner's Lane, and after threading the obscure streets which lay between Ludgate, St. Pauls, Cheapside, and the river, reached Bucklersbury.

Directly opposite the house of Ephraim Blake was a public house, in a corner of the parlour of this tavern, which parlour commanded a view of the street, Mr. Watkins, after having called for a pipe and a tankard, quietly established himself.

And from that corner he never moved for an instant. To those persons who occasionally dropped in, took their customary draughts of purl or canary-sack, he appeared to be a dull, heavy-looking customer enough—a man who was dissipating his brains in smoke, and washing down his ideas with strong ale. They, however, failed to perceive the cold, calculating, watchful eye, that watched unceasingly the opposite door, just as the lynx watches the fissure of some rock from whose caverned recesses it knows its prey will assuredly emerge.

Puff—puff—puff ! Up to the curiously ornamented ceiling of the low apartment go the thin blue rings of smoke, after they have issued from the bowl. These vapoury frames encircle pictures, which are surpassingly beautiful in the eyes of the Bow Street runner. Up—up—up they go ! Now, with one of his eyes, for the other is never off the door opposite, he sees in the shadowy mirror himself—a little innocent boy; the picture dissolves, and is, by the aid of a new puff, changed into the same boy committing his first crime—again the picture changes; and Watkins sees the very image of himself, a young man in a prison—another change, and he is, after having been associated with thieves, transformed into a hunter of criminals. One more strong puff, and denser is the smoke, and more defined the picture than any of those which have preceded it. Mr. Watkins observes the very fac simile of himself in the parlour which bears so close a

resemblance to that in which he sits, that he cannot possibly be in error, in search of Blood Money !

The last tableau was so extremely unpleasant in the contemplation thereof to the sensitive officer, that he dashed down his pipe, tossed off the remainder of his tankard, and looked more stern than was his wont. At this moment the door of the late miser's house opposite was cautiously and but partially opened, and the visage of Blueskin, which was familiar enough to Mr. Watkins, appeared.

Blueskin, after a cautious survey of the locality, made up his mind to allow his body to follow his head, and feeling quite sure that no one was watching, he made a desperate rush across the road, and in order to escape observation, dived recklessly into the tavern parlour.

"Saves my running arter you," muttered the delighted Bow Street runner to himself. "One wolunteerer is worth a score o' pressed chaps;" and feeling quite sure that his prey was safe in his toils, he comfortably settled himself again in his corner and refilled his pipe.

But he never lost sight of Blake, he was all eyes and ears, the slightest movement of the man whom Jonathan Wild had doomed, was noted by him. As well might a miserable mouse attempt to escape from the talons of a hungry cat, as Blueskin hope to elude the vigilance of Watkins.

After having partaken of some refreshment, Blueskin was about to depart, but he was prevented doing so by the Bow Street runner, who laid his heavy hand on his shoulder.

"You are my prisoner," said Watkins, "and you had better not make any resistance."

"On what charge?" demanded Blueskin, his face turning deadly pale, and his lip quivering with excitement.

"Robbery of an old gentleman in St. Martin's Lane," replied the constable, dexterously manacling his prisoner's hands. "If you like to prevent exposure," he continued, "you can ride to the round-house in a hackney coach. It might hurt your brother's feelin's, you know, if he saw you in my company."

Blueskin gladly acceded to this proposition, and a vehicle having been procured, Watkins conveyed his captive to St. Pauls' round-house, and there searched him.

To his great joy he found upon him the skirt of Handsome Jack's coat, containing the pocket, and in the latter the book and papers which Jonathan Wild had been so anxious to procure.

Locking up Blueskin, Watkins immediately proceeded to Jonathan Wild's office, and delivered to him the documents. The thief-taker's eyes twinkled with delight as he grasped the parchments, and after attentively perusing them, he carefully secured them about his person.

"And, now, what are we to do about Blueskin?" asked Watkins.

"You must take him before a magistrate, and get him lodged in the Compter for the present," replied Jonathan. "His fate must depend on circumstances; as yet I cannot decide upon it."

Watkins then, having received a handsome

gratuity from Wild, left the office. Jonathan, as soon as his back was turned, drew the parchments from his breast pocket, carefully copied each of them in one of his journals, and then deposited them in his pocket book.

That same night, Mr. Wriggleton Doom was seated in his dingy office in Grays Inn. He had been working with desperate energy during the whole of the day, as a number of parchments on the table beside him testified. The fire in the little grate burned brightly, and ever and anon, Mr. Doom would fling into it papers, which he watched with feverish anxiety as they were being converted into tinder. As the glare of the flames fell upon his careworn and haggard features, a smile of grim satisfaction flitted over them; and when the last of the condemned papers was consumed, he drew a deep breath, as though a mighty load had been removed from his heart and brain.

His clerk, Tim Snarley, was seated in the outer office, busily engaged in the interesting occupation of drawing from a ruler, which he had converted into an imaginary flute, a mysterious sort of melody. While thus occupied in the pursuit of music under difficulties, he was interrupted by the entrance of a stranger.

"I want to see Mr. Doom," said the new arrival, in a gruff voice.

"Busy—can't see any body," muttered Tim Snarley, blowing away at the ruler with redoubled energy.

"Take my name into your master, you infernal young villain," said the stranger, thrusting the ferule of his stick into Tim Snarley's ribs; an operation which immediately compelled that young gentleman to relinquish his musical studies.

"You must give it to me first," cried Tim, grinning at the strange visitor.

"My name is Wild—Jonathan Wild—d'ye hear?"

Tim Snarley's eyes, on hearing this, opened to a prodigious extent; the name of the dreaded thief-taker being perfectly familiar to him, although until now, he was entirely unacquainted with his person.

And he surveyed the notorious individual, much as we might suppose Lemuel Gulliver did the Brobdignegian gentleman, between whose thumb and fore finger he was writhing and struggling; for Wild was, in his way, a monster scarcely less terrible than any which we read of in fairy tales, or children's miraculous story books.

Respectfully asking Wild to be seated while he should inform his master that an interview was requested. Tim Snarley knocked at the door of Doom's private office, and received the usual summons, "Come in."

Cautiously opening the door just sufficiently wide to admit his body, Tim Snarley insinuated himself into the inner office, and with mouth wide open, and optics distended, stood before his master.

"Its quite impossible," said Mr. Doom, "quite impossible, Tim, I can see no one to night."

On hearing this, Tim commenced and went through a series of pantomimic movements. First he winked his right eye, then he pointed his left thumb over his left shoulder in the direction of the outer office, and, lastly, he placed the tip of his right forefinger on his mouth, thus ingeniously intimating to Mr. Wriggleton Doom, that at that precise moment some one of no little importance, and whom it would be quite as well to keep on good terms with, was not a hundred miles off.

"It's Mr. Wild—Mr. Jonathan Wild," said Tim Snarley, in a voice scarcely louder than a whisper, "and he says he must see you."

Doom sprang to his feet in an instant, hastily huddling together the parchments which lay upon his table, and threw them into a drawer which he carefully locked. He then resumed his seat, and placing a law book before him, affected to be deeply engaged in the perusal thereof.

"Request Mr. Wild to do me the favour of coming in," said Mr. Doom to Tim Snarley, who immediately vanished.

"My respects to you, Mr. Wild," said Doom, rising as Jonathan entered the private office; and he obsequiously placed a chair beside the fireplace for the illustrious thief-taker.

Doom exerted himself to the utmost to preserve an appearance of calmness, so that a superficial observer might have supposed him at that particular period in a calm and comfortable state of mind. But the practised eye of the man with whom he now had to do, at once detected beneath the apparently contented surface a strong and raging undercurrent of tumultuous passion; and the involuntary quiverings produced by nervous agitation.

"I believe, Mr. Doom," said Jonathan Wild, after a short pause, during which the lawyer had anxiously waited for Wild to commence the conversation, in order that he might gather some information which would enable him to shape his own course. "I believe that in the course of your professional duties, you have had some dealings with a person named Town?"

The Grays-Inn-lawyer was taken rather aback at this, but he gave no indications of surprise, he had imagined Wild's business to be of an entirely different kind, for on more than one occasion he had been employed by him either to procure the acquittal or condemnation of persons charged with grave offences.

"Why, yes, Mr. Wild," replied Doom, "I had the honour of acting for Sir James Town in various little matters, and—"

"Sir James Town is not the man I mean," said Wild, fixing his piercing eyes on Doom.

"Then whom do you refer to? I know of none other," remarked the lawyer, who now began to feel somewhat uncomfortable.

"Nonsense, Mr. Doom, it's of no use your trying to deceive me. Do you remember having signed a certain paper relative to the affairs of one Richard Town some months ago, in this very room?"

Doom at once unhesitatingly declared that he had not the slightest recollection of any such circumstance.

"A bad memory is convenient enough sometimes," said Wild, and he added, "If I am not mistaken, there were two persons, named James M'Cleane and Mary Young, who were witnesses to your signature."

"It's false," cried Doom, who now absolutely trembled with apprehension, as he remembered that the document to which Jonathan Wild referred, was the one which Handsome Jack had compelled him to sign, and which contained his confession of his nefarious doings in conjunction with Flitchman.

"Supposing I produced that document, would you deny your own hand writing?" asked Jonathan, as he slowly drew from his pocket the book which Watkins had obtained from Blueskin, and which it will be remembered had been abstracted from Handsome Jack by the bulldog at the house in Hanging Sword Alley.

"You might show a forged document, perhaps," said Doom, "but that would not be received as evidence in any court of law."

"With corroborative evidence it would though," coolly remarked Jonathan Wild, as he opened the pocket book and took from it several folded papers.

Doom at sight of these turned as pale as death, for on the outside of one of these documents he recognised the well-known hand-writing of Flitchman.

Wild then unfolded one of the papers; and, without relinquishing his hold of it, held it before Mr. Wriggleton Doom's astonished eyes.

"That I know you have seen before," he said, "it is the confession of your participation in a crime for which I could hang you, Lawyer Doom, and hang you I will, unless you deliver up to me all the other papers you have in your possession connected with this affair. You know I am not to be trifled with, and have a habit of keeping my word."

Doom lay back in his arm chair, his long bony hands locked in each other; he spoke not a word, but looked at Wild imploringly and with terror pourtrayed upon every feature.

"And this you have not seen," continued the remorseless thief-taker, exhibiting to his view a confession from Flitchman, with reference to the same transaction.

This was a fearful blow to the lawyer, and he writhed under its infliction. Summoning, however, all his energies to his aid, he assumed a tone and manner of indifference, while he said:—

"You may do your worst, Mr. Wild; I know you to be a relentless enemy—one who will stick at nothing in order to effect his purposes; but once for all, I tell you, that on me your threats will not produce the slightest effect; I will not do what you require of me."

Jonathan Wild, whilst the lawyer was speaking, had carefully replaced the documents in the pocket book, and the latter he placed on the table before him. The moment after he had done so, a knock was heard at the door, and Wild suddenly turned his head in that direction.

Doom, who had with greedy eyes watched every movement of the thief-taker, pounced on the pocket book the instant Jonathan Wild's attention was withdrawn. It was but the work of a moment to fling the book into the fire which was now blazing fiercely, and to thrust it with the poker into the very centre of the glowing coals.

As he was, with a desperate energy—for he knew his life depended on the result of his daring manœuvre—endeavouring to entirely destroy the pocket book, Jonathan Wild sprang upon him, and fiercely seizing him by the throat, hurled him to the other end of the room. He then endeavoured to rescue the, to him, precious papers from the fire, which had now converted the leather of the pocket book into a wrinkled, shapeless substance. All his efforts, however, were in vain; it had got so wedged amongst the cinders that it was impossible to extricate it; and Doom, with intense delight, observed that the very efforts which Jonathan Wild was making to recover the papers were only hastening their destruction.

The most fearful oaths and imprecations burst from Jonathan's lips as effort after effort proved fruitless. At this moment, when all seemed lost, he thrust his fingers between the bars in the hope of recovering his prize in that way, but a severe burn was all he gained by his movement. He was on the point of rushing upon Doom and strangling him in his fierce rage, when Tim Snarley, who had just before knocked at the door, opened it and entered.

"Water!—water!—a jug of water, boy—quick!" shouted Wild in a voice of thunder.

Tim rushed from the room, and instantly returned with the office pitcher. Wild snatched it from him, and without an instant's delay flung it on the fire, which was quickly extinguished.

Then he groped amongst the damp cinders until he found the pocket book, reduced externally to a cinder itself, and commanding the lad to withdraw, he sat down in order to examine what injury it had sustained.

Doom also crept to his chair, and with anxious eyes watched Wild's movement. From the appearance of the pocket book, he yet hoped that its contents might, if not entirely destroyed, be so much injured as to be useless to the man, who he could not but regard as his mortal enemy.

"Keep off—Doom—keep away, I tell you—and warn you too, for I'm not in a humour to be played with now, you treacherous villian. Dare but attempt to lift a finger, and I'll squeeze every breath of life out of your infernal carcase."

The fire had so hardened the leather of the book, that it was no easy matter to open it, and Wild was compelled to use a knife to effect his purpose. To his great joy, and Doom's extreme dismay, on removing this outer shell as it were, the papers within were found untouched by the fire, and only soiled by the water which had entered through the fissures of the cracked cover.

"Now, Mr. Doom," asked Wild, with a malicious chuckle, "if, as you just now said, you had nothing to do with these papers, I should very much like to know why you should have been so anxious to destroy them. You have put me to some pain and a good deal of trouble, but I'm not inclined to be played with, therefore, without any further palaver, just hand me all the documents you have in your possession connected with the 'Town' estates, or I shall call up Mr. Watkins, the Bow Street runner, who is at this moment awaiting my orders in the court-yard below."

Still the lawyer hesitated.

"Now, remember," continued Jonathan, taking out his watch, "heed what I say, if you do not place in my hands, in five minutes from this time, what I came for, and what sooner or later I am determined to have, I'll find those who will prosecute you for forgery, and before you are a day older, you shall be an inmate of the Marshalsea or the Compter."

"And what compensation will be made me, supposing I should consent to your demand?" asked the lawyer.

"I will make no conditions with so treacherous a viper as yourself," returned Jonathan Wild. "Come, sir, three minutes have already elapsed."

Wild then went to the window, lifted the sash and looked out.

"See him," he said to Doom;—and seizing the lawyer's arm, he led him to the window.

Doom looked down into the court-yard, and there he beheld Mr. Watkins, leaning against a pillar, with his arms folded and evidently retained for a special purpose by some one.

"You see the party to whose tender mercies I shall consign you in case you refuse to obey my commands," observed Jonathan, pointing to the Bow-Street runner.

Doom's face became of an ashy hue—he saw that Wild was not to be trifled with, and that his only chance of safety, for the present at least, was to deposit the required documents in Jonathan's hands. He therefore took from his bureau a roll of parchment, which he handed to the inexorable thief-taker.

Wild untied the tape which bound them together, and minutely examined them one by one. Satisfied at length that no deception had been practised on him by the lawyer, he again rolled them up, and leaning over the window-ledge whistled to the officer below.

Watkins heard the preconcerted signal, and looked upwards. Wild then by signs intimated, that as the object of his visit was accomplished, the attendance of the Bow-Street runner was no longer necessary; and to Mr. Wriggleton Doom's infinite satisfaction, that constable quitted his pillar, and disappeared under the dingy archway of the principal entrance-gate of Gray's-Inn.

Wild himself then bade Mr. Doom adieu, and marched off both the documents, congratulating himself on the successful termination of his adventure. The unhappy lawyer, however, by no means shared in those feelings of exultation.

He had no sooner been left alone in his office than he flung himself into his old office chair, and resting his sharp elbows on his knees, and burying his face in his hands, he surrendered himself to the most bitter and agonizing reflections.

His best hope was now gone,—the only influence which he possessed over Sir James Town had been taken from him. This distressed him terribly; but what puzzled him, and perplexed him sadly, and harrassed him more than anything else, was the fact that Jonathan Wild had in his possession the confession he had made of his iniquitous dealings in the matter of the Town title and estates.

How Wild could have become possessed of a paper, which at any moment he could produce, and by the crushing aid of which could effect his utter ruin, he found it impossible to conjecture. Well enough he knew, that the daring and resolute man who had compelled him to attach his signature thereto would have rather parted with his life's blood, than with a document of such vital importance to the rightful heir to the Town property. He felt himself encompassed with toils, after all his endeavours to entangle others in his snares, and trap them in his pitfalls. Though cunning beyond measure, he had overreached himself; and his reflections were of the most agonizing character.

The day was fast declining: for hours he had been sitting in the old chair—almost without motion—pondering on the perilous position in which he was placed.

Twilight succeeded to sunshine, and the deep shadows of the evening rendered objects in the quaint old office dim and indistinct; yet still there he sat, still and grim-looking as one of the stony-carved men whom we see in the dusty niches of old cathedrals.

A rap at the door roused him from his reverie.

Every noise alarmed him now, and that rap of the knuckles against the panneling of the door made his heart beat tumultuously. For some minutes he hesitated whether he should admit the party outside, or by his silence convey the impression that he was not within.

"It's only me," said a voice, which Doom knew belonged to his clerk, Tim Snarley; "and I want to know if I may go—'tis past nine o'clock."

The lawyer bade him enter, and informed him that as he himself had important business to attend to, he should remain some hours longer where he was; but he intimated, to Tim's great satisfaction, that that young gentleman was at liberty to depart, a permission of which he speedily availed himself.

Again the lawyer sought his chair, having first carefully locked and bolted himself in, and for a couple of hours longer he remained in deep meditation. At the end of that time, as though some idea had suddenly struck him, he rose from his seat, took down his hat and cloak from a peg, and quitted his chambers.

"It is the only way left me," he muttered. "Every door of escape but that one is shut, and I must even venture it, whatever the consequences may be;" and pressing his hat over his fevered brow as he spoke, he started hastily away and turned into Holborn.

The night had set in with storm and tempest —heavy and dark masses of cloud, piled bank upon bank, almost entirely obscured the light of the waning moon. Large heavy drops of rain pattered upon the pavement, and the thunder rumbled over head, like the sound of the spirit of the storm's chariot-wheels as they rolled through the angry heavens.

But wild and terrible as was the commotion of the elements, the storm which agitated them was as nothing to that which raged in Wriggleton Doom's bosom. That was fearful indeed —a convulsion which shook every fibre of his frame, and made his heart-strings quiver with agony.

Just as he reached the corner of Brook Street, he beheld a strange spectacle: four men were bearing on their shoulders—a coffin, uncovered by a pall;—these fellows almost trotted along, jolting their dismal burden as they went in a most unseemly manner. There were no mourners—not one, and amid the storm and gloom the strange funeral group rather resembled a spectral appearance than an actual reality.

Impelled by a feeling of curiosity for which he could not account, Doom followed the bearers of the coffin along Holborn, and through Shoe Lane to the gate of the pauper's burying ground of St. Andrews parish, into which gloomy place the men carried their burden.

Into this burying ground also went the lawyer.

A shallow grave had been prepared beforehand, and, without a prayer or a tear, the coffin was rudely lowered, or rather flung, into it. Just as it reached the bottom, Doom, looked towards the heavens, and beheld a wandering star shoot athwart the murky skies, and then become suddenly quenched in darkness.

He learned from the conversation of the men, who were indulging in ribald jokes as they flung the heavy clods on the coffin-lid, that the individual who had thus been buried at the hour of midnight, was a suicide. Doom thought of the wandering star which had been lost in gloom, like the unhappy wretch who had just descended to an unblest grave; and·then, shuddering, he quitted the place of graves and retraced his way through Holborn.

He looked anxiously about him for an apothecary's shop; but though he traversed the whole length of Oxford Street, not one could he find open at that late hour,—weary and distracted, he once more sought his chambers in Gray's Inn, and sank, when he entered them, on a couch, in a complete state of bodily and mental exhaustion.

Scarcely knowing what he was about he commenced ransacking his drawers, and from amongst the masses of documents therein deposited, he selected several bundles, which, without opening, he threw on the fire, which had not yet gone out,—he also drew from a secret recess in his private bureau other papers, which also were committed to the flames.

Then he sat down to his desk, wrote several letters, which he sealed with black wax, and placed them where they would certainly be seen by any one who entered the apartment in the morning.

Soon after he had finished these labours, the clock of a neighbouring church chimed the hour of three, the sound roused him out of a kind of reverie into which he had fallen, and he muttered aloud:—

"I would rather have procured that by means of which I should have slept away existence: but the time for regrets of that nature is now past. The desperate means of freeing myself from the perils which environ me must be taken, for once in Jonathan Wild's power, as I am, I am not safe for a moment. Before that church shall tell that another hour of time is gone, I shall have baffled the hatred of those who would pursue me to the death. I have———"

He could not conclude the sentence,—the feelings which agitated his bosom were so tremendously overpowering that, resolved as he was upon terminating his miserable existence, he shrank from a full contemplation of the awful mystery of death.

"What will the world say to-morrow morning, I wonder, when they hear that the respectable Mr. Wriggleton Doom has committed suicide?" he said with a grim and ghastly smile, and how Wild will curse me when he finds I have slipped through his fingers! but I have not time to spare now—courage! courage!"

He rose from his chair, searched about the room for something which he could not find, and then went into the apartment usually occupied by Tim Snarley.

There also he, for some time, groped about in vain, at length he observed a box containing some old account books, around which was a rope.

"That will do—the cord is none of the thickest to be sure, but I'm not heavy," he said, as he unfastened the knots and removed it from the box.

Then he withdrew the bolts of the door of the outer office, unlocked the door, so that Tim Snarley, on his arriving in the morning, might find no difficulty in getting in, and retired once more into his private room.

It was strange; the calmness with which the wretched man now went to work; he tried the strength of the cord as coolly as if he had been about to make use of it for some common and every-day purpose; and being, after repeated tests, satisfied that it would answer his purpose, he placed it on the table and then closely examined the ceiling in order to discover something to which he might fix it.

In a strong beam, overhead, he observed a hook from which, at some former period, the chain of a lamp had hung; Doom, standing on the table, passed the rope over this, and by way of experiment grasping the two extremities of the rope, he swung himself from his elevated position. Scarcely, however, had he trusted his entire weight to the hook than it was torn from the beam, and the lawyer fell heavily on the ground.

He was somewhat shaken by the fall, but he shrank not in the least from his fell purpose; he procured a hammer, and after great exertion, he again fixed the hook in the beam, and this time so securely that his utmost efforts could not displace it.

He then removed from his neck his cravat, and after a few experiments, succeeded in making a slip-knot noose at the end of the rope. With this frightful composure he placed it round his neck, and drew the knot tightly beneath his ear. Satisfied that all was so far right, he removed it, and fastened the upper part of the rope to the hook.

There was not a single moment of wavering— Doom, as perfectly in his senses as ever he had been during the whole course of his life, went as resolutely to work as though he had been engaged in his ordinary business. There might have been an inward tremour; but the man showed it no more than if he had been made of iron.

Immediately beneath the noose which now dangled from the hook in the beam he placed a low stool; and all his arrangements having been completed, he set himself down, and burying his face in his hands, appeared absorbed in profound meditation.

Who shall tell what were his thoughts? Who shall describe the memories of childhood — youth—manhood—which then, perhaps, phantom-like flitted through his brain.

In this half-dreamy state he continued for a long time, he was roused from it by the church clock striking.

" One, two, three," he counted aloud, " four, five, six, seven."

As the last sound smote his ear, he sprang from the chair and leaped on the stool which formed for him a fatal platform.

" No time to lose. My God! where have I been wandering all this time. I intended all to have been over long before this."

He now placed the noose once more round his neck, and with a firmly desperate hand, adjusted it as he had seen Jack Price do it at Tyburn.

Convulsively clenching his hands, and almost biting through his nether lip with his upper teeth, he, by a sudden movement, kicked away the stool from under him, and then hung suspended with his feet about a foot or so from the ground ; a few convulsive heavings of the shoulders and legs, and then all was still in that gloomy chamber.

*   *   *   *   *

" Master's very late this morning," said Tim Snarley to himself, as he ceased for a moment playing on his imaginary flute. " Very late." And in pursuance of his usual practice, Tim applied his eye to the little fissure in the partition, by means of which Sir James Town had on a previous occasion observed and heard a certain old lady's conversation with the lawyer.

To Tim's immense surprise, he saw on the wall opposite, the shadow of a man in a rather singular position—the substance, whatever it was that cast the shadow, he could not observe, but being of an inquiring disposition and not in the least degree superstitious, he, to ascertain the cause of the phenomenon, boldly proceeded to Mr. Doom's private office door and knocked briskly.

There was no answer—all within was as still as the grave.

Tim then cautiously withdrew the latch and peeped in. God! what a sight met his eye. His master was hanging from the beam, his face horribly distorted and discoloured, and the draught from the opening of the door causing the body to move, it gently swung round, so as to impress Tim with the idea that his master was about to speak with him.

Rushing down stairs the lad gave the alarm, and the porter of the hospital, after the lapse of a few minutes, had cut down the body of the lawyer; Tim had previously gone for a doctor.

———

CHAPTER XXXI.

THE NIGHT ATTACK ON PURLEY HALL.—HANDSOME JACK MEETS WITH A STRANGE ADVENTURE.

THE addition made to the gang by the enrolling of Hawkins as a member, which enrolment took place on the evening of his introduction to the Country House by Jenny Diver, was an important one, Hawkins possessing the reputation of being one of the most daring highwaymen and cracksmen of his day.

Nor was it long before an opportunity was afforded him of distinguishing himself among his new comrades ; for through the agency of Beauty Ellis, it was ascertained that a nobleman of high rank, with his bride and her immense dowry all in ready money, would shortly travel through Epping Forest on their way to town.

It was also known that, in consequence of the late frequent robberies in the Forest, the nobleman and his lady would be accompanied by a strong escort well armed ; and whom, therefore, it would be no easy matter to overpower. To take the matter therefore into consideration and to decide upon the best mode of getting possession of so rich a booty a council of the gang was held.

One party of M'Cleane's followers were for making a bold attack on the party as they passed through the Forest; but another, with which Hawkins sided, considering such a course of proceeding would be too perilous, proposed that the lord and his lady should be attacked during the night in their own dwelling, when resistence is less to be feared from their followers, who on such an occasion would, most probably, be incapacitated from active exertion.

" For my own part," said M'Cleane, " I confess I should prefer the road. How say you, Dick Flybynight?"

" Oh! the out of door work for me, Captain. I'm no great lover of grubbing about dark passages, and wrenching open strong boxes. No—no; give me the starry sky above, the green turf, or the smooth road below; and my own good mare under me, and then Dick Flybynight cares neither for man or devil."

" And I vote, too, for the road," cried Jenny Diver, whose recent exploit had made her so much in love with the highway department of business, that she began to consider her former doings, clever as they had been, as things rather small and undignified.

Handsome Jack did not agree with M'Cleane, but strongly recommended that the suggestion of Hawkins should be adopted; and after a long discussion it was determined that the proposed attack in the Forest should be given up.

" To you, then, Hawkins, as our newest member, shall be confided the management of this affair," said M'Cleane.

Hawkins expressed his acknowledgments for the honour conferred on him; and as no time was to be lost, for the nobleman was expected at this country mansion on the night but one

following, he immediately began to make his arrangements.

"It will be necessary for me to have three beside myself in this affair," said Hawkins. "Who volunteers?"

"I for one," cried Handsome Jack.

"Good," remarked Hawkins; "but I fear you are new to this sort of work. Never mind! if my directions are implicitly followed, there will be no fear of failure. Who else?"

"You shall not want for support, Hawkins," said Dick Flybynight, slapping the new member on the shoulder. "For once, I'll forswear horseflesh, blacken my face, and carry a dark lantern. Besides, I'm rather anxious to see how the bride will behave when disturbed from the dreams of her wedding night."

"Thanks!" exclaimed Hawkins, grasping Dick Flybynight warmly by the hand, "with

No. 19.

such companions as you, success is certain; but one more is required."

"Take me!" exclaimed Jenny Diver.

"No!" said M'Cleane. "I protest against that—there's another little affair to come off, in which I shall need your assistance. Besides, I am afraid your sympathy for the bride would render you too tenderhearted."

"Not so, Jem," exclaimed the Diver, with a hearty laugh. "I should enjoy the scene mightily, I assure you; but, since I am commanded, I readily yield you my obedience."

During the latter part of the conversation, Beauty Ellis had entered the room, and, to the surprise of all, when Jenny Diver had ceased speaking, he said, whilst a grin adorned his ugly countenance:—

"I wolunteers to go, Captain."

"You?" exclaimed M'Cleane. "Why, Beauty,

what the devil has made you so valiant all at once?"

"And why shouldn't I have a finger in the pie?" asked Beauty Ellis. "P'rhaps I knows a little more about Purley Hall, the place you wants to crack, than you think; and 'tis werry useful to know the vays about an old house like that in the dark."

"True," remarked Hawkins; "if Captain M'Cleane sees no objection to your forming one of my party, I shall be happy to enlist you; you can stand fire, and keep a close tongue, I suppose?"

"For his courage and fidelity I will answer," said M'Cleane, "though I cannot say much for his beauty."

"Thanks, noble Captain," said Beauty with as much delight as though M'Cleane had pronounced a panegyric on his personal beauty.

"Then, Master Hawkins, I shall now have an opportunity of seeing what Beauty Ellis can do."

These, and other preliminaries having been settled, Hawkins, on the following day, commenced making his preparations for the projected robbery. His first care was to proceed himself in person to the old house, and thoroughly reconnoitre it. He therefore assumed the disguise of a country gentleman, and on his arrival near the house, which was situated about half-a-mile from the small town of Ilford, he put up his horse at the White Swan, and entered the kitchen of the hostelry.

A queer room was that kitchen—it had a fireplace large enough to make a small parlour out of, and yet have some room to spare. How ruddy and comfortable the fire looked; how the leaping flashes made pictures of themselves in the polished pewter plates which in bright array decked the dresser. And how bright were the eyes of the buxom maid-servant who bustling about in all directions, appeared to be the presiding genius of the place.

Hawkins had not long seated himself in this comfortable place before his keen eye caught a sort of answering glance. Sitting in the chimney-corner was a heavy-built man dressed in a smock-frock and soiled breeches. There was nothing remarkable about him but one thing—and that was his restless roving eye which never reposed, but was always on guard.

He might have been a poacher, a picker-up of unconsidered hares; or a house-breaker—or anything bad; at least, so thought Mr. Hawkins, and that ingenious gentleman instantly selected as his confederate the heavy-built man.

Purley Hall was an old-fashioned mansion abounding with secret passages, winding stairs, dark chambers and gloomy ante-chambers. Externally it was by no means prepossessing in appearance; the front was of red brick, and gables shot up everywhere. Over the principal entrance were displayed the arms of the old family—a family which had inherited it for centuries. Taken altogether, the house looked like its owner, Lord Purley,—very eccentric.

There were great doings in Purley Hall, for the noble owner was expected to bring back with him a young bride. People in the neighbourhood said that she had been compelled to accept her lordly suitor, and the servants in the hall, the fat cook especially, pitied her. Quite wonderful was the gossip among the women, and the men too, respecting the wedding affair; and, when the carriage rolled up to the door, expectation was on tip-toe.

Lord Purley stepped from his elegant carriage in a proud and dignified way enough. His bride followed him, and as she passed through the ranks of obsequious domestics, blushing at her new position, she formed a strong contrast to her husband. Exquisitely shaped and radiant with youth and innocence, she appeared like a blooming flower beside a withered bough.

Lord Purley, to do honour to his nuptials, gave his domestics a grand supper that night. He wished to be alone with his wife, on that their first evening at home.

And in his gorgeous room, he gazed on the fair young creature beside him; he toyed with her, trifled with her. She appeared quite passive; and when the housekeeper—for she had not a bridesmaid, intimated that her ladyship's room was in order; she silently quitted the side of the Peer; and with a heart full of melancholy, ascended the staircase which led to the bridal chamber.

The ancient bridegroom was not long in following her—but into that sacred room we shall not intrude. The happy pair are shrowded from view—and to their dreams we leave them.

We must now narrate the proceedings of Hawkins and his companions—

An hour after midnight, three men stole cautiously across the lawn, which, like a verdant carpet spread itself before the front of the mansion.

These persons were, Hawkins—Handsome Jack—and Beauty Ellis.

Hawkins tried the front door with some implements of a very peculiar construction; but, although he exercised his utmost skill, he was baffled. The owner of the mansion had caused it to be lined with sheet iron, and through that hard barrier the centrebit could not penetrate.

Failing in this; the burglars, keeping within the shadow of the ancient mansion, proceeded stealthily towards its rear, and soon arrived at the windows of an apartment which looked upon the flower-garden.

"All's quiet," said Beauty Ellis, "very quiet; wonder what the old gen'leman upstairs would say, if he knew of our wedding-visit—the first he has had."

"We have no time for fun now," said Hawkins, "the window will do."

And, with the utmost dexterity, he removed a pane of glass from the window—this having been accomplished, the remainder of their task was comparatively easy; for, although the front of the mansion was in almost a fortified state, the rear was almost unprotected.

"It is all right," said Hawkins, as he gently pushed back the folding shutters. "Now, Jack, follow me; and you, Beauty Ellis, remain where you are, and keep watch."

"But I know the way of the house better than either of you do," said Beauty.

"True," observed Hawkins; "and as all seems safe, perhaps you may as well pilot us.

Where does the old fellow keep his plate-chest, I wonder?"

" In his bed-room," replied Beauty.

" The great object will be to get the dowry of the bride," remarked Handsome Jack.

" Right enough," retorted Hawkins; " but it is quite as well we should take all we can get—so let us see what is in this bureau?"

The bureau was an old-fashioned piece of furniture; and, although Hawkins exercised his utmost skill to force the lock, it for some time resisted his efforts; at length, however, his task was accomplished—and what a sight met the burglar's eyes!

Piled on every shelf were pieces of old-fashioned plate, which rejoiced the hearts of the robbers. Carefully removing these and putting them into a sack, a slight noise was accidentally made. Immediately after this occurrence, Beauty Ellis's face became pale with terror.

" Hush!" said he, " some one is coming down stairs. We are discovered."

And surely enough a footstep was heard as of some one cautiously approaching in the direction of the apartment where they were.

Hawkins hastily drew the shade over his dark lantern, and drawing a pistol from his pocket awaited the appearance of the intruder.

" No murder," whispered Handsome Jack. " I bargained for robbery alone—and, by G—, I'll not see blood shed."

Beauty Ellis quitted the room, and reconnoitred the staircase. The individual whose footsteps had alarmed him, was the old butler, who was gently descending the staircase.

Scarcely had he reached the bottom, before Beauty seized him with the grip of a giant with one hand, while, with the other, he pressed forcibly on the old man's throat, so as to entirely prevent him from giving an alarm.

He then dragged him into the parlour, and by signs intimated to him that his life would be taken if he made the slightest attempt at resistance. Handsome Jack and Hawkins then gagged him, and leaving Beauty to watch him, they ascended to the upper apartments.

" The bed-chamber must be somewhere hereabouts," said Hawkins; " I marked the windows of it yesterday, and am confident I am right—this one must be it."

They had arrived at a door of one of the sleeping-apartments. Hawkins drew from his pocket some skeleton keys; and, fortunately for him and his companion, at the very first trial, the lock was noiselessly picked.

The utmost caution was now necessary. Hawkins leading the way, they entered the bedroom, in which a wax taper was burning.

By its aid they could perceive the old Peer beside his young wife—he was in deep slumber. She also reposed; but her face was so buried in the pillow, that it could not be recognised.

On the dressing-table were several diamond rings, some other articles of jewellery, and two valuable gold watches—these were taken possession of by Hawkins, who seemed thoroughly determined to carry out his principle of taking all he could get.

The money, however, which had been the principal object of their visit could not be found.

Drawer after drawer was ransacked, but in vain: and the robbers were about to quit the apartment, when the bridegroom suddenly awoke.

To his surprise and consternation, he discovered that two men were in his chamber. Uttering a cry for assistance, he leaped from his bed, fled to his sword, and seemed determined to defend himself to the utmost.

The noise now awoke the fair partner of his pillow, and the scene which ensued was terrible.

Foaming with rage, the old man glared on Hawkins and Handsome Jack, and harshly commanded them to retire. His wife hid her face beneath the bedclothes, and screamed with affright.

" It's of no use to resist, old man," said Hawkins, levelling a pistol at the nobleman's head, " we have come for your money, and that money we will have; so no more need be said about it. Come, sir, your brains or the money which you received with your wife to-day?"

" Villains!" cried the old gentleman, still acting on the defensive; " but you shall hang for this;" and he attempted to grasp the bell-handle, but was prevented by Handsome Jack, who by a desperate movement disarmed him.

He was now completely at their mercy, and their first proceeding was to pinion his arms, and throw him on the richly-carpetted floor.

" Now by the God who made me," said Hawkins, " unless you discover where your gold is concealed, I'll cut your throat," and, as he spoke, he drew from his pocket a large clasp-knife.

For a long time the old man obstinately refused to satisfy them, but at length his fears induced him to point out where his dowry was concealed; it was in a strong iron chest which was under his bed.

This they soon opened, and from it they took several bags of gold, and some bundles of bank-notes. Having secured these, they were about to quit the chamber, when the bride, attracted by Handsome Jack's voice, looked steadily at him—uttered a fearful scream, and fell back half fainting on her lace-bordered pillow.

Handsome Jack also gazed into the face of the fair young creature, and as he identified her features, he quivered with surprise and terror.

For each knew the other The old gentleman's newly-married wife was no other than the very girl to whom Handsome Jack had been betrothed.

" Richard Town!" exclaimed the poor young creature. " Can it be possible that I see in you, who I had always till now considered the very soul of honour—a robber?"

" Emile!" was all that the wretched man could for a moment utter, so great was his astonishment; for his connexion with M'Cleane's gang had prevented his visiting of late her to whom he was affianced.

And, stung to the quick by his neglect,—she had, in a fit of spleen, accepted the hand of a man of title, for whom she cared not a straw; but of this Handsome Jack was entirely ignorant, or he never would have engaged in the enterprise of that night.

After his first astonishment at so singularly

unexpected a meeting had passed away, he rushed to the bedside and was about to support the bride, but she waved him away.

"Leave me!" she exclaimed, with indignation. "Leave my presence instantly—I once loved Richard Town, but with a midnight robber I hold no communion."

"Hawkins," cried Handsome Jack, "the money and other articles which we have just taken must be returned—I cannot rob her."

"It is rather unlikely that after all this risk I should consent to deliver up such a goodly amount of swag," remarked Hawkins. "You may, however," he added, "give back your share, if you choose; for my own part I must decline to part with what I have worked so hard to get."

"I must insist on your replacing the money in the chest—and the watches and other matters must be restored also; so let there be no more words about it," said Jack, firmly.

Hawkins again refused, and a quarrel ensued, which resulted in blows; taking advantage of this circumstance Lord Purley contrived to creep to the bell-rope which he pulled violently.

His summons was speedily obeyed—the gardener, who slept in an attic, dashed into the room, but on perceiving the burglars, as speedily withdrew.

"Giles—for God's sake ring the alarm bell," shouted Lord Purley, "or we shall all be murdered in cold blood." Fortunately the gardener possessed sufficient presence of mind to obey the order, and although Hawkins darted after him, he succeeded in reaching the turret in which the bell was hung.

Seizing the rope, he rang the alarm, and the stillness of the night was disturbed by its incessant peals. There were some farm-houses near the mansion, whose inhabitants instantly quitted their beds for the sake of ascertaining the reason of the disturbance.

The instant the bell sounded, Handsome Jack and Hawkins ceased their quarrel, and the latter was about to hasten from the house with his booty, when Jack seized him by the throat and forcibly detained him.

"Not one step do you move," he cried, "until you do as I command you. Restore the property."

As Hawkins still refused to do so, Handsome Jack, by force, dispossessed him of the treasure just as feet were heard ascending the stairs. To secure his own safety not a moment was to be lost, so, throwing the money and watches on the bed, he made for the window and boldly leaped from the balcony outside it.

Fortunately, he alighted on the turf below without sustaining any material injury, but he had only ran a few yards, when a stout farm-labourer put a stop to his further progress by roughly collaring him.

This man was forcibly dragging him to the house which he had just quitted, when Beauty Ellis, who had escaped, rushed to his rescue. With a single blow, Beauty felled the countryman, and Handsome Jack effected his escape.

Hawkins, however, fared differently. Overpowered by numbers, he was compelled to submit to his fate, and a constable having been sent for, he was dispatched in his custody to the nearest watchhouse.

CHAPTER XXXII.

HANDSOME JACK AND BEAUTY ELLIS MEET WITH A WINDFALL.—A SCENE ON THE ROAD. HOW THE BEAUTY GOT MORE THAN HE BARGAINED FOR, AND THE HAIRBREADTH ESCAPE OF BOTH.

RELEASED by the opportune interposition of Beauty Ellis, Handsome Jack made the best of his way, still in company of his liberator, to the "Country House."

That his feelings were anything but pleasant, may be very easily conceived. In the act of committing a desperate robbery, he had been detected and recognized by the very last person in the world he could have thought or desired to view him in so degraded a position; and what the consequences might be he shuddered to imagine. True, he considered Lady Purley herself might be induced to keep his secret in consequence of the love she formerly felt for him; but then, on the other hand, her husband would not be influenced by any such consideration; indeed, were he made acquainted with his bride's former engagement, supposing him still to be ignorant of it, he would perhaps be still more vindictive than if the attempted robbery of his mansion had taken place under ordinary circumstances.

Beauty Ellis, also, was deeply mortified at their want of success; and he was not a little surprised, when Handsome Jack informed him that it was through his interposition the money had been returned to its rightful owner.

"Werry ridicklus indeed, Handsome Jack, and pray what good have you done? You might just as well have had the swag, after you'd run all the risk, for if Hawkins chooses to peach—and its werry likely he may, the shiners would have got you safe out of the country at least. Besides, after all the trouble I had with that servant we gagged, I should have liked a few of the flimsies."

"By G—, I could not find it in my heart to rob her," said Handsome Jack; "but I'll make up your share, Beauty, as soon as I have had a few good jobs on the road; for as for this d—d sneaking into people's houses in dead of night, I'll have no more of it."

"Nonsense, Handsome Jack," exclaimed Beauty Ellis, "nonsense I say; now, my opinion is, that cracking a crib is a werry pleasant change from the highway practice. As to what you say about making up my loss, why, I accepts your offer, that is, if you should be able to keep your promise."

"Do you doubt me?" cried Handsome Jack, with a gesture of indignation.

"Yes, werry much indeed," returned the Beauty.

"I always understood that there was honour among thieves. Why should you distrust mine, for," and he spoke with great bitterness, "I'm now, more than ever one of that respectable fraternity."

" And so there is," remarked Beauty. "Your honour I do not question in the least, it is to your being able to fulfil your intentions, I question."

" How so?" asked Handsome Jack.

" Why, look here," the other replied. "Do you think it will be good for your health to stop at the ' Country House' just at the present. If, as I said, Hawkins should, to save his own neck, tell all he knows of the matter, your's and mine may be in danger, especially as he has been made a member of our fraternity. Why, he could lead the officers to the very spot and pounce on us like hawks on a pair of pigeons."

" True," remarked Handsome Jack. "I had not reckoned on that. What then is best to be done?"

" We shall have time enough at least to go to M'Cleane, and inform him of all that has taken place; indeed, it is absolutely necessary to do so in order to put him and the rest on their guard. Afterwards, we must be ruled by the Captain's advice."

This course was accordingly adopted, and they made the best of their way towards the " Country House."

After a long walk, and when they had arrived within a mile of the place of their destination, the sound of a horse's footsteps slowly advancing towards them from the direction of Highgate was heard.

Hastily concealing themselves, they awaited the arrival of the stranger who soon appeared in view. He was a burly, powerful-looking man ; saddle-bags hung on either side of his stout steed, and the but-end of a pistol projected from beneath the huge flaps of his heavy riding-coat; behind him, on the horse's crupper, was strapped a well - filled portmanteau.

" Here's a prize, mayhap, Handsome Jack," whispered Beauty Ellis, " if we have been unlucky once to-night, that is no reason we should be so again. What say you, shall we try our luck with the traveller?"

" I would not hesitate for a moment," replied Jack, if we were mounted on our good steeds; but how the devil, Beauty, should we manage to escape should the hue and cry be raised. Besides, yonder customer seems no chicken to deal with."

" But we are two to one," urged Beauty, "and for my own part, with such odds in our favour, I fear nothing. Besides, if we gain a prize now, it will go far to redeem our late misfortune in the eyes of the gang."

" Not quite two to one, Beauty," said Jack, " for I take it, that one horseman is a match for two men on foot."

" You hesitate," said Beauty, angrily, " then, by Heaven, I'll attack him single-handed," and the man drew a pistol from his belt.

" That you shall not," said Handsome Jack. " We came out together to share in a common danger, and curse me if I will desert you in a moment of peril." And Jack also drew forth his barkers, and looked at their priming.

" You seize the reins, and at the same moment I will endeavour to prevent the fellow's doing any mischief," said Handsome Jack.

" This is, indeed, a resolute blade, and we must not do things by halves.

By this time the traveller had arrived almost abreast the place where Handsome Jack and Beauty Ellis were concealed beneath the drooping branches of an oak tree. When he got a few yards past them, both the highwaymen as noiselessly as possible quitted their covert, and glided after him.

In another instant, and before the horseman could be aware of danger, Beauty Ellis, seized the reins of the horse, which being an animal of a fiery disposition, reared on its haunches so suddenly as almost to dismount its rider, who, however, did not fall from his seat, but with great presence of mind rapidly drew a horse-pistol, and levelling it at the head of Beauty Ellis, with a desperate oath, was just about to pull the trigger, when Handsome Jack threw up the arm of the attacked man with so much violence, by a blow from the barrel of his own weapon, that the horse-pistol was jerked from the hand of its owner and sent spinning to the side of the road.

Thus disarmed, the traveller so far as arms were concerned, was completely at the mercy of the highwaymen, but he struggled so violently that it was not until he was half-stunned by a blow on the head from the pistol of Beauty Ellis that he could be searched.

" Your money, watch, and whatever jewellery, you may have about you," said Handsome Jack, " or you move not from this spot alive; and see that you are quick about it."

" I'll see you both hanged first, you cowardly plundering villains," exclaimed the traveller, " if you possess yourselves of my property, you shall use force, for without that, you shall not have the value of a farthing."

As he said this, by one desperate effort, he broke from the grasp of the two robbers, and with one blow, sent Handsome Jack to the ground, where he lay for a moment as senseless as a log.

Beauty Ellis he was about to dispose of in a similar manner, but Jack's accomplice was now on his guard. Springing on his adversary, he struggled, and having thrown him, absolutely pinned him to the ground, and whilst laying on the fallen man, he besought Handsome Jack to assist him.

Jack soon recovered from the traveller's sledge-hammer-blow, and ran to the aid of Beauty, who, in his turn, was now almost overpowered. With some trouble, they bound him to a tree and gagged him, and then began ing his pockets.

From his fob they took a valuable gold watch, and in his pockets they found about three hundred pounds in Bank notes and about a score of guineas together with some silver, the latter they returned him, and then commenced searching his saddle-bags and portmanteau.

In these, however, they found nothing of value to them excepting an old pocket-book, which contained five more ten pound Bank bills and some letters and other papers; these latter the traveller begged they would return to him, a request with which the robbers immediately complied, observing, however, that on account of the resistance he had made he deserved no mercy at their hands.

The horseman's riding-gloves having dropped off in the struggle, Beauty Ellis observed that on one of his fingers was a large and very valuable diamond ring: the highwayman, seizing his hand, attempted to possess himself of it, but in consequence of the finger on which it was placed having become much swollen by reason of the blow which the man had bestowed on Handsome Jack, he found it impossible to withdraw it. To have it however, he was resolved.

"That ring I beg you will leave me, it is an old family relic which I much prize;" and in the hope of softening the hearts of the highwaymen, he added: "It was put on that finger by my wife as she lay on her death-bed, and I made a solemn vow that it should not quit this finger until I should be in a similar condition, and then only transmit it to my child. For God's sake, gentlemen, do not rob me then of this trifle."

"Trifle!" cried Beauty Ellis, who, as the reader is well enough aware, was never troubled by anything resembling tender feelings, "why it's worth forty or fifty pounds if it's worth a penny. Come, no humbug—off with it, or I shall be forced to use roughish means to get it."

In vain did Jack second the traveller's request—Beauty would not yield a jot, and still continued striving to detach the ring. At length rendered savage by disappointment, he roundly swore, that sooner than be baffled in his purpose he would cut off the finger itself."

The wretch drew his case-knife, and was actually about to carry his intention into practice, when his companion suggested that although the ring could not be taken from the finger with drawing it, it might be filed through in its thinest part. Beauty objected to the delay which would be incurred by the process; but Handsome Jack, who, as housebreakers are, was provided with a small file, had already set to work, and in a very few minutes the thin gold circlet was so divided that by a little bending backwards, it was removed easily from the finger.

As a last resource in order to recover the ring, the traveller offered fifty pounds to the robbers if they would leave it for him with Jonathan Wild, and assured them that no questions should be asked; but on this point neither would give any definite answer until they had communicated with Captain M'Cleane.

The robbers now, fearing as day was not far from breaking that it would not be safe to remain longer in the scene of their depredation, having first driven by a sharp whipping, the horse some distance from the spot, quitted the unfortunate victim of their wiles, and walked off as fast as possible in the direction of Highgate; but they had not got above half-a-mile when another horseman passed them.

This circumstance caused them but little uneasiness, as they imagined they should with ease reach the 'Country House' before the party who they had suffered to go by them unmolested should fall in with the one they had bound; but in this they were deceived.

For before they entered the outskirts of the little village of Highgate a horse in full gallop coming towards them was heard, and Beauty Ellis, turning pale with apprehension and drawing a pistol, exclaimed:—

"By G—, Jack, we are pursued, and must trust to cunning for our escape; if the fellow who is coming this way has freed and accompanied the man we bound, the matter may go hard with us."

"Then let us run for it," cried Jack; and off they started as though they ran a race for their lives, and which in fact they did.

Anxiously did they survey each side of the road, in the hope of discovering a way of escape into the fields, but for some distance, in that particular part of the road the latter was bounded on each side by two high park walls, which were so smooth that not the least footing on their sides could be obtained.

"Damnation!" muttered Handsome Jack between his clenched teeth, "when shall we get to the park-gate or the edge;" and still he and his companion increased their pace, although they were before making almost superhuman efforts.

Still nearer and nearer drew their pursuers, and just as the robbers gave themselves up for lost they arrived opposite one of the lodges of the park.

Uttering an exclamation of delight, they both ran to it and commenced scaling it.

This lodge-gate was one of those old-fashioned affairs which we occasionally see at the entrance to the mansions of Elizabeth's time. It was of a Gothic design, and constructed of open iron-work. To reach the top of it was easy enough. but when that was done a formidable obstacle, in a number of long iron spikes, which arose from and bristled around the upper portion, presented itself. Over these they must get to escape, and with a few lacerations Handsome Jack managed to clear the barrier, and descend to the other side in safety.

Beauty Ellis, whose short, thick-set, muscular form caused him not to be the most active in the world, was far less fortunate, and under other circumstances Handsome Jack would have been mightily amused by his lumbering and awkward attempts to clear the gate; but by dint of great exertion he reached the top, and was cautiously getting over the spikes, when the party pursuing them rode up.

It was the very man whom they had plundered, he having been, as might have been expected, relieved by the traveller seen by the highway-robbers.

His horse was going at such a rate of speed that it was some minutes after he passed the lodge before he could rein him in; but rapidly as he had passed the place he had seen the form of Beauty Ellis, and instantly recognised him.

The other horseman who had joined in the pursuit now came up, and the pair called on the escaping man to surrender himself—but that he declined doing, of course, and only made redoubled efforts in order to effect his escape.

Beauty's situation was extremely perilous, for he was so compelled to use both hands, that it was impossible for him to draw his pistol and defend himself, which he would gladly have done. Handsome Jack, however, flew to his assistance, and in order to intimidate the gentlemen fired at them from between the iron bars of the gate, but so agitated was he that he entirely missed his aim.

The shot was instantly returned by one of the pursuers also without effect; on seeing this the other rode up almost close to the wall adjoining the gate, so as to protect himself from Handsome Jack's weapon, and carefully levelling his own pistol, he deliberately fired it off, not six yards from the body of Beauty Ellis, who had by tremendous efforts succeeded in scaling the spikes, and was commencing the descent of the opposite side.

This time the shot told as was evinced by a shriek of pain, and then a volley of curses from Beauty Ellis, who, deprived of the use of one arm, and turning suddenly so faint that he could not support himself, fell heavily on the ground just inside the gate.

The instant he reached the turf, Handsome Jack rushed forward and dragged him behind the park-wall before the party who had wounded him could reload his weapon; but a new cause of alarm now troubled him, for the gentlemen commenced ringing with great violence the large bell of the porter's lodge.

"Fly and save yourself," said Beauty; "Don't wait for me—the fellow has winged me," and Ellis sank back half-fainting.

"Never," said Handsome Jack; "never shall it be said that I ran from a comrade in adversity. But cheer up," said he, "matters may not be so bad after all. Curse that bell, but I'll stop it. Would that I had thought of doing so before."

And stealing cautiously to the wire which led from the handle outside, to the alarm, he, by a powerful effort snapped it and prevented the bell from further sounding. But it was too late, for in a room of the lodge, which appeared to be a bed chamber, a light was suddenly seen, and a window was thrown open,—then the upper portion of a man in his night-shirt and cap made his appearance with a blunderbuss in his hand.

The robbers were thus hemmed in before and behind them; but still Handsome Jack did not despair. He drew Beauty Ellis within the cover of some shrubs under which he was completely hidden, and made himself better informed as to the nature of the wound from which the blood was streaming freely.

Two balls or slugs had evidently entered his right shoulder and were lodged there, but all he could then hastily do was to wrap his handkerchief tightly round the wounds: fortunately he succeeded in staunching the blood.

Whilst he was thus engaged he heard the man from the window enquire the reason of the disturbance.

"We order you to open the gates, in the king's name, and admit us. A daring highway-robbery has just been committed close by, and the villains have just escaped over this gate, they are somewhere inside and we are determined to capture them," said one of those outside.

On hearing this, the wife of the old lodge-keeper came forward in a terrible fright, and vowed that her husband should not venture from the house lest he should be himself murdered by the bloody villains: the keeper himself appeared, to Jack's great joy, to be no wise inclined to leave his snug quarters, and venture out in the dark where robbers might be concealed;—so he at once refused, and in hope of satisfying the applicants fired his blunderbuss at random among the trees below.

Still, however, the travellers demanded admission, and swore if not let in, they would go round to the owner of the estate at the principal entrance, and procure the lodge-keeper's dismissal for his conduct. This threat, especially as it was accompanied by an assertion that the estate owner was one of his particular friends produced some effect; for, muttering that he would be down immediately, the old fellow left the window, put on some garments, hastily reloaded his blunderbuss, and soon appeared at the front door, with his weapon in one hand and a large lantern and a bunch of keys in the other. After having carefully looked about him he ventured forth, and walked tremblingly along the winding gravel walk which led to the gate.

Handsome Jack, who knew that in Beauty Ellis's almost helpless state, he would certainly be discovered should the gentleman even institute a search within the gate, immediately made up his mind as to the best—indeed, the only course to be pursued.

Concealing himself behind one of the trees, which grew beside the winding walk, he awaited the passing by of the old keeper, and the moment after he passed the spot—his teeth chattering with cold and terror—he rushed on him, tore the blunderbuss from his feeble grasp, and commanded him on peril of his life to be silent.

He then deprived him of the keys, and dragging him across the lawn, fortunately came unexpectedly on a sort of shed, which the old man informed him, in answer to his demand, was a wood-house.

"Then show me the key in your bunch which opens this door," said Jack, peremptorily.

The old man unwillingly complied, and as the door turned on its hinges, Handsome Jack requested him to enter.

"For God's sake, Mr. Robber, don't murder a poor old man who never did you any harm," he exclaimed in faltering accents, as Jack presented his pistol to his head to enforce his commands; and the wretched creature fell on his knees and assumed an attitude of supplication.

"Your life is safe if you obey my commands, and not else," said Handsome Jack. "Let me hear—and I shall place a sentinel with you to see that you behave yourself—the slightest noise, and both you and your wife shall be worm's-meat before another hour has passed over your heads."

Then, bidding the old man to be seated, he locked the door on the outside, and ran to the spot where he had left Beauty Ellis concealed.

He found him much recovered, and led him to the wood-house, the door of which he again opened, and left him there in charge of the keeper, then hiding the blunderbuss in the thatch of the roof, he stole towards the entrance gate, to observe how matters went on.

He had scarcely come within sight of it, than he perceived the two gentlemen, who were tired of waiting for the lodge-keeper, following the example he and Beauty had set of scaling the gate. Involuntarily he raised his pistol, but a sudden thought flashed across his mind, and he returned the weapon to its place.

For he knew that the report of the pistol would indicate his whereabouts, and he wished it to be considered that he and his companion had made their escape across the grounds.

The gentlemen had no sooner made good their entry, than they made for the keeper's dwelling, but Handsome Jack had ran to it before them, and seeing the old woman at the window, informed her that he was one of the pursuers of the highwaymen, who had gone to the other gate of the park, her husband watching them, and requested her to send the other two gentlemen in the same direction.

Scarcely had he done this and again concealed himself, when the two men who were the real pursuers came up, and Handsome Jack had the gratification of seeing them start off in the direction of the other park-gate, which he knew must be at a considerable distance.

So far his ruse had succeeded admirably, but much yet remained to be done. Without losing a moment, therefore, he again ran to the wood-house, and whispered something to Beauty Ellis, who immediately followed him out. Again cautioning the terrified old man, they relocked the door and hastened to the gate by which they had entered.

To the gate the horses of the two gentlemen were tethered. Loosening them, Handsome Jack assisted Beauty Ellis to a seat on one of them, and then himself mounted the other. He had previously thrown the keys into a part of the shrubbery where he knew they would not be easily discovered.

They now put their steeds to the push, and instead of returning to Highgate at that time, they turned off into a byeway, and proceeded as fast as Beauty's wounds would permit him to London; in a remote street of which near Aldersgate, Jack called up a surgeon, and desired him to attend to Beauty's wounds, which had now become, from the jolting caused by the ride, excessively painful. Jack and his party, to account for the incident, invented a story to the effect that it had occured in a tavern brawl, and as the practitioner was well feed for extracting the two slugs, he did not care to make any particular enquiries.

While this operation was going on, Handsome Jack, on the pretext of taking his horse to a livery stable, of which there were then many in that vicinity, left the surgeon's and proceeded with them to a dealer in Smithfield, who believing that he and his friend were flying from bailiffs, and were anxious to dispose of them even at a sacrifice, as they wished to cross into France. Under the circumstances the animals fetched a sum far short of their value, and as Handsome Jack, who did not care to be seen too long at that early hour in their company, without much bargaining accepted the dealer's offer,

and returned to Beauty Ellis with forty more guineas in his purse.

During the whole of that day the two highwaymen deemed it prudent not to quit the city, —they therefore sought the shelter of a retired public-house, with the landlord of which Beauty Ellis had some acquaintance; the stable-keeper of whom, like our old friend Tony Bilkit, having formerly done a little in the free-trade line himself: and here they met with an unexpected adventure, which will be related in a future chapter.

CHAPTER XXXIII.

HOW MR. WATKINS FOILS HAWKINS, AND HOW HAWKINS IS ANYTHING BUT SATISFIED.— THE ESCAPE FROM NEWGATE.

WE left Hawkins after his capture at Purley Hall, on his way to the watchhouse. On his road thither, he indulged in the most violent execrations against his late companions; Handsome Jack especially, who he swore had deserted him. He made, too, the most desperate attempts to escape from his captors, but so strongly had they secured him, that he found all his strivings entirely fruitless.

On arriving at the watchhouse, he was at once transferred to that part of it called the "Little Ease," (the strongest and most uncomfortable part of the building as its name implies) and a constable kept guard outside its door, until he could be sent before a magistrate.

Within a few hours after he had been first incarcerated, he was removed, heavily ironed, and taken before a Bow Street magistrate, who having examined and adverted to the facts of the robbery, or rather burglary, for no booty was carried away, he was fully committed, although he obstinately refused to reveal his real name, to Newgate for

It so happened that an old acquaintance, Watkins, the Bow Street runner, was in court when Hawkins was placed in the dock, and he immediately recognized the prisoner as an old acquaintance.

Watkins, as soon as Hawkins was committed, whispered a few sentences in the ear of the magistrate, who requested that the prisoner might not yet be conveyed to Newgate, as he understood other charges would be preferred against him.

On hearing this, Hawkins literally gnashed his teeth with rage, for he had hoped to get clear of one charge, on the ground that he had carried away no property from, nor used personal violence at Purley Hall. Other charges, however, he knew well enough, might entirely crush him.

Hawkins was, for the present, removed to a cell connected with the justice-room, and while he lay therein ruminating on his desperate condition, he was visited by the Bow Street runner.

"Mornin', Mr. Hawkins," said the constable.

"That's not my name," said the prisoner, doggedly, to the officer.

"Ah!" no wonder as you're ashamed of it," remarked Watkins, "but you can't deceive me. Now, I'll bet a guinea, as you know mine, for we've met before I'm sure."

"Never saw your face before; and curse you it's not a very pleasant sight now," said Hawkins.

"Dare say not," rejoined the constable, drily, "there's werry few, Mr. Hawkins, of your perfession as is over fond of me. The first time I had the pleasure of seeing you vas when you were butler——"

"At Sir Dennis Drury's, down at Staines," cried Hawkins, who was for a moment thrown off his guard; but I'll swear I never saw you there."

"Werry good reason why—I took care never to let you—but when that heap of plate

No. 20.

was missing, I was down at Staines for the purpose of watching your movements. I knew well enough you was in that job, but I was a little too late, or I should have nabbed you then."

"Curse you! they could prove nothing against me," said the prisoner.

"No, they couldn't 'xactly, to be sure, but I knew as you did the job; and what I told Sir Dennis Drury made him believe you were the thief as well—d'ye think if he had thought you were innocent he would have discharged you?"

On hearing this, Hawkins made a spring on the constable, as though he would tear him limb from limb as a tiger might rend his prey; but the weight of his irons prevented him doing any real mischief. In an instant he was roughly seized by the constable and rudely thrown on the straw of his cell, where he lay foaming at the mouth with passion.

"Ha! would you, Hawkins?" said the Bow Street runner, with a triumphant chuckle. "Now, do you know, I think it's werry ungrateful of you to serve an old friend in that way. If you go on so, I wont do for you what perhaps I can do if I choose—help you out of the scrape you've managed to get into."

Drowning men, they say, catch at straws, and these few last words of Watkins, conveyed some hope to the mind of the prisoner.

"What the devil do you mean—and why don't you speak out?" said he.

"Why, as there's another charge hanging over you for robbing the north mail, along with two others. Do you know anything of this?"

As Watkins placed before the eyes of Hawkins a letter, the prisoner gazed upon it for a moment, turned deadly pale, and sank back groaning on his bed of straw.

"Whence got you that?" he at length gasped.

"It was handed to me by the Postmaster-General," replied Watkins.

The contents of this missive, which had so prostrated the hardy highwayman were as follows:—

"Sir,—I am one of those persons who robbed the north mail, which I am very sorry for; and to make amends, I will secure my two companions as soon as may be. He whose hand writing this shall appear to be, will, I hope, be entitled to the reward of his pardon."

To this letter no signature was appended, but Hawkins at once knew by the writing from whom it came.

"The d——d craven!" he exclaimed.

"So yer do know something of the affair then, Master Hawkins," remarked Watkins.

The prisoner had again unconsciously fallen into a trap of his own making, to get out of which uninjured was impossible.

"Is the writer of that letter apprehended?" he asked.

"No!" replied Watkins, "there's only one of the three who were concerned in the matter in limbo as yet, and that one is yourself; but they can't be at large much longer, for our scouts are out in all directions."

"I suppose then, the first who tells all about it will get the pardon?" said Hawkins.

"Sartinly, and I should advise you to look after your own good. Will you let the cat out of the bag?" asked the constable.

"I will reveal all I know at once," said Hawkins, hurriedly; for he trembled lest his comrade who had written the letter referred to, should be beforehand with him.

Watkins then took him again before the magistrate and requested a private interview, which was immediately granted; and Hawkins then, in the presence of the justice, made a confession and some discoveries, which were committed to writing by the clerk, and signed by the prisoner. Watkins then conveyed him back to his cell, and drew from him particulars necessary to be known in order to effect the capture of the other two parties implicated in the mail robbery.

These particulars he noted down in his pocket-book, and then said to the prisoner:—"You've done a good job for yourself, Hawkins; for as to that job, at least, your neck is in no danger."

"That job, at least!" The words conveyed anything but a pleasant idea to Hawkins' mind.

"Yes, that job," repeated Watkins.

"Why, won't my turning king's evidence on one charge, clear me of any other?"

"Lord bless you, Mr. Hawkins, why what could have put such a werry ridik'lus notion into your head? Why, there are two more charges, and heavy ones too, again you."

"Then can't I do in those cases as I've just done in this?" asked Hawkins.

"Can in one of 'em, if you chose—but not in 'tother," coolly remarked the runner.

"And why not?" demanded Hawkins, whose alarm and indignation at having been overreached, and anger with himself at not having made better terms, were excessive.

"'Cause 'tis impossible—how can a man turn king's evidence against his own flesh and blood?" replied Watkins.

"I don't quite understand you," said Hawkins, who fancied the constable referred by one's own flesh and blood to a relative. Now, the prisoner happened to have a brother who accompanied him in several of his robberies, and he assured Watkins that he should not feel the least reluctance to sacrifice that near relative, if by so doing he could benefit himself.

"Not the least doubt in the world that you would," returned Mr. Watkins; "but as I meant, you wouldn't be allowed to peach against yourself alone—that would only be a confession which might hang you as much as if twelve men in the box had declared you guilty."

Hawkins listened moodily, but said nothing; and Watkins continued:—

"Lord Bruce and the Earl of Burlington are sent for by the beak, and will presently be here; something about some money, watches, and a ring which you eased them of in Richmond Lane. There was only one in that little matter you know."

Watkins, with a sneer, now left the miserable man whom he had cajoled into a confession of one robbery, knowing, at the time, well enough that he could be indicted for others; but it was all in his way of business, and he hugged himself on his cleverness.

The Earl of Burlington and Lord Bruce having arrived, Hawkins was again placed at the bar—both noblemen swore to the best of their belief that the prisoner was the man who attacked them in Richmond Lane. Hawkins, however, roundly asserted that he was in another place at the time; and spying a liverystable keeper in the court, who resided in London Wall, he called that worthy, who on oath said, that on the night of the alleged robbery, the prisoner lodged in his house.

As the noblemen refused to swear particularly to the prisoner, who, when they were plundered, had crape over his face, although they recognized his voice, the justice was about to dismiss the case, as not being sufficiently proved, when Watkins again whispered in the magistrate's ear.

"Stay," said the justice, "call Israel Van Jacobi as a witness."

There was a bustling in the crowd, as a man pressed through it, and mounted the witness box.

On catching a glimpse of him, Hawkins changed colour, and convulsively grasped the railing of the dock.

The new witness was a queer-looking, little old man, dressed in a Jewish gaberdine, and leaning on a long gold-headed staff. His face was sufficiently indicative of his Israelitish extraction. Beneath two grey pent-house sort of eyebrows, black as jet, although the thin hair which streamed down his neck and his long beard were of a snowy whiteness, gleamed rather than shone two small grey eyes. His head was bowed with years, and over his aquiline nose, which more resembled a beak than aught else, a parchment-coloured skin was strained. The mouth was retracted and toothless, and his form trembled with feebleness as he stood before the justice.

"Your name?" enquired the clerk.

"Israel Van Jacobi," mumbled the Jew.

"Where do you reside?"

"At Amsterdam, vere I carries on the pusiness of von jewel merchand."

"And you visit this country to dispose of your gems every year?"

"I do."

"Swear him," said the magistrate.

The clerk handed to the old man, who then put on his hat, a copy of the Seven Books of Moses, and on those he made his affirmation.

"Do you know the prisoner at the bar?"

"Yesh, Mynheer, I haf sheen de shentleman before."

"Where?"

"At mein hans in Amsterdam."

"What dealings have you had with him?"

"Only von, sh'elp my Fader Apraham, Mynheer, and dat vas ven I prought a sapphire ring of him."

"It's a lie—the scoundrelly Jew swears falsely; I never saw him in all my life," said the prisoner.

"Ah! mein Gott," said Israel Van Jacobi, lifting up his withered hands. "Shentlemans, I haf got dat ring mit me now."

And fumbling among the folds of his gaberdine, the Jew drew forth a small jewel-case which he opened, and took from it a splendid sapphire ring, which the Earl of Burlington instantly identified as the one which had been stolen from him.

Again the Israelite distinctly and positively swore that Hawkins had sold it to him at his house in Amsterdam. And this evidence being deemed conclusive, the prisoner was at once committed for the highway robbery, greatly to the satisfaction of Mr. Watkins who received a handsome doceur from the Earl as the reward of his sagacity.

That evening, Hawkins was conveyed to Newgate, and thither we must accompany him.

After having been heavily ironed, he was placed in a cell on the ground-floor of the prison. This cell was the lowest of a tier of four,

and was one of the strongest in the whole gaol. The windows were double grated, iron bars were placed at intervals across the flue, and no precautions which were calculated to ensure the safe custody of those placed therein, seemed to have been neglected.

In this gloomy place he passed four wretched days, when his turn for trial came on—before, however, he was himself arraigned, he was placed in the witness-box, and his two companions in the robbery of the northern mail were placed at the bar. On Hawkins' testimony, coupled with that of the post-boys they were condemned and sentenced to be hanged and gibbetted on the spot of the robbery.

He was then himself placed in the dock, and indicted for the robbery in Richmond Lane, and being found guilty of this, he was again arraigned for the burglary at Purley Hall. A verdict of guilty in this case was also recorded, and he was told to prepare for an ignominious end, as in his case, although he had assisted to bring others to justice, he was so flagrant a criminal himself that mercy could not be extended to him.

When sentence was passed and he was being led away, he suddenly turned round and addressing the Bench, said:—

"May I request, my lord, as a dying man, one favour at your hands?"

"Name it," said the judge, "and if it be reasonable, you shall not be denied it."

"It is," said Hawkins, "that I may be confined in a condemned cell, separate from the men against whom I this morning gave evidence. They would in revenge murder me. And, if they went not so far as that, would effectually prevent me from preparing for my end."

"To that I cannot object—Jailer! let the prisoner be placed in a separate cell until the day of execution," said the judge.

In making the application, Hawkins did not so much fear the men he had been instrumental in condemning, as he would have the bench suppose. He had a great object in view in being alone in his place of confinement; an object which will ere long be apparent to the reader.

The cell into which he was now conveyed, was much smaller, and quite as secure as the one he had formerly occupied. But the doomed criminal was one of those who never will despair whilst a spark of life remains—all his thoughts were now bent on devising a mode by which he could escape from the vengeance of the law.

At a certain hour of the day he was allowed to walk in the yard of the prison. Men sentenced to death were not then, as now, rigidly confined to their humble cells until they went forth from them to the scaffold.

Fortunately for Hawkins, he was not destitute of money, and he was allowed to send out for what food and liquor he chose. Of the opportunities thus afforded him he determined to avail himself.

He had observed, during his walks, the regular arrival of a young woman, who visited the prison daily, and for a certain consideration, performed errand for those confined. Hawkins thought he had certainly seen the girl before, but could not exactly remember where. All of a sudden, however, he recognized her as a woman of the town whom he had formerly visited in the Almonry at Westminster.

It was no other than Sal the Gonnoff, who, to satisfy the incessant greedy extortions of old Mother Sin, resorted to this employment as a means of procuring ready money.

"Sall," said Hawkins to her quietly, as she passed close by him, "Sall, hist!"

"Who the devil are you?" asked the girl, and then looking him full in the face, she exclaimed, "Well, I'm d——d, if it isn't my old pal, Jack Hawkins. Why, they say you're safe for a dancing match—poor fellow!"

"Not if I can manage it—and if you'll help me, which you can," said Hawkins, slipping three guineas into Sal's hand.

"How?" asked Sal. "You know I will if I can—but what must I do?"

"Here's another shiner for you—procure me a small crowbar, one of that sort you know which unscrews into three or four pieces, you know where to get one—and secure this in some paper in your pocket. Then get Old Mother Sin to make a large loaf, but before it is baked put inside it a small thin file; you can bring this loaf openly into the gaol and give me as if from charity, with a bottle of spirits. The crowbar you will be able to slip into my pocket privately."

"And when must I bring them?" asked the girl.

"To-morrow—not a moment must be lost. So do not delay, Sal, for God's sake."

"Never fear, Jack, I will be in this place with what you require by noon to-morrow, be on the look out for me," and she strolled from Hawkins towards the other inmates of the prison.

On that night, Hawkins retired to his cell with a lighter heart than that with which he had quitted it in the morning. A hope almost amounting to a certainty that, difficult as the escape from the prison must and would be, he should effect it, elevated his spirits.

His first object was thoroughly to examine every portion of his cell, and ascertain its weakest part—if, indeed, a weak part there were. With this view, as soon as the turnkey had paid him his last visit for the night, he crept a little distance up the chimney, but his progress was soon stopped by iron bars which were placed across the aperture, and thrusting his arm through the narrow openings of these, he could feel others yet higher up. Not doubting but that these barriers were placed to a considerable height, he at once gave up all hope of finding egress in that quarter.

Next he examined the window, but two impediments, almost insurmountable, presented themselves; in the first place, the double grating was formed of massive bars of iron very deeply imbedded in holes dug in the solid stone; again, it looked into a court yard, where a night-guard was always posted. To escape by this window, therefore, was altogether out of the question.

Had his cell been on a third, or even on a second storey, his task would have been far less difficult than it now promised to be, for the sides of his cell were far thicker than those above it, and presented effectual barriers to his escape through them.

He was musing on his almost hopeless case, when a very slight circumstance, so slight that it is almost wonderful he should have noticed it, startled him.

It was but a slight dripping sound, as of drops of water falling at regular intervals on the floor of his cell. Common-place as this sound would have been to him under ordinary circumstances, it was as music to his ears now. He examined the stones, and there saw a small pool of moisture—looking up, he beheld the place from whence it issued—it oozed from the mortar between two of the stones of the arched roof.

He instantly surmised that the leads of the roof must be out of order, and that from some of the gutters the water must leak through the two cells above him until it reached the one in which he lay—if so, he thought there must be a weak part in the roof of his own cell, and to ascertain if this really were so, he placed his table on his bed, his chair again on that, by which means he found he could reach the ceiling with ease.

Trying the mortar between the interstices of the stones, he found it almost soft to his touch, two stones removed and he should gain the next cell, and by the same means he trusted to gain the outer leads.

Wearied with his exertions, which from the weight of his irons, were most exhausting, he descended and went to bed, but it was long before he slept. He woke in the morning with renewed hopes, and oh! how he longed for the arrival of noon and Sal the Gonnoff.

At the appointed hour she came, and had been fortunate enough to convey the articles through the porter's lodge unsuspected. By adroit management, she contrived to place them in Hawkins' possession; and never did miser clutch and worship gold so gladly as did that condemned criminal the implements by which he hoped to free himself.

He now longed for the arrival of night as much as he had before done for noon, and when again, he was left for twelve hours, he screwed together his crowbar, mounted again the chair and table, and found that he could easily remove the mortar all round the stone, but this he refrained from now doing lest the fissure might attract attention.

He now commenced to file away his irons, and so rapidly and dexterously did he work, that by the morning he had so weakened them that on the following night, which he fixed upon for his enterprise, a very little force would be sufficient to remove them. In order to hide the marks of the file, he chewed some bread, mixed it with soot from the chimney back, and plastered it in the places worked out by the file, which effectually concealed them.

The next day, pleading indisposition, he could not leave his cell, fearing that did he appear in the yard attention might be directed to his irons; and further to allay suspicion, he begged the religious services of the chaplain, who attended him for some hours.

The next evening at length arrived, and his last meal for the day being brought him, he pretended to retire to his bed. Just as the turnkey was leaving him, that functionary informed him that the Recorder of London had sent in his report to the King, and that the warrant for his execution, on the morning but one after, had arrived.

Hawkins affected great agony on hearing this; but no sooner had the turnkey turned his back, than he rose from his knees, on which he had thrown himself when he heard the awful intelligence, and after waiting a few moments, to be assured that all was silent, he set to work at his irons, and was very speedily released from them.

Now, then, he could work with ease, for he had only his wrist and ankle-irons remaining on him, and these did not much trouble him.

The clock from the neighbouring church of St. Sepulchres struck seven just as he had erected with his bed, table, and chair a temporary scaffold. There was yet sufficient light for him to work by, so taking a draught from the bottle of spirits which he had carefully preserved for this occasion, he at once mounted to the roof.

He commenced working the mortar all round the huge stone of the roof with his crowbar, and in the course of an hour he had the gratification of perceiving that the block slightly yielded to force. But now, an unforeseen difficulty occurred—the stone was directly above his head, and it might fall at an unexpected moment and crush him; and even supposing that he should escape destruction, it would cause such a noise as doubtless to alarm the officials.

To carry such a ponderous body on his shoulders, as he descended his frail stage which would scarcely support his own weight, was out of the question. What then was he to do?

He, after some consideration, determined to pry away the cement until the stone was all but detached; then remove his platform a little to one side, and after doubling his mattress and bed clothes on the floor immediately beneath it, to give it one finishing movement with the crowbar and let it drop on the soft body prepared to receive it. This, he trusted, would prevent noise or injury to himself.

On he went, cautiously, and gradually chipping the mortar away, bit by bit, and in about half an hour more, he conceived by the looseness of the stone that it was dangerous longer to work directly under it.

He therefore descended to the floor, moved his bed, table, and chair, and in the place where the former had stood, he arranged with great care the mattress, blankets, pillows, and sheets, so as to form a thick cushion.

Once more he mounted, and resolutely introduced his crowbar; but after about a quarter of an hour's work, although he could pass the tool through the crevice all round, the stone only moved laterally. He felt convinced that it was now unattached by cement, yet still to his surprise it did not fall from its bed.

Hawkins was perplexed at this, and for some time strove to ascertain the cause. At last, he could tell by feeling the crowbar, for it was now dark, that it did not go through the crevice which he made in quite a perpendicular direction, but so nearly to it, that he had not hitherto noticed the circumstance. The truth of the matter now flashed on his mind in an instant; the stone was very slightly wedge-shaped like the stones of an arch, and its upper surface evidently formed the flooring of the cell above. All the precautions, therefore, which he had taken that it might fall noiselessly were in vain, and some precious time had been thrown away. Had he waited until doomsday, the mass would not have dropped as he had imagined.

Again he placed his bed, table, and chair where they had before been, and mounting to the stone, he tried if he could push it upwards; to his great joy, he discovered that this was no difficult matter, for after a few efforts he succeeded by main strength in raising it so far, that, by a dexterous jerk, he threw it on its side on the floor above head.

The aperture, however, was scarcely large enough to admit his body; but quickly detaching a smaller stone he descended, and took some bread which he soaked in the spirits and rested himself for a few moments.

Two hours had been occupied in the work we have described, but much yet lay before him; his next care was to convert his sheets and rugs into ropes, which he very speedily did, and carefully coiling the length round his body, he prepared to squeeze himself through the hole in the ceiling.

This was no easy matter, but what will not a desperate man who is flying for his life accomplish? After prodigious efforts, Hawkins succeeded, and stood panting and bathed in perspiration on the floor of the second cell.

This was a far less secure place than the one he had just quitted—he saw that at a glance, and there were, too, a bed, table, and chair in it; guided by experience, he took it for granted that the third cell contained no occupant, like the second—so he at once determined again to break through the roof.

This last was by no means so difficult as the other had been; and therefore we need not describe his mode of accomplishing it. Suffice it to say, that by the aid of his trusty crowbar, he vanquished all difficulties, and as the clock chimed a quarter past ten, he had gained the uppermost cell.

The roof of this was flat, and from this circumstance, he judged that above it were leads. He therefore determined to try to gain them by way of the window which had only a single grating.

He then, with great care lest the noise should alarm the turnkeys in the yard below, began to file the lower and upper portions of the iron bars; this slow process occupied nearly an hour and a half, and then he wrenched four of them out, and looking through, he perceived that in the court-yard no one was stirring—all was as still as the grave.

Casting his glance upwards, he saw directly above him, and within reach, the large gutter-leads. About eight feet from him, on his right-hand, was a leaden water pipe with which it was connected, and which was fastened to the wall at regular intervals by strong semicircular bands of iron clamped into the joints of the wall itself.

If he could but reach that water pipe, he thought he should have little difficulty in mounting by its aid to the flat roof—but how to reach it—that was the question.

Beneath him, to the pavement of the prison-yard, was a depth of about forty feet, but in spite of this obstacle to a project he hastily formed, he was determined to put it into execution.

Seating himself on the stone sill of the window, he leant backwards with his face towards the skies, pressing his heels firmly against the wall of the cell to preserve his balance, he caught hold of the edge of the leaden gutter, which he found, by experiment, would support his weight; then packing his crowbar in his breast pocket, he laid hold of the fearful support, drew himself backwards out of the window, and the next moment he hung suspended by his hands from the gutter.

Hawkins was a man of prodigious strength, and to that alone he trusted; the slightest weakness or fear now would be fatal to him. Holding fast by one brawny fist he relieved the other, which he planted a few inches further on; and by thus going hand over hand, he arrived within two feet of the water pipe in safety, when, to his horror, he felt the spout above bending beneath his weight.

A profuse perspiration burst from every pore, and a feeling of faintness pervaded his entire frame, as he shudderingly gave a hasty glance downwards. God of heaven! still the leaden gutter yielded—for it was a part which no bracket supported. Hawkins saw that a moment's delay would be ruin, so with one desperate effort he, with his left hand, clutched at the lead above him a few inches nearer the pipe, and found that it yielded not an inch,

Then he relieved his right hand, and again he was successful; in another instant, his feet rested on the iron band of the water pipe, his chief peril was passed.

Here he was compelled, for a short time, to rest and recover his breath; this point gained, he, by means of the iron supports, mounted to the flat leads, on which he lay in a state of complete exhaustion; and with fingers that seemed permanently crooked and contracted from their death-grip of the edge of the gutter.

After he had a little recovered, his heart beat with delight to find that he was no longer between stone walls, and only the sky was above him. Oh! how sweet to him seemed the night breezes which fanned his cheeks—how delicious the feeling that he was almost as free as them.

On examining his position, he found that there was no way of getting from these top leads but by dropping to those of another part of the building, about ten feet below. Those once gained, he knew from previous observation, that he could without much difficulty enter a window the passage inside which communicated with the upper leads of Newgate.

Hawkins let his shoes down first with his blanket-rope, by means of which he would have let himself down, had there been anything to

which he could fix it, and then lowering himself as far as possible by grasping with his hands the edge of the parapet, he let go, and without making much noise descended in safety.

High above these leads, on one side, rose a lofty wall in which was a window, so low that by standing on tiptoe Hawkins could easily reach it. Being situated in the private passage through which the chaplain proceeded to the chapel, it was only protected by a single bar, which Hawkins speedily removed and entered. After passing a little way along it, he came to a descending flight of stairs, but convinced by this that he had taken the wrong turning he retraced his steps, and went in the opposite direction until he came to a door, the lock of which he, after much trouble, wrenched off.

He was now in the chapel, on the opposite side of which was another door, which also he forced, but before he passed through it, an unaccountable whim took possession of him, and returning to the condemned pew, he sat down in it for a few minutes.

" I wonder if I shall ever be in this d——d box again," he said to himself, as he rose to quit it.

He now mounted a winding stone staircase, and only one more barrier opposed his progress; this was a trap-door, the staple of which he filed away, and then raised it.

He was now about twelve feet above, and very near to, the roofs of the houses in Newgate Street, and he prepared to reach them. Only a low parapetted wall now separated him from freedom, but still the utmost caution had to be observed.

Uncoiling his blanket-rope from around his body, he looked anxiously about for something to fasten it to, but his search was fruitless. At one time he thought he would drive his crowbar into the wall and trust to that, but he remembered what it had already done for him, and he considered how precious it might be to him in future, and abandoned the idea. At last, he determined on prying away a stone from beneath the stone coping, so making a hole through which he could pass one end of his rope, and by passing it over the coping itself and tying it, make it answer his purpose; for it never would have done for him to have risked dropping on the roofs below him, which were not flat like those he had hitherto met with, but steep and studded with gables.

His task was soon completed, and in ten minutes more he was no longer a prisoner within the dreary walls of Newgate.

Slinking along the gutters, he presently arrived at an attic window, partially open. This he entered, and found himself in an uninhabited room where was a bed, on which he felt a strong inclination to repose after his tremendous exertions; but knowing well that the neighbourhood was too hot a one for him, he armed himself with his crowbar, and crept quietly down the stairs.

All the inhabitants of the house were buried in profound repose, and his feet were on the last flight of stairs, when, to his horror, he heard the alarm bell of the prison ring out shrill and clear.

He knew at once that his escape had been discovered.

The street without was all commotion, from where he stood, he could hear loud cries of "Watch!" and the announcement of a convict's flight. Had he been without, he would have seen lights glancing on the summit of the gaol, and dark forms passing to and fro.

Still the tumult increased, and the bed-room windows of the house in which he had sought refuge were thrown open, as the people rushed by he heard his own name passed from one to another, and he trembled with rage and apprehension.

"Had they but given me half an hour longer," he muttered, "all would have been right; but even as it is they shall not take me alive."

Presently the hubbub ceased, at least in that quarter, and thinking he now had a chance, he endeavoured to break open the street-door with his crowbar. The noise awakened the master of the house, who rushed down stairs in his night-shirt, and seeing Hawkins was about to seize him, when he received a blow from the crowbar which sent him bleeding to the floor.

"Now or never," cried the late prisoner, and with one desperate effort he burst open the door; looking cautiously out, and seeing no one but an old watchman near, he rushed out, and overthrew the guardian of the night, as he ran off in the direction of St. Paul's.

But before he arrived at the end of Newgate Street, the charlie had given the alarm, and Hawkins felt that he was pursued. He could hear the yells of the multitude behind, and fear added wings to his feet. Dashing into Cheapside, he turned down one of the narrow streets leading from that thoroughfare, and soon found a refuge in one of those labyrinths of lanes which lie between it and the river.

CHAPTER XXXIV.

M'CLEANE IS TORMENTED BY THE GREEN-EYED MONSTER.—THE ADVENTURES OF DICK FLYBYNIGHT WHILST ON A CRUISE OF DISCOVERY.

GREAT was the anxiety and consternation at the "Country House" at Highgate, when, after waiting many hours for the return of Handsome Jack, Hawkins, and Beauty Ellis, from the midnight expedition to Purley Hall, neither of those parties made their appearance.

M'Cleane, Jenny Diver, Dick Flybynight, and Gipsey Betty remained up in waiting for them until long after daylight, and then they retired to their beds, but not to sleep.

And during the whole of the following day the hours went laggingly along; for, although scouts were sent in all directions, no tidings of either of the three could be met with.

Towards evening, Jenny Diver vowed she could bear the suspense no longer, and volunteered to disguise herself and go in search, but

to this proposal M'Cleane would by no means accede.

"No! no!" said he "I almost fancy you are a trifle too anxious about Handsome Jack, Jenny—to tell you the truth, I did not much like your putting on men's clothes, and taking, a little time since, a midnight journey with him."

"Oh! Jem, Jem, this is too unkind of you," cried Jenny Diver, bursting into a flood of passionate tears.

"And your eagerness to accompany him to this robbery at Purley Hall also, was not much to my liking, I assure you," continued the Captain, not heeding the weeping girl.

"My God! M'Cleane, what have I done to deserve this? I have never regarded Handsome Jack but as a friend ——"

"Psha!" exclaimed M'Cleane petulantly, "that same friendship, girl, is rather ticklish and a dangerous thing when a good-looking fellow and a pretty wench profess it for each other—'tis apt to change its name and nature, and become love."

"I see how it is, Captain M'Cleane," said the girl proudly, and starting to her feet, her eyes flashing with scorn. "I see how it is, you are tired of me—is it not so?"

"I am vexed with you, and with everybody," was the sole reply, and M'Cleane himself rose, and paced the room. After a short time thus spent, he rang a small silver hand-bell, and the old hag, who in Beauty Ellis's absence acted as mistress, made her appearance.

"Send Dick Flybynight to me—instantly," he commanded.

The old woman glanced maliciously at Jenny, regarded the Captain for a moment, with a contemptuous smile, and retired.

"Dick," said M'Cleane, as Flybynight entered, "I have a commission for you to execute."

"Name it, Captain—whatever it be, it is yours to command, and mine to obey. But," as he observed the Diver's strangely altered countenance and swollen eyes, "what the devil's the matter with you, Jenny?"

"Leave that to me, Dick," said M'Cleane, "this way, I would speak with you in private."

"Captain M'Cleane, you need not remove from where you are. I will quit an apartment and presence, where I am no longer welcome." And she was retiring when M'Cleane exclaimed:—

"Remember your oath of obedience! Go to your own apartment, and remain there till I send for you."

Jenny left the room, and M'Cleane again rang the silver bell, which was, as before answered by the portress.

"On your peril," said he to her, "allow not Mistress Jenny to quit this house—remember, I place her for the present in your charge; but let her remain a close prisoner in her own apartment."

"And now, Dick," said the Captain, after the old portress, who was evidently delighted with the office of petty gaoler conferred upon her, had retired, "I wish you to disguise yourself and go wherever you think you may obtain tidings of the three members of our gang who are so strangely missing.   I know I can **trust** to your fidelity."

"Do you apprehend then," asked Dick Flybynight, "that any one amongst us is unfaithful?"

"I have my doubts—but it is not the way you take it, that my meaning lies; and, if you please, we will drop the subject."

Dick Flybynight bowed his head in submission.

"You had perhaps better go into the City, and drop in either at Jerry Laggum's, or at the crib in Fetter Lane, where Jenny played that pretty trick on Flitchman—Do you remember the place?"

"Well!" replied Dick.

"Perhaps you may find it serviceable to look into some of the old taverns about London Wall, but go to the Jolly Pedlars first; and remember that Jerry does not recognize you, for he is an infernal villain, and is, I have good reason to believe, in league with Jonathan Wild."

"I know to a surety that he is, for he was in company with Jonathan on the day his master, Tony Bilkit, was tucked up," remarked Dick.

"Now then—to your disguising; and when ready, come again to me, and should aught else occur to my mind, I will say more to you."

Dick Flybynight then went to an apartment in the "Country House," which was appropriated to a rather peculiar purpose. It was roomy, and contained from three to four hundred dresses of different kinds, suited both for males and females. From the robe of a prince to that of a beggar, all sorts of suits were there.   There was a grave physician's dress, from the cocked hat to the ivory-headed cane; here a lawyer's robes, and in another a peasant's rude covering; ladies of title, demi-reps, modest girls, tradesmen's wives, old women and young women might, in this strange place, so far as garments went, be speedily manufactured.   In short, there was not a single character of society for which a suitable dress was not provided.

Dick Flybynight, from this motley multitude of disguises, selected one which he thought best suited to his purpose, and speedily presented himself before M'Cleane.

"That will do, Dick," remarked the Captain.   "I'faith, man, you almost deceive my eyes, and they are not easily cheated, as you may perhaps know."

Dick no longer presented the appearance of a dashing highwayman.   The bold adventurer of the road had, as though by magic, metamorsised himself into a substantial country yeoman—a wig of reddish hair, thick and lanky, completely concealed his own raven locks; his graceful figure was covered with a rustic great coat of a sober grey hue; huge knee-buckles confined the extremities of his corded small-clothes, and heavy hobnailed shoes covered feet, which would have felt far more at home in jackboots.   In his hand he carried a stout ashen stick, and on his cheeks certain dies had conferred that healthy ruddiness, which the inhabitants of country places generally possess.

"I have naught, Dick, to add to what I just

now said, except an urgent request that you will use your utmost speed, for I much fear that the matter may be one of life and death," remarked M'Cleane.

Assuring his principal that neither time nor exertions should be wasted, Dick Flybynight bade adieu to the "Country House," and proceeded on foot, by way of Highgate Hill and Holloway, to Islington.

"Merry Islington," wore at that period a far different aspect to what it does at present. Its "Green" was a spacious surface of emerald sward, studded with leafy trees, beneath whose wide-branching foliage, on sunny and calm summer evenings, used to sit, enjoying their pipes, social cans, and comfortable chat, the sober citizens with their wives and children. The place was then a rural village, unconnected with the metropolis by long lines of brick and mortar edifices, for between the Angel and St. Paul's were shaded green lanes, in whose verdant marts young lovers wandered, and luxuriant fields, where cattle browsed quietly, and the evening birds sang; and where, instead of the rattle of omnibusses and the everlasting roar of our modern Babel, the musical tinkling of sheep-bells, the deep lowing of oxen, and such like rural sounds were heard.

During the day, the village was almost as quiet and drowsy-looking as are far away villages at the present time, if, indeed, in this age of railroads, there yet remain any rural places, where the shrill scream of the locomotive whistle has not been heard, a fact, in respect of which we entertain some doubts.   The chief signs of moving life in Islington were exhibited in the shape of groups of idlers who lounged about the road, or sat on benches in front of the various hostelries, drinking from huge tankards of ale, and smoking enormous quantities of tobacco; or, peradventure, by the presence of a party of rake-helly bloods from the neighbouring city, who, like our modern "fast" young men, had escaped from the vigilance of their parents or employers, for the purpose of "making a day of it" amongst the Johnny Raws.

In front of "the Sir John Oldcastle," one of the most famous hostelries of Islington, and on the borders of the "Green" a group of gossippers were assembled when Dick Flybynight arrived in the centre of the village.   Beneath the ample porch, sat in easy contentment, enjoying his pipe and morning draught of purl, the rosy-faced and fair round bellied host—Stephen Tapswill.   Opposite him, in all the dignity of office, likewise furnished with his can, was Nicholas Rook, the parish constable; and in the doorway stood Dame Tapswill, the vintner's wife, listening to the conversation that was going on.

The latter, as Dick Flybynight approached the porch, dropped a low curtsey and bade the visitor "Good Day."   Then, darting a look full of meaning at Nicholas Rook, she hinted to that worthy that he had better vacate his seat in favour of the new arrival, whom she obsequiously invited to accept it.

"What may it please you to take for your morning drink, my master?" courteously enquired the landlady, dropping a curtsey still

lower than before. " The Sir John Oldcastle, hath the best tap in all Islington, let the ' Angel' and the ' Peacock' brag as they may, though I say it that should not; and then, my master, there are strong waters, and real Nantz besides."

" A can of purl, good hostess," said Dick, who was rather annoyed at the loquacity of the landlady. " And see that it hath a well-spiced toast in it."

" For purl with a toast, my master," continued Dame Deborah Tapswill, " I warrant me, there be none like that brewed at the Sir John Oldcastle, let the ' Angel' and the ' Peacock' brag as they may. And then there are ——"

" Damn thy long tongue, Deborah!" exclaimed Stephen Tapswill; " do'st not see, wench,

that the worthy gentleman is dry? mayhap he hath not moistened his throat this morning, and the roads be dusty enough, I trow."

" Hoity-toity!" said the hostess, waxing wroth, " a pretty pass things be come to when such as thee shows off airs—an' it were not for thy wife, the Sir John Oldcastle might go without custom from Monday till Saturday, and the ' Angel' and the ' Peacock' might ——"

" I'd need be an angel to put up with such peacock-squalling as thine," muttered the hen-pecked vintner, as his better and, doubtless as he considered her, his bitter half, bustled into the kitchen to superintend the brewing of that beverage which should make the celestial being and the gaudy bird, whose effigies adorned the fronts of the rival houses, become, the former as envious as the devil himself, and the latter as crest-fallen as a vanquished monarch of the dunghill.

The dainty beverage soon made its appearance, foaming above the rim of the shining tankard, the frothy head foaming with nutmeg, cinnamon, and other spices. As Dick indulged in a long draught, the hostess intently watched him; and when he laid down the vessel with a satisfactory "Ha!" a smile of vanity spread itself over her jolly face—her triumph over the "Angel" and the "Peacock" was complete.

Dick Flybynight, refusing her pressing invitation to rest himself in her parlour, called for a pipe, and invited the host to join him in another tankard in one of the arbours, several of which constructed of light trellis-work and covered with creeping plants were placed on either side the hostelry, their doors, or rather entrances, for there were no means of closing them, fronting the road.

Stephen Tapswill was by no means loath to accede to Dick's proposal, and a double tankard having been speedily manufactured, the vintner and his guest were soon comfortably hob-nobbing together.

"Awful times, worthy master," remarked Stephen Tapswill, after a prodigious puffing with his long pipe. "Awful times these, when honest men can neither lie in bed without being murdered in their sleep, nor go about their lawful business without fear of a highwayman. Oh! Lord, what be the world come to?"

"You be groaning again, be ye, Master Tapswill?" said Nicholas Rook, the parish constable, who having heard Dick Flybynight's invitation to the landlord to drink, as was his usual custom in such cases, had watched for an opportunity of introducing himself, in order that he might procure a share of that drink which he never by any chance indulged in at his own expense.

"And enough to make one groan too, Nicky Rook, except, indeed, 'tis such as has cause to laugh at villainy of all kinds," remarked the landlord.

"How do you mean? I don't apprehend—that is to say, I don't comprehend you like?" asked Rook.

"I means this—as you lives by thieving and murder, and you can't deny it—you know you can't," said Tapswill, knocking the ashes out of the huge bowl of his pipe; "there, Master Rook, take a drink, and wash down that if you can!"

The constable was by no means slow to accept the invitation, and so long did the tankard linger at his lips that, as a portion of its contents descended his gullet a perfect intimacy appeared to be established between them. To all appearance, however, the draught had not extinguished his indignation, for, with a fiery visage, he turned upon Stephen, and demanded the reason why his moral character had been so villainously attacked?

"Live by thieving, quotha!" he muttered, as he unceremoniously seated himself by Dick Flybynight, and addressing the latter, Nicholas Rook said:—

"What would you say, worthy master, were your character so foully attacked? What would you do if any one said that you lived by robbery?"

"He should prove his words," replied Dick Flybynight; "aye, and I'd make him too."

Neither Stephen Tapswill nor Nicholas Rook understood Dick Flybynight's real meaning. There was, as the reader is well enough aware, no doubt whatever that had our doughty highwayman been accused of taking that which was not his own, he would have seized the earliest opportunity of affording the party who had made so serious an assertion, the means of proving it in his own person.

"D'ye hear what the gentleman says, Master Tapswill?" asked Rook.

"That I do, constable, and I will prove what I declared; and I'll declare it again, that you, Nicholas Rook, live by thieving."

"Do so then, master, if you can," cried Nicholas, who in a paroxysm of passion quite emptied the tankard, and then with a ferocious look, planted it upon the oaken table with such force that a proof impression of the rim was left on the hard wood.

"You won't deny—you can't deny as the parish pays you for taking up all the rogues and vagabonds—eh! Rook?" asked Stephen.

"That is true enough, Master Tapswill, but that don't prove I'm a rogue or a vagabond myself," replied the parish functionary.

"And you get your weekly pay for it?"

"That is true also."

"D'ye follow any other trade or calling, Master Nicholas Rook?"

"None," replied Nicky; "there's so much roguery for me to pull down, that I should like to know how I could find time for any other business?"

"Good!" remarked the vintner, with a chuckle of satisfaction.

"And you get your living by taking up thieves?" resumed Tapswill.

"Of course I do, master, and no harm neither," said Rook.

"Then you live, as I said, by thieving, and I ask this worthy gentleman if I am not in the right?"

Dick Flybynight thus appealed to, sided with the landlord, unconscious that this bit of pleasantry had been got up for the purpose of delaying him, and provoking him to order more drink; and also, that from time immemorial it had been a favorite diversion between the host and the constable when fortune favoured the former with a liberal-looking customer. As it was, he ordered another supply of the fluid, at which Rook rejoiced with exceeding joy.

"Think they'll hang him?" asked the vintner of Nicholas Rook.

"Safe enough, master, you see he was taken in the very act, and——"

"Hang who? my friend," interposed Dick Flybynight, carelessly.

"Jack Hawkins," replied the host, "him as was caught last night breaking into Purley Hall; and if they catch the two others they'll keep him company."

"They do say," observed Rook, "as the new Lady Purley knew one of the men who broke into her bed-room on her wedding night; and that her old husband swears he'll know him too."

At that moment, a man, wretchedly attired, with a bundle of execrably printed papers, walked to the part of the " Green " opposite where they were sitting, and commenced bawling out, " A full, true, and particular account of the daring robbery and bloody murder committed the night before at Purley Hall, with the capture of the notorious John Hawkins the highwayman and housebreaker."

Motioning the man to approach, Dick Flybynight drew a small coin from his pocket and purchased one of the papers; as the man left, Dick observed that he eyed him scrutinizingly. This made him feel rather uneasy, and this uneasiness increased when he observed the flying stationer turn after he had got to a little distance and again examine him from head to foot.

Dick Flybynight fancied he had seen the fellow somewhere before—indeed, he felt assured that he had done so; and fearful, therefore, that did he remain longer in the company of Stephen Tapswill and the constable, he might be involved in trouble of some kind, he bade both adieu, and pursued his journey.

Scarcely, however, had he reached Clerkenwell, when he felt a light tap on his shoulder, and turning round he perceived standing behind him the bill-seller.

" Did you think, Dick Flybynight, that your disguise could deceive me?" asked the man.

" You are mistaken, friend," remarked Dick, somewhat alarmed, but still preserving his coolness. " I have important business which will not brook delay. Let me pass."

" Too proud, eh, to speak to an old friend, but hark ye—I know you and perhaps can assist you in what I fancy to be your object just now. You are searching for three of your companions?"

Dick Flybynight was astounded; he, however, recovered himself, and was about to move onwards when the mysterious stranger stepped in front of him, and exclaimed:—

" One foot forward you do not go; and if you attempt to thwart my will, remember there is such a person as Jonathan Wild."

At the mention of this dreaded name, Dick Flybynight paused and felt somewhat uneasy, for he well knew that the thief-taker had scouts out in all directions, and that he himself was not to be trifled with.

" You must make me a solemn promise," said the stranger, " before I allow you to depart."

" Name it," said Dick, who now began to be seriously alarmed lest he should be recognised by any other parties.

" You know Mother Sin's house in the Almonry, I believe?" asked the stranger.

" I do, perfectly well," replied Dick.

" Then, to-morrow at midnight fail not to be there, and you will meet with one whose instructions you would do well to follow."

" How am I to know that no trap is intended?" asked Dick.

" If such were meant, what would hinder my calling assistance, which at the present moment is nearer at hand than you think for, and

handing you over at once to the constable? You need not fear—give me your word that you will be there?"

" I will," said Dick Flybynight.

" Enough," remarked the stranger, and now go your way.

This mysterious individual then quitted the highwayman, and the latter, puzzled and anxious respecting what had just passed, deliberated within himself whether he had not better return and inform Captain M'Cleane of the transaction. At length he decided on pursuing his journey to London, not even on his return mentioning the matter to his Chief, who, he feared, might possibly prevent him from keeping his appointment.

Threading as much as possible the bye-streets and lanes of the City, Dick Flybynight soon arrived at the Jolly Pedlars, which hostelry now displayed on its front in huge letters the name of Jerry Laggum as its landlord.

That worthy was behind his counter, busily engaged in dispensing strong waters of all kinds to his numerous customers. On Dick Flybynight's entrance, the highwayman was gratified by observing that he was not recognised, although it formed no part of his plan to conceal himself from Jerry. The recent encounter at Islington had made him fearful that he was not sufficiently disguised, but he was now reassured.

" A good day, my master," said Jerry Laggum. " And what drink would my worthy sir choose wherewith to wet his throttle?"

Dick, by way of reply, made a private signal to Jerry Laggum unobserved by the other people who happened to be in the hostelry; it was instantly understood by the vintner, who motioned Dick to the apartment behind the bar.

To the room Dick retired, and ordered a bowl of canary possett for himself and the landlord, who soon joined him.

" Why damn it, Dickon," said Jerry Laggum, " I'm right glad to see thee, but I confess thou didst most wonderfully disappoint me just now."

" In what manner?" asked Dick.

" Why thus," replied Jerry, " when I saw thee enter my shop, I began to calculate the depth of thy pockets; for verily I took thee for a grazier who had come to Smithfield with a well-lined purse, into which I hoped I might have dipped."

" Thou art as great a rogue as ever, and right worthy to succeed thy master," remarked Dick Flybynight, with a laugh; " but come, Jerry, I have a little business in hand, and require thy assistance."

Jerry Laggum protested that he would gladly do all in his power to aid so gallant a gentleman as Dick Flybynight, and then the latter informed him of the object of his visit.

" 'Tis a bad case that of Hawkins," remarked Jerry; " and nothing short of a miracle can save him—and if he peaches, depend on it the other two will stand a good chance of accompanying him to Tyburn."

" It is about his two pals that myself and M'Cleane are most especially anxious," said Dick Flybynight. " At present, it is of the utmost importance to know, whether they have escaped or are in custody."

"That can soon be known," remarked Jerry, "if you don't mind a guinea or two, I'll find a fellow who is a regular ferret in such matters as this, and if your friends are above ground, never fear but he will hunt them up."

Dick threw down a well-filled purse on the table, and said:—

"Take that Jerry Laggum, and reward this messenger of yours as you think fit, and retain the rest yourself—but no tricks remember—no hints to one Mr. Jonathan Wild."

"What is Jonathan Wild to me!" asked Jerry, pettishly.

"Oh! nothing particular," replied Dick; "only I thought you were very friendly just now, that's all." But observing that Jerry did not much relish the hint he had thrown out, he deemed it prudent to drop the subject.

"And where is this messenger of yours?" he enquired.

"Fortunately, he happens to be in the house at this very moment," replied Jerry; and ringing a bell, a drawer made his appearance.

"Send Rattling Raby to me, you will find him asleep most likely in the loft over the stable, for he was out all last night, and be quick with you," ordered the vintner.

"You must necessarily put confidence in Raby to some extent," remarked Jerry, "but you need be under no apprehensions—I will answer for his fidelity."

Dick Flybynight said nothing; but he could not help thinking that Mr. Jerry Laggum's proposed security was rather questionable.

It was not long before Rattling Raby made his appearance.

He was a middle-aged man of short stature, spare in figure, and lean in face. Two keen, dark, restless eyes glistened beneath a pair of bushy eyebrows, his nose was turned up as though it were perpetually scenting something, and the lips were bloodless and contracted. There was an expression of sagacity and cunning in the man's physiognomy, which he could not conceal, although he evidently sought to do so beneath an assumed look of simplicity. He appeared to be just the man for Dick Flybynight's purpose.

"Raby," said Jerry, "this gentleman has a little job in hand for you, for which, if you accomplish it cleverly, you will be well paid."

"Never fear then, master, but what Rattling Raby will do it if it is to be done. What is it?"

Dick then explained to Raby what the reader already is aware of, that his earnest desire was to know whether Handsome Jack and Beauty Ellis had escaped apprehension, and if they had been so fortunate, to know where he could find them.

"Only a pair of them, master?" asked Raby.

"But two—for unfortunately one of the party, a man named Hawkins, was apprehended, that I know for certain."

"And what sort of looking men are those whom you want me to look for?" asked Raby.

Dick described as nearly as possible the personal appearances of Handsome Jack and Beauty Ellis, and Raby assuring him that if two such men were lying by any where in London, he would undertake to unkennel them, after making a signal to his master to follow him, quitted the room.

But he did not quit the house, for he retired to Jerry Laggum's private room behind the bar, and there awaited the coming of his master.

No sooner had Rattling Raby quitted the presence of Dick Flybynight than Jerry Laggum proposed to refill the bowl of possett at his own expense, as a mark of respect (so he said) for his guest. As Dick was compelled to wait the return of Raby, he made no objection to this, and the vintner left the apartment for the purpose of preparing the beverage.

Before doing so, however, he joined Rattling Raby, or the "Rattler," as he was more frequently called, in the little back parlour.

"What now, Raby?" asked Jerry, "there's some deviltry going on, or you wouldn't grin so pleasantly."

"Enough to make one grin, master.—Why, I know where to drop on the men as Dick Flybynight wants, without any trouble whatever."

"The devil you do—you're a keener fellow than I took you to be; but who do you mean by Dick Flybynight?"

The Rattler chuckled with glee, and pointing his right thumb over his right shoulder in the direction of the parlour, said quietly:—

"The man within there—why he could not cheat me. I tell you, Master Jerry Laggum, I should have known him among a thousand at masquerade at Ranelagh even."

"Then keep your own counsel, Raby, d'ye hear? We must pluck the bird well ourselves, and make as much use of him as we can before we hand him over to you know who. But about these people he is in search of, where are they?"

"I was in their company this very morning, and saw one of 'em sell a horse in Smithfield," replied the Rattler, evasively.

"Then you had better go to them at once, Raby; and, hark ye, we must play a double game with this gallant within. Wild, you know, has offered a handsome reward to anyone who will discover to him where M'Cleane's gang have removed to from the 'Chapel.'"

"And Watkins, the Bow Street runner, is not a bit the less anxious to know," remarked the Rattler. "He won't forget in a hurry how the Captain served him in the dungeon."

"An opportunity now occurs of worming ourselves into the confidence of these people, and watching them to their stronghold. You proceed on your errand, persuade Handsome Jack and Beauty Ellis that it will not be safe for them to venture to their crib till nightfall, when you can make arrangements for dogging their footsteps. I will do the same by Dick Flybynight here, who, in a couple of hours time, shall be informed that you have returned after an unsuccessful search."

"Good!" said the Rattler, "now I'm off," and after tossing down his throat a bumper of Nantz to the success of his expedition, he left the Jolly Pedlars.

We left Handsome Jack and Beauty Ellis at

the livery-stable keeper's in London Wall, and there we must now rejoin them.

They were seated over a bowl of sack in a little dark room, anxiously waiting for the time when they should be enabled to quit their place of concealment and join their companions at the "Country House."

"D——d unlucky affair that at the Hall," said Handsome Jack, "I wonder what M'Cleane will say to it! However, there's one comfort, we shan't go home quite empty handed."

"What the devil shall I do with this diamond?" growled Beauty Ellis, as he surveyed the gem which he had obtained from the traveller, "if old Williams, the fence, hadn't been burnt in Hanging Sword Alley, I'd have taken it to him and made sure of twenty shiners; but now, I might as well have a piece of glass."

"Give it me," said Handsome Jack. "I'll give you twenty guineas for it."

"And what will you do with it?" asked Beauty.

"Restore it to the owner, if possible, as he seemed greatly to value it as a family relic," was the reply.

"Werry sentimental! but doing such a thing as that may get you into a precious deal of trouble, Handsome Jack. However, take the sparkler, and hand me the canaries;" and he transferred the diamond to Handsome Jack's possession.

"By heaven! Beauty," said Jack, after they had been sitting for some time in silence. "I can stand this no longer. You remain quietly here, whilst I take a stroll; my person is not known to the officers, and I shall run no risk. On no account do you leave until my return."

Beauty Ellis vainly attempted to persuade Handsome Jack from so rash a course. Listen to reason he would not; and he quitted the place.

Strolling through Aldersgate Street, he perceived in the window of a jeweller's shop a placard, the heading of which "Diamond Ring Lost—Handsome Reward," attracted his attention.

On more attentively perusing the document, he felt not the slightest doubt, from the description given of the stone, that it referred to the one which he then had in his possession. It had been taken from the gentleman to whom it belonged, much against his will, by Beauty Ellis, and he now determined to restore it.

But how to do so—that was the difficulty. It was stated in the placard, that no questions would be asked, but Handsome Jack well knew that such a condition was often a mere trap in which to catch the thief. Suddenly he remembered that perhaps he could, with less danger to himself, restore it to the owner through the medium of Jonathan Wild, and accordingly he proceeded to the office of the thief-taker in Newtoners Lane.

CHAPTER XXXV.

MR. DOOM MAKES A SECOND APPEARANCE ON THE STAGE OF LIFE; AND SIR JAMES TOWN, HIS FIRST APPEARANCE ON A PUBLIC PLATFORM.

As soon as Tim Snarley perfectly comprehended the state of affairs on that morning when he perceived his respected master, Mr. Wriggleton Doom, dangling from the ceiling, he as we have before stated, procured the assistance of the porter of Grays Inn, and then rushed boldly off in search of a surgeon.

"Well!" he muttered to himself, as he ran, "only to think now of that old rascal of a master of mine, so far forgetting himself as to disgrace a honourable perfession in this way. Might have saved himself the trouble too, for Jack Price would have been sure of him."

Panting and puffing he reached the door of a medical man, and knocked furiously at the door, presently a night-capped head appeared at one of the windows, for the worthy son of Æsculapius had been engaged during the previous night in helping a fellow-creature into the world, thus by one branch of practice making compensation for the occasional sending an unfortunate sinner out of it.

"You must come along with me directly," said Tim Snarley to the surgeon. "Master has hanged himself."

"Then I can be of no possible use," remarked the surgeon; "you'd better go to the undertaker, or the crowner, 'tis their business, not mine."

"You must come," screamed Tim, "Mr. Doom is ——"

"Doom—Doom—did you say?" asked the surgeon.

"Yes—yes!" replied Tim.

"Mr. Wriggleton Doom, the lawyer of Grays Inn?" asked the surgeon once more.

"That's the werry man," cried Tim, "so, for God's sake, come along."

"Mr. Doom may be d——d, as no doubt he is, as well as hanged," said the surgeon, with considerable warmth. "I'm very glad there's one scoundrel less in the world this morning. Go to some one else, boy, for curse me if I go to him, I could never get a fee from him when he was alive, and 'tisn't very likely I shall now he's dead."

And the surgeon slammed the window together so violently, that Tim saw it was of no use to persevere. Bestowing, therefore, as a parting benediction, a tremendous rap of the knocker, he hurried off in search of another practitioner, and fortunately soon found one, with whom he returned to the chambers.

The scene in the lawyer's private room was indeed a ghastly one. Lying extended on the floor was the long and gaunt figure of Mr. Wriggleton Doom, without either sense or motion. The porter had, with much difficulty, removed the cord from his neck, around which was now perceptible a livid ring. The face was swollen and puffed; from their deep sockets, the eyes protruded; and the slackened tongue was thrust out of the mouth. Tim

Snarley shuddered and shrank back as he beheld the fearful spectacle.

The surgeon immediately on his arrival removed the coat and waistcoat from the body, and laid his hand on the chest—it was yet warm. He then commanded strict silence, and placed his ear over the heart. After a few moments of anxious listening, he fancied he detected a slight pulsation, so feeble, as to be almost imperceptible; yet still he felt assured that life was not quite extinct, and forcing open the rigid jaws of the lawyer, he poured down his unresisting throat a few teaspoonfulls of some strong cordial.

Then he opened a vein in each arm, from which a little blood flowed; presently a cold sweat burst out all over the wretched man's body, and in about a quarter of an hour afterwards, a long laboured breath proclaimed that life still lingered.

With the greatest care Mr. Doom was then placed in a bed which had been hastily made up for the occasion, and continually supplied with stimulants; but it was long before his senses returned. When they did, he gazed stupidly and vacantly around him, and at length he recognized Tim Snarley.

"What's all this Tim—how came I here—what's the matter, eh?" he asked faintly.

"You ain't to say nuffin," said Tim, holding up his finger to his master, a thing he had never before dared to do.

"And my neck—how stiff it is," remarked the lawyer, whose entire consciousness had not returned.

"Should wonder if it wasn't," muttered Tim Snarley, "mine would, I know, if it had been stretched as yours has been."

"I feel choking—choking, Tim—there's a green flash of light before my eyes, and my brain is bursting—bursting Tim Snarley. Ha! there he is—there he is—save me—save me!"

"There's who? master," asked Tim. "Who d'ye mean, I don't see any body?"

"The devil!" shrieked the wretched lawyer, placing his hands before his eyes and sinking back on his pillow.

"Oh Lord! what d'ye frighten a poor fellow like that for, master?" exclaimed Tim Snarley, who was now in an agony of terror, and felt almost convinced that his satannic majesty was actually present.

It was evident that the lawyer, in his half-delirium, imagined he had overleaped the barrier which divides life from death; and was now in the world of darkness. The dim chamber in which he lay, was to him a hell, and Tim Snarley, his humble comforter and attendant, to his disordered imagination, assumed the appearance of that awful personage whom, for many years, Mr. Wriggleton Doom had so indefatigably served.

Gradually, the unhappy man arrived at a full consciousness of his situation. The fearful scene through which he had a few hours previously passed, returned to his memory with appalling force; and it was with a feeling of intense and bitter regret, he discovered that all his efforts, desperate as they had been, to escape from the trammels which fettered him, had proved vain.

He failed not to remember, too, that his recent attempt on his life would infallibly provoke inquiry and encourage suspicion; and he trembled as he thought that the very means he had taken to rid himself at once of his misery and his existence, might hurry on the exposure of his iniquities. These fearful anticipations and recollections so retarded his recovery that for days his life trembled in the balance; but his previous habits of rigid temperance, had so fortified his naturally strong constitution that, in spite of all, he gradually got better, though it was long before his system entirely recovered the shock which it had sustained.

We must now accompany Handsome Jack, who we left on his way to Newtoners Lane.

Having arrived at the office of Jonathan Wild, he was admitted by Abrahams, the Jew, who informed him that his master was from home.

"But," said the Israelite, "perhaps Mr. Vatsyourname, I could manage your leetle pusiness ash vell as Mishter Vild—Valk in."

Handsome Jack accepted the invitation, and was shown by the Jew into a small apartment opening from the passage, near the entrance-door. Motioning him to a seat, the Israelite scrutinized every feature of Handsome Jack, but he was evidently at fault, for he could not recognize his physiognomy.

"Vat can I do for you, mishter, is it a loss or a find you come about, eh?" asked Abraham.

"Here is a diamond," replied Handsome Jack, which fell in my way, and for which I have little doubt the owner will apply to Mr. Wild. On what terms am I to leave it here?"

"Vait a bit," said Abraham, and taking from an iron chest a large book, he leisurely put on a pair of huge spectacles, and opened it.

"Look here, mishter," he said, pointing with his skinny forefinger to the very last entry which had been made in the volume.

Handsome Jack read as directed, and to his astonishment perceived not only a minute account of the gem itself, but so correct a description of his own person and that of Beauty Ellis, that he involuntarily started and turned pale.

The Jew regarded him with a lynx-eye. He was so accustomed to negociations of this kind, that he felt not the slightest difficulty or hesitation in arriving at the conclusion that the individual before him was one of the two highwaymen who had committed the robbery.

"Vat might you want for the diamond, Mishter?" asked Abraham, as, apparently to confirm his suspicions, he compared the diamond with the description given of it in the book.

"Twenty guineas," replied Handsome Jack.

"Vat!" almost screamed the Jew. "Tventy guineash! I tell you vat I do mit you; look you, it isn't vorth more as ten shiners. I'll give you five, and take five mineself for not to know who prought it to Mishter Vild's. Don't you see?"

"Not exactly," replied Handsome Jack. "Why, I could have got four times what you offer at a goldsmith's not an hour since."

"And get grabbed into the bargain," sneered the Israelite.

"No," said Handsome Jack; "it was explicitly stated that no questions would be asked."

On hearing this, Abraham placed his forefinger alongside his prominent nose, winked his right optic in a most villainous manner, and elevated his shoulders and eyebrows doubtingly.

"Vell—and I vont ask no questions neither, mishter, if you come to mine terms; but if you don't, perhaps I shall be obliged to," replied the Jew.

"Ask as many as you please," remarked Handsome Jack, with some show of indignation. "I can, at least, refuse to answer them. Give me back the diamond. On second thoughts I will not dispose of it."

At this moment a knocking at the outer door was heard.

"Oh! you vont answer me—eh, mishter? Vait a leetel bit, and perhaps I may persuade you into a better humour. Somebody is come on pusiness just now. So, if you don't vant to be seen, just step into this closet, and look through the chink, and we'll talk over the matter presently."

The knocking was renewed, and Abraham hurried Handsome Jack into the closet, which, in reality, was a huge cupboard. Through some crevices in the wainscoting, he could command a tolerably good view of the room he had just left, and in his hiding-place he had not long been ensconced, when he observed Abraham usher in a gentleman, whom he called Sir Philip Aubrey.

The position of the new-comer was such as to prevent Handsome Jack from seeing his features; he could, however, distinctly hear the conversation which passed.

"Well, my worthy son of Abraham," said the stranger, "and has Mr. Wild heard anything of the business about which I called early this morning?"

"Ah! Sir Philip," exclaimed the Jew, "a vonderful shentleman—a vonderful man ish Mishter Vild to lay himshelf out so for the goot of the public."

"Very likely," remarked Sir Philip, "but I did not come here to listen to Mr. Wild's praises. Had I not heard that he was able to procure the restoration of stolen property, I should not have applied to him, my friend. But to business. Have you heard anything of my diamond?"

As Sir Philip spoke, he partially altered his position, and Handsome Jack had a full view of his face. He saw at a glance that the very man who he had robbed on the highway on his return from Purley Hall was before him.

"Yesh, Sir Philip," said Abraham, in reply to the question of the baronet, "dere ish some intelligence of the jewel as the rascals stole from you. And more than dat I knows vere almost to find de rogues themselves."

"Place them—or either of them before me," said Sir Philip Aubrey, "and you shall be well rewarded; but at present, for a most important purpose I require the diamond, and you must do all in your power to recover it."

Handsome Jack shuddered as he heard the last observation of the baronet. He felt himself to be utterly at the mercy of the Jew, and

expected every moment to be betrayed, but to give up the highwayman was not the policy of the crafty Abraham.

"Do you see this?" asked the Jew of Sir Philip Aubrey, as he placed before him the diamond which he had just received from Handsome Jack.

"I could swear to it amongst a million," replied Sir Philip, "if you will examine it closely, you will find a flaw in one of its facets."

"It is so," said Abraham, as he observed the peculiarity mentioned. "And I am happy, Sir Philip, to be enabled to restore you a jewel which you seem to value so highly."

Sir Philip Aubrey then placed a bank note for a considerable amount in Abraham's hand, and after assuring him, that if he succeeded in capturing the robbers, he should be handsomely rewarded, he took his departure, much to the relief of Handsome Jack, who, fearful that the Jew would betray him, had spent an anxious and a miserable quarter of an hour in his place of concealment.

"Come along out, mishter," said Abraham, as he opened the door, "you heard vat the shentlemans said, didn't you? See now, if I didn't take care that you should not be hurt. Vy, if Sir Philip had only known that one of the men as robbed him was close at hand, you'd have been afore the beak, ma tear."

This was so evidently true, that Handsome Jack had nothing to say, and only felt anxious to quit Newtoners Lane as speedily as possible.

"And what are you going to give me for the diamond?" he asked.

"Vell," said Abraham, "you know I oughtn't to give you anything considering how much I lost by not introducing you to Sir Philip Aubrey; but I don't like to be shabby or dishonourable, mishter, and as I hope ve may do a little more pusiness together, vy I'll give you five guineas, and Mishter Vild will plame me for being so liberal. There, take the shiners, and make haste away before Vild comes in, or perhaps ven he knows as much as I do, he vont let you go at all."

Handsome Jack saw that no better bargain could be made, and therefore appeared to be satisfied; indeed he was too glad to have escaped as he had, to stand upon bargaining; and being likewise desirous to avoid Jonathan Wild, after what the Jew had just intimated, he took the proffered money, and left the receiver's house.

No sooner had the door closed on him, than Abraham violently rang a bell, and almost instantly a lad of about sixteen years of age made his appearance.

The face of this boy was indicative of the most profound cunning mingled with malice. His figure was distorted, and he was of short stature, long ape-like arms dangled by his sides, and though he rather shambled than walked, he travelled along with considerable rapidity.

"Shadrach, you saw that gallant who left here just now?"

"I saw two, Master Abraham," replied the boy.

"I mean the one who an instant since left this room."

"Yes—I marked him," said Shadrach.

"Then follow him, and hark'ye, do not lose sight of him until he is housed; and you shall have, if you are successful, a golden guinea. What d'ye think of that, Shadrach?—a golden guinea all for yourself."

"Never fear, Master Abraham, I'll hunt him down," observed the boy; and seizing his hat, he darted from the house, and followed in the track of Handsome Jack, who, to use a sporting phrase, he speedily "sighted."

Unconscious that a spy was dogging his footsteps. Handsome Jack sauntered towards the Strand, and on entering that great thoroughfare he observed an unusual number of people proceeding in the direction of Charing.

At that period one of the places of public execution, and of other inferior and disgraceful punishments, was situated close to Charing Cross; and the pillory which was there placed, was the most illustrious among the many that graced, or rather disgraced the Capital—illustrious by reason of the remarkable evildoers who underwent ignominy in its wooden and unfriendly embrace.

On enquiry of some people who were hastening along the Strand, Handsome Jack learned that two men were to be exposed in the pillory that afternoon; and as time hung somewhat heavily on his hands, and he required something to banish the unpleasant thoughts which crowded on his mind, he determined to join the multitude, and view a spectacle which to him would present, if no other attraction, that, at least, of novelty.

Had the people, who were now hastening to Charing Cross been going to a fair or other place of amusement, they could not have been merrier or more joyous than they were. Coarse jests and gibes were bandied from lip to lip, lewd songs were roared out, and many a practical joke played off. The greater number were well supplied with missiles of various descriptions, which were intended as free-will offerings to the unfortunate beings who were about to undergo the punishment to which the law had sentenced them. Dead cats—putrid meat—rotten eggs, and all kinds of other things, seemed, for this especial occasion, to have been carefully collected from sewers and dunghills; pockets were crammed with stones, and not a few carried brickbats in their hands. Even the very women prepared to join in the inhuman sport of half-pelting to death a wretched, fettered, defenceless fellow-creature.

"Who are to be pillored this afternoon?" enquired Handsome Jack of a decent-looking tradesman, who leaned against the door-post of his shop, watching the multitude as they passed by.

"One of the knaves has committed perjury; the other has been convicted of common swindling; and to my mind the swindler is worse than the false swearer. A pox on the fellow for cheating honest traders," replied the shopkeeper.

As Handsome Jack drew nearer to Charing Cross, the crowd of people became denser and denser, and when within a hundred yards of the spot where the statue of Charles now stands, he found it utterly impossible to proceed further. Here he became wedged in the midst of the mob, and could neither move backward or in advance.

High above the heads of the crowd appeared the instrument of punishment and of torture. It consisted of a platform which turned on a pivot, at an elevation of about ten feet from the ground, from which rose a stout upright of timber, across which was fitted two boards connected by a strong hinge, and pierced with three semicircular notches, one large to admit the neck, and the others small to confine the wrists of the person punished, so that when the upper and lower portions were brought in contact, circular holes were formed, in short the machine was constructed in a similar manner to the stocks of our own time, only this difference being observed, that the neck and wrists were confined instead of the ankles.

Some time elapsed and the culprit not making his appearance, the mob began to grow impatient, and commenced pelting each other with the unsavoury missiles which they had intended for the swindler and the perjurer. At length, however, a movement in the crowd was observed, and the appearance of Jack Price, the common hangman, on the platform, was the signal for a cessation of hostilities.

Bowing low to the mob, the hangman politely requested the people not to commence their sport until he had secured the prisoner in the pillory; but his appeal was utterly disregarded, for no sooner had he made the appeal, than a shower of rotten eggs assailed him; and uproarious was the mirth of the multitude as Jack Ketch, spurted the nauseous matter from his mouth and wiped it from his half-blinded eyes.

The first prisoner was now, apparently more dead than alive, dragged up the steps and placed in the pillory—his head and hands being so fixed that he could not by any possibility shield himself. His legs alone were free, but the only use he could make of them was to plant them firmly on the scaffold, so as to ease his neck as far as possible, for a failure of the knees, by causing a sinking of the body, might produce suffocation.

At the first stroke of the bell of the church of St. Martin-in-the-Fields, as it announced the hour of four, the hangman having secured his victim, descended from the platform and took his place beneath it, where the apparatus for turning the machine was placed. And the moment the rotation commenced, what the thousands of spectators were pleased to call the "fun" began.

Then full in the unhappy perjurer's face were hurled stones, dead animals, putrid eggs, offal, and the most disgusting missiles. No sooner had he received a violent assault from one quarter, than the platform revolved, and a new battery was opened on him. There was no shelter—none—and no mercy, for the criminal had by false swearing been the means of sending several innocent youths to Tyburn merely for the sake of the blood-money. In ten minutes his countenance was so disfigured that his own mother could not have recognised him, and after he had been exposed half an hour the sheriff ordered him to be released in

order that he might undergo the remainder of his sentence.

An elbow-chair was then placed on the platform, and in it the perjurer was placed. Beside him stood a surgeon, and opposite him appeared the hangman with a long and keen knife in his hand.

Then an assistant forcibly drew the poor wretch's head on one side, and with one or two bungling sweeps of the weapon, the hangman cut off one ear close to the side of the head.

The same operation was then performed on the other ear, and then handed both the ears on a skewer to a sheriffs' officer, whose duty it was to receive them, and who immediately nailed them to the upright post.

Then, with a pair of scissors, Jack Price slit both his nostrils, and seared them with a hot iron; but the prisoner, who until now had undergone his punishment with undaunted courage, now fainted away, and by the direction of the surgeon he was removed to the Ship Tavern close by.

No. 22.

"Now for the gentleman," shouted the mob, as another victim ascended the platform.

The miserable man who now made his appearance, was pale as death, and appeared to feel most acutely the degraded position in which he was placed. Owing to a change in his position, Handsome Jack could not obtain a view of his face for some time, and when the hangman had fixed him in the apparatus and retired beneath, the victim's back was towards him.

But at the first turn of the pillory, the criminal's face was brought directly opposite his own, and to his surprise, he instantly recognized the features of the man who had robbed him of his inheritance.

The pilloried swindler was SIR JAMES TOWN!

Raising himself to his full height, he looked his wretched cousin full in the face, and at the same instant Sir James encountered the gaze of his injured relative.

In the face of Handsome Jack, scorn and

pity struggled for the mastery, but the features of the baronet became livid with emotion.

"Turn—turn!" he shrieked convulsively to the hangman. "Ten guineas if you turn me quickly."

A dead dog flung full in his face stopped him, and in another moment, not a feature of his face was discernable.

Sick at heart and struggling with a variety of emotions, Handsome Jack extricated himself from the crowd, and hurried back to the place where he had left Beauty Ellis, who was anxiously awaiting him.

But he was not aware of the fact that, from the moment that he left Jonathan Wild's office in Newtoners Lane, the boy Shadrach had never for a single moment lost sight of him.

CHAPTER XXXVI.

HANDSOME JACK GETS OUT OF THE FRYING PAN INTO THE FIRE. — AN AFFRAY AND ITS RESULTS. — THE MURDER IN THE ALMONRY. THE ASTROLOGER OUTWITTED.

BEAUTY ELLIS was just finishing his second bowl of possett, when Rattling Raby made his appearance.

"Who the devil would have thought of seeing you?" growled Beauty.

"Why, the truth is," remarked Raby, "I've brought a message from a gentleman as is particklarly anxious to see you."

"Who is that?" demanded Handsome Jack, who entered at the moment.

"A friend," said a well-known voice, at the sound of which Beauty Ellis, Handsome Jack, and Rattling Raby started and looked round in astonishment; and of the trio, none were more surprised than Rattling Raby, who to his surprise beheld the man who he supposed to be still in company with Jerry Laggum at the Jolly Pedlars.

Dick Flybynight, for it was indeed that individual, took a seat beside Handsome Jack, and seizing his opportunity—a moment when Rattling Raby's attention was drawn from them, whispered in his friend's ear:—

"Jack—beware! there is danger at hand. Be guided by my actions; when I quit the room, follow me; and hint to Beauty Ellis to do likewise. This fellow who came to you from Jerry Laggum's, is a spy of Jonathan Wild's."

"Come Raby," observed Dick Flybynight carelessly, "you must pledge our healths in a fresh bowl, afterwards we will talk on business matters."

Dick Flybynight rose and went to the vintner for the potation himself, observing, that he would have it brewed from right good materials, and not of such villainous compounds as were commonly palmed off on gentlemen."

The bowl was soon ready, and whilst conveying it to the apartment where his friends were, he dropped into it a small portion of a certain powder, some of which he always carried about his person.

Conveying, by signs to Handsome Jack and Beauty Ellis, the intimation that they must

not partake of the steaming potation, Dick Flybynight filled the glasses for himself and the rest.

The members of the fraternity only appeared to sip, but Rattling Raby, who was a thirsty soul, emptied his glass at a draught; and so often did he repeat the pleasing dose, that before long his head dropped on the table, and his stentorian breathing gave evidence of his insensibility to all that was passing around him.

"Now, then," said Dick, "if we wish to escape unwatched, now is our time."

The three then quitted the parlour, paid the reckoning at the bar, and informing the vintner that they would presently rejoin their friends who would wait for them, they quitted the house, and within two hours arrived safely at the "Country House," Highgate.

M'Cleane was in the large room of the establishment alone, when Handsome Jack and his two companions entered. Beauty Ellis and Dick Flybynight were heartily welcomed, but his reception of Handsome Jack was cold in the extreme.

"You seem offended, M'Cleane. I am not conscious of having given you cause to treat me thus," observed Handsome Jack.

"I once thought that you were an honourable man," said M'Cleane, with a sneer, "but I am deceived."

"Who dares impugn my honour?" exclaimed the exasperated Jack.

"I do—and with sufficient cause," replied M'Cleane, and he continued in cool, measured, sarcastic tones, "I little thought that the friend I sheltered would have proved a viper."

"Such language I hear from none, Captain M'Cleane," exclaimed Handsome Jack, as he drew his sword, and rushed on the Captain who was ready for him with his own weapon.

In vain did Dick Flybynight seek to heal the breach; the two men were furious and fought with desperate energy.

Although Handsome Jack missed his footing and fell, in an instant the sword of M'Cleane was pointed at his heart, which in his blind rage he would have pierced had not Jenny Diver rushed into the room, and distracted his attention.

"Back—Jenny—I command you!" said M'Cleane, his face pale with suppressed rage.

"Fool! madman!" exclaimed the girl, "put up your weapon—as God is my judge that man," pointing to Handsome Jack, "has never injured you in thought, word, or deed."

"A woman's trick," muttered M'Cleane, putting up his sword, "but I despise ye both."

"Hearken, M'Cleane," said Handsome Jack, "I know, spite of all this, that you have a noble soul, and sooner would I plunge my own weapon into my heart than allow my heart to beat falsely towards you. If, as I suspect, jealousy afflicts you, all I can do is to swear that I have given you no cause, and to pardon and pity you."

The mere mention of the word "pity," added to the rage of M'Cleane. His spirit was too proud to brook compassion from any one.

"Pity!" he exclaimed, "I would rather have a man's hate than his commisseration:—however, Jack, as you have, on the word of a man, denied that any ground for my suspicions existed, and as Jenny Diver here, seems rather somewhat indignant at my having suspected her, I freely confess myself to be in the wrong, and so let the affair drop. Jack—Jenny! there is a hand for each of you."

Handsome Jack, without hesitation, grasped the extended palm of M'Cleane cordially; but Jenny was not quite so placable; she stood aloof, biting her plump nether lip until the blood nearly burst its coral barrier, and her finely arched brows were knit into a frown.

"Come—come, Jenny," said Handsome Jack, "bear no malice—you see I do not—the best of us are apt to be mistaken."

Handsome Jack's entreaties were seconded by Dick Flybynight, harmony was speedily restored, and some sparkling wine having been quaffed, all were good friends again.

M'Cleane was now made acquainted with the adventures at Purley Hall, with the particulars of which the reader is already well acquainted. On hearing of the capture of Hawkins, the Captain was seriously alarmed, for the new member of the gang had not as yet given any proof of his utter devotion to the service of the fraternity, and therefore his fidelity could not be implicitly depended on. The adventure on the road, however, of Dick and Beauty Ellis, coupled with the booty it had obtained, somewhat consoled him.

"Since you disapprove, Jem, of my going on the road, I must even return to my old tricks," remarked Jenny Diver; "and, after all, I like practising in the streets and the theatres better than on the highway. To-morrow, I shall pay a visit to some of my old haunts, if you do not object, M'Cleane."

The Captain willingly gave his consent, and it was arranged that himself and the girl should go forth together in search of adventures on the following day.

We must now follow in the footsteps of the fugitive Hawkins, who, after his escape from Newgate, we left in one of the dark and ill-lighted streets which led from Cheapside to the Thames bank.

Relieved from the fear of immediate danger, he paused to take breath, and concealed himself in a dark passage which led to an obscure court. From the interior of one of these low habitations issued the sound of music and revelry; and from certain words which now and then reached his ear, Hawkins felt assured that he was close to one of those houses used as a rendezvous by the thieves of the metropolis.

With slow and stealthy steps he drew near to the low window, and looked in. A motley group was assembled there, consisting of persons of all ages and both sexes. All of them were clad in tattered garments, many were scarcely covered by raiment of any kind, and some of the children actually naked, were lying asleep on the floor of the dirty apartment. On the table were a quantity of mugs and cups, and a reeking odour of strong spirits and tobacco issued from the broken windows.

A villainous-looking one-eyed hag appeared to be the mistress of this choice establishment. The filthy garments she wore hung loosely about her figure, and allowed her shrivelled bosom to be fully exposed. A constant devotion to the dram bottle had purpled her nose and bloated her face; she was, in short, a harridan of the worst water.

Hawkins, determined to seek, for a time at least, a refuge in this abominable kennel, where he felt almost positive that he should not be recognized. Accordingly he gave a low tap at the door, which had the effect of causing the noise within to be instantly hushed, and the lights to be extinguished.

The door itself was not opened, but a window overhead was drawn aside, and the head of the woman we have described protruded therefrom.

"What's your business at this hour of the morning?" she asked in a voice the tones of which had that peculiar huskiness which dram-drinking alone produces.

"Food and shelter—and both as soon as possible," replied Hawkins, who was now thoroughly dead beaten by his terrific labours of the previous few hours.

"Go to a tavern then, my master, there are plenty open," remarked the half-suspicious woman; "but," she resumed, "there is a way of obtaining admission here—perhaps you know it."

Hawkins immediately uttered some words which to other ears sounded like mere jargon; they were, however, perfectly understood by her to whom they were addressed.

"Wait," she said, "and if you are on the dark lay, and can pay for the accommodation, we'll help you to a crib where the devil himself would not find you."

Hawkins intimated that the woman should be satisfied for the accommodation, and after a few moment's delay, the front door was cautiously opened, and he was admitted.

There, for the present, we must leave him, and return to another of the personages of our tale.

According to the arrangement to which we have already referred, M'Cleane and Jenny Diver, on the morning after the quarrel between the Captain and Handsome Jack, set out for London, trusting to chance for whatever booty fortune might fling in their way. Both were admirably disguised. On their arrival in Fetter Lane, they entered the shop of the vintner where they had some time previously met with Flitchman, and called for refreshment.

The little parlour was nearly filled with topers busily engaged in taking their morning draughts, and conversing on the topics of the day, the most interesting of which appeared to be the exploits of a famous highwayman who had just been committed for trial to Newgate.

Carefully avoiding asking any questions, although they were intensely desirous of knowing particulars, M'Cleane and Jenny Diver listened attentively to what was going on, and at length learned that their comrade Hawkins was the prisoner alluded to.

"And, 'tis said," remarked one of the company, "that he will turn king's man—naught but that can save him."

"Jenny," whispered M'Cleane, "I must see

to this, for if Hawkins loosens his tongue, we must even quit the 'Country House,' as we did the 'Chapel.' Whilst I go about, and pick up all I can, do you try your luck in the parks or the streets, and meet me in this place after dark."

This arrangement made, M'Cleane bade Jenny Diver farewell, and sauntered off in the direction of Westminster, Jenny taking her way towards London Bridge.

In the hope of acquiring some intelligence which might be useful, the Captain sought the Almonry and soon arrived at the domicile of Old Mother Sin; that respectable old lady herself opening the door to admit him.

In spite of M'Cleane's disguise, the hag knew him in a moment; she had lived too long among deceivers to be easily deceived herself.

"Welcome, valiant Captain," said the woman. "Why 'tis an age since I saw you." And seizing his hand, she roughly shook it. "This way—this way." And she led M'Cleane to a small apartment, on a table in the midst of which were a large bottle and a dram glass, which latter, Mother Sin instantly filled and presented to her visitor.

Concealing the real object of his visit, M'Cleane, as soon as he had tossed off the strong waters, enquired for Sal the Gonnoff.

"Ah! ah! Captain," said the old brothel-keeper, with a lecherous leer; "the same dog as ever after the girls, I declare! Sal is at home—but she has an old spark with her at present; a rare old hunks—an empty head and a full purse."

"It would not be full long if Jenny could fall in with him," muttered M'Cleane to himself, and he almost regretted he had not brought the Diver with him.

"And Flitchman?" enquired M'Cleane, "has he quite recovered from the sword-hurt which he received in Covent Garden?"

"Quite," remarked Mother Sin, "and anxious enough to see you, Captain—but hush! Sal's companion is coming down stairs."

As the old gentleman descended the rickety and creaking staircase, he indulged in hearty fits of laughter; M'Cleane fancied that he had heard his voice somewhere before, and became anxious to get a view of him. In order to do this, he squeezed himself behind the little parlour door, and peeped through the crevice between it and the wainscot of the room.

The instant he caught sight of the features of the old fellow, he recognized them as belonging to the waggish old gentleman whom he had deprived of his valuable wig on the occasion of his journey to Bristol in the waggon, and from whom he had had so narrow an escape at the Bristol hostelry.

The amorous old fellow, who was evidently on amazingly good terms with Mother Sin, drew a heavy canvas bag from his breeches pocket, and presented the harridan with two broad pieces.

"And what do you mean to leave for the girl," demanded the bawd; "why this hardly pays me for the room, which you have had a whole blessed night."

"Blessed, indeed! you may well say that, Mother Sin," said the waggish old gentleman, chucking the woman under her chin, "well—well—there's another guinea for yourself—I've satisfied Sal already."

"Sal! what did the worthy gentleman give you?" screamed the old wretch from the bottom of the staircase.

"Only a guinea, d—n his stingy old carcass," replied the girl, "he swore he hadn't got any more, but he says he'll call again."

But Mother Sin, like the other members of her profession, had but very little faith in the promises of the gay Lotharios who frequented her house. Turning the key in the lock, she fastened the door, and, with a tremendous oath, declared that the old gentleman should not depart until he had satisfied her.

But not one farthing more would the old gentleman consent to give, and his face became livid with rage as he found himself a prisoner.

"If you think to bully me," he said, "you are very much mistaken—look at this," and he drew a double-barrelled pistol from his pocket. "Ever since a scoundrelly highwayman plundered me, I never move without it, and, by G—d! if you obstruct me, I'll make you acquainted with its contents."

Still, however, Mother Sin stood with her back against the door, absolutely refusing to allow the man to depart unless he complied with her extortionate demands. At length, wound up to a pitch of frenzy, the old fellow endeavoured to force his way out, and in so doing one of the triggers of his pistol became entangled in some portion of the woman's dress, and the weapon was discharged.

A shriek from Mother Sin proclaimed that she was wounded, and M'Cleane, regardless of consequences, rushed forward to her assistance.

Encounters and brawls of this kind were common enough in the Almonry, and therefore no notice was taken by the neighbours when they heard the report of the pistol; had it, however, happened at night, curiosity might have been excited.

"Help—for G—d's sake, help! the villain has murdered me," cried the bawd; and M'Cleane, regardless of consequences, rushed to her assistance.

Alarmed at what had happened, the old gentleman was attempting to unfasten the door and escape, when M'Cleane grappled him by the arm, and dragged him back. In another instant he flung him on the floor, and wrenching his pistol from him, presented it at his head.

In the scuffle, M'Cleane's hat had fallen off, and the old gentleman's eyes were instantly rivetted upon him.

"My wig—by all that is wonderful!" he exclaimed, "I'd swear to it amongst a million—and you—yes, I'd swear to that also—are one of the rascals who stole it and its contents from me."

The old fellow was not far out in his judgment, when M'Cleane disguised himself that morning, he had selected the head covering from whose secret recesses he had, not many months before, abstracted such a goodly sum in bank notes.

"I'll hang you, by G—d!" screamed the old

man, now absolutely raving with rage; and he redoubled his efforts to free himself.

M'Cleane fully comprehended the dangerous position in which he was placed. To allow the old gentleman to depart was out of the question, and to let him remain where he was was almost equally hazardous, for so loudly did he call for assistance that the Captain every instant expected unwelcome visitors might arrive.

Fortunately, Mother Sin had only received a flesh wound, the ball having merely grazed her temple. Having now risen from the ground, she also, alarmed at the noise made by her customer, seized a towel and thrust it into the old fellow's mouth, and thus, by half-suffocating him, effectually prevented his cries from being heard.

"Curse him!" cried M'Cleane, who began to think that he had better make off, and he hinted as much to Mother Sin.

"No!" said the woman, emphatically; "not at least till you have helped me to lighten the old fool of some of his guineas, and of the flimsies he has in his fob—that is, if Sal the Gonnoff hasn't been beforehand with me." And thrusting her hand into the captive's breeches pocket, she abstracted the canvas bag of gold.

She then searched the fob, and found a roll of notes to a large amount, which she handed to M'Cleane with the observation, that he would find better means of disposing of them than she could; the Captain received them, stowed them carefully away, and was about to depart, leaving the plundered party to be further dealt with by the virago, when the old man, by a desperate effort, sprung to his feet, flung Mother Sin against the wainscoting, and rushed upon M'Cleane, who he gripped by the collar.

"You do not escape thus," cried the old gentleman. "I have sworn to see you hanged, and I'll keep my oath."

"Hands off, or it will be the worse for you," cried the Captain, "I do not want to shed your blood; but, by heaven! I will if you do not release me."

With the utmost tenacity, the old man retained his hold, and again he renewed his cries for assistance. At length, alarmed at the noise, the neighbours began to collect round the door.

At this moment, Sal the Gonnoff made her appearance, and lent her aid to drag the old fellow down a short flight of stairs which led to an underground cellar.

This effected, by Mother Sin's directions, she opened the door, and informed those who had gathered round it that one of the usual brawls had occurred, and that the young blood who had caused it by attempting to bilk her, had escaped by the back way.

Satisfied with this explanation, they departed, and the way was once more clear.

"Do you mean to murder as well as rob me?" cried the old man, "that you have dragged me to this hole?"

"No!" said M'Cleane, "on your giving me your word of honour that you will not mention to a living soul what has passed here—you shall depart at once."

"Return me my money, then, and I promise."

"I make no such conditions," said M'Cleane, "but here are the notes. This woman must do as she likes with the gold."

But this the brothel-keeper prized far too much to even dream of parting with it. Emboldened, however, by having recovered his notes, the old gentleman rushed upon her, and seized her fiercely by the throat.

"He's throttling me, Captain M'Cleane, help!—help! for G—d's sake!" screeched the woman, whose face grew purple, as the pressure on her throat was increased.

"M'Cleane! then was it that notorious villain who robbed me," cried the man, glaring on the Captain, without, however, relinquishing his grasp of the hag.

"D—n the woman's long tongue; would that she had been indeed choked before she had mentioned my name," said the Captain, as he drew his sword and commanded the gentleman to loose his hold of the woman.

"I'll never do so until she gives me back my money, or gives up her own breath—and as for you, Captain M'Cleane, I know you, you scapegrace too well, and I'll never lose sight of you until you're tied up like a dog."

"Fool!" exclaimed the Captain, as he rushed in the madness of anger on the unfortunate old man, who displayed more daring courage than M'Cleane would have given him credit for. "Fool! you court your own destruction—let the woman be released I say, or you shall repent it."

A grin of defiance was his only answer, as he grasped Mother Sin's neck so tightly that her eyes started from their sockets, and her tongue black and swollen, protruded from her mouth.

"There then—madman!" cried M'Cleane, as at one lunge he passed his rapier clean through the body of the old gentleman, who, relaxing his grasp, fell heavily upon the floor of the cellar, groaned once or twice, and then breathed no longer.

M'Cleane and Mother Sin gazed at each other in silent horror for a few minutes after the dreadful deed had been committed.

"He seemed to know me well," said the Captain; "and after all I only acted in self-defence, but what must we do with the body?"

"Let us search it first," suggested Mother Sin, who always, and in all circumstances, kept a keen eye on the main chance, and in accordance with her own recommendation she began to examine the pockets, from one of which she again drew forth the bundle of notes which she handed to M'Cleane.

"Here's a bulky pocket-book," she observed, as she took a well-stuffed leather case from the dead man's breast pocket. "I'm no scholar, Jem, you had better see if there's anything worth our keeping in it."

M'Cleane accordingly drew near the cellar-grating and opened it, it only contained papers, but one of these documents on being opened at once caused the highwayman to stagger and turn ghastly pale.

Hurrying the book into his pocket, he again asked the woman how they should dispose of the body? Without replying, she stooped, grasped an iron ring in the floor, after one or two efforts succeeded in raising a trap door.

"Look down," she said, to her companion.

M'Cleane stood on the edge of the well-like abyss, and gazed into its black depths, from whence a chill draught ascended, and a sound as of running water was heard. Peering into the gloomy place more attetively, he thought he could discern the dark waters far down, and he turned for explanation to Mother Sin.

"'Tis one of the deep sewers which communicate with the river," she said; "but it is so crooked that any large body like this (and she kicked the corpse) can never find its way to the river; it must rot first, and go piecemeal, so that there is no fear of its being discovered. Besides this, there are hundreds of other houses in Westminster which have an opening into this drain, and even should the body of this fool be discovered, who is to know that it came from here?"

"True," said M'Cleane, "the sooner the job is done the better," then, and with the help of Mother Sin, the yet warm body was dragged to the well's mouth.

"Stay," said M'Cleane, "I must have this signet ring from off his finger—I fancy I know the initials."

He soon disengaged it from the dead man's stiffening joints, and then, with a heavy plunge, the body fell into the sullen stream far beneath, and all was silent again save the montonous rippling of the stream as it washed against the banks of the sewer.

The trap door was again replaced, and all signs of having been taken up of late obliterated. Mother Sin and M'Cleane then adjourned to the apartment above and equally divided their plunder. Sal the Gonnoff being presented with a few guineas for the slight share she had taken in the transaction.

"And now," said M'Cleane, "I have some business to transact with Flitchman, who I hope has recovered from the effects of his wounds."

"Quite," replied the girl, and requesting the Captain to follow, she led the way up stairs towards the room in which the late confidential clerk of Mr. Doom still lay concealed.

There we must for the present leave them while we follow the fortunes of Jenny Diver who parted from M'Cleane in Fetter-lane.

The girl took her course through Fleet-street, intending to visit the neighbourhood of London Bridge, that great thoroughfare being generally so densely thronged that she seldom failed to be successful there in the practice of her profession.

She was walking leisurely round St. Paul's, when she observed just before her a lady dressed, like herself, in very fashionable attire; but there was a something in the gait of the female which struck her sharp eye as being artificial and assumed. Determined to satisfy herself whether her suspicions were correct or otherwise she took the opposite way when she reached Cheapside, hurried along for about five hundred yards and then crossing the road returned, and met the object of her enquiries, whom she looked full in the face.

"Tristram!" ejaculated Jenny Diver.

"Jenny!" exclaimed the stranger, whom the Diver had addressed by anything but a feminine apellation.

"Don't let us talk here," remarked Jenny. "Follow me when I turn down beside Bow Church," and she led the way, the stranger keeping her in sight. They had no sooner reached a secluded street which led to the water-side, and where there was but little of a thoroughfare, than the Diver burst into a fit of laughter and exclaimed:—

"What the devil means this disguise, Tristry, and where have you been this age? I have scarcely set eyes on you since the week after I arrived in London the first time."

"Caged in an infernal cell of Newgate, and only for crying the black list about the streets; but mayhap I didn't lose much by it, for I came out a trifle wiser than I was when I went in. By the way, Jenny, if you've nothing else to do just now, I'm about a job, and to tell you the truth I was on the look out for a companion."

"What is it?" asked Jenny.

"Did you never hear of one Doctor Trotter?" asked Tristram Savage.

"What—the famous fortune-teller and astrologer of Moorfields?" asked Jenny.

"The same," replied Tristram, "the fellow is an arch imposter, and manages by his cunning to amass immense sums of money. He is patronised entirely by women, indeed from fear of being plundered he never allows a man to enter his study unless he uses extraordinary precautions."

"I see through it now," said Jenny, "but if the conjuror is not less sharp-sighted than myself I fancy he will see your disguise; however to do you justice, you make a pretty woman enough, and had it not been for the awkwardness of your walk I too might have been deceived."

Jenny and Tristram then retired to a tavern hard by where they arranged their plans, and having fortified themselves with plenty of wine and manchets, they set out for the residence of the notorious Doctor Trottter in Moorfields.

The astrologer's door was opened to their summons by a diminutive negro, who was firmly believed by all the doctor's neighbours to be nearly related to a certain sable individual who resides in a place of rather high temperature; and also to be the familiar spirit through whose aid the astrologer performed his wonders. Grinning diabolically the imp conducted Jenny and her pretended female friend into the laboratory or study of Doctor Trotter.

The astrologer was a tall weazen-faced man, with red ferret looking eyes gleaming beneath a pair of shaggy eyebrows. A black velvet scull cap partially covered his bald head, and from beneath it streamed locks of iron grey hair. A long beard reached almost to his waist, where a broad belt, inscribed with mystical signs and characters, confined the folds of an ample scarlet robe trimmed at the neck, cuffs and skirt with dark fur.

Before him on the table was a huge book, with thick wooden covers, and massive antique clasps. Celestial globes, quadrants, compasses, and orreries were scattered about the room, and from the ceiling hung dried specimens of natural history. In one corner was fixed a grim skeleton, and the floor was littered all over with books and parchments.

"A fair morning to you, ladies," said the astrologer, rising and motioning our two adventurers to seats. "Wish you to learn the secrets of the future or the history of the past, for by means of my potent art I can reveal either."

"Most learned sir," said Tristram, "it is to have my nativity cast that I have come hither," and he placed a guinea in the philosopher's palm.

"Good!" remarked Doctor Trotter, "your hand. Ah! these lines which I see seem to belong rather to Mars than Venus."

Jenny could scarcely refrain from laughing outright, for being better acquainted with her companions sex than was Trotter with all his supernatural knowledge she thought so too.

The doctor then drew a scheme of the twelve houses and filled them with strange looking characters of signs, planets, and aspects, and in the square space in the middle of the parchment he wrote the following jargon.

"That the sun being the casp of the tenth house and Saturn within it, but five degrees from the casp it denoted a fit of sickness which would shortly afflict her; but then Mercury being in the eleventh house, just in the beginning of Sagittarius near Aquarius, and but six degrees from the body of Saturn, and mundane square to the Moon and Mars, it signified her speedy recovery from it. Again, Cancer, being in a zodiacil time to the Sun, Saturn and Mercury, she might depend on having a good husband in a short time, and moreover it was a sure sign that he who married her should be a very rich and thriving man."

The idea of marrying a man tickled Tristram Savage as much as the former blunder of Trotter had amused the Diver; but they had little time to waste in trifling.

Scarcely had the astrologer ended his predictions than Tristram Savage assailed him with the question—

"Can you tell what I am thinking of?"

Trotter looked surly at this, and replied that it was none of his profession to tell people's thoughts.

"Why then, I'll show them to you," said Savage, pulling a pistol from his pocket and clapping it to the doctor's breast.

"Submit!" he cried with an oath. "or you are a dead man." Tristram and Jenny then tied the unlucky fortune-teller neck and heels and gagged him. Then while Savage held the pistol before his face Jenny ransacked his pockets, from whence she took a gold watch, twenty guineas, and a silver tobacco box; and from some drawers which they forced open a number of rings and other valuables.

With them they got clear off; but as soon as the thieves had departed, the gagged and fettered fortune-teller floundering about on the floor raised such an alarm that those below verily believed that their master was having a combat with the devil and feared to fly to his assistance. However, at length they ventured to go to his aid; and though they immediately set off in pursuit of Jenny and Tristram those accomplished personages were far beyond the reach of detection.

Tristram Savage presented Jenny Diver with fifteen guineas as her share of the robbery, and with this booty the girl made the best of her way towards the place where she appointed to meet M'Cleane.

CHAPTER XXXVII.

BLUESKIN AND THE BLOOD-MONEY.—JONATHAN WILD GETS ON THE "RIGHT SCENT" AT LAST.—HANDSOME JACK IN PERIL.

As soon as Mr. Watkins, the Bow Street runner, had safely deposited Joseph Blake, or, as we shall in future style him, Blueskin, in St. Pauls' round-house, he bent his steps towards the residence of Jonathan Wild, and of that worthy received his reward, as in a former chapter we have recorded.

Then he proceeded to the residence of Sir John Fryer, the magistrate, and informed his worship of the capture he had made, requested that an order might be granted for removing his prisoner to Wood Street Compter.

This document having been procured, Watkins returned to the round-house, and after putting Blueskin in irons, called a hackney coach, and conveyed his prisoner to the vile receptacle in Wood Street, where he left him, after giving his victim a promise that he would request Jonathan Wild to call and see him.

Blueskin had been too long acquainted with Jonathan Wild, and had assisted him too often in the execution of his nefarious schemes on the destruction of others, not to entertain a suspicion that he also was likely to be a victim of foul play. He therefore determined to be extremely cautious in his proceedings. Of the robbery with which he was charged, he knew himself to be entirely innocent, but he was also aware, that many an innocent man had made his exit at Tyburn, through the means of blood-money. For thirty or forty pounds men could at that time be found, who would swear away a fellow-creature's life as calmly as they would eat their dinners.

On the following morning, Jonathan Wild visited Blueskin, so completely did this consummate hypocrite's face express grief and mortification at seeing the prisoner, that even the latter began to think his suspicions had been groundless.

"This is an unlucky job, Joe," said the thief-taker, "but depend on it I'll do all in my power to help you out of the scrape—though I confess, from what I have heard, that things look very dark."

"So help me G—d Wild. I know nothing of this matter. And you——"

He stopped himself abruptly—he was about to say, "and you know it well enough," but it occurred to him that Jonathan might have his fate in his hands, and that it would be impolitic to offend him, so he substituted for the words

he was about to utter so unguardedly:—
"And you will help me to prove it—will you not?"

"To prove that you are not guilty of this St. Martins Lane affair," replied Jonathan, gravely, and with a look of deep meaning, "it will be absolutely necessary to prove that some other party is. How can that be done—eh, Blueskin?"

"What are you going to do with Oaky and Levy?" insinuated, rather than asked Blueskin.

"Hum!" said Jonathan, "they're both in Newgate on a charge of shop-lifting, but that offence was committed long after your affairs." Wild laid an emphasis on the last two words, for it formed a part of his plan to induce Blueskin to believe that he considered him really guilty.

"There's only one way for your getting off, that I can see, and perhaps you'd object to that," remarked Wild, after a pause.

Jonathan owed a grudge to the two men whose names he had just mentioned, they had on some former occasion deeply offended him, and he was not the man either to forgive or forget an injury. It now occurred to him that by using Blueskin as a tool, he could effectually revenge himself upon them, and at the same time throw an additional chain around his wretched instrument.

"Only one way! what do you mean, Wild?" asked Blueskin.

"This," said Wild, "you must confess that you are guilty of this robbery, and swear that Oakey and Levy were your accomplices. I will take care to provide witnesses against them if necessary. Do you consent?"

"And if I do, what is to be my reward?" asked Blueskin.

"What! isn't an escape from the gallows enough?" demanded Jonathan Wild, with some show of anger, "however, I'll procure bail for you, and till then allow you three and sixpence a week whilst you are in prison; and more than that, when you get out, I'll take you into my service and confidence again."

"Well," said Blueskin, "I agree, and will perform my share of the business as soon as you like, for I am cursedly tired of lying here."

"By the way," remarked Jonathan Wild, "do you happen to know anything of the man in whose pocket you discovered the book containing those papers which Watkins found upon you?"

"A little — not much," replied Blueskin. "Why?"

"I had particular reasons for asking, and it would perhaps be as well for you to reply to me. How did you become possessed of that pocket-book which is now in my possession?"

Blueskin saw through Wild's designs, but he deemed it imprudent just then to thwart them; therefore he informed Jonathan of the incident in which the bull-dog of the house in Hanging Sword Alley had played so conspicuous a part.

Wild then quitted Blueskin, again assuring him that he would provide for his safety. How he performed his promise will be shown hereafter.

On leaving the gaol, Jonathan proceeded to Newtoners Lane where he found his man Abraham.

"Good news Mishter Vild," said the Jew, rubbing his hands and grinning so as to expose his yellow teeth, which rather resembled fangs, "capital news for you."

"What! is that she devil, Mary Milliner, dead—or Timothy Dunn nabbed for Mrs. Knap's murder in Grays Inn Gardens? or —"

"Ah! Mishter Vild, now you'd never guess it if you vas to try for a veek. Vat do you think—I've managed to find out vere to clap hand on the man that Mishter Ephraim Blake is looking after."

"The devil you have," exclaimed Wild, in surprise.

"Fact—s'help me Father Apraham!" said the Jew, with a chuckle, "more than dat, he vos in dis room not very long ago."

"Why in the fiend's name, then, didn't you keep him here?" said Jonathan, in a rage.

"'Cos I vonted to track the fox to his hole, and I've managed to do it," replied the Israelite, coolly and with an air of triumphant cunning.

"That man," said Wild, musingly, "once in my power, my fortune is made. The writings in the pocket-book found by Blueskin, would be invaluable to me, could I only find the owner, and manage to entangle him in the meshes of my net. Could I do this, by one bold stroke, I should secure enough to enable me to quit for ever the dangerous business in which I am now engaged."

Apparently without having heard him, the Jew, whose ears had been eagerly drinking in Jonathan Wild's muttered words, said:—
"He's a highwayman, Mishter Vild."

"Who?" asked Jonathan, with a start.

"The man vot saved the young vomans out of the burning house, and left his pocket-book in de dog's mouth," replied Abraham.

"Are you sure?" asked Wild, eagerly.

"As sure as I'm alive this blessed minute, Mishter Vild, and I can prove it too."

"How?" asked the thief-taker.

Abraham then related to Wild the particulars of Handsome Jack's transaction with him in the matter of the diamond, and also a detailed account of Sir Philip Aubrey's visit.

"It must be so," said Wild, as his countenance betrayed the diabolical exultation he felt. "This Richard Town, to whom these papers refer, in his distress has gone on the road to make his fortune. Now, then, if I can fix this robbery on him, how easy the task to send him to Tyburn at once, or make a compromise with him for his broad acres, and spare his life."

Wild, who had spies in all directions, was perfectly aware that Sir James Town, the cousin of Handsome Jack, had, after a course of swindling, been condemned to the pillory, and after the infliction of that part of his punishment, to be transported for life. He was also well aware that Richard Town was the rightful owner of the Town title and estates, and he now began to study the game which he determined to play.

As if to aid him in his plot, he had scarcely retired to his private room for the purpose of arranging his plans, than Abraham entered.

"Mishter Vild! more luck. Here's an old shentlemans and a lady vants to speak mit you —'tis Lord Purley."

"Oh! I know his lordship—'tis about that job at Purley hall, doubtless—admit them," said Wild.

Lord Purley, his young and beautiful wife leaning on his arm, hobbled into the office of the thief-taker, who, with obsequious respect, placed seats for them near the table.

"And to what chance," said Jonathan, "am I indebted for the honour of your lordship's visit?"

"To seek your assistance, Mr. Wild, in apprehending another of the daring villains who sacrilegiously, I may say, broke not only into my mansion but even into my bed-room on the night of my marriage with this lady," and he pointed to his bride, who, as Wild stared at her some what rudely, blushed, and hung down her head at the reference to so delicate a subject.

"One of them, a fellow called Hawkins, is already in gaol," remarked Wild.

"But I'll not be content until all three of the

No. 23.

wretches are there; and not even then. I'll not rest, sir, till they dangle from a gibbet!" and as he uttered these words the old Peer, with ferocious energy, thumped the ferule of his gold headed cane on the floor.

"Know you either of these two other men, my lord, or can you describe their personal appearances?" asked Jonathan, "or perhaps you were too alarmed to take particular notice."

"Alarmed, sir!—damme what d'ye mean by my being alarmed," cried the old lord, his face purple with rage at the idea of having his courage suspected. "No, Mr. Wild, I was as cool, sir, as I am at this moment."

Which, by-the-bye, was not saying much for his coolness, for down on the floor again, with more force than before, went the stick, and the old gentleman's face grew redder than ever.

"I cannot say though," continued he, "that I took particular notice of the villains; but Lady Purley did though, and greatly to my surprise and disgust as you may suppose, Mr.

Wild, her ladyship evidently knew one of them well enough, and had sufficient interest with him to induce him to return the property he had packed up ready to take away."

"Then, doubtless, Lady Purley will afford me the necessary information in order that I may trace out the robbers," remarked Wild, bowing as he spoke to the bride.

"'Tis to force her to do so that I brought her here," said Lord Purley. "Although I have laid my commands on her she obstinately refuses."

"And shall continue to do so, my lord," said her ladyship, speaking now for the first time.

"You hear her!' cried her husband, "and yet she could parley fast enough with a midnight robber," and address him by name."

"By name?" asked Jonathan Wild.

"By name, as I'm a living man and a peer of the realm," said Lord Purley, giving the latter part of his reply with a great show of dignity.

Lady Purley observed the satisfaction which was pourtrayed on Jonathan Wild's countenance when her husband volunteered this piece of information, and she trembled with fear lest she should be the unwilling and unconscious instrument of bringing her former lover to justice, and perhaps to an ignominious end.

"Do you remember the name?" asked Wild.

"Yes, one—the christian name—but not the other, to do the fellow justice, he was good looking enough; but there are so many dashing blades of the name of Richard that unless one knew, as Lady Purley does, his surname, it would be no easy matter to pick the rogue out. His companion was as ugly a fellow as I ever saw."

"Richard? was that the name of the robber," asked Wild, almost breathlessly, yet nevertheless exhibiting no symptoms of excitement.

"That was the name, and my wife, to her shame be it spoken, intimated that of yore there had been some love passages between them."

Again Lady Purley bent her head, bit her lip, and blushed, but did not deny what her old husband had hinted at.

It must be Richard Town thought Wild, as he remembered what had so lately taken place between himself and his man Abraham; indeed, so convinced was he in his own mind that it was as he suspected, that he almost gave Lord Purley a positive assurance of being able to discover the delinquent.

"For the which, if you do, you shall be well rewarded," said his lordship as he took his departure.

"Well rewarded," almost shouted Jonathan, as he flung himself back in his great leather arm-chair. "Well rewarded! aye, that I shall be if all be as I fancy it will be. Richard Town once in my power, his large fortune is irrecoverably mine; nothing can hinder it, for his cousin, who till lately held it, is a transported felon, and he himself amenable to the law and its extreme punishment—Abraham!"

The Jew instantly obeyed the summons of his master.

"The man of whom we were just now speaking must be got hold of by fair means or foul," said Wild. "There are ten guineas for the information you have already given me, and I shall not cease to be liberal; you know that I shall not."

Abraham pocketted the gold with infinite glee, and then saying, "Vel, Mishter Vild," stood quietly awaiting his master's further orders.

"You said you had tracked this fellow who brought Sir Philip Aubrey's diamond—who did you put on the scent?"

"Who but leetle Shadrach—sharp boy, Shadrach—vy, Mishter Vatkins might take lessons of him," replied Abraham with enthusiasm.

"And where did he trace the man to?" asked Jonathan.

"To a public-house, a little roadside tavern at Highgate," replied the Jew. "Shadrach saw him go in in company with a man as he picked up at a house in London Wall, a fellow, Shadrach says, with as ugly a face as the devil himself has got."

"Ah! another link to the chain; Lord Purley spoke of the other robber as being ugly," exclaimed Wild with manifest glee.

"It is all true, Mishter Vild," said the Jew.

"I must have my friend Watkins's assistance in this matter," said Wild, and after having himself examined Shadrach, he dismissed him to the kitchen below, and putting on his hat and cloak went himself in quest of the Bow Street runner.

CHAPTER XXXV.

THE WAY IN WHICH SIR JAMES TOWN WAS CAUGHT—THE REWARD OF MOTHER SINGLETON—CADGERS' HOME AND EXPLOITS OF HAWKINS—THE OLD MINT—RIVER PIRATES.

To account for the appearance of Sir James Town in the pillory in Charing Cross, it is necessary that we should partially retrace our steps.

After having been liberated from the Sponging house, the unfortunate baronet, who had been plucked of his last guinea by the infamous Wolland and his associates. entered with readiness into the schemes which the latter proposed, and consented to play a part, for which the position in society in which he had recently moved eminently fitted him.

As yet the news of the downfall had not been noised about in the fashionable world; and as he had now everything to gain and nothing to lose he resolved to play a desperate game.

The better to carry out the schemes of the gang who now made use of him as their tool, he dropped his real name and assumed an alias, and after taking expensive lodgings in Bond Street, he contrived by means of reports circulated by his confederates to make various tradesmen believe that he was a man of rank and fortune.

His plan was to order vast quantities of

goods, for which his mode of living easily gained him credit. No sooner, however, were applications for payment made, than it was discovered that the property had been disposed of at rates far below their value in order to procure ready cash. The extravagances in which he indulged perpetually hampered him, and these were much increased by the reckless squanderings of a dashing woman of the town, who lived with him as his wife.

Forced at length to quit Bond Street, he privately decamped and took apartments in Pimlico. He now assumed another name and gave himself out as the steward of a nobleman of high rank. The better to carry on nefarious business he likewise took a house in Westminster, in which he placed an agent, who ordered in goods as for the nobleman; and the tradesmen who delivered these goods were directed to leave their bills for the examination of the steward.

No sooner had the property being left in Westminster, than it was removed by Wolland and his gang and disposed of to the brokers. This game, however, could not continue long, and Town found it necessary for a time to quit London.

He now travelled into the country, and still assuming the character of a man of fortune, he managed by means of forged letters of introduction to become acquainted with country families of distinction; taking advantage of these intimacies he contrived to learn the names of the London tradesmen with whom the various parties dealt, and in their names he wrote for goods. These orders were invariably executed, and to secure the proceeds of his iniquitous proceedings he, by meeting the waggon's that conveyed the goods before they reached the places to which they were directed, obtained possession of them, and then by another conveyance returned them to London, where Wolland received and disposed of them.

It would be unnecessary here to trace further this portion of the career of the quondam Sir James. Suffice it to say, that for months both London and the country were equally laid under contributions by him; and that jeweller's, watchmaker's, silversmith's, lacemen, hosier's, hatter's, mercer's, &c., were frequent dupes to his artifices.

On his return to London, from one of these country excursions, he was informed by Wolland and the gang that he had at length become too notorious to allow of their further continuing their connection with him. In vain did he claim compensation for his past services; the villains who had used him as their tool, now that they found him worn out and valueless flung him aside and even disowned him; and with a blasted character, a shattered frame, and but a few guineas in his pocket, the once fashionable and much-courted Sir James Town found himself a homeless wanderer, and all but a vagabond in the streets of famous London.

As he stood near Temple Bar musing on his melancholy situation, he suddenly remembered that there was one friend at least to whom he thought he might apply, and following the impulse of the moment he strolled in the direction of Mother Singleton's.

That lady was seated in her luxurious boudoir, as fair, fascinating, and voluptuous-looking as ever, when Town was ushered into her presence.

"Ah! my dear Sir James," she exclaimed, "where on earth have you been this age?" and as she uttered these words the buxom beauty saluted her visitor with a kiss.

So then, all's right so far, thought Town, she has not as yet heard of my downfall and misdoings; and, in the exercise of the low cunning in which he had now become an adept, he began inwardly to speculate on how he could impose on the procuress.

"The old game, Sir James, the old game, I suppose. Ah! you naughty man," playfully remarked Mother Singleton, giving Town at the same time a tap on the face with her fan.

The gentleman smiled, and bestowed on the rather amorous lady of the house a look which she perfectly comprehended. He now determined to conceal his true position, as it seemed to be unknown to Mother Singleton, who seldom stirred from home, and knew little of what was passing in the world without. With her he could he thought, find at least a home for a time, during which he might be on the look out for some chance of bettering his fortunes.

"You have come at rather an unfortunate time, my dear Sir James," said Mother Singleton, "positively every one of my cages are at this moment as empty as that from which your pretty little bird escaped some time ago—you remember, do you not?"

"Perfectly well," replied Sir James, and with a low bow to the lady he said with an air of refined gallantry:—"but one charming bird is still left I perceive, and I cannot but remember when it was surrounded by other lovely creatures it appeared the maturest and the loveliest of all."

Mother Singleton, who also well remembered the disappointment on the occasion of the baronet's last visit, when he was hastily summoned from her by his servant, blushed through her rouge on hearing this compliment.

Although, as we have before intimated, the good lady was no longer young, the amorous flame still burned as fiercely in her bosom as ever, and it was rumoured that among the many gallants who visited her little Seraglio, there were not a few who preferred the riper charms of Madame to the budding beauties who fluttered about her. She, too, had her favorites, and among them was Sir James Town.

But it was not so much his person that found favour in her eyes as his title and his wealth, the latter especially, which induced her to smile upon him. The unexpected visit which he now paid her was especially gratifying; and, with a half-expressed hope that his stay at her house would not be of so short duration as the last had been, she produced and placed before Sir James some of the choicest and most exhilarating wines.

Mother Singleton's attire was fashioned so as rather to display than conceal her mature and ripened charms. A low boddice laced down the front scarcely confined two plump and panting globes that partly burst the barrier of snow white lace whose net-work spread over their ivory surfaces. A neck, fair as alabaster, if it was not exactly swan-like was yet graceful in its outline, supported her small well-shaped head. Her face was still beautiful, and now that desire had been kindled it beamed with unwonted animation. Discarding the frightful hooped petticoat which was then in fashion, she wore a loose robe, which, confined to her waist by a simple zone of gold tissue, displayed to advantage the roundness of her hips and the seductive proportion of her waist. From beneath her embroidered petticoat two fairy feet encased in slippers of ermine, "like little mice peeped in and out," and altogether, though Madame Singleton confessed to thirty-five, and had done so for ten years past, so that no doubt on that subject could possibly exist, she was an exceedingly dangerous personage whenever, as upon this occasion in the case of Town, she chose to unmask her battery of smiles, and from her fine eyes send forth glances that were absolutely killing.

All this was not, as may be supposed, without its influence on Town, who was rather of a susceptible nature where women were concerned. Exhilarated by the wine of which he had partaken freely and fascinated by the blandishments of his companion, he, when supper was over, seated himself by Mother Singleton's side, and commenced a series of dalliances which were as agreeable to the lady as to himself.

And so the night wore on; in whose society Town passed it need not be mentioned, the truth will easily be guessed by the reader.

Towards noon on the next day, Mother Singleton and her guest sat at breakfast in an apartment whose windows commanded a view of the street below.

The ex-baronet was busily engaged in discussing the many good things which were spread before him, and at the same time congratulating himself on his luck in having such comfortable quarters. He little thought, however, that the mistress of the house, like all her class, was speculating how she could make the most of him; for as we have already hinted she still believed him to be wealthy and prosperous.

As soon as a servant had removed the breakfast things, he laid a newspaper of that morning on the table before his mistress who, flinging herself on a couch began carelessly to peruse it.

Town in the meantime sauntered to the window, and surveyed the passers-by in the street below.

Suddenly Mother Singleton started and turned pale with astonishment, then the blood flew back to her cheeks, and her eyes appeared to flash with indignation. Again and again she perused the article, whatever it was, which seemed to cause her so much uneasiness, and then folding the paper, so that what she had been reading might not be seen by Town, she laid it on the table and excusing herself to her paramour quitted the room.

No sooner had she reached her own apartment than she burst into a paroxysm of rage, and rang her bell violently. A moment afterwards a black footboy entered the room.

"Take this," said she, "with all speed to the magistrates' office in Bow Street," and she handed the negro a letter which she had hurriedly written.

The lad instantly departed on his errand, and the Procuress, who by this time had a little composed herself, descended to the parlour, where she had left her lover.

"Sir James," said she with a smile, and a look from which every trace of anger was banished, "you were ever kind and generous, and I feel sure you would aid me if I required assistance."

"That indeed would I—I am sure you cannot doubt it," he remarked with fervour.

"Then you can do so now?" she exclaimed.

"In what manner?" asked Town.

"By advancing me a little money which you can well spare—the fact is," she continued, "that a miserly tradesman has just now threatened me with arrest unless I pay him a paltry hundred guineas to-day. Will you lend me that sum?"

Town was terribly perplexed by this application; if he refused at once to do so, the state of his finances might be suspected, and to comply with the request was impossible, for he had only seven or eight guineas in his possession; he plainly saw that his only course was to temporize.

"I have not so much about me," said Town; "but when I go into the City I will endeavour to procure it—surely the man will wait."

"Sir James Town used not to be in the habit of endeavouring to oblige a friend," remarked the lady coldly, and with something very much like a sneer on her lip, "there was a time when he could and would have drawn a cheque at once for the amount; but it would appear that times are changed."

"You surely do not doubt my willingness—my ability to serve you," exclaimed Town, somewhat alarmed at the altered appearance of his mistress.

"Look at that, hypocrite!" cried the Procuress, now absolutely boiling over with rage and indignation, and pointing to a certain portion of the paper on which she rested the tip of her fore finger, "and then tell me if I have not sufficient reason to doubt both as I do. But by Heaven I'll be revenged."

Town took up the paper and to his utter consternation read the following advertisement:—

TWO HUNDRED GUINEAS REWARD.
"The above sum is hereby offered for the apprehension of James Town, alias Sir James Town—(here followed a string of numerous other aliases being the names which he had assumed in both London and the country for the purpose of plunder)—against whom as a swindler and common cheat a warrant has been issued; and all persons are cautioned against harbouring the said James Town, as by so doing they will be guilty of felony.—Gatehouse, Westminster, 17—.

"Pitiful scoundrel!" said Mother Singleton, with a glance of ineffable scorn at the man, who now stood mute and thunder stricken before her, "and so, penniless beggar that you are, you dared to intrude your vile carcass into my house and so pollute my presence. No wonder that Sir James Town, the notorious swindler of many names could not lend me the hundred pounds."

The pretended necessity for the sum was, as may be supposed, a mere ruse on the part of the Procuress. The instant she had read the advertisement, her first burst of rage over, she resolved to pluck Town of all he possessed if possible, before he himself knew of the affair, and then, with the usual rapacity of the unprincipled class to which she belonged, to betray him for the sake of the reward offered for his apprehension.

Somewhat stung by the woman's taunts, Town reminded her of the vast sums he had lavished on her in former times.

"To secure your own gratification," retorted the Procuress; "but listen."

At that moment a thundering knock was heard at the street door, and Town turned as pale as a sheeted corpse.

"Woman!" said he, as the truth flashed upon him, "you have sold me;" and he was about to spring on her and inflict summary vengeance, when the door of the apartment flew open, and the black servant boy and an officer made their appearance.

Before, however, the constable caught sight of Town, the latter had hidden himself behind a large folding screen, close to a window that was open.

"Sarvant, Madam Singleton," said the officer, with a bow, "wot have you turned decoy duck—eh?"

"Look at this," and she showed Mr. Watkins, the Bow Street runner, the advertisement respecting Town.

"I've been on the look out for that chap this long time," said Watkins,—"Do you know where he is hiding!"

"Yes—not far off," replied the Procuress.

"You'd better tell me where, for if you harbour him you know you'll get into trouble. Now, s'pose you splits, and we share the reward—eh?"

"With all my heart; but I must have the money down if I do," replied Mother Singleton.

"The instant I lay hands on the fellow I'll give you a hundred guineas," said the Bow Street runner.

"Then look behind that screen," said the woman.

Watkins darted to the spot, another minute and he would have been too late, for Town was just on the point of jumping out of the window into the street below. Siezing him by the leg, the constable dragged him back, and handcuffed him.

"Werry happy to see you, Master Town, you've given me a precious lot of trouble I can tell you, so you may as well be quiet now, or it may be worse for you. Boy, go and call a coach; I suppose you'll pay for a ride to Bow Street, Sir James, for if we walk, you know,

that velvet coat of yours might suffer. Rotten eggs are plentiful enough."

Town took the hint, and requested, for he was unable to do so himself, Mr. Watkins to draw forth his purse from his pocket.

The constable soon did so, and emptied its contents on the table,—"one, two, three, four, five, six, seven," he counted. "Werry good, Mister, I'll take care of them for you, for you are going to a place where the rogues would'nt allow you to keep 'em long."

Town was obliged to submit; but at that moment he would have given worlds had he possessed them, for the ground beneath his feet to have opened and swallowed him up, so utterly fallen and degraded did he feel himself to be.

Watkins then drew from his breast pocket a huge greasy leather pocket book, from which he counted out one hundred and five pounds and handed it to the Procuress, whose eyes gleamed with a ferocious pleasure as she held them triumphantly before the prisoner's face. A few minutes afterwards a coach drew up to the door and Watkins departed with the bird he had snared.

Town, at the ensuing sessions at the Old Bailey, was tried and convicted. How his sentence was partly carried into effect at Charing Cross we have already seen. After he had been almost pelted to death, he was removed from the pillory and conveyed to Newgate, there to undergo a term of imprisonment prior to his being sent as a convict to the penal colonies.

We must now shift the scene, and crave the readers company while we introduce him to other characters and localities.

Hawkins having been admitted by the one-eyed hag into the house of refuge referred to in a preceding chapter, became, at once, an object of great interest to the people by whom the apartment, into which he was shown, was occupied.

His appearance might well have provoked curiosity. Haggard and wearied by his recent tremendous exertions, his face, where any of the skin could be discerned through the dust, which moistened by perspiration, begrimed his countenance, was of a hashy paleness; his hair was matted and filled with pulverized mortar, and his clothes torn almost to shreds. The man looked as though he had been hunted like a wild beast, as indeed he had, and as he sat down panting on the rude bench, he gaspingly asked for water.

A jug full of the pure element was brought him, and from it he drank a deep and delicious draught; then filling a pipe with an ample quantity of tobacco he commenced smoking vigorously.

"Here, mate, try this," said a thick-set, ruffianly looking fellow, who, sitting at the head of the table, appeared to be the principal personage of the party present.

As he spoke he filled a glass with raw brandy and handed it to Hawkins, who replied by a nod, and then gulped down the fiery beverage at a draught.

"If I don't make a mistake, my Ben Cul, we've met before," remarked the ruffianly looking man, after he had surveyed Hawkins's features and person.

"Perhaps so," rejoined Hawkins, "but if we have, you've mightily altered since then, or I should have remembered you too, most likely. Even, now, though your mug puzzles me, I fancy I've heard your voice before."

"Speak softly," said the stranger, "there are those amongst us who would betray you instantly if they only saw what I have just noticed," and the man's eye glanced in the direction of Hawkins's ancles.

"I see how it is, but never fear that I shall blow on you, man; however, it would be just as well though if you would cover those ugly articles till you can file them off."

In his haste and confusion the escaped burglar had forgotten that the iron rings to which the links of his fetters had been fastened still encircled his ancles. To the keen eye and quick comprehension of the stranger these at once told the story of a prison breaking.

Suddenly Hawkins remembered his companion;—a movement of the stranger had caused his face to be fully exposed to the light, and a deep scar on the left temple was visible.

"Now, I remember you, Harry," said Hawkins.

"For God's sake speak in a low tone," said the party thus addressed. "By the way, it would be as well for us to be on the move presently; but we must not go off so suddenly as to excite suspicion. As you say, my name is Harry, can you tell me, Harry what?"

"Sims," whispered Hawkins.

"Right!" exclaimed Sims, "and yours?"

"Hawkins—Jack Hawkins; you've heard news about me lately, I fancy."

"Such news as disposed me to believe that I should never have the pleasure of seeing you but once more in this world. Why, man, by this time, the street criers and Tyburn bullies are provided with true and correct copies of your last dying speech and confession. But, come, we'll have a bowl of punch in to treat the company with, and while they are carousing we can depart unmolested."

The old woman of the house eagerly clutched the guinea which Hawkins placed in her palm, and in the course of a short time she produced a steaming bowl of liquor, of which Hawkins invited those around him to partake.

The good will of the people around him was thus secured, and like bees flocking to a flower, the different individuals present who had been scattered about the room now gathered eagerly around the board.

They were a strange-looking set. Mendicants of all descriptions and thieves of all grades were there assembled together. Men who during the day had, in a state of utter stone-blindness, groped fearfully through the streets of the metropolis, imploring in whining voice christian charity, now, as if by magic, exhibited brilliant-looking optics, in which an oculist would have found it difficult to detect an imperfection. Others, who had painfully limped through the streets from dawn till dark, now, flinging aside their crutches (a whole bundle of which articles, of all sorts and sizes, stood in a corner of this common room)

walked briskly about, without even a trace of weakness. Faces which had shocked sensitive women and compassionate men by their cadaverous appearances, were now ruddy with health, and brightened by animal spirits. All disguises were thrown aside, and the privations of the day were amply compensated for by the enjoyments of the night.

Amongst the cadgers who figured in this crib, however, there were a few who did not seem to take part in the general merriment; for even in a society such as this some were poorer and more unfortunate than others. Seated despondingly by the fire was a tall gaunt figure, in whose face at least was written in unmistakeable characters, wretchedness and privation. Near him was a gloomy looking man, who sat with clasped hands, his chin drooping so as to touch his chest, and his brows knit with suppressed rage, and leaning over a table, as if he sought to find a temporary emancipation from his sorrows in slumber, who evidently belonged to that class of people who are so often described as having seen better days.

But each and all of these roused themselves when the invitation to join the punch party was given. The gaunt, hungry looking man, with a ghastly smile of satisfaction quitted his stool by the chimney corner; the gloomy gentleman unclasped his hands, and rubbed them with a feeble imitation of gleesomeness as he heard the summons to drink, and even the shabby-genteel individual roused himself, and began to think, that after all, the times were not so bad, when a fellow like him could get his drink without asking for it.

While they were enjoying themselves a woman joined the company. She had just returned from her daily begging expediton. Taking from a wallet which was slung from her neck and dangled at her left side, a quantity of victuals, she flung the provisions scornfully on a bench which ran along one side of the room.

"What luck, Bess?—why, you look as sour as the devil's vinegar cruet," said one of the jolly beggars.

"Pox on the scran," exclaimed the woman, "it's not that I wanted, and yet I could get scarcely anything else to-day; this is all I could manage to pick up in the hard line," and she exhibited a handful of copper money.

"Where's the kid, Bess? you should try that lay again," said one of the revellers.

"Cuss it!" said the brutal woman, "'twas well enough once, but 'tis too healthy now; however, I shall blind the brat, and then 'twill be good for another six months at least."

"Do what, Bess?" asked Sims.

"Blind it—make it dark—don't you understand?" asked the she-fiend, with something like a sneer at the ignorance of the questioner, and she added—

"If the young imp was three or four years older it might sham blindness, but that it can't do now; and as I can't afford to wait and keep it for nothing I must manage its eye myself; besides, nothing takes better than a blind babby, 'specially if it's a pretty one like

Nelly. Nance! a glass of gin," and she flung on the table the price of the liquor.

Hawkins, inured as he was to deeds of violence, and indeed of blood, could not avoid shuddering at the shameless barbarity of Hell-fire Bess, for so was the heartless creature called. To brain a man in the exercise of the duties of his profession, if resistance made such a course necessary, he never would have hesitated; but to torture an innocent babe for the sake of gain appeared to him to be a proceeding of so hellish a nature that he considered Hell-fire Bess worthy of her diabolical nick-name.

Improbable as it may appear, such expedients as that to which the diabolical woman referred were then, and we believe still are resorted to in order to call forth the sympathies of the charitable and humane.

Glass after glass of gin was eagerly swallowed by Bess, until at length her face became perfectly demoniacal in its expression. Stting on a low stool she smoked a short pipe for some time, and then rising went up a creaking staircase to a room over head, from whence she almost immediately returned with a sleeping infant in her arms.

Resuming her seat, she laid the child on its back in her lap; the slumbering child was as she had just intimated very lovely; light golden tresses clustered around its marble brow, and a smile appeared to lurk around the half-parted lips. No greater contrast could possibly have been witnessed than that afforded by the countenances of the innocent little one, and that of its horrible nurse.

Drawing a bottle from her pocket which was half-filled with a dark-coloured fluid, she attracted the attention of the company towards it.

"There's that in this bottle which after a few weeks use of it, would make you all grope about in darkness, though the noonday sun was shining over head."

"How the devil did you procure it, Bess?" enquired the old one-eyed hag of the house.

"There's only one person living as can prepare it, and that is a woman who can tell the virtues of every plant that grows; some of you knows her—'tis Old Nan of the Common."

"The she devil," muttered Hawkins, "I know her too well."

Hell-fire Bess then withdrew the cork from the phial, and cautiously lifting the eyelid of the child, let a single drop of the liquor fall upon the delicate and sensitive organ of sight. Apparently no pain was produced, but a singular effect was immediately visible. The pupil of the child's eye became enlarged to more than double its size, and looked like a dull black circle with a narrow rim of blue around it. The other eye was subjected to the same experiment and similar effects produced.

"When this has been done about a dozen times, Nan of the Common tells me," said Hell-fire Bess, "that the child will be dark to the day of its death."

The vile woman was about to replace the phial in her pocket, when actuated by a sudden impulse for which he could not account, Hawkins snatched it from her and threw it into the midst of the blazing fire, the sudden heat of which burst the bottle, and irrecoverably destroyed the fatal contents.

Like an enraged tigress, the savage woman flung down the infant and sprang upon Hawkins, who, however, was on his guard. Grasping her arms, he prevented her doing him any mischief; but she fixed her malignant eyes on him, and poured forth a volley of oaths and fearful execrations.

"Ha!" she exclaimed, as she espied around Hawkins's wrist the remains of the handcuffs, which in the struggle had become exposed, "I see it all; this is the first time you have been here, and by G— you are the man who has just escaped from Newgate, and for whom the watch are now searching."

Scarcely had these startling words being uttered than the guant figure silently quitted the table, and glided softly towards the entrance of the room from the lane.

Sims observed his movements, and quick as lightning ran and placed himself with his back to the door; then drawing a pistol he swore he would shoot him or any one else who dared to quit the apartment.

"As for you, you sneaking villain, you would betray me to the watch, would you, for the sake of a few pieces as you have betrayed others? But be careful, the slightest alarm given by you shall, by G— be your death warrant."

And with tremendous force he hurled the hungry-looking man from him, and dashed him against the opposite wall. In the meantime the confusion in the room so greatly increased that Hawkins became alarmed for his own safety; and his apprehensions were materially increased when a loud knocking was heard at the door.

"Never mind, Hell-fire Bess, I'll soon quiet her," remarked Sims, and putting his mouth to the virago's ear, he whispered in it a few words which, as if by magic, arrested the current of her passion and dispelled his fury.

"Who told you that, Harry?" she asked as she stood pale and trembling.

"No matter," he replied, "it is sufficient that I am in possession of your secret; a secret which I will only keep on the condition that you do not betray, nor suffer any one to betray this man who has sought shelter among us."

The woman gave a nod of assent, and then Sims, seizing Hawkins by the arm led, or rather dragged him through a narrow passage which led into a small enclosed space at the back of the house.

"This is no place for you," said Sims in a low tone of voice, "for if those people who are knocking at the door are, as I suspect, on the look out for you we had better make our escape over this wall. Not one of the people you have just left can be trusted with the exception of Hell-fire Bess, who is too much in my power to act contrary to my wishes."

Following the example of Sims, Hawkins scaled the wall of the little yard, and the two, after making a wide circuit in order to avoid falling in with the persons at the front door, and threading a number of intricate alleys, arrived in safety at the water-side.

Fortunately, a waterman chanced to be on the spot. Hastily stepping into his boat they directed him to convey them across the river, and they were soon landed near the Surrey end of London Bridge.

Sims now conducted his companion down the Borough High-street, as far as St. Georges' Church; near the door of that edifice he suddenly stopped.

"Were you ever in the Old Mint?" he asked.

"Never," replied Hawkins. "Whitefriars has always been my sanctuary when in trouble, and to that convenient refuge I was making when I fell in with you."

"You will be safer where I shall take you," observed Sims, "follow me, and I will initiate you into the mysteries of the place.

Crossing the road, Sims led the way to an extremely narrow opening, directly opposite to the church. On the wall of this thoroughfare was a battered old board fastened with a few rusty nails, on which was painted in rudely formed letters the name of the place—THE MINT.

In the Borough High-street all was, at that early hour of the morning, comparatively quiet; but once within the precincts of the Old Mint the sounds of dissipation and the signs of business were plainly enough heard and seen. The taverns, for the most part deserted during the day, were now crammed with company, for the beggars and thieves who made the locality their regular residence, had returned from their predatory travellings through the streets of London, and having disposed of their plunder to the fences and Jews of the place, were now recklessly squandering their ill-gotten gains.

Avoiding the revellers in these taverns, Sims and Hawkins with some difficulty threaded their way through the narrow thoroughfare, the middle of which was entirely filled by articles of domestic furniture of the most heterogenous appearance. There were bedsteads with the posts sawn down to mere stumps; easy chairs without seats; rickety tables with hinges round their edges, indicating that at some remote period they had been endowed with pairs of wings; and second-hand furniture of all descriptions; furniture which had very venerable looks, and which had evidently ministered to the wants, and some of the articles to the luxuries of former generations.

Opposite each separate heap of goods, Hawkins perceived a little door, opening into a gloomy cavern beyond, a sort of charnel house, filled with filthy bones, rusty pieces of iron, and heaps of fœtid rags. These receptacles appeared generally to be in charge of toothless old hags, with mob-caps fastened to their heads by means of faded black ribband; the said mob-cap being most probably guiltless of soap suds. Without exception, these unearthly looking hags had, each of them, between her red half-raw gums, a discoloured and foul remnant of a pipe, in the top of which a live cinder was placed to keep the tobacco from going out.

"Here we are at last," said Sims, as he stopped in front of one of the oldest-looking houses Hawkins had yet noticed.

It was an ancient, dingy-looking, wooden fabric, which looked as though for centuries past it had been going through the process of sure but imperceptible decay. The beams, which crossed each other like gigantic network on the front of the house, were black with the smoke and dirt of centuries; the windows, most of them having substitutes in the shape of old rags for glass, creaked and rattled again as the hollow-sounding night blasts swept by or against the casements; and the tall, dark stacks of chimneys, high up, frowned over all, and looked as though a sturdy puff of wind would send them crashing through roof-tree and rafter into the apartments below.

"You will meet with strange company, Hawkins, in the place to which I am about to conduct you," said Sims.

"It will not be the first time I have dropped into queer quarters, and after the place I escaped from to-night, any crib will be welcome," was the remark of the escaped convict.

"Savage, however, as my comrades are, they may be relied upon," observed Sims, "and," he added, "before you join them, it would be as well that you should decide whether you will become a member of our company."

"What can I do, but either go on the road again, which will be rather a desperate step, or turn cracksman altogether, which perhaps is the safer of the two?" asked Hawkins.

"If you will be guided by me, you will not venture on either of the courses you have alluded to," said Sims.

"Had any one but Harry Sims made such a sage observation," said Hawkins, " I should have fancied he was about to propose that I should turn honest man."

"The company to which I belong," said Sims, " number among them neither highwaymen nor housebreakers. What say you, my Ben Cull, to a cruise with us on the water?"

"I do not exactly comprehend you," remarked Hawkins.

"This then is the fact," said Sims. " I am Lieutenant of the Black Gang—an extensive society, one branch of which meets nightly in a secret chamber of the house at whose door we stand. In short, Hawkins, we are River Pirates, and you could not do better than join us, for you are so celebrated on land, that not the keenest-nosed constable will imagine that you have taken to the water."

"True!" observed Hawkins. "Lead on, Sims; at present I can have no choice: and will gladly make one of your company."

The ground-floor of the house, in front of which this conversation had taken place, was fitted up as a chandler's shop; but this, of course, was a mere blind, for the wretched-looking, hoary old man who stood behind the miserable counter, dealt in other articles than those which met the eye of the stranger.

The real proprietor of the house was Mother Sin of the Westminster Almonry, but she had enough to do in her own neighbourhood, and never, except on special occasions, appeared in the Mint. The old shopman was a ruined paramour of hers who had once been rich—now, in his adversity, he acted as her receiver-general, and well did the hoary old villain discharge his infamous office.

PORTRAIT OF JENNY DIVER.

"Now then," said Sims, and he opened the little half door which separated the shop from the lane.

"A friend, Mr. Blite, a friend of mine, and who will be one of yours too—Are the lambs in the fold, eh?"

"All of them, Lieutenant, every one, and I believe there's business on hand—Walk in."

Mr. Blite led the way into a little back parlour, in the side of which, opposite the entrance, was a huge framed picture of a warrior on horseback.

Many a tale could that little back parlour have told had bricks and mortar been vocal, for in it was transacted all the business of the then most notorious receiver of stolen goods in the whole metropolis. But as with the main incidents of our story these secret affairs are not necessarily connected, we shall follow the footsteps of Hawkins and Sims.

The former of these advanced to the picture of the soldier just referred to, and touched a secret spring on one side of the frame.

The frame then easily turned upon hinges, and swinging back, a door behind it was seen. Taking from his breast a key, which was attached to a black ribband, and suspended from his neck, Sims opened it, and beckoned Hawkins to follow. An instant afterwards both men were in a dark passage, and the door behind them and the picture having been replaced, Hawkins drew from his pocket a whistle which on applying to his lips emitted a low and peculiar sound.

The house was divided, as nearly as possible, into two equal portions; one being employed as a sort of receptacle for pledges which a regular pawnbroker would not accept, for in those days the representatives of the Lombards were far less strict than they now are; pledges made by famishing and drunken wretches who would rather sell themselves than go without their accustomed stimulant. And in this part of the building might be seen, ranged in rows on narrow shelves, without any distinctive mark, except mayhap a red chalk mark in the shape of a St. Andrew's cross, bundles of wearing apparel, carpenter's tools, laundress's flat irons, and even scrubbing brushes. Probably in the whole collection there was not a single article worth more than half-a-crown, and certainly there was not a single miserable pledge on which more than sixpence had been

24

advanced; and for that sixpence, sixpence per week had been demanded. The unfortunate who failed to redeem the goods, or to pay the interest at the end of the week, inevitably forfeited his property.

The other portion of the house was situated at the back of that last described, and was the place appropriated for the reception of stolen property, the traffic in which was the staple trade of the establishment; the chandlers shop, as we have already intimated, being but a convenient place by means of which admittance to the mysterious interior could be gained.

Rotten and dilapidated as this old house of the Mint appeared to be externally, it was strong and cunningly constructed within. Every one of its thick, massive walls were hollow; every one of its heavy-looking mouldings concealed the edges of a sliding panel in the grim pannelling of each gloomy room. There was scarcely a stone which did not conceal a trap door leading to some well-hole, or secret closet, or dreary winding passage; the very spout—people called it a water-spout—which ran from the summit of the tenement to its cellar, served a useful purpose, for into it flowed from secret channels, when alarm was given portable articles, such as watches and packages of jewellery, which by means of an ingenious contrivance descended unnoticed into the subterranean recesses of the cellar; which cellar itself had a secret corner in which was situated a door unseen save to the initiated.

Besides the little back parlour which we have already mentioned, Mr. Blite had another, situated three or four rooms deep further on; but very few were admitted into that apartment.

There were strange stories circulated, and hints of a gloomy character dropped respecting that mysterious chamber. Those were not wanting who would have sworn that many who had been seen to enter its door had never been known to have emerged therefrom. Men who had had lucky adventures on the road, or in houses at midnight, and who were laden with valuables, had gone to the Old House in the Mint to dispose of their plunder to Old Blite, but had never more been heard of. Of course, inquiries were never made—searches never instituted; and therefore, after a little time, the missing men and women were thought no more of.

The reply to the summons of Sims was made by a hideous-looking negro woman, who, holding a light above her head, came out of the darkness, and addressed Sims by name.

" Is Captain Fresnean ready ?" he asked.

"Ready!" exclaimed the negress, rolling her eyes and showing her yellow fangs. " Look here, Massa Sims ?"

Sims looked through a small grating in a door in the side of the subterranean passage, and a sight met his eye which made his blood curdle.

On the floor of a sort of cell lay the corpse of a man, from a wound in the forehead a dark crimson line marked the course in which recently a stream of blood flowed. The brow of the deceased was rigid and fierce even in death, as though an evil spirit had stamped its own likeness on his forehead in his last moments, and until decay should obliterate it, fixed it there.

Sims flew at once to the side of the prostrate Fresnean, and lifted his head.

" How did this happen !" he inquired, eagerly.

" Here come Philip—he tell you all," was the reply of the negress,

At this juncture a tall, muscular man, habited as a sailor, joined them.

" Bad job this, Lieutenant Sims," he said, " but it can't be helped. Those who will run great risks must meet with strange crosses—and our poor Captain Fresnean has found out that."

" How happened this ?" demanded Sims.

"Come inside, and I'll tell you Lieutenant— but who have you brought with you ?" asked Philip.

" A friend," was the reply.

After some other questions had been put and answered, Hawkins expressed his desire to join the Black Gang, and for the purpose of his initiation he was conveyed to the private place of meeting of the River Pirates.

CHAPTER XXXIX.

THE HEAD QUARTERS OF THE BLACK GANG.— HAWKINS BECOMES A RIVER PIRATE, AND TAKES LESSONS IN HIS NEW LINE OF BUSINESS —THE LOT DRAWING.

CONVENIENTLY situated near to the river-side was the house in a subterranean chamber of which met a secret and daring body of men who were known among themselves, though but partially known to the public, as THE BLACK GANG.

As in the case of Captain M'Cleane's band of freebooters on the land, a regular confederacy was organised amongst these pirates of the river. Their full body numbered little short of a hundred men.

They were for the most part individuals who had committed mutinous acts and daring deeds on the high seas, for which some of them had been transported but had managed to escape ; of others, whose predatory habits and intimate acquaintance as long-shore men, with the localities on the river sides, and the best places of concealment for the purposes of safety or plunder ; and of desperadoes like Hawkins and Sims, whose deeds of blood and violence had rendered their persons too familiar to the authorities on land, to allow of their making their appearance in the streets or on the highway with any degree of safety.

The house into which Sims entered, was a dim, ancient building, the upper portion of which seemed ready to fall into the street—but rotten and dilapidated as it appeared, it was so strongly built that the blasts of wind which made houses not so frail-looking as itself, to shake and totter again, had no effect on this other one than to whistle mournfully and drearily through the crannies and creaking casements, causing sounds as if a legion of evil spirits were within.

Indeed, there were not wanting those who declared with shuddering, that strange forms had been seen at the midnight hour at the windows, and that awful noises had been heard, as though heavy chains had been dragged down flights of stairs, and trailed along floors. Wild and unearthly shrieks, too, issued at times from the ancient dwelling, so that it is not to be wondered that its appearance was sombre and melancholy, and its interior all but deserted.

All but the huge underground apartment, in which the Black Gang held their midnight meetings.

Formerly, a monastic establishment had existed so near the Old House, that the secret passages which were common enough in buildings of that description, and which remained unclosed when the monastery itself was razed to the ground, were by a little adroit management easily made available for the purposes of the river pirates, by whom the existence of the subterranean labyrinth was accidentally discovered.

In one of their adventures, they had, it seems, after committing a daring robbery on board a ship in the pool, been closely chased by the boats of some Custom House officers, and, by chance, during the darkness, entered a tunnel-like opening, into which, at high tide, a few feet of water frequently flowed. About ten feet from its entrance, they found a very singularly constructed iron gateway, which, after much trouble they forced open, and within it concealed the booty they had just possessed themselves of.

Fortunately for them, the darkness prevented the Custom House officers from noticing them entering this place of refuge, which the pirates, foreseeing how useful it might in future be to them, determined to explore, for, however much it might merely resemble the opening of a sewer from the water, the structure of the masonry and of the gate just referred to, convinced them that it had been excavated for secret purposes.

A company of the most ingenious of their gang, thereupon were deputed to follow, if possible, the winding way, and, if possible, ascertain whither it led. This expedition was conducted with the greatest secrecy, and it was followed by entire success, for after traversing a long distance and encountering no branching-off passages, they came to another iron grate which also they forced, and a little beyond this a flight of stone steps terminated the secret way, and after mounting these a little way, their progress was finally impeded by a trap door, through the shrunken chinks of which they could distinctly see, by the aid of their torches, that the apartment into which it opened was uninhabited.

This was welcome information, and the door was soon burst open. The river pirates then found themselves in a huge ancient room, or rather hall, for it was of considerable dimensions. Its roof was low, and groined its arch-like form, and the absence of windows clearly shewing that it was beneath the level of the ground. Indeed, ever since they had left the river, they had been sensible of a gradual descent, and the stone staircase was short.

The main point now, was to ascertain in what part of Southwark they were. They therefore left the hall, and ascended a long flight of stone winding steps, which led them into an apartment, which in former times appeared to have formed the refectory or buttery of some large mansion. There were several windows in its sides secured by shutters, now covered with cobwebs; and a door, thick and massive, studded with huge headed iron nails, and set in a low and narrow stone archway.

Carefully removing a window shutter, for too much noise might have been made in forcing open the door, one of the gang looked through the grating of the window, and looking upward, saw the tower of St. George's Church soaring high above the many-gabled roofs of the houses. This landmark informed them of their whereabouts, and the leader of the party having filed away the bars of the window gained access to the dilapidated and deserted garden without, into which he easily descended, it being but a few feet beneath the stone sill of the window.

A little examination now led to the discovery that the house they had entered was situated in the Old Mint, and contained no living creatures save rats and mice, who harboured there by thousands, and would perhaps have numbered millions, had it not been from the circumstance that these loathsome creatures, in the absence of other food, lived principally on their own offspring and on the bodies of their weaker companions, whom they despatched as soon as they had lost the strength necessary to secure their preservation.

On a report of these discoveries being made to the full gang, it was determined that possession of the house itself should be secured, in order that they might establish it as their head quarters. This, by means of artful representation, which it is not necessary should be here particularised, was effected and an old pirate and his wife installed in the shop which formed a portion of its front in the Mint, for the sale of common articles so as to prevent suspicion, while the upper rooms were kept closed as before.

Having thus far explained the locality of the house and a portion of its internal construction, matters necessary to be known in order that what follows may be thoroughly comprehended, we will now follow Sims, Fresnean, Hawkins, and the negress into the hall, now no longer deserted and dreary, but filled with members of the formidable Black Gang.

These men, dark, violent-looking fellows—every one of them habited in the garb of a sailor, were seated at the sides of two long tables which ran parallel to each other along the whole length of the hall, and were connected at their upper ends by a cross table, behind the centre of which was a raised chair, seemingly and indeed appropriated to the chief of the Black Gang.

From the groined ceiling of the vaulted arch swung, by iron chains, large lamps, whose large wicks had completely blackened the roof and the upper portions of the sides and ends of the walls, and these lights threw a wild glare on the bronzed and whiskered countenances of the men below, most of whom seemed approaching a state of maudlin intoxication when Hawkins and the others made their appearance.

The walls all round the place were completely covered with weapons, so placed that every man could, in case of necessity, instantly grasp his own pistol and cutlasses. None of the men had arms on their persons, for so frequently had murders of a frightful character been committed in their drunken debauches, that a strict law had been passed on the subject—and so stringent were the regulations on this subject, that in a moment after Hawkins's entrance, and before a word was addressed to him, a man stepped forward and formally demanded his trusty crowbar, from which he had never parted, and which he now held in his hand.

The escaped convict on hearing the demand looked at Sims as though he imagined treachery was intended.

"Fear nothing," said the latter, "it is one of our laws which cannot be broken; you'll be as safe as I am," and Sims, as he spoke, placed his own sword and pistols in the hand of the person deputed to receive them.

Hawkins then followed his example, and stood unarmed and defenceless in the presence of the gang.

"Our comrade, Sims, has introduced a friend, who wishes to become one of us, Captain," said Philip Fresnean, approaching the Captain.

"Let him advance: he is welcome if he brings with him a stout frame and a daring heart," observed the head of the Black Gang.

Fresnean led the new comer forward.

The head of the gang rose, in order, apparently, that he might the better survey the candidate. He was a man of extraordinary height, standing full seven feet high, and being also of herculean proportions. His face had once being handsome, and even now it was not without some pretensions to good looks; but it had been bronzed by many a years exposure to sun and wind in all climates; and deep gashes here and there told of bloody conflicts and hair breadth escapes.

He wore a huge shaggy coat, confined at the waist by a belt, in which, as a symbol of his authority, was stuck a keen Italian Stiletto, highly ornamented at the hilt; and also a pair of small double barrelled pistols.

What the real name of the worthy was was unknown to any of the persons who acted under his directions; but from his desperate hardihood and unmitigated ferocity he had received the name of Captain Fury, which cognomen alone was known to the members of the Black Gang, and by the masters and crew of vessels frequenting the Thames, to whom, indeed, it was a name of fear.

"If by the words you have just made use of," said Hawkins, addressing Captain Fury, "you mean to ask whether I am daring enough to join in any enterprize you may command me to undertake, I have only to say that I have since last night accomplished a task which I challenge any man here to surpass."

And, as he spoke, he bared his wrists and ancles, and exhibited the massive rings from which he had so recently filed off his fetters.

"At eight o'clock," he resumed, "I was confined in one of Newgate's strong rooms—damn them! with hundreds of pounds weight of iron dangling from arms and legs; and with the aid only of a sharp file and that crowbar I burst three roofs, not the easiest work though, I can tell you scaled high walls, gained the street, and here I am."

"Bravo!" shouted a score of rough voices, and a dozen hands were stretched out to grasp that of the escaped convict.

Drink, too, was pressed upon him, and he partook liberally of strong spirits, many kegs of which were piled up against the sides of the hall; for it should be remarked that Captain Fury, to his profession of pirate added whenever opportunity offered that of smuggler also.

"Such as you are always welcome to me and my bold companions. You are willing, do you say, to become one of us?" asked Captain Fury.

"I am—nay, I feel anxious to join you," was Hawkins's reply.

"What say you, comrades, you have heard what the man has said. Are you of opinion that he may be admitted into our society," asked the Captain.

"We are—all! was the deep toned response of the gang.

"Then let the ceremonies of initiation be at once proceeded with," said Captain Fury.

Immediately on this order being given a semicircle was formed between the two parallel tables; the said semi-circle consisting of the oldest members of the gang. Captain Fury still retained his seat.

A large goblet nearly filled with red wine was brought and placed on a low stool; on either side of this were laid a dagger, a phial of deadly poison, a halter, a loaded pistol, and hideous looking human skulls, from which the hair had not yet all fallen away and which had an earthy and charnel like odour.

All the lights in the hall excepting the one which hung immediately over the low stool, and the fearful things placed thereupon, were then extinguished, and the red light now glaring on the instruments of death and on the grinning skull produced a fearful effect!

One of the gang, who had a rude lancet in his hand then commanded Hawkins to bare his left arm. This having been done he was made to kneel down, and the lancet having made an incison into one of the small veins at the bend of the elbow, the blood which streamed from the orifice was suffered to fall into the wine goblet, and when about a sixth part of pint had issued, the flow was stopped and the slight wound bandaged up.

"Lieutenant, administer the oath!" commanded Captain Fury.

Fresnean now requested Hawkins to repeat after him—

"I hereby, in the presence of God, man and devil, bind myself to serve as a free-trader in this gang. To obey my captain in all his commands, whether at the peril of my life or otherwise: to keep faithfully all his secrets, and never to betray those with whom I am associated. Also, to guard against all treachery; in the performance of my duties to spare neither friend or foe—young or old—man woman or child; and if guilty of traitorhood to agree to take my choice of halter, poison or dagger, and never until death to quit the Black Gang."

As soon as Hawkins repeated the words of this oath the goblet of mixed wine and blood was handed him, he was ordered to drink to the dregs the fearful mixture. The cord, the poison and the dagger were then exhibited to him; the halter being dropped over his neck, the poison phial placed to his lips, and the dagger's point placed to his breast. His hands also during the speaking of these words were placed on the hideous relic of mortality.

It was the head of a former member of the gang; pointing to it, Captain Fury informed Hawkins that the crime of which the man to whom it once belonged had been guilty had been a violation of his oath, and that his skull would be so used should he be guilty of a similar offence.

Fury then quitted his chair, advanced to the spot where Hawkins was still kneeling, and extending to him his hand exclaimed—

"Rise, John Hawkins, you are now fully admitted to all our privileges and subjected to all penalties. In the name of our company I hail you a free brother."

A loud cheer was now given, and successively every member of the gang grasped the hand of the new member in token of amity.

He was then instructed in the private signs, and passwords used by the fraternity, and now the whole of the initiatory ceremonies having concluded, Hawkins took his seat with the rest of his brethren, when his health was heartily drank and wishes for his prosperity expressed.

A scene of boisterous merriment ensued, during which Hawkins succeeded, with the assistance of a comrade, in getting rid of the fetters which still galled his wrists and ancles; and being now thoroughly tired out, he requested and obtained permission to retire for the night.

And soundly indeed did he repose when he did lose consciousness, for his first slumbers were broken and disturbed by fearful dreams of the hangman, the scaffold, and the ignominious death from which he had so miraculously escaped. It was broad noon next day when he awoke, and as he first surveyed the sides of his chamber he could not at once remember where he was, and thought he was still dreaming; but by degrees a full consciousness of his recent escape from the dismal condemned cell, and his present comparatively happy position dawned upon his mind, and leaping from his rude couch, he dressed himself and found his way to the hall where he played so extraordinary a part some few hours previously.

But few of the gang were present, the greater number of them having disguised themselves and departed in different directions for the purpose of gathering information, or of making observations which might aid them in the prosecution of their nefarious designs.

Having devoured a hearty meal, one of the Black Gang present gave him some instructions respecting their operations, a task of no great difficulty to be mastered by Hawkins, he having in early life been apprenticed to a ship trading between London and the Hague. On account of his wild and disolate habits he could be done nothing with on board, and he escaped long before his period of servitude had expired, and had had taken to the road.

One after another in the course of the evening the river pirates dropped in, and at length arrived Captain Fury himself. Immediately on their chief's making his appearance a shout of welcome greeted him; and a rude but substantial dinner, consisting almost exclusively of provisions which had been plundered from ships, dockyards, and from warehouses along the river side was partaken of. These viands were washed down by repeated draughts of liquor, and the mouth was beginning to grow 'fast and furious,' when at a signal from the Captain, every horn was ceased to be refilled, and he thus spoke—

"Comrades! I have news for you; but first let me hear the several reports of the scouts who have been abroad to-day, and then we will decide on the expedition for the evening."

"I have ascertained," said a short, thick set fellow, who had a most sinister expression of countenance, "that a Dutch galliot will come to an anchor off Purfleet to-morrow night."

"What is her cargo, know you that, Ben Trapper?" demanded Captain Fury.

"Spices and silk goods principally, with a goodly amount of provisions," replied Ben.

"Of provisions we have at present more than enough for some time to come; and as for spices and silks they are things we cannot use ourselves and should run too much risk in disposing of them. The Dutchman may be left alone."

"I hear," remarked a fellow called Will Devilskin, "that a large ship richly laden from the Indies is at Gravesend, and will come up with to-night's tide, and lie till morning off Greenwich or in Deptford Creek; but they say her crew is numerous—"

"And well armed no doubt," interposed Captain Fury. "I fear the risk would be too great to allow of us attacking her, so she must even follow the Dutchman."

The other members of the Black Gang who had been on the look-out then made their several reports; but some objection or other seemed to attach to all of them; for it was Fury's great object to run but little risk, as in so limited a place as their field of action—the river, it was absolutely necessary that their robberies should be effected with the utmost secrecy, and their retreats so managed as not to afford the slightest cue to their stronghold.

When all the rest had spoken, Captain Fury rose, and a respectful silence prevailed.

"I told you lads," said he, "that I had good news. All of you know that while we are overstocked with articles for the inside of our bellies, we are cursedly short of the yellow stuff which makes a capital lining for our pockets. Now I have just learned that this very night a small vessel richly laden with dollars, moidores, and such like glittering articles from the Spanish Main, will come up the river, and lie off Wapping stairs until morning."

A gleam of ferocious joy brightened the countenances of the buccaneers as they heard this, and as if by a common impulse they rose from their seats and gave three hearty cheers.

"But," resumed Captain Fury, "the gold and silver, and there is plenty of both, will be hard to get at, nevertheless, brave men may accomplish a good deal."

"Only lead us on, Captain," exclaimed the desperadoes, "and we'll fight like devils for such a prize."

"No—there must be no fighting; that is, if it can possibly be avoided; the thing must be managed quietly, for the flash and report of a pistol would be certain ruin to us. But it will will be time, comrades, to consider our plans when we have drawn lots for those who are to take part in the enterprise."

A number of bullets were then placed in a canvass bag, twelve of them being marked with a knife, so as to be distinguished from the others by sight, though not by touch, the whole number of bullets corresponded with the number of the gang present.

Then each man put his hand in the bag, and drew forth a single bullet, and Hawkins happened to be among those who drew marked ones, and consequently formed one of the band who were to attempt the plunder of the Spanish ship.

CHAPTER XL.

THE FOX MAY RUN LONG, YET HE MAY BE CAUGHT AT LAST—JENNY DIVER GETS INTO TROUBLE, AND TAKES A VOYAGE AT THE PUBLIC EXPENSE—HOW SHE RETURNS HOME, AND WHAT SHE DID THERE.

AFTER a short interview with Flitchman, in the house of Mother Sin, in the Almonry, he returned to the shop of the vintners in Fetter-lane according to his appointment, with Jenny Diver, and found the letter there awaiting him.

A perfect reconciliation had now taken place between the Captain and his mistress, and the letter was therefore somewhat disturbed at the troubled countenance of M'Cleane.

"Why what in heaven's name is the matter with you, Jem ?" asked the girl, who missed his caresses.

"A triffle, Jenny, a mere triffle—but the fact is I have been compelled to do that which my heart recoils from, but under circumstances which left me no choice to do otherwise—lend me your handkerchief, I have lost mine."

The girl did as he requested. M'Cleane then went to the door of the room, carefully locked it, and then returning, drew his rapier from his sheath—it was stained with blood !

"M'Cleane, my God, more bloodshed," exclaimed the Diver. "How is it, Jem, that you cannot manage matters more pleasantly, as I do ? But what have you been trawling with now ?"

"I have sent one to his account who would have hanged me had I not done so, he replied, as he carefully kissed his weapon. The old fellow knew me, and swore to send me to Tyburn, so I finished him."

"And his body ?" asked the girl.

"Is rotting in a sewer by this time, half eaten by rats, perchance, before now," he replied.

Having thoroughly cleaned his rapier from the fearful stains of human gore, he returned the hankerchief to Jenny, who shrinking almost from its contact, threw it into the fire, where it was instantly consumed.

"Fire tells no tales, Jem," said she. "Come, let us be going, but first see the wages of my day's work, and exhibiting the fifteen guineas, she somewhat amazed and restored the drooping spirits of M'Cleane, by detailing her adventure, in company with Tristam Savage, with Doctor Trotter the astrologer, of Moorfields.

M'Cleane also produced the notes which he had taken from the waggish old gentleman at Mother Sin's, but to his chagrin he found them on examination to be only bank post bills, payable only to the person from whom he had taken them, and in consequence perfectly useless to himself. Cursing his luck, he was about to throw them into the fire when Jenny Diver prevented him, and intimated that by means of a slight alteration, they might be passed off to the jews, who well enough knew how to get rid of such matters.

As soon as evening set in, the pair returned to the country house at Highgate, but the fraternity had now become so notorious a pest to all the neighbours round London, that M'Cleane and his gang were compelled to pursue for the present, an extremely curious line of proceeding.

Besides, what weighed heavily on the mind and spirits of M'Cleane was the capture of Hawkins, who, for all he knew, might betray them. When the news of his condemnation reached him, his apprehension was seriously increased, and what course to pursue in order to ensure safety, he knew not,

Several days after his return with Jenny, to the country house, from which he had not stirred out. Beauty Ellis entered with a peculiar grin of delight in his ugly countenace.

"Cheer-up, Captain, cheer-up," said Beauty, observing the distressed countenance of M'Cleane.

"What game's in the wind now, then ?" asked the Captain, "it must be something remarkably tempting to induce me to move from here to night."

"Need'nt stir a peg, but stay where you are, with pretty Mistress Jenny, and care for nobody, it's all right."

"What do you mean ?" asked M'Cleane.

"Glorious news ! that man who's just come from London has told us in the kitchen. Lord ! lord ! how little the bloak thought it was the best tidings I'd heard for many a day."

And Beauty Ellis, rubbed his hands, with an expression of supreme satisfaction as he added :—

"You'd give me fine guineas to known it, that you would, Capt'n."

"And it proves worth the money, five guineas you shall have," said M'Cleane. "Speak out man. Has Hawkins been hanged without wagging his tongue ?"

"No, it's better than that, better a good deal," said Beauty.

M'Cleane thought within himself nothing could have pleased him more : but at all events, Beauty Ellis had something good to tell, for he was not one of those who proceeded upon slight grounds, or was easily elated.

"Here, Beauty," he at length said, somewhat impatiently. "Out with your news, man, and here is a bumper to moisten your tongue, speak."

"Well then, noble Capt'n. Hawkins has broke prison, like a bold fellow as I always said he was, and he has'nt peached on one of us," said Ellis.

"Thank God," exclaimed M'Cleane, and a heavy weight was at once removed from his heart.

"He's got clean out from the condemned cell, and no tidings can be heard of him, Capt'n. All London, they say, is wondering at the daring deed."

"Well they may," remarked M'Cleane, "I thought no one but that young rascal, Jack Sheppard, could have accomplished such a fact. But are you sure the news is correct ?"

"Certain," replied Beauty Ellis, "for, besides the man who told, there was another in the tavern kitchen who had one of the sheriffs' bills offering a reward for his capture."

"There, then," said M'Cleane, "take them," and he placed five gold pieces in Ellis's hands, and Beauty, with intense satisfaction pocketed them, and then retired to the hostelry kitchen, there to pick up any other information on the subject, in the hope, doubtless of a further reward.

Jenny Diver, unlike M'Cleane, paid her daily visits to London, and seldom failed to return laden with plunder. She was, now, however compelled to resort to other modes of swindling, for her frequent appearance in the parks and at the various churches, as a pregnant woman, had attracted suspicion towards her; and her person began to attract rather inconvenient attention at the theatres.

Her scheme too for the robbery of private houses, and of credulous gentlemen had got wind, so that for the present, at least, and until the recollection of her deeds should blow over, she was frequently compelled to resort more to chance than cunning for her successes.

Jenny was one day walking in Drury-lane, on the look out for some one on whom to exercise her dexterity, when she observed a richly-dressed gentleman approaching her, a great number of persons were passing at the time, and just at the moment of the gentleman's passing her, she resorted to one of her old tricks, in an ungarded moment, and pretending to be seized with a fainting fit, staggered and fell on the footpath.

The gentleman perceiving her to be attired like a wife of the higher class of tradesmen, instantly flew to her assistance, and assisted her into a shop at hand, where a glass of water was procured. Politely apologizing to her intended victim for the freedom taken, and for trouble she gave, she begged him to see her to a hackney coach, which he professed his willingness to do, and offered her his arm, on which she leant rather heavily, as if feeling great weakness. So well did Jenny improve her opportunity that she succeeded in taking from the good man's waistcoat pocket a gold snuff-box, set with diamonds, and it was unmissed by him until a moment after he had handed her into the vehicle, and it had driven off.

Instantly it flashed upon his mind that he had heard of other robberies being committed under similar circumstances, and he doubted not but that he had been robbed by the celebrated female who had with so much dexterity hitherto contracted to baffle detection.

A hue and cry was instantly raised, and as hackney coaches on those days travelled at an exceeding slow rate, the one in which our heroine had taken refuge was speedily overtaken and stopped.

A constable was immediately sent for from Bow-street, and presently panting and puffing with fat and importance, who should arrive in obedience to the summons, but our old friend Mr. Watkins, the runner, who had an exceedingly keen nose for a thief, and who was as famous in his day, as Townshend and Leadbetter a few years ago, and as many of the detective police of the metropolis are in our own times.

So often had Jenny's face and person been described to Mr. Watkins, by parties who had been robbed, and by the traitor Blackmoor, during the negociation of the latter with the Bow-street runner, that the sharpe-eyed officer of justice saw at a glance that our fair whom he had been long and anxiously on the look out for was at last placed, by mere chance, within his grasp.

Jenny's usual self-confidence did not, however, desert her even on this awkward occasion.

Affecting to be highly indignant at the charge made against her, she uttered threats of legal pro-ceedings against those who had dared to stop her on the King's Highway; and even went so far as to insinuate that the object of the assault on her, as she called it, was to extort money from her through threats of prosecution on an unfounded charge; a practice by no means uncommon at that time; finding at length that all these threats failed to produce the effects she desired, she tried what persuasion would do, promising, herself, to call on the magistrates, after she had had an interview with her solicitor; and finding the proposition not being entertained for a moment, she availed herself of a woman's last resource in difficulty and delicate circumstances, and burst into a well managed flood of hysterical tears.

The tears of a pretty woman have put many a man off his guard when all the previous wiles, and seductive blandishments of his charmer have failed to touch his obdurate heart. Every body who has seen anything of "life" as it is called, must have it one time or another, have found out this. But there are exceptions to every rule, and there are men, who would not give up a point, even if their wives or sweethearts (in the case of the latter the struggle would be more difficult than in that of the former) were to become second Niobe's, and completely dissolve, flesh, blood, bones, beauty and all, into showers of tears.

The plundered gentleman himself, when he saw Jenny Diver's distress, somewhat relented, and tried to persuade himself that one so fair must of necessity be honest.

"I may after all have lost it," he said to the Bow-street runner, "and God forbid that I should charge an innocent lady with being a pickpocket. Perhaps she had better be suffered to go, for I can't swear she robbed me."

But alas! for the hardness and unbelief of those individuals whose business it is to catch and cage delinquents! The tears and sobs of Diver had not the slightest effect on the mind of Mr. Watkins. The girl might as well have appealed to the stones beneath her. As for the remark of the gentleman, the Bow-street runner expressed his opinion of it by thrusting rather contemptuously his tongue into the hollow of his cheek, and winking his right eye.

"Ah! master you do'nt know so much of the young woman as I do," said Watkins, "and I'll convince you of the truth of what I say, if you'll step into the coach, and come with me and the beauty to Bow-street office."

The gentleman, who was rather an undecided and weak minded, though amiable man enough, as it would seem, still hesitated, when Watkins who saw that he should, perhaps, loss a chance, observed:—

"If you wish to recover your snuff-box come with us, for I'll warrant the girl has it concealed about her."

The appeal to his breeches pocket decided the wavering man, and following Watkins, he entered the coach, which by the direction of the Bow-street runner, was driven to the justice room hard by.

The prisoners was conducted into a private room, and committed by Watkins to the charge of one of the most horrible specimens of woman-kind that could be imagined.

She was a female of about forty years of age, but her constant occupation of searcher of female prisoners, had furrowed her face with hard and harsh lines, until her aspect was most forbidding. The nature of her office had long ago deprived her of almost every trace of feeling, but she was not quite so dead to it as not to exhibit at least a show of it when her palm was covered with a broad piece of coin. But when no such bribe was bestowed, she executed the duties of her office with the utmost harshness. In figure she was tall and skinny, and her face and bony arms were frightfully scarred with the small pox.

"Mistress Varlup just sarch this young woman, and mind you she's a precious deep 'un. I almost wish I had the job myself," said Watkins, with a leer as he retired.

As soon as the constable had vanished, Jenny drew herself up to her full height, and proudly confronted the repulsive Mrs. Varlup.

"Hoity-toity—my fine lady ! that wont do here I can tell you; so let's have none of your airs and graces. Come, just let me help you to take off those fine furbelows of yours?"

"What mean you, woman, that I must remove my attire?" asked Jenny, with a contemptuous look.

"Woman, quotha ! who do you call woman, I'd have you know that Dorothy Varlup is as good as any cut-purse of them all, and a little better too for the matter of that. So no more fantastic fooleries—strip, I say."

Jenny still hesitated, and still stood with flashing eyes and lips compressed.

Perceiving her harsh commands the woman flew upon her like a tigeress, and seizing her hat tore it from her head and threw it disdainfully on the floor.

Weak as Mrs. Varlup looked she nevertheless possessed immense strength—every muscle was like a bundle of wires, and Jenny feeling herself to be like a mere lamb in the grip of a lioness, thought it wiser to try what pacific means would do.

With this intention she took out her purse and taking from it a guinea, placed it in Mrs. Varlup's horny palm.

"That is summut like reason," remarked the woman, "I'm civil enough, if people will only behave themselves—here, give me that purse," and snatching it from Jenny, she placed it in the searcher's cupboard.

"Return that—it is my own," demanded the girl.

"If it is you'll soon have it again," was Mrs. Varlup's sole reply.

Mrs. Varlup then commanded Jenny to remove from her person every article of dress, and as very unwillingly the girl did so, she examined each with the strictest minutensss to see if any stolen property was concealed in any of them. First the hat was looked into, then the outer dress was rummaged, then the quilted petticoat underwent examination, and now Jenny stood in her boddice, her breasts panting and fully exposed to view.

"That surely will do," said Jenny.

"No ; your boddice must be unlaced," this was done, and the article was removed, and the flannel petticoat next was loosened, and Jenny appeared in nothing but her chemise, which scarcely concealed her plump limbs.

Still nothing had been found, and the Diver was congratulating herself, when the searcher just lifting the border of her chemise so as to expose the upper portion of her stocking, thought she noticed something between the inner part of the lower portion of the young girls thigh and the silken hose.

Clapping one hand on the part, she insinuated the other between the soft silk and the yct softer flesh, and drew forth a gold snuff-box set with diamonds, for Jenny had small pockets made in the upper part of each stocking in which watches, trinkets, and such things could easily be hidden.

"You keep your pouncet box in rather an odd place, Madame," observed Mrs. Varlup, with a sneer.

"The whole of the money in that purse shall be yours, if you will let me go," said Jenny, now in real distress.

"No, Mrs. Varlup honest woman ! wouldn't hear of such a thing as allowing a cut-purse to escape," but she took privately while Jenny was dressing herself, five or six gold pieces from the purse and transferred them to a secret place of her own.

As soon as Jenny was attired, Mrs. Varlup called in Mr. Watkins, and delivered to him the half-emptied purse and snuff box, with the particulars of the place where she found the other.

"Well, now who'd ha' thought of looking for a sneezing case in such a werry curious place Really it hurts my feelings to take such a clever creature as you are afore a beak; but dooty must be done. Come along, Jenny, you sees I knows one of your names."

The girl was immediately led into the presence of the magistrate who was then sitting and Jenny Diver was committed to Newgate for trial on a charge of felony.

*   *   *   *

Never had the Court of the Old Bailey been crowded with such an assemblage of persons of all ranks, as on a certain day about two months after the scene in Drury Lane.

Not only the little gallery allotted to the use of strangers, but the body of the court from which little could be seen and less heard, but the spaces behind the jury boxes; the seats appropriated to the men of law, the deep window spaces, and even those portions of the bench not occupied by the judge himself, were thronged with curious folks, who were intensely eager to see one whose name and exploits had so often been the themes of wonder and in some cases almost of admiration.

As yet, the bar, on the ledge of which was strewed sweet smelling herbs, and over which was placed transverseley a looking-glass, so disposed as to reflect a broad light on the countenance of a prisoner under trial, was empty; but all eyes were strained in that direction.

It was the day appointed for the trial of the celebrated Jenny Diver.

A blast of trumpets announced the arrival of the Recorder of London, who, immediately after it had subsided, took his seat on the bench.

The usual preliminaries having been gone through, the Governor of Newgate placed Jenny Diver alias Mary Young to be placed at the bar, and curiosity was then at its highest pitch.

Jenny advanced to the front of the bar, and

PORTRAIT OF DICK FLYBYNIGHT.

She was then indicted and pleaded Not Guilty; and the case which was so simple in its details proceeded. Not the shadow of a doubt could exist on the minds of the jury as to the matter, and without a moments hesitation they returned a verdict of 'Guilty.'

Jenny knew that it was in vain to protest her innocence, she, therefore, assumed an air of penitence and threw herself on the mercy of the court, which sentenced her to seven years transportation.

Ever scheming, she, now that her removal from the country was certain, employed the property she was possessed of, and which was faithfully conveyed to her by M'Cleane, in the purchase of stolen effects. At that time the transportation system was far different to what it is now, and convicted persons sent to the American Colonies were allowed to be at perfect liberty when they got there if they paid a certain sum,

No. 25.

and were also permitted to take what goods they chose with them.

So industrious was our heroine that when she went on board the transport vessel, (after an affectionate parting with M'Cleane) she shipped a quantity of goods, nearly sufficient to load a waggon. The possession of this property secured her great respect—property generally does that—and during the voyage she enjoyed every possible convenience and accommodation. At length the vessel reached Virginia, where she disposed of her wares to good advantage, and having assumed a new name set up an establishment and lived in the first style of fashion.

Her wealth was speedily diminished, and in the course of a very few weeks, finding that with all her art she could not turn her talent to account in America she determined as soon as possible to return to England at any risk; and this resolution once formed she set about contriving the mode of carrying it into effect.

Among the circle of her Virginian acquaintance was a young gentleman who was about to embark for England, and now she exercised her arts with such effect that the young fellow became speedily enamoured of her, and consented to take her with him to London.

Secretly embarking, she gained the vessel in safety, and after a favourable voyage the ship came to an anchor off Gravesend; and now Jenny, who had grown tired of her swain after he had answered her purpose, determined to abscond.

Feigning indisposition, she declined accompanying the young man to London in the captain's boat, the latter wishing to deliver his papers to to his owners before the ship itself sailed up the river to the dock; but she expressed a desire to go on shore at Gravesend and procure medical assistance, and permission to do so was granted her by her lover, who promised to return to the vessel with the captain in the evening.

No sooner, however, had her protector left the ship than she transferred from his trunks to her own every article of value he possessed; and calling a boat she had her boxes lowered into it and was soon put ashore.

Once landed she knew well where to go to, for Gravesend then abounded with crumps, fences, and houses of bad repute. To one of these infamous receptacles she had her goods carried, and then she sent for a Dutchman with whom she had had frequent dealings in the course of her iniquitous career.

"Vy, Mishtress Jenny, mein Gott! who vas haf thought of seeing dat purty face of yourn, mein tear?" said Mynheer Von Tenbroek, lifting up his hands in unaffected surprise.

"Not you nor any one on this side of the water, I warrant me," replied Jenny; "but you see I didn't much like being away from my old friends, so I took French leave of the colonists and here I am."

"Ver goot, mein dear, vell now you come pack did you pring any pargains mit you? Ah! you vicked puss, yesh, vat a fool I vas to ask dat of a cleversh girl as you are," observed Mynheer Van Tenbroeh, in a persuasive tone.

"Yes—and I must have good prices, Mynheer, or you and I shant deal again. See here," said the Diver.

Mynheer Von Tenboeh examined the articles which Jenny had surreptitiously obtained, and by a series of the most cunning questions elucidated from her the manner in which she had obtained them.

"Vy, dey aint worth ver moch, and monish is dam scarce, mein Gott, tish pad times," exclaimed the Dutch Fence, "and dare ish so mosh risk too."

After much chaffering the Dutchman offered Jenny a price so much below that she had fixed upon as the lowest she would take, that she flatly refused to let them go and intimated her intention of taking them with her to London.

"You couldn't do it, mein tear," coolly observed Tenbroeh.

"Why not?" asked Jenny.

"Because der ish a whole posse of constables, and scores of the city train bands down in dish place searching for some river pirates, and if you vas seen mit sich poxes as dese dey might pounce on you."

"But I'm not a river pirate," said the girl.

"No; but you're vat is vorse, mein tear—a returned transport, mein tear—and if they caught you perhaps, dey vould squeeze dat purty neck of yours. Oh! mein Got dat vould be pad."

Jenny thought so too, and considering, moreover, that she was completely in the power of the fence, who, with perfect safety to himself, might where he so disposed secure the goods and hand her over to the authorities, she at once closed with him though at a considerable sacrifice, and received sixty guineas, for what was at the least worth, even in such a market, two hundred.

This accomplished, she purchased a small trunk, and bundling into it a little wearing apparel, she travelled to London inside a stage waggon, and at midnight, with about a hundred guineas in her pocket entered once more the mighty metropolis, there to commence anew her career of crime.

———

CHAPTER XLI.

WHICH IS FULL OF MYSTERY—MR. DOOM IN A NEW SPHERE OF LIFE ASSISTS JONATHAN WILD—PLOTTING AND PLOTTEES—DICK FLYBYNIGHT MEETS THE MYSTERIOUS STRANGER OF ISLINGTON—HANDSOME JACK MAKES A RESOLVE — A FLEET PARSON AND HIS VICARAGE.

WE must now retrace our steps, for so many are the scenes and characters which are connected with the incidents of our tale; and so sudden and frequent are the changes in the condition of the latter, that it would be absolutely impossible to maintain anything like consecutiveness. It will be our object, however, to be as lucid as may be, so that from a seeming complexity of narrative an harmonious whole may be produced.

The reader must now accompany us to an apartment, in a low, ill-looking habitation in the immediate neighbourhood of the Fleet prison.

The house was one of a class which has long since been swept away by the besom of improvement, and the strange scenes which were formerly enacted in it are now looked upon as almost belonging to the chronicles of romance alone. Nevertheless facts they were, and the perambulator of London who now travels through Faringdon-street, hears no longer the invitations which formerly resounded there.

At the summit of the first flight of a creaking staircase was an apartment whose walls and windows were begrimed with the smoke and dirt of years; in one corner of it was a low truckle bed, which served as a chair also, and near this was a ricketty table, on which were spread books, papers and parchments. The floor was also littered with such articles, and in a small rusty-barred fire-place gleamed faintly a few decaying embers.

It was evening, that is twilight, and objects were growing faint and indistinct, giving a ghostly character to the room; altogether it looked like a place where only bad deeds might be concocted and iniquitous schemes planned.

Two individuals sat in this place at the time we have chosen to introduce the reader to it. Both were individuals already well known to those who have perused these pages — the one was Mr. Wriggleton Doom, the attorney, late of Grays Inn,—the other was his clerk, Tim Snarley, who still clung to his old master, rascal as he was, in his altered fortunes, much as a dog will not forsake its owner, though that owner perhaps is a greater brute than itself.

Before, however, we proceed further, it will be necessary to mention somewhat of the history of Mr. Wriggleton Doom since his attempted suicide.

We have already stated that it was a long time before he recovered his mental faculties, those of his body were never entirely regained. Deeply did the unhappy man feel his degradation, the more so as his desperate attempt had caused many a tale respecting him to be told, which were highly prejudicial to his professional character, but which in all probability would never have been raked up but for the circumstances to which we have alluded.

Gradually he began to resume the practice of his profession; but it had so deplorably fallen off during his illness that now it scarcely yielded him a bare subsistence. What to do he knew not; even his professional brethren looked coldly upon him, and he entered and quitted Grays Inn Gardens unnoticed, if not visibly despised.

He was seated alone one evening in his now deserted office, musing upon his shattered fortunes when the knocker of his door sounded.

Mechanically he opened it, for Tim Snarley had gone to his favorite place of resort, the cockpit, in Westminster, and the burly and stalwart form of Jonathan Wild stood before him.

Doom started back in terror, it was the first time he had seen the thief-taker since the visit to him just before his attempt at suicide, and when Jonathan had obtained possession of the papers relating to the Town title and estates.

"Don't be frightened, Doom, I'm not come to hang you; by the way, you had nearly saved any one that job," said Wild entering, and carefully closing the door after him.

"Don't speak of that, Mr. Wild, for God's sake don't put me in mind of that or I shall do it again—indeed I shall," almost screamed the lawyer.

"No you wont," said Wild coolly, "nor any any one else either, if you do as I tell you—I mean, command you."

"I have found out a secret relating to this Richard Town, by means, of which, if you faithfully serve me you may banish all fear for the future and snap your finger at Jack Ketch," said Wild.

Wild then imparted to the lawyer a plot which he had contrived, which it would be premature to detail just in this place. Suffice it to say that Mr. Wriggleton Doom agreed to play his part in it, and Wild departed.

Finding after a time that his business grew still worse the lawyer abandoned his chambers in Grays Inn, and taking a downward step in his profession, sank from a practitioner of good repute, at least apparently so, in a regularly recog-

nized Inn of Court, to one of those disgraceful and dangerous creatures, a low sharping, pettifogging attorney; and fixed his place of business in a locality where none but those who would employ the very scum of the profession chose to resort.

We have seen him installed in his new office, where for a brief period we must leave him, in order to render clear a coming portion of the narrative.

It will be remembered that when Dick Flybynight was leaving the Sir John Oldcastle tavern, at Islington, he was accosted by a stranger, with whom he made an appointment to meet on the following night at Mother Sin's, in the Almonry.

Faithful to his promise he was at the brothel at the appointed time; the mysterious stranger was already there awaiting his appearance in a private room.

"It is well you are come," said the stranger, handing Dick a bumper of wine, "but before I proceed further, it may be as well to state that I only mentioned Wild in order to ensure your being here—with Jonathan I have nothing to do, nor would I—"

"Then what may your business be with me?" asked Dick Flybynight.

"It is to benefit a friend of yours, known to you by the name of Handsome Jack and to me as Richard Town."

Dick Flybynight was somewhat astonished at the stranger's intimate acquaintance with the real name of his friend, and this circumstance at once aroused his suspicions; for he was aware that Handsome Jack intended to prosecute his claim to the title, and he imagined the person present might be one whose evidence would be important, yet he determined to be cautious.

"You might have told me this at Islington the other day as well as now; what proof have you that you are what you represent yourself to be?" he asked.

"If I had told you then," was the reply, "you might have doubted me; and as to the proofs that I am interested in his welfare look at these papers."

Dick scrutinized the documents, and to his surprise beheld deeds which Handsome Jack had spoken to him of, and which were absolutely necessary to the recovery of his claims. He now no longer doubted.

"You are then satisfied; but there are other papers than these which might be procured, and they are in the possession of one Doom, a lawyer; but I have other news for your friend. He was enamoured of a young girl who is now Lady Purley."

"What then?" demanded Dick Flybynight.

"Tired of and disgusted with her old husband, who exceedingly ill-uses her on account of discovering a certain former acquaintance between her and Richard Town. She has been heard to express her inclination to leave him, and follow the fortunes of her former lover whatever they may be, if he proves bold enough to bear her from the old dotard's arms."

"I doubt not," said Dick Flybynight "but my friend will prove bold enough for the adventure if he thinks it advisable."

"For reasons of his own, I know for certain," continued the stranger, "that Doom would give up possession of all the papers he now has for a trifling annuity. What would there then be to prevent your friend quitting the dangerous life he now pursues, turning his property into funds, marrying his first love, and seeking with her fame and fortune in a distant land?"

"I will mention to him all you have told me this very night; with him must rest the decision of the matter."

"And further tell him that to-morrow evening, Lady Purley, who has authorized this communication—here is a ring, given to her by Richard Town, which she sends as a token," said the stranger, producing a small emerald ring—"will be sitting in a retired part of her garden, in a summer house in fact, to morrow evening for an hour after sunset. To cover her confusion, she will affect a resistance which must not be minded, and she may be by good management safely borne off."

"And whither can he convey her?" asked Dick.

"Where he chooses; but the lady is somewhat ticklish and insists on an immediate marriage. Surely he could at once carry her to the Fleet,—there are plenty of parsons there who for half a guinea would splice any one at any hour, and such unions are legal. If the thing is to be done at all no time must me lost."

After assuring Dick Flybynight that he would place the documents he then possessed in the hands of Lady Purley, the stranger departed, and Dick made the best of his way to the Country House, to inform his friend of what had just passed.

Handsome Jack was greatly startled at the intelligence, and at first knew not what course to adopt. His present mode of life was full of risks—risks which every day but increased. At times he suspected treachery; but the production of the documents and the ring, which latter the stranger had sent by Dick Flybynight, instantly disarmed his suspicions. Then, he thought, how could he with honour leave the gang? this question, however, was promptly replied to by the late quarrel and still remaining coolness between him and M'Cleane, and many of his scruples vanished.

But love at last decided the question. Amid all his wanderings he never ceased to love his Emila, and since that terrible scene in the bed-room he had been half maddened to know that another, whom she loved not, a hoary old dotard, riotted and revelled in her charms. All night he lay tossing on his pillow undecided what to do; but at mornings dawn he rose from his bed, his mind made up to release the idol of his heart from her accursed bondage and to fly with her to a foreign land, there to dwell in peace and security, leaving a useless title behind him.

Without mentioning his decision to any but Dick Flybynight, who promised strict silence, he at once proceeded to arrange his movements.

And now return we once more to the office of Mr. Doom.

"Tim," said the lawyer to his clerk, "take this note over the way to the Reverend Mr. Jawbone; you know him, and his place too, dont you?"

"Should like to know them as didn't know Parson Jawbone as know'd anythink," replied Tim, with a grin, "vy, I lost a crown to the old buffer, the other night in the cock-pit,—b'leve he bilked me, though."

"And ask for an answer mind," said Doom, not noticing Tim's libellous remarks on the character of one of the clergy.

Off went Tim Snarley; rushing across the road he scudded away a little in the direction of Holborn, and stopped before a house, at the door of which several low-looking fellows were smoking.

Over this door was a sign, on which was rudely painted a design representing six individuals. The centre figure was that of an exceedingly broad, red-faced, big-wigged, and jolly looking elderly gentleman, habited in full canonicals, and looking something like what one may imagine of a dissipated dean or a burly bishop of the last century. This worthy had a book in his left hand, and with his right he was joining the hands of a gentleman and lady, the former dressed in a plum-coloured coat, yellow breeches, silk stockings and a bag wig; and the latter habited in a hooped petticoat, quilted fardingale, a jaunty cap over her highly-powdered head, and high-heeled blue shoes, with red heels. Behind each of these last mentioned persons, were two individuals of seedy exteriors represented in the act of almost pushing one into the arms of the other; and in the rear of the parson was a groggy nosed clerk, out of whose mouth was seen to issue the word, "Amen." Beneath all was written in large letters—

"FLEETE MARRYAGES SOLEMNYZED HERE."

"Here's the shop," said Tim Snarley, after surveying the sign with apparently intense interest, "and these old bloaks smoking at the door, I s'pose are some of the blessed old fathers and mothers who gives the children away. Wonder if old Jawbone's at home," and diving under the low doorway he commenced mounting the staircase which in Tim Snarley's opinion resembled "a blessed corkscrew with no end to it."

But it had though, for it terminated in a door very high up indeed; and from between the chinks of the planks of which that doorway was formed streamed out dense clouds of smoke, which, had they not been strongly impregnated with the odour of tobacco, would have made Tim Snarley suppose that the inside was on fire. Painted on this door were the words—

"THE REVEREND ICHABOD JAWBONE."

"Well—I'm cert'nly surprised," said Tim to himself, "why he told me at the cock-pit as he was the Wiccar of Saint Pauls Cathedral, and here's a pretty place for a head of the church to live in."

Tim knocked at the door, and a heavy step was heard approaching it; it was not, however, opened.

"Who's there?" asked a husky voice.

"Here's a note for Parson Jawbone," said Tim,

"Who is it from?" asked the rough husky voice.

"From lawyer Doom, Parson Jawbone," replied the clerk.

The door was opened cautiously, for the Reverend Ichabod Jawbone had very particular reasons for not admitting every one who knocked, and a fac-simile of the reverend gentleman, canonicals and all appeared.

"Parson Jawbone! you young Imp of Beelzebub," said the reverend gentleman, "what the devil do you mean by speaking thus of one of the cloth. Curse your impudence, give me the note."

"Here you are Wiccar of Saint Pauls Cathedrel," said the unabashed Tim, as he handed him the missive.

"What d'ye mean, you blasted young hound—eh! what d'ye mean," roared the clergyman, as he shook Tim violently.

"What do I mean? why, didn't you say as you was that ven you did me out of my crown. Come let go, or I'll pitch into your old shins if you be a parson."

"Be off, you villain," roared Jawbone, thrusting the lad from him.

"Mr. Doom said I was to wait for an answer, and here I stops till I get it, so be quick will you," and planting his back against the door Tim stood in, for him, a very determined attitude.

Jawbone read the note, sent a verbal message that he would be with Mr. Doom in an hours time, and then Tim Snarley rushed down stairs, whistling all the way.

"Damned rogue, that Doom," muttered the Reverend Ichabod Jawbone, to himself as he resumed his pipe, and manufactured a fresh glass full of mahogany-coloured brandy and water, "what devil's work is he after now I wonder? but no matter, the fellow always pays well for his dirty jobs, and I can't afford to be very particular."

With this profound sentiment the meek and pious gentleman puffed away all the scruples he had, if indeed he had any, and settled into a doze, from which after enjoying it, if tremendous snoring be an evidence of somniferous enjoyment, for about half an hour he awoke, powdered his wig, brushed his clerical hat, and dusted the ashes of tobacco from his rusty-brown black breeches, and stumping solemnly down stairs, walked towards Mr. Doom's office.

"Welcome, my reverend friend," said the lawyer, in a bland voice, "pray be seated."

Tim had just borrowed a chair for the accommodation of the parson from a neighbouring tavern; but he had purposely selected one so remarkably weak in one of its legs which had been clumsily bandaged after a compound fracture, that he felt perfectly confident that it would not support the Reverend Ichabod Jawbone's ponderous weight.

"You are far more respectful towards the cloth, Mr. Doom, than your clerk is, I am very sorry to say; that fellow," pointing to Tim, "not having the fear of God and of my profession before his eyes, but just now vilely insulted me—"

"I didn't," interrupted Tim Snarley, "I only called him the Wiccar of Saint Paul's Cathedral—just what he said he was himself when we was together at the cock-pit."

At this moment the Reverend Ichabod Jawbone placed his body on the seat of the chair, but no sooner did the diseased leg feel the superincumbent weight than it yielded to the enormous pressure, and the Fleet parson sank to the ground with a crash and a shock which shook the building itself.

Tim Snarley burst into a fit of laughter, and Mr. Doom ran to the assistance of the fallen man, who, cursing inwardly and rubbing outwardly, sought a more secure resting place on the bed.

"Tim," said Mr. Doom, "you may leave us at present, and return in an hour—not longer."

Nothing loath, the boy seized his three cornered cap and sauntered into the court-yard of the Fleet prison to see the racquet-players; while so engaged he leaned against the angle of a wall, and heard two persons near him in conversation. They, however, were so situated, that though he could observe their persons and hear all they said, he could not be seen by them.

One of them was a tall, stout man, with a square countenance which he fancied he had seen somewhere before—it struck him at Doom's office in Gray's Inn—the other of a more slender make, but with traces of deep artfulness implanted in his countenance.

"Are you sure the scheme will succeed, and that he will take the bait?" asked the stout man.

"I am positive, Wild," remarked the other, "he will bring her here about midnight."

"What was the name of the man, Quilt, who you saw at Islington, and afterwards in the Almonry?"

"Dick Flybynight, Mr. Wild—he is one of M'Cleane's gang."

"And do you think, Quilt Arnold, this fellow has sufficient interest over Town to induce him to carry off the girl?"

"I doubt it not in the least, for he told me he was the most intimate friend Town had—and when he saw the ring, he even appeared eager to enter on the business."

"Ah! that was a master-stroke—the gaining possession of that ring!" observed Jonathan Wild, for he it was, the other was his man Quilt Arnold, who under the disguise of a lover of Lady Town's own maid had, in the absence of the family, managed to purloin it while his sweetheart was showing him over the mansion.

Quilt Arnold had also during his frequent visits to the maid learned as much of Lady Town's past history and present habits as had enabled him and Wild to concoct their abominable scheme.

"You had better see Doom, Quilt, and report progress, as it will not do for me to be seen in the matter."

"That I have already done, Mr. Wild, I was with him this morning, all is right in that quarter."

"Is the parson provided and instructed in the part he has to play in the matter?"

"Doom promised to see to that, and doubtless he has, for not half an hour since I saw his clerk take a note into Jawbone's lodgings."

"Good," said Wild, "there cannot be a better man than old Ichabod, if he's well paid, and that he must be. By the way, Quilt, you may as well let me have those deeds which I gave you to cajole Town's friend with a sight off."

"Here they are, Wild," said Quilt, as he restored the papers, and then the two moved off without having noticed Tim Snarley.

"So my blessed master is at his old tricks again," observed Tim, "well, of all the old villains I ever heard of he beats all. I'll see what's in the wind now—that's what I will. Midnight," one of these fellows said, "and there's a woman in the matter. It aint no good if such as Doom and Wild and Parson Jawbone are in it; but I'll find it out."

And with this soliloquy Tim Snarley bent his steps towards the office.

As he mounted the steps he met Parson Jawbone coming down in a smiling mood, and felt strongly inclined to stumble so as to throw the reverend gentleman off his balance; but resisted the temptation. and entered the office, where he found Mr. Doom extremely cheerful, a certain proof in Tim's mind, that some deviltry was in progress.

CHAPTER XLII.

THE ATTACK OF THE BLACK GANG ON THE SPANISH SHIP—FEARFUL ENCOUNTER.

THE attack on the richly laden galliott—laden with treasure from the Spanish Main—having been resolved upon, three hearty cheers for the success of the expedition were given both by those who were to take part in the perilous venture, and by those whom the result of the lot drawing had compelled to remain at home and prepare for the reception of the plunder if it should be acquired.

These latter, so far from being glad to be released from so hazardous a trip, rather regretted that they had not been fortunate enough to draw the marked bullets, for there was not one amongst that gang of lawless and desperate men who would not have preferred the excitement of the undertaking to the comparatively less dangers of the Home duty.

Many a hand was now employed in furnishing weapons, which from disuse had become partially rusted, or were otherwise out of order, in polishing locks, screwing in fresh flints, in sharpening cutlasses and daggers, or in preparing cartridges and securing belt-buckles, and in a score of other necessary occupations.

Others again were at work in muffling oars, and padding the runlets of the boats which were to be employed. Hawkins himself was engaged in curling up ropes or affixing them to grappling hooks, and Captain Fury himself presided over the employments of all.

Two long-boats and a smaller one was to be used; the former to carry the boarders, the latter, a swift little craft, to ply about as a watch boat, and to give the others an alarm if assistance should be seen proceeding from the shore, or indeed from any quarter.

This smaller boat was dispatched, with three men in her as soon as the shades of evening fell, in order that she might observe the movements of the custom-house and pilot's boats, and report thereon to Captain Fury, when he should have reached half-way from their hiding-place to the deserted vessel at Wapping.

In the various employments we have hinted at the evening passed quickly away, and the hour of ten arrived; it was agreed to drop down with the tide at eleven, which would enable them to get close to the Spaniard without much rowing; and it was also calculated that the rushing of the receding tide would materially assist them by preventing their approach being heard.

At half past ten all the preparations having been completed, Captain Fury, with a keen eye, minutely scrutinized the river, and having performed this important duty he directed his lieutenant, Fresnean, to summon all the men together.

Fresnean took from his breast a small silver tube which was attached to a silver chain round his neck and gave a shrill whistle. In an instant the whole of the Black Gang stood in a row before their chief.

"Call over the names, Lieutenant," commanded Fury."

This was promptly done, all were present, and the eyes of each glistened with ferocious excitement.

"Deliver the arms," was Captain Fury's next command.

To each man was then given a cutlass, which swung from a broad belt at his side—a dagger which was placed in the girdle—two pistols also stuck in the girdle, and a keen clasp knife suspended by a yarn round the neck; all only to be used in case of need.

"And now, my gallant comrades," said Captain Fury, "to-night we shall have a chance such as we have never before had of enriching every one of us, and of adding something to the general stock: but, my lads, to succeed you must strictly obey orders, and the first man who dares to disobey them I'll shoot him, by God, through the head as though he were a dog! Do not use your weapons unless compelled; but if your life is in danger sell it dearly. Remember we may do more by craft than by violence. The fellows we shall have to baffle are devils in their revenge, and should they get the upper hand of us would make mincemeat of every man jack of us in no time. Therefore let us give one hearty cheer, and then after a dram round—only one, but drink your skinsful if you like when you come back, let us to the boats, but if any one fears to follow me let him at once retreat. We will soon enough fill up his place."

A hearty cheer responded to the Captain's appeal; but not one present seemed inclined to show the white feather—all stood firmly as statues.

"'Tis well," said Fury, "and now success to our cruise."

The Captain drank off a bumper of Nantz, and all the others followed his example.

The order was then given 'to the boats.'

These lay concealed near the entrance of the subterranean passage from the river, and towards them in single file, led by Captain Fury and Lieutenant Fresnean, the men now proceeded. They soon reached the boats, and scarcely had they entered them when the heavens which had all day long been lowering and overcast, was suddenly lighted up by a flash of lightning, so vivid as almost to blind those who had but just emerged from the darkness of the subterranean passage, and it was directly followed by a terrific peal of thunder, which seemed directly overhead, and appeared to shake the ponderous buildings on either side of the river.

"Curse the lightning !" growled Captain Fury. "If it continues, 'twill be likely to spoil our sport, Let it thunder as much as it pleases, but I won't bargain for anything which would make our course seen from shore as plainly as if we went by daylight."

Flash after flash succeeded to each other in such rapid succession, that the whole river reflected the glare. To have ventured out while it lasted would have been madness, and to delay much longer would entirely prevent the adventure altogether, for the tide was rapidly ebbing, and soon it would leave their boats high and dry. Moreover, on the next day the Spanish galleon would sail up to the docks, and then an attack on her, from her nearness to the shores, would be an act of sheer madness.

As suddenly, however, as the storm arose, it died away—the lightning grew fainter and the thunder now bellowed in the distance, and from the ragged-edged tail of the departing thundercloud huge drops of rain fell and pattered on the surface of the water.

"As much of that as you please," said Fury, looking anxiously at the sky, and the more the better—for few of those hounds, the river guards, will care to wet their jackets. A bright fire-side, a buxom hostess, and a full tankard will better please them."

As if in accordordance with Captain Fury's wishes, the rain now began to pour down in torrents, and the dark canopy of the heavens became blacker and blacker every moment. Not the sound of an oar was heard on the waters, nothing indeed was audible, but the eddying flood itself, as it swept rapidly on towards the all-engulphing ocean.

"Quick, lads, or the tide will leave us—but before you move look well to your primings, and carefully keep your pans and flints from the wet."

This done, a few sturdy shoves sent the two boats into deep water. With the utmost caution, and indeed silence, the men now embarked, and pushed off into the stream, Captain Fury taking command and occupying the stern-sheets of the one, and his lieutenant, Philip Fresnean, that of the other.

The river ebbed so swiftly that the rudder alone was required to be used for some distance, but as the stream widened the current became less strong, and orders were given to ship the oars.

This was accomplished so quietly and simultaneously, that the Captain, in low terms, spoke to his men encouragingly.

"Bravo! boys, work thus together, and all will be well. Stay—what light is that—rest on your oars."

Every blade was instantly raised; and, unimpelled, the boats floated along slowly; acted on only by the tide.

The Captain's alarm was not groundless. On the Middlesex side, and close by the Tower stairs, the light as of a lantern was observed, and though the person who carried it could not be discerned, it was evident enough it was borne by some one who was descending the flight of steps, which led from the high bank towards the side and surface of the river.

At that moment, Captain Fury's small boat, the one which had been despatched some hours before came along-side, the person in command of her, too, had observed the strange light.

"Thank God you are here, Dick Devilskin," said Captain Fury. "Make the best of your way in the direction of that light, and meet us about five hundred yards on this side of the water. You see that large ship with th edark hull looming up?"

"I do, Captain," said Devilskin.

"There I will wait for you—but for God's sake be quick."

"As the lightning we had awhile ago," replied Dick Devilskin, and the men with him bending to their oars, the little boat glided noiselessly into the darkness, and was soon lost to view.

Fury and Fresnean now steered for the large ship, and gently glided within its broad shadow, where, perfectly unobserved, they awaited anxiously the return of Dick Devilskin.

Almost before the little watch-boat could have been expected back, it returned from its mission as silently as it had disappeared on it, and Dick Devilskin informed his chief in command that the light which had caused so much uneasiness, proceeded from a lantern borne by a party of Custom House officers who, after they had entered their boat, pulled away in the direction of Southwark stairs.

Dick was then directed to drop in the rear of the other two boats, and to keep a close watch lest the Custom's boat should follow in their wake, and intercept them as they returned from the Spanish ship to their hiding place.

The night was now everything that could be wished for their purpose. Heavy and dense masses of clouds, almost unbroken and charged with rain, swept slowly across the heavens shrouding from view the light of every star, and making, by their dark reflection, the turbid river below to appear like the stream of the fabled Styx. The rain fell incessantly, so that it required the utmost care on the part of the men to keep their ammunition dry; but this they contrived to do, and all were in high spirits at the prospect of a successful termination to an enterprise commenced under such auspicious circumstances.

Nothing was heard, as they floated down the Thames, but the striking of the quarters from the various church steeples which stood on either bank; the watch-bells on board the numberless ships in the stream; and the low rippling sound of the water as the tiny waves lapped against the bows of the boats. In this manner they proceeded, until by Captain Fury's calculation they came (for they still crept as closely as possible to the shore) nearly abreast of the place where the object of their pursuit lay.

And now commenced in good earnest the work which they came out to accomplish.

Steering his boat so that it should drift with the tide, and Fresnean following the example, the two gradually neared the Spanish vessel, but so pitch dark was it, that it was not until he was nearly close upon her, he saw her hull looming up through the obscurity, and her masts and spars faintly shadowed out and scarcely distinguishable from the thick atmosphere which surrounded them.

By dipping the blades of their powerful oars in the water, the pirates, by dexterous manoeuvres, kept their boats stationary while Fury and his lieutenant carefully surveyed the vessel. Not a soul could be discerned on deck, but a faint light was seen proceeding from one of the cabin windows, which Fury judged to be the captain's. Although, however, there was no appearance of a deck watch, neither the chief of the Black Gang nor his lieutenant for a moment doubted that there was one, but they surmised that he might, supposing there was little danger on such a night, from river sharks, have slunk into a place of shelter for the purpose of stealing an hour of repose.

"Fresnean," said Captain Fury, in a low voice, "drop down about a hundred yards below the bark, and then pull quietly up to her starboard side, and make yourself fast to her main chains. I'll do the same on the larboard here, and when you hear my whistle, board the Spaniard with two of your men, and I will meet you with three of mine by the main hatchway."

The boats parted company. Fresnean did as commanded, and Fury steered his boat, which, in a few moments, unsuspected by any one on board her, was alongside the Spanish galleon.

Selecting three men, Fury ordered them to take a last look at their weapons to make assurance doubly sure that all was right. Then he whispered to them these significant words:—

"A fortune for all, comrades! or a gibbet for every one of us at Execution Dock, or Cuckold's Point!"

In the meantime, Fresnean had dropped down the stream, and then, after his men pulling up with muffled oars, had secured his boat to the starboard main-chains.

Thus the Spanish ship's enemies lay on either side of her, ready to attack her at a moment's notice.

According to previous arrangement, should all prove quiet on board, Fury now, with the utmost caution, climed up the side of the ship; and without exposing his person any more than was absolutely necessary, surveyed, so far as it was possible he could do in the deep gloom, the deck of the vessel.

It was all but deserted and silent as the grave: to his great joy he espied the man on watch fast asleep under the long-boat, where he was sheltered from the wet; Fury, however, knew from long experience that the slumber of sailors is cat-like—that the slightest noise would awaken the man who so grossly neglected the duties of his post.

Slipping off his shoes, he clambered along the outside of the bulwarks, and made his way towards the bow of the vessel, until he arrived opposite the place where the ship's bell hung; he then clambered over, gained the deck, and untying the thick silk scarf from his neck, he noiselessly wound, and secured it round the clapper; an important movement, inasmuch as it would entirely prevent any alarm being rung, and assistance procured from vessels near.

Fury next clambered along the starboard side of the ship as he had before done on the other side, and soon getting to Fresnean's boat, dropped into it, and after a few moments' conversation, both, provided with ropes and a gag, crept stealthily on the Spaniard's deck, and with steps a noiseless as that of a Red Indian in his native solitudes, approached the still unconscious sentinel.

It was but the work of a moment to seize him, clap the gag in his mouth, and bind him hand and foot A pistol was presented to his head by Fury, and the surprised and terrified sailor was made to understand by signs, that if he made the slightest attempt to raise an alarm, he would be dispatched without mercy.

Leaving Fresnean to guard the prisoner. Captain Fury then proceeded aft in order to reconnoitre. So confident it seemed had the captain of the ship been of security, that it was evident he was a stranger; and one, too, who had so recently arrived as not to have been informed of the necessity of protecting his vessel from the numerous marauders who infested the river, who might well have been supposed to be tempted by so rich a freight as that which the San Salvador bore.

While he was endeavouring to ascertain the exact position of the captain's cabin, near to which he naturally supposed the treasure was deposited, Captain Fury observed a sky-light, on looking through which he could perceive everything in the cabin below, from the cieling of which swung a small and exquisitely-shaped silver lamp, the flame from which diffused a softened light through the place.

Fury started as a sight met his eye, for which he was totally unprepared. In his confusion, indeed, he had nearly thrown himself off his guard by an involuntary exclamation, but he quickly recovered himself, and again peered into the strange place as though his eager eyes would have never been sated with gazing.

It was not the place itself which so excited his interest and admiration, that itself was very beautiful and totally unlike anything he had before seen afloat. A moderately spacious cabin, seemed to have been converted into something between a bed-chamber and a boudoir, for it partook of the characteristic appearances of both, and was evidently constructed for the uses of one of the fair sex. This was further proved by the numberless elegant trifles which lay scattered here and there, and by a couch draperied with curtains of the finest texture, lined with pale rose coloured silk tissue, bordered with silver; and by a laced quilt of the most delicate workmanship. It was a nest in which one who was but a little lower than the angels in beauty could have fitly reposed.

And such an one was the sole inhabitant of this lovely chamber.

Before a silver crucifix, on either side of which two small wax tapers burned, which holy symbol stood in front of a small altar, curiously adorned with gold and precious stones, which reflected in a thousand gorgeous hues the light of the taper, and the whole of which rested on a high table, covered with a cloth of silver tissue elaborately wrought, knelt a young girl absorbed in devotion.

She could not have been more than seventeen years of age, though, as is commonly the case with the dark-eyed daughters of the South, her exquisitely rounded form was fully and perfectly developed; and this fact was the more palpable as the lady had cast off her outer clothing preparatory to her retiring to rest, and unconscious that the rude gaze of one of the other sex was upon her had loosened the other portions of her attire, thus revealing charms on which no man's eye had ever before rested; and in the abandonment of utter and sacred privacy allowing every beauty free to smile and swell as heaven pleased.

Her sable glossy hair, large flashing eyes, rich olive complexion, and voluptuous figure, proclaimed her a native of Spain. Fury, who was a passionate admirer of women, gazed on her with

intense delight, and it is a question whether he did not at that moment forget his craving for gold in the intense desire which burned within him to possess and revel in the charms of that beautiful creature. Had it not been for the fear of compromising his comrades, he would at once have abandoned his original design for the purpose of endeavouring to effect an entrance into the young girl's chamber; but warm as were his passions he had sufficient control over them to render them subservient to his reason, and therefore he determined whilst pursuing his original plan, to use every endeavour to capture and bear away to his secret habitation the prize which had so unexpectedly fallen in his way.

Returning to his lieutenant, he informed him of what he had seen, and told him of his hastily formed resolution.

"What! the bold Captain Fury captured by a

No. 26.

pair of black eyes?" exclaimed Fresnean, half in scorn.

"And such a tempting figure, Fresnean! by heaven to look on that delicious bosom of hers, all unconcealed as it was, reminding me of two snowy hills tipped with the rosy gleams of sunset, made the blood rush as furiously through my veins as the waters does round the vortex of the Maelstrom. Fresnean, I must possess her!"

"But the gold, Captain, surely you will not prefer the maiden to the moidores," said the lieutenant.

"I'd rather have her than an Argosy laden with gold and diamonds too; but, Fresnean, if a struggle ensues assist me in siezing her and half of my prize money shall be yours."

"Good!" remarked Philip, who cared more about virgin gold than virginity of another sort. "I'm your man," and he extended his hand to Fury.

An examination of the forecastle convinced the Captain that only four men were sleeping there; he therefore ordered two of his followers who he beckoned from the boats to stand guard over these, and to prevent their quitting their berths should they awake.

Then with the remainder of his gang—two men from the small boat, Dick Hellfire and Bloody Simon, having joined them—he proceeded to the door of the saloon of the young Spanish girl, and gently tapped thereat.

His summons was not replied to, and softly turning the handle of the door he opened it, and entered on tip-toe. The lamp was still burning, but the girl had retired to her bed, and was already sleeping the sleep of innocence. Fury gazed at her for an instant, and then bending down imprinted a kiss on her pouting, half-parted lips. Startled by this the girl awoke, and uttered a faint scream as she beheld a tall, to her it seemed a gigantic man at her bedside.

"For God's sake be silent," said Fury, "and no harm shall befall you," and he endeavoured to sieze the girl's hand, but she snatched it from him, and shrank beneath the bed-clothes in great fear.

"Guard this girl, and on no account suffer her to raise an alarm or leave her bed," said Fury to Hawkins, "and, hark ye!" he added, "touch or injure but one hair of her head, and by the God who made me you shall not leave this place alive!"

"Now for the Capitano," said Fury to his men, "one bold rush, lads, and the treasure will be ours."

The door of the Spanish Captain's cabin was directly opposite to that of the young lady's; but unlike hers it was bolted on the inside. A sudden and powerful application of the Captain's brawny shoulders to it, however, burst it open, and the chief of the Black Gang at the head of his men rushed in.

But they had not now to do with a weak girl. Starting from his bed the Spaniard leaped on the floor, and siezing a heavy cutlass prepared to defend himself to the last.

Desperately did he fight, calling all the while for assistance; but the numbers of his antagonists were too many for him to continue the struggle with any chance of success. At length exhausted with the loss of blood he sank on the floor, and exclaimed in tones of agony, "Holy virgin, preserve my child—my Isidora!"

"Fear not for her, Capitano," said Fury, "but I'll just trouble you to make a less noise, or I shall be compelled to muzzle you."

"Who are you, ruffians?" exclaimed the Spaniard.

"A milder term would suit us," observed Fury, "but come, we have no time to spare. Show us where you have stowed your treasure chests."

This, with an oath, the Captain of the galleon refused to do.

"Then I'll try if I cannot find means to make you," coolly observed Fury, and he quitted the cabin of the captain and entered that of Donna Isidora.

"Your father, lady, demands your presence. You shall be left alone for five minutes, at the end of that time I will return for you," said Fury.

Pale and trembling the poor girl quitted her couch, a thousand fears oppressing her, and her heart beating as though it would burst. Timid by nature she dreaded to move from the spot, but the thought that her beloved father, her sole parent was in danger, endued her with almost supernatural courage, and determined to sacrifice herself if necessary, in order to save him, she threw around her delicate limbs a loosely fitting robe, and awaited with extreme terror the return of Fury, whose daring trade she suspected, for as the daughter of a sailor she had heard many a fearful tale of terror respecting the freebooters of the deep, and she had, indeed, on one occasion with her father, narrowly escaped falling into the hands of one of those bands of sanguinary villains who infested the Spanish Main.

The Captain of the Black Gang again appeared and conducted her into her father's presence. Isidora was about to fly into her parent's arms, but Fury prevented her, and addressing the old man, said—

"Senor Capitano, I give you your choice; I and my comrades are determined to have your gold, if you refuse to show us where it is secreted I will not only ransack your vessel till I find it but carry off this girl and make you daughterless. Hawkins, remove the young lady to her own chamber."

Hawkins attempted to obey this savage order, but the wretched girl frantically prayed to be allowed to remain by her father's side. Fury, however, was inexorable, and Isidora was forcibly removed.

A general search was now commenced but without effect, so well had the boxes of gold and silver been concealed, and faithful to his trust, the Spaniard absolutely refused to reveal the spot where they lay. Fury was now rendered half mad by disappointment, and rushing into Isidora's cabin he dragged her forth, and commanded his men to take her up the companion stairs and force her into the boat.

This they were actually doing when the wretched father relented, as he saw his beloved child holding out her imploring arms to him who was incapable of defending her—the gold he could bear to lose but not his child.

"Spare her—spare my child," he screamed, "and I will do all you require."

Isidora was then brought back, and the Spaniard informed the Captain of the Black Gang that the specie was contained in six boxes and four barrels, which were stowed away in recesses beneath the cabin floor.

These valuable packages were speedily removed and transferred to the boats, when Fury approached the captain with a grin, and fastened him firmly to the ring of a locker with a rope.

Then he summoned forth the trembling Isidora and informed her she must depart with him, as he vowed he could not live without the society of one so lovely. In vain did the miserable girl pray for mercy, and her father supplicate that his child might not be taken from him. The cold-blooded monster, Fury, grasped the girl round the waist, after binding her mouth tightly with a handkerchief, and heedless of the ravings of her distracted father bore her on deck, and committed her to the care of Hawkins, who with the aid of his comrades dragged her into one of the boats.

Scarcely had they quitted the vessel, flushed

with their successes, before the sailors in the forecastle, alarmed by the bustle, awoke; and one of them saw the white robe of Isidora fluttering in the stern of a boat which was quitting the galleon. Rushing to the cabin he learned the state of affairs, and failing to sound an alarm by means of the bell, owing to its having been muffled, he and his fellows jumped into their boat and gave chase to the river pirates, leaving no one on board but the Capitano: for the mates and a portion of the crew had obtained on the previous afternoon leave of absence, and had not returned on board. An unfortunate circumstance for the owners of the treasure; but one of which Captain Fury was well enough aware, he having, by means of a deeply laid scheme and aided by confederates, contrived to make the men drunk, and thus prevented their returning to their duty.

The sailors of the Spanish vessel soon overtook the other, now heavily laden boats, and a desperate conflict ensued; for Isidora was looked upon by each sailor of the San Salvador as an angel of light, and there was not one among them who would not have sacrificed his hearts blood to save hers.

But what could they do, partially armed as they were, against such ruthless and desperate opponents? Short and bloody was the struggle, and when it terminated several of Captain Fury's men were severely wounded; but of the San Salvador's four brave and devoted mariners, one lay half-expiring across the thwarts of the boat, and the mutilated corpses of the other three floated slowly down the dark and eddying river.

"Pull, men, for God's sake pull! I see the Customs watch-boat behind us, and they evidently smell something," cried Captain Fury, whose brawny arm encircled the waist of his fluttering and half-insensible captive.

The men bent to their oars in good earnest for they now rowed for life or death. The boats flew through the water, as the stout spars quivered again from the lengthened strokes. A long line of foam churned in their wake, and every minute increased the distance between the pirates and their pursuers.

"Lay to, or we will fire into you," cried some one from the boat which was now some way astern.

"Fire and be damned!" exclaimed Fury, "it must be a good marksman who could manage to hit us now."

Then the sharp report of a musket was heard and a bullet struck the side of Captain Fury's boat.

"By God, though, that is too near to be agreeable," he said, and he once more urged the men to exert themselves to the utmost.

And now a new cause for alarm arose. Suddenly a ship's bell began ringing violently, and the alarm was taken up by one and another vessel until from one end of the pool to the other every bell was sending out its jangling sounds. Sounds too, as of men jumping into boats, were heard, and Fury began to feel somewhat uneasy.

"If any of the devil's imps should head us and cast us off from the secret entrance," he exclaimed, "we are lost. But we cannot be far off now. Ha! there it is, now then, my brave fellows, a dozen strokes steady and strong will make all right, and thank Heaven! I can no longer hear those bloodhounds behind."

The pursuing parties, indeed, seemed to have given up the chase, for, as Captain Fury intimated, the falling of their oars in the water could no longer be heard. Taking advantage of this, and with a heart somewhat lightened, the commander of the Black Gang steered his boat direct for the subterranean passage, and was closely followed by his lieutenant, Fresnean. In a few minutes both parties were shielded from observation within the bank, and there they remained for the purpose of listening.

In a short time the sound of oars, as if in pursuit, was again heard, and the shouts of Customhouse officers reached their ears: these came nearer and nearer, and presently those who would gladly have made them prisoners were abreast of them. It was so intensely dark, however, that they were not perceived, and they had the gratification of hearing the boat pass them and proceed towards London Bridge.

The utmost speed was now used in unloading the boats, and soon the vast amount of treasure which they had obtained was safely placed in the secret passage, from whence it was conveyed to the Hall of the Gang.

Captain Fury had not for a moment relinquished possession of the unfortunate young creature who had fallen into his hands. Up to the time of their reaching the secret way from the river to the interior of the pirate's den, terror had kept the poor girl mute, and she had not relinquished her hope of deliverance; but when the fearful man who had torn her from her father took her in his arms, stepped on shore with her, and carried her into the subterranean way, she burst into a wild shriek of despair, and the gloomy walls of the passage echoed her cries for succour. Heedless of this, now that he was certain the girl could not be heard, Captain Fury bore her along in spite of her struggles, and at length he reached the hall. By this time Isidora worn out by her passionate exclamations, and almost superhuman endeavours to free herself from the huge libertine's grasp, had again relapsed into a state of insensibility.

Fury immediately directed that the old woman who performed the necessary domestic duties of the place should be sent for, and as soon as she arrived he directed her to take charge of Isidora, and on no account to allow her to escape. As the hag gazed on the beautiful creature who lay pale and senseless before her, a grin of deep meaning spread over her face, and she bestowed an arch wink on the Captain. Isidora was then removed, still insensible, in the arms of Fury, who would suffer no one else to touch the fair Spaniard, to a bed-room; and having again cautioned the housekeeper, and given her directions to the effect that her captive was to want for nothing, he returned and once more joined the men under his command.

CHAPTER XLIII.

THE ABDUCTION OF LADY PURLEY—A MARRIAGE IN THE FLEET.

EVER since the memorable night when the daring attempt at robbery at Purley Hall was made by Handsome Jack, Hawkins and Beauty Ellis, the life of poor Lady Purley, in consequence of her having recognised in one of the midnight marauders her former suitor, had been one continued scene of almost unmitigated misery.

Old Lord Purley had used every effort which lay in his power in order to induce his bride to reveal the name of the individual to whom she had addressed herself in her bed-room but in vain. He had even gone so far as to threaten her, but this course also was unattended with success. Fortunately the ancient Peer's deafness had prevented him from hearing her mention Richard Town's name on the night alluded to, and there was no other way by which he could ascertain the secret.

Like most old men who marry young wives, Lord Purley soon became extremely jealous, although he had not the slightest reason in the universe for listening to the ' green-eyed monster.' Conscious, as he must have been, that at his time of life he was ill-fitted to discharge marital duties, he imagined that in the absence of those endearments which constitute the great charm of the connubial state, his wife would seek for enjoyment from other and forbidden sources. Never was a man more mistaken than was his lordship; if his lady did not feel so warmly towards him as young brides generally do towards their liege lords, she at least kept strictly in the path of duty, and endeavoured as much as possible to banish from her recollection all remembrance of him who had once possessed her young heart, and who had so fallen from the paths of rectitude and honour.

Glad to escape as much as possible from the society of the surly old nobleman, Lady Purley passed a considerable portion of her time in a small summer-house or grotto, which lay furthest from the mansion.

It was a lovely and secluded spot, embowered amongst the foliage of aromatic shrubs it afforded an admirable retreat; and so entirely secluded was it that a stranger might have passed within a few yards of it without ever suspecting its existence. Here, with books or her embroidery frame, Lady Purley wiled away many an hour which would otherwise have hung heavily on her hands, for Lord Purley's avaricious habits prevented him from seeing company, and between him and the neighbouring gentry, owing to his litigious propensities, anything but a good feeling existed.

It was to this summer house or grotto that Quilt Arnold referred in his interview with Dick Flybynight, at the house of Mother Sin in the Westminster Almonry.

Within a dozen yards of this little retreat was a doorway in the wall of the garden which communicated with a lane, and this lane led into the high road. There was no other way of exit from the garden than by this door, or by going through the stable-yard to the front of the house, or by passing through the mansion itself.

Return we now to Handsome Jack, who we left musing on the strange and unlooked for information which had been conveyed to him by Dick Flybynight.

Thoroughly acquainted as he imagined and believed he had been with the disposition and principles of the girl who, before he had plunged into his present reckless and dangerous course of life, he had fondly hoped one day to call his own; he was, it must be confessed, not a little surprised at hearing that she was willing, nay anxious to quit her husband clandestinely, even although that husband did not possess her affections.

However, he came to the conclusion that she had been driven to this extreme step by extraordinary circumstances, and he determined at all risks to engage in the enterprize. The sight of the ring which had been sent to him banished all scruples and he at once commenced making preparations for his singular expedition.

Adhering to his resolution not to inform Captain M'Cleane of his intentions he determined to secure the assistance of Dick Flybynight, for it was absolutely necessary that he should have some aid in the affair, and he knew no one who he thought would more willingly render it.

Nor was he mistaken, for on his seeking his friend, and craving his good offices, Dick grasped Handsome Jack's hand and exclaimed—

" Join you—aye, with all my heart and soul Jack; and I only wish that there was another pretty woman in the affair, that I might carry off a prize too. But seriously, Jack, do you mean when you have got possession of your little charmer to quit the road ?"

" Aye, that I do, Dick and the country too, for I imagine after the few escapades I have had that the air of a foreign clime might better agree with my constitution. If I stayed here I might, you know find myself riding towards Tyburn some fine morning."

" Well, damme," said Dick Flybynight, slapping his small clothes, " dangerous as the road is, upon my soul, I do not think that I could forsake its fascinations for the brightest eyed wench in Christendom. Egad, Jack ! what pleasure in life is there equal to having a dark sky above, a brave horse beneath, a well-laden traveller before you, and the courage to pluck him ? No—no, Jack, the road is my bride, and I must and will be faithful to her."

" Please yourself," replied Handsome Jack, " and now adieu until evening, when I shall expect you to meet me."

The friends then parted, having agreed on a place of rendezvous.

The whole of that day was spent by Handsome Jack in a state of intense excitement; in his breast there was a tremendous struggle between love and duty: love to Emilia, and his duty towards the gang to whom he had so recently vowed adherence, and which he felt he could not leave without a pang; but then on the other hand he reflected :—to what end will this course of life lead, it is better for me at once to break the charm which holds me than still to wear it, until it shall drag me down to perdition.

Alas ! Handsome Jack little knew how difficult it is to eradicate pernicious habits when once formed: the charm which bound him to his destiny was more firmly rivetted than he was at all willing to suspect.

*   *   *   *

Unconscious of the machinations which were to be brought into operation against her, the beautiful and youthful Lady Purley, on the evening of the day on which the above conversation between Handsome Jack and Dick Flybynight occurred, bent her steps as usual through the flower garden towards her favorite retreat.

It was the hour of sunset. The slanting beams of the sinking orb of day shed a mellow radiance on every surrounding object, and brightened as with a halo of glory the quaint twisted chimnies and gables of Purley Hall; all nature appeared to repose, for no sounds were heard save the crawing of rooks, high over head, as they winged their way homewards; the drowsy hum of some belated bee, or the distant and musical tinkling of sheep-bells. Every thing appeared to be serene, excepting the heart of the lovely lady as she paced the flower-bordered walks, for on her alabaster brow there was a settled sadness.

Lady Purley could not explain how it was—but on that particular evening a feeling of an undefined nature, and for which she could not account, oppressed her. It was as if a dark thunder cloud hung over her, which every minute threatened to burst, and overwhelm—perhaps destroy her entirely.

Lord Purley too, had been in a remarkably good humour that day, and had actually allowed the dinner to pass over without once taunting his lady, or referring to the mysterious recognition in the bridal chamber. So that on that score she had been in a measure relieved. What then could cause her remarkable depression of spirits now?

Some philosophers would have us believe, that on the approach of certain critical or eventful periods of our lives, vague, mysterious warnings which we cannot fully comprehend are given us, and these they term omens. Whether this be the case or not this is not the place to discuss the question, even had we the time or inclination to do so. Certain it is that Lady Purley, without being able to assign any cause for the phenomenon, felt a sort of pre-shadowing of coming evil; a dreamy impression that something dreadful was about to happen, and which it would not be possible for her to avert.

She at length reached the little grotto and sank on one of the sofas. A book was in her hands; but she found it impossible to confine her attention to its pages. No sooner did she attempt to peruse the beautiful poems they contained than her thoughts wandered far far away.

And whither did those wandering thoughts fly, and where did they repose?

On that eventful evening her whole former life passed as it were in review before her: she was again the happy girl, unconscious of other than parental love: she was once more the blushing maiden, listening to the first words of affection breathed from a lover's lips; she was, in imagination, the betrothed of Richard Town; the object of a pure, fervent, and manly attachment, which was as fervently responded to! But these daydreams passed away, and she half started as she remembered how her lover had abandoned himself to infamous company; how he had even violated the sanctity of her chamber; and how she was now the wife of a man whom she could not respect far less love.

Indulging in such reveries, Lady Purley remained that evening in the retired grotto longer than was her wont; for her husband had intimated his intention of sleeping alone that night, greatly it must be confessed to his young bride's satisfaction; and the evening, in addition, was unusually mild. The time was favorable to contemplation, for the young moon like a silver cresent rose above the lofty elms, and the dreamy influence of the hour gradually soothing her troubled spirit, she sank insensibly into a gentle slumber.

Leaving her to her dreams we must now return to Handsome Jack and Dick Flybynight.

"Strange animals are these women," remarked Dick, "why, here's a girl dying to jump into your arms, quit her ancient husband, and follow the fortunes of a highwayman, and yet she stipulates a little show of resistance. Damn it, Jack, these females are puzzles in petticoats."

"But you must remember, Dick," said Jack, "that she can scarcely help feeling abashed at taking such a step, and as your informant observed, Lady Purley will only assume a repugnance to be carried off the better to hide her confusion. But come, it is time we should be going —is all ready?"

"All," replied Dick, "the chaise, in charge of a trusty fellow, will be in the lane at the back of the garden at nine o'clock, by which time it will be quiet dark; here is the key of the door near the grotto, so that few obstacles will stand in our way: all you will have to do when you have got your charmer safe in the carriage will be to drive off to the Fleet as speedily as possible."

"But have you made the necessary arrangements respecting the documents with Doom? Curse the fellow! I half mistrust him now," remarked Jack.

"You need not, I have seen him," replied Dick, "and he promises solemnly, on Lady Purley's producing the documents which my informant at the Almonry was to place in her hands, that he will, for the consideration of a sum sufficient to provide him with a small annuity, give up the other papers in his possession. These parchments once in your hands a purchaser can soon be found, and you at liberty to seek your safety in flight."

"And how about the parson? I confess this Fleet marriage does not much please me," said Jack.

"That too is made all right; one Ichabod Jawbone has been engaged to make you and your mistress one. Doom has also seen to that matter," replied Dick.

The two friends now set out secretly from the Country House, at Highgate, and avoiding the high road, threaded several lanes on foot. At about a mile distant from the village, they found a man waiting their arrival with two horses.

Throwing the man a couple of guineas, Dick Flybynight requested him to call for the horses in three hours time, at a small roadside public-house, where he said he would leave them. Handsome Jack and Dick then mounted their nags, and in half-an-hour were within a quarter of a mile of Purley Hall.

They now dismounted, and according to the arrangement with the man who they had recently left, they placed their horses in charge of the landlord of a low hostelry, a man with whom Dick Flybynight was well acquainted and on whom he thought he could depend.

"A brave night, my worthy masters, for the knights of the road;" observed the tapster; "but wont your honours moisten your throats before you venture out?"

"Aye, Jenkyn, give us a cool tankard, man, as you may see by our leaving our horses, we go not on business to-night. But ask no questions, man, or thou mayest get a crack on thy sconce for thy impertinence. There take these two guineas, and let me see if they will keep that long tongue of thine still."

"That will it, my worthy master," replied Jenkyn, grinning with delight, "but have in the tankard."

Our two adventurers soon emptied the vessel, and then once more set out on foot.

A brisk walk soon brought them to the entrance of the lane, which, as we have before stated, ran at the back part of the garden of Purley Hall. Using now the utmost caution in their movements lest they should be observed by any of the servants belonging to the mansion, they crept within the shadow cast by the high wall, and soon reached the place, where hidden from view beneath the wide spreading branches of a stately oak, the post chaise was drawn up.

Having ascertained beyond a doubt that all the arrangements so far were complete, Handsome Jack commanded the driver to pay no attention to the struggles or resistance of the lady who he was about to place in the carriage, but to obey his orders only; promising him a handsome reward on her arrival at the Fleet.

As a matter of precaution the two highwaymen now proceeded to disguise their faces by covering them with black crape; their pistols were then looked to, and replaced in their belts, and drawing the key of the garden door from his pocket, Handsome Jack led the way to the private entrance to the garden.

With a trembling hand he placed the key in the lock: it grated slightly as he softly turned it round.

"Ah! I see you are a novice at this sort of work," observed Dick Flybynight, "never attempt to do a thing of this sort in so gingerly a manner. Why—Damn it man, that slow sort of work is the noisiest—now let me give you a lesson."

Taking the key from the hand of Handsome Jack, Dick Flybynight applied to its wards part of the contents of a small phial which he drew from his pocket, this liquid had the property of instantly dissolving the rust with which it was encrusted, for that door was but seldom used; he then placed the stem of a tobacco pipe in the keyhole, and poured into the bowl some more of the fluid; by a little skilful management, he thus continued to inject a quantity of the acid, for such it was, into the most intricate portions of the lock itself, and on those parts, it of course had an effect similar to that produced on the key—viz., the dissolving the rust of years. Then he plentifully

smeared the wards of the key with grease, and partially melting it by the flame of a match, he inserted it in the keyhole, gave a quick peculiar turn of his wrist, and without making the slightest noise—the bolt of the lock flew back.

Impatient to carry his plans into operation, Handsome Jack was about to push open the door, when he was again stopped by Dick Flybynight.

"Steady man, or you will ruin all," observed the latter, in a low voice, "do you not perceive that those old rusty hinges may tell tales—'tis well I came with you, or you might not only have lost your lady love, but have been trapped yourself into the bargain."

After performing the same operations on the hinges that he had previously done on the key and lock, Dick Flybynight gently pushed the door which yielded to the pressure, and the only obstacle to their entrance to the garden was removed.

The pair, Handsome Jack taking the lead, now with as much secrecy as possible, crept through the shrubbery. The moon was shining sufficiently bright to enable them to thread their way according to the instructions they had received with tolerable correctness. They had not gone far before, through an opening in the trees, they perceived the summer-house which was the goal of their expedition.

It was with indescribable feelings, that Handsome Jack approached this place; his emotion was so great that he felt a choking sensation, and his limbs tottered under him; but he speedily rallied, recovered his energies, and motioning Dick Flybynight to remain just outside the summer-house, he crept on tip-toe towards the door which was partly open.

Peeping in, he perceived a female form reclined on a sofa—a book had fallen from the sleeper's hand and lay on the floor; on listening intently, he could hear the regular respiration of the lady, who, by the mild light of the moon whose beams fell directly on her face and form, he recognized as his once devoted Emilia.

Handsome Jack felt somewhat surprised that on so critical an occasion she should have yielded to the influence of the drowsy god; but he felt also that he had little time to waste in surmises; so plucking up his courage, he boldly yet quietly entered the summer-house.

Light as his step was, however, it awakened the Lady Purley, who started from her couch in the utmost alarm at seeing a man near her; a faint scream escaped from her lips, and she was about to cry for assistance when Handsome Jack stepped back and closed the door.

"Be not alarmed, Emilia! it is only him whom you expected—all is ready for your flight," said Handsome Jack, as he removed the disguise from his features, and approached towards Lady Purley with extended hand.

"You here—Richard! Dare you again intrude yourself into my presence," observed the lady, on recognizing the voice and features of Handsome Jack. "Tell me, in pity's sake, why do you thus haunt me?"

And the unhappy lady, in the anguish of her feelings, clasped her hands, and looked imploringly into the face of her former lover.

"Come—come, Emilia," replied Jack, "this is no time for playing a part; you know you expected me, and the sooner we are off the better lest our flight may be prevented. I have no wish to make Lord Purley's acquaintance to night, therefore let us go."

"Flight! What mean you? I am bewildered; or am I still dreaming?" and Lady Purley pressed her hand against her marble brow as if to ascertain whether she was indeed awake. "Who presumed to speak to me of flight?"

"I did, Emilia ——"

"I beg, sir, that you will address me less familiarly," said her ladyship, drawing up her form to its full height and looking scornfully at the intruder. "And more, sir, I command you instantly to quit my presence."

Handsome Jack was rather confounded. He had been prepared for a little opposition on the part of the lady, but he had no idea that it would be carried to such an extent. Nevertheless, he still gave Lady Purley credit for merely acting a part, for he firmly believed that she had sought the summer-house at that late hour purposely to meet him.

"Does your ladyship know this emerald ring?" asked Handsome Jack, presenting to Lady Purley the trinket which Quilt Arnold had handed as a token to Dick Flybynight at Mother Sins.

"How came that in your possession? Yes, I know it too well—it was given to me in happier times by one in whose feelings of honour and delicacy I thought I could confide, but it seems I was bitterly mistaken; and thus I show my scorn both of the gift and the giver."

As she uttered these words, Lady Purley threw the ring on the ground and stamped violently on it. Handsome Jack became irritated, and thinking the lady was carrying matters a little too far, determined to bring matters to a conclusion. Whether Emilia was a party to the daring abduction or not, and he now began to suspect that there might be some mistake in the matter, he determined that, as he had gone so far, he would not retreat until he had accomplished the purpose for which he came.

Seizing Lady Purley round the waist, in spite of her struggles, he threw a large cloak with which he had come provided, over her head so as to stifle her screams, and lifting her like a feather in his arms, he rushed from the summer-house.

"So you've caught your turtle-dove," remarked Dick Flybynight as he joined the latter, and the two hastened from the garden.

"Yes; but 'twas harder work than I had bargained for," exclaimed Handsome Jack, "but we will talk of the matter by-and-bye—let us hasten to the carriage."

Lady Purley had fainted away, and when placed in the vehicle, and for some time afterwards, was in a state of insensibility. The fresh air, however, and the motion of the carriage restored her to consciousness, and a piercing cry burst from her lips as she discovered that she was being borne from her home by two men.

But her cries for succour were unheeded; the noise of the carriage wheels drowned them, and Dick Flybynight heeded them but little, believing as he did, that Lady Purley was only acting in accordance with a preconcerted plan.

On rolled the chaise, and fortunately for the two daring men who had accomplished the abduc-

tion of the unfortunate lady, the latter had become so exhausted by her struggles, and the intensity of her feelings that she was now incapable of raising any alarm as they passed through the streets, which were so ill-lighted that they escaped the scrutiny of the watch. Boldly taking the principal thoroughfares, they arrived about an hour after midnight in the neighbourhood of the Fleet, where, on a private signal being given by a man who was evidently on the look out for its arrival, the carriage stopped.

The Reverend Ichabod Jawbone was sitting alone in his room at midnight over a reeking bowl of punch, and sending forth from the bowl of a huge pipe, and from his mouth also, huge volumes of smoke when he heard a heavy step ascending the stairs which led to his dormitory.

Presently a knock was heard at the door, and as at that hour of the night the reverend gentleman felt assured that no importunate creditor would call on him he opened it without hesitation, and requested whoever it was outside to enter.

The person who now made his appearance was a stranger to the Fleet Parson, but the person and functions of the latter appeared to be extremely well known to Mr. Quilt Arnold, for it was that useful emissary of Jonathan Wild's who now sought an interview with him whom Tim Snarley described as the "Wiccar of Saint Pauls."

"May I ask what your business may be with me, good sir?" asked the parson, in his blandest voice, "perhaps you may require my services in the matrimonial line, if so, and the woman is below, I'll rivet you at once, for I have another job on hand, but can attend to you first—a guinea if you please."

"Yes, I know you've a little business to do presently, Mr. Jawbone, and it's about that I'm come."

"Then you don't want to enter into the holy state yourself," remarked Jawbone, with a sigh, for he had calculated fully on a guinea, as it seldom happened that he had other than matrimonial visitors at such an hour.

"I should imagine not," replied Quilt Arnold, "I made a fool of myself in that way years ago—thank God, I wasn't tied long though, for my wife was led to another sort of halter within two years of the time when I honoured her by giving her a right to assume my name."

"Then you mean to say that your wife was—"

"Hanged—parson Jawbone—hanged! there's no use mincing words you know; but as I was saying though, I'm not going to trouble you myself, I mean to have something to do with this marriage."

"In what way?" asked Jawbone.

"I'm to give the young woman away, and witness the marriage. Mr. Doom appointed me to that office; but I fancy as I shall have a tough job of it."

"How so?" asked the Fleet parson.

"Why, it is expected that the bride won't be quite so willing to be disposed of as the young fellow is to gain possession of her; but there's a mint of money in the way, Mr. Jawbone, if she's clenched all right and correct. Now do you think that there will be any difficulty on your part, if she can't be got to go through the service?"

"The lady must utter the responses," observed the parson.

"But she may speak them in so low a tone that you may not be able to hear distinctly. You are a little deaf are you not, reverend sir?"

This question was accompanied by the exhibition of a bank-note for twenty pounds, which Quilt Arnold temptingly displayed to the admiring eyes of the Reverend Ichabod Jawbone.

"Why, yes, I am seized with fits of deafness occasionally," said the parson, who saw plainly enough from which quarter the wind was blowing. "Indeed, I am now labouring under an affection of that kind."

"But," resumed Arnold, "should the young lady either from bashfulness, obstinacy, or any other cause, speak in so low a tone that your affliction will prevent you from hearing her, would not you be satisfied if I as her guardian repeated her replies to you in a louder tone?"

This time the twenty pound note was placed in the Reverend Mr. Jawbone's hand with an intimation that he might henceforward consider it to be a part of his personal property.

"Certainly, my excellent friend," said Jawbone, "without doubt; indeed I should feel amazingly obliged to you if you would so far assist me; for I verily believe that I should not be able to get through the service without some such aid."

So well did Parson Jawbone understand his cue that whilst making the last remark he actually looked deaf; and bending forward he put his hand to his ear so as to bring the sound of Arnold's voice into a focus, and begged him to speak a little louder.

"We may consider that matter arranged then," remarked Quilt Arnold.

"Quite—depend on it that you will find no difficulty; but as a matter of precaution, I think t would be as well for you to see my clerk, as he will have to be present on the occasion.

"I do not exactly see the necessity of so doing," remarked Arnold.

"But I do," said Parson Jawbone, with a look of inexpressible cunning. "Nathaniel Bang, who officiates here is no fool, rather a little of the other thing; you know what I mean, don't you?"

Quilt Arnold nodded an assent.

"Well then, is'nt it probable that he might be deaf too?—he's getting in years, and time brings infirmities. At all events it would be as well to ascertain the fact, as in case of his hearing been sharp, who knows but on some future occasion he may swear that the young woman never uttered a syllable?"

Arnold could not contradict this, so the old clerk was sent for and matters having been arranged to the satisfaction of all parties, Quilt took his departure and proceeded to report progress to Mr. Doom.

The lawyer and Jonathan Wild's agent in this nefarious transaction were still engaged in conversation, when footsteps were heard ascending towards the apartment in which they were seated.

The door opened, and a shabby looking man entered. He was attired in seedy black garments; his face was lean and cadaverous, and an expression of infinite cunning lurked among his sharp features.

"Have you brought the potion I ordered, Vardon?" asked Mr. Doom, with evident anxiety.

"Here it is," remarked the man, who, though so miserable looking and poverty stricken was a chemist of great talent, though a man of no principle, "I have had great difficulty in procuring the drugs necessary for its composition, and that has delayed me; but I warrant you, that it will effect the purpose you desire."

"Good," remarked the lawyer, as he took the phial which contained a fluid of a reddish brown colour, and now as to the directions for its use."

"Ten drops of that liquid infused into a glass of wine will so affect the person who partakes thereof, that memory for the time will be entirely destroyed, and but a confused idea of what is actually passing at the moment be retained in the mind."

"And a larger dose?"

"Would produce total insensibility."

"And were the quantity still further increased?" asked Doom, who appeared extremely anxious to obtain full particulars with respect to the contents of the phial, what would ensue?"

"Temporary madness, ending perhaps in inflammation of the brain and death," replied the chemist.

"Here is your fee," said the lawyer, as he placed two pieces of gold in the hand of Vardon, who apparently did not seem satisfied with the reward.

"You must understand," said he, addressing Mr. Doom, "that you have to purchase my silence as well as my drugs, and this sum is barely sufficient to remunerate me for the latter and for my time in making this singular preparation."

The lawyer saw that he had no other course to pursue than to act with greater liberality; he therefore further rewarded Vardon, who then retired.

Then placing the phial in a cupboard, he sat down opposite Arnold, and the pair listened in silence for the arrival of Handsome Jack and Lady Purley.

Two hours had elapsed since midnight when a carriage was heard to stop in the street below.

Hurrying to the window, Quilt Arnold looked out, and saw Dick Flybynight descend from the interior of the vehicle; he was followed by another man who bore in his arms something resembling a human figure wrapped in a cloak.

"Here they are at last," said Arnold. "Now then, Doom, while you manage the business here I will away to Parson Jawbones, and have all in readiness against you bring the parties over to the chapel."

Quilt Arnold then slunk down the staircase, and quitted the house.

Accompanied by his friend, Dick Flybynight, Handsome Jack now, still bearing Emilia in his arms, ascended to Doom's chamber, and laid his lovely burden on the truckle bed.

Lady Purley was still in a swooning state, but her lover having bathed her temples with water, she soon recovered, and staring wildly around demanded, in a faint voice to know where she was.

"With friends," replied Doom, "but pray compose yourself, you shall soon be at liberty, but it is necessary that some trifling business should be transacted which immediately concerns you, and which presently I will explain. In the

interval let me prevail on you to accept of a glass of wine."

Lady Purley, who was completely exhausted silently assented, and Doom withdrew to the cupboard, and after pouring ten drops of the fluid which the chemist had brought, into the glass, filled it up with wine and handed it to the lady, who unsuspectingly swallowed the whole.

The effect was instantaneous and most singular. Instead of referring to the past or asking further questions as to where she was or why she was brought thither she manifested a total unconcern, and when requested to rise and accompany Richard Town she unhesitatingly gave him her arm, and with him quitted Doom's office, and proceeded towards the chapel of Mr. Jawbone.

Handsome Jack who was utterly ignorant of the administration of the marvellous potion, was delighted at the change in Lady Purley's manners,

and now, more than ever, believed that her former reluctance had been but feigned. Without speaking, however, he conducted her under Doom's guidance to the Fleet parsons.

That reverend gentleman dressed in full canonicals with his clerk, and Mr. Quilt Arnold were waiting to receive them. Handsome Jack looked rather surprised when he cast his eye over the strange looking place in which the marriage ceremony was about to be performed, and well might he have been astonished.

It was a small chamber about twelve feet square, with bare plaster walls on which, here and there were stuck common tin sconces, in which some flaring tallow candles were stuck. At the upper end of the room was a small space railed off, in which was a table covered with a shabby white cloth, on which lay a book and some pens and ink bottle. One or two mats were placed in front of the railing, and this with three chairs completed the furniture and fittings up of Mr. Jawbone's chapel.

As it were, mechanically, Lady Purley, led by Handsome Jack walked towards the rail, behind which, book in hand, stood the Rev. Ichabod, who immediately commenced gabbling through the marriage service. It was evident that Lady Purley was unconscious of what was going on; her eyes had a fixed, unnatural glare; she appeared indeed, more like a piece of statuary or wax work than an animated being. Once only she gave a convulsive sort of shudder, it was when Handsome Jack slipped a ring on her finger. As for the responses, Mr. Jawbone's deafness was so distressing that he took it for granted they had been made, Quilt Arnold who acted as father or giver away of the bride, assuring him in a loud voice that the lady had uttered them. In due time the ceremony concluded, and Richard Town led his unconscious victim from the altar, after having received a certificate of the marriage, and inscribed his name together with that of Emilia in a book, and again with her returned to the office of Mr. Doom.

But the strange events which occurred there must form the subject of another chapter.

CHAPTER XLIV.

JENNY DIVER HAS A WINDFALL—DICK FLYBY-NIGHT AND BEAUTY ELLIS ARE GRATIFIED BY A DISAPPOINTMENT—M'CLEANE RECOVERS HIS LOST TREASURE.

FILLED with new hope, and something of a gainer by experience, Jenny Diver re-commenced her metropolitan campaign.

Her first care after her arrival in London was to seek after her old companions. With this intention she resolved to take an early opportunity of visiting the Country House at Highgate.

Ignorant of the many changes which had occurred during her absence, she fondly imagined that all had gone on prosperously, and indulged in fond anticipations of a meeting with Captain M'Cleane. Buoyed up with the feeling that her appearance would create a more agreeable surprise, if she accomplished some dashing act, she determined to disguise herself, and alone venture on the king's highway.

She had, as is already known to the reader, on one occasion distinguished herself in this line; but then she had Handsome Jack as a companion, now she determined to trust to her own energies alone.

Three nights after her arrival in London she set forth on her expedition; but knowing that by hiring a horse she should expose herself to great risk, she contented herself with procuring a man's dress, and a brace of pistols. She was so accustomed to this sort of masquerading that when she walked along the Holloway Road in the gloom of the evening, her air was such that not the most experienced constable would have detected in the stranger either Jenny Diver, the returned transport, or a footpad in search of adventures.

For some time she wandered along without meeting any one, and the girl began to imagine that her usual good fortune had deserted her, when she observed a private coach drive up to the door of a gentleman's house. Jenny was near enough to hear a conversation which passed between a man who had alighted from the vehicle and the coachman, although she could not herself be observed. The gentleman after entering the house re-appeared, and handed to the coachman a canvass bag, requesting him to take it to town, and deliver it with its contents at a certain goldsmiths whom he named.

Jenny Diver at once determined to possess herself of this bag, which she believed, from what she had seen and heard, contained valuable booty, She, therefore, with her usual quickness immediately resolved on a course of action and proceeded to put her scheme into practice.

The moment after the coachman had driven from the door of the gentleman's house, Jenny called to him, and enquired whether he was going to London, and having received a reply in the affirmative she offered him half a guinea for a seat in the vehicle, a proposition to which the fellow very willingly agreed, as the applicant appeared to be a gentleman, and in appearance not at all like any of the highwaymen who infested the neighbourhood of the metropolis.

Our heroine had so narrowly watched the movements of the coachman, that she had observed him deposit the bag which he had received from his master in the pocket of his breeches. The great object now was to obtain possession of it. The driver was a man of great stature and strength, and did not look like one who would be easily frightened. All her address, therefore, would be required to effect her purpose.

The vehicle had proceeded at a slow pace for about half a mile, when it arrived at a very secluded part of the road. Looking from the window, in order to ascertain if the coast was clear, Jenny saw that the highway was bounded on one side by a low edge, which separated it from a thickly planted orchard. Not a soul was in sight and, therefore, drawing one of her pistols from the place in which she had concealed it, she cocked it, and then pulling the check-string, called out to the coachman that she had forgotten something, and should relinquish her intention of riding into London.

The man, instantly pulled up his horses, descended from the box, and opened the door of the carriage.

He had no sooner done so than Jenny rose from her seat, and as she descended the steps pointed her pistol full in the face of the astonished coachman, who at first felt inclined to treat the matter as a remarkably pleasant joke.

He was, however, speedily undeceived, for the Diver laying her hand on his shoulder pressed the muzzle of her pistol so forcibly on the forehead of the coachman, that he felt as though a ring of ice was placed on his brow. This action was accompanied by a premptory request that he would instantly surrender possession of the bag of money which he carried.

The coachman, now somewhat recovered from his astonishment, stoutly denied that he possessed anything of value excepting his watch, which he tendered to Jenny, who dropped it carelessly into her coat pocket and repeated her demand.

And so persuasive was Jenny Diver's pistol, and so threatening her aspect, that after some hesitation, and with infinite reluctance, the stout driver drew forth from his pocket the canvass bag and handed it to Jenny, who then ordered him on peril of his life to remain where he was for the next ten minutes, assuring him if he attempted to give the slightest alarm that she had comrades at hand who would dispatch him on the instant.

Still presenting her pistol at the man whom she had plundered, Jenny retreated, walking backwards, towards the low edge, over which she managed to scramble and gained the orchard, under cover of the trees in which she contrived to effect her escape.

At the end of the orchard was a lane, which led by a circuitous route to the bottom of Highgate Hill. Taking it for granted that the coachman would speedily raise the Hue and Cry, she traversed the thoroughfare with the utmost speed and on emerging from it she had the gratification of discovering that all was quiet. She, therefore, without hesitation commenced the ascent of the hill

It was pitch dark, but every step of the road was familiar to her; and accordingly she made rapid progress on her journey. Within little more than half an hour she stood in front of the hostelry, which as we have in a former chapter stated served as a sort of blind, to conceal the real purposes of the gang commanded by M'Cleane.

So well was she disguised that she determined to introduce herself as a stranger, and pick up as much information as possible before she made herself known. Her return from the Colonies was not as yet, of course, known to her former associates, and therefore there would be little chance of their detecting her, before she herself should choose to throw off the mask.

As she stood gazing on the well-known spot the young girl was almost overpowered by her emotions. What might not, she thought, have happened since she had last been there? No one knew better than herself how precarious was the lives of those who resorted to the road as a means of living; and it was not only possible, but more than probable, that she should hear that some one or other of the gang had either, like herself, been exiled from the land of his or her birth, or had been more summarily disposed of on the dreary tree of Tyburn.

But her chief curiosity was to know what had become of her lover, M'Cleane, for whom she still cherished an almost romantic affection. Had he forgotten her? She almost feared that he might have consoled himself in her absence by returning to the embraces of his former flame, Madame Charlotte, who, she felt assured, would spare no pains to re-capture her once dear and devoted Captain. As she mused on this latter subject, Jenny Diver's eyes flashed with jealous fire, and her heart beat violently.

Stepping to the door of the inn she rapped on its dingy pannels with the butt-end of her pistol, and then immediately replaced the weapon in her pocket, so as to prevent its being observed.

The summons was speedily responded to by Beauty Ellis, who rose lazily from his seat in the chimney corner, where, with Dick Flybynight, he had been discussing a tankard of strong spiced ale.

At the first glance of her old acquaintance, Jenny Diver felt assured that she was not recognized; and she was well convinced that if she could manage to deceive the lynx eyes of the Beauty, she should find but little difficulty, if any, in personating an utter stranger in the presence of any other members of the confederacy.

"A good evening, my master," said Beauty, as his eyes lighted on the graceful, though somewhat petite figure of the stranger. "Will not your honour enter."

"I came for that purpose," replied Jenny, in an assumed tone. "Unfortunately I have been belated and lost my way; my servants too have missed me. Can I obtain refreshment and shelter here until the morning?"

"That can you, my worshipful master, and here," pointing to Dick Flybynight, "is a worshipful gentleman, who is also a guest, perhaps your honour would not object to join him over a friendly bowl."

Jenny with a graceful obeisance to Dick Flybynight, which was as graciously returned by the latter, intimated a willing assent to Ellis's proposal, and drawing from her pocket the canvass bag of guineas, which she had taken from the coachman, she took out a guinea and carelessly flung it on the oaken table.

The sight of the bag with its jingling contents was a matter of great interest both to Beauty and Dick. The former winked knowingly to the latter, and the dashing Flybynight almost imagined the shining treasure was already in his possession. Beauty Ellis's huge eyes sparkled with delight, and he showed the utmost politeness as he placed the steaming beverage before the person who had so liberally paid for it.

"You do well," observed Dick Flybynight, "to take shelter here, for you seem to be well provided with gold, and the neighbourhood is none of the honestest. Your health, worthy sir."

"Aye," remarked the disguised Jenny, "I have heard much respecting a gang of rogues who infest this quarter; however, I have little fear of them, as you may judge from the circumstance of my being here unattended and unarmed."

"Yet, judging from your appearance, friend," remarked Dick Flybynight, scanning as he spoke the stranger's figure from head to foot, "you would be likely to come off but second best should you chance to fall in with the redoubtable Captain M'Cleane."

"M'Cleane, who is he?" enquired Jenny, with an air of utter ignorance.

"Why, have you never heard of the most celebrated highwayman of his day?" returned Dick, enthusiastically. "I had thought that so bold a knight of the road could scarcely have failed to attract the attention if not excite the alarm of all who travelled at midnight with money in their purses, which they did not care to lose."

"It's true," remarked Jenny in a quiet tone, "that I have at this moment a large amount of gold in my possession; and it is equally true that I have not the slightest fear of the bold highwayman you have mentioned."

"You are brave indeed, sir," said Dick, "Captain M'Cleane I understand was never conquered but by one person, and that individual is now far away."

"Indeed," said Jenny, "and pray who may that conquering hero have been?"

"No hero at all," remarked Dick Flybynight, "it was only a woman."

"Only a woman," repeated Jenny Diver to herself, with a scarcely perceptible sneer on her finely curved upper lip, "and what may be the name of this redoubted heroine?"

"Jenny Diver," was the simple reply of Dick Flybynight.

"You said just now," remarked Jenny, "that the victor over M'Cleane was far away. What meant you by that?"

"Simply this," replied Dick, "her ladyship, who was devilish clever, made a slight mistake, and the big wigs, thinking she was rather too clever for the mother country, sent her off to illuminate the American Colonies. Most likely at this very moment the pretty Miss Diver is the mistress of a cotton planter or a tobacco grower."

Jenny Diver had a private opinion of her own that the speaker was quite wrong in his conjecture; but she prudently abstained from offering any opinion on the subject. Her curiosity, however, to know whether she still retained the affections of M'Cleane, induced her to put another question to Dick Flybynight—

"And think you that the damsel is yet remembered by the bold Captain?"

"I can answer for that, my noble master," said Beauty Ellis, "for I happen to know that since Jenny Diver's transportation, M'Cleane has showed himself out but seldom; and if what report says be true, his spirits have forsaken him, and his courage has evaporated."

"I will never believe that," cried Jenny. Then remembering that she had committed herself, she added—"I meant to say that I could not believe a woman should have so much influence over a man of courage and bravery as, by her mere absence, to subdue or destroy those valuable qualifications."

Here the conversation ceased, and Jenny asserting that she had changed her mind, announced her intention as the night was fine to resume her journey.

A signal given by Dick Flybynight to Beauty Ellis proclaimed that nothing could have pleased them better than the determination on the part of the stranger, who having also noticed the understanding which subsisted between Ellis and Dick, rose, and after discharging the reckoning, bade them a courteous good-night.

Jenny on quitting the tavern took the road in the direction of Barnett, and walked leisurely forward, fully convinced that the pair whom she had just left would before long join her.

Nor was she deceived; but before we follow her further we must return to Dick Flybynight and Beauty Ellis.

No sooner had the pretended traveller quitted them than they hurriedly armed and disguised themselves in huge cloaks, and then after rapidly traversing some bye-ways arrived at a point which, from previous enquiries, they knew their intended victim must pass.

Concealing themselves within the shadow of a high edge they listened intently, and before long heard the traveller approaching humming a song tune which was exceedingly popular at that day.

"Here comes the ruffler," said Dick Flybynight, "he will sing to a different tune presently or I'm much mistaken. Don't be violent, Beauty, I charge you; but take a lesson by me, and see how easy it is to pluck your bird without ruffling a feather."

At that moment, just as Jenny arrived opposite the spot where the highwaymen were concealed, Dick stepped forward and demanded the travellers money.

"And suppose I should not feel disposed to give it you, what then?" asked Jenny, with the utmost coolness.

"Then I'm sorry to say as you'll have a brace of bullets in your head," replied Beauty Ellis, exhibiting at the same time a horse pistol.

"Pooh!" observed Jenny, producing her own weapon, "I heed not your threats, and defy you to gain possession of the few score guineas which are in my pocket—Stand back!"

Dick Flybynight was rather staggered by this courageous conduct; but he took it for a mere contrivance to throw him off his guard, and again demanded the money.

Fearful that some interruption might take place, Dick Flybynight laid his hands on the shoulders of the traveller and was about forcibly to take the bag from his pocket, when he was greatly surprised by his intended victim bursting into a fit of laughter.

"You seem inclined to be merry, my master," remarked Beauty Ellis, "but it would be as well for you to remember that we have no time for joking. Come, Dick! it is high time this job was finished."

Again the stranger indulged in a silvery peal of merriment.

Dick Flybynight could not but fancy that he had heard the voice of the stranger before, but where he could not recollect. His doubts on the subject, however, were speedily set at rest.

"What, do you not know me, Dick?" asked Jenny, offering her hand to the astounded highwayman, who retreated a few steps, and surveyed the questioner in undisguised amazement.

"Did I not know that a certain person with whom I was once acquainted was some thousand of miles off I could almost swear that either Jenny Diver or the devil himself was now standing before me," exclaimed Dick Flybynight.

"Sir, you would not be far out in your reckoning so far as the girl is concerned," returned Jenny, removing her hat, and allowing the luxuriant tresses which had been concealed in its crown to fall in glossy waves over her shoulders.

Both Dick Flybynight and Beauty Ellis were not a little startled by this unlooked for appearance; and for some moments neither could speak. Beauty Ellis, who had no little superstition in his composition was actually alarmed, supposing that he beheld a ghost; but Jenny by a hearty shake of the hand soon convinced him that she was not only mortal flesh and blood, but as merry, as artful and as beautiful as ever.

"I thought I would have a diversion at your expense, before I visited the Country House," remarked Jenny, "you understand now, why I exhibited the bag of gold, which, by-the-bye, I picked up by chance on my way hither."

Jenny now, in reply to the eager questioning of Dick Flybynight and Beauty Ellis, related by what means she had been enabled to quit the Colonies and once more make her appearance on the scene of her former adventures and triumphs. Her narrative was listened to with eager curiosity, and it received the meed of hearty approbation from the listeners.

Jenny now proposed that they should return to the Country House, where the two men informed her that Captain M'Cleane then was.

They accordingly made the best of their way to that rendezvous; and Jenny having been secretly conveyed to the room in which the disguises of the gang were kept, selected from among the motley multitude of dresses, a favorite one which she had often before worn at the express desire of M'Cleane.

Thus altered, she rejoined Dick Flybynight who was so transported with delight on seeing their queen, as he termed her, once more among her faithful subjects, that he caught her in his arms, and ravished a kiss from her tempting rosy lips.

"M'Cleane is in his old apartment I suppose," asked Jenny, "or is he," she added with a voice which slightly faltered, "snug in the arms of his old flame—Madame Charlotte?"

Dick assured her that she had little to fear from the rivalry of the latter; and Jenny recovered her self-possession.

"I will go to Jem then, and surprise him," said Jenny Diver, and taking a small lamp, she bade Dick good night, and proceeded to the chamber of her former lover.

The door was slightly ajar so that she entered noiselessly. M'Cleane, who had recently undergone considerable fatigue, was buried in deep slumber; so profound indeed, that Jenny bent over him and imprinted a kiss on his cheek without awaking him.

She at first intended to have seated herself by his bedside until he should awaken and behold her; but with her usual caprice she all of a sudden changed her intentions, and determined to slip quietly into bed beside him.

Undressing herself, therefore, with the utmost caution, she placed the lamp so that the light from it would fall directly on her face, which was now suffused with a roseate blush.

Then she gently turned back the coverlet, and slid as quietly as possible into the bed, where for some moments she lay perfectly still; but as she grew warm her ardent transports were not to be controlled, and flinging her arms round M'Cleane's neck, she almost devoured him with kisses.

Thus roused from his slumber, M'Cleane gazed vacantly into the face of the fair girl who was lying beside him. For a few moments he believed himself to be dreaming, and it was not until he had rubbed his eyelids and pinched his flesh to convince himself that he was not still in the realms of visions, that he ascertained that something more substantial than a mere shadow shared his bed.

Once completely roused, he recognized the well-known features and arch smile of Jenny Diver. So great was his surprise, however, that he leaped out of bed, and continued gazing without uttering a word.

"Why, don't you know me, Jem, or have I grown so ugly since I last saw you that you are afraid of me. There was a time when I kept you in bed—not frightened you out of it."

"Do my eyes deceive me?" exclaimed M'Cleane, getting into bed again, "or do I again behold my incomparable Jenny Diver. "Yes—yes," he added, "it must be so; but tell me, how in Heaven's name have you managed to get back to England?"

"Easily enough, dear Jem, but to put you out of suspense I'll tell you presently the whole story; and after some warm embraces, the nature of which must be left to the imagination of the chaste reader, Jenny Diver gave the Captain a full, true, and particular account of her adventures abroad, and of the circumstances under which she had returned to her native shores.

Captain M'Cleane then, in his turn, informed Jenny Diver of all that had transpired during the period of her absence; and thus in love and conversation passed away the hours. It was long after the dawning of day when Jenny rested her head on the bosom of her lover, and closed her eyes in happy slumber: M'Cleane speedily followed her example, and to their dreams we will leave them while we record the doings of other personages who are intimately connected with our tale.

CHAPTER XLV.

CAPTAIN FURY IS REPULSED BY ISIDORA—THE DESTRUCTION OF THE BLACK GANG—RESCUE OF ISIDORA.

WHEN the young Spanish lady whom Captain Fury had carried off by violence from the Spanish galleon awoke from the swoon, or rather from the succession of fainting fits into which she fell after she had been conveyed to Captain Fury's apartment by old Mrs. Blite, she found herself alone.

Her first thoughts were how could she escape from the mysterious and fearful place into which she had been conveyed. To ascertain whether it was possible for her to rejoin her father, she at once rallied her energies, and proceeded carefully to examine the place, or rather prison in which she had been so cruelly incarcerated.

It was a square apartment, rudely though comfortably furnished, and lighted by a grated window close to the ceiling and consequently far above her head. By piling articles of furniture on the bed she contrived to so raise herself as to look through the bars, but so thick were they and so closely placed together that she could only distinguish through their interstices the roofs of some houses, and the spire of a neighbouring church.

This view, however, afforded her no information, for she had never been in London before, and consequently was totally unacquainted with the locality of the spot of her imprisonment. Even had she the means of escape, she should not know which way to direct her steps in search of her parent; for she had, it will be remembered, been brought from the river through the subterranean way, thus preventing her from noticing any land mark by which to judge of her course. Added to this, she was almost entirely ignorant of any other language than her own, and would have found it a matter of extreme difficulty to make herself understood by strangers.

The door next underwent her scrutiny, but

that was fast locked; evidently she had nothing to hope for from that quarter. She, therefore, in order to dissipate her melancholy as much as possible, once more mounted on her platform of table and chairs and leaning her head mournfully on her hand, she gazed with wistful eyes upon the sky which looked blue, bright and free beyond —anything she thought was better than to survey the barred door and lonely walls of her prison.

Her situation was indeed pitiable, she knew too well that she was in the midst of a band of ruffians, who would have no more compassion on her than a lion would feel for a lamb in its talons. In her innocence, however, the poor girl little dreamed of the base designs which Captain Fury harboured against her, for she had been brought up in so secluded a manner that her knowledge of the wickedness of mankind was limited in the extreme.

She had sat for more than an hour at her barred window, when the door of her cell opened, and Mrs. Blite made her appearance with some delicate viands and choice wines which Captain Fury had ordered to be procured for Isidora.

The instant the hag perceived the young girl gazing wistfully through the barred window, she commanded her in a harsh tone to come down, and with menacing gestures intimated that such conduct would not be allowed. Placing the food before Isidora, who apparently noticed it not, she quitted the apartment and the young Spanish girl was once more alone.

Instead of partaking of any refreshment she drew from her bosom a gold crucifix studded with precious stones, and holding it reverently before her eyes prayed devoutly to be delivered from the power of her enemies. While she was thus piously engaged the door once more revolved on its hinges, and the dreaded Captain Fury entered and bolted the door after him, so as to prevent any one interrupting the tete-a-tete he intended to have.

Fury had on this particular occasion attired himself with great care, in order to produce as favourable an impression on the young lady as possible; but it may easily be supposed that his huge frame, disfigured as it was by wounds, and the effects of a wandering and dissipated life, would be calculated to disgust and alarm rather than please or attract a delicate creature like the fair daughter of Spain. The Captain, however, who had his full share of vanity never in the least suspected this.

Fury, indeed, possessed one advantage, he had travelled in many parts of the world, and knew several languages, among them he was acquainted with the Spanish tongue, well enough to engage in fluent conversation. This was no slight cause of rejoicing to him as Isidora could not speak a word of English.

The reader will therefore understand that all conversations between Fury and his captive were in the language of the latter, although for obvious reasons we shall relate them in our own tongue.

The moment Isidora beheld Captain Fury enter she rose from her knees, and looking into his face with a most beseeching air, besought him with the utmost earnestness to allow her to return to her father.

"What, do you not think you can be happy with me, my pretty Isidora," said Fury, laying one of his huge hands on her shoulder. "No—no!" he added, shaking his head, "I ran rather too much risk in kidnapping you to let you escape so easily."

"But he will die," she exclaimed, bursting into tears, "and no one will be near to attend to him. Senor Capitano, I engage that the half of my fathers fortune shall be yours, if you will but place me in his arms, and I will for ever pray to the Virgin for your salvation."

"Bah!" cried Fury, "keep your prayers for me to yourself, or if you must chatter to the queen of Heaven as you furriner's call her, ask her to make you contented with your present situation for here you will remain, and understand as my companion."

The girl shrank into a corner of the room, and stretched forth her hands so as to warn him not to touch her; but heedless of the hint he advanced towards her, and rudely placed his arm round her waist, and sitting on the bed endeavoured to force her on his knee.

But she was stronger than he had anticipated, with a wild cry she burst from his embrace, shuddering and looking aghast as though a serpent had threatened to sting her. Her delicate form appeared to dilate; her dark eyes flashed fire from beneath their long silken lashes, and with compressed lips she muttered the word—'villain.'

"Come—come," said Fury, "if you will not listen to reason, means must be used to compel you to accede to my wishes," and again he attempted to grasp Isidora in his arms.

With the quickness of lightning she again eluded his grasp, and placing herself with her back against the wall of the cell, she drew from a concealed fold of her dress a small poignard with which she menaced the man who had so cruelly assailed her.

Captain Fury, however, merely laughed at what he considered her impotent attempts, and in derision drew forth his huge cutlass, and brandished it over his head.

"Advance but one step towards me, and this dagger shall find a sheath either in your breast or mine," exclaimed the Spanish girl, who by this time fully comprehended the delicate and dangerous nature of her position.

Seeing that she was so determined in her opposition to his infamous desires, Captain Fury determined for the present to leave his intended victim; he, therefore announced to her that he should visit her again in the course of a few hours, when he hoped he should find her in a more complaisant humour.

Fury then quitted the bed-chamber and joined his companions in the Hall of the Black Gang.

No sooner had her persecutor quitted her, than Isidora again revolved in her mind the possibility of making her escape from that dismal place. She perceived that force it would be impossible for her to use; therefore stratagem was the weapon which must be employed to accomplish her deliverance.

Taking from her pocket a small book of devotions, she tore a blank leaf from it, and wrote thereon, in Spanish, a slight account of herself, describing as well as she could the manner in which her father and herself had been treated. Then placing a gold coin in the paper she tied it up into a parcel and directed it at a venture to some charitable christian. This done, she mounted to the barred window, threw it as far as possible, and finally seated herself on the bedside to wait the result of her scheme.

When the Captain of the Black Gang rejoined his companions he was received with vociferous cheers, for at that meeting it had been arranged that a distribution of the wealth which had been taken from the unfortunate Spanish ship should take place.

Piled on the table lay heaps of gold and silver coin as well as ingots of both the precious metals. The eyes of the daring plunderers gleamed with savage joy as they looked on the glittering prize and all were impatient to receive their share of the plunder.

Fury having taken the seat of authority proceeded to arrange the distribution, each man according to the time he had been a member of the gang, receiving a certain share of the proceeds of the robbery. The ingots of the precious metals the Captain reserved for himself: soon was the table cleared, and the pockets of the robbers well filled; and now they prepared to give themselves up to drunkenness and revelry.

Hours passed in this manner, and even Fury forgot that other treasure which he had under lock and key, whilst he was under the influence of the bowl. Suddenly, however, he remembered in his cups that Isidora was still confined in his bed-chamber, and a drunken whim to exhibit her to his comrades entered into his brain.

Reeling along the hall he proceeded to Isidora's room, and on entering it found her still in the attitude of prayer; but still holding the dagger in her hand. By mere brute force he wrenched the weapon from her grasp, and then seizing the young girl round the waist he bore her triumphantly into the midst of his fierce and now furious comrades.

The animal passions of the robbers already excited by strong drinks were still further excited by the sight of the lovely Spaniard, who with dishevelled hair, torn robes, and timorous aspect now shrank in horror from the libertine glances which assailed her modesty from every side.

"There mates! what think you of this morsel which I have put by for myself? Why damn it, the girl is fool enough not to estimate properly the honour I am going to confer upon her by making her my mistress."

"It aint quite fair, Captain Fury, as you should keep that bit of dainty stuff all to yourself," said one of the gang, with a leer.

"Couldn't we go shares in her as well as in the gold, Captain?" demanded another, whom wine had somewhat plundered of his discretion.

"Aye, lads, after I have done with her, mayhap I'll then turn her over to some of you; but, harkye! if one of you dare to lay hands on the girl until I give permission that moment shall be his last."

It was well for Isidora that her ignorance of English prevented her understanding this barbarous speech. The rude manner, however, of the gang so alarmed her that her terrors could hardly have been increased.

Still the revelry went on, Isidora being forced to occupy a chair beside the Captain, who in-

dulged to a fearful extent in drink. Obscene songs were sung, and the grossest licentiousness indulged in. At length a pause in the revelry ensued, which was after some continuance disturbed by a novel and unlooked for circumstance.

* * * *

The plundering of the Spanish galleon, San Salvador, the brutal treatment of her Captain, and part of his crew, and more than all the forcible carrying off of his beautiful daughter, created an extraordinary sensation in the metropolis, especially among that portion of its inhabitants who were engaged in seafaring matters.

The watch-boats of the river, immediately on the circumstance becoming known, were filled with officers, who at once commenced the most rigid search; but investigations into the mysterious affair were materially aided by the step which Isidora, the young Spanish girl, had taken. Fortunately for her, it happened that the piece of paper which she had thrown from the window of her prison was picked up before it had been trampled on and lost in the mire: the document itself would have been but little cared for had it not been accompanied by the piece of gold. This secured attention to it, and ultimately led, by means which it is not necessary for us to define, to her deliverance.

While the Black Gang were in the height of their revelry, a noise as of fighting was heard proceeding from the direction of the house through which Hawkins and his companion had entered the strong-hold of the river pirates; and with a pale face, and an expression of the utmost terror on his countenance, Blite, the ancient warder of the desperadoes, rushed into the hall.

"Fly!" he exclaimed in a hoarse voice. "The Captain of the City Train Bands with a large party have made good their entrance into the Old Mint, and are already in my apartments searching for a girl who they swear is concealed here."

"Damnation!" muttered Fury, whom this intelligence completely sobered. "But the villains shall find no easy matter to surprise us. To arms, brave companions, to arms!"

Seizing a large cutlass, he hastily fastened its scabbard to his belt, in which he stuck two large pistols. The other members of the gang also speedily armed themselves, and prepared to meet the common danger.

That a desperate conflict was at hand could not be doubted, for scarcely had Fury and his men placed themselves in the attitude of defence, than the sound of approaching footsteps were heard; these gradually drew nearer and nearer, and suddenly with a tremendous crash the door was dashed from its hinges, and a number of the City Train Bands accompanied by a party of the Customs' officers armed to the teeth, rushed upon the pirates.

But the most striking figure among them, and one who seemed possessed by the very demon of revenge, was an old man, with his grey hair streaming in the damp; his eyes glaring like those of a maniac, and brandishing a glittering rapier. The instant the individual's eyes rested on the tall form of Captain Fury he impetuously rushed towards him; but his light weapon was instantly jerked from his hand by a stroke of the pirate's cutlass, and its owner lay at Fury's mercy.

"My child—my Isidora," exclaimed the wretched old man. "Villain, restore me my child."

A sneer was the only reply of Fury; but, at that moment, as if in answer to the agonizing prayer of the old man, a door leading into the apartment was dashed in by two of the soldiers, and in an instant Isidora rushed from the chamber of her imprisonment, and seeing her father, rushed towards him, and uttering a heart-piercing shriek, fell senseless in his arms.

The battle between the members of the Black Gang and their assailants now raged with the utmost fury. For a brief time victory hovered alternately over each party, but reinforced by additional numbers, the attacking party soon gained the advantage, seeing that the game was becoming desperate, Fury, with a wonderful energy once more rallied his followers, and endeavoured to animate them by his example; seeing, however, that capture or death was inevitable, he determined that, if he and his gang were destroyed, those who had been the means of vanquishing them should be involved in their ruin.

Seizing his opportunity, he retreated to the secret passage, and took from thence a small cask of gunpowder. To drive in the head of it with his heel was but the work of a moment; he then lifted it in his arms, and boldly marched with it into the centre of the hall where the conflict was still raging.

"To the river-passage, comrades," he shouted with a hoarse voice. "We may yet escape by the boats—I will be the last to leave this place."

On hearing this, a rush was instantly made by the pirates, but they were prevented from leaving their den by the officers, who now completely surrounded them.

Seeing this, Fury, with a terrible oath, approached the open cask of powder, which he had placed on a table, and firing a pistol into it, a fearful explosion instantly shook the building from its foundation to summit.

When the smoke had partially cleared away, a fearful spectacle presented itself. In every direction lay blackened and mutilated bodies, some yet retaining life; others, from which the vital spark had been miserably and suddenly banished; the walls and the ceiling were scorched and blackened, and the air was so vitiated from the effects of the explosion, that the miserable creatures who were yet alive, could scarcely inhale it.

Conspicuous amongst the corpses was the huge body of him who was the author of the fearful catastrophe. By the force of the explosion he had been hurled against the wall of the apartment with such tremendous force, that his skull was literally battered into fragments; his sinewy hand yet retained the pistol in its death-gripe, and on his grey brow there still lingered an expression of savage daring and ferocity. Near his body lay the mangled remains of Hawkins, the escaped culprit.

Almost by a miracle about half a dozen persons were saved, and were comparatively unhurt. Among these were the old Spanish Captain and his daughter. The blast, however, in that confined place had stunned them almost into unconsciousness, and rendered them for a time heedless one of the other, and a still greater danger which threatened them.

The building, as we have before intimated, was an excessively old one, and when the explosion occurred some old beams overhead, which were almost as inflammable as touchwood, took fire, and smouldered unobserved for some time. But as soon as the air, which came through the subterranean passage, began to circulate freely, the smouldering sparks were speedily converted into flame, which ran along the rafters, licking them as tongues of fire, and communicating the destructive element to other portions of the room.

Dense volumes of smoke which now rolled upwards and onwards speedily filled the entire building, and at length escaping by the doors and windows which opened on the narrow thoroughfare of the Old Mint, formed a gloomy canopy, like a sepulchral pall over the robbers stronghold; the alarm was given, but before assistance could be procured the flames roared along the winding passages, raged in every room and poured forth from every window, illuminating the whole neighbourhood.

Higher and still higher they ascended, until at length the leaping flames reached the roof, round the huge beams and rafters of which they wreathed like so many hissing serpents eager for their prey. Before long the covering of that devoted house fell in with a tremendous crash, and the hitherto dull, lurid glare was exchanged for a brilliant illumination.

When Isidora recovered from the fainting fit into which she had fallen, she shuddered to perceive the terrible and new evil which threatened her and her father. The old man also gradually revived: but was so horror-stricken at the prospect of perishing by fire that for some moments he gazed vacantly on the scene, unable either to aid himself or to render assistance to others. Fortunately for both father and daughter one of the Custom House officers had entirely overcome the effects of the tremendous shock, and this man at once endeavoured to rouse them from their stupor.

Seizing a case-bottle which escaped the general wreck, he ascertained that it contained some of that liquid for which the distilleries of Nantz was famous, and a small portion of which he poured down the throats of the strangers. The stimulant proved of the greatest service, for both the Capitano and Isidora were enabled to direct what little energies they possessed towards the means of escape.

Whilst still irresolute, and uncertain as to what course to pursue, Isidora drew the crucifix from her bosom, and kissing it, breathed an earnest supplication to the Virgin for their deliverance. As if in answer to her prayers, at that moment a thought flashed across her mind, and a smile of hope flitted across her countenance.

To quit the place where they were by the door through which her father and the officers had made their sudden entrance was now impossible, for the space beyond it was completely blocked up by still burning timbers. All means of egress, save the mysterious one by way of which she had been conveyed thither were therefore unavailable.

A stream of fresh air which fell upon her fevered cheek, indicated to her the situation of the entrance to the subterranean labyrinth. Grasping eagerly at the hope which this silent messenger conveyed to her mind, she dragged her parent to the side of the apartment, and there fortunately

discovered the entrance door which led to the secret way.

Once within this they were comparatively safe. They had not availed themselves of this providential place of refuge one moment too soon; for scarcely had they quitted the Hall of the Black Gang when the roof came crashing through the half-consumed floors, and literally buried the bodies of Fury and his comrades in a grave of fire. Shuddering as she observed the peril from which she had escaped, Isidora penetrated still further into the dark passage, and assisted by the officer who had already devoted himself to their service, the girl and the old man penetrated still further into the gloom of the passage.

Their progress was necessarily slow, and many were the bruises they received in stumbling against unseen projecting angles, and over casks, which in many places were piled near the wall.

No. 28.

At length, after a toilsome wandering, a gleam of light appeared in the distance, and the air seemed to be fresher and keener. Ten minutes more assured them that all danger was passed, for they stood on the brink of the river which swept onwards toward the sea.

The boats of the river-pirates were high and dry, and therefore useless to them; but by dint of hallowing and waving a handkerchief from the end of a long pole the attention of some boatmen was soon attracted, and speedily the Captain and his daughter were conveyed to their ship, the San Salvador; the old man almost reconciled to the loss of his treasure, now that he regained possession of, and rescued from what he considered to be a condition far worse than death itself, his beloved child.

The officer had no sooner seen his companions safely bestowed, than he at once proceeded to report to the authorities the strange events to which he had been a witness, and the calamity from which he had so wonderfully escaped.

CHAPTER XLVI.

LAWYER DOOM IS CAUGHT IN HIS OWN TRAP—FLITCHMAN'S REVENGE—THE LAWYER TAKES HIS LAST JOURNEY TO TYBURN.

IMMEDIATELY after the sham and forced marriage of Lady Purley, Richard Town and his still half insensible victim returned as we have seen to the office of the villainous lawyer, Mr. Doom.

The first thing he did was to use every endeavour to recover his bride from the stupor into which she had fallen. This was found to be no easy matter, but after some time the influences of the draught which Doom had obtained from the chemist, yielded to the stimulants administered, and Emilia awoke to full consciousness.

The important occurrence, however, which had just transpired seemed to her but as the result of a troubled dream, for her memory retained a dim perception of having been a principal in a marriage ceremony. Still, for some time, she could not persuade herself that it was sad reality.

But when once convinced of this, and fully alive to the perils of her situation, her indignation knew no bounds, and she bitterly rebuked her former lover, who, in his turn, was not a little surprised at the turn which affairs had taken. Appearing not to heed the denunciations which she heaped on his head, he demanded of her the papers which Quilt Arnold had informed Dick Flybynight she would bring with her; but to Handsome Jack's astonishment the lady not only denied that she had any documents in her possession but asserted that she had been forced against her own consent to quit her husband's house.

"What means this, Mr. Doom?" angrily demanded Handsome Jack of the lawyer, who sat coolly at a table, turning over some papers.

"How should I know," replied the lawyer, "I did not run away with the lady—did I?"

"But did not you authorize some agent of yours to inform me that you would find a purchaser for the estates of one Richard Town?" enquired Jack, with some uneasiness.

"Never;" replied the lawyer, "but here comes one who can perhaps give you some information on the subject."

The heavy tramp of some one ascending the stairs was now heard; in a moment afterwards the door opened, and a man of burly proportions made his appearance.

It was Jonathan Wild.

"You have arrived opportunely, Mr. Wild," remarked Doom. "Here is a gentleman who is making enquiries respecting some papers relating to the estates of one Richard Town, know you aught of the matter?"

"But little," observed Jonathan who had keenly scrutinized Handsome Jack," and yet that little may be important, for I happen myself to have some documents relating to this Town's affair, which came in rather a curious manner into my possession."

While saying this, Jonathan Wild drew from the breast pocket of his coat the pocket-book, which it will be remembered was in the possession of Handsome Jack when he rescued Jenny Diver from the fire at Williams's the Fence, in Hanging Sword Alley, and which was torn from him by the bull dog, Beelzebub.

No sooner had Handsome Jack's eyes lighted on it than he attempted to snatch it from the grasp of Wild, who, however, was too wary to allow himself to be dispossesed of it in this way.

"Not so fast, young man," said the thief taker coolly. "Before I part with this, certain conditions must be complied with. You seem mightily anxious to obtain it. May I ask why?"

"Because it is mine, that is all," replied Handsome Jack.

"Yours! then you are the Richard Town to whom these papers refer."

"I am," said Handsome Jack, who now perceived that he had somewhat committed himself. "But name your conditions," he added, as coolly as possible.

"That on condition of receiving a sufficient sum to enable you to proceed to some distant land, whence you may never return, you will legally assign over to me the whole of the property to which these deeds refer," was the proposition of Jonathan Wild.

"Never!" exclaimed Handsome Jack, casting a look of ineffable scorn on the thief taker. "There are means of compelling you to deliver me that book, and I warn you not to refuse to hand it to me,—you retain it at your peril."

Wild smiled contemptuously at Town as he thus spoke, and then approaching the door gave a low whistle.

Immediately afterwards the sound of several footsteps were heard ascending the stairs, but before they quite approached the office of Doom, Wild called out to them to halt.

"You little think," he said, turning to Handsome Jack, and pointing significantly to the dark staircase, "that I have the means at hand to enforce your consent if you remain obstinate. Here is a document which I have had already prepared —sign it and you are free—refuse and your ruin is certain and speedy."

"I refuse, let the consequences be what they may," said Handsome Jack. "Doom," he added, addressing that worthy, "you have been meddling in this villainous affair; but by the God who made me you shall suffer for this sooner or later."

The lawyer, who knew that Handsome Jack held now no longer the proofs of his forgery, took no notice of this ebullition of passion, and by looks defied the man who he had so terribly injured.

Another whistle from Jonathan Wild caused the footsteps again to be heard, and immediately afterwards a possee of Bow Street Officers, with Mr. Watkins at their head made their appearance in the room.

Handsome Jack surveyed the men for a moment and then drawing his sword prepared to defend himself.

"I believe, Madame," said Jonathan Wild to Lady Emilia Purley, "that you were brought hither against your own consent, and that you were no party to the vile outrage which has just been perpetrated against your person and liberty?"

"I have been cruelly treated; for God's sake save me," exclaimed the wretched lady, throwing herself at the feet of Jonathan.

"I will not only do so, Madame," said Jonathan, with seeming benevolence, "but I will restore you to your husband. Hearken! I hear a carriage drawing up below:—happening to hear of the iniquitous plot, though somewhat too late to prevent the false marriage, I at once sent an intimation to Lord Purley of your whereabouts, and here he comes to claim you."

It was as Wild said, for, bursting with fury, Lord Purley entered the room. The instant Lady Purley perceived him she rushed towards him and claimed his protection, but the exasperated Peer, who firmly believed that his young wife had willingly eloped from his house, rudely thrust her from him, and shrunk from her touch as though she had been a scorpion.

But he was soon undeceived, and then he vented his rage on him who had torn his wife from his arms. Gazing at Handsome Jack steadily, he at once recognized him as one of the men who had entered his bridal chamber on the night of his marriage, and he openly charged him with the commission of the burglary.

This was music to the ears of Jonathan Wild, who instantly suggested in a whisper to the Peer, that by giving him into custody on that charge, he might avoid the inconvenience and mortification of an exposure of his lady's flight; a circumstance which would not fail to create a vast deal of scandal in the fashionable world.

Lord Purley, who was morbidly sensitive when anything threatened to effect his dignity, eagerly embraced the proposal, and beckoning Watkins to his side he whispered a few words into that persons ear.

"Good!" muttered the Bow Street runner, and approaching Handsome Jack, he laid his hand on his shoulder and said—

"Richard Town, you are my prisoner—in the name of the king I require you to submit to my custody."

"Your prisoner!" demanded Handsome Jack, "on what charge dare you thus lay hands on me?"

"Why, on a werry awkward one, Mr. Town," replied the Bow Street runner, "you see as this honorable gentleman is ready to swear that you broke into his house in the dead of the night, which is not a werry honest way of doing business—so surrender."

A desperate struggle now took place, attracted by the noise of which, Dick Flybynight, who had been keeping watch below, entered Doom's office. By the time he had gained the room, however, Handsome Jack overpowered by numbers, had been disarmed and secured, and now stood panting, and glaring wildly on his captors.

A private signal from Handsome Jack brought Dick Flybynight to his side, and an earnest conference was held between the two. Fortunately, the person of Dick was unknown both to the officer and thief-taker, and he was permitted to communicate freely with his friend. The nature of their conversation will be understood when the events which followed it shall have been narrated.

Handsome Jack's capture having thus been effected, preparations were made for carrying him to the Compter for the night. Perceiving that he was about to be led off, he implored as a particular favor that he might be permitted to say a few words to Lady Purley in private.

"Not a word, save in my presence," exclaimed the stately Lord Purley, drawing himself up, "it is hardly possible," he added, "that I should allow her ladyship to hold secret intercourse with a thief and a robber, as this man has proved himself to be."

Handsome Jack's whole frame quivered with rage and indignation; but his regard for her whom he had so deeply though to a certain extent unintentionally injured, kept him within bounds, and he preferred speaking to Lady Purley though clogged by such a condition, rather than not have an opportunity of communicating with her at all.

He was now thoroughly convinced that he had been made a dupe of for the second time by the scoundrelly attorney Doom; and that Lady Purley had never once dreamed of quitting the house of her husband. Feeling how much misery he had thus brought upon one for whom he would most willingly sacrifice his own life, he was anxious to make all the reparation in his power; and, therefore, with a view to shield her as far as possible from the probable ill-treatment or unjust prejudices of her old husband, he openly avowed in the hearing of the latter, that the abduction of Lady Purley had been effected by force and entirely against her will and without her own consent.

He fancied that the lady thanked him with an expressive look for this vindication of herself, and this was some consolation in his fettered and perilous condition.

"Dick," whispered Handsome Jack, once more placing his mouth close to the ear of Dick Flybynight "fail not to visit Flitchman, at Mother Sin's; that man must be kept in our interest—he will expose the whole of Doom's knavery; but in the first place do what I requested you a few minutes since—all depends upon that."

"Now then, my master," said Mr. Watkins, touching his prisoner's arm, "this way," and the other officers surrounding him he was led from the apartment; and in less than half-an-hour afterwards Handsome Jack, the rightful heir to an ancient title and thousands of broad acres, lay on a wretched straw pallet in a common gaol.

Dick Flybynight lingered not a moment after the departure of his friend, who he watched until the wicket gate of the Compter concealed him from his eyes.

Then he returned towards the Fleet, and creeping stealthily up the stairs leading to Doom's office, listened at the door and ascertained that Jonathan Wild had not quitted the company of the lawyer.

At that door there was also another listener whom Dick Flybynight did not discover until he accidentally came into contact with him in the dark. This was Tim Snarley, who in accordance with the plan he had devised after hearing the conversation between Jonathan Wild and Quilt Arnold, in the Fleet Prison, had adopted this means of fathoming the secret of his rascally employer.

Seizing hold of the lad by the nape of the neck Dick forced him down stairs, whispering to him that he should be choked if he dared to raise an alarm. This, however, need not have given him any concern, for Tim Snarley was himself as desirous as Dick Flybynight could have had wished to avoid being detected in that place by his worthy master.

"What do you want of me?" asked the youth, looking into Dick's face which was now visible by the light of a lamp.

"To know why you were listening at that door, and to know who you are," replied Dick Flybynight.

"I'm Doom's clerk, and I wanted to know what devil's work he was up to now. Curse you, if you hadn't spoiled the fun I should have heard all by this time."

"You are no great friend of Mr. Doom's then, though you do serve him?" asked Dick Flybynight, keenly scrutinizing the lad's features by the aid of the lamp.

"Friend! what, of a man who would as soon cut my throat as eat his dinner; if I let my tongue tell half of what I know—no, no," said the boy, "devil's incarnate such as Doom are served from fear or interest not love."

It instantly occurred to Dick Flybynight that this lad would be of great use to him in carrying out some of the projects which he had already formed. Slipping, therefore, a piece of money into his hand he plied him with various questions, and then made him the promise of a liberal reward if he would on a future occasion relate all he knew of certain transactions in which his master had been concerned. To this proposition Tim Snarley willingly assented, for his love of money, which he squandered at cock-pits, was inordinate; and besides this, since the removal of his master from Gray's Inn, his services had been so miserably paid for, that the little attachment he had once felt, for the old attorney was well nigh at an end.

Placing himself within the shadow of an old house which was situated immediately opposite the office of the lawyer, Dick watched intently for the departure of Jonathan Wild from it. He had learned from Tim Snarley that Quilt Arnold had already taken his departure, so that it was certain the thief-taker would return homeward alone. This was exactly what Dick Flybynight desired.

Two o'clock sounded from the sonorous bell of St. Pauls Cathedral, and the deep tones were taken up, as it were, by those of a hundred other churches around, and still the lawyer and his companion appeared to be engaged in secret conclave, upon some matter of importance, for the highwayman could perceive by their shadow, which fell upon the window blind, that they were seated at a table, and apparently bending over it as if reading or examining documents. He began at last to fear that the person whose appearance in the street he was anxiously expecting, would not come forth until daylight, in which case his object would be frustrated; but just as he had almost given up hope he perceived that one of the men, who he knew must be Wild from the appearance of the shadow, had arisen from the table and put on his three cornered hat.

Presently the shadow disappeared, and the light also; immediately afterwards Mr. Doom was seen at the door, with the candle raised over his head, lighting out the thief-taker.

The moment Wild left Doom's door, Dick Flybynight, with stealthy, cat like steps, followed on his track. Carefully keeping close to the houses so as to be as much as possible within their deep shadow, he walked as far as the foot of Snow Hill, every moment getting nearer and nearer to Jonathan, who with all his wariness little suspected that his movements were watched. On arriving opposite Green Arbour Court, in the Old Bailey, the thief-taker paused for a moment and surveyed its gloomy walls with a grim satisfaction depicted on his countenance, an expression which was instantly exchanged for one of terror, as he felt himself grasped by the arms, which were pinioned as it were by some unseen person who dragged him by main force into the dark court, before he could recover sufficiently from his surprise to alarm the watch.

No sooner had he removed Jonathan from the public thoroughfare to a place where he was less likely to be detected by the guardians of the night than he forced him to the ground, another planting his knee on his broad chest, levelled a pistol at his head and threatened him with instant death if he moved hand or foot, or attempted to call the watch.

"Do you know who I am, you villain, and that I could hang you for this?" demanded the indignant thief-taker, his bloated face purple with rage.

"I've no time to answer questions," replied Dick, pressing still more firmly on Wild's chest, "but I'll trouble you to hand me a certain pocket book which you have in your possession, as I have taken a particular fancy to it, Mr. Wild."

"So then you do know who I am, villain; but you shall pay dearly for this."

A blow from the butt-end of Dick Flybynight's pistol on Wild's head, which would almost have fractured a bullock's, was the highwayman's only reply. This application to the thief taker's scull completely stunned him, and taking advantage of this apathetic state Dick commenced rummaging his pockets. His search was successful, for in a part of his dress, to which Handsome Jack had directed his attention, Flybynight found the pocket-book which he had ran so much risk to gain possession of.

Satisfied with the result of his adventure, Dick Flybynight did not care to search Wild's other pockets, so bestowing a parting kick on Jonathan who now gave intimations of returning consciousness, he plunged still further into the gloom of the court, and descending the rather dangerous Breakneck steps at its other end, he soon gained Farringdon Street once more, and then passing into Fleet Street, hastened to the Temple stairs, where, finding several boats he wrenched away the staple of the padlock which secured one of them to a post and jumping into it was fortunate enough to find a pair of oars, by means of which he crossed the river, and landed not far from Westminster Bridge, the tide having drifted him in that direction.

Leaving the boat to the mercy of the tide, he now made the best of his way to the Almonry, where he arrived just as the chimes of the abbey were playing four o'clock. A light in the low room on the side of the entrance convinced him that Mother Sin was still up, and without hesitation he gave the usual signal at the door.

The ancient bawd speedily appeared, and warmly welcomed Dick who she informed was lucky inasmuch as his old blowen Sal, the Gonnoff, was at that moment in bed, and for a wonder disengaged; but to Mother Sin's surprise, Dick Flybynight informed her that with affairs of love he should at that time have nothing to do, business of the utmost importance with her lodger, Flitchman, had brought him thither.

As, however, Dick did not omit to place in Mother Sin's willing hand the usual present that ancient and amiable lady was by no means dissatisfied; on the contrary, she possessed the utmost anxiety to serve Dick, and presented him with a dram of strong waters, without a dose of which, she had a decided opinion that no matter of any moment whatever could be transacted.

Dick Flybynight having received the proper directions mounted to the room occupied by the late clerk of the Grays Inn lawyer. Flitchman was in bed fast asleep, but the glare of Dick Flybynight's candle instantly awakened him, and he started up in the utmost alarm.

Dick, however, assured him that his visit was of a friendly nature, and having related to him the occurrences of the night, he observed—

"You are of course perfectly aware of all the circumstances connected with the forgery of Mr. Doom's—I may say also of yours. You cannot also fail to know that should the worst come to the worst your neck would be as much in peril as his."

A shudder and a nod from Flitchman indicated an assent to the uncomfortable assurance.

"Then there is but one way to save yourself. Do you mind sacrificing Doom?"

"Why should I?" asked Flitchman, fiercely, "did he scruple to attempt to murder me, by flinging me into the Thames? I scruple to hang him—no; so much the contrary, that if a word of mine could save him I would not utter it."

"Right!" remarked Dick. "Then in that case you must immediately inform on your old master, and have him apprehended. Besides your testimony I have here his own confession of his guilt," and taking from the pocket-book the paper Handsome Jack had forced the lawyer to sign, he showed it to Flitchman.

"To-morrow morning you must appear before a magistrate and not only accuse Doom of forgery, but you must at the same time admit your participation in this crime, and pray to be admitted king's evidence. This will not be refused, and you will be safe. If you refuse Doom will inevitably be your destruction."

Flitchman wearied out with anxiety, and fearing every moment to be captured, after some little consideration consented to these terms, and Dick Flybynight, after giving him some gold as an earnest of what he should hereafter receive, in order to enable him to procure a living here or abroad, left the Almonry.

Dick's first step on the following morning was to seek out Watkins, the Bow Street runner, who he well knew would gladly undertake the impeachment and capture of the lawyer, and conceal also the way in which he had become possessed of the necessary documents, if he received a proper

consideration, as a reward for his indefatigable exertions.

Nor was the highwayman deceived, for a well-filled purse so operated on Mr. Watkins's conscience that he promised to do all that was required of him, and Dick Flybynight quitted his presence, in order to hasten to Handsome Jack and inform him that his desire for revenge was likely to be amply satisfied.

The lawyer was seated at breakfast on the morning following the forced marriage of Lady Purley; and at an hour somewhat later than usual, when Tim Snarley entered the office, and informed him that Mr. Watkins, the Bow Street officer, desired to see him.

"About last night's business no doubt," muttered Mr. Doom. "Thank God, that matter's safe at last, I can snap my fingers at Sir Richard Town now, and when Wild gives me that cursed paper which I signed, as he promised, not a soul breathing can injure Wriggleton Doom."

"Mr. Watkins seems in a devil of a hurry," remarked Tim Snarley.

"Why, yes, my business is rather of a pressing nature," remarked the officer, who had closely followed the footsteps of Tim Snarley, and now walked unceremoniously into the room, "and," he added, rather mysteriously, "that business is with you, Mr. Doom."

"So I presume; but perhaps you will explain," remarked the lawyer.

"It's werry unpleasant, I assure you, werry grating to my feelings to inform you that you must accompany me to a magistrate; but dooty must be done, Mr. Doom, and here's my warrant for your apprehension."

Had a thunder bolt fallen at the feet of the attorney he could not have been more terribly astounded. Only a little time before he had been felicitating himself on his imaginary security; but at the very moment when the dark cloud which had so long hung over him seemed about to pass away, it had suddenly burst, and the deluge of wrath had fallen on his devoted head.

The lawyer turned ghastly pale and could scarcely credit the evidence of his senses:—as soon, however, as he had in some degree collected himself, he saw the full extent of the ruin which had overtaken him, and prepared to accompany the officer, leaving Tim Snarley in charge of his office.

No sooner had Watkins and his prisoner departed, than the clerk of the latter, who by no means astonished at the turn which affairs had taken, seized the ruler which lay upon the table, and played upon it, pantomimically, an exceedingly lively and joyous tune, dancing at the same time with surprising agility, and otherwise indulging in expressions of merriment. Then he snapped his fingers in a sort of ecstacy, swept the books from the table to the floor, jumped upon them, and finally he put on his hat, locked up the office, and sallied forth in the pleasant consciousness that he was now his own master.

We must, however, follow in the track of Mr. Doom. That worthy having undergone an examination before a magistrate was fully committed on the capital charge of forgery; his former clerk, Flitchman having been admitted king's evidence against him. Handsome Jack, who himself had not yet been committed to Newgate, was a principal witness against the unhappy lawyer, who at the ensuing sessions was found guilty and sentenced to death.

Before we revert to the other scenes and characters of our history, it may perhaps be advisable to follow up the story of one who has figured in it so frequently.

As soon as the awful sentence of the law had been pronounced on the miserable creature he sank into a state of almost hopeless despondency. Old and wretched as he was though, he still clung to life, and with his long bony hands firmly gripping the edge of the dock, he fell upon his knees and in the most abject terms implored mercy. Still shrieking for this boon, he was dragged forcibly away, and consigned to the horrors of the condemned cell.

There, it may easily be imagined, his reflections were of the most agonizing description. His whole career had been marked with iniquity, for the Town fraud was but one among many. The curses of orphans and widows rested upon his soul; and now, in the solitude of his dungeon with death staring him in the face, he buried his face in his hands and groaned in very bitterness of spirit.

Remorse, not repentance, was his sole companion. A continual course of crime had, as it were, so case hardened his heart, that it was only effected by the thunders of a terrible retribution. And so the few days of his miserable life passed away, and at length but a few short hours intervened between him and an ignominious death.

Vain were the exhortations of the chaplain—vain all the efforts of those who endeavoured to rouse him to a sense of his situation; but as the last hour drew near his apathy changed to extreme terror, and when he was led from the condemned cell into the press yard, where his irons were knocked off, his agitation was such, that he was obliged to be supported, and he was lifted into the fatal cart.

The day of his execution was quite a holiday with the people, who, in those days, always made it a rule to attend every criminal during his progress from the gloomy gate of Newgate to the still gloomier tree of Tyburn. On the present occasion the interest was much greater than usual, for to see a lawyer hanged was considered by the multitude a remarkable thing, especially as Mr. Doom had been a rather noted man in his profession.

Among the crowd, who at the door of Newgate awaited the forthcoming of the cart, was Tim Snarley, who by this time had set up in business on his own account in his old masters office. Doom, hovever, did not recognize him; but as the cart rolled slowly on one figure attracted his attention and made him shudder.

Close to the cart, and anxiously keeping up with it was the man, who had by his evidence fastened as it were the halter round Doom's neck. This individual glared on the unhappy lawyer with an absolutely fiendish aspect, and appeared to gloat over his mental and physical sufferings. None in all the crowd appeared so gratified as him by the spectacle, and no wonder, for a stern spirit of revenge urged him on—it was Flitchman!

The ex-clerk, in that hour of his triumph, remembered how Doom had endeavoured to plunge him beneath the dark waters of the Thames; and how he had hired an assassin to waylay him in Covent Garden. Safe from ill-consequences himself, all the bitterness of his nature now displayed itself, and almost hanging on to the vehicle of death he appeared to use every endeavour to harass the last moments of his late miserable old master.

On rolled the cart, surrounded by countless thousands; just opposite Grays Inn, where Doom had practised iniquity for so many years a temporary stoppage occurred, and the wretched culprit shook, as with an ague fit, when he for the last time surveyed the scene of so many of his crimes. To his frenzied imagination at that moment, gaunt faces appeared at the window of his office with reproachful looks; faces of the widows whom he robbed, of the orphans whom he had ruined. Sick at heart he closed his eyes, and again the cart moved forward.

He refused to drink of the bowl which was offered to him according to custom at the usual place; but notwithstanding, as he approached nearer to the place of execution his energies rallied surprisingly. His old hard nature revived, and in his inmost soul he resolved to exhibit as much fortitude during the last scene as possible. He even returned Flitchman's glance, with one as full of malice and hatred.

But this was only a temporary flushing up; for when they neared the gallows, by a sudden turn of the road, the victim suddenly caught a glimpse of the hideous apparatus, as black and grim, it turned up against the blue sky of morn. The sight instantly made him relapse into his former state of terror, and he swayed his body to and fro, moaning piteously.

His devotions ended, the old man was led up the ladder, from thence he was to be turned off. His face presented a horrible spectacle—it was ghastly and livid, and marked with the deep lines of terror. The nightcap he wore added to the grotesque misery of the picture: his trembling hands clutched the rongs of the ladder, and when the ropes had been fastened to the cross beam, and the hangman had descended, he could not throw himself off, but clung with a giant's strength to the bits of wood which now only intervened between him and death.

The mob, accustomed to see bold highwaymen and brave burglars leap off courageously, and die like trumps, grew rather indignant on witnessing this scene, and roared out lustily to the lawyer to "jump" and let the devil have his due at once, —but the terrified old man either heard or understood them not, for he still retained his hold. Vain were the exhortations of the Ordinary that he would submit to his fate—vain the assurance of the hangman that the matter was just a mere trifle, vain the commands of the sheriff himself—Mr. Doom seemed determined to prolong his life in spite of them all.

And he would have eked it out for some time longer had not Flitchman, who formed one of the circle immediately surrounding the gallows, suddenly darted forward, and seized the foot of the ladder.

Before any one could prevent him—he had grasped it in his strong arms, and forcibly dragged it from the gallows, so that its upper part no longer rested against, and was supported by the cross-beam. With a crash, it fell to the ground, and as it descended escaped from the gripe of Doom, who dangled struggling convulsively in mid air.

A loud shout rent the air whilst yet the poor wretch quivered in agony; and almost before his struggles had ceased the flying stationers were reaping a rich harvest by disposing of numerous copies of his "last dying speech and confession," albeit he had never made either; and the usual and regular sports of Hang Fair had already commenced.

CHAPTER XLVII.

CONDEMNATION OF BLUESKIN—MURDEROUS ATTACK ON JONATHAN WILD—THE FLIGHT FROM THE COUNTRY HOUSE—DISCLOSURES.

WE left Blueskin, it will be remembered, in Wood Street Compter, to which place he had been sent by Sir John Fryer, the magistrate, on a charge of having committed a robbery in St. Martin's Lane.

It had been arranged between Jonathan Wild and Blueskin that the latter should confess himself to be guilty of the robbery, which in reality, was not the case, in order that he might impeach two men against whom Jonathan Wild had a grudge as accomplices.

No sooner had Blueskin, against whom Wild felt no less hatred, on account of his having interfered with his plans, positively sworn that Oaky and Levy had in conjunction with himself perpetrated the street robbery in question, than the wily Jonathan proceeded to extort witnesses, who, for a certain amount of bloodmoney would swear to all three. He also exerted his influence secretly to prevent Blueskin being accepted as evidence for the crown, the consequence was that greatly to his surprise and terror, Blueskin, at the next Old Bailey Sessions, was with the other two men placed upon his trial, and his confession, concocted by the arch traitor Jonathan Wild, produced in evidence against him.

Blueskin made a vow of black revenge against Jonathan for this treachery—but how was it to be executed with effect? His legs were heavily ironed, and he was surrounded with guards,—still he determined to watch for an opportunity, and fortune appeared to favour his intentions.

Previous to receiving sentence, and while another trial was proceeding, Blueskin and his companions, who cursed him, and with good reason, as the author of all this misery, was removed to the room of the turnkey which was situated beneath the dock. Here they were furnished with food by their friends who were allowed to visit them, and from one of these, the now desperate man contrived to procure a large clasp knife.

This he concealed carefully in his bosom, determined, whatever the consequences might be, to be revenged upon Jonathan Wild if an opportunity occurred.

And before long, that opportunity was afforded him. When he was again placed at the bar, Blueskin peered intently into every nook and corner of the court in the hope of discovering one, who he now knew to be his mortal enemy. For some little time he failed to discover the thief-taker, but at length he beheld him enter the Court wearing an aspect of utter unconcern for the person whom he had so treacherously sacrificed.

In order to accomplish his desperate purpose, Blueskin endeavoured to banish from his countenance all traces of enmity towards the author of his present misfortune; and assuming a look of the deepest dejection, he watched intently for the purpose of catching the eye of the thief-taker. In this, he was for some time unsuccessful, for Wild rather avoided than courted the scrutiny of him whom he had thrown as it were into the very jaws of destruction. At length, however, a bustle in that part of the court which was situated behind the bar occurred, and attracted Jonathan's looks in that direction. Without intending it, his eyes thus met those of Blueskin, and the latter instantly made a private signal to Wild that he had something of importance to communicate to him.

The thief-taker, well aware that Blueskin was still in possession of many of his secrets; anxious also to persuade the latter that circumstances, which he had not been able to control, had caused matters to go contrary to his wishes and designs; and if possible to impress him with the notion that he, Wild, would still find means to procure him his liberty, immediately made his way through the dense crowd towards the place where the prisoner stood. Blueskin felt his blood boil with rage and indignation as Jonathan elbowed his way towards him; he thrust his hand beneath the waistcoat and grasped the handle of the concealed knife, but not a muscle of his countenance served to indicate the deadly design which lurked beneath.

At length Wild reached the dock, and Blueskin bent over him to hear what the thief-taker said: for the moment Jonathan came close to his victim, a deceptive smile lighted up his grim countenance, and addressed him in a low tone.

"You know better, Wild," said the prisoner with bitterness, in reply to something which Jonathan had said, "I am safely lagged now, and you know it."

"Nonsense, man," observed Jonathan, "why, Blueskin, my power is such that were the halter round your neck, I could slip you out of it; and even supposing things should come to the worst, and you kept your counsel, I could do you a good turn at the very last."

"In what way? I don't understand you," remarked Blueskin.

"You wouldn't like your body to be anatomized at Surgeons Hall, and your bones to be polished, and hung up in a cupboard, there to rattle on springs, instead of being decently buried in christian ground—would you?" asked Jonathan Wild.

Blueskin, ruffian as he was, shuddered as Jonathan Wild drew this imaginary picture, for strange as it may seem the most daring villains, who by their crimes made themselves amenable to the laws, felt much less terror of the gallows than of the scalpel of the dissector! To be sentenced to hang on a gibbet, and then rot away piecemeal, was thought to be rather a compliment to their daring and bravery than otherwise; but to be laid on the table of a dissecting room, and afterwards to be boxed ignominiously up, was considered a degredation by those men whom laws could not restrain, but whom a surgeons knife could fill with the utmost terror.

In reply to Wild's question, so adroitly put, Blueskin at the thought shuddered, and Wild, perceiving his emotion, continued :—

"And if they should scrag you, Blueskin, you shall have a decent burial in your own parish churchyard; for I'll provide you a coffin, and a hearse, and mourning coaches myself. But I'll not fail to do my utmost to prevent matters coming to such a pass.—You know my power, don't you."

"Your power !" almost hissed Blueskin into Jonathan Wild's ear; "your power ! yes, I know it too well, Wild. Your power ! You have had power enough to make me a villain : your power plunged me deeper and deeper into crime, whether I would damn myself or no : your power caused me to swear away the lives of Oaky and Levy : your power has doomed me to the gallows; and now your power could furnish me a paltry funeral. But let me tell you, villian, that I scorn you and your power alike."

Unaccustomed to be thus bearded as it were by those whom he kept in such infamous subjection, Jonathan Wild felt inclined to pour out the vials of his wrath on the head of the devoted Blueskin, but the presence of those in whose favour it was of so much importance he should stand high, restrained him within bounds, and he repressed the indignant remarks which he was about to make. But his brow, nevertheless darkened, and that peculiar expression of malice and revenge which once seen could never be forgotten, darkened his sinister countenance.

Jonathan, apparently, therefore, treating the tirade of Blueskin with contempt was about to quit the vicinity of the dock, when a circumstance almost unparalleled in the annals of criminal judicature occurred, which threw the Court, and the spectators into a state of utter consternation. For, taking advantage of the moment when Jonathan Wild passed immediately before the dock on his way to the vicinity of the witness-box where Wilkins and several other of his " blood-money " witnesses stood in a group, Blueskin leaned over the edge of the low partition which separated him from the spectators, as far as the weight of the irons which were attached to his legs would permit him, and suddenly threw his left arm round Wild's neck and dragged him towards the dock.

Then, with the rapidity of lightning and before his strange movement had been observed by any other than those immediately about that particular spot, Blueskin, having forced the head of the thief-taker backwards so as to expose his bare throat, drew across the latter, the blade of the knife which he had previously concealed. So suddenly yet so effectively had this been effected that it was not until the blood of the thief-taker spurted over the dresses of those about him, and until Jonathan Wild's face was ghastly pale and cadaverous, that what had happened was fully comprehended.

Scorning to conceal the daring deed, Blueskin triumphantly flourished the bloody weapon over his head, and then flung from him the half insensible body of Wild which was instantly borne, amidst the greatest confusion, from the Court to an adjoining tavern, where surgical assistance was promptly rendered. Fortunately for the

thief-taker the position of his would-be assasin had been such that in his sweep of the keen blade, it had failed to sever the larger bloodvessels of the neck, and almost by a miracle Wild escaped a doom, which at a later period of his life he often wished had been his. The thief-taker's end was destined to be of a far more ignominious character.

As for Blueskin he was immediately seized and doubly ironed. Without having any sentence passed upon him, he was again hurried away from the bar, and thrust into one of the foulest and most noisome dungeons of Newgate, where for the present we must leave him in order the follow the fortunes of other persons connected with our narrative.

We must now return to Captain M'Cleane who, it will be remembered we left at the Country House at Highgate, happy in the warm and unexpected embraces of Jenny Diver.

When the first transports of this unlooked for re-union had passed away on the following morning, Jenny suggested that a fresh campaign should be entered upon, as it was evident from various circumstances that the suspicion of certain parties had been attracted to the proceedings of the gang since they had met in their present quarters.

It was, therefore arranged that a grand meeting of the gang should be held on the following evening, and to evade suspicion as far as possible, Jenny advised M'Cleane to appoint their old place of abode—' The Chapel,' in the neighbourhood of Long Acre, as the place of rendezvous.

The services of Gipsey Betty were now put into requisition, and that young lady having disguised herself so completely that even the lynx eyes of Mr. Watkins would have failed to detect her, was dispatched to the different haunts in which it was almost certain the various members of the community would be found. Beauty Ellis was also sent off on a similar mission, so that M'Cleane fully calculated on a general meeting of the gang.

That night the Country House, at Highgate, was, as the chapel on a former occasion had been, temporarily abandoned, and a secret notice for those of the fraternity who might by chance visit the adjacent hostelry having been left, the private apartments of the Highgate establishment were closed, and the entrances to them carefully concealed.

*   *   *   *   *

It was approaching towards midnight on the evening of the day when the Country House, at Highgate, was evacuated, as that lonely man sat in an ancient room of a dilapidated house in Bucklersbury.

The remains of a miserable fire were smouldering in the small grate, rendered still smaller by the insertion of pieces of brick; and over these faint embers bent the figure of a man, who gazed intently between the bars, and appeared to be absorbed in thought. For some time he sat thus still as a statue, and it was not until a low and cautious knock at the street door resounded through the passage leading from the chamber where he was to the thoroughfare without, that he roused himself from his apparent unpleasant reverie.

After trimming the wick of his solitary lamp he took up the latter, and holding it over his head, crept towards the entrance gate and demanded who knocked? The reply was apparently satisfactory, for he immediately and with as little noise as possible withdrew the huge bolts, unlocked the door, and half opening it admitted a man, who was muffled up in a large cloak, which in connection with a slouched hat, effectually concealed his features and figure.

The inhabitant of the house was Ephraim Blake—the man to whom he had just given admission was his cousin, Blueskin.

"I cannot bid you welcome, Joseph Blake, though I must perforce grant you shelter; but let me warn you that you now cross this threshold for the last time. Follow me."

Without saying a word, Joseph Blake, or Blueskin, for it was indeed he, softly walked after his
No. 29.

cousin, and entered the chamber which the latter had but recently quitted. Ephraim Blake silently pointed to a chair, after sinking into one himself, and Blueskin, apparently much fatigued, availed himself of the hint.

"How do you think, Joseph Blake," asked Ephraim sternly, and looking daggers at his cousin, "how do you imagine that I can find gold time after time to lavish thus upon you; but I have now assisted you for the last time; my wealth has saved you from the gallows; what more would you?"

"It's true, cousin, and I thank you," growled Blueskin, "but it was for no love you bore me that you bribed the gaoler to leave the door of my cell unlocked. You feared that disgrace would attach to your name, and prevent your union with the broker's daughter, of Eastcheap, if your cousin swung from Tyburn Tree. But to come to the point, I want a purse of gold, and furnished with that I will relieve you of my presence and importunities for ever."

"Gold!" almost shrieked Ephraim Blake, "it is always gold; but what security can you give me that you will not further trouble me thus?"

"My word; I have naught else," said Blueskin surlily, "and remember time is precious; if you would not have your name disgraced, comply with my demands at once, for the hounds of of the law are, I fancy, already on my track."

"You must first show me the secret way to that infernal den near Long Acre, where I hear that I am likely to pounce on the miscreant who murdered my father," said Ephraim.

"It is true, the person of whom you speak is there," said Blueskin; "but your revenge may sleep, for the villain long since was sent to his last bed by a bullet. He is buried in the vaults of that very den as you call it."

"Show me his bones and I will believe you—otherwise I will not. Here are five hundred guineas in this bag, the moment I am satisfied by Watkins, the Bow Street runner, of the truth of what you assert, the sum shall be yours, and on no other condition."

"Come then," remarked Blueskin; "but supposing Watkins should re-capture me, how then?"

"I will guard against that," said Ephraim Blake, "the officer will do any mortal thing for gold?"

The pair then proceeded in the direction of the Chapel in Long Acre, but the events consequent on their visit must for the present remain unrevealed. In the interim we must partially retrace our steps, and account for the appearance of Blueskin outside the walls of Newgate.

The moment after the desperadoes murderous attempt on Jonathan Wild, he was, as we have seen, removed from the bar, and conveyed once more to the prison yard.

No sooner had his fellow prisoners been made acquainted with the particulars of the attack on the thief-taker than they raised Blueskin on their shoulders, and conducted him round the yard in triumph. Amongst that daring band of lawless men there was not one who did not hate as well as fear the extraordinary man who exercised so singular and powerful a control over their destinies. The conduct, therefore, of him who had so recklessly attempted to rid them of a tyrant, met with universal approbation, and Blueskin was suddenly invested by them with all the attributes of a hero.

Well aware that his late offence would be severely punished, and that no effort of Jonathan Wild's would now be spared to accomplish his destruction, Blueskin began to ponder in his mind the possibility of an escape from the prison. This he knew would be no easy matter, for the recent exploits of Hawkins had greatly increased the vigilance of the authorities of the prison. It happened, however, that he was not unprovided with gold, which had been advanced him by his miserly cousin, on condition that he would not avow his real name, and so disgrace his relative. Money in a prison, as well as elsewhere, generally works wonders; but to Blueskin's surprise, his bribes on the present occasion produced no other

effect than that of increasing the vigilance of his guardians.

It became evident, therefore, that some bold stroke must be resorted to if he would escape from confinement, and, therefore, he with great caution sounded the opinions of a few of the most desperate of his fellow prisoners, as to the practicability of gaining their liberty by creating a riot within the prison walls, and then, aided by their friends without, on whose assistance they knew they could safely reckon, effectually overcoming all opposition to their regaining their liberty.

The Old Bailey sessions, which were then sitting, would not, Blueskin knew be concluded for nine or ten days at least; and, as during that period a large number of the officers of the gaol were compelled to be in attendance in court, it was certain that those prisoners who remained in the yards and the cells would be less vigilantly guarded than at other times. Of course, therefore, the present time was the most favorable opportunity for a desperate dash at liberty, and after a consultation with several fellow-prisoners, others who had not hitherto been let into the secret were enlisted in the ranks of the insurgents, and through the medium of friends who visited them arrangements were made for assistance, the moment they got outside of the prison walls, should they be so far fortunate in their daring enterprise.

As at night all the prisoners were locked up in seperate cells, it was evident that the attempt at riot and escape must be made during that time which intervened between broad daylight and the hour of locking-up. As soon as this point had been settled, other parts of the scheme were discussed and decided upon, the arrangements of those who were to receive them on the outside of the walls were perfected, and Blueskin and about thirty other powerful and desperate men, anxiously awaited the moment when they should commence their proceedings.

Before detailing these, however, it is necessary to give some description of the difficulties which they had to surmount in their perilous adventure.

The conspirators were confined by day in a small yard into which their several cells opened. This yard was surrounded by a high and remarkably strong iron railing, surmounted with a kind of chevaux de frise, which it was next to impossible to scale unobserved under cover of darkness, and which in broad daylight served as an effectual barrier, as a view of it was commanded by the windows of several of the rooms appropriated to the uses of the prison.

From this court-yard a narrow passage led to another and a larger enclosure, which, in its turn communicated by a wicket-gate with the entrance lodge of the gaol. The great feat to be achieved, therefore, was the gaining this place unmolested; and that accomplished the remainder of their task would be comparatively easy.

By the unanimous consent of the parties who had entered into this conspiracy, Blueskin was honoured with the post of leader of the gang; and to the successful accomplishment of their purpose he now directed all his energies. An accidental circumstance which occurred between the determination of the project and its fulfilment, served materially to aid them, and the aid was more warmly welcomed inasmuch as it came from a totally unexpected quarter.

Blueskin was one morning smoking his pipe in the yard, and pondering on his scheme, when he observed a female enter amongst the other visitors, with whose person he thought he was acquainted.

On obtaining a nearer view of this individual he at once recognised her as Jonathan Wild's former mistress, Mary Milliner. It will be remembered that the thief-taker had, during a quarrel made a violent attack on the person of his paramour, and severed her ear from her head. After this a separation had taken place between the pair, and although Wild granted his former partner in iniquity a pension, her hatred toward the man who had so brutally mutilated her was unquenchable.

Blueskin, from his former intimate acquaintance with the thief-taker and his affairs, of course was well aware upon what terms Jonathan and Mary Milliner stood, and he rightly judged that in this woman he should meet with a valuable assistant. He, therefore, sought an opportunity of renewing his acquaintance with her, a no very difficult matter, as the offer of a dram, to which the lady was particularly partial, served as an introduction.

Mary Milliner, who had heard of Blueskin's daring attempt to murder Wild, entered heart and soul into Blueskin's scheme, after he had cautiously entrusted her with his secret. Through her agency he obtained several gags, some short iron bars, to serve as weapons of offence and defence, and, what to him and his comrades were worth their weight in gold, several small files. Milliner also undertook to find a place of refuge for Blueskin after his escape, and without much persuasion agreed to live under his protection in future.

The day on which the fate of the conspirators was to be decided at length arrived, and so secretly had the requisite preparations been made that not the slightest suspicion on the part of the authorities of the prison had been aroused. In the interim, it should have been stated, Blueskin had been summoned before the court and received sentence of transportation for life, the Recorder, who pronounced it, intimating that a milder punishment would have been awarded, but for the atrocious crime which he had been guilty of in the presence of the court itself. To this remark Blueskin, with his accustomed daring, replied that he only regretted one thing, and on being asked by the Recorder what that might be, he said he was only sorry that he had not fully accomplished his object, and so rid the world of an arch hypocrite and villain as Jonathan Wild.

As soon as the conspirators had been served with their breakfasts on the morning of the decided day, they by turns retired to their cells, and commenced their work by, as secretly as possible, filing their irons so far through that they could at the last moment easily free themselves from their encumbering weight. By taking regular turns in this occupation, the whole of them had by the evening accomplished this part of the business. Mary Milliner, punctual to her time, brought into the prison the last of the iron bars, for she could not venture to smuggle in more than one at a time, and assured Blueskin that

every preparation for his reception outside was complete. Thus nothing but the final stroke for liberty now remained to be made.

The prisoners were served with the last meal of this day at five o'clock in the evening; and at seven o'clock they were locked up in their respective cells. It was during this interval that the decisive step was to be taken, as at about half past six the twilight would be fast fading into darkness.

Six o'clock was tolled by the bell of Saint Sepulchre's Church, and the hourly turnkey made his usual tour of the prison yard in which Blueskin and his comrades appeared carelessly sauntering to and fro. The official glanced at the prisoners and having ascertained that all was right, left them, and proceeded to other parts of the building.

The prisoners knew they should be now alone until a quarter before seven o'clock, when another turnkey would visit them and conduct them to their dungeons. Time, therefore, was most precious, and to work they at once went.

To free themselves from their heavy irons was their first care. Blueskin and two others whom he had selected to aid him then put themselves at the head of three divisions of the gang, and huddling themselves together in order to conceal from inquisitive eyes the removal of their fetters, they impatiently, and with throbbing hearts awaited the coming of the prison official.

At length the chimes of Saint Sepulchres announced the wished for time, and scarcely had the echoes of the bells died away before the rattling of bolts and locks were heard, and the heavy footsteps of the turnkey approaching their locality were perceptible to the prisoners.

The turnkey appeared with a lantern in one hand and a huge bunch of keys dangling from and jingling in the other.

Perfectly unconscious of what had been going on, the turnkey entered the yard and was locking the gate after him, when Blueskin sprang upon him from behind and pinioned his arms securely, whilst at the same moment another forced a gag into his mouth, and effectually prevented him from calling out for assistance.

Throwing him on the ground, two of the gang dragged him by main force into one of the cells, and having selected the proper key from the bunch they securely locked him in, after threatening him with instant death if he attempted to raise an alarm. Then they held a brief consultation, and prepared for the most perilous part of their enterprise.

As no one appeared within sight, and as it was gradually becoming very dark, Blueskin determined at once to proceed, judging rightly as he afterwards ascertained, that the other turnkeys would at that hour be occupied by their duties in the various departments of the prison. Inserting, therefore, boldly the key of the gate in the lock he opened the barrier, and then leading the way he and his companions, silently and in single file like a procession of Indians, passed along the passage and gained admission into the second court-yard, which they found to be deserted, the turnkey they had just imprisoned having, previous to his visit to themselves, locked up its usual inhabitants for the night.

So quietly had they carried on their proceedings

that hitherto not the slightest alarm had been raised. Now, however, they could scarcely hope to complete their arrangements without a disturbance of some kind. What they feared most was the sounding of the prison alarum bell, which was hung in a turret immediately over the lodge, and the rope communicating with which terminated in the entrance lodge, so that it could be made to sound forth its harsh summons at any moment.

A brief pause now ensued, during which Blueskin crept quietly towards the door which opened from the lodge into the yard where they now were, and which as it happened was slightly ajar. Through the narrow opening he perceived two turnkeys seated at supper, and close to the shoulder of one of them dangled the end of the alarum bell-rope.

The backs of these men were towards them; Blueskin, therefore, directed two of the most stalwart ruffians of his gang to seize them immediately on their rushing into the room, and so prevent the rope being pulled. Scarcely had he issued these directions when he was startled by the sound of approaching footsteps, which he judged to be those of one of the turnkeys returning from his rounds. Should they be surprised in that situation all would, he knew, be lost; therefore he at once put himself at the head of the gang, and to the utter consternation of the two officials, they rushed into the lodge.

Blueskin, himself, took care whilst the turnkeys were being pinioned and gagged, to sever the rope close to the ceiling—a feat easily accomplished by mounting on a chair and a table. Then he hastily locked and bolted the door by which they had just entered, thus cutting off completely all communication between the place in which they then were and the other points of the prison. Only the wicket-gate now separated them from the open space without; but this was locked, and they could not find the key.

To add to their alarm, the turnkeys who had been locking up the prisoners had now returned, and surprised at the lodge-door being fastened were now thundering away at it. Fearing that an alarm would be given to the governor, and that this barrier would be forced, the daring ruffians ungagged those whom they had made prisoners, and, assuming most menacing aspects, swore that they would instantly murder them if they did not furnish them with the key of the gate. Faithful to their trust this they obstinately refused to do, and one of them hoping to bring assistance cried out to the turnkeys, who instantly rushed from the place in order to procure aid, it being now evident to them that a serious revolt had broken out in the gaol.

But dearly indeed did the miserable man pay for his impudent fidelity; for scarcely had the words of warning to his fellow servants left his lips, before Blueskin lifted, with a fearful oath, the iron bar with which he was armed, and then sent it with a dull crashing sound into the scull of the turnkey with a force which actually bent it. The walls of the apartment were instantly bespattered with blood and brains intermingled, and the quivering corpse of the turnkey fell on the hard stones, where it lay a fearful spectacle, waltering in its still flowing gore, which formed a rapidly congealing pool around it.

Struck with horror at the terrible fate of his companion, the other turnkey no longer persisted in his refusal to comply with the demands of the villains, and at once supplied them with the means of completing their escape. Apprehensive, however, that immediately after their departure this man would point out the direction in which they went, they, in the most brutal manner, again gagged him, and then bound him fast to the body of his dead companion. To make doubly sure of his not moving from where they had laid him, Blueskin resorted to an infernal contrivance which a mere casual circumstance at the moment suggested to him.

On the fire was a huge vessel filled with boiling water. To the iron handle of this Blueskin fastened one end of a rope, and so nearly balanced the vessel itself that the slightest movement in any direction, forward or sideways, would inevitably precipitate it and its boiling contents on the floor of the lodge. Dragging the corpse and its living companion close to the fender, the ruffian contrived so to connect them by means of the rope with the vessel referred to, that the slightest movement of the turnkey would precipitate the boiling water upon him. Satisfied that so far all was secure, Blueskin now proceeded to take the last step in his daring enterprise.

Inserting the huge key in the massive triple lock of the wicket gate, he turned it, and the bolts flew back with a dull grating sound; then he with great caution opened it a little way, and peeped anxiously through the chink to ascertain whether any persons likely to interrupt him and his fellows were loitering about. Luckily for him a drizzling rain was falling and but few persons were about; and those who were were hurried by the gate of the prison without particularly heeding it.

While thus engaged he saw on the opposite side of the open space of the Old Bailey, a woman standing within the entrance of one of the numerous alleys which abounded in that neighbourhood. A private signal assured him that this was Mary Milliner, and being convinced by this that all was right he no longer hesitated to venture forth. Before doing so, however, he directed his companions not to rush forth in a body but singly in order to avert suspicion from the watch should they be prowling about. In another moment he was outside the walls of Newgate.

Under cover of the darkness he crept within the shadow of the prison walls towards Smithfield, followed by Mary Milliner in the distance; and as soon as he reached one of the narrow thoroughfares leading towards Seacoal Lane, he plunged into it and waited for the woman who speedily joined him. Scarcely had they exchanged greetings when the bell of the prison was heard to ring out, and the hurried tramp of foot steps and the discordant sounds of the rattles of watchmen fell upon Blueskin's affrighted ear.

For a moment he stood as it were paralyzed; but his companion almost forcibly dragged him on until they reached the door of a low public-house into which they entered. Mary Milliner had prepared herself with a disguise for Blueskin, which he now rapidly put on, and so metamorphosed was he that he felt not the slightest hesitation in calling for a tankard of spiced ale and a pipe, with which he was regaling himself when a stranger entered the room, and announced that a great riot had just broken out in Newgate, and that the notorious Blueskin had managed to escape.

From the stranger it was also learned that his companions had been far less fortunate than himself. It appeared that immediately after the departure of their leader they rushed in one body from the prison into the street, a circumstance directly in opposition to his orders, and one which naturally attracted attention to them, in consequence of which a chase took place, which resulted in the capture of the whole.

Leaving Blueskin for the present, we must now once more pay a visit to the Chapel, in Long Acre, where in obedience to the summons of M'Cleane, all the members of the gang had assembled.

CHAPTER XLVIII.

BEAUTY ELLIS DISCOVERS A GOLD MINE—THE ROBBERY OF THE MINT.

IT was as yet unknown to the greater part of the comrades of M'Cleane that their old and clever companion Jenny Diver had managed to elude the vigilance of the law, and was once more on English ground. Great indeed, therefore, was their surprise when, as they sat assembled in their old place of rendezvous, Captain M'Cleane led her into the saloon and presented her to the gang.

The timely return of this young woman was considered by her comrades as an omen of good fortune, and this was indeed needed, for of late the community had not been as successful as of yore. This falling off of their luck was attributed to various causes, and indeed the object of their meeting at that very time was to devise some means of bettering their condition.

They had been now for so long a time absent from the Chapel, that after some discussion on the subject it was unanimously agreed that all cause for uneasiness as to its being their fixed place of residence, had passed away. It was, therefore, determined that it should from that hour be occupied as formerly, and so the stronghold was forthwith put into as complete a state of defence as possible without attracting attention. Madame Charlotte was once more reinstated in the hotel department, and, to his great joy, our old friend Beauty Ellis, resumed the office of porter to the establishment.

The occasion of the return of the gang to their old quarters was celebrated by a banquet on a most extravagant scale—so magnificent that even the splendours of by-gone times were almost surpassed. To this succeeded the merry dance and the jovial song, and the pleasures of the hour after business in reality commenced.

It would occupy by far too much time and space to relate in this place at any length the proceedings which occurred at this time. Suffice it to say that it was determined to prosecute their adventures both on the road and in the City with renewed vigour and additional caution. Only one circumstance damped their ardour, and that was the absence and perilous position of Handsome Jack.

To Dick Flybynight and Jenny Diver the fate of their old acquaintance was a source of real sorrow; but M'Cleane secretly rejoiced, for the demon of jealousy had not yet been quite drawn from his bosom. It was, however, on all sides determined that no pains should be spared which might effect his deliverance from the dangers by which he was environed.

"We must, however," said M'Cleane, "first consult our own security, for a hundred snares are laid for every one of us. I propose that before we engage in any enterprise which has for its aim his rescue, we should seek to line our strong-box which is now most cursedly empty. What say you, comrades?"

A general assent to the expressed opinion was given, and Beauty Ellis, conceiving the present moment to be a favorable one for mentioning a scheme of his own, asked permission to suggest a means of doing what Captain M'Cleane had recommended.

"Out with it, Beauty," said M'Cleane, "and don't stand grinning like one of those blackamoor's whom Jenny has left over the seas. What's in the wind now?"

"A brave chance," replied Beauty, "for those who have stout hearts to risk it; but great as that risk will certainly be it will be well worth the running."

"Speak out, Beauty, and don't tantalize us," cried Dick Flybynight, "you know well enough that not a man or woman amongst our company is white-livered. For my own part, I would venture into the head quarters of the Prince of Darkness himself, if there was a chance of getting a good haul of that gold which secures him to many subjects."

"To business, Beauty," said M'Cleane. "By Heaven our treasure chest is well nigh empty, and we must not stick at trifles—Proceed!"

Thus commanded, Ellis first poured out a goblet brimming full of canary, and having emptied it at a draught, said—

"What's the use of picking up gold by dribs—of obtaining a few score guineas or so by mere chance work, comrades, when it is in our power to dig into the mine itself, and work it bravely too?"

"You are really growing eloquent, Beauty," remarked Jenny Diver. "So far as I am concerned, I am decidedly of your opinion that a bold stroke for a large booty is preferable to your little peddling cut-purse affairs. But where is this mine of yours situated?"

"Not a hundred miles from the Tower," replied Beauty Ellis, with a mysterious grin.

"What, of London?" asked M'Cleane, with a somewhat incredulous air.

"The werry same," replied Ellis.

"Why you would not have us seize the crown, would you, Beauty, and claim some of the regalia as your share of the booty?" asked Dick Flybynight, with something like a sneer on his lip."

"Not so fast, Master Flybynight," returned Beauty. "Of what use would the king's crown be to any of us? None, I fancy; but what say you to dipping your hands into the government chests, and finding heaps of guineas ready coined for your use?"

"Enough of this talking in riddles," said M'Cleane. "Now then, Beauty, without further delay let us hear what you have to communicate; and rely on it that we will decide upon the course which shall seem most beneficial for all of us. If you have turned up a lucky card you shall not be unrewarded!"

The latter part of M'Cleane's address to him appeared to enliven the Beauty, who again moistened his parched throat, and entered at once into the marrow of his subject.

"You, all of you," he said, "have heard of the Mint. I don't mean, Ben Culls, that old, rotten, dingy, tumble down place in Southwark—a neighbourhood which I fancy nobody here is ignorant of—but the Mint where bars of gold and silver are turned into the king's coin, and kept in ironbound chests, from the fingers of such as us. Now, pals, I've often and often thought to myself that a fine haul might be made there if a few bold fellers had only the courage to try for it."

"But the treasure is too well guarded," observed M'Cleane.

"There, Captain, you are mistaken," remarked Beauty Ellis, interrupting him. "I always thought so too till yesterday, when by chance I learned to the contrary. In fact, by means of a little craft, the Mint may as easily be robbed as any gentleman's house in the united kingdom."

"But let us know how you became acquainted with this precious piece of news," said M'Cleane, who was still incredulous. "I always understood that a regular dragon-watch was kept over the mint; but if you can prove to the contrary, and show that there is any chance of an attempt to sack the Mint being successful, why I for one will not hesitate to attempt the feat, perilous as it must necessarily be."

"Why look you, Captain," said Beauty. "I dropped in at Jerry Laggum's last night, just to pick up what news I could, and while I was there an old acquaintance of mine, Tramping Ned, came in. Ned and I, in old times had been in many a nice job together, but I'd lost sight of him for months and months,—so, in course we was glad enought to fall together again."

"Proceed," said M'Cleane, after Beauty had once more moistened his throat, which appeared to be particularly and frequently afflicted with drought—"proceed, and d'ye hear, make your story as short as possible."

"I will, Captain," said Beauty. "Well, then, comrades, Tramping Ned and I began of course, to converse about old things, and I found out that my old pal had taken to the sneak line. I needn't tell you, mates, that that means he acted a sort of lion's perwider in nosing out jobs for cracksmen. Ned, somehow or other had, I saw with half an eye, got hold of some wallyable secret—so of course I took care to fill his glass pretty often, knowing well as he was one of those coves as can't keep a secret when they've got a skinful of drink. At last, sure enough, out it came.'

"And what was it, Beauty?" asked a dozen voices at once.

"Patience, Ben Culls, and you shall hear," replied Beauty Ellis, with a serio-comic kind of dignity in his manner, for he immagined that his importance in the gang now was, or ought to be greatly increased.

"It appeared from what Tramping Ned told me that through the influence of some nobleman to whom in former days he'd been a walley or summat of that sort, he had got a sittiwation in the Royal Mint. In course, the sight of such a power of money as was continually afore his eyes, warnt likely to make a feller like him feel honester than he was before, and he began to consider how he could lay his claws on some of the gold and silver, without being found out. But the devil of it was every time he and the other workmen left the place, they was obliged to be to strip themselves naked and submit to be sarched, from head to foot; so he found out that prigging wouldn't do no how, not in that way at best.

"Well Ned warnt to be done; so, werry much against his inclination, he managed to keep his fingers strait and determined to use his eyes instead of his hands for the present. For a long time this sort of bopeep went on, and at last he sees a chance for a heap of plunder to be carried off. And his errand to Jerry Laggam's last night was to see if he could not fall in with any of his old friends amongst the cracksman line who would go share and share with him in the job. As luck would have it he dropped on me."

"Good so far," remarked M'Cleane. "But now, Beauty, you must be a little more explicit, and rely upon it, if we take this affair in hand, and it should turn to be successful, you shall have a noble share for your part in this business."

"I know that, Captain," said Beauty Ellis, "and I should deserve it too—but I have yet something further to tell you of."

"We are all attention, Beauty," remarked M'Cleane. But before we chronicle Mr. Ellis's plan it will be necessary to make the reader acquainted with the locality of the old establishment marked out by the Beauty and his friend Tramping Ned, as a scene for the exercise of their predatory propensities.

Many years prior to the period in which the various scenes of this narrative are laid, the current coin of the real was manufactured, or struck within the precincts of the Tower of London; but the many political movements of the times requiring that nearly the whole of that building should be converted into prisons for those, suspected or convicted of state offences, the offices had been removed to a building situated on Tower Hill, not far distant from the site on which the Royal Mint now displays its commanding and well-guarded exterior. The building temporarily appointed to these important uses was an old mansion which had been formerly occupied by one of the Percy family. It was in this building that his Majesty's portrait was now stamped on all the gold, silver, and copper which found but a temporary shelter in too many of the purses of the lieges of England.

In this establishment, as a confidential servant, Tramping Ned had indeed, as Beauty Ellis informed his comrades, gained admittance; and so well had he employed the opportunities for observation afforded him that he had conceived a plan for immediately enriching himself, without at all attracting suspicion to his own conduct.

Having premised thus much we must again

listen to Beauty Ellis's developement of the plan suggested by his friend, Tramping Ned.

"To-morrow," said Beauty, with an air of mysterious confidence, " is the anniversary of the King's birthday, on which occasion there is always a holiday at the Mint. These holidays are rare enough, and it is only at such times that the establishment is only partially watched. Now Tramping Ned will be one of those retained on the premises, and for him and the rest within the walls a substantial supper will be provided. Ned proposes that a certain drug should be secretly infused into the potations, and while they are sleeping off its effects he should with the aid of a sentinel who he had managed to secure in his interest, give secret admission to those who will not depart until their pockets are so well lined with guineas and ingots that no second adventure of the kind will ever be necessary."

Beauty Ellis ceased, and after draining a bumper of Canary, uttered a satisfactory " Ha!" and then waited to see how his proposal had been received by M'Cleane and his companions.

"Why," remarked Dick Flybynight, " if all that Beauty has told us is correct, I for one volunteer to join a party in the expedition—to speak truth, I am growing weary of doing little or nothing. What say you, M'Cleane?"

"First of all the thing must be well considered, and our plans well matured. The time for preparation is devilish short, but nevertheless I fancy the attack may be made. What do you think of the business, Jenny?"

"That it ought to be done," was the girl's short and sharp reply. And she added:—"We have done more extraordinary things than this. I will answer for the success of the attack."

"Your prophecies, Jenny, generally turn out to be true," said the Captain. "And now," he added, " how say you, comrades, shall we determine on making a forcible entry into His Majesty's Mint to-morrow night or otherwise?"

An unanimous opinion in favour of the adventure was given, and the minor details of the robbery were at once planned; but as these will appear in their due order in the course of the narrative, it is unnecessary to mention them in this place.

During the following day each member of M'Cleane's gang was in high spirits, for the anticipation of a large booty was now more than usually cheering, their funds in consequence of a recent want of success in various quarters having reached a very low ebb. Indeed so much terror had the depredations of M'Cleane and his companions excited in the suburbs of the metropolis, that scarcely any one ventured out who had money in their possession without being well armed, or otherwise protected from lawless men.

As soon as it was dark, on the evening of the intended robbery, Jenny Diver, disguised as a country woman left the precincts of the Chapel; and making her way through Fleet Street and Cheapside, soon reached Upper Thames Street, from whence she emerged on Tower Hill.

In the centre of that open space there was a huge bonfire, and many of the surrounding houses were illuminated in honor of the Royal birth-day. In the bustle and confusion incident to such a time she passed on unrecognized, and on reaching a tavern near the Minories, she entered it and turned into a small room which branched off to the left from the passage.

Sitting by the chimney corner was a man smoking. The moment Jenny entered he removed the pipe from his lips and laid it on the table before him. No sooner had he made this movement which a stranger would never have noticed, then Jenny Diver took another pipe from a heap which stood on the mantel-piece, and laid the stem of it across that of the strangers.

"Good!" remarked the latter, " I am the person whom you expected to meet here."

"Tramping Ned?" asked Jenny in a low tone.

"The same," replied the man, "and now to business; but first let me procure you a drain, for the night is somewhat of the keenest."

A glass of right good Nantz having been placed before Jenny, the stranger or rather Tramping Ned, informed the young woman that he had told the wife of the porter of the Mint, (who himself was luckily laid up with the gout) that he expected a cousin from the country that evening, and had begged of her to let her pass through the gates to see him. "I need not tell you," said he, " that you must be my cousin for the time; and faith if you turn out to be as daring as you are pretty, I shall have no occasion to be ashamed of the relationship."

Jenny smiled at the compliment, but gently pushed aside the payer of it, who, being of a rather amorous disposition, had attempted to snatch a kiss from the girl's rosy lips.

Tramping Ned then furnished the young woman with other directions, and took his departure for the Mint, requesting Jenny to follow him in about half-an-hour from that time.

Punctual to her appointment Jenny Diver appeared at the little wicket-gate which was constructed in the large and massive doors of the important and extensive building.

In answer to her summons the small gate was opened, and a withered old woman, palsied, and half-blind made her appearance and demanded the business of the person without.

"I pray you, good woman, is Edward Burbidge to be found here?" asked Jenny in a voice, feigned, to represent the speech of an awkward country girl.

"Be you his cousin, young woman?" asked the old lady.

"The same at your service, good mother; and here in this basket are some fat capons of which I crave your acceptance, together with a flask of rare metheglin."

"Come in and welcome, honey," said the old lady, " Ned hath spoken of thee. And so, girl, thou'rt come to London to see the rejoicings. All our knaves too are gone to the bonfire; but come, for I warrant Ned is dying to see thee, and I warrant me thou hast a sneaking kindness for him."

The old crone chuckled at her own humour; and having carefully closed the wicket, led the way to her own room which was just inside the great gates.

Tramping Ned was now summoned and introduced to his cousin, whom he affected to meet with great affection. Then he begged the portress to allow his relative to remain with her until he should be able to quit the Mint and show her the fireworks. Having obtained a ready assent he left the room for the ostensible purpose of joining his companions who were revelling in the guard-room.

So well did Jenny manœuvre that she speedily wheedled herself into the good graces of the portress, and everything seemed to promise a successful termination to her part of the enterprise. At a distance she could hear the noise of the guards and others, who were banquetting; but these sounds grew gradually less frequent and loud, and at length ceased altogether. Then she felt assured that the narcotic of Tramping Ned was doing its works, and she herself prepared for action.

The little wooden clock in the hall of the portress had just struck the hour of nine, when Jenny's quick ear caught the sound of a shrill whistle from without: again she listened; it was repeated, and then flinging off the cloak she approached the old woman and suddenly whipped a gag into her mouth, which effectually prevented her raising an alarm.

Threatening her with instant death if she resisted Jenny next, with cords she had brought, securely fastened her arms and legs to the high-backed arm-chair; and then wrenching the keys from her ferocious grip, she selected the one which she had seen the portress lock the wicket with, and immediately ran to and opened that little gate.

"Quick, Jem, quick, all well so far, but lose not a moment," cried Jenny, as M'Cleane, followed by Dick Flybynight and Beauty Ellis glided within the portal, which Jenny speedily closed and locked.

Before the girl had done speaking, Tramping Ned who also had heard the signal whistle was beside them, and by signs requested them to follow him. He then took the keys from Jenny's hand, and left her in charge of the terrified portress.

Leading them through a court-yard, Ned came to a low archway in which was a door, which with one of the keys on the bunch he easily opened; this door admitted them into the ground story of one of the towers of the ancient edifice, from whence they passed through a long passage into a square chamber which communicated by a flight of stone stairs with the extensive vaults underneath.

Here Tramping Ned drew from his pocket a huge key that he had contrived to purloin from the office of the chamberlain, and with it he easily opened the lock into which he inserted it; but, greatly to his surprise the door still refused in spite of the united strength of the robbers to move on its hinges. On inspection it was discovered that there were two locks, one above and one beneath the one they had forced; and Ned suddenly remembered that the keys of these were deposited in the hands of two of the warders, in order that the treasure-vaults should never be visited save by three parties at one and the same time.

"What in the devil's name is to be done now?" asked M'Cleane of Tramping Ned, "to get the other keys is impossible, and the door appears too strong to be forced."

"Yes; by tools such as cracksmen are in the habit of using," remarked Tramping Ned; "but a thought strikes me,—and fortunately the people

above are so sound asleep that the noise of our operations will not disturb them. At all events we must run the hazard."

Ned then drew from his pocket a powder-flask, and made a tube out of a piece of paper. One end of the latter he inserted into the keyhole of one locks, and sending a quantity of gunpowder through it he speedily filled the whole of the hollow portions of the interior with the combustible article: then he fitted a match tightly in the aperture, and after having repeated the same process with the other lock he directed his companions to withdraw to the extremity of the passage.

After applying a candle to the extremity of each match which he had previously rubbed over with fine gunpowder to prevent the light being extinguished, he also drew back, and with intense anxiety awaited the result of his manœuvre.

Scarcely had he rejoined his companions before the fire communicated with the powder within the locks, and a slight explosion occured—the pent-up passage and the comparatively unconfined space in which the explosive material was placed, preventing any noise which could be heard above. The force exerted, however, was, as Tramping Ned had calculated, sufficiently great to tear the frame of the massive locks from the door to which they were fastened, and consequently to allow of its being opened without further trouble.

A short passage now led them into the vaults, where the sight which met their eyes made them almost delirious with joy.

Piled on each other, reached, from the stone paving of the vault to its arched and groined ceiling, boxes bound with iron, and marked on the outside with the amount of gold or silver contained therein.

In the recesses of the wall were ranged hundreds of ingots of uncoined gold and silver, and kegs of foreign bullion were heaped in pyramids in every direction. The wealth of a nation was treasured up in that singular place, and it only remained for the daring men who had so far desperately forced their way hitherto to choose as to which booty they would seize upon.

After a few moments' consideration, M'Cleane ordered some of the boxes to be forced open, which was no easy matter: but this once accomplished, he saw that in a very short time enough to enrich them for life might be secured. The robbers therefore commenced filling their pockets with gold coin of the realm, of which in a brief time they secured an immense sum. Each man, when he had stowed away as much as he could well support, then filled up the interstices of his jack-boots with the shining coin, and some even unrolled their neckerchiefs, and converted them into belts to hold guineas, which belts they secured round their waists.

"We had best be off with what we have," said Tramping Ned, "for the sentinel will be placed on guard at eleven o'clock, and it is now past ten —if we do not quit the Mint before long, we shall only leave it for the Tower opposite."

M'Cleane felt the force of the remark, and seizing one of the gold ingots, an example which was followed by each of the gang, he led the way out of the vault. The rest followed him, and before long they had all reached the court-yard in

safety, and soon rejoined Jenny Diver in the old portress's room.

Half dead with fright the old crone was still sitting bound in her chair, and Jenny Diver mounting guard over her. Leaving her in that position the gang, accompanied by Tramping Ned, who had now formally joined the ranks, quitted the place in all haste, but avoiding all chance of attracting notice. In this design they were greatly favored by the crowded state of Tower Hill; and so without further adventure they, in separate parties, made for the neighbourhood of Long Acre.

Before, however, they could reach and find sanctuary in the Chapel, an unexpected event transpired, which, as it seriously affected the future fortunes of the gang, deserves more attention than can possibly be paid to it at the fag end of a Chapter.

No. 30.

CHAPTER XLXIX.

JENNY DIVER EXPERIENCES THE TRUTH OF THE ADAGE 'THAT IT IS A LONG LANE WHICH HAS NO TURNING'—HER LAST EXPLOIT.

IF we were inclined to moralize or to inflict a page or so of sentiment, we might in this part of our narrative be extremely pathetic, and set forth such wise lessons that doubtless great improvement and edification would result.

We have, however, to do with events; to others we leave the duty of improving them. In accordance with this plan it is necessary that, like faithful chroniclers, we should record the waning fortunes and final achievements of one who has borne a rather prominent part in the adventures recorded in the foregoing pages. We refer to that paragon of pickpockets, Jenny Diver.

When M'Cleane and his companions quitted the Mint, Jenny purposely avoided returning homeward in their company, and, therefore, as it was yet comparatively early, sauntered leisurely through the streets; her brilliant eyes wandering in every direction in the hope of meeting with some chance of distinguishing herself, and of displaying her abilities in her own particular line, in which she was still as yet unrivalled.

It appeared to the Diver that the part she had sustained in the Mint affair had not been one calculated to confer any particular credit upon her; and as ambition was one of her guiding stars she ardently hoped for an opportunity of performing some brilliant achievement before she rejoined M'Cleane and his companions. It was, therefore, with undissembled delight, that just as she reached Saint Pauls Churchyard, she beheld a gaily dressed young gentleman descend from a hackney carriage, and walk down Ludgate Street.

Still wearing her disguise of a country girl, she determined to keep up the character in every respect, and to attract the attention of the gentleman, who was evidently a young rake upon town, towards her. She lightly tripped past him, displaying at the time, by an arch movement, an ancle and part of a leg whose exquisite shape would have kindled the flames of desire in the bosom of an Anchorite.

As she intended, the bait took effect, for as she was hurrying on she felt herself seized round the waist, and uttering a faint cry of alarm, she turned round and looked with a well-assumed air of terror in the face of the gentleman who appeared ravished with her beauty. Jenny perceived at once that the fish was nibbling the bait which she had angled with; but to preserve appearances she struggled as if to free herself, contriving artfully at the same time to so disarrange her dress as to exhihit to the wanton gaze of the gallant a portion of her plump and panting bosom, which now appeared exposed to view.

The stranger was, as may be expected, not a little excited at this display of Jenny's charms, the more so as he believed it to be perfectly unintentional on the young girl's part. So well, indeed, did Jenny Diver assume the part of an unsophisticated country lass that the town gallant was completely taken in, and he began on the instant to open his lottery of fond glances, ogles, and lecherous smiles.

Jenny was not slow to observe that her artifice had succeeded, and she prepared by putting on an additional air of modesty to effect a conquest. At a glance she perceived that her intended victim was one of those confirmed rakes who, palled by enjoyment found in the arms of women habituated to the trade of prostitution, sought for the additional excitement only afforded by the destruction of youth and innocence. Her cue, therefore, evidently was to assume all the timidity of one over whom the arts of deceitful man had never as yet triumphed.

When the gentleman had folded her in his arms, and bestowed a hearty kiss on her pouting lips, Jenny, in pursuance of her plan, affected an air of the most indignant modesty, and attempted to disengage herself from his rapturous embrace, exclaiming at the same time in doleful accents against the diabolical artifices of mankind. These ejaculations, however, produced not the slightest effect on her innamorata, who by dint of coaxing ultimately so far overcame her scruples and her modesty as to induce her to walk quietly beside him.

"Ah!" exclaimed Jenny, "Mother down in the country often used to tell me of the wickedness and arts of London gentlemen, and warn me against their wiles;—and well it was she did, for I plainly see, sir, that you would fain be a poor virtuous girl's destruction."

"But my little rural angel," remarked the gallant, "would you not rather be decked in silks and satins and adorned with jewels, and have a carriage to ride in like that one which has just passed us, than tramp through the mud and mire of London Streets."

"Why, yes; of course," replied Jenny with an air of rusticity, "but I shall never be a fine lady; I'm going to look for a place, sir."

She curtsied awkwardly and was just about to depart when near the spot where Fleet Street commences, when her admirer besought her forgiveness, and entreated her company to join in a tankard of sack possett at one of the neighbouring Fleet taverns.

This was just the thing which Jenny Diver could most have desired; but carefully concealing her exultation, she made many objections to entering a house of public entertainment,—objections which the gallant gradually overcame, and with many blushes Jenny was led into a vintner's and seated herself beside her companion, who, prior to ordering a draught, whispered a word or two in the ears of the host.

Seated in the same apartment was a man with a burly figure, a rubicund visage, and a besotted appearance generally. His dress was of a clerical cut, but seedy in the extreme, and his rusty wig was half pushed off his shining bald head.

Scarcely had Jenny and the gallant been seated when this worthy, who had eyed them on their entrance much as a shark surveys its victim ere he swallows it, rose from his seat, and staggering towards them pipe in hand, said, in thick and stammering tones—

"If you want to be spliced, young people, I beg to say that here's the man that can splice you for life as quick and cheap as ce'r a parson in the Fleet. A guinea, my noble gentleman, and a bowl of punch, is all I shall charge you, and so give me the word for here I am at your immediate service."

"And who the devil are you?" demanded the gallant.

"Ichabod Jawbone—the Re-reverend Ichabod J-jawbone. Damn the words, they won't trip over my tongue somehow to-night! Fleet Parson and Vicar Extraordinary of Saint Pauls," muttered the half drunken clergyman, for such indeed he was, though sufficiently degraded it must be allowed.

"The last pair I tied together I had a deal more for," he hiccupped. "One was a real lady called Purley, and her new husband was one Richard Town, otherwise Handsome Jack."

On Jenny Diver hearing this she slightly started and listened eagerly. Jawbone, however, said no more in connection with her old companion, and she was afraid to ask any questions lest she should by exhibiting her acquaintance with her former comrade, show more knowledge of metropolitan matters than a raw country girl should possess, and so defeat the object she at that particular time had in view.

The mention of a Fleet marriage seemed mightily to please Jenny's gallant, and a notion immediately struck him which, if carried out, he imagined would greatly facilitate the accomplishment of his designs upon the pretty country girl.

Affecting to be struck so forcibly by her beauty and artlessness that he could not exist without her, the gallant announced himself to be a man of quality and fortune, and professed his willingness to throw himself at Jenny's feet, and share all he possessed in the world with her.

Secretly delighted at the progress of affairs, Jenny became less and less coy; but positively refused to listen to the advances of her lover unless he threw around her virtue the shield of lawful matrimony, and excited by the strong beverage of which he had partaken by no means sparingly he consented to this, in the hope that by a union, which his wealth would easily enable him to set aside, he should at once be admitted to revel in the yet unrifled charms of the blooming rustic.

"Harkye, Parson Jawbone, or whatever your name may be," said the gallant to the Fleet functionary in a whisper, "this wench with whom I have accidentally fallen in is not to be snared in the usual way; but, by God, I must possess her. Now, if you will hook us together without witnesses, and in the names I will give you, I will pay you ten guineas; but all your skill will be necessary to persuade the girl that the marriage is legal."

"Never fear," replied Jawbone, who for gold would have sold the soul of his own father,— "leave all to me, and you shall revel in the embraces of the buxom beauty. She is not the first who I have had to palaver; and by the way if you want to be accommodated with a bridal chamber I happen to have a friend who will be glad to receive you. I suppose you will only want a room for one night."

"That is all," replied the rake. "After the flower is plucked I shall care but little what becomes of it. It will be no easy matter for the girl to find out her husband, (and the worthless wretch indulged in a hearty laugh) in this huge City. And indeed, if she did, who would believe her story, which, of course, it would be to your interest to contradict?"

"Ah!—who indeed?" ejaculated Parson Jawbone, with a villainous wink; "but, my noble sir, if the job is to be done had we not better proceed at once, or your charmer may alter her mind."

A nod of assent was given by Lord Martingale for such was the name of the Peer; although for the occasion he assumed the name of Sir Harry Bradford.

It would be needless to mention at any length the steps which his lordship took to induce Jenny Diver to submit under such peculiar circumstances to a private marriage. No one knew better than our heroine that the ceremony itself would not make the slightest difference to her, inasmuch as she only regarded it as a means of accomplishing the object she had in view. To blind her intended victim when he broached the subject to her she blushed, hesitated and seemed to be covered with confusion; but after much persuasion she yielded a reluctant assent, and secretly rejoicing at her success, timidly approached the altar, where, book in hand, stood the Reverend Ichabod Jawbone.

Little thought, at that moment, the false and designing Lord Martingale, that whilst he had been cunningly contriving a pit-fall for another that a snare was also laid for himself.

Before the ceremony commenced, Jenny requested a word with her intended, and when he gave his attention, she said—

"Before we proceed, would it not be better that I should know what you will settle upon me, for as a poor country girl I have nothing; and if you love me as much as you say, surely you would not have me disgrace my station."

"By no means," replied the nobleman, "and as an earnest I here present you with this purse and these rings," handing her a large sum in gold and notes, and some valuable diamonds. "To-morrow, you shall be attired in a style becoming the wife of Sir Harry Bradford.

"Is it not the custom for ladies of title to wear a watch?" giggled Jenny, surveying with envious eyes a superb gold repeater, which Lord Martingale at the moment drew from his fob.

"Take this and welcome," said the impatient bridegroom, "to-morrow a chain of gold shall be appended to it," and he gallantly attached the watch to Jenny's waistband, the girl appearing as much pleased with her finery as though she had never in her life beheld such things before.

"Now then, all ready I believe. By the way, my charmer, I do not know your name, I have already told you mine. What will you call yourself?"

"Jane Old, an' it please you, Sir Harry," replied Jenny, with a blush and a curtsey.

"Old—Old," repeated the baronet. "Why, gad zounds, methinks Young would suit you better, for I never knew aught so tender so misnamed before," and he chuckled mightily at his own miserable attempt at wit.

But how little did he suspect that he had by chance stumbled on the real name of the person who he was about to espouse. This, however, was but one of the mistakes into which, in his scheme for destroying Jenny's innocence, he was destined to fall.

Everything having been arranged to Jenny's satisfaction, the ceremony was proceeded with, and the Reverend Ichabod Jawbone presented Jenny a certificate of the marriage, which in reality was as worthless as the filthy scrap of paper on which it was written. However, Jenny carefully placed it in her bosom and assumed an appearance of satisfaction.

"And now, my charmer," said the newly made husband, "through the good offices of our reverend friend here, a lodging will be found for us at once where we can repose for the night—let us depart."

This arrangement, however, did not at all suit Jenny Diver, who had already provided for such an expected contingency in her own fertile mind. Blushing, therefore, as if with excess of virgin innocence she modestly hinted that on an occasion so trying to a young maiden, she should prefer lying at the house of a distant relative of hers, a worthy and excellent widow lady, to whose house, indeed, she was journeying when she chanced to fall in with her admirer.

Careless where the marriage was to be consummated so that it was happily, the now impatient bridegrom enquired as to the whereabouts of the respected relative of the young woman's resided.

In Westminster—in a part known as the Almonry," replied Jenny Diver, adding, " indeed, sir, I only know the place by name, for as yet I have not well acquainted myself with the different parts of the town."

"So I should suppose," remarked the gallant " for the place you speak of is none of the most fashionable ; at least so I believe, for I only know it from report, having never visited it."

Jenny was overjoyed to hear this admission, as it assured her that her dupe would not be likely to recognize the person to whom she was about to introduce him.

"But how are we to find our way, my charmer ?" asked the rake.

" Once by Westminster Abbey," replied Jenny, " I doubt not but I shall be able to find my way to my aunt's dwelling, so minutely has she described the way to it, from the building I have mentioned.'

"Then we had better drive thither at once," said Sir Harry, and a man was sent to procure a hackney coach, into which when it arrived the gallant handed in the blushing bride, and the vehicle slowly rolled along towards Westminster Abbey.

There they alighted and discharged the driver, after the latter had pointed out to them the direction in which they should proceed. Pretending to pick out her way by certain signs which had been described to her, Jenny Diver threaded the dark and narrow streets, and before long they arrived opposite a house to which we have before now, conducted the reader, and which was no other than that occupied by that ancient and respectable lady, Mother Sin, whom Jenny had resolved to pass off for her relative for the occasion.

"Here is the dwelling of my aunt," said Jenny; " but as it will be necessary and only respectful to her to apprise her of the happy change in my situation. I will first speak to her in private and then introduce you as my husband."

To this proposal the bridegroom could not very well object, although he seemed not much to relish parting with his prize for a moment. However, he assented, and Jenny tripping to the door, knocked, and was at once admitted, leaving her swain in the street without.

This movement was of course a ruse of Jenny's in order to secure an opportunity of informing the old procuress of all that had transpired, and also of schooling her in the part she was to sustain. Mother Sin was an apt scholar enough when her interests were concerned, and she speedily understood and agreed to act in concert with the artful Diver, who, as soon as Mother Sin had hastily changed her costume for some attire of a more sober description, and more in character with the affair in hand, emerged from the house and joined her spouse, who stood quivering with excitement in front of it.

"Thank God, all is well," said Jenny, " my aunt at first chid me severely for taking such a hasty step without consulting her, for she much feared that I had fallen a victim to one of those villains with which the town swarms. But on exhibiting my certificate of marriage and the presents which you have bestowed on me, she was at once satisfied, and now anxiously waits to welcome you."

Sir Harry was overjoyed at this statement, for he was a fool as well as a rascal and believed every word Jenny said.

Following the girl he entered Mother Sin's abode, and was ushered into the private apartment of that lady, which had been hurriedly set into something like order. The dram bottle and glass had been shoved into a corner cupboard, and in their place on the table was a huge prayer-book with a pair of spectacles laid upon the open leaves, to give an impression to the visitor that the worthy and pious lady of the house had been attending to the affairs of her soul prior to her departure to rest. Mother Sin was up to all such trickeries and frequently practised them, and to give her credit she usually so conducted herself as to cause little or no suspicion in the minds of the keenest observers.

In due course the bawd made her appearance, and was presented to Sir Harry, who insisted, after the usual courtesies had passed, on ordering a supper at a neighbouring tavern, to which, by the way, neither Jenny nor her respected relative objected, as it afforded them additional opportunities of carrying out their scheme.

Cheerfully did the old lady pledge the health of the newly married couple, and with turned-up eyes, piously did she pray for her dear niece's happiness. But when her spirits had been enlivened by a few glasses of generous wine, she unconsciously forgot her grace and matronly character so far as to indulge in certain rather warm allusions to the position and duties of the bridegroom, which made that gentleman feel somewhat restless, and at the same time a little surprised at the intimate knowledge of nuptial matters exhibited by his beloved wife's " maiden" aunt.

"Now, my dear," said Mother Sin, very significantly to Jenny, after a somewhat prolonged sitting over the potent liquor, " had you not better go to — to —"

"To bed, my angel," said Sir Harry, supplying the word which it appeared Mother Sin's sense of delicacy would scarcely allow her to utter.

"Yes, Sir Harry, that is what I meant, the poor child is tired I am sure, and her situation is somewhat strange ; but I will act as her bridesmaid, and when all is ready I will inform you. Ah ! you naughty man !" she added, as she held up her finger to the bridegroom, who by a peculiar look gave her to understand that he hoped she would allow him to join his beautiful young wife as speedily as possible.

Mother Sin and Jenny Diver then quitted the parlour, the latter putting on an air of bashfulness, as her gallant politely handed her to the foot of the staircase which led to her bed-chamber. No sooner, however, had they entered the room and bolted themselves in, than the pair sank each into a chair, and indulged in fits of immoderate laughter.

Jenny then presented Mother Sin with ten guineas, and instead of undressing and retiring to bed, attired herself in a cloak, lent her by the bawd, which completely covered her dress. The old lady then conducted her by a sliding pannel into an adjoining room, and then after once more rehearsing the part she was now to perform, she quitted Jenny and descended to the expectant bridegroom.

"Is my lady in bed ?" he asked anxiously.

"She is," replied the old bawd; "but the dear timid creature is so extremely shamefaced that she entreats as a favour that you will divest yourself of your attire in the dressing-room which adjoins your bed chamber, and that you will not take a light with you into her presence. Poor child ! she will soon get used to the presence of a man in his shirt ; but you know, my dear sir, that girls are timid at first, so I hope you will accede to her request."

"Certainly, by all means," said the baronet, who would have walked a mile in a state of complete nudity for the sake of enjoying such a delicate feast at the end of it. By all means, my dear madame, suffer me to salute you as my new and respected relative, and then I pray you to conduct me to the ante chamber."

The salute was given and received with some show of reluctance, and then Mother Sin led the way up stairs and showed the baronet into a small room, a door from which led to another, in which he was informed his bride now lay bedded and waiting his arrival. Mother Sin with a wicked look then retired, and the enamoured swain speedily divested himself of his garments, and passed on to the supposed bridal chamber.

The place was in utter darkness, and as the room was one of large dimensions he was some time groping about before he could discover in in what part the bedstead was situated. Not a sound indicated its exact situation ; and at this the anxious man did not much wonder as he supposed that the excessive modesty of the bride kept her in such a state of total silence. At length in his groping about he stumbled against one of the pillars of a four-poster which he anxiously clutched.

The night was none of the warmest, and the gentleman shivered from the effects of his peregrinations. Longing, therefore, to warm his half chilled frame in the embraces of his dulcinea he uttered a low sound as if to call her attention to the very interesting fact that her devoted admirer was about to claim the rights of a husband. No reply was, however given, and he stood somewhat puzzled at the foot of the bed.

"Certainly the girl has lost her wits," he muttered to himself, and then screwing up his courage to the sticking point, he felt his way to the bedside, and summoning up all his courage prepared stealthily and gently to enter it.

But to his unutterable surprise his hand fell not on the soft warm bosom of a beautiful girl, but on a rough chin and a most unmistakedly bushy whisker ; and in less time than it occupies in the telling the astonished bridegroom felt himself kicked from the bed to the floor, and when there suffered from the violent pressure of a strong man's hand upon his throat.

"The devil !" exclaimed the unlucky mortal, who had been so suddenly ejected from his pro-mised paradise, that he could not but think that the sable gentleman must have had a hand in the matter. "The devil ! murder ! thieves ! fire !" he shouted.

"Another word and I'll brain you," cried a rough voice. "And so you thought to cheat a poor girl did you; but by God if you do not come down pretty handsomely you shall be exposed for this."

The man with the bushy whiskers and the gruff voice then forced the baronet into an arm-chair and again vowed vengeance against him if he attempted to move ; but this precaution was well nigh useless, for the victim was so paralysed by fear, surprise and disappointment that he was absolutely incapable of stirring a limb.

The stranger then procured a light by kindling some powder and tinder in the pan of his pistols, and Flitchman, in a threatening attitude, stood revealed to the eyes of the trembling captive.

"Ha ! is it you, my Lord Martingale," exclaimed Flitchman, peering curiously into the face of the person who had passed himself off to Jenny Diver as a baronet. "Methinks, my lord, we have met before."

"We have," replied Martingale, "you were formerly a clerk to one Mr. Doom, a lawyer of Gray's Inn."

"The same," observed Flitchman, "but I warn you that you had best forget that part of the business or it may be the worse for you. The affair of to-night will not at all redound to your credit, so it would be as well to keep your own counsel too with respect to that part of the business."

Martingale, who was one of the rakehelly bloods of the day, felt that placed in such a ticklish position, it would be advisable for him to get out of the scrape in the easiest manner possible. He, therefore, promised on condition of his clothes being restored, and he himself set at liberty, to maintain a perfect silence with regard to the adventure in which he had been engaged.

Flitchman retired from the bed-room and in the course of a few moments re-appeared with the garments of the amorous peer ; but greatly to the chagrin of the latter he found that his pockets had been rifled, and now he clearly saw through the trick which had been played off on him. Mortified beyond description, he inwardly swore to be revenged ; but he carefully avoided giving utterance even to the semblance of a threat.

Crest-fallen and abashed, Lord Martingale slunk down the very same staircase which he had so recently mounted as lightly as if he was soaring on the wings of love. At the door, Flitchman presented him with his sword, minus its diamond hilt, which his guide jocosely remarked would remunerate him for the inconvenience he had been put to by having had his rest disturbed ; and then the poor duped nobleman, robbed of all his property saving the clothes on his back found himself alone in the unknown and perilous precincts of the Almonry of Westminster.

———

CHAPTER L.

JENNY DIVER AND MOTHER SIN GET INTO TROUBLE

No sooner had Jenny Diver crept through the sliding panel, than Mother Sin carefully replaced it in the wainscott, so as completely to conceal all traces of the passage by which the girl had got out of the intended bridal chamber, after having introduced Flitchman into the bed to personate anything rather than a soft and yielding bride; and for which service he was well paid by the liberal Jenny Diver.

On counting over gains, Jenny Diver discovered that her nights' adventure had yielded her a sum amounting to nearly a hundred pounds, exclusive of the watch and jewellery, which were both extremely valuable. As the young girl considered that she should run too great a risk by attempting to dispose of them herself, she suffered herself to be persuaded by Mother Sin to entrust them with her for sale; and then determining not to return to M'Cleane until the following day she accepted of a bed in the procuresses house.

In the meantime Lord Martingale was wending his way through the dirty and dingy purlieus of Westminster towards his residence in Picadilly. The peer was a man of a deeply revengeful disposition, and when he began to get cool and after all danger to his person had ceased to exist, he began to consider whether he could not contrive a plan for recovering his property, some part of which as heir boons he highly valued.

It would be easy enough he imagined to stop the mouth of Parson Jawbone by a handsome present, and a threat of transportation for illegally marrying, and in that case, supposing the wedding affair was brought on the carpet who was to prove the matter? A story of his having been decoyed into the house in the Almonry on some pretext or other could be easily trumped up; and at length he determined to make a bold stroke, and attempt to turn the tables on those who had duped him.

With this object in view, his lordship, on arriving at Charing Cross, bent his steps toward Newtoners Lane, for the purpose of at once giving information of the robbery to Jonathan Wild. Late or rather early as the honr was, he found the thief-taker at his office, and an ample fee at once secured an immediate and private interview.

In stating his case to Jonathan, the Peer carefully avoided making any reference to the Fleet Street affair; but alleged that he had casually picked up with the wench who had plundered him in the street, and at her request he had accompanied her to the house in the Almonry, the situation of which he so accurately described that Wild immediately felt assured it must be the habitation of Mother Sin.

"The wonder is that you escaped with your life, my lord," remarked Jonathan, "there are tales afloat of mysterious disappearances of gentlemen who have been seen to enter the dwelling but who were never known to leave it. I have long had my eye on this woman, and now that an opportunity occurs of applying for a search-warrant, a thorough hunt shall take place. But what kind of a girl was it who took you there?"

Lord Martingale's powers of description were again called into requisition, and so well did he pourtray our heroine's appearance and manners, that coupling what he heard with the ingenious stratagem by which she escaped, Wild, after musing for a moment, exclaimed—

"It must be either that jade Jenny Diver or the devil. And now I think of it Abraham informed me that he suspected she had returned from transportation."

Jonathan Wild requested Martingale to call on him on the evening of the following day, when he hoped, he said, to give him some information concerning his lost valuables.

The Peer then took his departure, and a few hours afterwards he knocked at the door of Parson Jawbone, who was not a little surprised at his haggared and anxious appearance.

The worthy ' Vicar of Saint Pauls ' was, for a wonder, sober enough to comprehend the story of the man whom he had married on the previous evening, and the reverend gentleman having an inordinate affection for gold, a few pieces of that valuable metal procured from him a solemn promise that what had transpired should never be made known.

Martingale now felt convinced that he need not fear any exposure on that score, and he returned to his own home, there to await the course of events.

The instant Lord Martingale had quitted Jonathan Wild's house, the latter summoned to his presence his trusty servant, Abraham, who, when he entered the private office, beheld his rascally master chuckling and rubbing his hands together as if in high glee.

"Any goot newsh, Mishter Vild?" asked Abraham, with a cringing air and a roguish twinkle in his eye.

"You know the house of that old she devil Mother Sin, in the Almonry?" asked Wild of Abraham.

"Vere the old shentlemans vas lost and supposhed to be scragged?" asked the crafty son of the tribe of Moses.

"The same," replied Wild, "now I have to do a job there which admits of no delay. Go at once to Bow Street and bring Mr. Watkins hither, and in your way call also in Shire Lane and direct Quilt Arnold to come to me without a moments delay, or the bird I am looking for will have flown."

"It shall be done, Mishter Vild," said Abraham, and he hastened from the place to execute the order he had received.

In the course of an hour Watkins, Quilt Arnold, Abraham and Jonathan Wild were assembled in the sanctum of the latter, where they held a consultation, after which, having armed themselves to the teeth, they left Newtoners Lane and proceed to Bow Street, where Watkins called up a justice who lived in the neighbourhood and procured a search warrant. This effected, they all directed their steps towards the residence of the unsuspecting Mother Sin.

The grey dawn of early morning was just revealing indistinctly the countless towers, and spires of the metropolis, when Wild and his three companions entered the precincts of the Almonry, almost every house in which was as familiar without and within to the thief-taker's eye as his own, for there was scarcely a dwelling in the neighbourhood which in his professional capacity he had not had at some time or other occasion to visit, for the whole neighbourhood was the then head quarters of roguery in the metropolis.

Scenting out the house as instinctively as a blood-hound detects his prey, Wild led the party through the labyrinth of narrow streets, until at length he suddenly stopped opposite Mother Sin's domicile.

Not a light appeared in any of the windows, and Watkins and Wild were convinced from appearances that the people within had retired to their beds. Jonathan then directed Arnold and Watkins to go round and guard the side door which communicated with the house from a narrow passage, and he himself with his man Abraham took up their posts at the front entrance. Having thus disposed their forces, they were all readiness for the accomplishment of their purpose.

Mother Sin, Jenny Diver, Flitchman, Sal the Gonnoff and the other inmates were deep in slumber when they were awakened by a thundering knock at the front door, and a demand for admission. On looking from her bedroom window Mother Sin beheld Jonathan Wild, who requested to be admitted for the purpose of searching for a thief whom he named. Certain that no such person was beneath her roof, yet fearing to refuse Wild, whose vengeance she dared not brave, the bawd, after much hesitation, half-dressed herself and ran for Jenny, whom she hid in her own bed. Then she descended the stairs and opened the door, immediately on which the thief-taker and his man Abraham, followed by Watkins and Quilt Arnold, whom they had summoned from the side door by a whistle, rushed inside, greatly to the terror of Mother Sin who had not before perceived them.

"Werry sorry to disturb you, Ma'am," said Watkins, with an awkward grimace, "but business is business at all hours. This ere paper empowers me to make a search in your werry convenient house, so if you wallys your own safety you won't hide nothing. Let's go to the bedrooms first," and he exhibited to Mother Sin's eyes the search warrant.

Seeing that opposition was of no use the old bawd led the way up stairs, and on arriving at the door of her own chamber she hinted that it was her own apartment and hoped the gentlemen would not think it necessary to search there. Mr. Watkins and Wild, however, appeared to think an inspection was necessary, but they merely glanced round and greatly to Jenny Diver's relief, they quitted the room, the door of which Wild locked and put the key in his pocket.

"Had a gen'lman here awhile ago, Ma'am," remarked Mr. Watkins, " and I believe he left a watch and some fal lals of trinkets behind him, perhaps you can put your hands on them."

Mother Sin swore that Watkins was mistaken, for not a soul but herself and her usual lodgers, who roused from their beds now surrounded her in their night-dresses, had been beneath her roof that night. Wild and the rest, however, would not believe her, and a general ransacking now commenced.

But vain was their search until at length, Watkins suddenly thrusting his hand into the bosom of Mrs. Sin, pulled therefrom a watch, which his practised eye had detected concealed there. On the case was a coronet, and the runner knew he was on the right scent.

"Suppose we search the cellar," said Watkins and ordering Mother Sin to follow them, they went down stairs for that purpose.

A terrible shudder passed over the frame of the procuress as she saw Watkins draw from his pocket a long cord with a triple hook fastened to one end of it, and then lift the trap-door which covered up the well leading to the sewer.

"I've heer'd," remarked the officer coolly, " that people hide their money bags and other things too, in such places, so I'll try whether I shall be lucky enough to fish up anything," continued the Bow Street runner, as, to the infinite horror of Mother Sin, he lowered the grappling hook into the well, and let it sink with a splash into the dark waters beneath.

Several times did Watkins draw it up but nothing adhered to the hook but the filth and ooze of the noisome sewer. At last, however, a heap of cloth with buttons attached thereto came to light, and Watkins minutely examined it.

"Queer place to find a gentleman's coat in," remarked Watkins, as he turned the dirty garment over ; " but where one part of the dress is the rest may be also—let us try again," and once more he let down the hook.

It seemed to hold something and now the officer found it impossible to drag whatever it was fastened in by his own power. Arnold lent his aid, and then by great exertion, a shapeless mass of something was drawn up and thrown on the floor of the cellar.

"My God! it's a dead man," exclaimed Watkins. "There has been murder here Wild, seize Mother Sin, for this must be some of her damnable doings."

But the step Watkins had ordered to be taken was unnecessary, for immediately on the discovery of the body the miserable woman with a fearful shriek had fallen senseless on the ground.

The body was then carefully inspected, and from the marks of violence yet perceptible on it, the man, whoever he was had evidently been murdered. Mother Sin was removed up stairs, and Abraham was placed as a guard over her whilst the search in the room of Mother Sin was resumed.

But there they found nothing to connect her with the suspected murder, and the men were about to quit the apartment, when Wild, more by chance than otherwise, threw back the clothes from the procuresses bed, and to the surprise of all Jenny Diver was discovered crouched up at the bottom of the huge bedstead.

"Who the devil have we here?" said Jonathan, throwing the light from his lantern full upon the frightened girl's face.

One glance was sufficient. He instantly recognised Jenny Diver, who he had seen when she was tried at the Old Bailey, and laying his hand on her shoulder, made her his prisoner.

"On what charge dare you detain me?" asked the girl with spirit, but in reality her heart sank within her.

"For robbing from the person of a gentleman not three hours ago—and also for returning before your time from transportation," replied

Wild, eyeing the girl with a look of demoniacal satisfaction. He then searched her, and in her pockets discovered the gold she had deprived Lord Martingale of.

"This will be a rare night's work, or I am mightily mistaken," remarked Wild to the Bow Street runner,—a remark with the truth of which that functionary appeared entirely to coincide. They then consulted as to what steps should next be taken, and finally Mother Sin and Jenny Diver were conveyed to the Compter in a hackney coach by Watkins and Abraham, whilst Wild and Arnold remained to guard the house; and to wait for the return of the Bow Street runner, when they proposed to resume their search in the sewer.

In accordance with this resolve, a minute and searching investigation of the Old House in the Almonry was instituted, and it became evident that the body of the unfortunate gentleman which had been brought to light by the officer was not the only one which had been committed to that horrible and dark receptacle. No paper or property of any description were discovered upon the corpse; but, nevertheless, a verdict of "Wilful Murder" was returned against Mother Sin, who was ordered to be detained a prisoner until evidence to connect her with the dreadful deed could be procured.

Wild now experienced transports of exultation at having captured so notorious an offender as Jenny Diver; and the Bow Street runner looked forward to receiving something handsome as the reward of his vigilance. In the meantime Jenny was in a state of despair; and when the news of her capture, which spread over the town like wildfire, reached M'Cleane and his comrades at the Chapel, the greatest consternation was excited.

Great indeed was the tribulation of the Captain, for he really felt greatly attached to the girl, in whose society he had performed so many feats of predatory dexterity, and in whose arms he had enjoyed such delicious transports. His regret, too, was vastly different to that which he had formerly felt when other members of his gang had been laid by the heels in prison, inasmuch, as in Jenny's case he felt not the slightest apprehension that the caged bird would utter a single note which might involve her comrades in her own disaster. Jenny's character for faithfulness to those around her was well established, and on this account a more than usual sorrow was felt for the loss of so valuable a member of the gang.

M'Cleane was, in a word, completely at fault. He knew not what course was best to pursue to aid Jenny, the damning charge against whom was her return from transportation. The other charge might have been got over, but the Captain felt that this was too serious a matter to be trifled with. To add to his embarrassments, the robbery at the mint had made a most prodigious stir and he greatly feared that Jenny might be recognised when brought up for examination, as the young woman who had gagged the portress, and so lead to his own detection.

At all risks he determined not to desert Jenny in her day of adversity; and to do all in his power to aid her in escaping from her too probable fate. How he succeeded we shall see in the end.

On the day succeeding that on which Mother Sin and Jenny had been apprehended in the Almonry, our heroine was taken before a justice of the peace, at Bow Street, where she was first examined on a charge of having robbed Lord Martingale.

His lordship, when he made his appearance in the witness box to substantiate his charge, entered into a statement which had everything in it but truth to recommend it to the magistrate, who happened to be a friend of the nobleman's, and therefore, of course, took all he said for gospel. Not a word did the Peer say about the Fleet marriage—not a word respecting his willing visit to the false relative of the prisoner. He merely asserted that Jenny Diver accosted him in the public thoroughfare, induced him by her arts to accompany her to the brothel, and that when there she plundered him of the property laid in the indictment.

"Look at this paper, your worship," said Jenny when called upon to speak, "I am that man's lawful wife."

A murmur of astonishment ran through the court as the girl thus spoke. Lord Martingale assumed an air of the utmost surprise, and a sneer of incredulity curled his rather handsome lip.

Jenny here handed to the magistrate a paper —the one she had received from Parson Jawbone, purporting to be certificate of her marriage with a baronet. The justice after examining the document beckoned Watkins, the Bow Street runner to him, and placing a warrant in his hand immediately dispatched him in search of the self-styled Vicar of Saint Pauls.

In about half-an-hour that worthy individual made his appearance, and on being questioned by the magistrate, promptly swore that he had never seen either the gentleman or the prisoner before in his life, and that as for marrying them the charge was perfectly absurd.

Lord Martingale drew himself up with an air of triumph, and the justice was about to intimate to the Peer that he might retire, when Tim Snarley stepped forward, and pulling his firelock, said to the magistrate—

"It aint no such thing, yer Vershup, I seed Parson Jawbone unite that gen'man and that young 'ooman at the bar there in holy matrimony myself; for I'd been a watching the proceedings of that old rascal in the Cossack for some time, and happened to creep into his chapel as he calls it while he was at his dirty work—marrying them two."

"What say you to this?" asked the magistrate of the rather confused clergyman.

Jawbone promptly denied the statement of Tim Snarley, but the justice fearing to altogether dismiss the matter bound over the Parson to appear whenever called upon, and then committed Jenny Diver to take her trial for the alleged robbery of the baronet.

The girl was about to be removed from the bar when Jonathan Wild's burly form was seen by Jenny conspicuous among the crowd. The thief-taker's eye met her own, an expression of diabolical malice was on his countenance as he surveyed his victim. The Diver had hitherto conducted herself with great fortitude, but when she observed Wild lean forward and hand a written paper to the clerk of the court, she felt a sudden tremor steal over her, and she was compelled to

hold by the railing of the bar to prevent herself from sinking on the floor of the court.

The Clerk of the Court for a moment perused the paper, shook his head gravely as he glanced from it to the prisoner, and then passed it to the justice who presided in the seat above him. This functionary also gazed earnestly at the prisoner and then sank back in his chair as if to await further proceedings.

"Let Jonathan Wild be sworn," said the clerk.

The thief-taker stepped forward and entered the witness-box. A dead silence prevailed in court as he took the book in his hand. When he had kissed it the judge asked him if he knew the prisoner at the bar?

"I do," was the stern and decided answer of Jonathan.

"What is her name?"

"Mary Young, alias Jenny Diver," was th reply.

"Has she been before convicted?" was the next question.

"She has, and was lately sentenced to transportation at the Old Bailey.

"And her term of banishment has not yet expired?" asked the justice.

"It has not," said Jonathan, "and there is another witness to prove the prisoner to be the person who was sent, as Mary Young, to the American Colonies."

Mr. Watkins, the Bow Street runner, was next called, and he sufficiently corroborated the evidence of Jonathan Wild to induce the magistrate to commit Jenny Diver for trial on the charge of returning from transportation—a capital offence.

Before Jenny was removed from the bar, she glanced anxiously round the court, evidently in the hope of seeing some one known to her; but after vainly prying into every part and corner of it, she turned away disappointed and sick at heart. Not a pitying eye was there: not one whom she knew; and in the bitterness of her heart she accused M'Cleane and her companions of ingratitude.

At that time the prisoners committed for trial were not altogether cut off from communication with others, the moment they were removed from the dock. In pursuance of the usual plan of proceeding, the girl was taken into an adjoining apartment which was crowded with curious spectators, to whom the far-famed Jenny Diver was an object of vast curiosity. At that time, too, notorious criminals were often exposed to the public gaze, for the sake of benefitting those in whose custody they were placed; and many a broad, bright guinea did Mr. Watkins pocket that day by the exhibition of his lovely and unfortunate captive.

Among those who gazed at the prisoner, much as people gaze at a wild beast in the den of a menagerie, was one who suddenly and by a secret sign attracted the attention of Jenny Diver. Could she be mistaken? No! She was not then altogether forsaken, for she was confident that in the laced and ruffled gallant who effected to examine her features and figure, just as he would have scanned the points of a horse, she saw no other than her lover and friend, Captain M'Cleane. And so it proved, but unfortunately for both no opportunity of profiting by the recognition took place, and Jenny Diver was hurried off to Newgate there to await her trial.

In her distress we must for the present leave her, while we return to Handsome Jack.

It will be remembered that we left the unfortunate dupe of Jonathan Wild's devices on his straw bed in the Compter, to which place he had been conveyed by Watkins, the Bow Street runner, after the mock-marriage of Lady Purley, on a charge of having, in company of other parties not in custody, burglariously entered Purley Hall with intention to plunder.

The reflections of the unfortunate young man, as he tossed himself uneasily on his wretched bed were of the most agonizing description. Through the long dreary hours of the night he recalled to memory the strange events of his past history; and when he reflected on what he was and what he might have been, his mind became almost distracted. The bitterest reminescence of all was the rememberance of the late scene with his once beloved and still virtuous Emilia, and the thought of what she might be doomed to suffer from the severity of her jealous husband tortured him beyond description. At length, wearied with utter misery, sleep visited him, and for a few hours he slept only to awake to a renewed and still more poignant sense of his misery.

The first tidings which yielded him any satisfaction were those which informed him of the apprehension of Doom, the lawyer. As we have already stated prior to he himself having been committed for trial, he was examined as a witness in the attorney's case. So far he was revenged; but the death of the man, who had in connection with James Town driven him to adopt such a desperate course of life as that which had ended in a prison, had caused an additional exposure.

It was true, all the former obstacles which prevented his resuming his title and recovering his estates were now removed; but in their place a far more insuperable bar at present existed, for the offended laws of his country now stood between him and his hereditary rights, and in the event of a conviction every farthing would be claimed by the crown, and the whole of the Town estates would be confiscated.

From his cousin whom he last saw in the pillory at Charing Cross he had now nothing to fear; and he bitterly remembered that had he but patiently waited instead of having given way to his headstrong passions he would at that moment have been moving in his own proper sphere among the brilliant circles of fashion. Regret, however, was useless, and as Handsome Jack was not one to be quietly down in despair, he began after the first shock of his imprisonment was over to revolve in his mind some schemes for extricating himself from the awkward situation in which he was placed.

That Jonathan Wild would use every endeavour to procure his conviction and consequent death Handsome Jack was perfectly well assured; he determined within himself, therefore, that rather than the thief-taker should profit by him he would attempt a manœuvre by means of which, if successful, he should secure his life and procure his liberty by making a tremendous sacrifice. But what sacrifice will not a man make to preserve life? Scarcely had the project entered into Handsome Jack's head before he began to act upon it.

In his imprisonment he was frequently visited by Dick Flybynight who he employed to seek out an attorney who could be relied upon. Such a person was soon ferretted out by the highwayman, and by him introduced to Handsome Jack in his cell.

It will be perfectly unnecessary for us to chronicle all that passed at the various interviews which took place between the man of law and his client, suffice it to say that the latter proposed an arrangement with Lord Purley which should have the effect of preventing the attendance of his lordship as a witness upon his trial. The particulars of that arrangement may be thus briefly stated.

It was well known that if Lord Purley entertained the slightest affection for any one thing in this world, it was for money. Gold was his deity; and to and for it he would sacrifice anything short of his life.

On this weak side it was thought he might be assailable, and Handsome Jack, therefore, executed a power of attorney and offered the half of his property to Lord Purley on condition of his temporarily quitting the country, so as to render his appearing against him at the Old Bailey impossible. To stimulate the attorney entrusted with this very delicate business to use his utmost endeavours to effect an amicable arrangement a thousand pounds were secured to him.

Lord Purley was seated in his library one morning after breakfast, severely lecturing his wife for some presumed indiscretion, when his footman announced that Mr. Smoothton Sharp, of the Inner Temple, desired an interview with him.

Motioning to his wife to quit the library, he ordered the lawyer to be admitted, and that gentleman, with a most profound obeisance to the magniloquent Peer, entered.

After the usual courtesies, the Peer requested to know to what circumstance he was indebted for the honour of Mr. Sharp's visit, for the old gentleman was exceedingly polite, and would not have been guilty of a breach of etiquette for the world.

"I have heard, my lord," insinuated the man of law, "that your lordship is desirous of becoming the owner of some estates immediately adjoining your own parks."

Mr. Sharp had ascertained such to be the fact beyond doubt prior to his visit to Lord Purley.

"True, sir," replied the Peer, "but I fancy there is a small chance of my obtaining them. If I mistake not they will before long become the property of the crown, and as I am not in favor with the minister, much as I should desire it, I shall not be allowed to bargain for it."

"But supposing, my lord, that on certain conditions they were at once offered you, and you thought proper to accept of those terms, you need not trouble the minister or any one else in the matter."

"Exactly so, sir; but nothing will prevent the conviction of the person, Town, to whom the property belongs. I am the principal—nay the only witness (for Lady Purley obstinately vows that she will not enter the court) against the fellow. I do not, therefore, see what you are driving at," said Lord Purley.

"Possibly not," remarked Mr. Sharp, "but you will better understand me when I state that by this act of attorney I am empowered on one condition to place you at once and without any trouble or a farthings expense on your part in full and undisputed possession of the property in question."

Lord Purley stared as if he believed the lawyer was mad; but at length he became convinced that his offer was in good earnest and he immediately understood the matter.

At first his lordship hesitated and talked of duty to the public and all that sort of thing; then he walked to the window and surveyed the prospect, and thought how pleasant it would be to call all the broad lands which spread away as far as the eye could see his own; then he cheated himself into the belief that he should be doing a humane act in saving a fellow creatures life: avarice whispered to him how much his possessions would be increased; and he suddenly remembered that her ladyship's health was extremely delicate, and that her physician had recommended the air of France. Finally on receiving an assurance that the real state of matters should be kept a profound secret he acceded to the proposition, pocketted the necessary title deeds and the next day he and his wife were on their way to the French capital.

Jonathan Wild was kept in utter ignorance of all this affair, and greatly to that worthy's chagrin he was served with a legal notice to deliver up the remaining documents relating to the Town property which remained in his possession. This however he refused to do until compelled by subsequent events.

Greatly relieved from the terrors which had haunted him ever since his apprehension, Handsome Jack now regained, in a great degree, his usual health, and he looked forward without apprehension to his coming trial, which, as the reader will readily surmise resulted in an acquittal.

Unbounded was the rage of Wild when he discovered the absence from England of Lord Purley. He had played a deep and he believed a successful game in respect of the Town estates; but just when he thought he had a prize within his grasp it had been snatched from him. Fortunately for Handsome Jack the thief-taker had not been enabled to rake up any other charge against him, but the wily wretch determined to watch his future movements with the utmost scrutiny in the hope of being revenged by his destruction for the disappointment he had suffered.

The moment Handsome Jack was acquitted for want of evidence, he authorized his lawyer to dispose of the remainder of his property, and to convert everything into money, announcing it to be his intention to quit a country in which his name was tainted with crime. He then determined to pay a farewell visit to M'Cleane and his old comrades, whom he could not bear to abandon without a sort of affectionate farewell, much as he now determined to relinquish the pursuits into which he had, whilst associated with them, been hurried.

We must, however, leave for the present Handsome Jack to his reflections, and return to Jenny Diver, whose lucky star was hidden by a cloud of gloom, and which, to all appearance was about to set for ever.

Public curiosity had been raised to a great height on the occasion of Jenny Diver's making her first appearance in the dock of the Old Bailey; but the sensation then produced was absolutely nothing when compared with that which agitated the town when it became known that one so notorious had had the hardihood to return from her banishment, and again practise her deceptions on the public.

Dexterity of a superior order, in whatever class of persons it may be found, is certain to beget a certain sort of admiration, and the fame of our heroine having for so long a time been hinted abroad she became at once the lion of the day, and the place of her confinement was visited by hundreds of persons who were intensely anxious to behold the woman, who by her wonderful powers of deception had raised herself to the very pinnacle of her nefarious profession.

In losing Jenny Diver M'Cleane felt that he had been deprived of his right hand, and as much from gratitude as from love towards the partner of his bed he determined that not an effort to facilitate her escape should be neglected. But so closely watched was the prisoner that all his schemes were found to be useless, and at length the day of the trial drew near.

In the interval which had occurred between the apprehension of Mother Sin and the commencement of the Old Bailey sessions, Mr. Watkins, the Bow Street runner, had exerted all his sagacity in order to discover who the old gentleman was whose body he had discovered in the drain beneath the old house in the Almonry, and a considerable reward was offered to any one who should afford correct information on the subject.

While sitting one day disguised in a tavern near the Old Bailey, to which place he had been for the purpose of seeing Jenny Diver, M'Cleane's eye happened to fall upon the bill announcing the reward. Suddenly he remembered that on the occasion of the murder he had possessed himself of a pocket-book belonging to the deceased, which contained papers that explained who the unfortunate man was. It now struck him that, although in producing them he should run no small risk himself, he might, should matters come to the worst with Jenny Diver, make some sort of compromise with the authorities by means of which the girl's life might be saved. But this he felt must be brought about by sacrificing Mother Sin, the only person beside himself and Sal, the Gonnoff, who were cognizant of the horrible tragedy which had been enacted in the cellar. To act as a traitor was extremely repugnant to his feelings, but the case was desperate; and besides he apprehended that the old procuress might be before-hand with him. M'Cleane, therefore, resolved to be mainly guided by the course of events, and in the event of real danger to Jenny Diver to abandon the late owner of the house in the Almonry to her fate.

On the morning of the eventful day which was to decide her fate, Jenny Diver arose early, and and as on a former occasion spent not a little time in decorating her pretty person, no body being better convinced than she was that appearances went very far. Jurymen were but men after all she thought, and no more than any other mortals insensible to the power of beauty. Indeed on the occasion of this which might be called her fatal toilet, she might rather have been supposed by lookers on to have been preparing for the ball—the theatre, or some fashionable assembly, and not for the grim court of the Old Bailey and the dread company therein assembled.

At length the work of beautifying came to an end, and in spite of her perilous situation, Jenny could not help displaying a smile of exultation as she surveyed herself in the glass. She indeed looked charming. The little coquettish patches, which it was then the prevailing fashion of the day to wear, she had so arranged that really they gave to her animated countenance quite a killing appearance. Her confinement, prohibiting her as it had from her usual out of door exercise, had somewhat paled her cheek, but the judicious application of some famous cosmetics had artfully supplied the place of nature. In conformity with her usual extravagance she attired herself in a new and splendid dress constructed in the very height of the fashion of the day; a natty little hat with a feather graced her well shaped head, and high-heeled shoes completed her costume. In her gloved hand she held a fan, which she playfully flirted, and a superb gold chain dangling from her neck was attached to a watch of the same precious metal richly coloured with precious stones.

Densely crowded was the court of the Old on the day when it was known the far-famed criminal would once more be arraigned. Every avenue leading to the place of justice was thronged by the nobility and gentry, many of whom had been victimized by our heroine, though the fear of exposure had prevented their appearing as prosecutors. Ladies of rank and title struggled or places, and large fees gladdened the hearts of the Old Bailey officials. The affair was thought to be as good as a play, rather better indeed, as the principal actor in the scene was to be no maniac personage but a real criminal, who doubtless would undergo anything but a maniac punishment!

It was a proud day for Mr. Watkins, the Bow Street runner! That gentleman to whose sagacity Jenny Diver was in a great measure indebted for her misfortunes, had, like his unfortunate captive, expended no little time and pains on the decoration of his portly person. Indeed the occasions of the Old Bailey sessions were quite festivals with him and of all the class to which he belonged; seasons when they appeared in all their glory as little heroes, though it must be confessed, as conquerors on rather a small scale. In the button-hole of his gold-laced official coat, the constable wore a huge bunch of flowers the prevailing colours of which were of a colour which was almost rivalled in intensity of hue by his jolly cheeks, and the fiery tip of his rubicund nose. On a gold banded three cornered hat was displayed a cockade of enormous size composed of purple and white ribbons; and, as a further mark of authority, his ample corporation was encased in a scarlet waistcoat; and in his hand he carried a long white wand in place of the staff which was his usual companion.

The Recorder entered the hall of justice amid a flourish of trumpets, and the formalities of the court began. The jury was sworn, and a number of trifling cases disposed of; so trifling that the impatient gallants and ladies present felt not the slightest simpathy for the unfortunates who had not been daring enough to commit crimes which would excite admiration or interest. It is only your great criminals who can make a man of quality curious, or cause a lady's heart to flutter in her fair bosom. At length, however, the gaoler was ordered to place Mother Sin and Jenny Diver at the bar in order that they might plead.

The old procuress first made her appearance, and a universal shudder of disgust ran through the court as she advanced to the front of the bar. Her aspect was absolutely hideous, for since her incarceration in the prison she had given up freely to dissipation, and her bleared eyes, flushed and bloated face, and unsteady gait indicated the effects of habitual intemperance. The traces of a foul and frightful disease too were sufficiently evident, now that she had for some time been deprived of the benefit of those powerful drugs with which she had been accustomed to check its ravages. The damp of the prison had greatly aggravated the progress of the disease; her nose was almost flattened on her face, owing to the bones and cartilages of that feature having been slowly eaten as it were away: the flesh of her cheeks was of the color and consistence of dough, and scars, here and there on the hag's wrinkled neck, showed where ulcerous sores had burrowed and broken. Mother Sin no longer exhibited her former reckless and impudent air, she was now completely cowed and overwhelmed with terror, and her feeble limbs almost refused to sustain her weight. Shudderingly she looked round the court, but not one sympathising look did she encounter; and clinging with both hands to the railing of the dock for support she sank on her knees and blubbered for mercy.

Far different was the appearance and bearing of Jenny Diver, who in a few seconds after Mother Sin's appearance joined her in the dock. We have already described our heroines dress, and it is not, therefore, necessary to again revert to it further than to remark that amid the beauties of high birth and breeding who bent their looks curiously, and it may be added enviously upon her, none shone more brilliantly than the fair prisoner at the bar, whose surpassing beauty was set off to great additional advantage by the appearance of the hideous creature who stood next to her. In truth, Jenny appeared as much at her ease in the dock as if she had been in a drawing-room. When she first met the fixed gaze of the multitude it is true she felt for a moment abashed, or rather she assumed the appearance of such an emotion, and curtsied with the most innocent and winning grace to the bench. This done, she modestly cast down her eyes and awaited as it seemed with humility the further proceedings.

A subdued murmur of admiration ran through the court as the crowd gazed on the fair creature whose life depended on the issue of that day's trial. The prevailing sentiment felt was pity that one so young—so beautiful and so fascinating should be placed in such a fearful position. Even the Recorder himself was observed to relax his rigid and severe features when he surveyed her through his spectacles, and the flinty-hearted lawyers themselves felt softened by so unwonted a spectacle.

Mother Sin was first called upon to plead to an indictment charging her with having been concerned in the murder of a gentleman whose name was unknown. To this the old hag pleaded in piteous tones—'Not Guilty,' avowing at the same time that if mercy was extended to her she would name the person who had indeed committed the crime. To this, however, the judge refused to listen, and the old lady was dragged, howling, to the back of the dock.

Jenny Diver was then called upon, and the clerk of the arraigns having notified the charge to her, she pleaded—'Not Guilty,' to the accusation of robbing Lord Martingale. With respect to the charge of returning from transportation she could not well deny it, as her own personal appearance in the court furnished abundant proof of the fact. She positively asserted, however, that she had been informed by official parties in the colonies that she was at liberty to return to England, and on that information had done so.

The trial for the robbery of the nobleman was then proceeded with, and as the Peer chanced to be connected with some individuals high in office, it may easily be supposed that his own version of the tale was listened to, and that Jenny Diver's account of the Fleet marriage was treated as an impudent forgery. Aid, however, was at hand which Jenny little dreamed of.

Lord Martingale was descending from the witness box after having, by denying the little affair in the Fleet, grossly perjured himself, when a shrill voice was heard from the body of the court to exclaim—

"Make way, good people, make way, and let me be examined, for that swaggering ruffler has just sworn to as big lies as ever the devil coined; make way I tell you."

The middling classes, then as now, were only too happy to catch a nobleman slipping, they, therefore, squeezed themselves closer together so as to allow the speaker to push his way towards the witness-box. The lad, for it was our old acquaintance Tim Snarley, was, however, rather rudely repulsed by the all-important Mr. Watkins.

"Get out of my vay, old scarlet veskit," said Tim, indignantly, "and don't stop a member of the legal purfession in the exercise of his dooties," thrusting by the Bow Street runner at the same moment so rudely that he crushed the magnificent bouquet, which adorned the officers coat, into a flat, shapeless state. Nor did he cease to struggle on until he attracted the attention of the Recorder himself who demanded the meaning of the disturbance.

"Give me the oath, and I'll say what I know," said Tim Snarley, mounting the steps to the witness box.

"What do you know of this affair?" demanded the Recorder, after Tim Snarley had been sworn.

"This," replied Tim Snarley, "that that bloak in the lace ruffles, who stood here only a minute since swore falsely when he declared that he was never married to the young lady at the bar."

Jenny's eyes flashed with joy,—how the witness, however, became acquainted with the affair she was utterly at a loss to know.

Tim Snarley then swore that on the night of the alleged robbery he had for other purposes been employed in watching the movements of one Parson Jawbone, a notorious Fleet Parson, and that while so engaged he from his hiding-place had witnessed the prosecutor united to the prisoner.

"Let this man, Jawbone, be sent for," said the judge.

And accordingly in a very short time the Rev. Ichabod Jawbone, in the custody of an officer, was brought into court. A debauch of the previous night had not by any means contributed to the dignity of his appearance, and in this respect he presented a striking contrast to the ruddy and prim looking Lord Mayor's Chaplain who occupied a seat on the bench. On being questioned by the court he stoutly denied that he had performed any such ceremony, or that he had ever seen the prisoner before; a statement at which the reader will not much wonder when he is informed that for celebrating such a ceremony he had committed an illegal act, which rendered him on conviction liable to be transported for the remainder of his life.

Tim Snarley, thus baffled, solaced himself by turning up the whites of his eyes towards heaven in unaffected horror at such a shoking exhibition of moral depravity; and by uttering various exclamations of a no very complimentary character respecting the wickedness both of Lord Martingale and the Wiccar of St. Pauls; but he was speedily silenced by Mr. Watkins, who laid his heavy hand on his shoulder and then placed him beside Jenny in the dock.

To Tim Snarley's utter consternation, the Recorder then addressing him in very severe tones pointed out the enormity of the crime of which he had been guilty, and then and there committed him to take his trial for wilful and corrupt perjury; a circumstance which appeared to be productive of extreme gratification to Lord Martingale, and Parson Jawbone, as well as to the Bow Street runner, who had golden reasons for not disobliging the Peer.

And here we may as well interrupt the narrative a moment to state that within one month from that time, Poor Tim Snarley might have been seen dolefully riding up Holborn Hill towards a suspicious looking piece of mechanism which had previously been erected at the end of Hatton Garden, and which was called a pillory: and that there for the space of one hour by Saint Andrews Clock he endured the peltings of the pittiless crowd, until the last semblance of humanity had been battered from his visage, and all for telling the truth. Tim Snarley to his dying day, never forgot the hard lesson he on that occasion learned; and candour compels us to state that he was never after known to attempt doing a good natured action. He grew up a soured man, and revenged himself on the world for the injury he had sustained. Like his old master, Doom, he became a consummate rogue and told lies by the million, because he had been pilloried for speaking the truth.

As may be imagined, the interference of Tim Snarley in the manner we have just recorded, rather injured than otherwise the person for whose benefit it had been intended, and after a brief trial our poor heroine had the mortification of hearing the foreman of the jury utter the unpleasant word 'Guilty.' She, however, wonderfully maintained her fortitude, though her heart in reality sank within her, and hope almost for the first time in her life seemed to abandon her.

No sooner had the above verdict been recorded than an officer of the court produced the record of her former conviction and sentence of transportation; and the young woman having been proved to be the same who had been formerly banished by the Bow Street runner, she was asked what she had to say why sentence of death should not be passed upon her?

At this fearful moment a dead silence prevailed in court, and many of the females present were visibly affected. Jenny Diver, however, preserved her tranquil bearing, and only answered for the purpose of asking mercy on behalf of her child, for during her intercourse with M'Cleane a boy had been ushered into the world. A perfect mistress of effect the Diver had contrived that the woman whom she had engaged to nurse her offspring should be near her during the trial, and she seized the opportunity when making her last appeal of taking it from the nurse and pressing it to her own bosom.

But she might as well have appealed to the stones beneath her feet as to that severe judge who had tried her. Without heeding her petition he composed his features into a stern severity of expression; put on the fatal black cap, and then in slow measured tones which rang like a death-knell through the court, he expatiated on the enormity of the crimes of Jenny Diver, and then, with as much coolness as though he were pronouncing the doom of a brute, he sentenced her to be hanged by the neck, and concluded by a kind of mock prayer that God would have mercy on her soul!

After kissing the infant, Jenny Diver replaced it in the arms of the nurse and was then conducted from the dock to the condemned cell by the turnkey.

*　　*　　*　　*　　*

Morning in London! The day is not ushered in as in the country by rural sounds and sights, but still the time has its distinctive features—features which are observable at no other period during the twenty four hours.

Morning in London! In the outskirts of the huge city hundreds of conveyances of all descriptions, lading with the various produce of the country around are slowly moving towards the different markets. Now, drowsy watchmen extinguish their lights and creep home to their beds, there to slumber through the day. Now the very shops begin to awake; and in front of them half-awake 'prentices stretch their arms or lazily remove the shutters. Now, slipshod servant maids gossip at the street doors with the milkman, or discuss among themselves the affairs of their master and mistress. Now is heard the cheerful sound of the muffin bell, and the thousand cries of the metropolis ring out clear and distinct in the fresh morning air. As yet the huge pall of smoke has not spread itself over the vast Babylon of brick and mortar, and the sunshine visits the streets and lanes for a brief season. Families meet around the cheerful breakfast table, and thousands upon thousands, refreshed by the tranquil slumbers of the night, begin the day with new hopes and new prospects of success.

But morning in London, wears not for all the same cheerful aspect. Let us glance at another part of the picture. Sitting in a narrow cell on the edge of a miserable bed is a woman, in all the prime of her strength and beauty. On her lap is a still slumbering infant, whose features she is regarding with the most intense anxiety; none but a mother could bend so lovingly over it. Near her, resting on a stool, with her back against the wall, doses the nurse who had brought the babe to that fearful place. Through the high and grated windows the slant beams of early sunshine fall upon and gild the opposite wall of the cell, rendering the surrounding gloom still more doleful. The child opens its mild blue eyes, and gazes in mute wonder on its mother, who it has so seldom seen that it is unconscious of the relationship. A smile plays on its rosy lips as it looks into the beautiful face which bends above it, and as if by instinct it stretches out its little arms. Moved by the sight the young woman catches it up, and pressing it to her beating heart sheds a flood of bitter, bitter tears.

The young mother reader is Jenny Diver, who has awoke to see the rising of that sun which shall set over her clay cold corpse, to behold her last morning on earth. The child she fondles is her neglected babe, now rendered by the near approach of death so terribly precious! So broke the morning for her; not bringing with it life, joy, and healing on its radiant wings, but the awful and dread realities of death and judgment.

The nurse awoke, she was a plain, good sort of woman enough, and had had charge of the child almost from its birth, for Jenny Diver's multifarious engagements had never allowed her opportunities of attending to the duties of a mother. To this person Jenny now once more committed the fruit of her illicit love, with the strongest injunctions that it might be brought up to pursue other courses than those which after many escapes had ended in her own destruction. With these requests the woman promised implicit compliance, and Jenny made arrangements which secured her payment for her services. This matter arranged she bade a heart-breaking farewell to the little creature, and the door of her cell shut it out from her sight for ever.

To M'Cleane who had been incessant in his endeavours to save her from her ignominious fate, she had already bidden adieu. The particulars of their parting interview we have foreborne to detail suffice it to say that it was of a most tender and painful description. At her own request M'Cleane presented her with a lock of his hair which she requested might be enclosed in her coffin, and the Captain also possessed himself of one of her raven tresses which he swore should accompany him to his grave. He also promised to watch over their innocent child and to avoid bringing it up in the ways of crime.

The clock of Saint Sepulchre's Church had just struck the hour of ten when the door of the condemned cell was opened, and the sheriffs in their robes appeared in the narrow passage. Jenny knew their errand too well, and rising from her bedside announced that she was ready. She was then led from the condemned cell into the press-yard where two other doomed individuals were already standing. One of them, a young man, who was undergoing the ceremony of having his irons knocked off; and the other, Mother Sin, as hardened as ever, and evidently in a state of intoxication, for to inspire her with a false courage the miserable wretch had been during the whole of the previous night drowning reflections in frequent libations of her favorite liquor, with which she had been supplied through the connivance of the well-paid turnkeys.

All the preliminary preparations having been completed, Mother Sin and the male prisoner were placed in the cart, each of them seated on a coffin. Jenny Diver occupied a mourning coach, for which she had paid handsomely, and at a given signal the immense folding doors of Newgate having been thrown back, the dismal procession moved forward to the dull sound of St. Sepulchres bell which tolled the service of the dead over the living.

Tremendous was the excitement when the two vehicles first appeared in the open space in front of the prison. Mother Sin, who had long been notorious to the Town for her abominable practices was at once assailed with the rankest abuse, as well as by a shower of missiles of all descriptions, which compelled the hangman, who rode in front of the vehicle, to descend from his exposed position, and induced the sheriff to order his javelin men to charge among the crowd. This, however was but of little avail, and at length it was found necessary to remove the procuress from the open cart and place her in the coach beside Jenny Diver, who generously afforded her the protection she so much needed.

The instant this step had been taken, the yellings, hootings, and peltings ceased, for a strong

sympathy was felt for our heroine by the mob, who are always ready to admire daring of any kind. Her beauty too, of which such exaggerated statements had gone abroad, had excited the most intense curiosity to behold her; but Jenny who appeared to be truly penitent for her offences, buried her face in her handkerchief and carefully concealed it from view.

Thousands upon thousands crowded the great thoroughfare of Holborn, and the windows of every house were crammed with curious spectators. At Saint Giles's a temporary stoppage took place, and the ordinary who accompanied Jenny took advantage of the momentary cessation of the tumult to exhort Jenny to impeach those accomplices with whom she had so long been associated in the commission of crime.

"Never!" was Jenny Diver's indignant reply. "I am ready to pay the penalty of my offences, but it shall never be said of me that in my last moments I turned traitor."

At that moment Jenny happened to look from the window of the carriage, and a countenance she knew but too well met her glance.

Unconsciously she uttered a slight exclamation which induced Mother Sin to turn her eyes in the same direction. She also observed the person who had attracted Jenny's notice, in spite of the assumed disguise worn by the individual in the crowd.

"Seize him—seize him!" exclaimed the old procuress, pointing him out, "there is the man who committed the murder, and then flung the body in the water. Seize him I say, he has the old man's pocket-book to prove my innocence."

"Back, woman!" cried Jenny Diver thrusting with almost supernatural strength, the hag back into her seat; but too late to prevent the attention of the populace being drawn towards the stranger pointed out by Mother Sin. A look full of meaning from Jenny conveyed to M'Cleane, for it was indeed him, the danger of his situation and quickly returning a grateful glance, he instantly plunged into the thickest of the crowd and was lost to view; but the lynx eyes of Jonathan Wild and Watkins the officer, had caught a glance of his face, and both of these worthies had heard Mother Sin's denunciations. Like hounds which had just caught the trace of blood they rejoiced, and each inwardly determined not to lose the scent until they should have ran down their human prey.

Jenny Diver clasped her hands with unaffected joy when she became assured of her favorites escape. For her own part, she would rather have died twenty deaths than he should have been captured at such a time. Mother Sin, on the contrary, blasphemed horribly, and in louder tones than ever asserted her innocence.

On they went, the crowd still following and hemming them in on every side, and becoming denser and denser every moment. The bright noonday sun shone as brilliantly over head as if sorrow and suffering had never visited the world. Merrily sang the lark in mid-air for they had now left behind them the dense mass of buildings and were travelling along a road bordered by suburban meadows. The greater number of the people present wore holiday clothes, and looked happy and cheerful, just for all the world as if the occasion which called them together had been one of joyous excitement; the officials were busy and big with importance, and even the finisher of the law himself seemed in rather better spirits than usual, which, however, might be easily accounted for inasmuch as he had had a jovial bowl on the way and was looking forward to a triple fee.

A sudden halt and a low buz of excitement rises from the crowd, now the carriage moves a few yards further on—now it again stops and the javelin men surround it, a dead silence prevails, and at some signal, unseen by Jenny Diver, every head is uncovered. A shudder runs through her delicate frame; she well knows, although she does not see it, that the dreary gallows tree is close to her—her time she feels is come !

Mastering her emotions as well as possible, she looked out from the coach window. Aye! there indeed it was, rising black and grim above her head. The blood left her cheek as she beheld the instrument of death, and for a moment the weakness of the woman and the mortal triumphed.

But not for long; the pang passed away and she calmly awaited her doom. Mother Sin, however, now absolutely raved with rage and terror, and when the door of the coach was opened she had literally to be dragged from it. Not so, Jenny Diver, without a word she followed the sheriff who led the way to the short flight of steps by which she had to mount the cart.

The moment Jenny appeared on the plank which was placed across the sides of the vehicle, a murmur of admiration and sorrow ran like wildfire through the vast assembly. The extreme paleness of her countenance, added perhaps to her beauty, and she looked more like the inhabitant of another sphere than of a notorious criminal about to expiate her many crimes. Her last act was to acknowledge to the ordinary that she sincerely repented her misdeeds, and then she stood beneath the fatal beam whilst the rope was being adjusted round the necks of her wretched companions.

The hanging apparatus of that day was but a clumsy contrivance compared with that which modern civilization has brought into general use, and in consequence thereof the sufferings of criminals were often painfully prolonged by their having to witness the launching of their companions into eternity before they themselves were turned off. The ingenious drop does away with all such delays in our time. On the occasion we are now describing Mother Sin and the man were the first to suffer, and the moment the woman was dragged by the rope from the plank as the cart moved away, a loud cheer of exultation burst from the crowd. Then the hangman proceeded to complete his awful work, and the signal having been given, the horse gave a spring forward, the wheels rapidly revolved and Jenny Diver, after a a few struggles, closed for ever her eventful and most extraordinary career.

A deep sigh was heaved from almost every breast as she quivered in her last agony; and a piercing shriek of despair, not from a woman's lips, rang loud and shrilly over all. Hundreds looked to see from whence the sound proceeded but none could discover the source. Could Jenny Diver have heard it she would have recognized in that involuntary expression of agony the lamentation of James M'Cleane.

CHAPTER LI.

THE GRAVE-DIGGER IN SPITE OF HIMSELF— EPHRAIM BLAKE'S FATAL CURIOSITY — THE MYSTERIOUS POCKET BOOK.

THE execution of one of the most celebrated and successful members of M'Cleane's gang could not fail to produce the most serious consequences. For the loss of the bright-eyed accomplished creature herself the deepest sorrow was felt, especially by M'Cleane, who, as we have seen, having failed in all his attempts to deliver Jenny Diver from the danger by which she was surrounded, witnessed her last appearance on the stage of the world.

Nor did his attachment cease with her last breath. In accordance with previous arrangements, a hearse was in waiting at a short distance from the fearful scene of her execution, and immediately on its being cut down Dick Flybynight and Gipsey Betty, who had completely disguised themselves, made an application to the sheriff in the character of friends of the criminal, for the body to be delivered up to them. As it was only in cases of murder that culprits were doomed to the horrors of the dissecting room, no objection was made on the part of the city authorities, and accordingly the young girl's mortal remains were given up.

The hearse containing the corpse was placed in the yard of a neighbouring tavern until darkness should have set in; and then with all possible privacy it was removed to the churchyard of St. Pancras, where, in the presence of M'Cleane and two or three others it was interred. No ceremony was performed, and when the last shovel full of heavy mould had been thrown into the unblessed grave the few mourners quitted the melancholy place with a sigh and returned to the Chapel.

We must now return to Blueskin who, it will be remembered by the reader, we left on his way to the head quarters of the gang in Long Acre, in company with his cousin Ephraim Blake.

The son of the miser so far from allowing his revengeful feelings against the man who had murdered his father to die, did all that lay in his power to cherish them. The story which his cousin had told him of Blackmoor's mysterious death and burial in the vaults of the Chapel, in the Acre, he believed to be merely a fiction got up for the purpose of deceiving him, and it was to convince himself by occular demonstration that he now was about to venture into the very strong hold of the mysterious gang who had so long been the terror of London.

Just before the arrival of Blake and Blueskin at the secret entrance of the Chapel, two men might have been seen stealthily creeping within the deep shadow of the opposite houses, keenly watching it, and keeping their persons secured as much as possible from observation.

These were Watkins, the Bow Street runner, and Jonathan Wild.

Not contented with having captured and hunt to the death one of the most formidable members of the lawless confederacy, these bloodhounds now sought to secure other victims for the purpose of enriching themselves. The escape of Handsome Jack from their clutches had been a matter of the most profound mortification to both of them, but Wild was not a man to be easily discouraged. Baffled in one direction, he sought to accomplish his designs by the more assiduously working in another quarter.

They had not been long in their place of concealment when they were joined by a third party, a man. It was Flitchman, who, forgetful of the obligations under which he lay to M'Cleane, had yielded to the offers of Watkins and Wild and communicated information to them which greatly perilled the safety of his benefactor.

"You say Mother Sin saw M'Cleane take a pocket-book from the murdered man; are you sure that he always carries it about his person?" asked Watkins.

"He never parts with it," replied Flitchman, "I had my information from Gipsey Betty, a few nights since."

"Good!" remarked Watkins, "we must manage to secure it; who knows on what scent it may set us?"

"You know the porter as he is called, Flitchman; while we watch here for M'Cleane's return you pay a visit to him, and see if he is to be bought. That fellow once our friend the whole gang will be in our power."

With cautious step, Flitchman quitted his employers for the purpose of endeavouring to corrupt Beauty Ellis. On his making the private signal he was immediately admitted; but to his utter surprise no sooner was the door fastened behind him than the porter bluntly informed him that he was fully acquainted with his treachery and that he must consider himself a prisoner.

Flitchman, with a dreadful oath, denied that he had done anything to merit such treatment; but Beauty Ellis only grinned a disbelief of his assertions, and advised him to be silent. The treacherous wretch, however, persisted in his declarations of innocence.

"And so yer vanted to bribe me, did yer?—werry odd if you had," observed Beauty indignantly.

"No! I never had any idea of such a thing," exclaimed Flitchman.

"Liar—infamous liar," exclaimed Gipsey Betty, who made her appearance from a dark corner of the apartment, where she had hitherto been concealed, "I heard you not an hour ago make the bargain with Watkins and Jonathan Wild in the house of Jerry Laggum, more than that, the written promise of Jonathan to give you a hundred guineas and provide you a free passage to the Colonies, as the reward of your rascality, is now in your pocket."

Flitchman turned very pale and his knees trembled. With a strength which no one would have supposed the girl possessed, Gipsey Betty, whose indignation was thoroughly aroused, flew upon him, and held him by the throat, for her quick eye had observed him fumbling in his breast, and she suspected he was about to draw forth and secrete elsewhere or swallow the proof of his guilt.

With the energy of despair the detected man dashed the girl from him, but the instant her hold was loosened Beauty Ellis sprang upon the fellow, and with one powerful hand held him as in a vice. The other he thrust into the inside pocket of his coat, and drew forth a paper which he handed to Gipsey Betty.

"This is it," exclaimed the girl. "Would that the Captain were here."

Scarcely had she uttered the words before M'Cleane stood himself before him, he having entered by way of the shaft alluded to in former chapters.

"I would rather," said M'Cleane, after he had heard the charge against Flitchman, "not be judge in this matter. I leave all to you, Dick," and turning on his heel he left the place.

The trial was brief enough, the facts of the case were proved, and sentence of death was passed in due form.

"Take him away," said Dick Flybynight, impetuously, and inform me when all is ready.

After summoning two or three of the subordinate members of the gang, Beauty Ellis formed them into a sort of procession, heading it himself, directing Flitchman to follow him he led the way towards the interior of the building.

Before, however, reaching the saloon, Ellis turned aside into a vaulted passage, and after descending a flight of winding stone stairs they reached that part of the Chapel in which were situated the cells of the Secret Tribunal.

In the small space outside these gloomy receptacles was a stone slab in the shape of a grave stone, which evidently had been recently placed there. Beauty Ellis grasped Flitchman's arm and drew him close to it; then directing the light of the lantern upon it, an inscription was visible, and the trembling prisoner read these words.—"The grave of a Traitor."

"The bloak underneath got his deserts; and werry proper too: and now you're a goin' to have yourn," hissed Beauty Ellis into Flitchman's ear; but you shall have your choice as you've heard. Now, will you dig your own grave, and then be tucked in with a bullet, or shall we put you into one of those cells there and brick up the door on you?"

Flitchman was speechless! either alternative was horrible; but he saw no way of escape from them. The idea of being immured living in a tomb was more horrible in the contemplation than a speedy death. The miserable man in the moment of agony remembered the tales he had heard of nuns convicted of having broken their vows of chastity who had been encased in such a fearful way, and shuddered at the very thought of undergoing similar torture. Turning an imploring look on the scowling faces around him, faces rendered doubly fearful by the fitful light of the lanterns they carried, he saw that to implore mercy would be utterly useless, and in the desperate hope that assistance might possibly arrive from Wild and Watkins who must be waiting, he knew for him without, he signified his desire to be dispatched after he should have prepared the receptacle in which his body was to rot, unvisited by mourner or friend.

Taking a spade he prepared to commence digging his own grave! By means of a crowbar the stone slab, that covered the earth beneath which lay the remains of Blackmoor was removed and Flitchman was commanded to dig, but he drew back and hesitated.

"This is horrible!" he muttered. "Surely you will not compel me to re-open the grave of another! Common humanity—"

"That be damned; dont know what it means,"

sneered Beauty Ellis, "the hole in which one villain lies is good enough for another."

Forced to prosecute his loathsome task, Flitchman now shovelled out the heavy mould, but as slowly as possible for the reason we have already mentioned. As he got deeper a horrible stench began to pervade the place, and he grew sick as he remembered that within a very short time his now active body would be in that pestiferous charnel house. A sickness came over him, a mortal agony shook his entire frame, and he would have fallen headlong in the pit had not a slight sound caught his ear, and half revived the spark of hope which was dying fast within his heaving bosom.

The sound, whatever it was, seemed not to have reached other ears than his own, for on his momentary cessation from his terrible labour, Beauty Ellis, with a fearful oath, commanded him to resume it.

At length a sufficient depth, in the opinion of the man who superintended the proceedings, was attained, and Flitchman now almost dead through breathing the dank air of the charnel house, was ordered to come forth and stand on its brink.

A messenger was then dispatched for Dick Flybynight, who immediately answered the summons. He held in his hand a large horse-pistol, which he loaded with a double charge, and then from his pocket he drew a small canvass bag in which were leaden bullets, corresponding to the numbers of those present. Of these bullets one was marked in a peculiar manner.

"Flitchman" said Dick Flybynight, sternly, "you have been guilty of a crime which never meets with pardon here. I give you five minutes to prepare yourself; make the best use of your time, for it is short. Now then, comrades, let us draw lots and see who will have the honour of punishing a traitor."

Before drawing, however, Beauty Ellis requested that he might be allowed to officiate; but to this Flybynight would not accede. The bag was then passed round, and each man drew a bullet. On examining them by the light of the lantern, Dick discovered that he himself had selected the marked bullet.

The time allotted to the doomed man passed rapidly, and having in vain attempted to prolong it, he was dragged by Beauty Ellis to the brink of the excavation.

Dick Flybynight deliberately raised the pistol, when a hand was laid upon his arm, and looking round he beheld Handsome Jack. The suddenness of the visit of the latter somewhat startled him, and dropping his arm he embraced his friend. For the moment he disregarded the object of his revenge, and this delay heralded another unexpected occurrence.

Leaving the party around the new made grave, we must now return to Ephraim Blake and his cousin Blueskin.

The latter being well acquainted with every way of entrance into the Chapel had conducted his cousin Ephraim to one of them, and at the very time when Flitchman commenced the ghastly work upon which we have seen him employed, the two were cautiously threading their way through one of the subterranean passages of that singular place.

Whilst groping their way, the sound of voices startled them, and the better to conceal themselves they extinguished the light in the lantern which they carried. Proceeding further onward, they at last came to part of the passage from which owing to the damp some small stones had fallen out, and through the chinks so made, struggled a feeble ray of light.

Here they anxiously watched the proceedings of Flybynight and the others of the gang to whom we must return.

All this time, that is while Dick Flybynight was explaining the position of affairs to Handsome Jack, the miserable man, Flitchman, stood shivering with mortal agony on the brink of his own grave. His respite however, was but of short duration, for Beauty Ellis, who was impatient to witness the punishment of the condemned one, reminded him who had been selected to perform the office of executioner, that Captain M'Cleane would not be well pleased if the matter were further delayed.

"Stand aside, Jack," said Dick Flybynight to his friend with whom he had just been conversing, and at the same time he withdrew a few paces from Flitchman, and levelled the pistol directly at his heart.

"Mercy—mercy!" shrieked the culprit, falling on his knees and imploring the humane interference of Handsome Jack, in whose features he fancied that he could discern some expression of horrer at the tragedy about to be enacted.

"Can no indulgence be extended to the man?" asked Handsome Jack, who, however, we may during the remainder of our narrative more correctly denominate Richard Town, the latter remembering that Flitchman had been instrumental in bringing Doom, the iniquitous lawyer to justice.

"Nothing," replied Dick sternly, and the sharp clicks of the pistol as he cocked both the locks was heard.

"One—two—three!" and then the report of a pistol was heard, and the vault was filled with smoke.

But when it partially cleared away, to the utter astonishment of those present, the prisoner stood erect and uninjured on the brink of his self made grave, and Dick Flybynight's arm hung powerless by his side, the pistol which he had so recently grasped lying undischarged on the floor at his feet.

Scarcely had the party recovered from the surprise into which they had been thrown, when the discharge of another pistol startled them, the flash from which appeared to issue from the wall of the subterranean place. This time the ball from the mysterious quarter was more terrible than the former one in its effects, for, simultaneously with the report of the weapon from which it had been discharged, Beauty Ellis, who stood close beside Richard Town, gloating malignantly over the distorted features of Flitchman, suddenly sprang convulsively, with a shrill cry, several feet from the floor, and then fell upon it a corpse. A ball had penetrated the very centre of his forehead, and had lodged in his brain, inflicting on him the very fate he was so desirous of seeing awarded to another.

"In the name of the devil and all his legions, what mystery is this?" exclaimed Dick Flybynight for the moment forgetting his prisoner, and rushing to that part of the vault of the Secret Tribunal from whence the death-dealing messenger for Beauty Ellis had been dispatched. Then the crack in the crevice was perceptible, and the idea that a piece of treachery, similar to that which Blackmoor had been engaged in on a former occasion, and with which the reader is well acquainted, had been perpetrated flashed upon his fertile mind.

"You shall not escape, however, at any rate," said Dick, as with his left hand, for the ball from the first pistol which was discharged had broken the bone of his right arm, he picked up his pistol; then absolutely rushing upon Flitchman, and putting the muzzles of both barrels close to his breast he discharged them almost at the same instant into his body.

A wild shriek rang through the vault, rising high and shrill above the dull sounds produced by the pistol, and then with his arms convulsively tossed above his head, Flitchman fell backwards into the horrible cavity prepared by himself for his reception.

To account for this unlooked for occurrence, it will be necessary that the reader should once more return with us to Ephraim Blake and his cousin Blueskin.

We have seen that through the chink in the side of the vault of the Secret Tribunal they watched the preparations for the destruction of the unfortunate Flitchman. To Blueskin himself these proceedings were intelligible enough, but Ephraim Blake regarded them with intense curiosity, not unmixed with horror for he felt that his own situation, should he be discovered, would be little less enviable than that of the individual he beheld awaiting the execution of his sentence. Determined, however, that should he be dragged from the place of his concealment, he would sell his life dearly, he grasped his pistols, and held them in readiness for instant use.

Whilst thus situated he suddenly beheld Richard Town, and the sight acted like a charm upon him. His features grew pale with excitement; a fiendish rage took possession of his heart, and made his frame quiver with a demoniacal desire for revenge; he glared upon Town with joy, for he recognized the man who had assisted the murderer of his father, the miser of Bucklersbury to escape from the gallows, whom he afterwards saw in the act of rescuing Jenny Diver from the fire at the house of Williams the Fence, in Hanging Sword Alley, and for whom he had offered a large sum to his cousin Blueskin. Regardless at that moment of wild revengeful feeling of his own safety he lifted his pistol and, in spite of the efforts of his companion, fired it at Town whom it missed, wounding, as we have seen, Dick Flybynight in the arm. Maddened at his failure again he discharged his weapon and owing to the tremulousness of his hand again he missed his mark and killed Beauty Ellis.

"Damnation! Ephraim—what have you done?" exclaimed Blueskin, "but if you choose to be made mincemeat of yourself, I am not inclined to have my carcase hacked," and he dragged forcibly away his cousin from the aperture to which Dick Flybynight was rushing.

At that moment the devil or one of his imps whispered a diabolical suggestion in the ear of Blueskin.

He remembered that his cousin was wealthy—that to guard against the casualties of the public funds he kept his money in his house, and that none but himself resided there. What was there to hinder him at that moment from sacrificing him and then proceeding to his residence and possessing himself of his property? The question suggested itself in the very nick of time, for Flybynight and Town were commencing a search for them, and in a moment more they would be discovered. Unwilling, however, to shed blood, he determined on stunning him so that he would inevitably be found by his pursuers, who would not fail to dispatch him. He, therefore, with one blow of the butt end of his pistol felled Ephraim Blake to the earth, and then flew as quickly as possible from the place and safely regained the street.

Not long was it before Ephraim Blake was found by Dick. His career was speedily closed. A few thrusts of a rapier finished what his cousin had begun, and then his body was flung into the grave beside the still quivering body of Flitchman.

"This man could not have come hither alone," remarked Dick Flybynight, after they had made an ineffectual search for others who they suspected were concealed. "Be that as it may," he added, "this is no place now for us," and giving directions to his men to follow him, he supported himself on Richard Town's arm, for he felt himself somewhat weak from the effects of his wound, and they both hastened to join M'Cleane.

They found the Captain in a private apartment busily employed in removing a large stone with a ring in its centre, and which had hitherto been so carefully concealed that its existence had been known to M'Cleane alone. After Dick Flybynight had reported the proceedings in the vault, and M'Cleane had welcomed Richard Town, he carefully closed the door and in a low voice said—

"It is as I thought; evil days are at hand, and for this I have been preparing as you see."

"What! by digging a grave for yourself, Captain?" asked Dick, pointing to the cavity.

"Not quite that," replied M'Cleane; "but the fact is, Dick, we must at once and for a long time quit the Chapel:—the fates are against us. Look at this pocket-book, it was formerly in the possession of the man who was murdered at Mother Sin's, and it contains documents which one day may be worth far more than their weight in gold, for they relate to the secret history of the most exalted personages. The murdered man was Dr. M'Cleane, Chaplain to a British Embassy and my uncle, such I discovered by the merest chance."

Both Town and Flybynight uttered an exclamation of surprise.

"And these papers, which it is not safe for me to have about me, I am about to conceal here until the time shall come when they may be of value," continued the Captain, depositing as he spoke the pocket book and its contents in the secret place, and then closing it up so as to hide all traces of its existence.

"So you are going to quit England?" said M'Cleane to Richard Town.

"For ever," replied his late comrade, "would that you and Dick would join me. This mode of life must end—"

"At Tyburn Tree you would say. I know it; but it cannot be helped now, so farewell, and God speed you Richard Town. Linger not here or you may again be snared, for the bloodhounds are at our doors."

And bidding an affectionate farewell to his two friends, Richard Town departed from the Chapel.

CONCLUSION.

HAVING thus so far traced the footsteps and fortunes of the principal personages of our narrative, it now only remains for us, with as much brevity as possible, to refer to those of whose ultimate career we are as yet ignorant.

In accordance with his determination, Captain M'Cleane quitted the Chapel, and embarked for the continent, where for a long time he was eminently successful. Suddenly, however, he disappeared from the scene of his exploits, and his fate became shrouded in mystery, which, at a future time we may withdraw.

Dick Flybynight fell a victim to the malice of Jonathan Wild, and in company with Gipsey Betty suffered at that dreadful place where so many of his companions in crime had preceded him.

Blueskin was transported for a robbery in Wych Street, the ill-gotten wealth he had procured from his cousin's house having been speedily squandered amongst his dissolute companions.

Madam Charlotte, deprived of her situation in the hotel department of the Chapel, removed with the property she had acquired to the Almonry, where she rented the house formerly occupied by Mother Sin. There, with Sal the Gonnoff she became one of the most notorious procuresses in that quarter of the metropolis. As for Mother Singleton, she perished by her own hand, soon after the disappearance of Sir James Town.

Jonathan Wild and his men still pursued their nefarious occupation; but this is not the place for recording their later adventures. On a future occasion the story of their career will be resumed and concluded.

As if to show that while vice assuredly leads to a disgraceful end, virtuous repentance may avert such a terrible catastrophe, Richard Town's after life may be referred to. On quitting his native land he adopted new courses; as a soldier he won honourable laurels, which amply covered his former errors. His old love for Lady Purley never died, and when the ancient lord died he again wooed and won the object of his affections. His old age was happy and serene.

Thus have we brought our tale to a close, and happy shall we be if the object we had in view when we commenced it, viz: that of attracting to the paths of honour, by pointing out the dangers of dishonesty and crime, have been accomplished.

THE END.

www.ingramcontent.com/pod-product-compliance
Lightning Source LLC
Chambersburg PA
CBHW080720290626
47170CB00017B/2806